SEASONS OF DESIRE

by *Arielle Briar*

published by
Nocturnis Productions
P.O. Box 9635
North Amherst, MA 01059-9635

Seasons of Desire is a work of fiction. Any resemblance between the characters depicted herein and real persons, either living or dead, is unintentional and purely coincidental. Likewise, while towns, streets, and various geographical features of New England are referred to by name, all shops, bars, guesthouses, and other businesses in these stories are entirely the products of the author's imagination. They are not intended to depict actual sites or commercial enterprises.

Contents

Springambols

Her fertile lips rest between my boughs

Breath rouses the pink bud

Capers and grows

The banal miracle restores my body

like the tired earth

Willing to risk disclosure

for a moment's beauty

To end, to start deep, without boundaries

Seasons of Desire

No rain. No traffic. The frigid March wind scraped my prickling cheeks and newly shaven scalp like a rusty blade. I shoved my duffle bag into my van and slammed the back door. Ten minutes later, I was on the Mass Pike. With any luck, I'd be in Connecticut before dark.

It was time to go. I'd known that for a long while. Occasionally I fantasized about leaving New England entirely, just packing everything up and hitting the road for California, but I knew I'd never go through with it. People who made the move told me they couldn't stand it out west, where the year was just one long, unbroken season. Eventually they all came back. Maybe the Puritans bred some kind of homing instinct into us, just so we wouldn't start to enjoy ourselves too much in a sunnier climate somewhere. Besides, I didn't think my old van would make it past the Midwestern states, and from what I'd heard, the flatlands were no place for an obvious butch like me.

I lifted my eyes to the rearview mirror just in time to see Lowell's dingy silhouette sink from sight. I wondered if Jack Kerouac had felt the same sense of relief when he left family, brick, and toxic fumes behind and went on the road for the first time.

Having spent my whole life in the factory capital of Massachusetts, I'd been hearing about Kerouac from the time I could read. And I have to admit, he was one guy I could relate to. If he'd been alive when I was growing up, we probably would have moved in the same depressing circles. My mom worked in a plastics factory, and, like the Kerouacs before us, we were always worried about money or making sure no one saw my dad drunk. And I had something else in common with Kerouac: people who knew me never called me Jackie or Jacquelyn. They just called me Jacq. Luckily, it had been about five and a half years since I'd finished high school and had to correct a teacher about what to call me besides "dyke."

Eventually, the dismal scenery along the highway gave way to trees and steep walls of jagged grey rock. Fresh cold air gusted through my open window. Cranking up the tape deck, I glanced at the map spread open on the passenger seat. Instinctively, I checked the rearview mirror for cops before I pumped the gas pedal. I just couldn't wait to play.

Sage

I got to Waterbury that evening and headed for my ex's place, where I planned to hang out for a couple of days until I got settled. Unfortunately, in Waterbury, I found Lowell's identical twin brother. A dull brown color tainted everything, and a tacky mammoth crucifix rose up in the distance. The houses perched on the hillside matched the placement of the gravestones nearby. There wasn't a bud in sight on any of the trees or neglected flowerbeds. When I got out of the van and headed up the steps of the apartment house, I got a whiff of the air. Apparently pollution had taken its toll here, as well.

To my surprise, there was no answer when I knocked on my ex's door. That was strange–I hadn't been able to reach her by phone for about a week, either. I'd figured she was sleeping over at her new girlfriend's place. Maybe she was over there now.

I was about to leave and come back later when a middle-aged guy with a beer belly and a faded tattoo on his arm stepped out of the apartment next door.

"You Jack?" He squinted at my dark crew cut and camouflage pants. I guess he'd been expecting a guy, and he still wasn't sure if he'd found one or not.

"Yeah," I said cautiously.

"Here," he said, handing me a folded note. "Gal who used to live here said to keep an eye out for you. Told me to give you this when you showed up."

I waited until he'd shuffled back into his own apartment before I opened and read it.

Babe, the scribbly handwriting announced, *I've gone to stay with my new lover in New York. Things really bite at the moment. My parents found out that I'm gay, so they told the landlord and cut off the rent money. Hope you can find another place to stay on such short notice! Hugs–Sue.*

"Shit!" I crumpled it up in my fist. Reliable and dependable Sue wasn't, but I never figured her for vindictive. She could at least have given me a phone number or directions to the nearest lesbian flophouse. What the hell was I going to do now?

I fumed for a while, then decided to make the best of the situation. Since I was already here, I figured I could get some cheap food and maybe a thrill or two before I moved on.

That night, I parked in an isolated suburban area and slept in the back of my van. It was cold, but I wore sweats and my leather jacket and wrapped myself in two sleeping bags, so I managed okay. In the morning, I went to a small grocery store because I didn't want to waste any of the few hundred bucks I'd saved up on eating out.

For once, my tightfisted habits paid off. While I was in the store, I saw a woman about my age standing in the produce aisle, her tousled brown curls cradling her clear-skinned face. Though she apparently worked there, at the moment she was preoccupied with sampling the grapes. I was entranced by her moist lips as she looked around and popped the bright green orbs into her mouth one by one. The color matched the apron she wore, and I casually walked around her, trying to see if she wore a nameplate. Unfortunately, she didn't.

While I was still watching, she polished off the last of the grapes, wiped her hands on her apron, and headed for the back of the store. Soon she came back carrying a wooden crate of apples. She began sorting them out and placing them on the shelves with a bored expression.

Magnetized, I approached her. "Uh, I was wondering if those were organic," I stammered. I didn't really know what I was talking about, but Sue was a vegetarian and spent most of her time lecturing me about stuff like that. All fruits and vegetables seemed pretty much the same to me, but at least the question gave me a chance to admire her up close.

She laughed. "In this place? You've got to be kidding. Try the co-op three blocks down." When I didn't move, she turned and gave me the once over herself. "Maybe you'd like these. Farm fresh, the box says, though they sure aren't local." A mischievous smile played across those luscious lips, and her amethyst eyes glittered as she handed me two shiny yellow apples.

"Speaking of local, is there anything interesting to see around here?" I asked. Weighing the large fruits in my hand, I eyed the pyramid she was building with the others.

"Like I said, you've got to be kidding. Waterbury's a pit, as you probably noticed. Still, there are some stimulating people–if you know where to look."

I moved a bit closer. "You wouldn't have time to show me, would you?"

She paused, wiping her hands on her apron again. Her tone grew skeptical. "Well, I don't have a car, if that's what you're interested in."

"That's okay. I already have one of those."

"Oh. In that case, you can meet me at the bar sometime. I'll give you the guided tour, which should take about five minutes." Grinning, she reached into her apron pocket, pulled out another grape, and popped it into that plush mouth of hers. I envied that grape. "After that, we'd have to find something *better* to do."

"I can't wait," I replied, not hiding my enthusiasm for her.

Later that night, I followed her directions to the bar she'd mentioned. It was a real dive, filled mostly with gay men, though a few older butches were shooting pool in the corner. No one spoke to me, so I sat drinking beer for a while. Grape Girl never showed up.

The next day, I went back to the store and found her sticking price tags on cans of chicken noodle soup. She smiled and shrugged when I said I must have missed her at the bar.

"I don't always go there," she said, her voice maddeningly casual. "Sometimes I just prefer a quiet evening at home."

"I'm still waiting for that five-minute tour," I said.

"Maybe tonight," she replied, laughing.

I killed time all day until it was dark enough to head to the bar. Once again, there was no sign of her, and I knew she'd just been playing me. Annoyed that I'd wasted my whole day waiting to see her, I sipped the icy suds and watched the people around me.

Most of them, both men and women, were in couples, leaning close and trading intimate whispers. Some danced together as the jukebox played. Others simply propped their elbows against the bar, like I was doing, and scanned the crowd hungrily.

After a while, I decided that my beer tasted flat. I signaled to the bartender, intending to complain until she exchanged my half-full bottle for another. When I raised my arm, warm fingers slipped around the crook in my elbow. I let it drop again.

"I made it this time," she said, looking up at me. "You were so into your own thoughts that you didn't even see me come in."

"You're right. I didn't." I noticed again how generous her round breasts were, sort of like the firm apples we'd held in the store. Her lips were smeared with cherry-red lipstick. I knew it would get all over my own mouth if I kissed her. "I wondered if you'd ever get here. I was about to give up on you."

"I almost didn't come. Then I got a feeling that you were here waiting for me."

I wasn't sure how to respond to that, so I just asked

her if she wanted a beer.

"Oh, it's all right." She shrugged. "I'm not a big drinker."

I downed the rest of my glass, ignoring the bitter taste. "You know, you never told me your name."

"It's Sage." She smiled and seemed to focus on the corner of my mouth. "Like the plant. Or like wisdom."

"I'm Jacq," I said, instinctively wiping my lips with the back of my hand.

"Can I offer you a cigarette?" She slipped a flat silver case out of the doll-sized leather purse she carried. "I know it's not cool nowadays, but I don't really care. I like the taste."

"Okay. Thanks." I took the cigarette from her and put the corked tip between my moistened lips. Menthol, I noticed. Too sweet for me, but I didn't complain.

She took out a neon blue lighter and proceeded to light my cigarette as well as her own. I watched her lipstick imprint the slim brown filter as pale billows of smoke rose between us.

"Remember the tour you promised me?" I prompted.

I watched the words coming out of her mouth and barely heard them at all. "Oh, well, I'm afraid there isn't much to see around here. It's just your typical New England industrial town."

"That much I gathered. So what do you do for fun?"

"This is it," she responded with a dry laugh and blew smoke through her teeth.

"You hang out here a lot?" I was curious to know if she slept around much. Not that it would deter me from becoming her next lover if she did. For some reason, I just wanted to know.

"I don't know. I go through phases."

Thoughts of that soft mouth fogged my mind while I tried to keep up with the conversation. But it was becoming more difficult with the noise and the music playing loudly. I took a last puff and stubbed out my unfinished cigarette in a nearby ashtray.

"Sure I can't I get you some beer?" I offered. By now I was pretty sure she was interested in me, so I hoped she'd offer me a trip to her place instead.

"Maybe later," she said, which I still took as a good sign. "For now, why don't we just dance instead? I love to dance."

"Definitely," I replied.

We got up, and that Jewel song *Foolish Games* started playing. Sage, who was slightly shorter than I was, rested her head on my shoulder as she allowed my fingers to stroke her curly brown tresses. Her hair smelled of jasmine.

I blew into her ear. Her breasts were two soft pillows that burrowed into my own. My hands massaged the small of her back while she hugged my hips. My mouth brushed her smooth forehead naturally, like we'd held each other many times before.

I closed my eyes so I could pretend no one was around except the two of us, holding each other and swaying to Jewel's smooth voice. Our feet barely moved. I sensed the hardening of her nipples through my t-shirt.

My hand traveled up her back, and I felt smooth shoulder blades, but no bra strap. I held her tighter, maneuvering her toward the back of the bar. Sage followed my lead, and we moved into an isolated corner.

Finally my tongue parted those luscious lips and slid inside that moist, lipstick-painted pout. Sage put her arms around my neck and kissed me back with her whole mouth. She tasted like nicotine and grapes.

My lips roamed her sweet face, concentrating on her glossy temples and the edges of her hairline, now moistened by a faint gleam of sweat. Sage released a baby animal's moan of delight, and I felt her small tongue dart against mine. My palms slipped down her hips. Chills raged through me despite the heat we'd generated.

I steered her back against the pinball machine and sensed a presence next to us. I didn't want to interrupt our dance, but a woman's shrill voice shattered the calm that had settled over my body.

"That's enough, Nancy!"

I opened my eyes and pulled back from Sage. The intruder was an attractive butch, her fists balled up on her hips and her dark eyes flashing anger. "I'm jealous, all right? It worked. Stop torturing me."

"Get away from me, Jane," Sage retorted, grabbing me by the hand. "Jacq, take me away from her!"

I looked from Jane's tight face back to Sage's, and decided that her suggestion made sense. Towing Sage along after me, I raced to my car. I could still taste her on my mouth.

"Where should I go?" I asked as I floored the gas pedal.

"Take a right and go straight up the hill. The view is unbelievable, even at night." Sage was looking at me with wide-open eyes. "Hurry!"

As we pulled away, I saw Jane rush out of the bar and stand on the curb, shouting at us. I didn't ask Sage any questions.

Ten minutes later, we arrived at the top of a steep, sloping road that seemed to go nowhere except out into the vast darkness. I pulled over, cut the lights, and waited, but no one had followed us. The stars above and the city below shimmered, the white lights matching the glimmer in her eyes.

I scooted closer to her. "You're very attractive, Sage. You have the nicest lips. You're worth stealing," I murmured as my mouth moved onto hers.

She still tasted sweet, and her cheek burned hot against my clammy skin. We kissed hard, but I wanted much more, much faster. I broke away for a second and pulled her into the roomy back of the van.

On the mat I used for a bed, we got back to business. Sage groaned and nibbled my lip, sucking it into her wet mouth. I lost myself in her as our kisses became more and more audible. When her tongue snaked up and curved around my ear, I moved my hands to her breasts.

"I'm so glad you saved me from Jane," she blurted.

"Mmm," I responded absentmindedly, my hand poised at her nipple.

"From the minute I saw you, I knew this was meant to be."

"Mmm," I murmured again.

"I know we'll be together forever," she said, breathing heavily and pushing herself into me.

I could have ignored that comment as nothing but

the spontaneous overflow of raging hormones, but when she clamped onto me more tightly than a rusty vise and plunged her tongue almost to the recesses of my brain, I had to do a double-take. I felt like she would suffocate me with her tongue. I broke away.

"What is it, honey?" she asked, sitting up beside me.

Again those red lips, smeared crazily with lipstick now, beckoned. "Nothing," I said, shaking off a nervous feeling.

"I want you to be honest with me, Jacq," she announced. "I want to know exactly how you feel about me."

"Feel?" I repeated, raking a hand through my spiky hair. "What do you mean?"

"Just what I said, of course." Her cheeks flushed until I could see their color change even in the dim light.

"What do you mean? I like you, Sage. I already told you that."

"And that's it?"

"Well, sure it is. We barely know each other."

"What difference does that make? Don't you feel that there's some kind of connection between us? I picked up on it right away. That's why you came back to the store, isn't it? I waited a whole day to be sure."

I didn't bother to hide my exasperation. "Look, I thought you were a free spirit. I thought you wanted me the same way I wanted you."

Her face grew darker, and she crossed her arms across her chest. Her anger crushed those soft breasts flat. "I'm an Aquarius," she said huskily, "and yes, I do. All the same, I know when I'm in love."

"Whoa," I said, making a cutting motion in the air

with my hand.

"Aren't you looking for love, Jacq? Aren't you?" she demanded. Suddenly she brought her arms up and lifted her t-shirt. Two bare, perfectly formed breasts loomed in front of me. Their sweetness almost tempted me to lie.

I got hold of myself with an effort. "I think love is great, but it's not really something I'm into. I guess I prefer just to enjoy the moment." I could see her puffing up with emotion, so I quickly added, "Is that so bad?"

"You're a heartless beast," she sobbed, pushing the shirt down again. "Love is special. It's rare, and beautiful. How can you push it away?"

I shook my head again. This chick was getting nuttier by the minute. "We all have to make choices, Sage–or Nancy, I should say. Look at you and Jane. Did you love her, too? You obviously don't feel that way anymore. You chose not to."

"It's Sage, and it's none of your business." Her breathy voice rose with each word. "I'm not a slut if that's what you're implying."

"Hey, let's be realistic! I don't even have an apartment. I'm just passing through town, sleeping in my van. I showed up here because I was hoping that my ex could put me up for a few days."

"Jane told me about people like you," Sage–or maybe it really was Nancy this time–hissed. "I thought you had feelings for me. I had no idea you were such a user."

"Do you want me to take you home?"

By the light of the stars, I saw the droplets glisten on her face. "Make love to me, Jacq, please. I know you care about me, too, and you know it. You're just afraid of being hurt. But I'll never hurt you, I swear it."

"Sage, there's no way I can do that now." I knew I sounded cold, but I always preferred honesty. "I like you and find you attractive," I repeated, even though neither statement was really accurate by then. "I'm just not interested in love. I'm sorry if you got the wrong idea."

She looked away, and her hands shook slightly. "All right, take me home. I live just down the road."

We sat in silence throughout the short drive. The small Cape Cod she called home was blue with white shutters, and a new Chevy sat in the driveway. Jane, the woman from the bar, watched us from behind a curtain. I fought off the temptation to wave to her.

Sage glared at me and got out without saying goodbye, banging the van door behind her.

My body was still revved up from Sage's promise but lack of delivery. I caught a few hours of restless sleep and hit the road at daybreak.

Luci

The first week of April found me in upstate Vermont, renting a room in an old farmhouse. The place had once been a dairy farm, but had fallen on hard times and into the hands of some dyke vegetarians. They had since declared it "women's land" and turned it into a cross between a country co-op and a '70s-style hippie commune. Though the tye-dyed clothes and suds-free shampoo were a bit much for me, I liked the fact that I could work off part of the rent and eat home-grown produce for free. Under those conditions, I was willing to put up with the compost heap outside the front door and the chickens pecking outside my window at daybreak.

I met Luci on a warm Spring evening, just after the first buds appeared on the trees. I remember it was a Friday, because that's when I got turned down for the delivery job at Zio's Pizza. It wasn't that I was dead-set on a career hauling greasy cardboard boxes around some two-horse town, but my cash was getting low and I thought I should replenish my roll. From what I'd heard, Zio had been advertising for someone reliable for over a month. Just the same, he took one look at my masculine haircut and attire and turned me down without missing a beat. I've always preferred rejection to pretension, but the whole scene put me in a foul mood.

I got home at about eight that evening. Luckily, none of my nutritionally correct housemates were around, so I went straight to the fridge for one of the beers I kept stashed there. It had been raining outside, and my hands were wet and slippery as I fumbled with the bottle opener. For some reason, I couldn't seem to get the cap off. Memories of the fruitless job hunts, the homophobic stares, and the total lack of sex boiled over inside me.

I barked out a stream of filth and smashed the fucking bottle against the counter. Glass flew. A searing pain flashed up my arm, and my hand spurted bright red blood. Cursing again, I grabbed a towel and pressed it to my slashed palm. When my head began to swim, and the blood gushed faster, I started to get scared.

Fighting my panic, I tied an old washcloth around my hand, crawled into the van, and drove myself to the nearest emergency room. By the time I got there, the road was fading in and out, and the hypnotic glare of the parking lot lights blinded me. The van stuttered and wove around a series of parked cars, then screeched to an abrupt halt when its front bumper plowed into a light pole. Everything went black for a moment–or, more accurately, a dark, wet red.

Through this mental haze, I saw Luci for the first time. She stood at my side, helping the doctor–some man whose face I can't remember–stop the blood from spurting all over my clothes, the vinyl seats in the van, and the pavement. Somehow I ended up on a table in a pristine white room, surrounded by harsh light. The room was filled with people, but I only focused on Luci.

"She's losing a lot of blood," Luci said to the man, who bent down to work on me. I lost consciousness as soon as I felt the first prick of the stitches.

The next time I opened my eyes, Luci was holding my left hand. It surprised me that I wasn't in a lot of pain, especially when I looked at her face. She had cherubic, rosy cheeks unmarred by any make-up, soft pink lips, and grey eyes framed by small oval lenses. As my vision became less blurry, I began to see the fine lines around her mouth and eyelids. I guessed she was in her early forties.

Eventually everyone else left the room, leaving her to fuss around me.

"How did this happen to you, Jacquelyn?" she asked, somewhat sternly.

"Call me Jacq," I responded in a groggy voice. "Actually, it's kind of embarrassing. I was opening this beer bottle, and. . . ah. . . things just got out of control."

"I assume it wasn't the first one you'd ever opened," she said.

I stifled a smirk. "You got that right."

The doctor returned, and the two stepped away to confer privately. "The doctor says we can release you tonight," Luci said when she came back, "but first I need to know how you're going to get home. You realize your car isn't in any better shape than you are."

"I don't know." I shrugged, feeling defensive about my van. I hoped it wasn't too badly damaged or I'd be one step closer to homelessness. "I guess I'll hitchhike. It's only a few miles."

"You really are something." Luci shook her head. "I'll call you a cab."

"No, don't. I'll call a friend to get me," I lied.

The next time I saw her was out in the parking lot about an hour later. I was trying to repair my smashed left headlight with only one hand. I guess the steady stream of curses that escaped my lips attracted her attention.

Luci walked up to me with that same critical expression. "Look, I'm going home for the night. Would you like to come with me? I have a feeling it's the only way I'll be able to keep an eye on you–and prevent you from killing yourself."

Much as I hated to admit it, I was in no shape to refuse her–and I didn't really want to. On the way to her place, I found myself admiring the strawberry blonde curls she kept in a tight bun at the back of her neck, and the delicate backs of her small hands.

Eventually she led me into a large condo she apparently shared with no one. While I leaned against the foyer wall, feeling out of place, Luci unfolded the couch in the living room. Soon she had it all set up with crisp paisley sheets and fluffy pillows. I lay down, my head swimming, while Luci fixed us each a cup of tea. Finally she sat down in a rocking chair opposite me.

I took a sip of the tea, which tasted like herbal-scented dirt, fantasizing about the cold bottle of suds I never even got a taste of. "You don't happen to have a beer, do you?"

"Are you an alcoholic?" she asked, lifting a silky brow.

I found myself shifting uncomfortably in the bed. "You're pretty direct," I retorted. "My father is an alcoholic. I just like a beer every once in a while."

"Well, Jacquelyn–Jacq–let's get this out in the open. I don't have any alcohol in the house, and I wouldn't give you any if I did."

"Fine. I'm sorry I brought it up." A long silence stretched between us. I gulped the rest of my tea, trying not to taste it. I felt grubby and stressed out, not necessarily in that order. "Do you mind if I hop in your bath for a while?"

"You'll have to keep your arm dry."

"I can manage that."

She led me to the bathroom and ran the hot water while I fumbled with the buttons on my shirt. It was a lot harder than I'd expected with only one hand. When she saw me struggling, Luci stepped forward and helped me undo each one.

I felt kind of embarrassed about letting Luci undress me, but I figured that a nurse would think nothing of it. To my surprise, I heard her breathing became more and more ragged, and I caught her trying not to stare at my breasts. All the same, her eyes kept drifting back to them.

With aching slowness, Luci slipped off my underwear and stuck them, along with the rest of my things, in the washing machine in the corner. Turning back to me, she helped me into the tub with a strength I wouldn't have attributed to someone of her small stature.

I leaned my head against the polished tiles as the hot water made me more and more dizzy. For a moment, Luci's eyes traveled down my body as I lay floating. We were silent. Thick steam spread around us, blurring the room.

"Remember to keep your arm dry." Luci dipped her soft hands into the water beside me, wielding a bar of soap. I wrinkled my nose; to me it smelled like the tea. She lathered me slowly, starting with my breasts and moving around to my back. As she leaned over me, her cheek brushed my face.

I waited while Luci smeared my shoulders with scented foam and dabbed some under my arms. Her hands made hypnotic, circular motions on my pink skin while they slowly drifted back to my breasts. Each gentle touch drew the tension out through my pores.

Soon my nipples stood out straight and hard, anticipating her touch, but she rubbed her way around them without ever touching that dark, sensitive flesh.

I heard myself sigh with disappointment. She looked into my eyes, but said nothing. Her short nails skimmed my abs, then hesitated.

She avoided my pubic region the same way she had my breasts, even though it was begging for her fingers, and went instead to my thighs and shins. I closed my eyes as she rubbed the bottoms of my tired feet. I could feel every nerve there tingling, aching for her fingers to press down harder.

My body still throbbed as, without a word, Luci helped me out of the bath and toweled me down. She helped me into one of her old nightgowns, one that was much more feminine than anything I'd usually be caught dead in, and tucked me back into my fold-out bed. I lay there a long time after she'd retreated to her bedroom and closed the door. My slashed hand beat like a drum.

In the morning, I woke up to find Luci preparing a delicious breakfast. As I'd suspected, she took good care of herself. Rather than the sugary cereal and sludge-like instant coffee I usually wolfed down before heading out the door, Luci provided my grateful stomach with wheat toast, freshly squeezed orange juice, and gourmet coffee.

"I hope you weren't expecting Michelob," she said, eyeing me as I filled and gulped down a second cup.

I shook my head. "Before noon, it has to be Rolling Rock or nothing."

"You can tease me all you want, but I get very concerned when I see younger lesbians like you indulging in such self-destructive behavior."

"What do you mean, 'like me'? You don't know

anything about me." I put down my cup and thrust out my lower lip.

"You'd be surprised. I've been out a lot longer than you, Jacqueline, and I've seen it again and again. You try to hurt yourself just to prove something to the rest of the world. The sad thing is, the world doesn't care. Not even other lesbians care–not for the most part, at least. I was lucky enough to recognize early on what that whole bar culture was really all about. I knew I had a lot more to offer, both to myself and to other people. I have a feeling you do, too."

I stabbed my fork into the last hunk of mushroom-and-red-pepper omelet, downed it in a quick, angry swallow, and pushed my chair out from under the table.

"I've got to go," I said. "How far is it to the hospital?"

"About a mile and half," she said calmly. My outburst didn't seem to affect her at all, which ticked me off all the more.

"I'll walk back."

I stormed through the living room, past the sofa bed where I'd spent the night, and out the front door. I purposely didn't thank her.

"Come back to the emergency room in a few days and I'll check your stitches," Luci called after me. "Don't want them getting infected."

Luci didn't follow me, and it turned out to be a miserable walk back down the hill. I had to have my van towed for repairs, though at least the Triple A guy drove me back to the farm. My housemates gave me a little static about my not being able to do my chores, and the rest of the beers I had stashed in the fridge mysteriously disappeared.

I found out that it was going to take a week and three hundred dollars to get the van back, effectively marooning me at the farm. I spent the days cooped up in my room, brooding. Occasionally my housemates would bring up their latest tofu concoction and watch me wince while I ate it.

About a week later, Luci called to tell me that if I didn't come in to the hospital to get my stitches checked, she was going to send a doctor over to do a house call at my expense. I had to go in anyway, to show proof of indigence so they wouldn't slam me with a four-thousand-dollar bill. The next afternoon, I hitchhiked to the hospital.

Although she wore a self-satisfied grin when she saw me, Luci looked even cuter than I remembered. She'd done her hair differently, letting her light curls hang down to frame her intelligent eyes. "So you came after all," she said, undoing my bandages with a brisk, businesslike air. She looked relieved when she examined my wound.

"I guess all that alcohol flowing through my veins kept the cut sanitary," I taunted her.

All she did was shake her head. It seemed like she did that a lot. "You are one impossible young woman, Jacqueline."

"You're much too generous with your flattery."

"All right, let me show how nice I can be. Can I take you out for some pizza? You look thinner than when I last saw you."

I was going to refuse, but I just couldn't take another supper of braised dandelion leaves and undercooked barley. So I accepted her offer, even though I resented her bossy habits.

I hung around the hospital, reading magazines and browsing in the gift shop, until it was time for her to get off duty. Then I followed her down to her car without saying much. When we passed by the pizza place that had turned me down, I started to say something nasty about it. To my astonishment, she pulled over and parked right in front of it.

I wouldn't get out of the car. "No way, Luci. I'm not going in here. Those bastards wouldn't give me a job because I looked too butch."

Luci sighed and rested her hands on top of the steering wheel. For a minute I thought she was going to bang her head against it in frustration. But I should have known better than that.

"Jacq, you need to go of this attitude. You're never going to grow up if you don't face up to your own insecurity. Just let it roll off you. Besides, it's the only pizza joint in town, and they have the best pepperoni you've ever tasted."

I sat there for a while with my arms crossed and my lower lip thrust out. My stomach was already growling with hunger. "Fine," I finally grumbled. "Since you're buying, I won't argue."

We went in, ordered, and sat down at a booth. The guy who turned me down wasn't there, but to my shock there was this other butch tending the counter instead. So the bastard just liked her better than me. I didn't know whether to be happy or even more offended that the rejection had been totally personal. I sat there with a dark cloud covering my face until the pizza arrived. I had to admit that it looked and smelled delicious. The butch smiled when she set it down between us. I didn't dare ask for a beer.

"Why don't you let me get you some work at the hospital?" Luci asked, ignoring my scowl. She used a plastic knife to divide the pizza into six equal wedges. "That way I could keep an eye on you."

I was too hungry to argue at first, but once I got some hot pizza in me, I felt bolder. "Luci, you weird me out. I mean, if you're looking for someone to take care of, I'm not interested. I wouldn't mind sleeping with you, but all you want is a freakin' puppy dog."

"Don't be so hard on me," she snapped. "I was once a lot like you, you know. I just want to protect you from all the rejections and the unhappiness, something no one ever did for me."

The butch at the counter was now watching us with interest. I fell silent, munching another slice of pizza. Luci seemed to have finished. She just sat there and watched me. Her napkin and plastic utensils lay in a neat arrangement on her plate. Rather than waste the last few slices of pizza, she asked the butch to wrap it up for us.

"You can take the leftovers home with you," Luci told me as we drove out to the farm. "It's probably hard for you to cook with your hand like that."

"Yeah," I agreed. I was grateful to her for thinking of that. I'd been too angry.

Luci's face changed a little when I motioned for her to pull up at the farmhouse. "This is where you live?" she asked. Her voice was about an octave higher than it had been before.

"Well, it's not the Taj Mahal, but it's cheap and

comfortable," I shot back, not sure why I was so desperate to defend the place.

"I see," said Luci, stepping primly out of the car. She'd taken about five steps toward the house when the ramshackle kitchen door banged open and a squat, dark shape came streaking through the twilight at us. Luci screamed as powerful teeth wrenched the bag of pizza from her hand, nearly lopping off two of her fingers in the process.

The grizzled creature dashed past Luci's car, its hindquarters noisily impacting the fender, then skittered out into the road. We heard another crash, and one of my housemates dashed out in pursuit. "Alice B. Toklas! Naughty goat!" she screamed. "Come back here!"

"Hey!" I shouted after her. "Why is that damn thing in the kitchen again?" Luci stood frozen in shock and disbelief. Her hand was stretched out as if the bag of pizza were still in it. "Don't worry," I said, patting her rigid arm until she lowered it. "They don't like to keep her tied up. She's more annoying than dangerous." I figured she'd understand that I meant the goat and not my roommate.

When she'd recovered, I took her inside and served her a cup of tea at the rickety kitchen table. I could see that she was all too aware of the difference between the farmhouse and her own scrupulously tidy condo. Outside, the chickens scratched noisily at the crabgrass, and the wind blew foul-smelling dust through the window.

"I can't believe you never got gangrene from this place." She took a few sips of her tea and pushed the cracked mug to one side. She reached across the table and grasped my unbandaged hand. "Look," she blurted, "why don't you come and live with me for a while, until you find a cleaner place?"

I gaped at her. "Jesus, Luci, do you think I'm a damn nun? You want me to move in with you when you won't even kiss me?"

"Is that the problem?"

Suddenly, Luci stood up and came around the side of the table. I saw passion flare in her eyes as she bent and carefully wrapped her arms around me so as not to hurt my arm. She rubbed her cheek against mine, her skin soft and fragrant against my own.

Luci kissed me gently, reverently. There was something so intense about her desire for me that I felt myself get very wet.

I kissed her back more passionately and plunged my tongue between her perfect white teeth. She gasped and tugged her mouth away, then held me tightly, whispering, "Oh, baby, oh, baby." Her hand caressed my head. I never felt so loved, so comforted.

She made small kisses all over my face and neck while my body poured sweat. Standing on shaky legs, I pulled her into the next room and onto the couch. When I reached for the buttons of her blouse, though, she resisted me.

"No, Jacq, not here."

I was dumbfounded. "Are you fucking dysfunctional or just trying to torture me?"

Sitting up, she smoothed down her shirt. Her mouth became a tight, dark line. "You're too smart to use that kind of language, Jacqueline."

"You mean this kind?" I let out a string of epithets that made Luci's face go from bright pink to several shades of crimson.

She sighed. "Look, I just don't think we should have sex right away. Kissing you was–was wonderful. We need to go slower."

"Oh, I understand. No sex but you want me to fucking move in with you. What the fuck is your game, Luci?"

"Relax, please. You'll hurt your arm."

Just to annoy her, I gesticulated wildly at the door. I thought I could feel my new bandage coming loose. "Get out. I'm not in the mood to be your daughter."

"Fine. I'm going." She heaved herself to her feet. Halfway across the room, she stopped and looked back at me. "Promise me you won't drink."

"Mind your own goddamn business. I'm still a free human being as far as I know, and I'll do what I damn well please!"

"I'm sorry. I think you are unbelievably attractive. I want you very much–but I just think we should wait."

I turned my back on her. "Goodbye," I said without glancing back.

She left, and I didn't see her again until I went to get my stitches out. She waited outside the examination room while the same male doctor attended to me, and she was still there when I came out. I was too angry to talk to her, though.

I got even more pissed off when the State Health Department showed up to do a surprise inspection on the farm. My roommates were in tears for days, and one of them stashed the goat in her bedroom for fear it would be kidnapped. While we were waiting for the official verdict, Luci called again and asked if I'd changed my mind. I began to wonder if she'd squealed on the co-op just so I'd give in to her. But I wasn't going to let her tell me what to do. I could take care of myself.

The Department of Health closed down the farm, giving us a week to vacate. The next day, I cleaned the last of my cash from my sock drawer and went down to get my van out of hock. Before I could count out the rumpled bills, the guy at the garage told me it was all taken care of and gave me back the keys.

When I got home, Luci called and offered the same solution to my difficulties. "Move in here," she coaxed. "I'll take care of you."

I asked her not to call back and hung up. Three days later, I packed up and moved on.

Emily

On the outskirts of Portland, Maine, I finally found a job in construction, which I liked because I could wear anything I wanted. I moved into an apartment with a bunch of women who'd stuck up an ad in a supermarket. They were all het, which made no difference to me, though I got a little sick of them bringing in all these sleazy guys to screw.

There was one other woman on the construction site. Emily was long, lean, and attractive, though I figured she was straight because of her long hair and the fact that she had a kid. She'd been doing construction work ever since she dropped out of high school eleven years earlier.

One afternoon on our lunch hour, she told me that she'd just bought a house.

"I've been saving for years," she bubbled, "and it's the nicest place I've ever lived in. Of course, it's not brand new or anything, and it's not in the best neighborhood. But it's got three bedrooms, and I'm going to finish the basement myself."

I nodded. "Construction know-how has its advantages."

"Sure does," she answered. "You oughta come over and see the place."

"Sure," I said. "Thanks for the offer."

I figured that she'd just said it to be nice, and nothing would really come of it. But Emily seemed to be turning something over in her mind. "You know, I could pay you for your time if you wanted to come over and help me out this weekend. I don't have a lot saved up, but I could get it done a lot faster."

"I won't take your money, Emily. But I'd be happy to help you."

She seemed relieved. Whether it was because I'd refused payment or agreed to help her at all, I couldn't tell. "Great! Dakota is going to her father's place this weekend, so I can make you a home-cooked supper afterward."

Saturday turned out to be a sunny, breezy day, and I found myself looking forward to giving her a hand. Her house was a run-down Victorian wedged tightly between two others. Though her neighbors were obviously poor, they seemed to take pride in their houses, decorating their porches with delicate wind chimes and boxed flowers. It reminded me a little of the neighborhood I'd grown up in.

Little Dakota opened the door the second I knocked, like she'd been waiting for me. She wore long sunny braids with two bows at the bottoms and a freckly smile. While she sized me up, she wagged her head to and fro and gnawed her bubble gum like a calf chewing its cud.

"Are you a boy or a girl?" she demanded.

Emily opened the door just as I was about to put the little brat in her place. She looked especially attractive with her paint-splattered overalls and a red bandanna tying her long hair back. The color brought out the cornflower blue of her eyes, which widened at her daughter's rudeness. Exasperated, she grabbed Dakota's wrist and pulled her into the house.

"Dakota, that's enough! I told you if you want to stay, you'll have to behave. Please come in, Jacq. Have a seat until I get Dakota taken care of."

I followed them into the house. I watched Emily scold her in the hallway while I sat in the living room. I have to admit, the two of them looked adorable, glaring at one another to see whose will would win out. "Go outside and play," Emily finally growled.

"No, I won't! I waited the whole morning to talk to Jacq!" Soon she stomped back into the living room, flinging her slight body onto my lap. "Do you like to play catch or Barbies?"

"Well, if I had to choose it would be catch."

"I knew you were fun! I just knew it!" she chirped. "Wait right here!"

In moments, Dakota dragged every type of ball I

could have imagined in a netted bag, thumping down the stairs before Emily could stop her. We ended up playing a little with each one, and I have to say the kid charmed me with her tomboy ways until Emily brought her over to the neighbor's.

"Sorry about that," Emily apologized. "Her dad didn't show up for visitation. He's not the most reliable guy. I hope she didn't get on your nerves."

"Actually, she reminded me of myself when I was that age. Maybe I just haven't changed all that much."

Emily sighed. "I spoil her too much. But she's always so sure of herself that I just give in. Did your mom do the same thing?"

"My mom didn't have much choice."

"Neither do I. Well, now that I've taken care of her for a while, why don't we get to work?"

"Okay," I agreed.

We got right to the dry-walling. "This is a cute place you've got, Emily," I complimented her.

"Thanks, I love it," she responded with a big grin, passing me the heavy bucket with a look of gratitude. "It's really nice of you to help me out."

"Oh, I think it's fun, really. I love building stuff and fixing up houses and all."

"Mmm. . . . Jacq, do you mind if I ask you something personal?"

"Shoot."

"Have you heard the guys, you know, talking about me behind my back at the site? Did they ever tell you anything about. . . um. . . about me and Dakota's father?"

"Never. Why would they?"

"Oh, okay. I just wondered."

We worked in silence for a while. When I glanced over at her, she was biting her lip. "Have they been bothering you, Emily?"

"Well, I don't know. The other day, Pete and a few of the others started making some comments about how I got my ex-boyfriend fired. They think it was my fault, but it was really because he's a damn drunk."

I stopped what I was doing and watched her face intently. "Don't let them get to you."

"You don't know how guilty I feel," she went on, as though she hadn't heard me. "I tried to get him to stop, but he kept on drinking, and one time he even hit me. And his friends still blame me." I heard a catch in her voice. She kept working to distract herself, not looking at me any more.

"I know what you're going through," I said.

She paused. "Your boyfriend was like that?"

"Boyfriend? No boyfriends for me, thanks. No, I was talking about my father."

"Really? Did he ever hurt you?"

"He tried to once, but I hit him back and he never did it again. After that, he kept to himself, sitting in the back room with a bottle in his hand. It was like he became invisible. "

"What about your mom?"

I shrugged. "She was kind of invisible, too."

"That must have been so hard for you," she said, and I saw tears gather in the corners of her eyes.

"Well, it taught me to be independent, you know. Anyway, those guys shouldn't take it out on you. You can get them in big trouble, and they know it."

"I was a little intimidated at the time." She licked

her lips.

"Don't worry. I'll be your witness if you need me."

She reached over and gave my arm a squeeze. "Thanks."

By suppertime, we were both beat. Emily warmed up some chicken cacciatore and brought out a bottle of red wine. It was a nice dinner. Afterward, we sat on the couch, polishing off the wine and watching TV.

Emily looked really cute with her bangs falling over her forehead and her eyes half closed, leaning her head back on the old plaid sofa. I wasn't thinking much about it when I reached out and stroked her face. My fingers traced the outline of her distinctive cheekbone.

She sat up and blinked at me like I'd scared her. I immediately regretted what I'd done. "I'm sorry, Emily. I didn't mean to offend you. You just looked so sweet, and I. . . I'm sorry." Nervously I checked my paint-spattered watch. "It's late. I've got to go."

"I. . . you just startled me," she replied in a sleepy voice. But she didn't object to my leaving. "Hey, I really appreciate your help."

"Oh, forget it. Thanks for supper. See you Monday," I called out and closed the door behind me.

I left red-faced and wondering if she'd ever be friends with me again. Well, it wasn't the first time I'd gotten carried away with a straight chick, and I was pretty sure it wouldn't be the last.

The van broke down on Sunday, so I didn't have time to worry about Emily until late Monday afternoon at the site, when I spotted Pete following her to the row of blue porta-potties. I hurried over and found that the guys had cornered her.

"Pete, what's the trouble?" I asked.

"No trouble," he spat. "We were just kidding around. It's none of your damned business, dyke."

Emily was leaning against the shed, her arms wrapped across her chest. "You guys need to lay off me," she said. "Just leave me alone. Joe got fired because he nearly dropped a girder from two floors up. It wasn't my fault he was drunk on the job!"

"You coulda helped him," Pete insisted. The other men nodded in agreement. "Coulda got him sobered up."

"I couldn't stop him from drinking. I tried!"

Pete just glared, so I stepped between them. "I think Emily made herself very clear, Pete. Joe had the problem, not her."

"You just don't get it," Pete fumed. "First she kicked him out of the house and hit him up for half his wages to support that kid of hers. Then she turned around and took away his fuckin' job. What the hell is he supposed to do now? He can't even afford to find work now!"

"Probably couldn't anyway," one of Pete's goons commented. "Too many dykes around to take his place."

"Yeah, and in more ways than one," another of them guffawed, leering at Emily.

Furious, I stepped up to Pete and lifted my hands in front of me. I wasn't threatening him, not exactly, but I think he got the idea that I could take care of myself–not to mention Emily and Dakota, if it came to that.

"Listen up," I said. "You assholes need to mind your own business. If you give Emily any more trouble around here, you'll have me to deal with. You might just find yourself propping up the bar with your old buddy instead of having your own job to get to."

Pete's hands snapped into fists. "Fine, we're going," he mumbled. "But I still say you shoulda done som'thin'."

"How about an apology?" I demanded.

"Whatever," Pete said, and they ambled away as the whistle blew for quitting time. Emily was still shaking, but she also looked relieved.

"Thanks, Jacq. That was really great of you."

I was still seething. "Don't worry about it. Guys like that really piss me off sometimes."

"Well, I thought you were great." She averted her gaze for a minute, like she was going shy on me. "Listen, you want to come over to my place for a beer?" she offered. "I can give you a lift home afterward."

Since my van was still on the fritz, I accepted.

We drove over to her house in silence. Dakota was still next door at her babysitter's, and the house was quiet and cool inside. Emily rummaged in the fridge for two beers, then turned to me and swallowed. "Hey, I'm sorry for the other night."

"Nah, I'm the one who's sorry. I know you're straight. I just got a little buzzed and lost myself somehow." I laughed uncomfortably. "You are very attractive, and I'm only flesh and blood, you know–but I hope you don't think I helped you out just to sleep with you. I want us to be friends. Really." I stopped when I felt myself rambling on.

"I'm glad you're my friend, Jacq," she commented suddenly.

"Me, too."

We drank our beers on the sofa. We didn't say much until Emily unexpectedly reached out and gave me a big hug.

"Jacq, thanks for today. I felt so much better with you there."

"I told you, it's okay." Emily smelled of the construction site and the sweat she'd accumulated from working hard all day. I couldn't have been more turned on. When she finally pulled away, her face lingered in front of mine for a second, her full lips only inches from my own. I had to physically will myself not to kiss her.

Then she was hugging me again and sobbing quietly on my shoulder. "I don't know why I'm crying. I just got freaked by the way they wouldn't leave me alone. It was so weird."

"It's okay," I responded, stroking her soft hair. "Maybe you should take a self-defense class. You'd get a lot more confident."

Her tears ran down my neck and pooled in the crease between my breasts. For a long moment she looked up at me, our eyes locked. Her breathing became heavier, my own more shallow. Emily moved closer to my lips. I couldn't stop myself. Our mouths met gently, then moved away and waited.

After a moment's pause, she leaned over and kissed me hard, pushing her body against mine. I responded by pushing open her dry lips and exploring the surface of her wet tongue. It touched, caressed, and ignited my own.

"Oh, Jacq, just hold me," she said, lifting her face

away and leaning her head against my shoulder. I held her for a long time, stroking her back.

I don't know how far things might have gone, but just then we heard the screen door slam. Emily jerked upright in my arms with an almost guilty look on her face as Dakota raced into the living room.

"Hey, you didn't tell me Jacq was going to be here!" she chirped. She flew past her mother and landed right in my lap, wrapping her little arms around my sweaty neck and giving me a possessive squeeze. "Jacq, are you going to stay for dinner? Can she, Mom?"

"Well, I suppose so. But maybe you should ask her if she wants to first."

"Please, Jacq? Please. Please?" Dakota bounced up and down on my legs and nearly hugged the breath out of me. When I could get my vocal chords to work again, I agreed.

Dakota wouldn't stop talking to me while the three of us wolfed down burgers, French fries, and soda. This time, Emily didn't interrupt her. She just kept looking at me and then at the kid with this weird, almost sappy expression on her face.

Finally, I wiped my mouth and stood up. Before I was out of the kitchen, Dakota hopped off her chair, ran right up to me, and blurted out, "Jacq, why don't you stay here all the time? My mom really likes you—and I do, too."

This time Emily did intercede. Her face was red as she sent Dakota off to the backyard to play.

"I'm sorry about her, Jacq. It's just that since her father left, we don't have many friends over. She gets a little carried away."

"Don't worry about it," I said, then shoved my hands in my pockets. "Guess I ought to get going now."

"I can drive you home, remember?"

I shrugged. "That's okay. I'll just walk to the bus stop."

She seemed a little sad, but she didn't argue with me. "See you at work, then."

"Bye," I said. I went out the front door so Dakota wouldn't see me leave. For some reason, I didn't want to disappoint her.

For the rest of the summer, Emily and I stayed close, but I never went back to her house or kissed her again. I figured she was really bi–she did have a kid, after all–and I decided not to stick around. She was kind of hurt when I decided to move on, but she understood.

Dex

By fall, I'd had enough of Maine, with its cold, unpredictable weather and people. I thought I'd find something better somewhere else. So I packed my stuff and headed south.

About two hours into the drive, I glanced at the side of the road and spotted this woman about my age, wearing the same butch haircut I did. When she saw me through the windshield, she smiled and waved at me like she needed a ride.

Normally, I wouldn't bother stopping, but it was a crisp October evening, and there she was with this knapsack and a worn J. Crew barn jacket, looking right at me, so I stopped and rolled down the passenger-side window. Her eyes had the look of someone who hadn't had a good night's sleep, dark and hollow. Her lips were parched from the wind, and she rubbed her hands together.

"I'm heading south. Does that suit you?" I called down to her.

"Anywhere's fine."

"Hop in," I told her, and that was the first time I saw Dex smile. It was a tired smile, but one of relief and strength. Two shallow dimples framed her mouth, and thread-like laugh lines tugged at the corners of her sharp amber eyes.

She stretched out next to me with a sigh. I was curious about her, but I didn't want to pry. So there we were, riding the long strip of highway, looking straight ahead without talking.

We had driven about ten miles before I decided to break the ice. "Would you like some decaf? I made a whole thermos of the stuff."

"Sure," she answered.

I pointed to the thermos under her feet. She poured some into the screw-off cup, took a sip, and licked her lips. "That's the best decaf I've ever had."

"Well, glad you like it. I can't take the caffeine. It makes me hyper and I'm already that way by nature."

"I actually haven't had any real coffee since I was with Jan. She always did the cooking. I just fixed her computer, which broke down fairly often."

"Oh, you work with computers?" I was intrigued, and a little disappointed, because I'd pegged her as someone who worked with her hands. I just assumed she was like me for some reason.

"Yeah, I do computer tech work. I didn't go to college, but I still got better pay than Jan, even though she had an M.A. in Biology from Tufts. She lives in Cambridge now with a very nice woman. We had three happy years, one pretty bad one, and the last was terrible."

"That's too bad," I said, but inside I was glad she was free.

"I guess so, but I'm okay with it now. I'm so glad to be on my own again."

"I know what you mean. By the way, do you have somewhere you'd like me to drop you?"

"No, I don't have anywhere in mind, wherever you happen to stop will be fine. Does that shock you?"

I laughed. "Nah, I'm kind of a drifter myself. I like to feel free, too, not tied to anyone or any place."

"I'm with you. I feel like those five years with Jan are a blur. But listen, any time you get the urge to be by yourself, just let me know. I won't be offended."

Somehow that short ride Dex needed turned into a full-blown vacation. We traveled down and across the state, stopping at every national park and rocky beach we found. We climbed scenic trails side by side and sat on the precipices in silence, just looking down at rolling hills and twisting rivers. Sometimes we got so close to the edge it felt like we could have taken wing and glided to the rocky ground below.

Day after day, adventure found us. Rabid racoons and moose as big as my van stared at us as we sipped imported beer and bullshitted about life. Skittish hikers and lightning-fast snakes hid from us when we blew smoke at them. At night, we curled up in separate sleeping bags and fell asleep in the middle of a conversation. But I'd never had so much fun.

One time, vicious storm winds sent us running for the van, which rocked on its wheels like a sailboat in the eye of a hurricane. Rain mixed with ice pelted my windshield so hard that we huddled in the back of the van, afraid the glass might shatter.

Neither one of us was particularly afraid or needed comfort. It was just the moment, the feelings that swept us away. Before I knew exactly what was happening, I felt her warm breath against my left cheek, quite close to my mouth. It was like nothing I'd experienced before–gentle, slow, enticing.

I turned my face to hers and her lips melted against mine. That first kiss burst through me like wildfire. I placed my hand on her breast. Dex gasped and pulled me on top of her, peeling my flannel shirt off me. Wordlessly her mouth clamped down on my hardened nipples, worshiping my rigid pink buds with her tongue.

Groaning, I lifted her own top over her head. She barely paused as she slipped her arms free, still sucking my nipples like she'd never tasted a woman before. I could feel myself getting wet as she nudged her face lower, gliding her tongue along the valley between my breasts and down to my pelvis.

"Yes, yes," I murmured. I arched my back like a cat.

We rolled over on the sleeping bag, and Dex confidently covered my body with hers. Together, we squirmed out of the rest of our clothes, and I felt an incredible freedom when she finally slipped my soaking panties down my legs and off. My clit pounded with a need I'd never known I had as her impatient mouth closed around my drenched bush.

She flicked her tongue harder and harder against my engorged clit, then guided one of my hands into the creamy fuzz between her legs. Her blazing pussy seemed to swallow me up, and she moaned and thrashed her hips when I eased my first two fingers inside her fiery cavern. She was so wet that my hand was immediately soaked with her stickiness. Hot shivers wracked both our bodies.

Sooner than I would have liked, I felt my own climax approach, swelling through me with a thunderous pressure that matched the storm outside. I howled as an explosive orgasm blazed through my torso and legs. When I heard Dex moan and felt her start bucking against my body, I began plunging my fingers into her much faster. My thumb buffed her clit as fast as I could.

She drank and sucked and tongued me until I cried out incoherently, spasming, freezing, and spasming again. I felt her wet pussy closing around my fingers like a fist, gripping and squeezing them until my muscles ached. Finally she lifted her head back and let out a shriek of ecstasy.

"Oh! Oh, yes! Don't stop! That's fantastic!" she wailed. Her screams gave way to a series of low, inarticulate yelps as her orgasm tore through her. Her skin turned the color of fire, and her nipples jabbed the air like twin spearpoints.

My hand still inside her, we fell back together. Exhausted and sweating, we used our discarded clothing for pillows and snuggled up side by side. Dex lay almost totally still, panting and looking at me, stroking my head while I rested it on her moist pubes.

When I could breathe normally again, I hoisted myself up and wriggled my tongue along the damp but sweet-smelling skin at her neck. My nub was still throbbing with the aftermath of the magnificent climax she had given me.

"Oh, that was so good," I whispered in her ear. "So good."

Her response was to flash a smile that intoxicated me more than a whole case of beer. My response was to make love to her again.

We ended up spending the rest of the fall in an old house in Northampton, making love and jogging at the track at Smith, then going back to the apartment and making love again. My lips, fingers, and palms all had Dex's special scent imbedded in them. Sometimes, when she wasn't around, I'd rub my hands all over my lips and breasts, pretending that she was there with me. Dex's smell was my personal aromatherapy.

Her every touch seared my core. I lost my sense of self inside her. All I wanted to do was eat her, drink her, and suck her until she came over and over.

There was no denying that I was in love.

All through the autumn, I kept myself from saying those terrifying words. But come November, Dex said she wanted to go back to Boston. I wanted to beg her to stay, but I knew better.

Finally, a few days before she was set to leave, we were sitting on the old screen porch of the house. The weather was getting colder every day, and the damp air tasted of snow. Pretty soon there'd be nothing to do but stay in the house, snuggle under soft blankets, and watch the drifts pile up

My skin prickled. I stared vacantly down the oak-lined street and clenched my jaw so tightly that a pain spread though my head. Dex noticed, and frowned.

"It's not like you to be tense. Did something happen today?"

"No, I was just–I mean, I took Blondie to the vet for her shots today, remember?"

"Oh, yeah." Blondie, our newly adopted feline companion, nuzzled our legs as we spoke. Dex stopped massaging me and petted the cat, and Blondie purred softly.

"Well, Blondie seems to have recovered. Now let's see what we can we do for her mom." A glint of lust sparked in Dex's playful eyes. "I'll massage your back, and you'll feel better," she offered. I turned around obediently. She started to massage my shoulders, kneading deeply.

Her touch ignited me. I turned and brushed my kiss against her slim neck and maneuvered my right hand to her breast. Dex sighed contentedly when I lifted my face and entered her luscious mouth with my tongue. She kissed me harder, and her hands found my aching nipples under my sweatshirt.

She flicked them back and forth, took a breath, and muttered, "You are so fucking sexy, Jacq. I can't stop thinking about you."

The warmth of her hand went right to my heart. "Oh, it's so good to be with you, baby, so good," I responded. My other hand was under her shirt now, making soft scratches along her spine, something I knew turned her on.

Dex bit my neck and sucked hard. I felt the hickey immediately form, but she'd already moved on to make another. I sank against her, closing my eyes. Her touch spoke to me even though she wouldn't express her love. Her tongue licked me when her words were scarce. But I didn't care about words. All that mattered were the feelings that coursed through me, keeping me endlessly on fire for her. It had become so easy for me to anticipate her next feeling or thought, to know just how to please her. This is love, I thought.

I understood her well enough to know that any note of desperation on my part would send her running in the opposite direction. I knew I should keep quiet and wait until she asked me to come with her, but I didn't have the luxury of time. My heart was beating a mile a minute.

That was when I lost my head and broke from her. Our lips were millimeters apart. I could feel her heat on my face.

I took a deep breath and just blurted it out.

"Dex, I need to tell you that I love you." Sweat was pouring down the back of my neck. I was self-conscious of my face, my tone, my every limb. The thought of losing her deadened me inside. "Let me go back to Boston with you."

The moment my words registered on her, Dex jerked her head back and dropped her hands from my body. At the same time, Blondie jumped onto my lap and nuzzled my breast with her soft head. I stroked her yellow-orange fur over and over. My hands shook, and she knew something was wrong. Her little heart thumped faster, her tail stood up, and she eyed Dex suspiciously.

"Jacq, where is this coming from?" Dex asked and stood up. Her sharp gaze never left my face. Blondie scowled at her and hunched her thin shoulders as if she were preparing to pounce. Noticing, Dex bent over to pet her. "C'mon, Blondie."

Blondie lashed out and scratched her. Long bloody streaks appeared on her forearm, and Dex yelped and grasped herself in pain. "Shit, what's the matter with you, Blondie? I was just going to pet you."

I admit I was gloating a little when Dex went in the kitchen to wash off. I sat there and stroked the cat.

"Come in here," she called. I got up, and Blondie ran off after a squirrel.

I dragged myself into the kitchen. The screen door slammed. The harsh flourescent light flickered over our heads. Dex sat at the table, looking pale and vulnerable. Her bangs hung over her eyes. I stood next to her and stroked her misshapen hair. "Are you okay?"

"I'm all right," she answered, staring into space.

"I've been wanting to tell you this ever since you said you wanted to go back," I said quietly. "But I was afraid."

"I'm surprised," Dex answered, shaking her head.

"I thought you might be."

I went to the fridge and got us both beers, but I didn't sit down next to her. The brew tasted bitter. Dex took a sip and then splashed some on her bloodied arm. She winced with pain. "You always said you were a free spirit."

"I am. I'm making a choice," I said.

Puzzled, Dex searched my face for some kind of understanding.

"I tried not to say it. I tried not to need you so much."

She stood up and shielded herself with her hands.

"Oh, Jacq. What do you want me to say? I have to be on my own. I need to be free. You need to be free, too. You told me so, damn it!"

The tears rolled down my face. I moved to her side, ready in case she wanted to reach out for me. "You're hurting me," I sobbed. "Doesn't that matter to you, Dex?"

Dex lowered her voice, but her hands stayed where they were. "Jacq, when we met I told you I wanted to be free–just like you. I haven't changed. I never saw you changing."

"I have changed, even if you didn't see it," I answered.

She shook her head. "Jacq, it's not like we won't see each other. I'll come back–eventually."

My eyes burned with rage, my hands trembled. "You bitch!" I whispered. "You're not listening to me at all!"

Dex's eyes narrowed. "Don't look at me like I've fucking misled you. You told me you were a drifter, too. I thought that's what kept us connected." She raised her clenched hands above my face. "You're clinging, you're clinging. I never thought you would."

I had no answer for her, nor would the right explanation make a difference. I took off and ran for a long time. Nothing mattered to me any more.

When I got back, Dex had gone. I went upstairs and sat on the bed until I heard a noise somewhere in the house.

"Dex?" I called out, rushing down the stairs. My voice carried down the darkened hallway. But only Blondie sat there, staring at me and meticulously licking her fur.

I went back to the sagging feather bed and lay alone in our chilly rented house. As winter quietly approached, I waited.

Sculpting Her Passion

She walked into *La Place* in Stamford with a bounce in her step and a flush on her cheeks. I imagined I could smell the spring breeze in her hair as she crossed the foyer toward me. Her buoyant aura and almost self-conscious smile captivated the artist in me. Though we'd come together for purely professional reasons, I recognized her as the sort of woman whose friendship could bring great pleasure to others.

When she approached me and extended her hand warmly, I took the opportunity to study her in more detail. Her nut-brown hair was a bit too long, in need of a styling. She was a head taller than I, and maybe fifteen pounds heavier, but of course I'd always been too thin. Her eyes betrayed fine laugh lines that added character to her round, smooth face, and the reflection in those lucid amber orbs redirected my gaze inward. In those deep pools, I saw the image of myself as she must have seen me: urbane, well-dressed, but with something missing inside. I knew that what it was had been missing for too long.

"I'm Brooke," she said, though of course I already knew that. What I still wasn't sure about was how she'd gotten wind of my new sculpture studio, and why she'd decided to profile my work for the Sunday newspaper's Arts and Leisure section. It was my first interview of any kind, but I tried to come off like a seasoned pro as I returned her handshake and suggested that we adjourn to the hotel café. There, over cappuccino, what I had expected would be a dull afternoon, with me trying to explain my sculpture without sounding narcissistic or inane, turned into the kind of conversation that quickened the pulse in my head. By the time we headed back to my studio, where her staff photographer was due to meet us, I found myself thinking about my techniques, my perspective, even the whole way I looked at my art, in an entirely new way.

When we parted, I was exhausted, but felt confident she really understood and liked my work–not to mention me. I was flying so high that I guess I should have expected a letdown when the article came out the following week. Maybe all that attention had swelled my head, but when I read the piece, I was stunned to find no evidence of the connection I'd felt to her. Her words were slick, glossy, and so impersonal that I had to double-check the byline to be sure she was the one who had written it.

Maybe I had just been another job to her, I thought, relegating the paper to the back of my file drawer. I pushed all thoughts of Brooke from my mind and got back to work on the project I'd started. It was an abstract rendition of a woman's body, sort of like Brooke's but softened by my half-acknowledged fantasies of her. I couldn't help thinking it was one of the finest pieces I'd ever done. At least I'd have that, I consoled myself.

I would have left things there, but a few days later, Brooke called to ask how I'd liked her piece.

"It was all right," I said. My guarded tone didn't fool her for a moment.

"Okay, so I can tell it wasn't exactly what you expected. I was afraid this might happen when you said it was your first interview. I didn't want to say anything at the time, but sometimes it's necessary to put a more general spin on things when you're writing for the layman."

"A commercial spin, you mean." I bit off the words a bit more harshly than I'd intended. I expected Brooke to react defensively, but to my surprise she laughed. I wasn't sure if that made me feel better or more angry.

"Look, Val, I loved your work. And I'm telling you that this article will boost your sales like crazy. If it doesn't, I will personally make sure you get a free full page ad in next week's Sunday edition. How's that? Are you still annoyed with me?"

"Well, I never really was," I muttered. Actually, my vehement reaction had begun to puzzle even me. I was a little embarrassed to admit to myself how much I'd wanted to impress Brooke, and I felt disappointed that I hadn't done just that.

She ended up inviting me to lunch that very day. She bought, and I apologized for my hypersensitivity. Before long, we were chatting like old friends, and I felt that same nervous energy buzzing through my veins. When the meal was over, she suggested that we get together again to scout museums or attend the theater. I quickly agreed.

During the month that followed, Brooke and I began to go on regular outings, and I was forced to apologize to her as I noticed that my sales shot up, just as she'd predicted. After a short time, I realized that I felt much more for her than friendship, but didn't know how she might react to that kind of interest. Despite the time we'd spent together, I hadn't learned much at all about her private life. Yet desire ate at me until I could hardly stand the uncertainty.

One Saturday morning, I woke up with the aftereffects of an exquisitely erotic dream still coursing through my body. As I lay on my futon, idly caressing my erect, aching nipples, I decided it was time I broached the subject openly.

An hour later, I knocked at her door holding a bag of breakfast pastries and flavored gourmet coffee. Brooke answered wearing a white terry robe, clearly just out of the shower. Her skin glowed, the curve of her generous cleavage swelling against the soft fabric as a veil of steam wafted from her.

When she recognized me, her eyes widened in her flushed face. "Val!"

"Thought I'd surprise you with breakfast," I said, holding up the bag. I was about to say something else when a flash of movement inside her apartment caught my eye. Suddenly, an exquisite blonde stepped up behind Brooke, wearing nothing but a smirk and a peach-colored bath towel.

I felt like I'd just been belted in the stomach. "Oh, I'm sorry." I gulped. "I had no idea you had company. I'll. . . ah. . . we can get together another time."

As I stood there cursing myself, Brooke blushed more deeply and slid her arms around herself, as embarrassed as if she'd been cheating on me. My thoughts raced desperately. Was this blonde interloper a lover, an ex, or just a weekend indulgence? I was even more confused when I turned to leave, and Brooke grabbed my arm.

"Val, don't go. I'd like you so meet someone," she said. I didn't protest as she drew me inside and closed the door. "This is Mika," she said. Her tone explained everything and nothing at the same time.

I nodded politely and attempted to smile. Mika responded by tilting her head and flashing a row of perfect teeth that were probably the only straight thing about her.

I fought back an intense urge to smack that angry grin right off of her admittedly lovely face. Instead, I smiled inwardly at the notion that Mika perceived me as a rival for Brooke's attention.

Maybe she knew more about Brooke's feelings for me than I did, but that wouldn't be saying much. I concentrated on getting through this three-sided misery, vowing to rip the pink triangle off my bumper when I got downstairs.

In the meantime, Brooke had taken out a ceramic dish and was arranging crullers and danishes in a neat circular pattern. She lay the plate on a table in the middle of her white, spotless kitchen. When she noticed that I'd brought only two capped paper cups, she bent hastily over the coffee pot.

The whole time, Mika just sat there, her fluffy towel half undone. She picked up a pastry and nibbled delicately at it, like she wanted to show me what a beautiful body she had–and planned to keep. In the end, I was more disappointed in Brooke's taste in insecure women than I was threatened by this half-naked temptress.

However, the whole scenario of Brooke bedding her instead of me ruined my appetite. I quietly sipped my coffee from a "Connecticut Is For Lovers" mug and waited for Brooke to create some type of socially acceptable atmosphere. For once though, she seemed at a loss for words. In the end it was Mika who began chattering endlessly about the doctoral thesis she was writing, a study of indigenous people from some remote jungle of Central Africa.

It dawned on me that Brooke's punishment for choosing Mika over me would be spending more than five minutes at a time with her. I guessed Mika must be a damn good lover for Brooke to put up with such arrogance. But pretty soon the idea of Mika making love to Brooke incensed me to the point where I just couldn't sit there any more without shaking things up a bit. I waited for a lull in the one-sided conversation, which came when Mika bent to take another birdlike nibble from her doughnut. I set down my mug and looked from her to Brooke.

"So," I asked outright, "are you two a couple, or are you just having a lowdown, dirty affair?"

Coolly Mika licked the chocolate glaze from her perfectly manicured fingers. "Is this where I'm supposed to ask, 'why don't you join us, Val, and find out?'"

"Don't flatter yourself, Mika," I retorted. My face felt hot. "I'm not that desperate."

The color in Brooke's cheeks had risen as well, but this time she made no attempt to stop me as I pushed my chair back from the table, got up, and walked out.

During the next few days, she left several messages on my machine, asking me to call her, but I didn't bother. I had no intention of competing for her affections. I knew I had no right to think that she had any special loyalty to me, but my feelings had become so strong that I couldn't be her friend any more. Eventually, she stopped calling.

I plunged headlong into my sculpting and dated only occasionally, vowing to be more up front about my feelings for the next woman that came along. The ones I met were terrific in bed, but not very stimulating out of it. I remained single, and vowed to keep it that way.

Suddenly, after a whole year without any communication from her, I received a phone call from the newspaper Brooke worked for. I listened, astonished, as the stranger on the other end offered me a commission to make a sculpture for their office courtyard. I had a strong feeling she was behind it, and my instincts told me to run. Still, the project was so lucrative I couldn't turn it down. Soon I was hard at work in my studio, all those feelings of intimacy flooding back as images of her face and soft body throbbed in my head. The fact that I'd been given a second chance wasn't lost on me. This time, if the opportunity presented itself, I planned to let Brooke know exactly how I felt about her. Then I'd step back and let her make an informed choice for herself.

It took about a week for her to show up. She came to my studio unannounced and sneaked behind me while I was concentrating on the job at hand. When she cleared her throat, I looked up and saw a much different Brooke than the one I remembered. Her lean body was encased in black silk harem pants and a matching mesh blouse over a sleek red shell. Her dark hair was much shorter, framing a face that seemed to glow with a new sophistication and confidence.

For the moment, I was struck speechless.

She spoke first. "Val, don't be angry that I didn't let

you know I was coming. I was across the street buying something and couldn't resist stopping in to see the sculpture." Her gaze swept over the twisted hunk of metal in front of me. I'd been worried that its abstract nature was too much of a departure for me, that I wouldn't be able to carry it off successfully. But Brooke sucked in an admiring breath that I recognized as genuine.

"Oh, it looks wonderful." Her face softened, and that same admiring gaze traveled over me. "And so do you."

"I've seen better days," I said somewhat nervously, wiping my hands with a towel. My face was streaked with sweat, and my lopsided ponytail was coming undone. Still, my happiness at seeing her overwhelmed my vanity. "By the way, you're the one who looks terrific."

Grinning, she whisked her fingers through her cropped hair. "Well, I figured it was high time I made a few changes."

I returned her smile, untied my smock, and tossed it onto the floor. "I'm really glad to see you. . . and your timing is perfect. I was just about to take a break. Why don't you join me?"

To my delight, she agreed, and I got out my handy jar of instant coffee. Brooke seemed to be turning something over in her mind while I rinsed out two mugs and plugged in the hot pot I kept on my workbench.

"I suppose I'm the one who owes you a cup of coffee. I don't think it's ever tasted the same to me since I saw you the last time." She looked at me wistfully, and neither of us said anything else until we were sitting across from each other on two big floor cushions, holding our cups and avoiding each other's eyes.

After a while, I felt my heart pounding, and I began to suspect that she could actually hear it. I cleared my throat and took the plunge.

"Listen, Brooke, I'm sorry we fell out of touch for so long, but it was difficult for me. The truth is that I wanted more than friendship from you, and I just assumed you were interested in me in the same way. When I found out there was someone else, especially someone like Mika. . . ."

Brooke held up a hand to silence me. "I'm almost ashamed to get into that–except to tell you that I did a lot of thinking after that whole disaster at my apartment. You couldn't have realized how unresolved my feelings for Mika were at the time. I'd been involved with her for a year before you and I met. I wanted to leave her, but somehow she'd convinced me that once she was gone, there wouldn't be anyone else."

"And you believed that? Even when you knew how I felt?"

"But that's just the thing, Val. I couldn't be sure how you felt. Sure, I knew you were interested, but what if I dropped Mika for you, and things didn't work out? She wouldn't have come back, and I would have been alone again. At the time, that seemed like the most terrible fate in the world."

"It's partly my fault." I sighed, my eyes locked on hers. "I should have been more open about how much you meant. . . mean. . . to me."

Brooke licked her lips, but continued to meet my stare. "Well, that's all over with now. Once you were gone, I realized how tired I was of living in Mika's version of reality. I realized that I needed to break free of her, to figure out what really mattered to me. After she and I broke up, I spent a lot of time alone–until I could admit to myself that it wasn't so bad, that I could make it on my own if I had to. For the first time, things started to fall into place. That's when I knew I had to find you again, to make things right. I wanted to make sure you weren't still angry, so I pushed that sculpture idea through before I showed up."

I couldn't help smiling. "I figured you had something to do with that." It was funny–after a year of fantasizing about exactly this conversation, I was still at a loss for an adequate response. As I struggled to find the words, I put down my cup and took her hand instead. "In case you haven't guessed, I'm not angry."

I felt her relax. Her eyes lingered on my face, and our connection gradually resumed as if nothing had separated us. I sensed that familiar longing build inside me, but this time I wanted her to make the first move. Part of me was still afraid.

"I missed you." Brooke loosened my hair and laced her fingers through it. I felt I was being swept away. "Your face is still as beautiful as one of your sculptures," she whispered, trailing her palm down over my cheek. My body went weak, and I instinctively leaned my head back.

I twisted my fingers through hers, bending close. Suddenly she moved my hair aside, kissing the nape of my neck. I pulled her close to me in a long-awaited embrace. We held on tightly, and I lost myself in the softness of her clothed breasts as they meshed with my own.

Swept away, I nuzzled her muscled shoulder with my now-flaming cheek. Before I knew what was happening, she began to bite my shoulder. I responded with all the ardor I'd suppressed so long. I plunged my tongue between her perfect teeth, entwined it with hers.

"Do you realize how much I want you right now?" My words were only a shade above a moan.

"I do," she murmured.

"Yeah?" I taunted. "Show me, Brooke, show me."

Brooke reached up and grabbed a new drop cloth off my workbench, then spread it on the floor beside us. She pulled me down next to her, and her lips and fingers grazed my face, my hair, my neck. I sighed, squeezing my body against hers, and lost myself in the unrestrained blaze of her desire.

After a while, I couldn't bear the constriction of our clothes. I began to strip her. "I want to see if you're as beautiful as I imagined you to be," I muttered.

Watching her reactions, I lifted my hands to the buttons of her blouse and undid them. I pushed the garment down her arms, peeled the red shell off over her head, then reached around to unhook her bra. It popped open with ease. My eyes stared at her large, soft globes and fully erect nipples. I smiled as I slid down the waistband of her panties and eased the black lace from her creamy thighs.

She stretched out on the cloth, naked before me. In my fantasies, I had always imagined her as embarrassed and self-conscious at that moment. Instead, real life proved more satisfying, for I found her delightfully confident and aggressive. She quickly relieved me of my own t-shirt and bra, planting small kisses on every inch of newly bared skin. My breasts tingled with anticipation. Then, with aching slowness, she freed me of my jeans and panties. It seemed as if she wanted the moment to last forever.

Brooke dropped her hand onto the curve of my hip as she inspected my naked self. "You have an enchanting body, Val. But I always knew you would."

She kissed me again, more passionately than before. Her hands slid everywhere: along my spine and buttocks, over my belly and thighs. Everywhere, in fact, except where I was itching for her to touch.

I teased her back by fluttering butterfly caresses on her inner thighs, brushing my lips against her soft hairs and traveling up her stomach to her bobbing breasts. I squeezed one of her breasts with my left hand, and the other I kissed and licked until her hard nipple poked deep into my mouth.

I sucked it as hard as I could. Brooke moaned with pleasure and started to move her hand back and forth over my pubic mound, her touch gentle and sure. Soon it was my turn to shiver with pleasure.

I was creaming freely now, and Brooke's palm became glossy every time it passed near my streaming cleft. I tipped my head back, half-closing my eyes with pleasure as my clitoris gradually stood up and demanded her attention. Brooke obliged by increasing the sweep and pressure of her stroke.

"You're exquisite," she muttered in my ear, but her voice sounded like it was coming from another room. My head filled with the hammering of my own wild, throbbing pulse as her brazen fingers touched me directly. I felt the muscles in my thighs contract and ripple with enjoyment.

She maneuvered me flat on my back and lowered herself over me. Her long, satiny legs stretched out alongside mine, while her thick dark curls sank onto my own triangle like a mound of feathers. She leaned forward to lick my breasts, swirling her tongue over each nipple until both grew rigid with desire.

Almost before I knew what was happening, she swung around full-length and nestled her hot center over my face while her fingers slid over my bulging feminine pearl. Swiftly she plunged them inside my dripping slit.

I opened my mouth and sucked in Brooke's rich melted honey. At the same time she slowly began to explore me, probing my deeper recesses until my whole body screamed silently with pleasure. I raked my clipped nails against Brooke's bare torso and her sleek thighs, murmuring with delight.

Intoxicated by Brooke's nectar, I hammered my tongue against her engorged, pulsating bud, all the while manipulating her hot folds with my nose. "Beautiful," I gasped when I paused. "You're everything I imagined."

"You are, too." She breathed deeply, her breath ragged with passion. "That feels so right." Her feminine muscles sucked me back like a small, starving mouth as a shuddering spasm raked through her. I could tell that she was fighting it back, off a serious orgasm, desperately waiting for me to catch up.

She didn't have to hold back very long. Her tongue

entered me, sliding in and out so urgently that tremors rose inside me, rocking my hips and searing the insides of my spread legs. A burning sensation collected in my center, but I set my teeth and bit it back. I was determined to give Brooke exactly what she needed. Gingerly I added one finger, and then two, to the mix.

Brooke howled as raw desire burned through her torso and legs, lifting her up. I continued to tongue her as fervently as I could until she fell back against the floor with a scream as the final vestiges of control deserted her. My hand felt like it had become part of her. Her hot lips still enveloped it, scalding my flesh.

Brooke must have sensed how close I was, because she suddenly bore down on me in a frenzy. Her tongue foraged through me again and again, sinking as deeply inside as I ever imagined anyone could go. She even cried out as if to give voice to my own exhilaration.

I clenched my knees together as the heat squeezed through me, my thighs molding around her now-disheveled coiffure. I rocked back and forth, cries of pleasure and relief escaping my throat.

When I had finished, my legs fell open around her. She propped herself up on my belly. "Oh, Val," Brooke groaned, watching me. "You're gorgeous when you come."

"You're pretty stunning yourself," I managed to gasp. "A real work of art."

Brooke sat up slowly. She hovered over my spent body, watching my ribs rise and fall as I panted in exhaustion. A series of sweet aftershocks rippled up and down my spine as she caressed every hot nook and steaming cranny of my passion-drenched body.

I wiped my face with the back of my hand and sank back in exhaustion, rolling onto my stomach. Soon I felt Brooke's hands massaging my shoulders, turning me on all over again.

"You know," Brooke said after a while, teasing me with her fingers as well as her voice, "I want to ask you about that sculpture you're working on. It's a little on the abstract side, but I can't help thinking there's something familiar about it."

"Oh, really?" I asked innocently. "What do you mean?"

She blushed deeply, slid her arms around her drawn-up legs, and looked down at her painted toenails. "It's just that it reminds me of something. . . . I can't put my finger on it."

Though I was trying to keep a straight face, I suddenly burst out in a grin that gave it all away.

"Well, I can," I said, touching her breast. "Don't be shocked if your co-workers gain a new appreciation for your finest qualities once it's on display." I raked my eyes over her glistening body, its sleek curves and swells almost a perfect match for the ones that graced my statue.

She leaned over me, laughing, and we proceeded to put our mouths to artistic uses we could only have discovered together.

One Perfect Night

For my thirtieth birthday last year, my girlfriend Celia bought me something I'd been longing for: a brand-new, high-powered computer that did practically everything but brew the morning coffee–and I wasn't so sure that, with practice, I couldn't eventually coax it to do that!

I also got a subscription to one of those on-line services where people of all persuasions can post messages and chat "live" about their most personal experiences. . . and fantasies.

I'm still not exactly sure what took me to the "single lesbians" message board, since I had been happy with Celia for two years and she'd just spent all that money on me. But it was like I took on a whole new identity whenever I became "Stardust," my screen persona, and clicked into that magical, uninhibited cyberworld.

I'd been dipping into the chat boards for about a week when I met "Astarte." Her fanciful screen name immediately swept me away to a sunlit ancient world by the sea. There, naked women danced and writhed in tribute to their shimmering goddess. Soon my fingers were stumbling over the keyboard in my haste to become one of those women.

The next few days were lost in a blur of sizzling messages and unrestrained appetite. My hands would sweat as I described every imagined flick of my tongue against her pulsing center, and she would respond by recounting every vivid twist of her fingers in my own pussy. Soon I was actually in the habit of sitting naked at my desk as I waited for her to page me, my hips heaving around my hand as I orgasmed to the imagined clash of primeval cymbals and wooden ceremonial flutes.

Finally, one day, I knew things had reached the point of no return. I begged her to meet me in person so we could satisfy our lust for real. At that point, she admitted that she wasn't free–she'd been living with another woman for several years, and had no intention of leaving her. But the encounters she'd shared with me, she confessed, had been the hottest and most satisfying she'd even experienced. I told her about my girlfriend, and how she had almost ceased to exist in my life the day I'd hooked up with Astarte.

Clearly, we were in a dilemma. In the end, we called one another on the phone and decided to meet–for one night only–in a city hotel that lay within traveling distance for both of us. On the appointed day, I made some excuse to Celia about an old college friend being in town, fighting my guilt when she kissed me and told me to have a good time. I drove at what was surely an unsafe speed to the rendezvous point and waited in the hotel bar for my erstwhile goddess to arrive.

I knew her the instant she walked in. She was tall and red-haired, as she had already informed me, with hips and breasts that made my mouth–as well as another, more secret part of me–water. Her sea-green eyes glowed with lust and recognition the moment she noticed me.

"Ashley?" I whispered, for she'd told me her real name when we'd finalized the arrangements to meet.

"Yes," she said with a smile, extending her slender hand. I shivered when we touched in greeting. "Welcome to our one perfect night."

I clung to her fingers a bit longer than was really necessary. We gazed at each other, nearly speechless with desire, and hurried to the elevator to avoid tearing each other's clothes off right there in the crowded lounge.

We exercised no such restraint when the elevator doors slid shut. Ashley enfolded me in a desperate embrace, her teeth grazing my lips and her fingertips prodding the insides of my thighs. In turn, I raised my hands to cup her full, warm breasts, my thumbs softly flicking her nipples. At the same time, moving as if by instinct, I nudged my leg between hers. As she began to breathe heavily, I flexed my thigh muscles against her hot pubic mound.

My heart was throbbing in tune with my pussy as we stumbled to our room and practically fell inside, peeling each other's clothes off in a frenzy of desire. I was struck dumb with excitement as I gaped at her exposed body, then blushed as she lifted my chin and kissed me deeply.

"You're lovely," she whispered as her lips played softly over mine. "Just as I expected."

I pressed my naked body to hers. Our damp bushes melted together as we luxuriated in the velvet blend of skin on skin. I sucked in my breath at the special tickle of her pubic hair against the crevice of my thigh. Even my knees ached with desire.

"You're everything I imagined, too," I said huskily. The din of my pulse nearly drowned out my words. In response, Ashley's fingers dipped between my fringed outer lips. I sagged against her as her tongue, cool and flavored with mint, plunged between my teeth. I opened my mouth, yielding for a moment, then bared my teeth and left her lips stinging with pleasure.

She toyed with my small, taut nipples, then bent to arouse them with her palms. She caressed my upper body in a circular motion, moving from my shoulders around to my rib cage, back over my breasts, and down again. I moaned, tilted my hips into hers, and rubbed my bush against hers hungrily.

"I need you inside me," I wheezed, wriggling my hand into the lower curve of her buttocks. I stretched out my fingers and coated the tips in her sizzling juices. I longed to taste her nectar, but I couldn't bear to let go of her even that long.

"I want you just as much," she whispered, then sank to her knees. My hands slipped reluctantly from between her legs and strayed into her long hair as she began to explore, orally, the insides of both of my legs. She worked her way down until she was kissing the tops of my feet, then lapped her way up again. By the time she got bolder, I was already rigid, breathing hard, my head thrown back in abandon. Ashley jabbed her tongue into my folds and lifted my pearl free of its burning, fleshy hood.

"Oh, yes," I gasped, squeezing my thighs around her bobbing head. The moisture that slicked her face now smeared my own. Tendrils of wet heat penetrated my body like a writhing mass of tongues and fingers.

"More," I wheezed. "Harder! Yes!"

Eager to please, Ashley lapped and prodded me with

increasing vigor until I shuddered, quaking against her face. My nails dug into her scalp as she wrapped both arms around my hips and guided me onto the carpeted floor. When I was sprawled out on my back, she plunged her whole head between my legs. She nuzzled my clit with her nose and kissed between my legs as if the lips there hid a tiny mouth.

I cried out, gritting my teeth and squeezing my eyes shut as I tried to savor every marvelous feeling her leisurely ministrations aroused. I gasped for breath through wide-open lips, my back tense and my legs straight out as convulsions of pleasure rippled through me.

"Almost there," I choked out. "Almost–"

Ashley kept at me with firm, quick, constant movements, ultimately taking my swollen clit between her lips and shaking it gently until stabs of pleasure shot all the way up to my nipples. She finished me off by planting her palm fully over my mound, stroking one or two fingers over my clit with gentle pressure. When I came, it felt like I was cresting one long, reeling wave of passion that lifted my body clear off the rug.

I grew quiet as my orgasm faded, my whimpers of delight giving way to a deeply satisfying tranquility that silenced the turmoil inside me.

"That was wonderful," I said, cuddling up next to her on the floor. As a fresh need built inside me, I swept my hand over her bush and felt its outer muscles contract with fresh arousal. I ravaged the side of her neck, alternating urgent kisses with gentle bites.

Ashley trembled and arched her back as the warmth

of my mouth against her hard nipples forced her to cry out in want. When my body moved to cover hers, she parted her thighs and raised her hips. My hand moved abruptly to address her need.

"Teach me to please you," I begged. Her lips curved into a smile against my collarbone as my manipulation of her most sensitive area grew fierce. Choking with need, unable to ignore the agony of desire, Ashley seized my hand and crushed it to her hot center. Her passion crested within a matter of moments, leaving both of us gasping and tangled together as if we'd been shipwrecked.

"Sorry–I wanted to draw it out longer," I apologized, tracing the russet outline of her pliant nipple. Far from disappointed, Ashley sat up and smiled.

"Don't worry about it. I was just too turned on to hold out." As I blushed with pride, she squeezed my own tit playfully. "Besides. . . quantity can sometimes compensate for quality. Would you care for a shower?"

She jumped to her feet, pulling me along with her, and led me to the immaculate hotel bathroom. I self-consciously arranged some towels by the sink while Ashley bent to adjust the spray. Pretty soon the mirror in front of me fogged up, and I knew the water was as hot as we were. I stepped behind the curtain to find Ashley waiting for me.

She wasted no time. As soon as I approached her, she covered my body with hers. One hand groped my breasts and the other slid into the crack between my buttocks. I responded by cupping her in my right hand and massaging her hot folds as the soothing spray of the shower thrummed against us and slicked down our hair.

Groaning hoarsely, I lowered my hand until my index finger found her center. Again driven by some instinct that seemed to awaken in me spontaneously, I slid it around the rim, teasing and rubbing. She leaned against the tiles, her face partially obscured by a cloud of hot steam, while I slid to my knees without removing my finger. I burrowed the lower part of my face into her and snaked the pointed tip of my tongue in and out of her drooling crevice.

"I love the taste of you," I whispered. It was true. The juices that oozed around my tongue were tart and sugary.

My first few strokes probed her clitoris, arousing it to a rigid little triangle. The next few moved lower and jabbed inside her tender flesh until it closed up. It felt as if she wanted to capture my flickering tongue, hold it prisoner until it yielded every possible pleasure.

She ground her buttocks against the tiled wall, her hips rolling and shuddering as the onset of the orgasm disoriented her. Meanwhile, I kept moving my index finger in and out, setting up a rhythm so that one of her two pleasure zones was continually penetrated or rubbed. She moaned and thrashed and humped her hips against my steam-reddened flesh.

Finally, Ashley gasped and stiffened, and I closed my mouth over her and sucked hard. My fingers raked her wet hairs as she pumped out her passion right there against the tiles, banging back and forth and howling like it would never stop.

It did stop, of course, and all too soon. I sank back against the tiles, which seemed cool compared to the rest of my body, and turned my face to the warm spray that gushed from the nozzle. The whole shower smelled like sex, and I imagined that gallons of her secret nectar, delicious and sticky, were flowing down over us. My head buzzed with the sheer forbiddenness of it all.

We soaked there a while, then stepped out of the shower and towel-dried each other. I spent a long time wiping and patting at the insides of her thighs, using the raised texture of the plush towel to give her a little post-orgasmic thrill.

"My legs are still shaking," she murmured. A smile of pleasure made her face glow.

"One perfect night," I said as she leaned over to kiss me. "And it's not over yet."

It wasn't. When we were dry enough, we moved over to the bed and rubbed, fingered, and tongued each other to more orgasms than either of us had ever enjoyed in a single bout of passion.

The next morning, I kissed her goodbye and watched from the window as she headed for the hotel parking lot. Could we really bear to stay away from each other forever? For me, at least, the challenge would be anything but easy. I could only hope that, at some point during the lonely days and nights ahead, she'd begin to feel the same.

Meanwhile, in the back of my mind, I heard the crash of ancient cymbals once again.

Summerapture

Devoured by her smile

Her ceaseless tongue singed my yielding body

Thrashed and willed me toward ecstasy

Flames surged

Fierce shudders consumed

Used me, made me

Burn only for her scented dew

As wet, thirsty lips drowned

My regret

Venetian Blinds

I've always hated Venetian blinds. I can never see out of them and usually end up slicing my fingers on their sharp edges.

Cautiously I twist the rusty metal and scrutinize the sidewalk below, but Tazha doesn't materialize. I step back and listen to the mellow breeze bang the metal strips against the window sill.

Agitated, I leave my Provincetown guest house and hurry to the water's edge below. There's no sign of her there, either, only seagulls wheeling and cawing overhead.

I'm on my way back to my room when a woman ambles toward me. From her walk, she seems young and vibrant. Her cropped blonde hair sticks to her temples, and her bikini top accentuates her boyish chest. She doesn't appeal to me, and I don't know why I'm watching her.

When she's right in front of me, I notice that her buoyant step is more of a drunken stagger. Angry tattoos cover her skin. Pierces line her abdomen and face. Pausing, she smiles and inhales the crisp ocean air.

Up close, she appears like a Halloween skeleton. Her stained teeth seem too large for her face, and her bony arms and legs twitch like dry sticks tossed into a campfire. I hurry away, repulsed, as she giggles and begins to talk to herself.

When I'm back in my room, my anxiety returns. I must check again to see if my patient is still staking out my guesthouse. I reach for the blinds, slashing my fingertips as I predicted. I have to wrench the tangled chords and twist my neck to see outside at all.

Miraculously, this time I manage to get a glimpse of her. She's down on the shore behind the guesthouse, collecting shells. Tazha loves to collect things. She bends to examine a large pink specimen. She is stiff but graceful, like an antique porcelain doll.

A shiver courses through my body. As her psychiatrist, I know that Tazha depends on me, but I also know that she needs more than therapy to heal. At first, I was upset that she followed me on my vacation, but now I feel better. At least I can keep an eye on her in case she is not well. She has been so fragile lately. Even as my torn hand aches and the blood oozes, I can't stop looking at her.

I watch her fingers caress the pearly interior of the shell, then drop it into her beach bag. When she gets up, her long amber tresses billow in all directions like the gusts of careening sand. Her slim hand rakes her curls behind her ears, away from her pale face. I imitate the movement without thinking and feel my wet blood on my cheek.

She searches for more shells and has just crouched down to inspect one when a small wave douses her feet and ankles unexpectedly. She jumps back and looks up, as if she knows someone watches her. Her gaze lights on my window, blaming me for the interruption. I pull back, out of sight, and feel the sweat drip between my breasts. After a few minutes, she shrugs and wanders away.

She must be waiting for me. That familiar lust

returns to my belly, and my mind fights the guilt.

Finally, the blinds crimp and block my vision. By the time I untangle them, I've lost sight of her. I hurry to put on my sandals, then clatter down the wooden steps to the beach. Soon I'm taking long strides, almost running through the soft, shifting dunes to find Tazha. I rush up and down the shore, but I can't find her. Moving onto the crowded midday streets, I continue my search.

At one point, I zero in on a woman coming out of a candy shop, but as she gets closer, I realize she is not Tazha. Undeterred, I check the library, the cafes, and make one more long trek down Commercial Street to check for her in the small specialty shops. She is lost among the throngs that stroll up and down.

I know she'll find me again soon, so I decide to prepare myself better for our possible meeting. I stop at a sportswear store when I notice a designer bathing suit I know will flatter my youthful figure. The price is exorbitant, but it makes me look ten years younger. I buy it and go back to my room to try on my purchase. I am happy that I spent the money as I gaze into the full length mirror and turn from side to side.

The lavender brings out the colored speckles in my dark blue eyes. The spandex accentuates my flat belly and long legs that I keep in shape by often not eating. I don't do this on purpose, but only when I am thinking about Tazha. Just the thought of her brings back both the fire–and the worry.

I put on make-up, a new habit of mine, adding some purplish eye shadow to match my new bathing suit. I add a bit of rouge and cover-up to hide the lines that have been more visible lately. I gather together some articles I have promised to edit for a prominent psychiatry journal, then call my office in Boston to check for messages. There are none. My secretary promises to record any calls from Tazha.

I place the paperwork in a bag, carry it down to my Audi, and drive to the beach at Race Point. Somehow I have a feeling she'll show up there this afternoon.

Soon after I arrive at the beach, my skin begins to burn. The editing bores me. The sun and the noisy passers-by begin to bother me. I rummage through my bag and take a Valium to relax. Now maybe I can concentrate on my work.

I come to the end of the first batch of articles. I wonder how some writers can make the human being seem uninteresting, and decide to read just one more so I can go out to dinner later. *Counter-transference: The Need to be Needed* is the condescending title.

Deep down, I hope it will solve my dilemma. The thesis is simple enough. *The therapist's ego, her need for love and admiration, taints her perception of the patient's issues.* Well, there is nothing new in that premise. There is more I need to know. *The problem reaches its most critical stage when the therapist's perception of herself and how the patient feels about her become disturbed.* This seems too simple a solution. My own feelings seem so complicated.

I know Tazha regards me highly, but this only makes my emotions more intense. She is twenty-four, and I will be forty-three in a month. I never got involved with a patient before this. I am sick with myself.

Still she haunts me like a phantom of lust, a mirror of my own depravity. I think of the many offers I've had from other women lately. All of them were sexy, but none had Tazha's brilliant mind or her pitiful need for my love. I know I'm an egotist, but the way she looks at me, with all the adoration of a schoolgirl, intoxicates me.

I try to think of my vacation plans: the midnight cruise, the whale watch, the bars and dancing I'd planned to enjoy, but Tazha intrudes on my thoughts again. I look down at the tranquilizers and try to remember how many I've taken. It could not have been many since I feel so tense. I take another half a tablet and lower my wide-brimmed hat over my eyes. I push myself to focus on the waves hitting the shore, the seagulls wheeling overhead, anything but Tazha.

I'm tired, so tired. . . .

A sudden coolness wafts across my bare shoulders, and I jerk awake. Tazha is finally at my side. She comes in and out of focus as my eyes adjust to the twilight.

"I wanted to see you," she says in an excited voice. "Your secretary told me you were spending the day at the beach. I searched all day for you."

I wonder if I'm dreaming as I squint into the sun. White and dark spots dance in my head for a moment.

"Dr. Ransenbach, I couldn't be without you this week. My mother is harping at me again. I can't get anything done. I feel so depressed." She talks rapidly, wiping the sweat from her brow. "You missed me, didn't you?"

"Are you taking the anti-depressants I prescribed?" I sit up, becoming tense myself. Tazha wears teal blue shorts and a colored top that matches her eyes and the sea.

The waves crash nearby. "I don't need them. I told you that already. I just need you," she answers and takes hold of my hand.

I want to push her away. I want to call another therapist to intervene. I want to ask her to go back home. But all I can think about is the pressure of her fingers on mine, inches from my throbbing breast. The sun has burnt my will, along with my skin, to a crisp.

"Here," I say, handing Tazha the after-sun cream I keep in my bag. I bought it in Europe the summer before. "Please rub this on my back."

Tazha turns her attention to my steaming back and gently massages the ointment into my scorched flesh. At the same time, she blows cool air along my spine. "Better?" she asks.

I answer her with a sigh of relief and pleasure, then watch the brandied orange sun melt into the approaching evening. There is no need to run from her now. I want to flow into her like the sun into the churning sea. Only then will she be cured of her unhappiness.

She seems to guess what I am thinking, because the pace of her breathing increases. "Doctor Ransenbach, what are those articles about?" she inquires, looking down at the papers that have spilled from my bag.

"All kinds of writings about different psychiatric

issues," I answer, growing impatient. My core pulsates with want. "Very boring, especially to the layman."

"This one you've underlined a lot. Tell me about it," she demands, still stroking my shoulder and arm with one hand and holding the article with the other. When I hesitate, she reads it to herself. Then she stiffens and pulls away. "This is such crap. Look at us. You love me, I love you, and it has nothing to do with this counter-transference shit. We just need each other. You still need me, don't you, Doctor?"

"Yes, Tazha."

"Is that good?" she says.

My eyes burn with the sight of her. "Yes."

She laughs. "I mean the cream. Does your skin feel better?"

"It does. I like it a lot." My voice grows suddenly husky as I bask in the touch of her hands against the sides of my breasts. "I like you a lot, Tazha."

"I think you want me, don't you?" She asks the question so casually that she might be asking about cloud formations.

"Why do you ask that? Do you want me, Tazha?" My hands tremble as I form the words.

She grins. "Oh, I've gotten excited many times, thinking about having sex with you."

"Somehow that doesn't surprise me," I respond with equal frankness.

"I never had the guts to tell you this, but I touch myself thinking about you." She still wears that devilish smile.

I am paralyzed from want. My body is an inferno.

Maddeningly, she changes the subject. "Why don't we take a swim?" she says, then gets up and pulls me along.

"You're not wearing a bathing suit," I comment.

"Yes, I am." She strips off her top and shorts to reveal her naked body. I can see raised bumps on her nipples and the shadowed indentation of her navel. Tazha is breathing hard as my gaze travels lower.

Valium mixed with lust makes me giddy. I feel like the basest animal and the most alive woman on this vast earth.

Her eyes narrow, she flashes me a crooked smile, and then she moves toward me. I step closer but don't touch, afraid that I might implode. She grabs my hand anyway. I bend my face to kiss her.

Tazha avoids me and pulls me to the waves. Together we enter the dark surf up to our hips. My body is so hot that the icy water torments me. The strong current tries to knock me off my feet. My torso shudders and clenches with cold.

Tazha floats up to me and presses her body against mine. She touches the straps of my bathing suit. "The purple matches your eyes," she murmurs. She holds my hand and brushes the top of it with her mouth. Her skin is softer than angels' wings but her incisors gnash my flesh.

My body stiffens with pain and pleasure. I am frightened. I know I could lose my license, my place on the board of the psychiatric journal. I've worked hard, so hard to overcome the sexism and the homophobia. And here I stand on the edge of this vast abyss, willing to risk everything just to touch her. I become dizzy and nauseated from anxiety. Indecision makes me speechless. I grip her other hand and look out at the endless sea, throbbing.

Tazha deserts me for a short swim. She appears superhuman, untouched by the frigid temperature. I float on my back and close my eyes. Weightless, I glide to no specific destination as the numbness sinks in. I still manage to hope that the cold will invigorate my rational side.

Tazha's arms slide around my waist, and the back of my head rests on her belly. Her silky legs slide under my buttocks. I turn my face to her stomach, duck my head under the water, and nuzzle her. She pushes her hips into my mouth, sliding her jagged fingernails through my hair. I dissolve into her.

Gasping, I come up for air, but Tazha pulls me back beneath the freezing surface. Her icy mouth clamps over mine. This is a lovely torture. The freezing water seeps into my hot skin. I struggle to hold my breath as her tongue plummets between my teeth.

Tazha's lust seems to overwhelm her, and she holds me under the water. Soon she lifts her mouth and breaks the surface, while I fight to bring my head up. Panic floods my senses. She won't let me breathe. Tazha is strong, and I begin to swallow copious amounts of the icy brine. Through the cloudy water, I catch a distorted glimpse of her monstrous expression. Her fingers clench my throat while she pounds my head with her tight fist.

I choke and struggle against her grip, aroused but

desperate. Finally, I manage to kick out and displace her thin legs, forcing her to lose her grip on me. I push my mouth to the surface and gasp for breath, still fighting her off with my arms. A wave crashes over me, propelling my limp body away from her. She runs from the water while I drift to shore like a beached dolphin.

My face is in the wet sand. My limbs are exhausted. There is so much salt in my eyes that I can no longer see Tazha. I try to summon a shout, to ask her why she has committed this brutal act. I am enraged at her and at myself.

Slowly, I regain my strength. But the Valium and fight have exhausted me. I close my eyes, but at the same time, I struggle to get up so Tazha can't come back and finish me off. I don't know how much time passes.

I spend a while collecting the contents of my bag, which Tazha has dumped out on the sand. I'm too disoriented to notice if anything is missing. I manage to locate my car keys and squeeze them in my clammy fist while I stagger to the parking lot.

I sigh with relief when I discover my Audi still intact. Then rage boils through me. I want her to pay for this, but I cannot contact the police or I will suffer the consequences. No, I must find her myself.

I drive slowly, scanning the road for any sign of her. I doubt she had a chance to make it back to town on foot. But she could be anywhere along the deserted highway, anywhere in the tree-lined dunes.

I wrack my brain to think where she might be. I park at the end of town and walk along Commercial Street, looking for her in the bars. Once again, I cannot find her.

I am ready to give up when I catch my own reflection in the window of a restaurant. My new bathing suit is dirty and the shoulder straps droop. Seaweed protrudes from its arm and leg holes. Sand sticks to my burnt skin. My hair stands up every which way. As I stare at myself, my pupils grow and squirm like dark beetles. I realize I am on the brink.

Behind the window, she sits dining alone in the candle-lit restaurant. Heedless of my appearance, I rush in to confront her. The maître d' sees me and tries to pull me away. Avoiding his grasp, I rush to her table, my fists raised in fury. Tazha looks up in surprise.

I have just opened my mouth when a waitress steps in front of me and sets Tazha's bill and Visa receipt down on her table.

"Thank you, Dr. Ransenbach," she says, never noticing me. "Come again!"

Cruise Control

I held the phone away from my ear as the shrill voice jabbered on and on. "Yes, Mr. Remington, I'm working on it now," I promised, forcing the impatience from my voice. "Yes, I know you've got to get to Newport Beach tomorrow. Yes, Mr. Remington, girls like us usually fix cars very quickly. I'm finishing it now. Thanks for your call. . . . "

I was glad he hung up on me so I could get back under the hood of his damn BMW. In their view of the world, I guess, the owners of luxury vehicles shouldn't be subjected to inconveniences like radiator leaks or conked-out air conditioners. Lucky for them I love to fix their cars.

I didn't even mind working overtime that night. I was happy to be alone so I could concentrate on the task at hand, though thanks to the weather it was slow going. A dense summer haze hung low overhead, muddling the Boston skyline. Prickly heat penetrated every corner of the garage, withering even the shadows on the wall.

Just before 8:00, I looked up and saw a sleek pink Mercedes glide by the front of the shop. The figure in the driver's seat sat silhouetted behind a tinted grey window.

I jumped to my feet, a thick knot forming in my stomach, as the vehicle slowed almost to a complete stop. Then it speeded up and headed straight for the open garage door. Powerful headlights flashed across my face as I threw down my tools and made a run for it.

Tires squealed against concrete as the Mercedes skidded inside and swerved directly into my path.

A blast of arctic air rushed from the open driver's side door, followed by a tall figure in a full-length leopard-print coat. Nothing ever went wrong with the Ice Princess' air conditioning.

"Damn it, Kitty," I yelped as lavender driving gloves seized me in a vise-like grip. "Get your hands off me, you oversexed she-ape!"

Laughing, Kitty thrust her six-foot frame against me, wedging me between her hip and the soda machine, unzipped the front of my uniform, and groped my breasts roughly. I could hardly believe that her vulgar behavior had ever turned me on.

"Don't tease me by saying you don't want me back," she breathed against my neck. Her sharp teeth nipped playfully at my flesh. "I can't believe I mean nothing to you now. I know you've missed our games as much as I have."

"Stop it!" I shouted, wriggling beneath the weight of her body. Between the slobbering lips clamped over mine, and the oppressive heat from the coat and her body, I was about to pass out.

"Hey!" A shout from the back of the shop made us both freeze. The acoustics made the voice sound deeper and more threatening than I knew it was. I looked up and saw Maria Cruz, our garage's new supervisor, striding toward us with a bag of take-out food in her arms. Her dark eyes flashed with anger. "What the hell's going on here?"

"And who is this charming creature?" Kitty

demanded, both hands still mashing my tits. I was more than a little embarrassed to be caught with my uniform open like that, especially since I wasn't wearing anything under it. I'd imagined baring my body for Maria plenty of times, but Kitty sure as hell hadn't played a prominent part in my fantasies.

"This is my boss," I said in a lame voice. "We call her Cruise."

Kitty's plucked brows took wing on her high, narrow forehead. Then she gave Cruise a contemptuous snort. "Well, my dear, I can't deny your way with words. On occasion I can be intrigued by ruffians with silver tongues, but I'm afraid I'm a bit busy just now."

Laughing, she bent down to snap at my neck vampire-style. At that point, I heard the bag of food hit the concrete and felt Kitty being lifted off me. She didn't want to let go and gave me a petulant shove into the soda machine. Cruise caught me before I could slip to the floor, then stepped in front to shield me.

Kitty hovered in front of us, her fingers spread menacingly. Her face had turned as purple as her gloves. "Oh, now I get it! This grease-monkey bitch has been greasing your panties, hasn't she?"

"Kitty, that's enough! There's nothing going on between Cruise and me. You just have to accept the fact that I don't want to see you again!"

"Sounds clear enough to me," Cruise said, folding her arms and planting her feet. "Now take off and let my employee get back to her work."

Hissing with fury, Kitty raised the flaps of her coat as if preparing to take flight on furred wings. Teeth bared,

she launched herself at Cruise like a gigantic fanged
moth swooping straight for a porch light. I watched,
stunned, as Cruise caught a flailing purple fist in each
hand and pushed forward. Kitty let out an ear-splitting
shriek when her butt hit the floor with a bang.

Livid, she climbed back to her feet. She tottered on
the one stiletto heel that had survived the fray. "This is
assault and battery, and I promise you'll be hearing
from my lawyers!"

"Fine," said Cruise. "And while you're at it, you
might ask your lawyer the legal definition of
trespassing."

Kitty turned on me next, though she backed off a
little when Cruise adjusted her position accordingly.
"All right, Dee, if that's how you want it," she snarled.
"You'll have to beg me to take you back after this."

Cruise's protective stance gave me courage. "I think
you ought to call it a night, Kitty, don't you?"

Kitty didn't bother to search for her lost heel. Instead,
she hobbled to her Mercedes in a huff and slammed the
door on her leopard coat. The tawny fur that stuck out
dragged through a nasty grease puddle as she hit the gas
and sped away.

I burst into nervous laughter once we were alone
again. Cruise wrapped her sinewy arm around my slight
shoulder and tugged me against her. "You okay?"

"Yeah," I said. In answer to the unspoken question in
her eyes, I shrugged. "I never thought Kitty would pull
something like that. I mean, it's been weeks since I've
spoken to her, but she just won't accept that it's over
between us."

Cruise laughed and dropped her arm to her side. "Well, she's not the first customer to think that a beautiful lady mechanic is destined for only one type of fuel injection. Listen, why don't you come into my office and take it easy for a while? I brought back some Chinese take out, and you're welcome to share whatever survived the fight."

"Thanks." I said. Cruise led me to her neatly organized desk and filled a paper plate with fried rice, sesame chicken, and a crushed egg roll.

"Funny she thought that we were together," she commented between bites. "In fact, I didn't even know that you were gay. I've been out since I was a teenager, but I can never tell about other people."

"Yeah, I know what you mean. I. . . uh. . . I guess I suspected that about you, but I've been wrong before. I don't like to make assumptions."

"I wish I'd known about you earlier," she said thoughtfully, then seemed to shake off an uncomfortable feeling. "Well, listen, if she shows up here again, just yell and I'll get the cops on her leopard-print butt. Do you think she might be waiting around out there somewhere? I can follow you home in the tow truck if you want."

"It's okay," I said. "Luckily, I never told her where I lived. We always just went to her place."

"Smart move." She nodded, and didn't push the issue any more that night. I was apprehensive because I felt attracted to her, but the night's events had soured me on any type of involvement at work. Still, I couldn't stop my eyes from drifting to the generous globes that bulged against the zipper of her uniform.

I'm not sure how it happened, or who made the first move. All of a sudden, Cruise and I were leaning toward each other over our half-finished plates of Chinese food.

Plush lips yielded to mine as Cruise kissed me back hard, opening her teeth and tonguing me. Our grease-splattered uniforms whispered together, and I could feel her stiff nipples prod my own.

"I probably should get back to the cars now," I said. "That Remington guy has already called me three times about his Beemer."

"Okay." She started collecting the empty plates and Chinese food containers and stuffing them back in the bag. "I've got some paperwork to finish up in here. Just yell if you need anything."

"I will," I promised. Then I hurried off, determined to finish at least one thing I'd started that night.

Though Cruise made a few attempts to talk with me, I kept my distance for the next few days. I was torn about wrecking the fantastic work environment I knew I'd never find anywhere else. Still, as much as I tried to avoid her, my resolve wore down like new treads on bad pavement. No matter how I tried, all I could think about was kissing her full mouth just one more time.

A week later, my emotional gauge was wound up so tight that I thought it would blow any second. Cruise and I worked late that evening, while the temperature hovered somewhere in the high eighties. We avoided each other except to make small talk or exchange tools.

Just as we were about to close, we got an emergency road call from a hysterical-sounding woman. There was smoke billowing out from under her hood, she sobbed. Could we bring the tow truck right away? The location she named was well out of our usual area, way out past an old industrial dumping zone. Normally we would have referred the call to someone closer, but Cruise said she didn't want to leave a woman stranded out in such a deserted area. She asked if I'd come with her, so I nodded and climbed into the truck. While we drove, I couldn't look at her. She didn't say much to me, either.

When we got to the area the caller had described, we looked around but couldn't see a car anywhere, disabled or otherwise.

"I don't get it," Cruise said, sweeping her high beams across one pitted stretch of concrete after another. We rolled to stop beside some rusty barrels and a twisted heap of metal that had once been an expensive piece of paving equipment. "She said she was right here."

"Maybe she got it to turn over after all. Or someone came along and gave her a jump."

"That's what I'm afraid of." Cruise clenched her jaw. "A woman alone can get into some real trouble, breaking down in a place like this."

"Yeah," I agreed. Despite the heat, I shivered as I squinted into the hazy darkness. Scorching city nights did seem to bring some unsavory characters out of their lairs.

"Still, there's no reason to assume the worst. Maybe

she pulled up a little farther and stopped again. We'll drive around some more and look for her."

We did just that, rolling up and down the dingy street. Cruise even talked to the state troopers on her cab radio, but they knew nothing of a stalled car, or any other type of disturbance, in the vicinity. The dispatcher promised to check with all units in the area and get back to us promptly.

"Well, that's that," Cruise grumbled, hooking the mike back to the dash. "Either she got her car going, or the whole thing was a hoax from beginning to end."

"I guess we'll have to wait for the cops to get back to us," I said.

"Yep."

We sat there for what seemed like hours, while the air in the tow truck grew heavy and the radio remained silent. The whole time, Cruise seemed to be turning something over in her mind. Suddenly she leaned forward and placed her hand on my thigh. The movement startled me so much I almost jumped up from my seat.

"Look," she said in a gruff voice, "I've been attracted to you since the first day we met. I get the sense that you're afraid of me, and I don't want you to be."

"It's. . . it's not you I'm afraid of," I said huskily. My chest began to hurt, and not just because of the thick air around us. "It's just. . . . "

"This?" she asked, bending forward to kiss me, as hard and as long as she had in her office that night.

I moaned and moved close to her. I placed my trembling hands on her chest and rested my mouth on the nape of her neck. "Yeah, this. Cruise, how can I say it? You make me crazy for you."

"You don't have to say it. I know exactly what you're feeling." She bit my ear and then stuck her tongue inside it, sending a shudder all through me. The contrast between her soft body and our rough contact made me dizzy with lust. I unzipped her uniform, delighted to find that she hadn't bothered to wear a bra either. I kissed my way down those luscious bare breasts.

Cruise slipped her arms out of her oil-splattered uniform, letting me caress her shoulders and back while I lowered my mouth to her steely nubs. I moaned with desire as I tasted her sweat.

She undid my overalls, too, and a wicked grin crossed her face when my own tits bobbed free. Her fingers went right for them, squeezing and caressing.

Soon Cruise flipped down the seat so we could lie comfortably together. She immediately took the opportunity to get on top of me so that we lay bumper to bumper, locked in lust.

I pulled her uniform down to her ankles, and she kicked it off along with her socks and boots. I wheeled my way over her tight stomach, tracing a path over her hip bones and licking my way down to her taut thighs.

Then to my surprise, Cruise said, "I've got a great tool to show you."

She bent over and opened the big metal toolbox she kept under the seat. From among the wrenches, pliers, and balls of wire, she extracted a fleshy-textured, strap-on dildo, which she promptly parked it between her legs and buckled it tight.

She grinned. "I've been saving this for a special occasion."

"And this is it?"

"You bet. I promise you'll remember this night forever, Dee."

I knew she was right when she began to strip me completely, making small bites on every newly uncovered bit of skin. Then she began to remove my slick panties and murmured when she found how lubed and ready I was. My engine had been warming for way too long.

She propped herself on her strong arms, stroking the insides of my legs with her fleshy wrench. The dildo was warm from the night air and its nearness to Cruise's body.

The straps around her hips scraped my outer lips, tugging at my hairs. As the blood rushed to my overheating groin, Cruise revved me up even more, leaning forward and teasing me with light tool-strokes on my inner lips, opening me for her.

She put the key halfway into the ignition, waiting for my engine to turn over. I pushed my hips into her and forced the rest of the dildo up me. At first, her thrusts were slow but thorough. She propelled in and out of me with measured precision. Then her strokes picked up steam, and she pumped in and out of me like a souped-up piston. My throbbing crevice swallowed every inch of rubber.

At that point, my body ignited and my butt swerved, lifted, and crashed back down on the leather seat again and again. Ecstasy shook me inside out as I gasped, moaned, and twitched my way to oblivion.

The second it was over, I wanted her all over again. But she was already extracting herself and undoing the straps of the harness.

"Did I live up to my promise?"

"With every stroke, Cruise."

My playful expression turned naughty. With a quick motion, I pushed her down on the seat. Then I grabbed the discarded dildo and wedged my head between her legs. Her groans became audible as her personal store of vulvaline slicked my face in vast gobs.

I licked my way across her moist inner thighs all the way to her thick, dark pubes, rubbing my face all over her. She groaned when I inserted my agile tongue inside her.

Cruise's face and body dripped with rivulets of sweat as she grabbed my head to hurry my tongue-thrusts. I could feel her stiff clit palpitating against my tingling lips.

I took the dildo and gently prodded her, keeping my tongue moving at the same time. When I sensed that her muscles were relaxing, I drove the dildo all the way up her. Her muscles contracted around it, forcing it farther up her. A perverse smile crossed her lips, motivating more boldness on my part. I moved the toy around in a counter-clockwise motion. Her hips followed my lead and ground in the opposite direction to maximize her pleasure.

"Harder, damn it! I'm there! I'm fucking there!"

I quickened my pace and widened the expanse of my

tongue as much as possible to cover more of her sensitive flesh. My face became red and chafed, but her lush cream salved me.

Then she really began to smoke. Her body reeled, and she lifted her hips full force into my mouth. I kept thrusting the dildo in and out of her while my tongue pushed her over the edge.

Her fingers dug into my shoulders as Cruise bucked and jerked, burning that rubber cylinder right off its shaft-mount until wave after orgasmic wave surged through her.

When she began to slow down, I extracted the dildo but kept up the tonguing until she lay back, panting and stroking my sweaty back. Finally, I slid my tongue out of her and turned my head to the side, resting my right cheek on her still pulsating body and gasping for breath.

We'd reluctantly slipped our clothes back on and were kissing again when we heard tires rumbling on loose gravel. Behind us, a horn started honking like crazy.

"What the hell is that all about?" I scowled, twisting around in the seat. A pair of blinding headlights blocked my view. My pulse began to hammer. Had some homicidal nut targeted us, too?

Apparently so. I groaned when the headlights cut out and I saw a familiar pink Mercedes wedged up behind the back of our truck. The bottom dropped out of my stomach as I realized who was behind that crank call to the garage.

"You sluts!" Kitty screamed as she leaped from her

car, the sides of her tight lavender dress nearly splitting in the process. Wielding her cell phone like a piece of artillery, she lunged for Cruise's window and started banging on it. "Do you screw all your employees or just my woman?" The points of her shoes made staccato noises, like shots from a BB gun, as she kicked at Cruise's door. "Come on! Get out of there and fight!"

When Cruise didn't respond, Kitty moved around to my side and continued her tirade there. Cruise turned to me, her voice low. "Keep talking to her," she said, then opened the door quietly and crawled under the tow truck.

"Cruise–" I yelped, but she was already gone. My heart raced faster and sweat gathered under my clothes. How could she leave me alone with Kitty ranting and raving only inches from my face? Still, I couldn't afford to show my fear. So I looked straight at her and raised my voice so she could hear me through the closed window.

"Kitty, listen! This jealousy thing has got to end. We've got to end. I've thought about it, and there's no way it can work. I'm just not kinky enough for you!"

"You sure had a different side to you a couple of months ago, lover. What happened? Cruise does you better? Is that it? Answer me, you little vixen!" She started banging on my window so hard I thought it would shatter.

I almost wept with relief when Cruise cracked open the driver's side door and silently slipped back behind the wheel.

"Cruise, what are we going to do?" I whispered, but

she just winked, started the engine, and slowly pulled away. Still shouting, Kitty stumbled alongside us on her awkward spiked heels.

"You miserable, good-for-nothing lesbo carjackers!" she ranted. "You'll hear from my attorneys about this! Get back here with my baby!"

I couldn't figure out what she was going about until I glanced in the rearview mirror and saw the Mercedes securely fastened to the back of our truck.

As we rolled out onto the highway, Kitty dropped farther and farther back, waving her cell phone in our direction and screaming like a banshee in heat.

"Are we just going to leave her there?" I asked. Though I tried to sound scandalized, I couldn't keep the wicked smile off my lips.

"Let her call for a limo. By the time she gets back to the garage it'll be closed up tight till tomorrow. She can deal with the emergency road call paperwork–and fees–in the morning."

Her hand moved up my thigh. I couldn't remember why I had ever resisted her. Grinning, I leaned over and let her lips and fingers drive me to ecstasy all over again.

Bitter Cream

Rivulets of sweat dripped down the back of my uniform and slithered between my breasts. The constant clang of plates dumped by the waitresses on the metal counter pounded at my temples. When I escaped the steamy kitchen, I had to swerve to avoid a male customer's out-thrust hand, which lunged at my ass for the third time that night.

As usual, the air conditioning was on the blink, and it was the middle of a scorching July in Newport, Rhode Island, vacation capital in Hell. Day after day, hundreds of rude tourists, rowdy teenagers, and mud-splattered little leaguers marched into The Creamery and demanded quick service.

I'd thought of quitting more than once that summer, but instead I became even more determined to stick it out through August, after which I would head out to enroll in the State University's pre-med program. So, pent up and frazzled, I steeled myself and went through the motions, served the lardy food and thawed ice cream, scrubbed away layers of grime, and trudged back to my parents' little run-down house. All my personal energy was set aside for the future.

When I met Beth for the first time, she was standing in the kitchen with her auburn hair pinned up and laughter in her shrewd grey eyes. When I admitted that I'd never been a waitress before, she grasped my hand and promised to look after me. Her small fingers felt warm and sweaty in mine. For some reason, her heat flooded my whole body.

We shared the night shift for months, and soon developed an easy working relationship. Whenever there was a lull, we'd gossip about the other waitress, Viola, whom we suspected of making it with both the owner and the customers. While we joked, Beth imitated Viola by pushing her breasts forward and thrusting her butt in reverse. I couldn't stop laughing.

One night, I told Beth that I was planning to be pre-med in the Fall.

"I had no idea you were leaving," she said, speaking more quickly than usual. "I'm really happy for you. I'm hoping to get an M.B.A. myself. I figure I'll save up for a couple more years, then start applying to some of the smaller schools. Someone will take me eventually."

"I'm sure they will, Beth. Of course, I won't be gone for good. My parents are still here, and I'll need to do some part-time work during the vacations and stuff. Will you be leaving when you go to school?"

"I don't know. Maybe. Would you miss me?" she asked. Her eyes opened wide. I wondered if she understood how I attached I was to her.

"Yes, I would miss you very much."

We were interrupted by a customer, and the conversation dangled between us for weeks. Then one night I happened to stroll outside and saw her get into her red pickup. As I watched her drive away, I saw the rainbow sticker on her bumper for the first time.

The following day we were both off, and I spotted her at a small park near the beach. I felt a stab when I saw her embrace an attractive dark-haired woman. I didn't know what to do with the strange feelings that boiled up inside me.

I remembered how I had reacted when she'd shaken my hand that first time. I realized I'd been watching her a lot. I'd noticed how her athletic body bent like a graceful reed in a soft breeze when she leaned over to pick up the dishes. I'd noticed how bright her smile was, how tight the muscles in her arms were. I'd even noticed how her small breasts bounced to the rhythm of her sensual gait, her tray precisely balanced on one muscular shoulder.

The evening after I'd seen her with the woman in the park, I didn't know how to act with her. I kept thinking of her full lips, imagining what it would be like to taste her, to experience her warm breath on my chin and neck. I thought about begging her to teach me what women do together, although I was starting to get some pretty creative ideas myself.

The next thing I knew, my watch showed one in the morning and the cook was waving goodbye. The two of us were left by ourselves to close up. I was straightening up the sundae bar when I dropped a carton of ice cream, which split as it hit the carpet. Beth came over and got on the floor with me to help me clean up the mess. Laughing, she licked maple walnut off her fingers.

"This is my favorite flavor," she smiled like a little girl sneaking a treat.

"Mine, too," I said, looking into her twinkling eyes. She was so adorable at that moment, with the ice cream dripping down her fingers and her pink tongue licking them off, that I began licking her fingers, too. Then I grew bolder and started sucking the ice cream off them.

After three or four slurps, I moved to the corner of her luscious mouth, and she kissed me back.

The sweetness of that first kiss was unbearable. We kept tonguing each other while the ice cream got all over us. Nothing mattered except the way we wanted each other.

"I thought you were straight, Annie. Are you sure this is what you want?" she mumbled and gasped in between kisses.

"Beth, don't stop. Teach me. I want you more than anything."

Her mouth clamped down on mine again, but this time her fingers went straight for my blouse. I moaned as she undid each of my buttons and then unhooked my bra. My breasts bounced free and brushed against her cool skin.

"Mmmm," I groaned as my stiff nipple jabbed her palm. "You–you don't know how I've wanted this. I'll never be the same, Beth."

"I don't want you to change," she responded, stroking my sticky bangs from my face and gazing intently into my eyes as she cradled me.

Suddenly, I remembered seeing her the day before. My heart raced. "Wait," I said, pulling away. "Before we do this. . . I need to know about that woman in the park. Who is she–to you, I mean? Your lover?"

She shook her head. "No, we dated but it didn't work out. I guess I was too crushed out on you, but I thought you were straighter than straight." Beth caressed my cheek with her sticky hand. Then she frowned. "Are you sure about this? I don't want you to change your mind and hurt me."

"Never. I swear it."

She kissed me again with her whole tongue, then swept it down my neck to my aching breasts. Her mouth found what it wanted. Her sucking became insistent, and her tongue melted into my nipple. I lay back on the floor and felt the sticky ice cream seep into my back. Beth crawled on top of me. Instinctively, I lifted my hips and mashed myself into her.

"I'm going to teach you everything, Annie, everything," she whispered. "But for your first lesson, you won't need all these clothes."

She proceeded to remove every stitch of my clothing, including my saturated panties, then covered her hands in the spilled ice cream. I giggled as she rubbed the sticky stuff all over me, dipping her fingers between my legs every once in a while to tease me.

After that, she got a devilish look in her eyes and reached up to the sundae bar. In no time, she had me decked out in whipped cream, warm fudge sauce, nuts, and a cute cherry to match my engorged button.

Beth dove in like she was satisfying a long-repressed sweet tooth. With aching slowness, she ate her way past my tingling inner thighs, through my decked-out mound, all the way to my steaming inner folds, lapping the concoction as she went. With each nibble, her hands groped and pinched my swollen nipples. Her face was covered with the frothy, sugar-glazed coatings.

When she slid her tongue into my tender crevice, probing and thrusting, all the blood in my body rushed to that point. I became light-headed and giddy with intensifying desire.

"Yes, I'm almost. . . . Yes!" I croaked, rolling my head from side to side in complete abandon. Beth licked me faster and deeper, forcing me right up to the edge of my desire's ragged peak. As I spiraled over the edge, I grasped her shell-like ears and pushed her harder into me. My body lifted so high off the floor that I was practically doing a back-bend into her mouth.

Despite my contortions, Beth didn't let up for a second. Soon I began to explode, twisting and turning my pelvis to the tempo of her thrusting mouth. The sweetest ripples I'd ever felt surged through my nervous system, blowing all my fuses and draining the strength from my body. Toward the end, I thought I felt Beth's lips break into a satisfied smile against my skin. But by then I was back on the floor, gasping and sweating.

Fighting to catch my breath, I reached out and pulled her on top of me. She kissed me again, and I tasted sundae fixings along with my own cream. I'd never savored anything so delicious. At that point, all I wanted was to give Beth the same joy she'd given me.

I undid her uniform top and pushed up her bra. Her pink nipples beckoned my curious mouth. Slowly, I planted my mouth on the pointed tip, sampling that sensuous scoop of flesh for the first time. When I sucked harder, she groaned with pleasure.

I peeled off her uniform and found her whole body flushed with lust. Her taut flesh glistened with the sweat of desires unmet.

Beth braced herself with her hands, which she placed just under my arms. All her weight was strategically centered as she positioned herself on top of me.

My personal creamery started to overflow as she massaged me with her rigid woman-pearl. Nothing had ever felt so right. I grabbed her snug rear end and crushed her into me. Beth helped, thrusting back at me and circling her hips on mine with long, drawn-out movements. She stiffened as her urgency increased.

"Come on, baby. Come for me like you never did before," she coaxed.

"Yes, Beth, it's what I want–you're what I want!"

My burning lips pressed into her shoulder, and my hands traveled down her back. Her rocking motions became faster and rougher, her breathing frantic. Gasping, I clutched at her with all my strength and rode the candy-scented wave that crashed over us, lifted us, and hurled us down again.

Afterward, Beth lay on top of me, her cheek next to my beating heart. Our bodies were totally covered in melted ice cream, sticky chocolate sauce, and the dripping remains of the whipped cream. Nothing had ever felt so sensual.

"No regrets?" she asked.

"Only one," I said as I settled my mouth against her neck and took a long, slow lick. "I regret not doing this sooner."

Beth laughed and bent down to kiss me again.

The rest of the summer was a blur of intense sex and emotions. Passions I'd never experienced with men exploded every time Beth and I were together, and it seemed like we couldn't be together enough. At work, we'd trade hungry stares and brush up against each other until it was all we could do not to dash for the storage closet in the pantry. Once we really did go out to her truck and get down on the floor so our heads wouldn't show in the window. There we kissed and tongued each other until the whole truck was as soggy as a sauna. When our break was over, we smoothed out our clothes and returned to the restaurant. No one suspected a thing.

As the weeks wore on, I began crossing off the days on the old wall calendar by the cash register. Sometimes I did it in front of Beth, but she never seemed to notice. The only person who mentioned it was Viola.

"Bet you can't wait to blow this popsicle stand, huh, Annie? Probably forget all about us, slaving away in here while you're off doing brain surgery somewhere." She laughed, apparently trying to picture me wielding a scalpel. "Make sure you come back and leave us a big tip."

"Don't worry," I said, looking straight at Beth, who busied herself by refilling a row of coffee pots. "I won't forget any of you."

In the third week of August, I quit the Creamery. It was time for me to head for the city, to find an apartment and start my new life. I decided to ask Beth to come with me.

I asked her late Sunday night, right after we'd made love in her apartment bedroom.

"I don't think that would be a good idea," she said in a flat voice.

"Why not? I love you. It makes perfect sense."

She sighed, then rolled over on the pillow. "It would ruin what we have, Annie. We'd start noticing every ugly thing about one another, and then all this closeness would become resentment."

"Why?" I asked, dumbfounded.

"Well, for one thing," she scowled, "you're going to be a doctor. I'm going to be a friggin' waitress for the rest of my life."

"But I thought you wanted to get out of this rut as much as I did. You want your M.B.A.–why not start it now? You can find a job in Providence and split the bills with me. We'd get by."

Beth shook her head. Her own cheeks were flushed, but not with passion. "Oh, Annie, you didn't think I was serious about that, did you? I just made it up so you wouldn't think I was as intellectually challenged as everyone else down at the restaurant. In case you haven't noticed, Annie. I don't read. I watch videos, for god's sake!"

"Then you don't want to leave Newport?" My voice was a strangled whisper.

"Honey, most of us will never leave. Who knows? Maybe you won't either, in the end. After all, your folks will still be here."

"It's so strange," I murmured, close to tears. "I remember how you begged me not to hurt you."

She didn't answer. Instead, she switched the lights off and turned herself away from me.

"Can't we resolve this, Beth?"

"Not tonight. I'm too tired," she said. "I guess you've forgotten what it's like to work those late shifts."

She pretended to sleep after that. I left.

The next day felt long and aimless, now that I had

no job to go to, but I forced myself not to drive down to the restaurant. Instead, I moped around the house, working intermittently on my packing. The phone never rang.

By the end of the afternoon, I couldn't bear to be away from her. Begging her to be with me just one more time seemed undignified, but eventually my need overpowered me.

I bought a bouquet of white carnations, her favorites, and walked to her apartment. I wanted to tell her I'd been too impulsive because I loved her so much. The words played out in my head as I walked up the rickety stairs to her place.

The apartment was locked, but I used the key she'd given me. I didn't think she'd mind. A light was on in the bedroom, and the door was ajar. I started to rush in, then stopped dead in my tracks.

Beth lay sobbing on her unmade bed. I walked in with the flowers. She sat up and looked at me, her eyes bleary and red. "Thanks."

"Beth, what is it? Can I do something for you?"

She shook her head and shielded her face with one hand. "No. I'm fine."

My voice started to crack, too. "Beth, I miss you already," I blurted, moving to sit on the bed. She barely moved. "I can't stand being without you, even for one day. How can I face the rest of my life like this? Tell me what to say so you'll come with me."

"You and I are different. I don't want you to get bored with me. I prefer to end this before I see disgust in your eyes, Annie."

"Well, I won't let you end it like this." I reached for her and cradled her in my arms. "Especially when I know you don't really want to."

"I don't," she confessed, then pushed herself off my shoulder. Undaunted, I reached for her again. Eventually she gave in to me, and her sobs melted into frenzied kisses. Her body seemed to dissolve into mine.

When it was over, we lay naked together, with Beth looking up at the ceiling and me staring at her lovely face.

Toying With Me

For months, my girlfriend and I had been planning our trip to Provincetown. My imagination was filled with pictures of the two of us embracing in the dunes and caressing one another as we waded in the cold surf. Then, two days before we were set to leave, she stunned me by dumping me for another woman. I've never been the kind to sit and pine, so I ended up on vacation by myself.

Like all the other tourists, I trod the picturesque main street with the fresh, salty wind in my nostrils as a virtual procession of proud, sexy lesbians came strutting past me. I felt like I'd found paradise, except for one problem: all the women I found myself attracted to had already paired off. As I watched them smooch, cuddle, and steal kisses on the doorsteps of restaurants and guesthouses, my nether regions started to burn for some action I had no idea how to find. I was growing more lonely and more frustrated by the minute.

Finally, on my third or fourth pass through town, I spotted a doorway I'd missed before. It sat nestled in the basement of another shop, partially obscured by a wrought-iron fence. I raised my brows at the gaudily painted sign, which combined a frank announcement of the store's wares with a coy, abstract rendition of the bodily areas it aspired to serve.

Well, this was a day for firsts, and I'd never even seen an all-woman sex shop before, never mind browse in one. So I took a deep breath, scooted down the worn stone steps, and ducked inside.

The dim, cool interior proved a relief from the bright sunlight and sweltering heat outside. So did the fact that I was the only customer, and the lone salesgirl sat in the corner with her back to me, reading a lesbian magazine. The full-color photos I spied over her shoulder left nothing to the imagination. When my eyes adjusted, I sidled over to the back wall and started to browse a rack of vibrators and dildos. I'd never really gone in for things like that, preferring a sex partner I could share coffee with in the morning. Still, this was Provincetown, and I hadn't exactly come here to catch up on my knitting. I figured that a second-hand orgasm would be better than none at all.

I soon became engrossed in weighing and squeezing the various products, almost as if I were in the produce section of some naughty grocery store. I nearly jumped when I heard the salegirl's voice pipe up beside me.

"Hi, I'm Hannah. Find everything you need?" she chirped. Fighting back a blush, I dropped a big green dildo hewn in the shape of a frolicking dolphin and flashed her a nonchalant smile.

I liked what I saw. She seemed about my age, twenty-three, but apparently took a more experimental approach to fashion. Her tight spandex halter top was tied above her navel, while black army boots matched the thick leather belt looped through her cut-offs. A small, tasteful gold ring glinted in the left side of her nose.

"Just browsing, really," I said in a flirtatious tone, hoping my voice sounded more confident than I felt. "I only got here this morning."

I immediately regretted this inane *non sequitur*, but Hannah didn't seem to notice. Instead, she offered a conspiratorial grin. "So, have you checked out Big Ben?"

When I looked blank, she moved to a nearby display case, slid open a glass door, and picked up an enormous hunk of rubber. She held it out between us, and I found myself staring at a double-headed dildo. Its surface was mottled, almost like blue marble, its shape contorted into a lopsided *V.* One of the dual shafts was significantly shorter and blunter than the other, while the bottom had been flattened so that Big Ben could sit upright.

"Big Ben has been ergonomically designed to allow both participants maximum pleasure," Hannah explained in the deadpan voice of a tour guide, casually turning the dildo around and nestling the stubbier head against the crotch of her cut-offs. I found it hard to meet her eyes when she pointed the longer shaft at me. "The shorter end is for the partner doing the thrusting. The longer one provides extra-deep penetration for the recipient," she went on. Then, apparently to make sure I understood, she began to perform a seesawing motion with her hips. I felt my panties suddenly grow damp.

"Uh. . . sounds great," I said, my eyes roving over her tanned body and spiky, beach-lightened hair. I imagined that her bush would be that same sandy color, too, and that her lush body, when naked, would smell like the ocean. I steeled my nerves and took a chance. "In fact, I'd be tempted to buy it if I had anyone to share it with."

She arched a brow. "I'd be happy to give you a

demonstration." I stood stunned as she locked up the shop and pulled down the blinds. Dazed, I followed her through a bead curtain and into a small storage area, where a little cot was already set up.

"Won't you get in trouble?"

"Nah. The manager likes for us to have first-hand knowledge of all our products." Hastily, Hannah stripped off her skimpy outfit, then turned and did the same for me. She held up Big Ben like a trophy and winked. "OK, let's get him nice and wet first."

Almost reverently, she placed the dildo on the narrow bed and knelt, then bent over to suck it deep into her mouth. Her blazing blue eyes trained on me, she lathered it up with her tongue. Gooseflesh broke out all over my naked body as I sank to my knees as well. Hannah stretched her arms across the thin mattress, took my breasts in her warm hands and strummed my erect nipples with her thumbs.

Taking a long, deep breath, I bent slowly forward and sheathed Big Ben with my mouth. Instead of reaching for Hannah's tits, which were really too small and perky for feeling up at that distance, I slipped my hands under the bed and started stroking my nails across the tops of her thighs. Her flesh trembled and tightened under my touch, and even though her mouth was full of dildo, I could hear her moan with arousal.

We knelt there for several minutes, slicking up Big Ben and, more indirectly, each other. We were soon bobbing up and down in tandem like ancient warrior-women venerating some makeshift fertility shrine. Finally, Hannah announced that we were ready to proceed. With the skill of a professional (which I suppose she was), she leapfrogged onto the cot and spread her legs wide.

My mouth watered again at the sight of those flared pussy-lips, thatched with sparse gold hair as I'd predicted and already ringed with thick, musky lubrication. "Let's get started," I whispered.

Without hesitation, Hannah scooted herself over the shorter of the two heads. "I'll take this end," she said, and fitted the blue rubber dome neatly into her hole. Though it looked at least three inches wide, it vanished inside her without a hitch.

"Are you sure?" I asked, nervously contemplating the longer shaft that would soon come plunging into me.

"'Tis better to give than to receive," Hannah joked. "Besides, I promised you an official demonstration, so I need to be in the driver's seat."

I shivered when she put her hands on my flushed thighs and spread them apart until I felt the muscles catch. I felt more than a little self-conscious to crouch there exposed like that, but I was also incredibly turned on. My sauce was drooling out so fast that a steaming waterfall was flowing straight down the insides of my quivering thighs. I imagined that Big Ben would slither all the way into me with only the slightest nudge.

My vulnerable pose was apparently turning Hannah on, too. Breathing hard, she fitted the other head of that double-headed monster to my throbbing pussy-rim. My hips rolled forward, and I felt the tender circumference of my wet hole clench and contract as her fingers brushed past it. I braced myself by putting both hands on her shoulders, then lifted my butt as she tilted her body to fuck me.

I held my breath, overcome with shudders of pleasure as Hannah started rocking up and down on her end of the dildo. The thick tube pushing into my scalding tunnel felt almost unbearably delectable as her first few motions shoved about three inches of Big Ben into my frothing core. Every time she pushed forward, another inch or so would snake into my convulsing depths.

"Oh, yes," I groaned, clutching desperately at her shoulder blades as hot torrents of passion boiled through me.

Hannah pumped forward again, her fists clutching the sides of the cot for balance and torque. "You're nice and tight," she grunted. "Sometimes that makes it feel even better."

"It's pretty incredible so far," I agreed.

As Hannah writhed in front of me, a trickle of sweat beaded up to trickle sensuously into the flexing valley between her small breasts. As my eyes followed the glowing bead down the length of her torso and watched it seep into her scruffy pubic bush, I felt myself expand and gulp the last section of Big Ben's slippery shank.

When the flat rubber base touched my ass-cheeks, I failed to suppress an outright wail of lust and satisfaction. Already I could feel a series of telltale tremors building inside me. My inner muscles, too, were rejoicing, aching deliciously as they clamped down on the welcome invader.

When I was fully sheathed, Hannah gave a little cry of triumph. Her eyes were half-closed, and as her little thrusts intensified, I could see that she was also on the brink of orgasm. Moaning, she encircled my bare waist with one hand, then reached out to use the other on my bud.

"Oh, Hannah, that's beautiful," I gushed–in every sense of the word–as her fingertips polished my pearl gently, yet intently. She worked me over as if the world's most precious diamond lay nestled between my wet red folds.

It sure didn't take long for the double-whammy of her fingers and Big Ben's internal massage to ignite my innermost fuses. My whole body went rigid as what seemed like two separate streaks of hot white power shot out from my clit and my core to connect in my trembling center.

"Wow!" I screamed. "Harder!"

"Yeah, yeah," she gasped. Eyes squeezed shut, Hannah pumped her hips faster. "Me, too."

At that point, pure instinct took over in both of us. We matched each other's fevered lunges stroke for stroke, driving the twin rubber heads into our bodies in perfect, steaming sync.

"Do it," Hannah cheered me on, her voice cracking as she too began to twitch all over. My entire upper body became paralyzed with ecstasy as I exploded again and again. My pussy was squeezing the rubber shank so hard I imagined that I might actually snap it half and trap it inside my willing body forever. Waves of pleasure more powerful than the ones on the beach rushed up my spine until even my neck muscles tingled. Though I'm not usually a sweaty person, burning droplets poured down my back and sizzled against my skin.

Hannah came even longer than I did, whooping and writhing and creaming all over that unyielding rubber stem. When I had finished, her finger left my clit and fastened instead on my nipple, pinching and pressing it with total abandon. The sensation, coming so soon after my raucous detonation, almost sent me right back over the edge. It would have, I'm sure, if the protracted excitement of my pussy closing in on itself hadn't worn my excitable nerves to a frazzle.

When the last tremors faded, and I slowly regained control of my body, I slumped back on the narrow cot, propping myself up on my elbows. With a knowing smile, Hannah extracted Big Ben from my stretched-out hole. My rim seemed to grab regretfully at it, and my copious juices made a squishy, sucking noise around the heated rubber.

"Good one?" Hannah asked as she parted her legs and slid out Ben's shorter limb. Her fleshy folds were red and sticky, and I could see them almost visibly pulsing from the aftershocks.

"The best," I managed to groan before flopping flat on my back. I wasn't exaggerating, either. My blood and nerves were still singing with joy, and my skin burned brighter and hotter than the sun on white sand.

Hannah stretched out the opposite way, with her feet next to my head, so that the small bed could accommodate us both. I took advantage of that fact by sucking two of her tan little toes into my mouth. She laughed softly and plopped the now-sticky Big Ben on her stomach.

"So, do you want to buy him?"

"Mmm," I said dreamily, extracting my tongue from between her toes, "I'm not sure."

She wriggled her foot happily against my lips, her fingers creeping up to dip into my wet center. I shuddered as fresh appetite surged in me.

"Damn, and I thought my sales pitch was more convincing."

I shrugged, mostly as an excuse to trap her fingers where they were still lodged. "Well, I don't think I could really make an informed decision until I try him out the other way around."

Without missing a beat, Hannah slid her first two fingers all the way back inside me. I had a feeling she wasn't finding me quite so tight anymore. "Guess I'll have to give you another demonstration, then. How about tomorrow?"

"How about right now?" I suggested.

She happily agreed.

Falloving

My burnished heart pines

Nestled amid night cravings

Days that smolder for you

Felled by your exit

I am bare. Yearning you hadn't

Left me to define

Want's halting remains

And the caress you left behind

Losing Track

Half the college was there to cheer me, and the rest of the women's track team, on. I breathed deeply, straightened my number, and jammed my feet in place. When the gun went off, I sprinted faster than ever before, slicing the wind with my every leap. Multicolored leaves swirled above me like an earthy kaleidoscope. I wanted to win more than anything. The crowd roared as I neared the finish line, my breath burning in my lungs, edging out the fierce-eyed competitor at my side.

Then, at the last second, Meg passed me.

While I limped to the locker room alone, my aching head slumped on my chest, I heard someone rush up behind me and felt familiar, sweaty arms slide around me. "God, you're sexy when you run like that."

I gritted my teeth. "I know you beat me. You don't have to gloat about it."

Meg blinked in surprise and dropped back a step. "Jeez, Daria, I barely won. It's not like you've never beaten me," she responded, still panting from the run. "Just cut the crap. Everyone is watching us."

She was right: our teammates were looking in our direction and whispering to one another. "I don't give a damn," I yelled back.

"You'd better take your little drama somewhere private." I heard an authoritative voice above the crowd noises. Colt, the graduate student who was our assistant coach, stood at my side. "We're all on the same side here, remember?"

I blushed and lowered my eyes. "Yeah, okay, sorry," I grumbled. "I lost it for a minute."

"Tomorrow we're going to start working out together every day," Colt said. "Next meet you'll finish first in at least one event. I guarantee it."

I finally managed to smile weakly. "Thanks, Colt."

"You both did great. Now stop being so hard on yourself and hit the showers."

Meg, the rest of the team, and I all started for the locker room, jogging slowly to work out the kinks in our muscles. About halfway there, Meg paused and looked back over her shoulder at me. I averted my head and avoided her gaze. Shrugging, she turned to a friend and chatted while they trotted along. With a sense of relief, I dropped back until the two of them had disappeared ahead of me.

The next day, as promised, Colt and I met at six in the morning. When I looked at her rock-hard body in action, I understood the value of cross-training. She whacked my ass in greeting and handed me an energy bar. "No breakfast, right?"

I laughed and chomped the whole thing down in three bites. We did some stretches and then hit the track.

I struggled to keep up with her. "You're really fast."

"So are you. You don't have to win every damn race to prove it."

"I know. I just hate losing to Meg."

"Daria, she really cares about you."

"I know, but she makes me insecure. She's so damn . . . *good.*"

"It's your decision to feel that way, hon," Colt said,

scowling. When I didn't respond, she fixed me with a sharp stare. "Would you prefer to go out with a loser so you can feel superior?"

"I know how it sounds," I snapped. "It's just that she has a 3.9. She volunteers at the women's shelter. She's got a perfect body."

"That would explain why you like her."

"Oh, you know what I mean. She never fucks up. I always have to fight to keep up with her. It's always been like that."

"Are you afraid she'll dump you?"

"No! You don't get it, do you, Colt?"

"I do get it. You need to grow up and communicate your fears to Meg and stop embarrassing her in front of everybody. Discipline yourself."

My face dropped into a sulk. "Whatever."

We ran the rest of the way in silence, though at the end I did promise to meet her the next day with a better attitude. It wasn't that I really meant it, but I was afraid she'd get me kicked off the team or something.

The gym seemed particularly oppressive the next afternoon. The heat was on for some inexplicable reason, and tinny speakers piped out crappy top 40's music. Tense, I rowed to the repetitive beat until I felt my quads begin to tighten. The pain made me wince and gasp.

"Having trouble with your leg?" Meg's voice asked suddenly. I started, so caught up in my thoughts of her that I hadn't noticed her come in.

"I'm all right," I stammered. "Just sore."

She nodded and walked past me, raking her fingers through her spiky bleached blonde hair while she debated which machine to use. With a determined look, she mounted the stairmaster. I resumed my rowing.

Soon I caught her staring at me while she worked out. Whenever I looked at her face, though, she turned her sharp eyes away. Beads of sweat coursed down her neck and disappeared between her small breasts. Still I kept heaving my shoulders, ignoring the pain that burned through my body like a fever.

"Daria, let up when it starts to hurt, for god's sake!" Meg yelled. She stepped off the machine and flew toward me. Her hands clamped over mine to prevent me from taking another stroke.

I felt the warmth of her face on my neck. "You're putting too much pressure on your back," she said, kneading my tense shoulders. "Why don't you try it like this instead?" Her muscular arms moved down to hug my breasts. My nipples stiffened with anticipation. "Now lean against me and pull your abs in tight." Meg's brow furrowed with concentration.

My breathing more audible, I began to row again. Meg's hands slipped down to my lower belly. She spread her fingers over my abs and then slid them to my quads. "Just as I suspected—you're much too tense."

"That's an understatement!"

I was so lost in her touch that I didn't hear her response. Even when she pulled back and released me, I still felt the hot impression of her body on mine. I was about to turn and kiss her when she jumped up and fled like Joseph from the Egyptian Princess.

Damn her, I thought, standing and kneading my sore

muscles with frustrated fingers. It was like she'd been put on earth just to mess up my life.

Only if you let her, I reminded myself sternly. Then I winced and started rowing again.

I devoted the rest of the day to my coursework, then settled down to a long, solitary evening in my room. The hours dragged by while I tried to read, then study, then watch TV without the slightest focus. I was about to give up and turn in when I heard a knock at my door.

She stood there in a Spandex pullover and faded black jeans. Neither did much to hide the tight muscles that rippled along her chiseled arms and long, sinewy legs.

"Meg," I said. We barely made it to the bed.

I'd always loved to look at Meg naked. The space between her legs was only sparsely covered with blonde down, so light that it looked almost silver. Those wispy tendrils glistened with moisture as she gazed at the sweaty body I hastily bared for her.

Her hands groped my breasts, fingers tickling my sensitive nipples like withering grass in autumn. Meg tweaked my hardening buds playfully, sending quivers through my torso. Her palms molded my skin to her grasp. I responded, crushing my chest into her. Then my own hands reached for her breasts. They felt like warm pudding, liquefying into my greedy palms.

I loved the feel of her weight on my body as her lust melted into my own. She spread her legs wider to give me easy access to her treasures. Soft blonde down stuck to my face as I rubbed my cheeks back and forth over her doused outer lips.

She murmured helplessly as I put my right hand under her and tilted her pelvis, and then the rest of her, up toward my movements. Her warm breasts plunged against my own.

We thrust and squirmed together, our heartbeats throbbing in sync as the beginnings of a mutual orgasm sizzled through our systems.

When she was right on the edge, I smiled and pulled back for a moment. "Tell me," I said. "Tell me how good I am for you."

"It's true," she wheezed, twisting her hands through my hair. "You're the best, Daria. Don't stop!"

Satisfied, I tantalized her with a few quick strokes of my tongue. Then I took a deep breath, tensed, and plunged my whole face into the maddening sweetness that was Meg.

Early the next morning, I left Meg asleep in my narrow dorm bed, pulled on my sweats, and headed for the track. I was determined to get there before Colt did and before Meg had the chance to sidetrack me like she probably intended.

My laps improved when I shifted my focus to the autumn foliage, aglitter with cool autumn dew, that encircled the track. The warm colors and burnished tones relaxed me. The run, the beauty, the feelings inside me came together. My strides took on a will of their own. My spirits lifted in a classic runner's high, as if I were flying along with those floating leaves, part of something bigger than me.

The more I lost myself, the more I felt connected to myself–like a carefree, child running through her own playground. I realized that wanting Meg was only a part of me. No matter how much I wanted her, there was so much more to who I was.

Then I rounded the next curve and felt her eyes drill twin holes through my back. I tried to distract myself, to concentrate on the meet coming up, on the weekend or the leaves. I forced myself not to glance back at her, not to take my eyes off the thin white line that marked my finish.

The moment I crossed it, I felt a sudden stab in my right shinbone. Cursing in pain, I sat down hard in the grass. Stretching my foot out, I clutched my calf in both hands.

I'm not sure how long I sat there, my leg throbbing with pain and my eyes blazing with tears. When I felt Colt's concerned touch on my damp spine, my muscles tensed even more.

"I'm doing okay," I insisted. Trying not to wince, I kneaded my strained peroneal.

Colt bent over and got a feel of my leg. "You're okay. Just stay off it for a while."

Meg stood next to her. "I would have stopped her if I'd known," she said. Her eyes were fixed on my face, but she talked about me as if I weren't even there.

Colt straightened up, rubbing her worried forehead between thumb and forefinger. "Meg, get Daria home and don't let her out of your sight until she has screamed and yelled enough to de-stress for a while. I need a break from the both of you."

"You don't have to bother," I said, brushing the sand

off my legs after Colt had stormed away. Still, I grasped the hand Meg stretched out to me. Pain flashed all the way up my leg, and she wrapped her arm around me tightly. She stood motionless, only inches away. The healthy, musky scent of her body made me dizzy with lust.

I clung to Meg, afraid of falling, afraid she'd never let go. We didn't speak until we stumbled back into my room, where she sat me down on the futon. She didn't look up while her soft hands massaged my shins.

"I really wish you wouldn't do this," I said. My teeth were clenched, and not just from the pain. I heard Meg sigh with irritation.

"Why are you so angry at me all the time? I try so hard to make you happy."

Tears spilled down my cheeks, stinging my skin. "It's just. . . it's just that you're so perfect." I bit off the words, then clenched my teeth as another wave of pain swept through me.

Meg rocked back on her heels and gaped up at me as if I'd gone mad. At that moment, I wondered if maybe I had. Wanting her and resenting her were so tangled together in my mind that I couldn't tell one from the other any more. Maybe they really were one and the same.

"As if!" she blurted, the words spilling out in an accusatory torrent. "You're the one who always needs to be perfect. I always feel like I need to do my very best at every thing we do together. If I screw up even once, you'll leave me."

"You're afraid?"

"Yes," she said. Her eyes were moist. "Yes."

"Oh, Meg, I thought you were competing with me all the time and that I had to keep up with you." My face reddened.

"Is that what you think?" My resolve to keep my hands off her melted away, and I slipped my fingers through her silky hair. Gently I tilted her head back, forcing her to look at me. My eyes searched hers, but found only love and admiration there.

"I wouldn't change anything about you," she answered. "You believe that, don't you?" I bit my lip, and she frowned. "You seem like you're hurting again. Is it your leg?"

"Kind of. I mean, I guess I'm going to be out of things for a while. The next few meets, at least."

"Does that bother you?"

I pulled her close to me, crushing her head into my breasts, nuzzling my chin against the top of her head. "Not as much as I thought it would."

"I'll quit, too, if you want. I mean it, Daria. Just say the word. You mean way more to me than any of Colt's 'discipline' and all that other crap. I want to be with you–even if we never hit the track again."

"No," I said. "You're too good at it to quit, especially because of me. I want you to run. I want you to win." I tipped her head back, caressing her brows with my fingers, and flashed her a mischievous smile. "But most of all, I want to make you come again."

Meg laughed, her face warm beneath my stroking fingers. "Well, I'm sure as hell not gonna stop you!"

"Glad we can agree on that," I said, then hobbled to my feet and stripped off my sports bra and shorts.

Her breath became husky as she unabashedly stared

at my breasts and the soggy curls adorning my pubic triangle.

I had just opened my lips to say something else when she kissed me—not softly, but with her whole, hungry mouth. I kissed her back, clutching her steely buttocks and crushing her groin into mine. I felt her heat blaze through her clothes and invade my body.

She didn't resist as I stripped her as naked as I was. I couldn't get enough of her concrete abs, sculpted arms, and the long, honey-colored pubes that tickled my hot thigh. When I was finished admiring her with my eyes, I bit her shoulders, her neck. I stroked and caressed her like I was polishing a marble statue's glossy limbs.

Meg moved her hands slowly down my inner thighs. Her strokes felt like caterpillars' marching feet. It seemed to go on forever, while I moved my hands up to caress her velvet globes. I was more than halfway over the edge when she knelt down and positioned her mouth on my hot center.

Her tongue, I knew from experience, was as athletic as the rest of her. It didn't disappoint me this time, either, danced over my outer lips, parted my drenched hairs, and lapped at my bud. Then she moved lower, spearing the pulsing cleft between my legs. My hands went through her hair and crushed her head to me.

I couldn't tell how long we stayed like that, while Meg licked, tongued, and caressed me to the threshold of pure ecstasy. Climax hit me swift and hard, like an atomic explosion. Victory rockets shot through my head in a searing, unbroken blaze. My mind was a blur, and my body was shaking. We melted together in pure liquid lust.

The pain in my leg seemed to disappear as we tumbled onto the bed and I stretched out alongside her, using my hands, my lips, my whole body to pleasure her. It wasn't difficult, giving her the same exquisite pleasure she'd given me. I followed her lead, just as I'd learned to do out on the track. By the time the shaking stopped, a crimson blush had spread across her chest and abs, and a low moaning sound escaped her lips. My body ached, my mind already filled with even bolder fantasies we could enjoy together.

As it turned out, my optimism proved more than justified. My leg healed quickly, thanks to Meg's constant massages, and I returned to the team more quickly than even Colt had expected. For the rest of the season, Meg and I excelled on the team–not as competitors, but as each other's biggest support. By the end of the term, we'd won every meet and even the state championship. When people asked Colt how we did it, she smiled and said that she considered incentive the key to success. I'm sure it took all her willpower not to look over and wink at us.

The truth was that before every race, Meg and I would work each other over until we were both about to come. Then we'd stop, rush to the meet, and run our asses off so we could get home and jump back into bed together. Talk about motivation!

Leaf the Butches to Me

A job transfer brought me to New Hampshire during the first week of autumn, when the foliage season transformed my new town into a collage of nutmeg brown, apple red, and sunlit yellow. Every journey outdoors, however brief, was a treat for the senses. The first few weeks, I had no time for a social life. Each time I passed a couple frolicking in a soft pile of leaves or sauntering past a pumpkin-strewn field with their arms around each other's waist, my determination to find someone myself intensified. So the moment I heard about an upcoming nature walk for singles, I rushed right to the sports shop to buy a pair of hiking boots and a backpack!

The group was scheduled to meet on the shore of a stunningly beautiful lake. It was a perfect afternoon, a warm Indian summer having pushed the temperature up to almost seventy degrees. I was almost unbearably horny, and I strategically chose an outfit that showed it.

My firm breasts bounced free under my cotton tank top, and my high-cut denim shorts displayed the muscular thighs I worked hard to keep in shape. I arrived early, determined to get first crack at any promising prospects.

As it turned out, I was in luck. In spite of the balmy weather, or perhaps because of it, only two other hikers showed up. Both of them were attractive single women who introduced themselves as Darryl and Stevie.

It was hard to say which of them I found more appealing. Darryl had reddish-brown hair the color of the turning leaves. Muscles rippled all over her compact body, which seemed as taut as a coiled spring. From the way she looked me over, I had a feeling I had already gained her approval.

Stevie was taller and darker, with serious eyes and a sensual mouth that looked like it could cause serious tremors in some lucky woman's nether regions. The two of them worked together in a local insurance firm, they explained, and had founded the hiking group in hopes of meeting women who shared their athletic interests.

"Well, I guess you'll have to settle for just me," I joked, arching my back a little so that my nipples popped up like two fingertips under my top. The left one pointed at Darryl, and the right at Stevie. The two of them smiled admiringly–first at me, and then at each other. What happened after that, I suppose, was inevitable.

We had hiked about a mile up the mountain when Darryl suggested we find a secluded spot and take a break. We sat in a circle, sipping from our canteens and admiring the breathtaking scenery. I slurped at my water bottle more energetically, my tongue still parched for a taste of honey.

"Beautiful, isn't it?' Darryl asked, flashing me a smile that made my aching pussy flutter. "Makes you want to chuck it all and just get close to nature for a while." Shifting her rear end enticingly, she shot a knowing glance at Stevie. "You look like the adventurous type, Holly," she said. "There's a great secluded trail over there. Ever take a foliage hike in the nude?"

It was really the last thing I'd expected her to suggest, but I was intrigued enough to agree. Darryl stood up and opened her backpack, her excited eyes never leaving mine, and began to strip while I stared appreciatively.

Naked, Darryl looked like a woman born to frolic naked in a primeval forest somewhere. Her chiseled legs and triangle were all dusted with a downy mat of hair the same color as the dried needles at our feet.

Stevie happily followed her lead, revealing an equally well-muscled physique. Before long they were both standing in front of me wearing only their hiking boots. I welcomed the cue to strip myself, because the sight of them standing there like that made me remember what I had been missing.

I pulled off my top first, rolling it into a ball and shoving it in my pack. Then, after taking a deep breath to calm my throbbing pulse, I undid my boots and pushed my jeans down. I could see the women shifting their feet as they stared at my damp blonde bush, the lower hairs already streaked with my thick syrup and my clit poking out of my crease like a bright red berry.

"Be sure to watch out for brambles," Stevie said helpfully, and the three of us set off on our naughty nature walk.

To my surprise, being naked under the clear, open sky was almost as much of a turn-on as watching Darryl and Stevie stroll alongside me. The crisp, fresh air tickled my skin like playful fingers, and the sunlight glittering through the trees warmed my skin like a lover held close. Before long, my clit was so hard that it felt like I'd gotten a pebble from the trail lodged between my pussy-lips.

Before long, I was no longer looking at the leaves,

and I was pretty damn sure they weren't, either. Abruptly cutting away from the trail, I plunked myself down under a tree with my naked legs spread wide. I slipped my fingers through my wet pussy hairs and tilted my head seductively.

"So what's the story, you two?" I challenged. "Are you just interested in admiring Mother Nature, or in taking full advantage of her charms?"

Darryl's face broke into an impish grin. "Thought you'd never ask." Without further ado, she followed me over to the tree and held out her hands. I slipped off my back and grasped them, and she helped me gently to my feet. Stevie closed in on my left as I settled my back against the birch tree, which was smooth enough that the bark didn't bite into my bare skin.

After she put down her own pack, Darryl got down on her knees in front of me and slid her fingers into my wet bush. She murmured happily as she burrowed her face between my pulsating thighs, inhaling the powerful scent of my arousal. By then, my juices were flowing so fast that the aroma filled my nostrils, too, edging out the earthier smells of the trail.

I moaned when she started circling her tongue over my aching pussy, lapping at the outside of my swollen lips. Now and then the point of her tongue snaked out and brushed against my protruding clit, making me shudder so deeply that the tree swayed behind me. Waves of pleasure blew through me like the mellow autumn breeze.

Meanwhile, on my left, Stevie drifted closer and reached around so she could feel up my tits. As her fingers roved over my rigid buds, pinching and twisting, I could feel her wet pussy drooling over my leg. I shifted my hips a little, hoping to slide my fingers inside her, but I was careful not to move too far. After all, I had no intention of dislodging Darryl's tongue! Stevie's clit finally came to rest on the side of my thigh near my bush. Our juices mixed together as she used my muscular leg to pleasure herself.

I couldn't stop myself from crying out when Darryl finally parted my cleft with her lips and burrowed her tongue deep inside my steamy folds. I moaned and hunched forward, feeling it skid through the fluids that had gathered around my hole. Stevie's fingers clamped around my tits, coaxing a second, breathier moan from my lungs. It felt like my nipples had inflated to the size of pine cones under her expert coaxing.

"Oh, yeah," I moaned as Darryl went to work, flexing my clit back and forth with her tongue. My syrup was flowing down my legs like sap from a maple tree, and she was slurping it up as fast as it came. "I think I'm about to come–"

I could feel the imprint of her smile against my bush as she pulled back, her lower lip still melded to my clit. My pussy started doing flip-flops trying to recapture her talented tongue.

"Not just yet," she teased. I could feel her gently moving me away from the tree. My hand found its mark, and I slid my fingers easily into her drooling hole. Luckily, the movement pressed my pussy back into Darryl's face. I ground myself against her mouth as she sucked in a deep breath and dove on my pleasure-button with renewed vigor.

Currents of ecstasy were racing up and down my

body with such ferocity that I could barely keep my balance. "Stevie, put your fingers inside me," I gasped. She hastened to comply, cupping my ass in with her right palm and moving positioning her other hand to enter me. I could hear her rapid breath in my ear as she leaned in close and slid her left hand down between my legs, poking her fingers up into my wet slit. My pussy ignited as the twin sensations of her hand and Darryl's mouth rubbing it deliciously raw.

While Darryl continued to tongue my clit, Stevie pushed upward until she was rummaging around in my hole. Finally she parted my cleft with her thumbs, massaging my rim while she settled three fingers against the hot opening. My whole body spasmed with excitement.

Her spread fingers massaged my deepest regions. That exquisite sensation, combined with Darryl's energetic tonguing, soon had every muscle in the lower half of my body shuddering and clenching. I balanced myself with my arms, tilting between Stevie's rigid fingers and Darryl's thrusting tongue. I howled freely while all three of us groaned and thrust and ground together under the sparkling canopy of the sun-drenched leaves.

Before long, I was coming and coming hard. My hips twisted and rolled, my spasming pussy clutched at Stevie's forceful fingering, and my clit seemed to strike sparks against Darryl's full mouth. She strained forward on her knees, pushing her face against me, riding my mound until my pussy-lips convulsed. I felt a glob of my sticky fluid roll onto her tongue, and felt her lips curve into a smile as she began sucking me dry.

While a cool breeze stirred around us, Darryl's lips brought my clit to a second, smaller climax. Sensing that Darryl was on the verge, I intensified my finger motions, burying them in her up to my knuckles. She opened her thighs so that her clit rubbed against my palm. "Don't stop," she wheezed, though she must have known that I had no intention of doing so! "Oh, yeah, that's great!"

While she came, howling and thrashing, I fucked her with my fingers as energetically as she had done to me with her tongue. Her clit slapped against my palm, her thick syrup trickling down my fingertips.

Meanwhile, Stevie rode my thigh like a cowgirl, flinging her head back in ecstasy, whooping and hollering. When her eruption had died down, she leaned over and sucked my tits while the golden leaves fluttered down around us, blanketing us in fragrant moisture.

Exhausted, Darryl nestled her head between my thighs and gasped for breath. Stevie fell back on a bed of dry leaves. We sat together for a long time, all of us damp with each other's warm moisture.

"This has been a beautiful day," I murmured, taking a handful of leaves and letting them drop, fluttering, over my swollen nipples. They drifted between my legs, the juice there making a few of them stick to my skin. It made them laugh, and Darryl reached over to brush them away. As she did, she snaked her fingers through my pussy hair.

"Wait till we go cross-country skiing together," she beamed. "It just so happens that Stevie and I know a great trail for that, too."

Touch & Go

The way she touched me this morning

Today I follow the red trails. Today her comfort eludes me. My curled knees dig into the soft flesh of my belly. A down pillow smothers my heated face. My ass-cheeks are spread wide. Long, angry lines burn along my spine, remnants of her scratches, while her tongue flings me along the clouds, suspended between lust and ashes.

I ride.

Lightning flashes across the battleground in my head. Ice tingles against my wet skin. The first wave overtakes pain, both past and present. The next drowns my resistance to the pleasure as sleek wings carry me higher.

I crash.

She lets go of my tingling feet and that familiar, wistful smile crosses her glistening mouth. My want covers her face. Her auburn hair falls soft across her shoulders. She knows, but still her wide hazel eyes wait for my throat to open to the tremors of release. I roll to my left side and hold my breath.

My silence enrages her. "Was that a good one? Can you say something for once?"

I gasp and turn over. Her flesh feels strangely cold as I take hold of her arm and pull her on top of me. We lie nipple to nipple while my dry lips captures hers. Slicing between bared teeth, our tongues struggle. I tilt my pelvis so her big, folded clit rakes mine. Holding her hips, I rotate her to the throb of my desire.

"Do it hard," I say.

Kimberly's body twists and grinds into me like a shovel, digging and gouging with harsh staccato movements. We shove at each other, burrowing into the heat, demanding satisfaction. She bends and bites my shoulder. I cry out and slam myself higher. She pushes me back to the mattress like a lioness overpowering her prey. But I struggle, hoisting her in the air with my hips.

"You'll come for me, all right. You'll scream my name!" she hisses, wrestling me into the comforter until I retreat.

I feel a chaotic fear that I may come for Kimberly, that I will lose myself in the deepest part of her, swallowed by her power. I begin to flail my arms aimlessly. She catches my wrists in her sweaty fingers and pins me down. Her voice purrs as I weaken. "You're my baby. You make me want you so bad. C'mon, be good to me."

Her mouth latches onto my nipple, and she sucks me too hard. I wince.

Next she assails my need with her stiff clit, teasing my opening with exact circular movements. Her touch is like a burgeoning cyclone inside me, widening and spinning. She snares my neck and feasts on my will to resist her. "Oh, Kim, stop, don't stop, stop, don't stop." I hear my voice repeat the words. It sounds distant, like it's coming from another room.

She slips her thigh between my legs, and I hump her like a vile animal, sliding up and down faster and faster. "Yes, that's the way, baby. Yeah, do my leg! Cream it!"

The way she went off alone, six months ago, for the fourth time

"I'm not interested in your trauma issues, Jade. I don't want to hear where you're at in your healing process," Kimberly tells me, laying naked and fingering herself. "I just want to get off without seeing all this horrible pain on your face."

"I've always loved your compassionate side, dearest."

"Damn, I was almost there," she mutters and pulls her shining hand to her face. She sucks her juices off her fingers, one at a time. "You're driving me crazy. I've had it. I'm breaking up with you."

I throw on a t-shirt. "Again? This is getting tedious." I rise from my bed and glide to the mirror. "If you hate me so much, why do you keep coming back for more?" I shrug and start brushing my hair.

Kimberly bangs the pillow. "Get back over here. Do you mean that I'm as afraid of intimacy as you are? Maybe that's why I keep coming back to you, but I don't care to analyze it, chopping every feeling up and gluing it back together like you with your constant narcissism." When I don't respond, Kimberly hammers the wall with her fist. "You always act like you're the only one who ever suffers!"

I can see the reflection of her red, hardened face. Slowly I turn around and look at her.

"I haven't met a lesbian who hasn't been screwed over by someone somewhere. And you know what, Jade? They work through it. They don't hate themselves for wanting a woman, and they don't feel sorry about it, either."

"Is the lecture of the day over with, professor? Because it's Saturday, and I'd like to relax, all right?"

"You don't know the meaning of the fucking word," she snaps.

"I am not going to continue this fight," I say. "If you want to be with someone else, go ahead. I can't have sex the way you want it right now."

"I've been a damn saint, supporting you, listening to you, propping you up. For a year of my life I've put your needs ahead of mine, Jade, but I've had it." She pulls a stray pillow over her middle and bites her lip. Her voice softens. "You've got to move on. You could be happy if you just let yourself live in the moment. Why don't you try it for once in your life?"

"I'm all right."

"That's not good enough. Can't you stop punishing yourself and be with me? Be with me, baby. I love you." She pulls me back to the bed. Hot tears roll down my face as I lay my head on her soft breasts. Kim holds me and licks them away. Her fingers glide through my long hair onto my back, caressing me. I feel my anger dissipate in her hands. The loneliness subsides, though I know that it's just an illusion.

The first time we touched, six months before she went off alone

I arrive with a bottle of red wine clutched in my clammy hands. They aren't the only part of me that sweats. My brand-new black leather pants are a lot warmer than they looked in the boutique. The rigid seams chafe my legs mercilessly.

Boisterous female laughter spills into the staircase while I trudge up to the third floor. The door stands ajar, and a college-aged woman with bright pink jagged hair and a gargoyle tattoo on her shoulder waves me inside. She looks down at my new pants and gives me a thumbs-up. "Cool," she says, and I'm glad I'd spent the money after all. I can live with a little raw skin.

I move past her and wander through the apartment, finding a lumpy bean bag sofa in the corner. A woman stands by herself nearby. She wears oval, wire-framed glasses and holds a can of soda in her hand. She watches the crowd, separate and thoughtful. She is about to smile at me when I turn my face away.

I have to sit carefully because of my tight pants, but a glass of spiked punch calms my nerves a little. I also watch the crowd of dykes milling around us. They all look pretty happy, flirting and drinking and wolfing down crackers and vegetable sticks.

I nibble on a few myself, then see two girls in the opposite corner. One, a petite and feminine blonde, sprawls across her butch girlfriend's lap. Slowly, her hand creeps inside the butch's crisp white t-shirt. As she raises the hem, I see the silver flash of a nipple ring and feel myself blush. Nervously, I down some more punch.

Just as my gaze bores in on the couple, the woman with the soda approaches. She looks at the couple I watch and laughs. "Can you believe them?"

"Yeah, they're really going at it," I answer, not looking around, not really knowing what to say. I don't want to watch, yet I can't help it. I'm not the sort of person who would do such a thing. Yet more than anything, I want to be.

The butch maneuvers her hand through a tear in the blonde's jeans. I am transfixed at her agility, at the response from the woman she fingers. Her eyes are closed, her face flushed, her head thrown back. A wicked smile plays across her parted lips.

Unexpectedly, I feel a shiver of desire course from my hardening nipples all the way down my body. The tight pants make the feeling more intense. Suddenly my breathing grows attrited, and I rock back and forth. A vivid picture flashes through my mind: I am stretched out naked, letting the butch finger me while the lecherous femme watches.

The woman with the soda startles me back into reality. "They sure are something, huh? That must be wild, to show yourself off to a whole roomful of people."

I am red with embarrassment when I pull myself together. Just then I notice that a few other guests are getting in on the act–kissing more openly, touching more brazenly. One woman takes the ice cubes from her drink and presses them to her girlfriend's clothed chest. The damp fabric clings to the rigid peaks of her nipples.

I take another gulp of punch and turn to her. Sweat runs down my armpits and spine. I feel it slick my thighs and the space between my breasts. My pulse palpitates in my veins.

"I wish I could be that daring."

She smiles, her lips moist and full. I imagine they would taste like the cherry cola she still clings to. "No? You don't look all that shy to me."

"I don't?"

"Nope."

"But you approached me."

"Yes, I did," she says. The blonde has finished coming now, and lies curled up in the butch's lap to rest. The pair with the ice cube moves off into the kitchen, maybe for a fresh supply.

"Kiss me," I whisper, wanting to feel her sensitive face close to mine.

She moves closer. Our lips touch.

Taut Chords

Mmmm. My body hummed. Molly's melodic voice reverberated in my head, the half-recalled wisps of her song shackling me softly to her. My emotions were knotted tighter than the steel strings on her guitar. I took a deep breath and tried to relax as I sat at the end of the bar, sipping a Tequila Sunrise. Every woman in the crowd seemed to stare at me with those consuming blue eyes I remembered so well.

Three years before, during the fall semester of my freshman year at Brown, I had studied acoustic guitar with Molly. A junior at the time, she was a talented lead singer in a local band. She taught me to feel the melody, not just follow the notes. Though I never acknowledged it, not even to myself, my week began to center around my hour-long lesson with her.

On one of those long-awaited Tuesday nights, I was just about to leave when I got a call from my mother.

"Cari, how are you? I wanted to let you know we took care of the payment for school."

"Thanks," I replied, trying not to sound resentful about my continued dependence on them. "How are you and Dad?"

"We're fine," she said. Then she reverted to her native Korean, a habit of hers whenever she got anxious. "Cari, are you still involved with that nice Catholic group on campus?"

"Mom, I've got to go. I'll call you later," I sighed.

"Cari, promise me you're hanging around with good kids. I'm worried about you."

"I promise. Don't worry about anything."

I donned my coat and woolen gloves, wondering if she'd ever accept my need for independence–both from her and from her whole way of living. Then I rushed to Molly's apartment, wanting to see her more than ever, wondering if she felt the same.

When I got there, I could barely concentrate on the lesson. For one thing, the heat in her apartment had broken down, causing me to shiver. Molly's nipples had hardened under her thin sweater. I tried not to look at her sweet breasts and wondered, in frustration, why she wasn't wearing a coat like I was.

Half an hour later, Molly realized that my attention had evaporated and called it a night. I didn't want to go, and I guess it showed, because instead of saying our goodbyes, we sat around and talked.

"You know, Cari, you're really good," Molly said, stroking my guitar. "Have you ever thought about going onstage yourself?"

"I've thought about it. . . but I'm too shy," I responded, lowering my eyes.

"You could get past that. I did."

I looked up at her in astonishment."You were shy?"

"Well, more like nervous about putting myself out there, exposing my feelings," she said, twisting her chilled hands together and rubbing the pink flesh.

"Yes, it's hard to let go," I sighed. "I suppose I've always wanted to do my own stuff. How does the music come to you?"

"I'll tell you a weird story. I usually don't talk about it because people who aren't creative think I'm totally whacked out. But you know that song I wrote about the lonely girl in the rain?"

"Yeah."

"I was in the front seat of the bus one rainy day, and there was this really beautiful woman sitting across from me. Something was bothering her, but she was trying not to let it show. I just sat there and watched her, listening to the wipers slap back and forth on the windshield. I started thinking that maybe they'd washed away her tears along with the rain. That was when that song just came to me."

I nodded, lost in the intense, vivid blue of her eyes. When Molly talked about something she cared about, her whole face seemed to glow.

"It's kind of like stepping outside myself when that happens," she went on, probably seeing that I had nothing to add. "It's the same when I'm up there onstage, singing about what I feel and believe in. I feel less. . . you know, isolated."

"Somehow I never thought of you feeling that kind of loneliness."

"Oh, I have plenty of friends and stuff, but real closeness is hard to find," she replied. Then she looked away, picking idly at my guitar strings. "When I'm up there singing, it's like I can sense this connection." Her face became wistful, like she was on stage at that very moment, and only I was there with her.

"I envy you," I said. "I wish I had the guts to be that vulnerable."

"You've got it in you, Cari. Just let go of the fear and you can do anything you want to." Molly laid her hand on mine, but let it linger this time. Then, like an afterthought, she self-consciously pulled it away. "I hope I didn't bore you."

"No, really. I'm flattered that you feel you can talk to me about your music."

She smiled and looked at the clock. "It's getting late. Are you safe going back to the dorm now?"

"It's no big deal," I replied, saying one thing but at the same time praying that she would ask me to sleep over and share her big brass bed. At least I was putting my Catholic education to good use, I thought.

"You're welcome to stay over, you know. I rented a video yesterday, and we could watch it together."

She seemed so comfortable that I was sure she never suspected my feelings. But at the same time, I hoped she was playing innocent the way I was, pretending that she was inviting me to nothing more than a private slumber party. My mouth was dry with nervousness, but I nodded casually. "Sure, that sounds great."

I slipped on the flannel nightgown she handed me, and crawled into the bed she slept in night after night. Molly disappeared into the bathroom. Soon she came out wearing a similar flannel nightgown, although hers was more frayed at the hem. Scented steam floated off her when she turned on the VCR. Molly quickly got under the thick quilt, at arm's length from me.

"Hope you like the movie. It's pretty hot. Maybe it will inspire the janitor to do something about the temperature in here." She punctuated her joke with a nervous laugh.

My heartbeat accelerated when her foot brushed against mine. "I guess we'll keep each other warm," I commented, unguardedly expressing my thoughts aloud. She looked at me intently, then turned back to the TV. The movie was some erotic thriller, but I could hardly follow the plot. Every time the hero pressed up against the heroine and kissed her, I imagined Molly doing the same thing to me.

The cold increased, prompting us to inch toward one another. About halfway through the movie, almost without thinking, I leaned my head on Molly's soft shoulder, pressing up against her alabaster neck. Her body went stiff, but a moment later she lay her head on mine.

I dozed until the end titles rolled on the screen. Molly turned to me in order to comment on the movie. I lifted my head, and her lips unexpectedly brushed my cheek. My whole body lurched. After only a moment's hesitation, our lips met for the first time.

When she tugged away, she was gasping for breath. "I feel so close to you," she confessed.

"Me too, Molly. Let me show you how close. I can't stand it any more." I breathed back. But I was unable to completely eradicate thoughts of my strict, conservative parents. "No one has to know."

The pair of us caught fire. I lifted her nightie. My tongue explored her shoulder blades, traveled down her ribs, and into the soft, secret place below. With quick, supple movements she slipped off my clothing as well.

I lost myself in pure pleasure, in Molly. I savored her nipples and kneaded her smooth, pliant flesh. The rougher my touch became, the more she seemed to like it. Her hips rotated with each frenzied push of my hands. Then she reached for me, too.

Our lovemaking seemed to flow magically. We knew by instinct exactly what to do to please each other. Afterward, we lay with our arms around one another, so satisfied that we fell asleep immediately.

The freezing temperature woke me at dawn the next morning. I lay on my side and watched Molly's chest heave peacefully, her face as sweet and artless as a saint's. I realized it was she I worshiped more than any god or priest. But the voice of my mother, begging, "Promise me, Cari," filled me with guilt.

I dressed quietly, assuming she was still asleep. While I buttoned my coat, I saw her watching me with eyes full of want. All I wanted was to get undressed all over again. But I didn't.

"I just can't do this again, Mol." I shook with cold and lust for her. "I feel too guilty."

Molly folded her arms over her still naked chest. "You can leave, Cari, but I know you'll never find anyone who will make you as happy as I did last night. I think you know that, too."

"I'm sorry," I said. The sorrow was for me more than her. Holding back hot tears, I left. I remembered to take my guitar. There would be no more Tuesday night lessons.

After I finished college, I got a job in a nearby legal firm, swearing off sex altogether. But though I tried to ignore the intensity of my memories of her, I couldn't. The closeness we'd shared, the taste of her mouth, the feel of her succulent body never left me.

One day in early November, I was on my way to work, glancing at the usual billboards and dreading Thanksgiving at my parents' house, when I saw a poster advertising a new, all-female rock group. They were playing at The Well, a popular lesbian-owned club in Providence, that very weekend. Startled, I moved in for a closer look. Sure enough: there was Molly in the forefront of the picture!

At that moment, I felt more alive than I had in years. I noted the address of the club and thought about nothing else for the rest of the week. And now here I was. But would she remember me? Or if she did, would she still want me? I was willing to risk anything to find out.

I held my breath as the group filed onstage, and abruptly she was right before me. Her tight leather skirt rode up her narrow hips, and her long legs kept the beat while her husky alto held us rapt with attention.

The crowd seemed to vanish. My heart drummed to the bounce of her breasts, the lilt of her song. I thought I saw a flash of recognition in her face while she belted out another song, but I wasn't sure.

When their set ended and the band left the stage, I knew what I had to do. I approached the owner and asked if I could speak with the lead singer, explaining that I was a friend. Of course she was skeptical, but I begged her to just tell her that Cari was waiting for her by the bar.

The minutes seemed like hours as I sat at the bar, shredding a paper napkin into tinier and tinier pieces. Then, to my relief, Molly appeared beside me, alone. I was dying to put my arms around her, but the coldness I sensed in her made me hold back.

"Molly? It's great to see you again. Can I buy you a drink?"

"All right." Those eyes that had haunted me looked like icy ponds so frozen over they would never thaw. She sat down. I felt my stomach knot.

The waitress brought the drinks, but it took a few sips before I could say anything. "Molly, I'm sorry. I was wrong and repressed and confused."

She rocked her drink back and forth on the bar, imprinting the wood with interlocking wet circles. "You hurt me a lot, Cari. Whatever you were feeling back then, I don't believe you were thinking of me."

"I can't excuse what I did. I can only say I wish you would let me make it up to you." I gulped down my drink and struggled to still the nervous puzzing in my head. "Are you. . . are you with someone now?"

She shook her head. "What does that matter? You have your life, I have mine. It's not perfect, but it's what I want. I have to get going."

When she started to slide off the barstool, I grabbed her arm. "Why did you come out here to see me if you don't have a shred of feeling left for me?"

"I never said I didn't have feelings for you. But I just don't trust you with them." She pulled away.

"Please, Mol, I still love you. I never stopped. It was so hard. . . with my parents and all that other crap. I was so young. I didn't know what I wanted. I've missed you so much. Won't you please just think about it?" I held my hands clenched at my sides.

"See you around," she said. Then she turned and made her way through the crowd.

I went home, too. What other choice was there? But I wasn't finished with Molly yet. Of that I was certain.

By the time Thanksgiving rolled around, I'd never felt so despondent. My mother took it pretty well, I guess, when I explained that I had to work and couldn't come home that year. She argued with me but I wouldn't budge.

Instead, I decided I'd try to see Molly one last time. I went back to The Well and basically bribed the owner to call Molly down for a quick look at a new singer who wanted to audition the following evening. It cost me extra to become that new singer myself, but I knew it just might be the best money I'd ever spent.

I stayed up the entire night writing a song of my own for Molly. I have to admit that no words did her justice, so a lot of them were about how empty I felt without her, and how deeply I longed for a second chance with her. The next day, I had not only a song, but I finally had the nerve to sing it.

I arrived early and sat in a shadowy corner to watch Molly come in. Again she was alone. I was elated. She sat at a table by herself, politely ignoring a few women who tried to pick her up. Still, every time one would approach her, I'd hold my breath.

At about ten, the club owner announced me. I looked at Molly as I walked out, clinging to the same guitar she'd once held in her arms. She suppressed a smile. My eyes never left her as I sang, and the tears that rolled down my face were the first I'd ever shed in public. By the last note, I saw her own cheeks glisten as the small audience applauded. I got down from the stage and sat down across from her. Briefly I remembered the story she'd told me about the crying woman on the bus. Maybe one day she'd write a song like that about me. Or maybe I'd have to write it myself.

"I love you, Mol. Please let me. . . ." I reached over

and grasped her soft hand. She didn't fight me this time, just got up and pulled me behind her. We crossed the bar and headed into a small dressing room at the back.

As we faced each other next to the bulb-framed mirror, the years seemed to spin away in a breathless rush. It was like we were college students again, cuddling close in that big brass bed. Her gaze surreptitiously raked my body. I felt her closeness between my legs.

"Molly, you were right, so right. No one ever made me feel the way I did with you." I sobbed while I caressed her smooth cheeks. "Will you let me make it up to you?"

Our bodies moved together as naturally as they had all those years ago, and I entwined my arms around her. Without a moment's hesitation, I brushed the hair from Molly's face and kissed her, opening my mouth wide and delicately thrusting my tongue at hers.

I rocked back and forth, holding her, and she began to sashay against me. I eased her face between Molly's supple breasts, caressed her with my cheeks as we danced to the rhythm of an imaginary beat. Her body against mine made me dizzy from want.

Soon she pushed me onto the couch in the corner. I stripped Molly of her leather skirt and panties, and she kicked off her shoes, ripping the buttons off my blouse in the process. Molly grinned while I maneuvered her bent legs and moved my face right up to hers.

"You've certainly changed for the better, Cari. Can I ask you what happened?" she panted.

"I adore you. That's all," I held her firmly and lifted my torso onto hers. "I never forgot you. You inspire me to be myself," I whispered into her ear and then licked it.

"I've missed *you*," she told me.

My hand drifted over her shoulder. I kneaded the tight muscles there while she kissed me. Drawing her closer, my tongue slipped along the roof of her mouth, my free hand moving down her breasts. She arched her back, pressing her body closer. Her thighs felt slick when my fingers gently moved between her legs.

Overcome, I slid down and hoisted her up, shoving her swollen pearl against my open mouth. I used my lips and nose to ease back the hot skin that sheathed her pounding center, then bore down with the point of my tongue.

Her tense muscles responded by closing around me. Her secret lips seemed to whimper with contentment as I drove deeply inside her. She was so hot, Molly began to break loose then and there, writhing with abandon.

When the first stabs of heat streaked up and down the length of her body, I knew that she had reached that magical peak I'd waited three years for us to ascend together. Molly's hips went rigid against my face, and her legs clamped around my head.

"Cari," she gasped, just before her passion overtook her.

"I love you," I exclaimed and bent my head back to her body. We rocked together, lost in the cadence of our own private song.

Winterising

Friction ignites icy burns

Chills my skin to

Spark and blush

Flare and beg

An Insatiable freeze

Twists tightens melts

Cold stirs me to fire

Control me

Winter Flames

You couldn't see the ground, and the snow kept falling, melting, and icing over the roads. It was a typical February in the heart of New Hampshire.

That winter, my writing had become my sole passion. I spent the long, dark nights alone, working and sipping organic tea, and I rarely left the house or the computer except to buy some groceries at the small convenience store near my home. Of course Sunni, my Siamese cat, was a comfort, but the only person I spoke with was the store's owner.

Felicia was an attractive woman in her early forties, about ten years older than I was. Although she's a native New Englander, she's not the least bit standoffish. Her warm personality charmed every customer. I found myself drawn to her bright smile even on days when nothing else seemed worth caring about.

After a few months, I started going in to pick up an item or two every day, just so I could see her. Sometimes I'd ask her to show me where various items were so I could breathe in her vanilla musk cologne. Other times I'd ask her to reach something to me so our hands would brush together. Thoughts of her flooded my sleep and my daydreams alike. More than once I had to stop myself from pulling up and parking outside the store just to get a glimpse of her. Finally, I found an outlet in my writing and began my newest work with her barely disguised as the main character.

While I wrote, I tried to keep away from the store completely. That worked fairly well until one stormy evening, when I ran out of cat food. The roads were glare ice, so I walked to the store and arrived half-frozen.

Felicia greeted me with an enthusiasm I found surprising.

"Hey, where have you been keeping?" she asked, squeezing both my hands in hers. "I've missed you."

My heart hammered as I hastily chose a can of cat food and fumbled with my change purse. "Well, I . . . uh . . . I've been kind of involved with my novel and I wasn't eating much for a while."

She nodded. "You do look thin. In fact, today you bear a strong resemblance to an icicle." I smiled, and she laughed. "Look, you've been my only customer for hours, and I'm about to close down because of the weather. Why don't you let me cook supper for you tonight?"

"I need to get home with the cat food," I said. "Sunni's probably clawing my sofa to shreds."

"She'll be all right for a few hours, won't she?"

"Well. . . ." I fidgeted nervously. Sunni had already eaten that day, and I'd left her plenty of water. She certainly wasn't as destructive as I'd made her out to be. Still, I wasn't sure which prospect was more unnerving: spending a frustrated evening alone, or putting myself in a situation where my feelings for her would be all too obvious to us both.

"Come on." Felicia grinned, picked up an extra can of Kitti Vittles, and tossed them into my bag. "I'm running a two-for-one special tonight. All my dinner guests can double their purchase at no extra price. That's a deal I don't think Sunni would object to."

A writer at a loss for words, I stammered out a yes.

Her cozy brick house lay right around the corner from the store. From the outside it looked very modest, but once she opened the door that led directly to the living room, I was impressed at how she'd created the illusion of a wide, spacious atmosphere.

"You look frozen," Felicia said, and I had to admit that I felt that way, too. My fingers and toes were numb, and my jaw ached from my chattering teeth. "Why don't you sit down and let me fix you some hot chocolate? It'll defrost you while I make dinner."

I thanked her and sat quietly while she bustled in the kitchen. Despite Felicia's attentiveness, I was unsure of her sexual preferences. Maybe her friendliness was just an expression of her warm personality. Still, I liked her so very much. I clung to my hopes like a drowning woman to a floating matchstick.

I managed to get through an hour of conversation and a whole plate of pasta primavera without shedding a single ray of light on the mystery at hand. I had nearly given up on my gaydar skills when I struck gold.

"How about some music?" she asked.

"As long as it's something soft and relaxing." Given the state of my nerves, I didn't know if I could bear a withering blast of heavy metal or the heartbroken wails of some crooning cowpoke.

"Exactly what I was going to suggest." She broke into an enormous smile as she got up. "I'll be back in a second."

She hurried to her stereo in the next room, and a moment later the mellow strains of k.d. lang flooded the house. It was all I could do not to jump up and embrace her in relief.

Felicia didn't return to her chair, as I expected, but moved over to stand beside mine. My whole body went

₃ warm brown eyes searched mine.

√hy do I make you so uncomfortable, Ivy?" she said
a soft, almost hesitant voice.

"I don't know what you mean," I said.

"I think you do." Sighing, she raked a hand through
her shoulder-length brown locks. "Every time I try to get
close to you, you pull away. I know you're a really
private person and all. . . but I really want to be your
friend."

I felt like my heart was about to crash through my
chest. Icy fear gripped my limbs like I was back out in
the blizzard. I forced my lips to part, forced myself to
answer her.

"Only my friend, Felicia?" I asked huskily.

It seemed to take forever for her to come closer, bend
down, and embrace me. I buried my face in her ample
breasts while she kissed my brown curls and stroked my
thin back. "No, Ivy. I want to give you much more than
friendship. Why have you made it so hard for me?"

"I'm sorry, Felicia. I was afraid," I responded. Then I
lost my train of thought as Felicia's sensual lips came
down hard on my own. I felt my whole body liquify in
her tight grasp, and my mouth seemed to melt beneath
the probing of her wet tongue.

Felicia's mouth looked swollen and red when,
reluctantly, she broke away from me. "Are you afraid
now?" she whispered.

In place of an answer, my hand went under her fuzzy
sweater and traced along her waist. With slow-moving
caresses, I stroked my way up to the breasts I'd been
longing to touch for so long and undid her bra. Her
heavy breasts fell into my palm, molding immediately

to my grasp, while her lips went to the nape of my neck. She flicked her tongue over the tiny hairs there, sending quivers through my sweating limbs.

Her body trembled and pushed against my hands. "Come with me," she whispered. "I need you so much."

I stood on shaking legs, and Felicia led me to her beautifully decorated bedroom. There, again, she covered my mouth with hers. The desire we'd bottled up for the past few months exploded when we fell onto her feather bed. I practically shredded off her sweater and jeans, while she peeled me out of my clothes with such slow, sensual movements that I feared I'd go mad. When we were both naked, Felicia lay back and smiled at me. She waited calmly for me to touch her.

For the first time, my eyes took in every inch of her luscious body. It was everything I'd imagined. Her creamy throat and sculpted shoulders gave way to two generous mountains on her chest, each topped with a delicious, erect peak that invited me to climb its pink perfection. Below, her soft torso shuddered with every deep, excited breath she took. Her sturdy legs parted to expose a semi-shaved valley already damp with desire.

I crawled on top of her, and we rubbed our naked bodies together like two sticks ready to spark into one blaze. Without hesitation, I latched my lusty mouth onto one lovely areola, then ravished her swelled nipple. She tasted like vanilla and woman, all warmed, all melted together in my mouth. Felicia groaned and pushed her chest up into my face. As she writhed and twisted in my arms, she seethed with an almost tangible excitement.

I drew a figure eight with my tongue from breast to breast, then licked my way down to her burning belly.

Meanwhile, her hands gripped my breasts and her thumbs strummed my erect nipples. She lifted each to her mouth and let her tongue flick them, the wet jabs thrilling me with pleasure. Raw passion blazed through our bodies as she suckled me softly.

I arched my back, nearly wild with lust, and caught a glimpse of her face. She looked incredibly lovely, with her soft hair draped over my sprawling limbs, her red lips clamped around my ruddy left nipple. I stroked the silky strands on her head with one hand and fondled the warm curls of her pubes with my other. Her private lips were as silky as her hairs, and my fingers tingled with the soft sensations.

We soon maneuvered ourselves into a sixty-nine position, but with a twist: I lifted my body and strategically placed myself so that my clitoris was on top of her hard right nipple. While she lapped around my thighs, my pelvis slowly rotated on her breast. Hunching my hips, I stroked her gently at first and then more roughly. While I teased her nipple with my swelling bud, I slipped my fingertips into her moist crease.

The nipple-massage grew more intense as I spread her open and bent my head to her hot center. Flame-like, my tongue darted out to kindle her palpitating wick. Felicia thrashed and rolled as if she were possessed, and I felt a special thrill when I realized that, at least for now, she was–by me. I circled and pressed, chafing my pearl against Felicia's nipple with increasing zeal.

"Harder!" she rasped. I immediately did what she asked, plunging my mouth against her with rougher strokes. Her hips buffeted my face, and the stony pearl between her legs wrestled with my tongue.

Then Felicia ignited, clasping my hair and calling my name as heat consumed her body. Smoldering like a bonfire, she lifted her breast to my hot core as smaller, hotter bursts of passion rippled visibly through her flushed body. I felt incredibly powerful as I coaxed the woman who had been a distant fantasy only hours before, to a second, and then a third vigorous climax.

She must have decided that she wanted me to come with her, because all of a sudden she hoisted her head so that her mouth touched and nuzzled me. The feel of her soft, full lips whisking over me pushed own emotions close to the edge. Excitedly she put her tongue to work and entered me with two fingers, thrusting inside me as far as she could. I swerved back and forth, ready to explode as I smashed myself onto her.

A conflagration engulfed my body. I writhed and moaned, twisting my head back and forth, my rigid nipples raking her legs. When she tugged her head away, Felicia left a trail of hickeys and bites along my inner thighs, sending me through another whirlwind of orgasms.

For a long time after we fell away from each other, neither of us could move. When Felicia recovered, she propped her head up on a few fluffy pillows. The white cases made it look as though she were resting on the piles of snow outside her window. I didn't think she'd ever looked more beautiful to me than she did at that moment.

"Still think I'm hard to get close to?" I joked.

"I've decided that you're just a little shy." She laughed and licked some of my leftover nectar off her lips and chin. "But that's something we can work on together."

"I guess you're right." A blush and a smile crept over my face simultaneously. Warmth welled up inside me, and I snuggled close against her to enjoy it. It was a change of inner climate I'd written about, but never experienced until then.

When she leaned over to kiss me, I knew that Felicia and I could both look forward to a steaming hot winter in icy New Hampshire.

Plunging into the Millennium

"Look, Lena, it's almost Christmas, and Baker and Stone are forty percent inflated this quarter. You're making a big mistake to invest now," I said, confronting her in front of the entire board. I regretted it as soon as I got the words were out. Everyone in the room either coughed or stifled a smirk.

Lena's dark eyes flashed, and her perfect white teeth clenched. I steeled myself for the tongue lashing I knew I deserved.

Lena turned a page in her leather binder and smiled. "Perhaps I neglected to give you the latest numbers, Cheryl. Why don't I update you after the meeting?" Our fellow other board members visibly relaxed when she wrapped up her report without incident.

For the rest of the meeting, I could barely contain my embarrassment over my behavior. To tell the truth, I wasn't even sure why I'd done what I had. Around my office, no one challenged Lena's opinion–not in the open, anyway. It was an unspoken rule.

Later, I was summoned to Lena's spacious corner office. I knew what she was going to say–that whatever our shared preferences, she was still my supervisor. Before she had a chance to lace into me, I held up my hand.

"I want to apologize for that whole scene, Lena," I said, barely able to meet her gaze. "It's no excuse, I know, but I just found out that Nikki is sleeping with Ted in Accounting."

Lena smiled sympathetically. "I hate to say it, Cheryl, so I won't."

"I know, I know, you warned me about her," I

replied, then bit my lip.

"What you need, honey, is a woman who's sure about what she wants. Nikki's just playing–with you, with herself. I saw that from the minute I met her."

I smiled in spite of myself and the mixed feelings about my ex-girlfriend that still tormented me in quiet moments. "I know. I remember."

Lena must have noticed the gloomy look that stole across my face, because she suddenly leaned forward and fixed me with a penetrating stare. "Listen, Cheryl, the holidays are no time to be moping around alone. Why don't I make New Year's reservations for the two of us at Heavenly Hot Tubs?"

I wasn't sure how to react. I'd come to her office expecting to get chewed out, and here she was asking me out! "Gee, Lena, I don't know."

"You don't have to answer right now. I'll make the reservation anyway." Smiling, she began to shuffle papers on her desk. I took that gesture as my clue to leave. "Somehow, I just know you'll be starting the millennium off right."

I didn't answer as I stumbled out of her office and went back to my own cubicle in a daze. To be honest, I didn't want to do anything on New Year's Eve except sit around and feel sorry for myself. I wasn't about to let Lena, however pleasant an evening with her might have been, cheat me out of a perfectly good pity party!

When I got home, the first thing I did was run to the answering machine. My heart almost skipped a beat when I saw the message light blinking. I pressed the button with a shaking finger, only to hear a droning male voice remind me that my car was scheduled for an oil change right after the holiday.

For a long time, I sat on the sofa practicing all the things I'd say to Nikki when she finally did call. Then I dialed Lena's home number, told her I'd be going to the hot tubs with her after all, and hung up before she had time to respond.

"I don't know if this idea of yours is going to work, Lena," I said as she drove me across town to the upscale spa. "Nikki hasn't called me even once since we broke up, even though I hear it isn't working out with Ted. I feel so depressed, all I want is to stay away from everybody and stuff my face with Rocky Road."

"Oh, Cheryl, that's the worst way to nurse a broken heart," she advised me. "The point is to pamper, not abuse, yourself until you're over it."

I couldn't help returning her smile. I intended for our connection to remain purely platonic, but I'd begun to doubt my ability to resist her. Earlier that evening, she'd treated me to a delicious lobster dinner at a trendy restaurant in the Back Bay. Though our table overlooked the harbor, I found myself watching her.

Okay, so Lena was a little older than I was–probably in her mid-forties–but her rich alto voice, ebony eyes, and the light sprinkling of grey in her otherwise jet-black hair had begun to win me over. Several times, I couldn't help thinking how distinguished she looked in the mellow glow of the restaurant lighting. Unlike Nikki, Lena wasn't some fly-by-night piece of fluff but a mature, sexy woman. Very sexy, I decided as I bit into a sinful chocolate-drenched dessert.

By eleven o'clock, we were at Heavenly Hot Tubs, walking up the wooden spiral steps. Lena had reserved a particularly pleasant space, with live ferns, tastefully patterned wall paneling and a bright red tub that quietly exhaled steam at our feet. Lena closed the cubicle door and latched it, then strode to a small shower set into the corner and tugged aside the curtain.

"Rinse off here first," she instructed me, arranging our towels side-by-side on two wall pegs. I watched as she casually stripped.

She looked stunning without her clothes on–tall and somewhat lean, with nipples the size and color of walnuts, her bronzed skin shimmering in a faint haze of steam. I couldn't help wondering, as I took off my own clothes, if she'd think me flabby and out of shape. I had to admit that I was.

If she did, she was too gracious to say anything. I forced myself not to look up until she'd scrubbed herself under the brisk spray and wrapped a towel around herself.

"Your turn," she said. Her voice held a challenge. Swallowing, I ducked in and did the same. When I emerged, she was kneeling by the tub to turn on the water jets. Soon the rushing sound of flowing hot water filled the room, and I felt the tickle of sweat on my forehead.

I couldn't help stealing another glance at her firm legs and the silky cloud of jet-black hair between them, not to mention her round, well-proportioned breasts as she slipped into the bubbles and motioned for me to do likewise. Her eyes followed my body as it descended into the warmth.

"Feel good?" she asked, sinking in the hot water up to her neck. Nodding, I did the same. "If you press right up against these," she told me, and indicated the little holes emitting the jets of water, "the bubbles will make rings on your skin, almost like hickeys."

"That's weird." I experimented, and decided that the sensation did indeed feel like a little mouth sucking hard on the tender flesh of my back. It wasn't unpleasant, but it caused some numbness after a few moments in one position. For this reason I struck out and allowed myself to bob freely in the current, my nipples breaking the surface every now and then. I could feel the tender skin contract a little each time they left the water. I couldn't help but wonder if Lena could see that, too.

While I paddled around, Lena leaned back and closed her eyes. "What we need now is a glass of champagne on a floating tray," she mused.

"I'm dizzy enough already!" I laughed nervously. Lena opened her eyes again. Her gaze was everything I could hope for: long, slow, and hungry. I knew what she was going to do even before she reached out under the water and wriggled her long fingers between my thighs.

Now it was my turn to close my eyes and surrender to her gentle and obviously experienced manipulation. I let go of the tub and floated right next to her.

"You were right, Lena," I whispered, twisting around in the frothy water to slide my hands along her trim sides. My fingers traced the smooth indentations between her ribs. "This does beat cramming my mouth with potato chips and ice cream."

"You seem to be feeling a lot better now," Lena agreed as she swivelled and took me in her arms. Her hot, naked breasts tickled me, turning me on in a way nothing ever had before. I moved to taste her mouth, at first lightly and then with a deep, driving thirst.

Lena seemed pleased with my forwardness. Her mouth opened farther, yielding completely, then suddenly turned aggressive. Her tongue skimmed inside my lips, then retracted as she bared her teeth and worked me over until my entire face was stinging with pleasure.

Her hands, meanwhile, were busy arousing the lower portions of my body. One massaged my right collarbone and the other stroked the billowing strands of hair against the tingling flesh of my thigh. I ached for her fingers to close around my breast and slide into my hot core, but she was in no hurry and waited until my need was at its most sweetly torturous peak.

"I told you I knew exactly what you needed," Lena soothed me with her voice, as I continued to luxuriate in the hum of the water, the velvet blend of soft skin with soft skin, and the tickle of her own special hair against my leg.

"You were right," I said against the side of her breast, then let my palms caress her upper body in a circular motion, moving from her shoulders around to her rib cage, then back over her breasts and down again.

Anxious to satisfy at least part of the lust burning my body, I lifted one appetizing breast above the water and closed my lips around it. When I teased the nipple with my tongue, I had the intense pleasure of feeling it stiffen against the sides of my mouth.

At last, her hands began to address my desire. Gently

moving my thighs apart, she inserted the tips of her index and middle fingers. I arched against the pressure of her hand, and my fingers dug into her shoulders as I moved to straddle her.

"Wait," she instructed gently, and eased my hands out to either side until they were touching the tiled rim of the tub. "Float on your back. Here, I'll help you." Since I was too far gone to even consider resisting, I allowed her to arrange my body so that it bobbed in front of her, my knees bent over her shoulders. I stretched out my arms to brace myself so my face wouldn't accidentally duck under the water.

Although I was already rigid, breathing hard with need, Lena took extra time to explore, orally, the insides of both my thighs and nibbled at the burning folds of flesh that guarded my middle. Then, after what seemed hours of teasing, she flicked her tongue against the soft, pulsating flesh of my engorged center with increasing vigor as I writhed and cried out for her to push me over my edge.

Still she kept at me, pressing harder and harder with her entire mouth and even her nose until, feeling an explosive wave of heat and pleasure rush over and through me, I cried out and shuddered, bucking against her face in total abandon. Though I often see stars when I come, I'd never experienced the two successive bursts of intense light, followed by darkness, that flashed against my tightly closed eyelids.

She released me, and I let my feet sink to the bottom of the tub. We floated a moment, catching our breath and bumping against one another in contentment.

"That was amazing," I said. "I even thought I saw

lightning!"

Lena laughed and bent forward, and I felt her tongue probe my mouth again, playfully. Gathering my last bit of strength, I sucked back until she shivered and broke away.

"I'm afraid it wasn't lightning," she said. "It was our five-minute warning. Time's almost up."

"You're kidding!" I couldn't believe it. "That was a whole hour?"

"I'm afraid so. We shouldn't stay in any longer for the sake of our skin." She held up the tips of her fingers, which already had that wrinkled look one gets from staying in any tub too long.

"It's a funny thing," I observed, after tipping my head back a moment to allow it to clear. "I can't remember being so thirsty."

Lena hoisted herself out of the tub and sat on the edge, still dangling her feet in the bubbles. My eyes drank in her glistening skin and hair with renewed appreciation and lust. "There's only one way to quench that," she advised as I climbed out as well. "You'll have to come back to my place and drink some of that floating champagne. It's almost midnight, you know."

She took my hand and pulled me to a standing position. My fingers strayed over her bare arm. "Somehow," I raised my eyebrow at her suggestively, "I think this is going to be a millennium to remember."

Safe Haven

The impotent sun barely dents the wintry dawn air. Nonetheless, the thin light that scintillates through my runty window wakes me. That familiar, perpetual want clamors inside me. Still half-asleep, I throw off my patchwork quilt and lift my t-shirt.

I begin my morning ritual by clamping two fingers onto my right nipple. It stiffens while I pinch the soft flesh roughly. Sweat pours from my taut limbs despite the minimal heat in my single dorm room. My mouth goes dry when my other thumb and forefinger reach between my legs. At first, I tease my outer lips slowly. Then I quicken my movements, exposing the slick inner flesh.

I stimulate my other breast now, leaving both nipples red and tingling. The fingers release my swollen desire, rub and then desert me. My hips jut forward, chasing myself, and my wet palm crushes the tiny bundle of nerves in my center.

Nothing can stop me from watching her mouth speak words I have no power to comprehend. She licks her lips and brushes a curl from her face. Dissembling innocence, I touch my hand to her slim, muscular shoulder. Her eyes hold mine in a mutual trance.

I thrust two fingers into my hollow and explore my layers and folds. I massage each glossy crevice, kneading the tender skin and sliding deeper and deeper inside my oblivion. The sweet torment that manacles my senses only scratches the surface of my insatiable hunger.

Suddenly, shyly, she kisses me. I return with a passionate French kiss, tracing the tops of her teeth with my hungry tongue. Her hands move down my back, caressing my spine. We are breast to breast, our hearts nearly bursting with anticipation. My hand grasps her tit, brushing against her ribs. She gasps with pleasure, pushing her well-rounded globe into my hand.

I lunge inside myself at a furious pace, grating the walls of my emptiness. Adding a practiced circular motion, my fingers climb into the narrow recesses. They reach and rub, tantalize and then satiate my raw, undulating nerves.

I maneuver Andi to my canopy bed. In one swift move she turns me over and is on top of me, biting my neck, undoing my bra.

"Baby, you're so beautiful. Tell me how much you want me," I repeat over and over, leaning my head back.

"Oh, Rachel, I do, really I do," she replies in a deep, husky voice.

My body freezes, then spasms and twists. My mind whirls and crashes. My hand drips. I lift myself off the bed over and over while a crimson blush takes over my flesh.

Climax is cruelly abrupt, and it leaves me even more hungry for her. I shake my head in an attempt to return to the all-too-real expectations of the day. It takes an effort to get up and splash cold water on my face, dress in layers, and walk across the campus to my morning class. Snowflakes melt on my coat while I plod through the ankle-deep drifts.

Once again, my thoughts again wander to Andi, and how I hoped she'd follow me to college after our high school graduation. Instead, she stunned me by signing up for the National Guard, saying that this way she can finance her own degree a few years down the road. Then her face had clouded over and she'd confessed her real motives.

We're too young, she said, and shouldn't be tied down. Both of us needed to see other people for a while, and then if we were meant to be, we would be. I didn't force the issue, both because she was a year older than I was and because I thought I would lose her forever. The weeks, and then the months, and now the entire fall semester had slipped by, and still she hadn't called. Remembering her words now chills me as deeply as the blustering wind.

The loss of Andi has affected me more deeply than even I thought it would. I finished my first semester without doing particularly well in any of my classes, though luckily I didn't actually fail anything. Partly to make up for my lackluster performance, I'd decide to take a couple of credits during J-term instead of staying home and feeling sorry for myself. I returned after Christmas to find that very few students have stayed around. I enjoy the quiet of the snow-blanketed campus. Once in a while I feel that familiar sadness return, so I take long walks next to the frozen pond, sampling mouthfuls of frigid air.

One evening, I decide it's time for me to get out and meet some new people—or, to be more precise, some new women. In the library, I locate a gay women's guide to the Northeast and call the only exclusively lesbian bar listed. It's a few towns away, so the gravel-voiced woman on the phone gives me detailed directions while I jot them down on a piece of notebook paper. When I'm ready to go that evening, I fold it up and tuck it into my coat pocket. Deep snowdrifts slash at my ankles as I trudge from my dorm to the student parking lot.

Mine is the only car there. A shiny layer of ice and snow glistens on the hood and the pavement. By the light of the stars, I wrestle the car door open. I find myself fighting off an image of Andi's face as I slide into the driver's seat and stick my keys in the ignition. I have to get her out of my mind, I think. It's time to make a fresh start, to open myself up to the possibilities. Somehow, somewhere, there's got to be another woman I could learn to care about.

I jam my foot on the brake and wrench the key much harder than I need to. The engine sputters out an angry laugh. Then it flops over and lies silent, mocking.

Again and again I hit the starter. But the engine, like my heart, is frozen.

I walk to the outdoor phone and call campus security. They promise to send someone right away, so I stand beside the car shivering until, at last, the marked patrol unit rolls up beside me.

The woman who steps out of the vehicle takes me by surprise. Officer Jean Blake is twentyish, tall, and broad-shouldered. Her short brown hair holds just a touch of ginger. She is compassionate as I explain about my car.

"Probably a dead battery," she says. "Let me pop the hood for you and take a look."

When I reach into my coat pocket and hand her my

keys, the paper with directions to the bar flutter to the ground between us. Blushing, I bend over to retrieve them, but Jean is too quick for me. We stand up together, each of us clutching a corner of the sheet. When our eyes meet, I can tell that she has identified my destination.

"It's a little cold to be heading all the way out there tonight," she says, and I feel her warm breath flutter on my wet cheek. "That place isn't in the best neighborhood. What if your car breaks down again?"

Red-faced, I shrug. Is she laughing at me? Judging me? No—it's empathy I see in those clear grey eyes.

"I just feel like I have to get out," I reply, trying to keep the nervousness out of my voice. "This place is dead. One more night in my room and I'm afraid I'll go stir crazy."

"I know what you mean." Jean nods, then checks her watch and shifts from one booted foot to the other. "Listen, I'm off duty in an hour. What do you say I take you someplace a little nicer? That way neither one of us will have to worry about you getting stranded."

Though her invitation catches me by surprise, I don't have to do much soul-searching before I accept. After all, wasn't my original plan to go out and meet someone new? So far, it seems to be succeeding, though not in the way I expected.

Jean and I make arrangements to meet later, discreetly, by the front gate of the college. After she jump-starts my car, she advises me to let it run a while, then leaves to answer another distress call. Alone again, I sit in the driver's seat, shove my hands in my pockets, and listen to the engine purr. I am relieved when it drowns out, at least for the time being, Andi's voice in my head.

Jean shows up as promised, in street clothes now, and I let her drive me to a small country inn about fifteen miles from campus. I'm not sure if this is so her colleagues won't see us, but I push such thoughts out of my mind and focus on our conversation. I tell her about my classes, my life in the dorm, the trouble I've had fitting in with the other students, who seem hopelessly young and naive to me. I don't mention Andi. Jean tells me about the courses she's taking in Criminal Justice at a nearby state college in hopes of becoming a full-time Corrections Officer one day. The nation's prisons, especially the ones for women, are badly in need of reform, she assures me.

Since I've never met anyone who's been in prison, I have no response. Jean also tells me about her lover, Pam, who couldn't adjust to her long hours on duty and the fact that, as a security guard, she is required to carry a gun. I nod and murmur. Meanwhile, I can't help but picture Andi, dressed in army fatigues and carrying an M-16 rifle.

Back in the car, Jean asks if I'd like to see her apartment. While she is looking at me, I feel a familiar tension between my legs, so I agree.

Jean's apartment is modestly furnished, immaculately clean. She hangs up my coat. We sit on the couch. Before the silence gets uncomfortable, she reaches out and takes my hand.

We kiss gently at first. I hold my breath in awe when

my mouth opens to her moist, probing tongue. Her lips remind me almost painfully of Andi's, and I break away.

Slowly, Jean slides her arm around my shoulder. Her fingers massage my muscles to soothe them, and lust clouds her expression. She draws me closer. Heat wraps us together.

I respond as if I have stepped into a sensuous dream, sliding my fingers along the sides of her head, stroking her sexy soft ears, pressing my demanding body fully against hers. Her strong breasts fit neatly between my fuller ones, her right thigh nudges between my legs.

Her fingers move to the buttons of my shirt. "Please let me undress you," she moans between half-starved kisses.

"Yes, yes," I murmur back, seeing Andi's fingers on my breasts, my own hands now sneaking under the smoldering shell of her light sweater. I reach under her bra to cup her stiffening nipples, pink and hard as the first buds of spring.

She gropes for the button of my jeans while I move one hand down her trim stomach and into the downy warmth between her legs. Gradually, without disrupting our increasingly urgent caresses, we slide onto the sofa. Jean, being the officer, takes charge like Andi used to. She crawls over me, relieving me of the rest of my clothing and covering each newly bared expanse of skin with gentle, teasing little kisses and bites.

When I am naked, she hurriedly strips off the rest of her own clothing, and I moan with satisfaction when she finally plunges her fingers into my bush, weaving them back and forth with an almost primitive fury. Our mutual urgency tells a story. It's been a long time for both of us.

Jean draws her fingers partially out, then hastily slides them in again. I begin pinching her blushing left tit with one hand and seeking a path inside her with the other. We moan together as ecstasy washes over us.

Jean's lips leave the hollow between my breasts and brush lightly over my bellybutton on their way down. I ache, anticipating what is about to happen. I am not disappointed as I feel her lips press into me. Though I long to preserve the feel of every soft flick and flutter of her flesh on mine, her tongue drives me relentlessly forward.

Orgasm blazes through my torso and sears its way down my legs. I cry out and clutch at her scalp. Jean pulls her head away softly, then crawls forward on her elbows until her body lies across mine. My fingers seek her heat, and I put everything I have into rubbing her. It goes on and on, and my arm begins to stiffen and ache as she bucks against my body. Finally she lifts her head back and lets out a cry of ecstasy as her own passion peaks.

We pull ourselves around so that we are lying side by side. My tongue lazily slips along the damp but fragrant skin at her neck. I continue to throb as my climax fades.

"I'm really glad your car broke down tonight," she says, snuggling her head against my left breast.

"Me, too," I say. My voice sounds distant to my own ears as I drift off to sleep, feeling more secure than I have in a long time. Then Jean's heartbeat, thudding soft against my side, reminds me of the way Andi's used to feel.

A week has passed since that night in Jean's apartment. The two of us are still seeing each other, though of course we have to be discreet because of her job. One night, unexpectedly, she shows up at my dorm room after her shift.

"You were right," she says, grinning. "It is really dead around here after dark. I don't think anyone even saw me come in."

I return her smile, then pull her inside. She wraps her arms around me, drawing me to her for a long kiss. Slowly, our clothes drop away and she begins to massage me, moistening my skin with her warm mouth.

Our wet centers are almost kissing as we fall to the bed. Arms and legs entwined, we flail together with a kind of desperate need. Once or twice our engorged buds touch, and a fiery current races through us both.

I grate my hips on hers with strong, sensuous strokes until her body blushes all over and she begs me to push harder and faster. In no time, she stifles a moan and quivers while a sweet torment fills her.

Next I open my legs as Jean straddles me in a sixty-nine position, nuzzling her neck with my thighs. I gasp when her mouth fuses with the wettest part of my body. My fingers wriggle into her flesh, and she drives her face against me, lunging harder and harder until the fevered shivers rake my body.

Gratefully I lose myself in Jean. For hours I go on smelling her, tasting her, too intoxicated to think about anything else. Even Andi.

Much later, as we lie awake just before dawn, I tell

Jean about Andi.

"You still think about her sometimes, don't you?" she asks. "When we're together, I mean."

"I won't lie to you," I respond. The words tear at my chest as I speak them, but Jean seems strangely unaffected. She takes it somewhat philosophically.

"Exes are like that sometimes," she agrees. "They get under your skin. Gnaw at you."

"Was it like that with Pam?" I ask hopefully.

Jean shakes her head and pulls the blanket up over her exposed right nipple. "Nah. When Pam moved out, it was over between us. Too much stuff went down. I realized it even then."

When I don't respond, she swings her legs out of bed and hunts for her clothes.

Her voice is soft. "Look, I've got to go. Can't let anyone find me here in the morning."

"Okay," I say, though I really don't want her to leave.

"I hope you can work this thing out about Andi," she says, slipping away in the near-darkness. It sounds uncomfortably like a goodbye. I lie there, alone and naked, in the bed. Before I can find my voice again, Jean is gone.

I'm too ashamed of myself to call Jean for a few days. Then, one Friday morning right before breakfast, the hall phone rings. Since I'm the only one living on my floor during J-term, I throw on a robe and head out to pick it up.

Stunned, I recognize the voice, but can't help thinking that I've really lost it. My emotions alternate from joy to rage and back again.

"Andi—I can't believe it's you!"

"Believe it, baby. I just got home from boot camp. The first thing I did when I walked through the door was call you."

"Why now? Why not—before?" I manage to whisper. All the time, I can picture her grinning down at the phone with that familiar full-lipped smile of hers.

"Never mind that. We'll talk about it later." She pauses and takes a deep breath. "Baby, I'm so, so sorry."

"Why did you leave me?" I ask, suddenly afraid that she might bolt. "I've thought of you every day since then."

"I was scared then, petrified—but I'm not anymore." Her voice is thick with emotion. I imagine that I can hear her wiping the tears from her face. "I'm here now, and I want to see you. Let me make it right."

"See me where?" I ask cautiously.

"I worked it all out on the map. There's this little motel with a diner right off of Route 10, about thirty miles north of your college. That would be about halfway for both of us. Why don't we both leave right now and meet there? Then we can. . . you know, we can stay overnight and work things out." When I hesitate, she lets out her breath in a hiss. "Please, Rachel. I need you so much."

Her intensity hypnotizes me, just like it did before she left me. At that moment, I want her so much nothing else matters.

"I'll be there," I promise.

My head spins as I tear through my room, tossing clothes and necessities into an overnight bag. I don't even bother to wear socks—just step into my boots and run out to the parking lot. More snow has fallen during the night, and my feet are soaked long before I am inside my car.

"Andi," I whisper, tasting her name on my tongue. "I'm on my way, Andi. Please, please wait for me this time."

I haven't put my gloves on, either, and my fingers shake as I jam the key into the slot and twist it ferociously.

Nothing.

"No!" I pound the wheel, and then the whole steering column, with both fists. "No, damn you, no!" Before long I get out and start pounding the hood of the car, too. The cold has numbed me to the quick.

Gradually, my eyes focus on the security phone at the edge of the lot. I remember when I first picked it up, remember how much colder the wind was that night. I never did get to that lesbian bar I'd copied down the directions to. Jean hadn't brought it up again, either.

I check my watch, wiping a grey mist off the crystal. How long will Andi wait for me at the motel? An hour? Two hours? Not nearly as long as I waited for her. That would take months—five months and three days, to be precise.

Inside the boots, my bare toes have lost all feeling as I walk back to my dorm and crawl into my bed. I lift the pillow to my face and catch a fleeting nuance of Jean's subtle scent, a souvenir of the night she spent with me, here in the room. This time, when the tears fall, I know they're not for Andi, but for what my own foolishness has almost cost me.

By the time I'm warm again, it's almost lunchtime. I force my voice to remain steady as I walk to the hall phone and ask the operator to send Officer Blake down to the student parking lot.

"Tell her that I need some help with my car again," I explain. "There's no hurry."

"It may take her a while," the dispatcher says, irritated. "She's out on another call just now."

"That's okay," I reply, picturing Jean's face when she receives my page. "Tell her I'll be happy to wait."

Too Long

She was walking down the sidewalk toward me. Her hair looked loose and soft like something from a shampoo commercial. Her ten-year-old blue sailor coat was bundled around her, held at the neck by her hand to she fight off the stiff Provincetown wind. She wore the black kidskin gloves I gave her last Christmas.

I couldn't tell if she saw me. My first thought was to duck into one of the shops along Commercial Street, but then there was no reason to do that. We'd parted more or less amicably–no yelling or angry accusations, just an agreement to go our separate ways.

I hadn't seen her since the day I left the house, after four years of sometimes painful, sometimes joyful, cohabitation. I had never really wanted to live with her, but I needed a place to go, and at the time I moved in it seemed to make some sort of sense. She could be the most generous and kind person I could imagine, and at the same time utterly vindictive and superficial. I never knew what she would be. And she could turn from Jekyll to Hyde in an eyeblink.

"Hey! What are you doing here?" she said when she saw me looking directly at her. Her eyes seemed to spark, or maybe it was my imagination. "Are you with anyone?" she looked both hopeful and disinterested at the same time, as only she could.

"Nope," I answered. "I came here alone. How about you?"

"Nope, me either. Do you want to have a cup of tea somewhere? I need to get out of this wind."

"Sure," I said. "I don't have anything special to do. I just took a few days for myself before I start a new job."

We settled ourselves at a table, coats on the empty chairs, cigarettes out. I realized it had been about eight months since I'd seen her.

"You look great," she said. "I see being single agrees with you. You are single, aren't you?"

"Yeah, I am. How about you?" Something in me wanted to hear she was alone, that she hadn't replaced me.

"I haven't even dated." She said this with the same honest face she always had when she lied to me. She stirred her tea and the small talk continued: stories about work, her friends, her life without me. "I still miss you," she said and seemed sincere. "I listen for your car at night, the sound of it coming up the hill, after I've gone to bed. Sometimes I hear you in the kitchen. Then I discover it's just house sounds or maybe a ghost." She looked at me in a way I'd before, sad and touched perhaps. She meant what she was saying. It's just that I wasn't buying it.

"Oh, you will. It just hasn't been enough time yet. I'll go away."

"The bed's so empty. I reach out for you at night or I listen for your breathing." I felt the steady pressure of her leg against mine under the table.

This was getting way too heavy. This was supposed to be a vacation, not a trip down memory lane.

"Well," I said, reaching for my cigarettes and the check, "this has been great. I never expected to run into you here."

It would be so easy, I thought, so very easy to slip

back into the past, go back and try to save all the good parts, but I didn't want the bad parts. I didn't want that ever again.

"Where are you staying?" she asked.

"Over at Victoria House. I love the hot tub, you know."

"What's your room number?"

"I'm in 24, second floor." I supposed this meant she'd come by for another chat.

"I'm in 36."

Done.

Sometimes a moment occurs when you just know what will happen, when you can write the scenario, and if you don't want it, then you have to fight fate with all your will. But then maybe I did want it. Nights were cold. I hadn't been with a woman since that wild butch with the brush cut brought her handcuffs to my apartment and wanted to play police lineup. Whew! That was a little intense. Thank heaven she never called again, though it was fun. Still, that was a few months ago now, and I could think of worse ways to spend a frosty January night in Ptown.

Though it was only 5:30, the sun was already down and the street lights were already on. Shops were still decorated from the holidays, but the cold was so bitter that we walked as quickly as we could. The wind had picked up and was twisting the street decorations into a frenzy. Her shoulder nudged mine when we turned the corner onto the side street where the hotel was. If we'd only been like this more often when we were together, maybe we wouldn't be apart now.

"I hope you don't mind," she said, "if I spend the

evening with you." Her voice was low as we climbed the steps of the old mansion, "Unless you have other plans." It was so like her to say something like that, insinuating more meaning than I cared to think about. But I didn't want to think, in fact. I felt her warm breath on my face the second we were in the hallway next to her room.

The room was toasty warm and welcoming. I removed my coat and threw it in the chair where she put hers. She was already sitting on the bed with her hand on the TV remote. Some things never change, I thought. Surprisingly, she put it down. "I'm not in the mood for television. How about you? Your cheeks are red from the cold. Let me warm you up."

I hadn't spoken since we left the restaurant. Now was the moment to change things, rewrite the script if I was going to. I fought the anticipatory void filling my emotions. At that point, my rational side rebelled but my wishful thinking won out. My mind went blank, and I pulled her to her feet. I kissed her first, sucking her lower lip hard and jostling her against the paneled wall, pressing her torso against me.

She threw her head back and a feline smile crossed her inviting lips. I eased my tongue between her teeth. Hers met mine and slowly explored my parched mouth. She put her hand on my back, crushing my body even harder into hers.

Then she shoved me onto the bed, got on top of me, and rubbed me. I could feel my whole being heating in response to her unbridled desire for me. In one motion, I slipped off her sweater and for the umteenth time admired her firm, small tits that beckoned me like tangy passion fruits. I clasped them in my hungry hands.

In seconds, she pulled my top off, too. She moaned when she got hold of my larger breasts, squeezing them with obvious delight. Then she licked her way down my torso and undid my jeans. I pulled hers off as well. Panting, we rolled on top of each other, naked and free.

She wasted no time in getting what she wanted and maneuvered herself so that her aroused folds lay directly on my face. She proceeded to go down on me at the same time, licking and sucking me.

We coupled with an intensity that had been missing since our early days together. She moaned when my tongue thrust deeply into her. She used her finger and her mouth on me, sliding it inside me, imitating my intense movements.

We came together, another thing that had almost never happened since the old days, twisting and jerking like we were huddled in a small dinghy during a violent ocean storm. If we had been, we would have overturned it as a virtual tidal wave roared through both of us.

It ended with both of us heaving and looking at each other. She hugged me, kissed the tip of my nose, and settled down to sleep, wrapping herself so tightly in the blankets that there were none left for me.

I watched her pensively, and that hollow feeling I'd had just before the lust won me over returned. I stared at her with a somewhat overwrought yearning, trying to love her as she lay dozing, her mouth slightly open. But this time a smothering feeling overtook me.

I got up wordlessly and dressed, taking pains not to disturb her. It wouldn't have mattered anyway. She had now fallen into a deep slumber. I went back to my own room.

I sat at the desk, took out pen and paper, and wrote several drafts of a letter to her, a letter that resembled the one I'd sent her when I'd left her the first time. I spent well over an hour trying to capture the words that would finally end it between us, the words that would release each of us from the other. But each attempt only added to the crumpled wads in the wastebasket.

Finally, I decided to confront her in person. I owed it to the both of us. I went down to her room, but it was locked and silent. When I crossed through the foyer, I noticed a letter in my box.

I opened it with an ache of premonition and a sense of relief, expecting long, convoluted pleas from her. But all the note said was, "Goodbye."

For the first time, she'd surprised me. I found the housegirl folding sheets in front of the downstairs linen closet, and I asked if she were still a guest. The housegirl shrugged and told me she'd checked out a few hours earlier.

I stumbled outside, back into the cold, on feet of lead. As I walked along Commercial Street, though, that familiar barrenness returned. I wondered if any woman could ever fill me the way I'd once imagined she could. And did it really matter?

By the time I returned to the guesthouse, I'd decided that maybe her good-bye didn't mean she'd left for good. Maybe this time, we would be apart for only a short, lonely while.

Additional copies of **Seasons of Desire** may be ordered from Nocturnis Productions for $13.95 plus $4.00 postage and handling. We also offer quantity discounts for qualified retailers.

To receive updates on upcoming Nocturnis Productions, please send a self-addressed stamped envelope to us at P.O. Box 9635, N. Amherst, MA 01375. We welcome all readers' comments!

THE MASSACRE IN HISTORY

War and Genocide
General Editor: Omer Bartov, Rutgers University

THE MASSACRE IN HISTORY

EDITED BY
MARK LEVENE AND PENNY ROBERTS

Berghahn Books
New York • Oxford

First published in 1999 by

Berghahn Books

Editorial offices:
55 John Street, 3rd Floor, New York, NY 10038, USA
3 NewTec Place, Magdalen Road, Oxford OX4 1RE, UK

Library of Congress Cataloging-in-Publication Data
The massacre in history / edited by Mark Levene and Penny
Roberts.
    p.   cm.
Includes bibliographical references and index.
ISBN 1-57181-935-5 (pbk. paper)
ISBN 1-57181-934-7 (hbk. paper)
1. Massacres.   I. Levene, Mark, 1953- .   II. Roberts, Penny.
III Series.
D24 .M37 1999   97-38276
940.54'05--dc21   CIP

British Library Cataloguing in Publication Data
A catalogue record for this book is available
from the British Library.

Printed in the United States on acid-free paper.

For Ala, Kathy and Clare

In Memory of Callum MacDonald
1947-1997

CONTENTS

LIST OF FIGURES

LIST OF ABBREVIATIONS

AVNOJ	Anti-Fascist Council of the Liberation of Yugoslavia
BBS	Bureau of Biological Survey (U.S.)
CIA	Central Intelligence Agency (U.S.)
CPP	Croatian Peasant Party
ETA	*Euzkadi ta Azkatasuna* (Basque Separatist Organization)
HDZ	Croatian Democratic Union
IRA	Irish Republican Army
JNA	Yugoslav National Army
KMT	*Kuomintang* (National People's Party, China)
NATO	North Atlantic Treaty Organization
NDH	Independent State of Croatia
NSC	National Security Council (U.S.)
PARC	Predatory Animal and Rodent Control Service (U.S.)
PKI	Communist Party of Indonesia
RPKAD	Resimem Para Kommando Angkatan Darat (Indonesian army commandos)
SUBNOR	League to Commemorate the Fighters of the National Liberation War (Yugoslavia)
UNS	Unit II of the *ustash*i security force

PREFACE AND ACKNOWLEDGEMENTS

It is not possible for any collection of essays to add up to a definitive statement on a subject. This issue is broached with regard to *The Massacre in History* primarily because the selection of suitable essays for it has proved to be something of an emotional minefield. To include discussion of one celebrated massacre is potentially to exclude another, or to put it another way, to demote an event which some might consider to be of great historical import. The subject of massacre often involves passionate partisanship. Even, perhaps especially, among historians.

So we include this preface to clarify what we consider the purpose of this volume to be. *The Massacre In History* grew out of a conference at the University of Warwick in March 1995. Six papers covered a time-span from the eleventh century to the early 1990s, ranging spatially from Western Europe to China and back to the Balkans, and including discussion of issues as varied as the artistic depiction of massacre in the late-medieval period, the role of personal testimonies as a form of counter-evidence to standard interpretations of an early-modern cause célèbre, to an analysis of the historiography associated with a notorious Second World War killing site, the politicization of which has contributed to the breakup of a contemporary state. This broad scope was quite intentional. We wanted to provide a framework in which historians could offer fresh, often disparate approaches to a subject too often treated only in a sensationalist manner, and to show how current debates and discourses in the historical discipline might be applied to it. History, in other words, could teach us something about massacre. Likewise, massacre could teach us something about history.

The success of the conference led to our decision to develop our material into a volume and to commission seven further essays to consider aspects of, or perspectives on the subject, which, because of time constraints, had been neglected in the conference. The massacre of animals was one area which we felt particularly needed historical examination. Another was the relationship between massacre and genocide, as well as that between massacre and social change. These examples alone suggested to us that we were not dealing with a subject which readily supplied cut-and-dried answers, but rather one which was a seriously contested arena. A further requirement in enlisting these additional contributions was to fill in some of the chronological and geographical gaps created by our original broad remit. With only thirteen essays to juggle with there were inevitably some losers, one geographical casualty being the Middle East. Nevertheless, the inclusion of essays on the Americas, Africa, the Caucasus, China and South East Asia, in addition to a central core on the British Isles and Western Europe, is a conscious attempt to create balance, as is the approximate numerical balance between early-modern and modern case-studies.

However, the real bone of contention remains: which case-studies? Those who might have sought an Oradour, a Lidice, a Katyn, or a Babi Yar may, doubtless, be disappointed. Or equally, to continue this very contemporary plaint, an Amritsar, a Sharpeville or a Tiananmen Square. This, surely, is at the nub of the problem. When we come to this subject, most of us have an axe to grind; one which more often than not takes us back over well-worn ground or even round in circles. What we conversely have sought to do is both give an airing to important case-studies and arguments which have rarely been considered or which get lost in a noisier polemic, while attempting to come at some of the more contentious issues and 'famous' cases from new perspectives.

Take the most obvious reference point for a Western audience: massacres committed in the Second World War by the Nazis, most particularly the extermination of European Jewry. Simply citing this example, however, raises a series of pitfalls, not least because the Holocaust today is not perceived to be part of a history of massacre so much as a subject entirely in a class of its own. On one level it could be argued that we have thus simply circumvented the issue by omitting an appropriate case-study. And it is true that one of our considerations has been not to replicate a category of massacre which has been covered extensively elsewhere. The Holocaust is a subject on which a vast amount has been written in recent years. Yet its centrality will not go away. Which is perhaps why four of the essays herein deal with some of the historical debates and issues thrown up by it. Shenfield examines what we mean by genocide as opposed to massacre. Dedering provides further context and cross-reference with an examination of an *earlier* German genocide. MacDonald considers Christopher Browning's recent critique of Nazi atrocities in his *Ordinary Men* with reference to a near-contemporary Far Eastern case-study. And, finally, Okey considers the death camp killings committed by both a Nazi satellite state and counter-killings by its adversaries, from the perspective of their post-war evaluation and memorialization by both Communist and post-Communist regimes.

None of this adds up to a comprehenisive treatment of the Holocaust or, indeed, of the huge history of massacre as a whole. But our remit was never to compile a straightforward chronology nor a consensual pecking order of most (in)famous examples. Instead what we hope we have achieved is something more interesting and valuable. First, perhaps, a recognition that in a world beset with so much violence and mass killing, the roots of that violence have to be studied historically as well as in other ways. Secondly, that while such interpretative analysis cannot offer ready-made, straightforward or glib solutions – not least because of the fluid, open and contested nature of the subject itself – it can nevertheless provide insights into some of the most perplexing, as well as most distasteful aspects of our communal, cultural and political selves.

We are grateful to the University of Warwick Humanities Research Centre for its support and thus for providing the initial impetus to this project. Peter Coates also specifically wishes to thank the University of Bristol Arts Faculty Research Fund for support given in preparing his contribution.

This volume inevitably carries a strong Warwick imprint. In addition to its direct contributors we would particularly like to thank Keith and Claire Brewster, Rebecca Earle, John King, Peter Marshall, Iain Smith, and Guy Thomson for ideas as well as suggestions which have brought together further outstanding contributors from both sides of the Atlantic as well as South Africa. Above all we wish to acknowledge with gratitude the tireless support of our colleague, Sarah Richardson, without whom our diverse collection of computer discs would have remained just that. Many thanks also to another colleague, Tim Lockley, on this same score, to Jenny Ivory for utter endurance, and to Sarah Miles, Barbara Newson and Marian Berghahn at Berghahn Books for their patience and for enabling this volume to see the light of day.

A final two words: Callum MacDonald. Callum was a guiding light in the original conference, his enthusiasm and encouragement opening the window to a whole range of future collaborative projects. At the time we were not aware that his particular contribution would also be his swansong. His untimely death has robbed the department of one of its leading, most gifted and productive scholars and the world of a truly noble and generous spirit. This volume is dedicated to his wife, Ala, and daughters, Kathy and Clare, in his fond memory.

Mark Levene and Penny Roberts

INTRODUCTION

Mark Levene

The news is awash with bloody massacre. Not a day passes but some atrocity committed somewhere in the world appears in our newspapers or on our television screens to horrify us. Rwanda, Burundi, Algeria, Srebrenica; as the stories get closer to home the less able are we to pass them off as something that happens only 'out there'. The massacres near Srebrenica in July 1995, possibly the largest in Europe since the end of the Second World War, might just still be far enough away to dismiss as another of those appalling things that distant, not quite civilized tribes,or clans, or warring peoples do to each other. Politicians and pundits might rationalize them as the unfortunate outcome of one-sided military conflicts. Some might even invoke history. 'The conflict in Bosnia', stated the then Prime Minister, John Major, in a House of Commons speech in 1993, 'was a product of impersonal and inevitable historical forces beyond anyone's control.'[1] Were these his private thoughts too, I wonder, after a lone gunman in March 1996 walked into a school in the Scottish town of Dunblane and shot to death sixteen little children and their teacher? The media, on this occasion, was reduced to clutching for explanations less from politicians, more from psychiatrists or churchmen. People mumbled about evil, many more were reduced to stunned silence.[2]

Dunblane was, of course, not Srebrenica. Nor Srebrenica the Holocaust. The disparities and the dissimilarities between them must limit, if not render dubious any attempt to find common characterstics, common causation. Theorizing, one-sided mass killing would somehow have to take into account all the variables; scale, context, modes of delivery, above all, perhaps, the motivation behind each massacre. Yet our Janus-like horror combined with fascination with all mass killing does seem to posit a range of awkward, difficult questions not simply about the perpetrators and their victims but more keenly about our biological, cultural, social and political selves. Are massacres the outcome of nature or nurture? Are we predetermined to be violent as part of our biological make-up? Or is 'man's inhumanity to man' the outcome of a particular wrong turning in our development ? Is there an overarching explanation, for instance, patriarchy, which might proffer that the victimizers, in the last analysis, have always been men and their main victims, women? Or are we talking about aberrations which, by rights, should not happen in 'civilized' societies at all and thus are throwbacks to some primitive time when life was 'nasty, brutish and short'? Is this, however, too general an approach? Is it only some men who are responsible for atrocity, who, for whatever reason, are ill in the head, or perhaps whose heads have been addled by too much alcohol, or ideology, or religion? A hundred years before John Major's speech on Bosnia, the French foreign minister, Hanotaux, shrugged off the growing wave of anti-Armenian massacres in the Ottoman empire as 'one of those thousand incidents of struggle between Christians and Muslims'.[3] Does it make us feel better, perhaps, if we rationalize such events as the dysfunction of other people's societies, not our own? Are Balkan, Central African or Central Asian peoples so locked into 'ancient hatreds' that they are inevitably massacre-prone in a way people like ourselves are not? Or is this just another example of Western ethnocentricism; of a failure to understand our own recent history and society and by extension, to make connections, even, perhaps, to accept our coresponsibility for massacres past and present elsewhere?

While there will always be more questions than answers to the causes of massacre, the long-term repercussions of a Srebrenica, or indeed a Dunblane, demand that they cannot be simply sidestepped. It has become fashionable to argue that the nature of killing has changed since Hiroshima and Auschwitz; that thanks to rapidly advancing technologies and their systematization within organized, rational bureaucratic systems, those who press a button from a launching pad, or fill in schedules for the transportation of prisoners from a transit camp to an extermination one, can be involved in a killing process without being in any sense physically or emotionally connected to their victims. This detachment, this distancing; it has been argued, enables or compounds both the depersonalization and dehumanization of the victims, thus making their hands off dispatch all the more easy, plausible and even sanitized.[4] Yet this version of modernity must sit uneasily with some contemporary realities. The

Rwandan genocide of 1994 is simply the most striking example of hands on, low technology, and entirely messy mass killing perpetrated by men, and sometimes women, who yesterday were neighbours, even friends.[5] Perhaps something has changed. Perhaps the great political shift that has happened in the last few years with the collapse of the Soviet empire and the last vestiges of bipolarism is in some way responsible. Or, perhaps, it has simply opened our eyes not so much to the nature of change but to threads of a malodorous continuity previously on the periphery of our vision.

Is this a juncture, then, at which a study of history, and the place of massacre within it, might offer not so much solace but possibly some signposts, some guide or map as to where we are coming from, if not necessarily to where we might be going? History is resonant with massacre. Refer, in Britain, to a Glencoe, a Culloden, or a Peterloo and they will frequently evoke strong reactions, even though these events were many generations ago. Massacres have deep meaning, they are part of people's consciousness, even their 'folk' memory. The problem is that what is evocative for one group of people may be viewed in a quite different way by another. Our identification is always with the victims, as if we were the victims, never with the perpetrators. As such, massacre is a very contested, and a contentious arena. One man's bloodbath becomes another's just desserts, or possibly something which was little more than a street brawl, where it happened at all. Massacre, real or imagined, can be the rallying cry for a people or nation aggrieved, and thereby can potentially cast a shadow, possibly for generations or even centuries, over intercommunal or even interstate relations.

If these aspects suggest massacre can help give a shape to history, it also implies that the emphasis here may not be on what 'actually' happened so much as how it was remembered. For the historian, this may be valuable as an indicator of collective, possibly cross-generational anxieties and resentments yet, as Mark Greengrass and Robin Okey show in this volume, highly problematic. Not only may the 'memory', in such instances, become a tool for political manipulation but often at the expense of other competing 'memories', usually held by opposing groups, or enemies, which are duly relativized into lesser, subsidiary events, involving lesser numbers of fatalities, where they are not airbrushed out of existence altogether.

What is the historian's role in this? Can he or she adjudicate between competing versions of the truth? Does this not take into account the possibility that the historian might also be partisan? Is not the correct thing to do to dispense with the mythic transformation that the 'massacre' has undergone to return to as thorough and comprehensive an investigation as is possible of the event itself?

Perhaps some of the problems inherent in this discussion may indicate why historians sometimes fight shy of the subject. Ugly, vicious events, often appearing to lack clear delineation or logic, massacres throw off course where they do not completely skewer any project which seeks to chart through precise information and data the long-term transformation of societies, economies and polities. Nor do apparently pathological, even sado-masochistic tendencies obviously complement the historian's penchant for the 'objective' fact or rational deduction. Yet history, after all, involves empirical observation of societies more often than not in conflict and crisis. It is, amongst other things, about relationships of power and unequal ones at that. Ensuing tensions, frequently leading to violence cannot be ignored or sidestepped; on the contrary they are absolutely integral to understanding how history 'works'. As such, charting the incidence or, obversely, avoidance of massacre, may indeed throw light on a town, or region, or country's political, social, or economic development. The way such events are either rationalized, justified or condemned may tell us much about the *mentalité* of a people – or peoples – as may the manner in which 'the massacre' becomes embedded and depicted within their respective cultures.

The thirteen essays in this volume, then, relate the subject of massacre from the medieval period to the present to a much wider range of historical discourses. Issues of gender, race, class, religion, and the too often forgotten relationships between man and animals all appear in this volume. So, more glaringly, does the issue of war. Some essays, such as that by John Edwards and Callum MacDonald are concerned with the anatomy of particular 'massacres' but in order to explore some broader intercommunal or interstate dynamic. Sometimes, as in the essays by Mark Greengrass and Robert Levine, it is not so much the massacre itself which is the focus but the way it was recorded or remembered by eyewitnesses, participants or victims, the aim here being to open a window onto the mores of deeply fractured or rapidly changing societies. *The Massacre in History*, in other words, is not designed to either celebrate or provide inventory for the largest or most famous massacres, though they will be found aplenty in these pages. Indeed, it is well to remember, on this score, that the vast majority are mostly forgotten or even unknown, in the latter case usually because they happened in out of the way places so that they could not be properly reported and, or, because the perpetrators had a vested interest in their denial or cover-up.

Stephen Shenfield, Tilman Dedering, John Gittings and Robin Okey chart some other modern instances of these 'forgotten' massacres. In the case of the Circassians and Hereros, Shenfield and Dedering argue that the systematic scope and scale of the massacres involved make the term 'genocide' a more appropriate and accurate definition of these events. Putting aside what constitutes a genocide,[6] this introduction cannot proceed without attempting to consider what constitutes a massacre.

Defining Our Terms: Extending the Debate

All massacre is violence, but not all violence is massacre. Do we therefore need to have some critical number of fatalities from a victim group before we have arrived at our destination? Is this what differentiaties disturbances or riots from the 'real thing'? Are there occasions, as John Edwards implies, when calling such events massacre, is really to misconstrue them? Alternatively, is the number of perpetrators also important? Will Coster, for instance, argues that a mass killing committed by a single individual is not a massacre. This would negate my earlier reference to Dunblane and, for that matter, the killing of twenty-nine Palestinian Muslim worshippers, by Baruch Goldstein, in Israeli-occupied Hebron, in February 1994, though the media had no reservations in reporting these events as such. Seeking fuller elucidation from a dictionary, moreover, is only partially helpful. An old French word of uncertain origin, massacre, suggests my dictionary, involves the violent, cruel, wanton or indiscriminate killing of large numbers of human beings or animals. It can imply mutilation or mangling of those killed. Colloquially, it is also a term we use for a shambles, a defeat in a game, or even in major political event, as witnessed in the crushing Conservative defeat at the hands of Labour, in May 1997.[7]

If the dictionary, therefore, sidesteps the issue of numbers, either of perpetrators or victims, it also fails to spell out other critical ingredients. One surely is the relationship at the point of delivery between those killing and those being killed. A massacre is when a group of animals or people lacking in self-defence, at least at that given moment, are killed – usually by another group (Coster's point is a valid though not easily resolvable one) who have the physical means, the power, with which to undertake the killing without physical danger to themselves. A massacre is unquestionably a one-sided affair and those slaughtered are usually thus perceived of as victims; even as innocents. This would allow for military massacre, as for instance after Culloden, when the remnants of a defeated army are cut down in flight; a Saint Valentine's Day massacre when one group of gangsters liquidates another; or a series of communal massacres, the killing of thousands of Ibos in Northern Nigeria in 1965, for instance, involving the violent death of men and women, including old people and babies, whom we might consider to be in the fullest sense 'innocents'. All this assumes quite specific spatial and temporal dimensions. Massacre implies an event which takes place in a limited, though not defined geographical arena, as well as in a limited, though again not clearly defined time period.

The technology of modern destruction, however, does raise some problems if not for the concept of massacre itself then, perhaps, for our perception of it. Can we talk, for instance, of massacre from the air, *à la* Guernica, Dresden or for that matter, Hiroshima? If that is so, does this not raise further questions about not only the physical proximity between those who do the massacring and those who are massacred but also about their physical and indeed emotional connectedness? I must confess my mental image of a massacre is of the St Bartholomew's day type; a thoroughly hot-blooded, 'hands on' affair in which the killers not only slaughter hundreds of people many of whom they personally know but with mostly crude, low-level technology. The massacre is complete when the targeted victims are either all dead or the perpetrators' emotional energy is spent. A recent film, *La Reine Margot*,[8] confirmed my mental image of St Batholomew's until it was pointed out to me how idealized – and eroticized – this thoroughly modern depiction was; full of naked yet never corpulent or diseased bodies, bloody but never overtly mutilated, always somehow managing even in death to strike a pose. In contrast, Laura Jacobus makes it abundantly clear that depictions of massacre in art or drama, are very dependent on broader cultural currents and mores which, in turn, are prone to change over time. The frequency with which 'The Massacre of the Innocents' was painted or engraved in the European High Middle Ages may thus remain a constant but the way the focus of violence in these portrayals increasingly centred on the children's mothers, marks a shift, argues Jacobus, towards a more misogynistic culture.

At stake here is the nature – and credentials – of 'civilized' society itself. If it is prone to fantasies about sadoerotic killing it is more difficult to argue that massacre, when it does occur, represents either a breakdown in its value system or some sort of societal dysfunction. On the contrary, one might choose to construe from this that massacre does have a place within a 'civilized' societal or political order, that far from connoting unpredictability, chaos, or a reversion to atavistic impulses we are actually dealing with a critical element in 'a utilitarian calculus',[9] a considered, if albeit crude, instrument of social and political control. Nor need we see this in terms only of power relationships between men and women, though violence against women in the form of mass rape may play a very specific functional role in the perpetration of massacres. Callum

MacDonald's analysis of what has become known as the 'Rape of Nanking' (of which literal rape was an intrinsic element), thus pits commonly held views of a wave of barbaric, mindless killings by a Japanese army which was deemed to be out of control with the counter-argument that it was let loose on the Nanking population, in 1937, in a quite calculated way and with much broader policy intentions for the subjugation of China in mind.

If this sort of mass violence is really the prerogative of the most organized and powerful states the role of massacre, paradoxically, may be necessary to our understanding of civilization. Yet our modern perception usually rebels at the mere notion. Raphael Lemkin, the international jurist who coined the term genocide in 1944, during the Nazi rampage across Europe, deemed it to be associated with the overthrow of civilization in favour of a reversion to barbarism.[10] But from where does this idea emanate? In the classical world, the Greeks disputed a commonality between themselves and those they perceived to be less developed peoples by denoting them as barbarians. The idea that only barbarians, or to use another loaded term, savages, commit atrocities but civilized people do not is a convenient one even when it is manifestly untrue. Simply witness the way classical religious rites of sacrificial mass slaughter – of animals – evolved into Roman 'games' in which animals and humans were regularly consumed by their thousands to feed an insatiable public appetite for blood spectacle.[11] Yet both ancient Greek prejudice and latter-day Roman spectator sport implicitly seem to point to a time in a deeper past when all men were 'savages', that is, when all mankind was to greater or lesser degrees dependent on slaughter in order to survive.

Common Roots: The Massacre of Animals

To propose that the contemporary idea of massacre is not only based upon, but has its authentic roots in prehistory is admittedly both speculative and controversial given that the experts do not agree on the nature of the earliest hunter-gatherer societies. Having said that a number of archeologists and paleoecologists do argue that the killing of animals by early man was pursued so vigorously and wantonly that a range of fauna throughout entire continents were rapidly depleted if not wiped out.[12] Whether or not one accepts the available evidence as proof of prehistoric man's proclivity to massacre animals not only to live but for the sheer bloodlust of it, one is on much stronger ground with the more recent historical record.

We do not know, of course, if Elizabethan English seamen were responding to some deep atavistic impulse when, confronted by docile penguins, their first reaction was to indiscriminately slaughter them.[13] What we do know is that killing wild animals was, as Peter Coates shows in his essay on that hated predator, *par excellence*, the wolf, pursued with overwhelming passion yet always accompanied by a battery of justifications. In seventeenth-century England, for instance, no one seems to have batted an eyelid as children massacred birds, squirrels and frogs. The maintenance of man's preindustrial wellbeing was indeed premised on this slaughter, necessity demanding that any creature which challenged man's control of crops and domestic animals was vermin and thereby subject to extermination without mercy.

But domesticated animals could be targets too. Before an age of urban sensibilities about animal suffering, stray dogs and cats as alleged disease or plague-carriers were particular targets of the civil authorities.[14] If this added public health to the list of rationalizations for killing animals there was always more to it than simply necessity. For instance, carnival in many French regions, was a time for the massacre of animal effigies associated with the rich – piglets and partridges were particularly popular – in a brief orgy of common people's wish fulfilment. The actual slaughter of dogs and cats, at carnival or any other time of year, added to the fun, though it could also serve to relieve some other social frustration.[15] Some animals in sporting massacres were, of course, off limits to the general populace. Game had been so depleted by perpetual massacre that conservation of their young or the confining of the killing to a regular season, became, until the twentieth century, the almost exclusive preserve of a hunting and shooting aristocracy, who, incidently, but tellingly, rationalized the carnage on the grounds that it kept them in trim for fighting war.[16]

No such constraints existed as Europeans 'discovered' new worlds in the Americas and the Antipodes. Slaughter of beasts on land and sea was pursued for their inherent commercial value and to make way for domesticated breeds. But indigenous peoples who had previously learnt and had deeply embedded in their cultures the wisdom of conservation against rapacity also became caught up in these movements, as in the northern Americas in the seventeenth and eighteenth centuries, where the beaver was hunted almost to extinction to supply seemingly unquenchable European markets with its fashionable pelts.[17] From the perspective of ecological history this type of massacre may have had profound consequences indeed. Without the dambuilding beaver, traditional watercourses and watersheds were radically dislocated and disrupted while the almost exclusively white man's near extermination of the formerly teeming herds of bison, in the following century, was to rapidly bring to a terminus both the sustenance and independence of the plains Indians.[18] If the last event was at least noticed and remarked upon, the point here is that animal killing, whether as the domesticated 'sheep to slaughter' or the wolf or fox exterminated in its lair, is so deeply ingrained in our human cultures; so taken for granted, that it informs our very notion of massacre. The clue lies in language.

A 'massacre' in the old French, notes Mark Greengrass, meant a butcher's chopping block, thereby finding its way into more general circulation via the archetypal St Bartholomew's example of what butchers do. The language of massacre is significant in other contexts too. A noble-led military detachment 'killed the peasants like swine' as an insurrection in Dauphiné, in 1580, was bloodily extinguished.[19] Twelve hundred Armenians killed in Harput in a great wave of massacres in 1895, were, reported a Turkish soldier home, simply food for the dogs.[20] When the Vietcong shot or clubbed to death at least three thousand civilians in Hué, during the 1968 Tet offensive, they dealt with them in the same way as 'they would get rid of poisonous snakes'.[21] Most tellingly, perhaps, a barracks where peasants had been killed in army operations in El Quiché, Guatemala in 1982, was described by a witness as 'like a butcher's slaughterhouse for animals'.[22]

It should not surprise us, then, that traditional techniques for the entrapment of animals have also been used against human prey since time immemorial; that in recent history conquistadors and later other European settlers in the Americas used dogs in manhunts against fleeing natives,[23] that, during the Second World War, the *Einsatzgruppen* and other German units did the same against Jews, Gypsies and others hiding from deportation to the camps,[24] that, in 1831, the British authorities instituted an island-wide 'pheasant drive' against the last surviving aborigines in Tasmania.[25] Nor that in some massacres, such as that which took place at Aintab, in Aleppo province of the Ottoman empire, in early 1896, it was the experts in killing and cutting up animals, the butchers and tanners, who, armed with clubs and cleavers did the slaughtering, only stopping for midday prayers.[26] But do these illustrations prove the point that massacre entails a reversion to savagery?

Civilization versus Savagery

A traditional Western perspective on history would certainly have us recall the carnage and destruction wrought by those it would perceive as the barbarians. It is the Attilas not the Romans who thus become the guilty party or, later, the Mongol hordes led by a Chinghis or a Timur. In the latter case there is plenty of evidence to confirm that the scale of human – and civilization – extermination over a huge area of Central Asia, the Near East and Northern India was so massive that the historian Arnold Toynbee felt impelled to comment that Timur in a span of twenty-four years (between 1379 and 1403) perpetrated as many horrors as the last five Assyrian kings achieved in the space of one hundred and twenty.[27] The comparison is instructive. Timur, like another great destroyer, Shaka, the early nineteenth-century founder of the Zulu people, may indeed, through the sheer scale of his killing have changed the course of history. But the respective agendas of a Timur or Shaka were not to wreak havoc and destruction for its own sake but rather to create conditions for their own supremely strong, centralized states.[28] These in turn, were to provide for a perpetual peace and stability, in other words, exactly what the Assyrian empire claimed as its justification every time it sent its armies to exterminate any rebels or other contenders who dared challenge its authority.

If the 'barbarians' massacred en route to becoming great civilizations while the great civilizations massacred in order to perpetuate themselves, where does that leave Lemkin's view of a Nazi Germany reverting to some earlier stage of savagery? Doubtless the Nazis would have unequivocally rejected Lemkin's proposition, just as the historian A.T. Olmstead did, in 1932, for the Assyrians and Romans, when he described them not so much as wolves of war but shepherd dogs of civilization.[29] Moreover, Olmstead's portrayal of the Assyrian system, with its massacres of rebel provinces and cities justified on the grounds of the preservation of a 'sacred order', sounds uncannily like the Japanese version of why it was necessary to brutally subjugate China and its other far-flung conquered territories.

But there is surely something not only distasteful but actually rather unsatisfactory here. All the above imperial 'civilizations' could only maintain power by a high degree of militarization coupled with an undiluted willingness to resort to terror. In resource and manpower terms such systems are inevitably expensive to maintain and hence likely to be fiscally onerous on subject populations. The result is likely to be a vicious circle in which the state has to be constantly vigilant against the possibility that the tables might be turned on it by those on the periphery, or by 'barbarian' groups, or even more advanced civilizations beyond, ready and willing to ride in to extirpate it. As the possibility of negotiation with these parties is excluded from the rules the only option is to carry on massacring. But is this, then, a statement not so much of strength but of ultimate weakness?

This may be particularly true because massacre is not a finely tuned instrument of control but an extremely fissile, potentially uncontrollable one. Once perpetrated it has a habit of becoming endemic, as, for instance, the Greek city states, in the phase of the Peloponnesian wars between 420 and 416 BC, found to their cost.[30] Admittedly, the states in question were rather evenly balanced. To perpetrate massacre with impunity it is necessary to have an absolute 'monopoly of violence'. Rome, certainly, had this for considerable periods, when it was not wracked by internal conflict. But after its fall, such a monopoly proved for all of its successors to be elusive. Clawing back the monopoly became associated with a long march towards modernity, a paradox given that modern states, at least in their domestic arrangements, are supposed to be ruled not by military coercion but the force of law. But this, surely, is doubly paradoxical as any state which could meet these conditions would not need to resort to violence at all. Its strength would be based on its societal cohesion and on the willingness of its constituent elements to always resolve disputes by negotiation. If this is so, the resort to massacre is a statement less of a state whose power is unfettered but of one whose power is diffused, or fragmented, or unsure of itself, or frightened of the fact that the power which it thinks it ought to have is illusory or slipping out of its control.

State and People

Let us return to that classic example from the early modern period, the St Bartholomew's Day massacre, perpetrated against Huguenots in Paris in 1572, the main focus of the essay by Mark Greengrass. Historians are unable to agree on its exact causes. Was it a premeditated attempt by the Crown to quash the growing power of the Huguenots or a knee-jerk, panic response to a botched assassination attempt on Coligny, their noble leader? Were the real instigators the princely Guise family and their motivation primarily one of personal vendetta against Coligny's Montmorency family or were they in fact part of a much bigger, international Catholic conspiracy, with the Spanish, in the wings, pulling the strings? What do we make of apparently contradictory oral and written commands given by, or at the behest of, the King, Charles IX, and where does communal participation in the killing, by Catholics against their Huguenot neighbours, fit, if anywhere, into this picture?[31]

Whatever one makes of these unresolved aspects, and whoever we exactly blame for it, it seems clear that the massacre was indicative not of power at the centre but rather, of the lack of it.

Moreover, if it was a gamble aimed at the reinstatement of the Crown's authority, it dramatically failed. France, instead, plunged into a further round of prolonged civil war punctuated by foreign intervention. Confused circumstances, Byzantine conspiracies, contradictory signals, often seem to lead to this type of tragedy. Robin Clifton charts another attempted coup, in Ireland, supposedly in the name of the king, in 1641, which also went calamitously wrong. And John Gittings provides a further example, four hundred years after St Bartholomew's but with similar ingredients to it, with the exception that the Indonesian army, who unleashed the counter-coup massacre, were able, in so doing, to definitively reassert state power albeit with a radically different domestic and foreign policy agenda to that which had formerly pertained.

If these particular massacres seem, on one level, to be outcomes of power struggles within weak or crisis-laden states, they also pose further questions about tensions between the state and particular elements of society. In Indonesia, as in France, directed nationwide killings were largely focused on specific sections of the populace, in the former, Communists or people aligned to communist-led organizations, in the latter, professing Huguenots, their families and sympathizers. Does this suggest that domestic massacre occurs when societal tensions can no longer be contained or mediated by state authority? Does massacre by the State resolve the problem by eliminating the perceived problematic elements, providing the framework for a new societal coherence and direction? Alternatively, does it simply prepare the ground for new societal tensions?

If there is something of a circular argument here it is possibly because there is no simple answer. The resort to, or avoidance of massacre may ultimately depend on the specific political, cultural and economic arrangements of a society but more critically on its ability to either withstand or to ride forces of change. Demographic explosion or implosion, ecological degradation, economic fluctuation may all play their part in testing a society's resilience but these or other factors may also throw up dynamic social, political or religious movements which seek to adapt to or possibly resist change. An area like maritime Flanders in the mid-fourteenth century, for instance, experienced dramatic population growth and urbanization which helped exacerbate resentments against high tax and tithes. In conditions of acute social deprivation, populist insurrectionary movements emerged which in turn were met by bloody state repression. This pattern persisted for decades without any obvious resolution.[32]

Whether peasant jacqueries, urban disorders or sectarian quests for an imminent millenium posed a direct challenge to an always, at best, diffused state authority, in medieval or early modern Europe, is, however, something of a moot point. Millenarian leaders from the eleventh-century crusades through to Thomas Muntzer, in the 1520s and beyond, certainly prophesied and preached an apocalyptic wipe-out of the rich and ungodly while some of them did attempt to act out their chiliastic vision.[33] But rarely were such movements sufficiently focused or effective enough to be able to overthrow the status quo and replace it with something entirely different, even when as later, in the Taipeng rebellion, of mid-nineteenth-century China, they mobilized on a truly massive scale.[34]

Indeed, in the premodern world it was the rebellious, the heretical, or merely the advocates of social renewal, not the magistrates representing political authority who had most cause to fear the imminence of extermination. Defending the status quo, even a changing status quo, was the bottom line for all regimes in power and even when weak they would mobilize all the forces at their disposal to crush real or imaginary challengers. Imaginary, more often than not, because many of the movements in question had opted not to take over society but to opt out of it altogether. Perhaps it is in the very fact that Cathars in thirteenth-century Provence or the late nineteenth-century Brazilian religious community at Canudos, described in the chapter by Robert M. Levine, offered a viable alternative to a corrupt, discredited or crisis-ridden mainstream which explains the virulence with which authorities set about destroying them. The fact that the Canudos example took place so recently suggests, moreover, that such violent relationships of power have not been subdued by modernity. Certainly, here, as in the European High Middle Ages, the State both fed and enlarged upon more widespread anxieties about the alleged communistic, even anarchic tendencies of the community, including (indeed focusing) on its sexual practices, to justify its reassertion of authority.

Collective group deviance (again real or imagined) in such circumstances thus become sufficient grounds for massacre. Repudiating violence and insisting on one's quietist credentials is not a sufficient defence, as Christian schismatic sects, in the pre-Enlightenment era, have nearly always found to their cost. But the way in which the authorities might be able to whip up hatred against an out-group begs a whole series of further questions as to the societal basis for massacre. Does, for instance, this sort of massacre need an input from the State at all? Could it be, sometimes, that massacre is a function of grass-roots fears, anxieties or even violent impulses which find their focus, or alternatively are projected onto a convenient out-group?

Victims and Instruments of the State

The classic group one might associate with this sort of victimization, at least in a European context, are the Jews. Isolated in the pre-modern period from the rest of society, Jews were paradoxically entitled to protection from direct physical violence by the civil authorities, on explicit order from the church. This did not prevent Jews from being utterly vilified as demonic, bloodthirsty villains who, among other things, preyed murderously upon innocent Christian children for alleged ritual purposes.[35] Nor at critical junctures did the civil authorities intervene when elements of the populace attacked them. But why these popular anti-Semitic outbursts occurred at particular times, and not at others, may lead us into a debate, not necessarily, or entirely about Jewish-Gentile relations, so much as about wider societal crises which the state was unable or unwilling to control.

Hans Rogger, in an important examination of the sequence of pogroms between 1881 and 1906,[36] for instance, has challenged the conventional wisdom that these particular anti-Jewish disturbances were manipulated into existence by a tsarist regime frantically attempting to deflect attention away from its own bankruptcy. Tsarism was implicated but in the negative sense that its traditional restraints and controls on Jewish occupational and economic mobility were not working. The *pogromschiki* themselves were, thus, not a state sponsored 'rent a crowd' but elements of a native population, mostly in the Ukraine and Bessarabia, which felt genuinely threatened by the arrival of Jews from other areas of the restricted but heavily overcrowded Pale of Settlement. In identifying the geographical specificity of the pogroms Rogger crossreferenced them to largely contemparaneous anti-black, anti-Chinese and anti-Mexican riots especially in the cities of the northern and western U.S.A. where a settled white working class 'got in its retaliation first', so to speak, against incoming ethnic groups who were perceived to be competing with, and thereby undermining, its established economic position. In all these cases the state was not directly responsible, nor did it need to fabricate resentments which were already culturally embedded and ready to be expressed in virulently racist terms. Intriguingly, one could read similar processes at work, as described in this volume by John Edwards, with regard to late fifteenth-century Spain, again with Jews or crypto-Jews as the victim out-group, or much later, in a northern Nigeria of the 1960s, where incoming Ibos were set upon murderously by the local population.[37]

However, if the Rogger thesis seems to provide explanation for a certain type of massacre phenomenon, linked to rapid economic change and social dislocation, invariably taking place in a urban setting, a note of caution may be necessary. The mortality figures in these disturbances vary widely. At one end, the late eleventh- and twelfth-century anti-Jewish mob violence does seem to have been significant, though the degree to which death was directly the result of these disorders, or rather of postdisturbance trauma, especially through exposure and exhaustion in flight, is illuminated by Robin Clifton's evaluation of causes of deaths in the comparable case of the 1641 Irish 'massacres'. At the other end, however, it is debateable whether many of the pre-1903 Russian pogroms can be genuinely classified as 'massacres' at all. Thousands of Jews were beaten up, or raped, while the damage to property was extensive. Of their psychological impact on the Jewish collective consciousness there can be no doubt, helping to foment radical responses which repudiated a century of striving for assimilation and integration into the Gentile mainstream.[38] But there was no serious loss of life until the 1903 Kishinev pogrom and the sequence which followed the collapse of the Russian revolution of 1905, and then the Tsarist apparatus, or at least specific elements within it do seem to have been directly implicated.[39]

This might suggest that enraged popular actors armed with local grievances against a perceived out-group are not sufficient unto themselves to wreak sustained and effective massacre. They require assistance from some higher, more powerful authority. This may be in the form of commission, direct arming, logistical support, propaganda and disinformation to neutralize onlookers and witnesses, as well as omission, involving assurances that their actions will not be impeded either by local or more senior forces of law and order plus, equally importantly, guarantees that they will be protected from prosecution after the event. The essay by Allan Macinnes suggests that in seventeenth-century Scottish Gaeldom at least some of these ingredients were critical to a series of massacres which, despite their popular association with cross-generational clan feuding, also specifically arose out of licences from the Crown, giving to certain clan chiefs a remit to carry fire and sword to clan neighbours in the State's bad books. While such licences were not supposed to give their holders *carte blanche* powers of indiscriminate revenge, examples of cold-blooded and premeditated slaughter, most infamously at Glencoe in 1692, in fact point to the Crown having a direct interest and involvement in the outcome. Two centuries on, the post-1905 pogroms were committed by a much more shadowy and, as Rogger decribes it, protofascistic body, the Black Hundreds, operating on the fringes of society. Yet like the Campbells at Glencoe, the violence they perpetrated with impunity suggests a definite

accord with the State, or elements within it, which, in certain key
respects, was not only at odds with aspects of social change but also
prepared to countenance those known for their addiction to violence to provide it with a solution.[40]

But the very existence of these accords again throws into relief
the problem of authority. A weak discredited tsarism may have felt
it necessary to turn to ultra-right-wing elements, because it had
nowhere else to go. Better to ride and channel such forces rather
than to be engulfed by them. Assuming of course that the State is
strong enough to ride them. But in legitimizing violence perpetrated
by one element of society against another, especially where these elements might be characterized in ethnic or religious terms, a polity
risks throwing overboard a pre-existing, if precarious balance
between them and, in so doing, potentially endangers its own security, even long-term survival. It may be, in such circumstances, that
it believes that the point of no return has already been passed, that
the balance has already been destroyed and its own position become
already too much in jeopardy. When the Ottoman Sultan, Abdul
Hamid armed and unleashed Kurdish tribesmen against Armenians
throughout the empire's heartlands in the mid-1890s, inaugurating
massacres which presaged a total genocide twenty years later, he
may well have perceived this to be his position. Alternatively, we
may read these events, as those in neighbouring tsarist Russia, not
as proof of a ruler's prescience but rather of persistent failure to recognize a systemic malfunction.

Culture and 'Otherness'

This discussion still, admittedly, leaves some problem areas largely
unresolved. If the finger of culpability is pointing back again towards
the State could one not equally argue that the reason a sultan or tsar
might specifically target Armenians or Jews as an outlet for societal
frustrations is because he shares popular antipathies towards these
groups? Armenians and Jews, historically, are in socioeconomic, religious and cultural terms rather different from the peoples amongst
whom they have dwelt. Might one not then take group 'otherness' as
one's central point of departure to explain communal massacres in
essentially cultural or ethnic terms? One would, after all, not need to
go too far in the modern world to find abundant examples to
endorse this thesis. At the microlevel, moreover, there is evidence
that emotion-laden objections to group difference can directly lead
to violence. Anti-Jewish pogroms in the middle ages often started in
holy week with some horror story about Jews allegedly 'desecrating'

a ritual wafer, while in the French wars of religion Huguenots might be massacred simply for refusing to kneel before a statue of the Virgin Mary or for not attending mass.[41]

At stake here is not the victims' actual behaviour but their alleged blasphemy in the eye of the beholder. Out of a perceived distinction between those who worship or comport themselves 'correctly', the 'us' who are pure and honourable and the 'them' who are unclean and commit unspeakable, animal-like acts – a tellingly universal accusation – emerges a demand that the alleged pollution has to be sacrificially 'cleansed'. Many writers have noted the dehumanization of the 'other' in this mental process. But it also seems to involve major collective anxieties about the 'us' really being the perceived, contaminated 'them'. The anatomy of communal massacres often seems to bear this out where the act of killing turns on efforts to 'exorcize' evil. Specific rituals of killing, mutilation, disembowelling, even sometimes cannibalism, characterize this 'purifying' response as do drowning the victims or setting them on fire. The fact that Muslim religious leaders, in Ottoman Anatolia, in the 1890s, encouraged their congregations to attack Armenian Christians in their churches after Friday night religious prayers, or that massacres of Tutsis by their Rwandan Hutu neighbours, in 1994, repeatedly took place, likewise, in churches, is surely indicative of this symbolic purpose.[42]

But how far should we take this argument? It is clear with regard to the essays by Mark Greengrass and Robin Clifton that Catholics and Protestants, in early modern Europe, hated each other as a matter of faith. This was, after all, the ideological faultline which divided western and central Europe throughout this period. But to go on from this to suggest that some cultures, or religions, are in themselves more predisposed to incite hatred of nonbelievers, schismatics or outsiders, than others, and that this may be an explanation of why they then massacre them, is itself an invitation to controversy. Vahakn Dadrian's recent assertions with regard to the Armenian genocide, that the warrior values of the Turk combined with those of Islam to produce a culture of massacre, fall within this category.[43] So, too, more famously, do Daniel Goldhagen's attempts to explain the participation of many ordinary Germans in the Holocaust in terms of a 'cultural cognitive model'; that is, a particularly lethal brand of anti-Semitism peculiar to German society.[44]

Isolating a special 'cultural' ingredient in this way, especially one which appears to be fixed and immutable, may seem tantamount to a discovery of the first importance. Moreover, if it can be demonstrated that groups from other cultures respond to the same stimuli in an entirely different way, the prosecuting case might seem conclusive. It has often been remarked, for instance, that the Italian army operating alongside the German Wehrmacht in the Balkans, between 1941 and 1943, did not participate in the latter's massacres of Jews, Gypsies, Greeks and Serbs and rarely initiated its own.[45] It may be that Italian culture did begin with a different set of premises about its relationship to these peoples and that this was significant in its conduct of war in the Balkans. But to go a step further and suggest that Italians, because of their cultural make-up, were innately less prone to killing people than, say Germans, would have to take into account the gusto and brio with which Mussolini's armies killed thousands of tribespeople in Cyrenaica and Abyssinia, in the 1920s and 1930s.[46]

Arguments based on culture, to the exclusion of other factors, have a habit of falling down in this way. So do others more inclined towards a sociobiological approach. To suggest, as Theodor Adorno attempted, soon after the Second World War, and others have done since,[47] that warfare provides particular opportunities for individuals with sadistic or pathological leanings, has to account for the fact that in particular circumstances most 'normal' people seem to be capable of gratutious sadism.[48] The distinction between the Japanese addicted to a warrior cult of Bushido and Cambodians or Balinese, so often characterized in the West as 'gentle' people,[49] falls away in the light of massacres, even genocide, committed by them all.

None of this signifies that we have to dismiss either biological or cultural criteria in their entirety. Michael Ignatieff has noted how every time he arrived at a road-block in war-torn Bosnia there was an almost palpable whiff of male testosterone;[50] the road-blocks were usually manned by gun-toting young men. Similarly, nobody would deny that most of the atrocities committed in the 1994 Rwandan genocide, and in other recent massacres in the Great Lakes region of Central Africa, were committed by active males in their late teens and early twenties. Biology linked to machismo does provide the necessary vehicle by which most massacres are perpetrated. Add further cultural prompts, for instance, real or fictional narratives mostly imbibed from the screen, and one has the possibility for quite ordinary American 'boys next door' to translate what they understood to be 'this Nazi kind of thing ... what the Germans did to the Jews',[51] into a four-hour orgy of rape, sodomy, sexual mutilation, scalping, and the slicing off of limbs, tongues and ears in the infamous My Lai massacre in Vietnam.

Such projections or suggestibilities, however, explain very little about why and when massacres occur. Only in very specific contexts do our young would-be warriors get the opportunity to play out their fantasies and or indulge their hyperactive bodies to murderous effect. For the historian this question of context must remain paramount. Ethnic or cultural antipathies may exist without ever leading to massacre,[52] just as screen violence mostly does not lead to mimesis. While the potential for the enactment of a My Lai may lie in all of us, only exhausted, disorientated and certainly extremely frightened army units are likely to vent their pent up frustrations on a supposedly hostile population in this particular sort of atrocity. Similarly, while the massacres of the French wars of religion could certainly not have occurred without grass roots antipathies of Catholics for Huguenots and vice versa, equally they would have been unthinkable if the State had been strong, single-minded, willing and able to protect its subjects, of whatever disposition. Instead, its prevarication, ambivalence and loss of central authority provided the necessary vacuum for the playing out of confessional violence.

Modernity and the End to Massacre?

The inherent structural weaknesses of the pre-modern State may explain a context within which massacre might sometimes occur but they also bring us to a central paradox of our argument. The modern State, by contrast, as well as by definition, is supposed to be an internally pacified one. Violence by diffused proxy, warrant, or commission is not only outlawed but redundant, not least, because the principle by which such a state operates demands that there can be no hierarchy of punishment. As all the State's members are its citizens, it follows that each is equally entitled to the protection of its law, even when, accused of transgressing that law, they are being judged by it. There ought, therefore, in such a 'civil society' to be no arbitrary, exemplary or rough justice, no place for mob rule, hired killers, or vigilantes: only for policemen, law courts and prisons. It is only these duly authorized and constituted bodies, holding a mandate from a state which is itself the expression of the 'general will', and acting according to publicly recognized and agreed procedures and rules who have the legitimation with which to punish offenders. If this might involve violence, this is because society has deemed it necessary for its wellbeing, just in the same way as it mandates the State to provide the means of violence – military forces – in order to protect itself against external threats.

If giving the State, in Weber's famous dictum, a 'monopoly of violence'[53] thus sounds like the individual and community's best safeguard against the threat of massacre the historical question it still begs is how was this supposed compact between society and

state arrived at? Focusing on a crucial event in the French revolution, the September 1792 massacres in Paris, Brian Singer has not
only proposed to locate a 'rupture' with the state-societal relations
of the former *ancien régime* but has even suggested that the 'form'
of killing involved – out-of-sight dispatch on the orders of
improvized tribunals – might provide evidence of the transition
towards its legalized institutionalization.[54] But herein lies part of
our paradox. Even supposing that we accept the argument that
modern state 'justice' emerged out of the body, and will, of the people – or to use a more potent revolutionary term 'nation' – Singer's
1792 case study, far from anticipating a terminus to massacre
instead simply poses a different, potentially more lethal thrust to its
logic. The revolution, in principle, conferred citizenship on everybody but then, quite literally, took it away, in the case of the
September massacres, from the common thieves, prostitutes, forgers
and vagrants who were its main victims. Social deviants had
become not only 'enemies of the revolution' but 'enemies of the
people'. And having debarred one group, in this way from what
genocide scholar, Helen Fein, calls the State's 'universe of obligation'[55] the list could presumably be lengthened to exclude any other
social, religious, ethnic or political grouping found to be politically
dangerous or socially wanting. As it was the State, moreover, which
decided who was 'in' and who was 'out' and with the apparatus of
violence now manifestly centralized in its own hands, its inhabitants
might consider themselves to be more, not less, vulnerable to violent
death than they had ever been previously.

One might rejoinder that it was only particular types of regime,
mostly those like the Jacobins, or the Bolsheviks, who had either
sought or found themselves at the head of revolutionary overthrows
of the old order where this danger to the populace was ever present.
Certainly, in the twentieth century it has been so-called totalitarian
regimes, with agendas for the rapid and, if necessary, forced-pace
transformation of society who have been most fixated on the idea of
the 'general will', and hence most troubled by what they have perceived to be problems of social heterogeneity.[56] And it is these same
regimes who have most readily resorted to massacre, deportation or
genocide to solve it.[57]

But, herein, lies the second part of our paradox. The reason the
Bolsheviks and their Stalinist successors, the Turkish Ittihad, the
Khmer Rouge, the Iraqi (and Syrian) Ba'athists, and the Ethiopian
Dergue waded quite literally through their people's blood was
because their idea of the 'general will' was founded on a fiction.
Their actual support bases were small, the mass of their populations
largely indifferent, if not actively hostile to their programmes and

they were additionally beset by serious external opposition. Not all totalitarian regimes had small support bases. Both the Nazis and Mao's Chinese Communist Party could be taken to be important exceptions. All, however, set themselves impossible, visionary goals which inevitably ran aground on unsurmountable obstacles. If these states, in other words, aspired to be not only strong and unfettered but harmonious and streamlined what their attempts at this realization highlighted was rather the highly unstable, crisis-ridden nature of their existences.

Far from modernity having freed such states from the limitations of traditional power relationships they found themselves, in some sense, locked into its embrace. To wrench themselves free again they either had to mobilize particular sections of society to support their agenda against those who were hostile or perceived to be so, or literally create new cadres, fashioned in their own image, who would function not according to the constituted rules of the modern citizen State, but covertly and by subterfuge, as a 'state within a state'. The Jacobin *armées revolutionaires*[58] sent out into the countryside, in 1793, to defend the 'people' against the people might be taken as both an example of the former, and a harbinger of the militias and youth movements formed to defend states and revolutions in more recent times. Similarly, Jacobin *comités de surveillance* might be little more than a puny, protoversion of the secret police apparatuses which, fully expanded, equipped and militarized as a Nazi Reich Security Main Office, a Stalinist NKVD, or a Saddamist Mukhabarat, would be ready and capable to undertake truly systematic liquidations of the state's alleged enemies.[59]

It would be a mistake, however, to assume that only fully fledged totalitarian regimes have been perpetrators of massacre in the modern age. Where they have not been able to mobilize paramilitary or military forces sufficiently effectively to eliminate opposition, other authoritarian regimes have resorted to forms of diffused violence. Gittings on Indonesia charts how the generals in their initial 1965 bid for power subcontracted Ansors – auxiliaries – in the form of Muslim paramilitary youth groups, to hunt down and destroy supposed Communists, thus also deflecting responsibility for the ensuing massacres from themselves. Weaker regimes still, have increasingly come to rely on the 'ethnic card', looking to survive in power by mobilizing support from the dominant ethnic group within otherwise multi-ethnic societies, or one or more groups they can rely on, even where these are not demographically dominant, or again, initiating a policy of divide and rule between such groups. Thus, institutionalized, this ethnic stratification has been seen by some scholars as the major contemporary cause of world conflicts, often leading, within some states, to endemic violence, even geno-cide.[60] The antidote to these conflicts, so the argument goes, is to be found in a genuine commitment to human rights, the rule of law and and in a striving towards the realization of pluralist, tolerant and democratic societies.[61] For which, one supposes, read the West.

Certainly, most Western states do have a relatively massacre-free recent track record. The French and other Western European police force responses to student revolt in 1968, for instance, compares very favourably with the contemparaneous student massacre perpe-trated by state authorities in Mexico city, or more recently in Tiananmen square, Beijing.[62] But self-congratulation on this score, might make us pause to ponder on 'Bloody Sunday' when fourteen unarmed civil rights protesters were shot down, by British para-troopers, in Londonderry in January 1972, a mere quarter of a century ago.[63]

Such an event must inevitably raise questions, not only about the stability and integrity of a supposedly consensual, well-adjusted modern Western state but in so doing about the very nature of its political and social control mechanisms.[64] The fact that a 'Bloody Sunday' is rare – certainly compared with more overtly police states – does not automatically consign it, as politicians might prefer, to the bin of unfortunate and regrettable aberrations. The British govern-ment's continuing sensitivity, on this score, may itself be instructive in throwing light on the inherently weak or contradictory points in its self-image. As for the massacre itself, the fact that it happened on an island with a long legacy of violence and coercion by British col-onizers against its native inhabitants, cannot go unremarked.

Limiting Massacre and Its Avoidance

In the three essays of this volume tackling aspects of massacre in the British Isles of the seventeenth century, there is considerable refer-ence to rules of military engagement designed to prevent massacres, but which, nevertheless, broke down, or were ignored, most persis-tently and disastrously in the hinterlands of the crown's rule, namely in Gaelic Scotland and Ireland.

Limits on soldiery exercising unrestrained butchery against defeated opponents in the wake of battle and against unarmed non-combatants developed out of Christian ethics of the middle ages and particularly theories associated with the concept of 'just war'.[65] Though these constraints did not apply to certain circumstances, for instance, when a town refused to accept the guarantees of a besieg-ing commander that its inhabitants would be spared in the event of its capture, so far as they existed, they were generally accepted as a correct code of practice and more often than not adhered to, even in very vicious civil conflicts. Moreover, their practice was developed and refined in the age of enlightenment to the point that by the time of the First World War, clear international guidelines were in place, most obviously in the form of the Hague Convention of 1907 ensuring that the defeated prisoner of war and the innocent civilian had 'nothing to fear' from the victor in warfare.[66]

These agreed codes started looking decidedly ragged, however, when army commanders felt that they were dealing not with people like 'us' but rather 'others' who could not be trusted to fight by the rules or, alternatively, were not worthy of their protection in the first place. These sort of rationalizations were particularly common on the part of Anglo-Scottish soldiery with regard to the Catholic Irish and Gaelic Highlanders but also, as Shenfield and Dedering note, as justification for some quite appalling nineteenth and early twentieth-century massacres committed by Russian and German armies in their imperial advance. Here, we seem to be back in the realm of the civilized versus savage, the novelty being that the latter now were more or less anybody who stood in the way of a Western version of 'progress'.

What began with the dehumanization or more accurately 'animalization' of peoples[67] on the periphery of the emerging nation-states of the seventeenth-century eastern Atlantic seaboard[68] was, thus, extended to the Americas and beyond with horrendous consequences. Attempts to give native peoples the same protection as those to which Europeans were entitled, were certainly made, most famously by Spanish jurists, in a series of debates before Charles V, in the 1550s. Interestingly, here as later, much of the argument of their advocates revolved around whether the indigenes were indeed 'savage' or whether their societies were, in their own way, 'civilized' sovereign 'nations'.[69] Most Western juridicial opinion, however, either repudiated these notions or ensured that they were ultimately overturned. The fact that the indigenes had a habit of responding to Western conquest and colonization by attacking settlers' livestock, property and persons, moreover, only confirmed the conventional wisdom that they were indeed backward primitives, or, in the view of evangelical Protestant settlers, that they stood in the way of God's will to tame the wilderness.[70]

Survival for the conquered thus only seemed to be on offer if they accepted their subjugated status and embraced the 'civilizing mission' of their conquerors. Late nineteenth-century racist and social Darwinian 'wisdoms' certainly buttressed a Western imperial understanding of this 'natural' order in which superior white men ruled and the inferior races knew their place. Westerners, however, were not alone in concocting these sort of pseudoscientific justifications for empire. The Japanese, as MacDonald shows, had their own version of the civilizing mission, in which their superiority, supposedly founded on their martial attributes, was contrasted with the childlike nature of the Chinese. It followed that what the Japanese did in 1930s China was for its people's own good. And if the Chinese misbehaved – as naughty children sometimes do – they had to be taught a lesson.

The persistent overkill employed by imperial powers in responding to native resistance and revolt may be, in part, a symptom of the degree to which they had swallowed their own conclusions. Imperial authorities often seemed to be genuinely shocked when the natives struck back. The fact that on occasions, such as in the late 1870s, their forces were even wiped out in veritable massacres – General Custer's cavalry at the Little Big Horn at the hands of plains Indians, a British contingent at Isandhlwana in the first Zulu war – served only to endorse the conviction that the only way of dealing with such 'outrages' was to respond against the perpetrators and their people with the iron fist.[71] In 1899 the British objected to the proposals of the Hague Convention to outlaw dum-dum bullets on the grounds that nothing less would stop 'savages' in Mahdist Sudan or the North-West Frontier.[72] Twenty years later, General Dyer was fêted, in many quarters, as the 'Saviour of Punjab' when he took 'purely disciplinary action' against what he believed to be both the onset of a general uprising in British India and a repeat of the 1857 mutiny.[73] His 'action' consisted of the premeditated, and cold-blooded shooting down of over a thousand people – which left at least three hundred dead – at an entirely peaceful meeting in Amritsar, in what is probably the most egregious single episode in British imperial history.

If military commanders repeatedly found grounds for ignoring their own codes of 'humane' conduct when it came to the natives 'out there', such wilful disregard is also observable in cases of partisan or guerrilla struggles closer to home. That such warfare pitted non-uniformed combatants against regular soldiery confused the issue in the minds of the latter and led to charges that they were having to deal not simply with an unseen but an illegitimate enemy. In an early example of this new encounter, Napoleonic troops in the Peninsular wars, in Spain, found increasingly that they were facing not so much an army of irregulars but more an entire population. Perhaps for the first time in modern European history a conqueror faced the spectre of people's war, a struggle which because it was conducted from the village level could not be obviously defeated and because it was also sustained and directed from the grass roots carried with it genuinely social as well as national liberationist implications. No code or convention of traditional military practice protected armed non-uniformed combatants from slaughter in the event of capture. But the inability to determine who was combatant and who not, plus the very resilience of the struggle itself, led the French to respond more and more indiscriminately. Executions of villagers became a feature of their collective reprisals. So too did a policy of scorched earth which, in denying shelter and bringing starvation to entire regions, was in its own way as brutal as direct massacre.[74] By the time of the Second World War such collective punishments had become standard operating procedure for many armies of occupation.[75]

Underlying these developments were undoubtedly often racist assumptions about 'enemy' populations which enabled soldiers to participate in massacres while leaving the sense of their own civilized behaviour unimpaired. But their response was also complicated by other factors. German soldiers advancing through Belgium in 1914, for instance, were not only highly stressed because of the fear of being fired upon but also indignant that the populace were so hostile to them.[76] Thus, time and time again, in twentieth-century conflict, commanders justified dispensing with the rule book in order to massacre noncombatants with impunity by claiming that, (i) resistance to the army of occupation was fundamentally misplaced, (ii) insurgents did not fight a clean, open war but killed their soldiers surreptitiously and cruelly, (iii) this allegedly barbarous and cowardly behaviour was indicative of an illegitimate nation which had no right to exist. Yet the post-1945 proliferation of national liberationist struggles either against colonial rule, or perceived forms of neo-imperial hegemony, ensured that these sorts of military reprisals (which had made the Wehrmacht and Japanese Imperial Army notorious) were developed and refined by armies worldwide, into textbook responses. Mao Tse-tung saw his partisan armies swimming like fish in a peasant sea. Counter-insurgency doctrine strove to drain it. The results were 'dirty' wars in which armies committed reprisals and their opponents commited counter-reprisals against any group believed to be collaborating with the 'enemy'. In either case, it was civilian, most rural, peasant populations who suffered the full brunt of massacre.[77]

Presenting Massacre to the World

The proliferation of military massacre in the post-1945 era was doubly paradoxical, given that it was this same world which was, for the first time, emerging as an international system of nation-states governed by a United Nations charter not only intended to outlaw violent disputes between member states but also to guarantee the human rights of those living in them, including that most cherished 'right'; to live. This supposed victory of Western enlightenment thought was, however, entirely pyrrhic. Power relations, at the macrolevel, were actually determined by the ideological and political contest between the United States and Soviet Union and while this remained a Cold War in terms of direct military, including nuclear confrontation, at its peripheries it affected and infected the vast majority of other disputes, however local in origin.

One result was that the presentation of atrocities in which one or other 'side' was implicated became part of an accompanying propaganda war, often of megaphone proportions. As Noam Chomsky, a well-known thorn in the side of the U.S. version, has suggested, there were three types of atrocities which mattered in this war: 'constructive', i.e. those which served U.S. interests; 'benign', which were irrelevant to its concerns; and 'nefarious,' which could be blamed on official enemies. To prove his point Chomsky went to considerable lengths to chart the scope and scale of Western media reportage of one such 'nefarious' bloodbath, the autogenocide committed by the Khmer Rouge in Cambodia, between 1975 and 1978, in contrast with its almost total silence on an almost simultaneous bloodbath in East Timor which, Chomsky charged, was equally horrendous, but as committed by Indonesian allies of the U.S. fell into the 'constructive' category.[78]

Chomsky's findings posed a whole series of questions about the nature and function of news in supposedly democratic societies, particularly its relationship to political structures. But it could be argued that the roots of what Chomsky was describing go much deeper than anything specifically Cold War in origin. What the printed page or moving picture could do was convert propagandist statements, or sometimes simply insinuations, into canonical wisdoms. In 1875 Gladstone's pamphlet, *The Bulgarian Horrors and the Question of the East*, sold 200,000 copies in just a month. It described the massacres of possibly fifteen thousand villagers by Turkish bashibazouk irregulars in retaliation for a failed Bulgarian uprising.[79] The atrocities did happen. And many more were to follow. But the indignation which the pamphlet aroused and which Gladstone utilized to heap opprobrium on a Disraeli government which was supporting the Turks, centred on the fact that the victims had been Christians. Henceforth, Muslim Turks always killed Christians. The fact that self-styled *komitacis* – 'freedom-fighters' – armed bands of 'Christian' Serb, Greeks and Bulgarians were busily massacring Muslims never seemed to enter into the equation. Nor that the persistent and widespread nature of such atrocities, not only in the Balkans but in other areas of the Ottoman empire, was, in large part, due to the destabilizing interference of the Great Powers, Britain included.

The appropriate adage might be that people believe what they want to believe. But where a state or other body has a vested interest in the matter, narratives of victimhood provide particular opportunities for constructing, or reinforcing a sense of endangered group belonging or identity. The media's role is to provide the martyrological evidence. In the Serb-Croat war, in 1991, Radio Television Belgrade repeatedly presented pictures of Croat atrocities against Serbs in battle-scarred Vukovar, which were actually pictures of Croats killed by Serb shelling.[80] A little later, during the height of the fighting in Bosnia, viewers were led to believe that footage of mass rape perpetrated by Serb militiamen on Muslim women was actually perpetrated by Muslim militiamen on Serbian women.[81] All through this period, the television served up a diet of historical horror stories, if not fascist *ustashi* murdering defenceless Serbs in the Second World War, then jihad-frenzied Turks and Bosnian Muslims doing the same, in the previous century.

At stake here is not whether a particular event in history did or did not happen but the way its has been either mythologized and, or repackaged to serve a latter day political agenda. A sense of belonging to an embattled nation, threatened with constant annihilation may well have provided the frame – and indeed stimulus – for gullible young men to join paramilitary outfits such as warlord Arkan's 'Tigers', and participate in Bosnian roundups, ethnic cleansings, mass executions and rapes while all the time imagining themselves to be heroic Chetniks struggling against internationally powerful yet malevolent forces, with, of course, the covert blessing and promises of protection from the Serbian state authorities. Add to this unholy mix, one or more adversarial political players with a version of the same historical events, or variation of them, but leading to quite opposite 'truths' and one has the basis not just for conflicting victim syndromes but for a potential dynamic of massacre played out across generations, even centuries.

What is thus disheartening is not simply the way that history itself, as Robin Okey's essay spotlights, is sometimes used either very selectively, or entirely disingenuously, as a tool for conscious distortion but the awareness that once embedded in the collective memory of a group or nation, it may be impossible to realign. The problem may be doubly complicated where an awareness of past victimization can be taken to be a legitimate ingredient in one's self-image. To deny this, for instance, to Jews, would be tantamount to a denial of the Holocaust. But to deny that the massacres at Deir

Yassin or Sabra-Shatila are part of Palestinian self-perception would be equally ill-conceived. The problem thus arises when these separate, though hardly unrelated, tragedies intersect in respective agenda-driven Israeli and Palestinian reworkings of their significance; where all Palestinians, or indeed all Arabs, are demonized as latter-day Nazis intent on a rerun of the Holocaust, or alternatively, where all Israelis, or indeed all Jews are part of some Zionist-cum-American imperialist conspiracy whose aim is the subjugation, if not Hitlerite annihilation of Arabs.[82]

Breaking out from a seamless web of massacre may thus require people to face up to, or even challenge their official state version of history. This, however, can normally only be contemplated where there is an independent media and, or, scholars are genuinely free to evaluate uncensored archival evidence. The Israeli response to the Sabra-Shatila massacres in Beirut, perpetrated in September 1982 by Phalangist militia acting under the protective umbrella of an invading Israeli army is perhaps instructive on the former score. In spite of rigorous army censorship news of the massacres did filter out rapidly from Lebanon via both the press corps and members of the Israeli army itself. This in turn precipitated an almost spontaneous mass rally of up to 400,000 Israelis in the largest single protest demonstration in the country's history forcing the Begin government to set up a judicial enquiry to investigate the events surrounding the massacre.[83]

Though the findings of the Commission stopped short of implicating the whole government in these events, and certainly failed to halt its invasion of Lebanon, the Israeli response to Sabra-Shatila nevertheless represents an example of an essentially democratic society facing up to unpleasant, even unpalatable truths about itself. Undoubtedly, in this case, the massacre posed a direct and unacceptable challenge to its cherished self-perception as a nation, in a peculiar sense founded on victimhood. But other pluralist societies, often emerging out of periods of straitjacketed social conformity have found coming to terms with experiences in their recent past equally painful and problematic. It has taken many years and much soul-searching for France to confront some home truths about its Vichy regime, how not only did most French people not join the *maquis*, but indeed how many of them collaborated with German deportations of Jews or actively participated in the *milice* (the Vichy militia) elimination of resistance fighters.[84] Still with France, the Harkis who fought alongside the French in their colonial war in Algeria a decade later, but were left to their genocidal fate, remains a much less debated skeleton in the cupboard.[85] Spain, Greece, Argentina, even post-1991 Iraqi Kurdistan, represent further examples of societies, whose increasing openness has also opened up old wounds.[86]

This may be because a previous 'closed' regime had airbrushed out of existence tendencies which it did not like or felt threatened by, pointing, usually, to the massacre, incarceration or deportation of its advocates. Or it may be, because the record is more complicated still, that the victims were not after all 'whiter than white' but while still engaged in some civil war-like struggle, committed their own atrocities, even against those who were meant to be their friends or allies. If moral distinctions between who are the 'good' and who the 'bad' start becoming blurred at this point, the narrative becomes further muddied when it is discovered that a foreign power may have supported, or even manipulated, one side against the other for its own ends, or been directly responsible for particular atrocities.

On one level, East European societies, as they have emerged out of the grip of Soviet domination, may be less traumatized by similar revelations, given that almost any official pre-1989 version of recent events is likely to have been taken with a pinch of salt. Nobody in Poland, for instance, believed the Soviet government's explanation that the more than four thousand bodies of Polish officers found murdered at Katyn, near Smolensk, during the Second World War, was the work of the Germans who uncovered them,[87] even though the Germans had committed massive anti-Polish atrocities of their own. This sort of scepticism, however, if pertinent in the case of Katyn, can have its own drawbacks. If the Soviets are, for instance, the big bogey, a dualist narrative might demand that anybody who struggled against them is a patriotic and saintly hero. The result in contemporary Rumania is the rehabilitation of Marshal Antonescu, the wartime anti-Communist leader who aligned the country with the Axis powers. Yet his responsiblity for a major, independently motivated Rumanian participation in the Holocaust is either downplayed or completely denied.[88]

Changing the Goalposts: The Role of Technology

With the Holocaust, we seem to have arrived at another, entirely distinct terminus for considering massacre; one, indeed, where we obviate the problem altogether by calling our subject something else. A witness who ought to know; the Auschwitz commandant, Rudolf Hoess, writing his autobiography in a Polish prison cell, in the winter of 1946-47, recalled the mass exterminations thus: 'I must admit openly that the gassings had a calming effect on me ... I was always horrified of death by firing squads, especially when I thought of the huge numbers of women and children who would have to be killed. I had had enough of hostage executions, and the mass killings by firing squad ordered by Himmler and Heydrich. Now I was at ease. We were all saved from these bloodbaths.'[89]

So, according to Hoess, what happened in the gas chambers at Auschwitz-Birkenau were not 'bloodbaths'. They were rather, something altogether more humane, death yes, but without trauma or mutilation, blood and guts. Hoess was entirely wrong on at least some of these ingredients. Nevertheless, his idea that what was happening was 'different'; that the Nazi application of modern rational calculation to the problem of mass killing – including cleaning up afterwards – and in which science and technology both provided the answers and, in the context of the killing operation the skilled technicians, has become a sort of latter-day wisdom.[90] Yet while recent Holocaust research would dispute these assumptions, not least because a significant proportion of the killing was perpetrated by the traditional, messy method of mass execution by firing squad[91] – replicating in so doing the majority of the Nazi non-Jewish wartime massacres – the idea that technology could distance the perpetrator from his victim has undoubtedly changed the face and contours of some modern massacre.

It was the mass, industrial production of rifles, and the annihilatory use to which they were put against the American bison which, perhaps, best illustrates this new departure. The .55 calibre Sharp model with a kill accuracy of fifteen hundred yards enabled an entirely systematic and emotionally detached slaughter of thirteen million great beasts to begin in earnest.[92] The mechanized destruction of animals with little or no danger to the killers, however, could also be applied to human affairs. Enfield rifles might be supplemented by Gatling, Maxim or later Hotchkiss machine guns, thereby transforming colonial wars, fought by often tiny units of white men, into veritable massacres of their numerous but anciently armed opponents.[93] The arrival of Winchester repeating rifles in Ottoman warfare between Turks and their rebelling subjects, in the mid-1870s, also expanded the scope of annihilatory irregular warfare.[94] But herein lies a complication. If the new weaponry found its way into the hands of the 'insurgents' and if 'they' ambushed 'you', or alternatively 'you' attempted to dislodge 'them' from their defensive positions, it might be your side which was 'massacred'. Furthermore, the application of superior mass fire power towards a limited area was to turn the frontal assaults of the First World War into bloody foregone conclusions. The Somme, where the British suffered sixty thousand casualties on the first day of their disastrous 1916 offensive, became literally a byword for pointless sacrifice.[95] In the circumstances the only thing to do was keep ahead of the arms race and ensure that your opponents were several notches down the technological rung. The Abyssinian campaign, launched by the Italians, in October 1935, maintained this trajectory, the engagements with the opposing Ethiopians being, with occasional hiccoughs, a one-sided war of annihilation, culminating in events at Lake Ashangi, the following March. Here, lavish use of mustard gas, combined with artillery-fired incendiary shells and aerial bombing led to the slaughter of twenty-thousand feudal levies, leading one observer to comment, 'It was no longer a war for the Italian airmen – it was a game. ... It was a massacre.'[96]

Fifty-five years later, in the Gulf War, 'allied' airmen repeated the feat when they literally wiped out already defeated Iraqi troops fleeing down the Basra road from Kuwait, in what was popularly – and tellingly – referred to as a 'turkey shoot'. Critical comment noted how Western media abetted the U.S. and British military in their press conference version of this event by presenting it as a victory for laser-guided weaponry.[97] By concentrating on the hi-tech and precision weaponry aspects of the war, this type of presentation thus enabled television viewers 'back home' to understand what they were seeing on their screens as something clean, sanitized and literally abstract.

Past Spectacle – Future Nightmare?

At the end of the millenium this media conjuring trick is all the more disturbing because, through technology (in this case satellite communication), an ever-increasing public are enabled to become no longer simply bystanders but literally participants in massacre 'as it is happening': 'virtual reality' yet removed from actual bloodshed.[98] Stock Western explanations for its 1990-91 intervention in the Gulf were as tardy and flawed as their media 'TV War' presentation of its results. Saddam Hussein, moreover, was not only allowed to survive but to commit mass, sweeping atrocities against his own people, practically under the noses of the allied forces.[99]

Yet Gulf War events are also significant in the fact that they provide the exception to the rule of global trends in the 1990s. The 'new world order', trumpeted by the United States, is none other than an international system of nation-states linked to a Western-dominated global economy, presided over and regulated by itself. In 1991 it was this system that ensured not only that Kuwait would be 'liberated' from Iraqi invasion, but, with the unusual proviso of Kurdish breathing space in the north, that Iraq would retain its integrity. The nation-state remains on paper and in the UN rule book sacrosanct.

Or does it? As I am writing, huge NATO air attacks on Serbia, in response to massacres and massive ethnic cleansing perpetrated against ethnic Albanians in its Kosovo province, seem to augur a radically new approach to the issue. Non-interference in the domestic affairs of fellow sovereign states, when they commit gross human rights violations, may no longer be accepted practice. Yet in reacting to the Kosovo challenge as they have done, Western powers are clearly heading into entirely uncharted waters. Not least because the internationalization of conflict often leads to its geographical spread, just as massacre itself in one country persistently produces knock-on effects on its neighbours. The recent collapse of Zaire is a classic illustration. Catalysed as it was by the Rwandan genocide for which, at the very least, Western states were in part responsible, they conspicuously sat on their hands both throughout it and the ensuing destabilization of the whole Central African Region.[100] Nor have other states in Africa, such as Sierra Leone, Liberia and Angola, where central authority has become equally if not more redundant, and which have for years been plunged into fragmented, often warlord-controlled zones of instability, lawlessness – and massacre – been rescued either by Western military power or its economic largesse.[101]

These seem to be the sorts of conflict in which the West – particularly after the fiasco of United States intervention in Somalia with all its resonances of Vietnam – does not wish to become embroiled, and the United Nations, without their wherewithal, can do nothing. Yet independent analysis confirms that these are the very conflicts which are proliferating, with consequences which include environmental breakdown, movements of refugees and famine on a truly massive scale.[102] Whether the United States-led response to Kosovo thus represents a blip in its avowed abnegation of the role of world policeman, or perhaps only its partial restoration in regions perceived by it, and its Western allies, as being of primary concern to their interests, of one thing we can be sure: so long as the state breakdown remains 'out there', we, in the West, can continue, by turns, to be fascinated and horrified by the symptoms, as seen on our television screens while sleeping safely in our beds at night.

Or, again, can we? The Western states' 'monopoly of violence' is no longer, if it ever was, vouchsafed. Its citizenry can be attacked by 'mindless' terrorists, from foreign countries but also by 'mindless' terrorists from home, as happened, out of the blue, in Oklahoma City in March 1996, when a bomb blew a federal building apart and left 168 people dead. The present-day Attilas may have confused if not bizarre grievances but, if the Oklahoma bombing is anything to go by, they can also be home-spun, apple-pie Americans.[103]

It is thus not only in countries like Albania where literal state collapse has left a surfeit of advanced weaponry in the hands of the populace. In a host of countries, Western ones included, mafiosi and drug barons (as well as more 'traditional' terrorists of the IRA and ETA type) have been able to plug into an arms technology and arms trade dominated by Western exporter nations, to eliminate interlopers on their perceived turf, in a growing, increasingly drug-related, 'black' economy, or to conduct more agenda-focused, but indiscriminate, terror campaigns. In a society like the U.S., however, the ownership of such weapons is not only legitimate, it is widely diffused among the population. Self-styled militias train for the day when imminent nuclear war or government collapse will give them a *raison d'être*, many of them millenarian bible literalists awaiting these events as signs of the approaching *tremendum*.[104] But others have more mundane reasons for being armed; to defend their property and wealth against a burgeoning underclass.

In less sophisticated countries social divisions between rich and poor may be so institutionalized that when the poor protest or rebel, the apparatus of state automatically goes into action to liquidate them. When this happened in El Salvador in 1932, it was called quite simply Matanza – massacre. Matanza One was, however, followed in the early 1980s by Matanza Two,[105] suggesting that the only way its U.S.-backed, cross-generational, powerholding élite know how to respond to social grievance is by wiping out the protestors.

But as the pace of globalizing change transforms more and more societies, so the differentiation between 'haves' and 'have nots' rather than diminishing is becoming increasingly blatant. Social, often regional disparities, which, as Robert Levine demonstrates, were explosive in end-of-nineteenth-century Brazil, carry equal potency at our own *fin de siècle*. The poor, the deprived, the visionary millenarians, even lone avengers with some personal grudge, seem to have access to an abundant means of violence as never before. The rich, in turn are increasingly retreating into safer suburbs or even stockaded enclaves where, isolated if not besieged, they rely not on the official forces of law and order but private security firms. The power of the State, it seems, is increasingly seeping away. Looking at some of the symptoms: at present-day Algeria, South Africa or Israel-Palestine, or even at Hebron, Dunblane, and Denver, will the historian a hundred years from now see so much spilt blood as ephemeral aberrations peculiar to those societies at that given moment, or as pointers to a more general breakdown?

Notes

1. Quoted in Noel Malcolm, *Bosnia: A Short History* (London and Basingstoke, 1994), xix.

2. 'Making Sense of Dunblane', *The Independent*, 15 March 1996, Henry Porter, 'Reason Eclipsed by Evil', *The Guardian*, 17 March 1996.

3. Vahakn N. Dadrian, *The History of the Armenian Genocide, Ethnic Conflict from the Balkans to Anatolia to the Caucasus* (Oxford, 1996), 78.

4. For examples, see Raul Hilberg, *The Destruction of the European Jews* (revised edn, 3 vols. New York, 1985); Robert Jay Lifton and Eric Markusen,*The Genocidal Mentality: Nazi Holocaust and Nuclear Threat* (New York, 1990); Zygmunt Bauman, *Modernity and the Holocaust* (Oxford, 1989); Eric Markusen and David Kopf, *The Holocaust and Strategic Bombing, Genocide and Total War in the 20th Century* (Boulder, San Francisco, Oxford, 1995).

5. African Rights, *Rwanda: Death, Despair and Defiance* (London, 1994); Gerard Prunier, *The Rwanda Crisis 1959-1994: History of a Genocide* (New York, 1995).

6. This is a subject in its own right. For introductions see Leo Kuper, *Genocide: Its Political Use in the 20th Century* (New Haven, 1981); Helen Fein, 'Genocide: A Sociological Perspective', *Current Sociology*, 38, 1 (1990): 1-111; Frank Chalk and Kurt Jonassohn, *The History and Sociology of Genocide* (New Haven, 1990); George D. Andrepoulos, ed., *Genocide, Conceptual and Historical Dimensions* (Philadelphia, 1994).

7. *Collins Dictionary of the English Language* (2nd edn, London and Glasgow, 1986), 947.

8. *La Reine Margot* (1994), directed by Patrice Chéreau, Renn Productions et al. See also Guy Austin, *Contemporary French Cinema* (Manchester, 1996), 167-69, who notes the film's allusions to civil war and religious intolerance in contemporary Bosnia.

9. Brian Singer, 'Violence in the French Revolution: Forms of Ingestion/Forms of Expulsion', in Ferenc Feher, ed., *The French Revolution and the Birth of Modernity* (Berkeley, Los Angeles, 1990), 150.

10. Raphael Lemkin, *Axis Rule in Occupied Europe* (Washington, DC, 1944).

11. Eric Carlton, *Massacres: An Historical Perspective* (Aldershot, 1994), 62-68.

12. See Paul Martin, 'The Discovery of America', *Science*, 179 (1973): 969-73. Also 'In Search of the Noble Savage', BBC *Horizon* programme, broadcast 27 January 1992, thanks to Peter Coates for transcript.

13. Keith Thomas, *Man and the Natural World, Changing Attitudes in England 1500-1800* (London, 1983), 275.

14. Thomas, *Man*, 275; Mark Jenner, 'The Great Dog Massacre', in W. G. Naphy and P. Roberts, eds, *Fear in Early Modern Society* (Manchester, 1997), 44-61.

15. Emmanuel Le Roy Ladurie, *Carnival in Romans: A People's Uprising at Romans, 1579-1580* (London, 1979), 287, 295; Robert Darnton, 'Workers Revolt: The Great Cat Massacre of the Rue Saint-Severin', in *The Great Cat Massacre and Other Episodes in French Cultural History* (London, 1984), 79-104.

16. Thomas, *Man*, 143-150, 183.

17. See William Cronon, *Changes in the Land: Indians, Colonists and the Ecology of New England* (New York, 1983).

18. Robert M. Utley, *The Indian Frontier of the American West, 1846-1890* (Albuquerque, 1984), 229.

19. Ladurie, *Carnival*, 238.

20. Dadrian, *History*, 159.

21. Stanley Karnow, *Vietnam, A History* (London, 1991), 543.

22. Ricardo Falla, *Massacres in the Jungle: Ixcan, Guatemala, 1975-1982* (Boulder, San Francisco, Oxford, 1994), 161.

23. David Stannard, *American Holocaust: The Conquest of the New World* (London, 1992), 102-7.

24. Christopher Browning, *Ordinary Men, Reserve Police Battalion 101 and the Final Solution in Poland* (New York, 1992), 123-32; Daniel Jonah Goldhagen, *Hitler's Willing Executioners: Ordinary Germans and the Holocaust* (London, 1996), 234-38.

25. Robert Hughes, *The Fatal Shore: A History of the Transportation of Convicts to Australia, 1787-1868* (London, 1987), 420-21.

26. Dadrian, *History*, 148.

27. Quoted in Kuper, *Genocide*, 12. Harold Lamb, *Tamerlane the Earth Shaker* (New York, 1932), 61-63, claims that 'along the belt of Arabic-Iranian civilisation, four-fifths of the population was eradicated'.

28. On Shaka see E. V. Walter, *Terror and Resistance: A Study of Political Violence* (Oxford, 1969), chaps. 6, 7 and 8.

29. A. T. Olmstead, *History of Assyria* (New York, 1923), 654. See also Michael Freeman, 'Genocide, Civilisation and Modernity', *British Journal of Sociology*, 46 (1995): 207-23.

30. Carlton, *Massacres*, 38-46.

31. Penny Roberts, 'Marlowe's "The Massacre at Paris"; an Historical Perspective', *Renaissance Studies*, 9 (1995): 430-41, for a review of the literature.

32. Norman Cohn, *The Pursuit of the Millenium: Revolutionary Milleniarians and Mystical Anarchists of the Middle Ages* (London, 1970), 104-5.

33. Ibid., 241-51.

34. John King Fairbank, *The Great Chinese Revolution, 1800-1985* (New York, 1987) notes that the combined effects associated with the suppressions of Taiping and other rebellions reduced the Chinese population from 410 million in 1850 to 350 million in 1873.

35. Joshua Trachtenberg, *The Devil and the Jews: the Medieval Conception of the Jews and its Relation to Modern Anti-Semitism* (2nd edn, Philadelphia and Jerusalem, 1983), chaps. 8, 9 and 10.

36. Hans Rogger, 'Conclusion and Overview', in John D. Klier and Shlomo Lambroza, eds, *Pogroms, Anti-Jewish Violence in Modern Russian History* (Cambridge, 1992), 314-72.

37. A. H. M Kirk-Greene, *Crisis and Conflict in Nigeria: A Documentary Source Book, 1966-1970* (London, 1971), vol. 1, 62-67.

38. Jonathan Frankel, *Prophecy and Politics: Socialism, Nationalism and the Russian Jews, 1862-1917* (Cambridge, 1981).

39. Shlomo Lambroza, 'The Pogroms of 1903-1906', in Klier and Lambroza, eds, *Pogroms*, 195-247.

40. Hans Rogger, *Jewish Policies and Right-wing Politics in Imperial Russia* (Berkeley, 1986), chaps. 7 and 8.

41. Trachtenberg, Devil and the Jews, 117, 144; Penny Roberts, *A City in Conflict: Troyes during the French Wars of Religion* (Manchester, 1996), 84.

42. Dadrian, History, 150; Christopher Walker, *Armenia: Survival of a Nation* (New York, 1980) 156-164; African Rights, *Rwanda*, chaps. 12 and 13. See also Natalie Zemon Davis, 'The rites of violence', chap. 6 of her *Society and Culture in Early Modern France* (Stanford and London, 1975).

43. Dadrian, *History*, 121-27.

44. Goldhagen, *Hitler's Willing Executioners*, 33-34.

45. Jonathan Steinberg, *All or Nothing: The Axis and the Holocaust, 1941-1943* (London, 1990), Part 11, 'Explanations'; Mark Mazower, *Inside Hitler's*

Greece: The Experience of Occupation, 1941-44 (New Haven and London, 1993).

46. Giorgio Rochat, 'La repressione della resistenza in Cirenaica (1930-31)', *Il Movimento di Liberazione in Italia*, 110 (1973). Also his *Militari e Politici nella Preparazione della Campagna d'Etiopa* (Milan, 1971).

47. T. W. Adorno, *The Authoritarian Personality* (New York and London, 1950).

48. See Stanley Milgram, *Obedience to Authority: An Experimental View* (New York, 1974).

49. See Michael Vickery, *Cambodia, 1975-1982* (Boston, 1984), chap. 1, 'The Gentle Land', for an interesting analysis.

50. Michael Ignatieff, 'Nationalism and Gender', 7 November 1995, University of Warwick Radcliffe Lecture series: 'Ethnicity, Nationalism and Statehood'. See also his, *Blood and Belonging: Journeys into the New Nationalism* (London, 1994).

51. Philip Knightley, 'This Nazi Kind of Thing', *New Statesmen/Society*, 15 May 1992. See also Michael Bilton and Kevin Sim, *Four Hours at My Lai: A War Crime and its Aftermath* (London, 1991).

52. Notes Professor Wladyslaw Bartoszewski, 'A large number of people can be antagonistic towards another national group but it does not mean there has to be some ultimate reckoning.', in Antony Polonsky, ed., *My Brother's Keeper: Recent Polish Debates on the Holocaust* (London, 1990), 227.

53. Anthony Giddens, *The Nation-State and Violence* (Cambridge, 1985), 18-19.

54. Singer, 'Violence', 150-73.

55. Helen Fein, 'Scenarios of Genocide: Models of Genocide and Critical Responses', in Israel W. Charny, ed., *Toward the Understanding and Prevention of Genocide: Proceedings of the International Conference on the Holocaust and Genocide* (Boulder and London, 1984), 3-31.

56. See Jacob L. Talmon, *The Origins of Totalitarian Democracy* (New York, 1961) for Jacobin connections, but also Gwynne Lewis, *The French Revolution, Rethinking the Debate* (London and New York, 1993), 111, for a vociferous rebuttal of this line of reasoning.

57. For exponents of the connection between totalitarian ideology and state-sponsored massacre, see Irving Louis Horowitz, *Taking Lives: Genocide and State Power* (Brunswick, NJ, 1980); R. J. Rummel, 'Democide in Totalitarian States: Mortacracies and Megamurders', in Israel W. Charny, ed., *The Widening Circle of Genocide*, vol. 3 of *Genocide: A Critical Bibliographical Review* (New Brunswick and London, 1994), 3-39; Robert F. Melson, *Revolution and Genocide: On the Origins of the Armenian Genocide and the Holocaust* (Chicago, 1992).

58. See Richard Cobb, *The People's Armies* (New Haven, 1987), 5-6.

59. Helmut Krausnick and Martin Broszat, *Anatomy of the SS State* (London, 1970); Ronald Hingley, *The Russian Secret Police: Muscovite, Imperial Russian and Soviet Political Security Operations* (New York, 1970); Samir al-Khalil, *Republic of Fear: Saddam's Iraq* (London, 1989).

60. Crawford White, *The Politics of Cultural Pluralism* (Madison and London, 1976); Kuper, *Genocide*; John McGarry and Brendan O'Leary, eds, *The Politics of Ethnic Conflict Regulation: Case Studies of Protracted Ethnic Conflicts* (London and New York, 1993); Human Rights Watch, *Slaughter among Neighbours, The Political Origins of Communal Violence* (New Haven, 1995), for examples.

61. See Horowitz, *Taking Lives*, and Rummel, 'Democide', for expositions of this view.

62. See Elena Poniatowska, *Massacre in Mexico* (Columbia, Missouri and London, 1975); Zhengyuan Fu, *Autocratic Tradition and Chinese Politics* (Cambridge, 1993) chap. 17.

63. Carol Ackroyd, Karen Margolis, Jonathan Rosenhead, Tim Shallice, *The Technology of Political Control* (London, 1977), 36-37.

64. Ibid., esp. chap. 15, 'Riot Control'.

65. Michael Walzer, *Just and Unjust Wars* (London, 1978).

66. Geoffrey Best, *Humanity in Warfare* (New York, 1980), 53.

67. See Thomas, *Man*, 134, on the medieval concept of *homo ferus*: 'wild man'.

68. Not only Gaelic highlanders. See Alfred W.Crosby, *Ecological Imperialism: The Biological Expansion of Europe, 900-1900* (Cambridge, 1986), 81-93, on the fate of the Guanches of the Canary Islands.

69. Lewis Hanke, *All Mankind is One: A Study of the Disputation between Bartholomé de las Casas and Juan Gimes de Sepulveda in 1550 on the Intellectual and Religious Capacity of American Indians* (Dekalb, Ill., 1974).

70. See Stannard, *American Holocaust*, 146, 241, for examples.

71. See Utley, *Indian Frontier*, 184; Jeff Guy, *The Destruction of the Zulu Kingdom: The Civil War in Zululand, 1879-1884* (London, 1979). More generally see V. G. Kiernan, *European Empires from Conquest to Collapse, 1815-1960* (Leicester, 1982).

72. Best, *Humanity*, 162.

73. See Alfred Draper, *The Amritsar Massacre: Twilight of the Raj* (London, 1985), 14.

74. Best, *Humanity*, 117.

75. See Omer Bartov, *The Eastern Front, 1941-45: German Troops and the Barbarisation of Warfare* (London, 1985); H. Krausnick, *Hitlers Einsatzgruppen: Die Truppen des Weltanschauungskrieges, 1938-1942* (Frankfurt-am-Main, 1985); Mazower, *Inside Hitler's Greece*, 173-78: John Dower, *War without Mercy: Race and Power in the Pacific War* (London, 1986).

76. John Horne and Alan Kramer, 'German "Atrocities" and Franco-German Opinion 1914: The Evidence of German Soldiers' Diaries', *Journal of Modern History*, 66 (1994): 34-78.

77. See Sir Robert Thomson, *Defeating Communist Insurgency* (New York, 1966), for the anti-insurgent view. Noam Chomsky, *Turning the Tide: U.S. Intervention in Central America and the Struggle for Peace* (Boston, 1985), for some of the results.

78. See Milan Rai, *Chomsky's Politics* (London and New York, 1995), 27-28. For further potent examples see Callum MacDonald, 'So Terrible a Liberation: The UN Occupation of North Korea', *Bulletin of Concerned Asian Scholars*, 23 (1991): 3-19; Mark Danner, *The Massacre at El Mozote* (New York, 1984).

79. M. S. Anderson, *The Eastern Question, 1774-1923* (London, 1966), 184.

80. Paul Parin, 'Open Wounds, Ethnopsychoanalytical Reflections on the Wars in Former Yugoslavia', in Alexandra Stiglmayer, ed., *Mass Rape: The War against Women in Bosnia-Herzegovina* (Lincoln, Neb., and London, 1994), 35-43.

81. Catherine A. MacKinnon, 'Turning Rape into Pornography: Postmodern Genocide', in Stiglmayer, *Mass Rape*, 76.

82. See Helen Fein, 'Political Functions of Genocide Comparison', in Ronnie Landau, ed., *Remembering for the Future* (Oxford, 1988), suppl. vol., 124-27; Mark Levene, 'Yesterday's Victims, Today's Perpetrators?: Considerations on Peoples and Territories within the former Ottoman empire', *Terrorism and Political Violence*, 6 (1994): 444-61.

83. Robert Fisk, *Pity the Nation: Lebanon at War* (Oxford, 1990), 383-84; Ze'ev Schiff and Ehud Ya'ari, *Israel's Lebanon War* (New York, 1984), 281-82, 301-2.

84. Henry Rousso, *Le Syndrome de Vichy (1944-198...)* (Paris, 1987).

85. Martin Evans, *Memories of Resistance: French Opposition to the Algerian War* (Leamington Spa, 1997).

86. See Mazower, *Inside Hitler's Greece*, 372-77; José B. Monleon, ed., *Del Franquismo a la Postmodernidad Cultural Espanola, 1975-1990* (Madrid, 1990): Comision Nacional sobre la Desaparicion de Personas, *Nunca Mas* (London, 1986); Kanan Makiya, *Cruelty and Silence: War, Tyranny, Uprising and the Arab World* (London, 1992), 144-45.

87. Nikolai Tolstoy, *Stalin's Secret War* (London, 1981), 182-88.

88. Radu Ioanid, 'Romania', in David S. Wyman, ed., *The World Reacts to the Holocaust* (Baltimore and London, 1996), 251-52.

89. Quoted in Markusen and Kopf, *Holocaust*, 234.

90. Hilberg, *Destruction*, is the forerunner of this trend though he himself also extensively charts the barbarity of the massacres, round-ups and deportations.

91. In addition to Goldhagen, *Hitler's Willing Executioners*, and Browning, *Ordinary Men*, see Dina Porat, 'The Holocaust in Lithuania: Some Unique Aspects', and Jonathan Steinberg, 'Types of Genocide? Croatians, Serbs and Jews, 1941-5', in David Cesarani, ed., *The Final Solution: Origins and Implementation* (London, 1994).

92. Utley, *Indian Frontier*, 229; David Lavender, *The American West* (London, 1969), 411-13.

93. Kiernan, *European Empires*, 124-25.

94. James J. Reid, 'Total War: the Annihilation Ethic and the Armenian Genocide, 1870-1918', in Richard G. Hovannisian, ed., *The Armenian Genocide: History, Politics, Ethics* (New York, 1992), 35.

95. Martin Middlebrook, *The First Day of the Somme: 1 July 1916* (London, 1971).

96. Quoted in Markusen and Kopf, *Holocaust*, 106.

97. Maggie O'Kane, 'Bloodless Words, Bloody War', *The Guardian*, 16 December 1995.

98. Martin Bell, *Newsnight* interview, BBC2, 2 July 1996.

99. See Haim Bresheeth and Nira Yuval-Davis, eds, *The Gulf War and the New World Order* (London, 1991); Jochen Hippler, *Pax Americana? Hegemony or Decline* (London and Boulder, 1994); Makiya, *Cruelty and Silence*, 57-104.

100. See Richard Dowden's terrifying forecast that this would happen in, 'A Wound at the Heart of Africa', *The Independent*, 11 May 1994. Also Victoria Brittain, 'Why Zaire is more than another little African war', *The Guardian*, 28 December 1997; Barry Crawford 'From Arusha to Goma: How the West started the war in Rwanda', *Africa Direct*, (1997), http://jb world.jbs.st-louis.mo.us/history/causes/crawford.html. Thanks to Joshua Ryan-Collins for the Crawford article.

101. Robert D. Kaplan, 'The Coming Anarchy', *Atlantic Monthly*, February 1994, 44-74.

102. *Sipri Annual 1995* (Stockholm, 1996). See also Thomas Fraser Homer-Dixon, 'On the Threshold: Environmental Changes as Causes of Acute Conflict', *International Security* (fall 1991), 76-116.

103. Alex Duval Smith, '"Patriot" who hated US', *The Guardian*, 3 June 1997. More generally see Walter Laqueur, *The Age of Terrorism* (2nd edn, Boston, Toronto, London, 1987).

104. See Michael Barkun, *Religion and the Racist Right: The Origins of the Christian Identity Movement* (Chapel Hill, 1994).

105. Thomas Anderson, *Matanza* (Lincoln, Neb., 1971); Chomsky, *Turning the Tide*, chaps. 1, 2 and 3.

CHAPTER 1

MOTHERHOOD AND MASSACRE

THE MASSACRE OF THE INNOCENTS IN LATE-MEDIEVAL ART AND DRAMA

Laura Jacobus

... Herod, when he saw that he had been tricked by the wise men, was in a furious rage, and he sent and killed all the male children in Bethlehem and all in that region who were two years old or under ... Then was fulfilled what was spoken by the prophet Jeremiah: A voice was heard in Ramah, wailing and loud lamentation, Rachel weeping for her children: she refused to be consoled, because they were no more. [Matthew 2, 16-19]

This was the sparse biblical narrative which provided the basis for medieval dramatists and artists to create their versions of the Massacre of the Innocents. Their efforts were to develop in two apparently contradictory directions – tragedy and comedy – and this chapter explores each in turn. The use of examples is necessarily selective, ranging over several countries and five centuries, but it will suggest that one constant feature of the material under consideration is that the Massacre of the Innocents was perceived as 'a women's problem'.

The earliest known dramatic representations of the Massacre occur in liturgical church dramas around the eleventh century, and they treat the theme in such a way as to underline its theological significance. The message of the ecclesiastical dramatists was that the Massacre was all part of God's plan for human salvation; it fulfilled the prophecy of Jeremiah (cited in the passage above by Matthew) and was explained in the Revelations of John (14, 1-6). The prophet

Jeremiah's stress on Rachel's inconsolable grief was understood to presage the grief of the Virgin Mary at the Crucifixion. The evangelist John revealed that the Innocents numbered 144,000 and were to be 'redeemed from mankind as first fruits for God and for the Lamb'. They were honoured in this way because they 'have not defiled themselves with women, for they are chaste'. These two texts, central to the liturgy on Holy Innocents' Day, established women's God-given roles: women mother, women grieve, and women defile.

A number of recorded performances of the Massacre of the Innocents survive, and from these it is possible to build up a composite picture of a 'typical' eleventh-century representation.[1] Nonnaturalistic conventions prevailed. The plays were performed in church by clerics and were sung in Latin plainchant. They used dialogue lifted and adapted from scripture, and minimal costuming or *mise-en-scène*. Texts often call these performances the *Ordo Rachelis* (the ceremony of Rachel) which indicates their quasi-liturgical character. A typical *Ordo Rachelis* might begin with a scene of Herod ranting in the manner of a pantomime 'baddy'. This element of farce was present at the origins of the liturgical drama, for it seems to have been felt appropriate to portray non-Christians and the enemies of Christ as being ridiculously over the top. The implications of this will be considered later. However, the massacre itself was staged in a different manner, in which the serious, symbolic importance of the event was heightened by solemn ritual.

Youthful choristers, dressed in white liturgical garments (albs or stoles) would process into the church, singing the praises of the Holy Lamb of God and perhaps carrying a banner with the image of the Lamb to convey this idea to non-Latin speakers. Because early texts rarely include many stage directions, it is difficult to be sure how the deaths of the Innocents were staged, but it is clear that naturalistic violence was not shown. For example, in an eleventh or twelfth-century *Ordo Rachelis* from Freising, we learn that a soldier slays each boy with the words, 'Know death, boy', which suggests that the choristers simply dropped dead on command.[2] At Laon and Fleury, the only indication that something is amiss comes when the choristers and a cleric representing an angel sing a responsory from the office of matins on Innocents' Day, chosen to draw attention to the miraculous nature of the events. The innocent choristers sing the line, 'Why do you not defend our blood?', and the angel delivers the theologically-sound cold comfort that they should wait a bit for they will rejoin their brothers (in heaven).[3]

The divine plan thus having been executed, the mothers grieve in fulfilment of Jeremiah's prophecy. At Fleury, they apparently witness the massacre and, being excluded from the knowledge of God's plan, attempt in their ignorance to stop it. 'We pray you spare the tender lives of our babies', they sing repeatedly in plainchant. Elsewhere, the mothers arrive *post facto* on the scene and begin lamenting. Chief among them is the figure of Rachel, accompanied by women who attempt to console her without success. Her companions ask her, 'Why do you weep, Virgin mother, lovely in your sorrow, you in whose countenance Jacob delights?' Given that Rachel, of all the Jewish matriarchs, is the one most vividly characterized by her sexual appetite, the reference to her as 'Virgin mother' can only be understood as an attempt to draw a typological parallel between Rachel and the mother of Christ. The parallel is confirmed by Rachel's own reply, 'My spirit is troubled within me', which is a quotation from the lauds of Good Friday, evoking the sorrow of the Virgin Mary at the foot of the Cross.

Thus, several themes emerge in these liturgical representations of the Massacre of the Innocents. They are saturated with the theological message of redemption, and the dramatic potential of the narrative is made subordinate to the demands of didactic clarity. Three fairly distinct episodes result:

1. the raging of Herod the pagan, who is shut out from the scheme of salvation;
2. the serene deaths of the Innocents, who, following the Lamb of God, will shortly ascend to heaven;
3. the lamentations of Rachel and her female companions, who can think only of their immediate loss, although for the audience they recall by association the more transcendent grief of the Virgin Mary at the Crucifixion.

A similar separation of episodes is seen in an ivory plaque from Lorraine or northeastern France which dates from the later half of the eleventh century and once covered a gospel book (Figures 1.1 and 1.2). At Herod's instigation the children are killed in the first panel. The nature of the medium necessitates the graphic depiction of violence which was merely evoked in the *Ordo Rachelis*. However the meaning of the event is subtly conveyed, for as the babies are being helplessly dashed to the ground, they nevertheless appear to fly upwards, their bodies in the shape of the cross.

Women are marginalized in the first panel, but the second is devoted to the depiction of their grief, corresponding to the later episode of the *Ordo Rachelis*. Rachel features centrally, a dead child on her lap (much as later images of the Virgin were to show her grieving over the body of Christ on her lap in the *Pietà*). Those around her weep and attempt to console her, as foretold by Jeremiah.

Figure 1.1 *The Massacre of the Innocents,* detail of ivory plaque. Lorraine/Northeast France, second half of the eleventh century (Trustees of the Victoria and Albert Museum, London)

Figure 1.2 *Rachel Weeping,* detail of ivory plaque. Lorraine/Northeast France, second half of the eleventh century (Trustees of the Victoria and Albert Museum, London)

In such early representations of the Massacre of the Innocents there appears to be quite a close correspondence between art and drama. By the thirteenth century, however, it seems as if the theological element in representations of the Massacre of the Innocents was becoming less clear. Instead, the story's dramatic potential as a scene of human tragedy was being exploited, particularly in the visual arts. The episodic clarity found in the *Ordo Rachelis* and in the Romanesque ivories gave way to a tendency to represent the Massacre of the Innocents as a single scene, in which Herod, his soldiers and the mothers were brought into direct relationship.

One can explain this development partly in terms of changes in art over the period. The later middle ages saw the creation of new forms of public, didactic art in the churches, as the potential of the visual arts to educate the illiterate was exploited with renewed vigour by the church. Narrative cycles brought the scriptures to the laity on every available surface: in stained glass and mural decoration, sculpture on church façades and portals, or on church furnishings. The need for visual economy, to incorporate as extensive a narrative as possible on a limited surface, probably contributed to the compression of the Massacre of the Innocents from three or two scenes, to one.

Alongside this purely artistic account of the development, other trends may be discerned. The growth of public narrative art in the churches can be related to the wider efforts of the church to involve itself, indeed impose itself, on aspects of lay life which had once been of lesser concern to it. Marriage was one such aspect. Early Christian writings had decried the married state and regarded those within it as having jeopardized their access to heaven through the loss of their virginity. However, in the twelfth century marriage was declared a sacrament, and hence subject to clerical control. With regard to women, a spate of moral treatises emanated from the church from the thirteenth century onwards, to take account of this new situation.[4] These generally communicated the message that while virginity was best, and the enforced chastity of widowhood was next best, marriage and motherhood did not make a woman irredeemable. The Virgin Mary herself had been a mother.

Though an ideology of motherhood was not articulated as such during this period, it may be sensed in sermons' and devotional texts' assertions and assumptions about the naturalness of maternal feeling. Traditional maternal practices which contradicted this assumption, such as abortion, infanticide or child abandonment, were condemned. Conversely, breastfeeding was promoted from the pulpit through sermons and through visual images such as that of the nursing Madonna. This was partly in order to counter the widespread practice of employing a wet-nurse.[5]

Thirteenth and fourteenth-century representations of the Massacre of the Innocents, which give a more prominent role to the mothers, may be seen in the context of these ideas. The theologically important figure of Rachel disappears from the visual arts, and perhaps plays a much-reduced role in dramatic performances.[6] She is subsumed into images of collective or individual maternal grief. These lack the theological associations of earlier representations, but contain strong social messages on the theme of motherhood.

Giotto's frescoes in the Arena Chapel in Padua (executed c.1304-6) illustrate these points with greater subtlety than most. The *Massacre of the Innocents* is adjacent to a scene of the *Nativity,* which when viewed in conjunction with the *Massacre*, enhances its meaning (Figures 1.3 and 1.4). In the Nativity, the love between mother and child is beautifully conveyed by their physical relationship; they gaze into each other's eyes, and together they inscribe a circle in the composition, expressive of their perfect closeness. The circle is completed by another woman, who is often interpreted as a midwife. However this is unlikely, as the Virgin is clearly handing the child to the woman, and not the other way round. I would argue that she represents a kind of 'Everywoman' through whom female viewers are invited to share in the joys of maternal love. Support for such a view is found in a women's devotional book of the period, the *Meditations on the Life of Christ*, which enjoins the reader to imagine herself shortly after the birth of Christ, visiting the Virgin and begging to be allowed to hold the child for a while.[7]

In the adjacent scene of massacre, a group of mothers join in entreaty, recalling the chorus in the *Ordo Rachelis* who implore the soldiers to 'spare the tender lives of our babies'. Two mothers try to hold onto their babies who are being wrenched away by the soldiers. In this act the symbolic circle of maternal love that was established in the preceding composition is shattered into a series of broken arcs, traceable in the bodylines of the babies and their executioners. By these means, Giotto subtly suggests the parallel between the love felt by the mothers of the Innocents, and the sublime love felt by the mother of Christ.

At about the same time, in the pulpit at San Andrea in Pistoia (completed in 1301), preachers could point to exemplary scenes of maternal feeling carved by Giotto's contemporary Giovanni Pisano (Figures 1.5 and 1.6). In the scene of the *Nativity*, the Virgin tenderly leans over and lifts a blanket to regard her sleeping child. In the contrasting scene of the *Massacre of the Innocents* we see women, dishevelled and anguished, apparently attempting to breastfeed their dead babies back to life. With a subtlety that matches that of Giotto, Giovanni Pisano heightens the contrast by

Figure 1.3 Giotto, *The Nativity,* fresco. Arena Chapel, Padua, c.1305 (Musei Civici Padova)

Figure 1.4 Giotto, *The Massacre of the Innocents,* fresco. Arena Chapel, Padua, c.1305 (Musei Civici Padova)

Figure 1.5 Giovanni Pisano, *The Nativity,* detail of marble relief, part of pulpit. S. Andrea, Pistoia, 1301 (Soprintendenza per i beni artistici e storici, Firenze)

Figure 1.6 Giovanni Pisano, *The Massacre of the Innocents,* marble relief, part of pulpit. S. Andrea, Pistoia, 1301 (Soprintendenza per i beni artistici e storici, Firenze)

almost subliminal means. Whilst the peace of the Nativity is rendered through the softest, most refined carving, the savagery of the Massacre is crudely hacked into the stone.

Similar scenes occur in many fourteenth-century paintings and relief sculptures. In one typical fresco in the Sienese Church of San Clemente ai Servi, probably painted by Pietro Lorenzetti in the 1330s, we see women tearing their hair and scatching their cheeks in an exact display of contemporary mourning gestures (Figure 1.7). Women in medieval Italy took on the role of enacting social grief in death rituals which involved an inversion of normal social behaviour; conventional restraints on their movements, dress and speech were abandoned as women howled and flailed their arms, and tore their clothes and hair and lacerated their cheeks.[8] When such customs were reflected in depictions of the Massacre of the Innocents, the brutal realism served to heighten women's identification with events. However, such apparent realism also served to heighten the contrast between ordinary mothers and the Mother of God. The Virgin Mary was never depicted in such an undignified abandon of grief at the death of her son; at the foot of the Cross she generally clasped her hands together, and sometimes swooned. Ordinary mothers, unable to match the sublime feelings she experienced in her mind, were impelled to express their lesser natures through their bodies.

Figure 1.7 Pietro Lorenzetti, *The Massacre of the Innocents,* fresco. Santa Maria dei Servi, Siena, 1330s[?] (Soprintendenza per i beni artistici e storici, Siena)

Extravagant displays of maternal grief had an affective power which the church was keen to exploit at various points in its history. It did so again in the sixteenth century when the Counter-Reformation spawned the growth of pilgrimage sites filled with waxwork-like tableaux, notably the gruesomely realistic Chapel of the Holy Innocents at Varallo in Northern Italy.[9] However, during the fifteenth century, in Italy at least, the stress on maternal grief in images of the Massacre of the Innocents seems reduced and the depiction of women's traditional mourning practices becomes rarer. The abandonment of such a potent representational formula requires explanation, and the reasons for this change may be sought in the swings in intellectual and artistic fashion which generally go under the guise of the rise of Renaissance humanism.

Notions of propriety were changing under the influence of humanist ideas. Emotional restraint was praised, and while this was most strongly articulated in relation to male behaviour, it had its effect too on women's behaviour. Extravagant displays of grief came to be considered unfeminine according to codes of proper feminine behaviour, even while such instability was supposed to be the product of women's female natures. From Petrarch onwards, there were calls for women to restrict their traditional mourning to the home, often backed up by legislation confining them there.[10] Such considerations may well have contributed to the reduction of grief display in contemporary images of the Massacre.

A further contributory factor, as the fifteenth century progressed, was the domination of new aesthetic ideals in the visual arts – once again under the influence of humanism. Artists came to be praised for their ability to work in a way that recalled the achievements of ancient art. An artist's ability to depict the human body in violent activity, realistically and excitingly *all'antica*, became one way of judging his merits. Ancient battle reliefs were particularly admired, but few New Testament subjects (which were still the painters' stock-in-trade) afforded the artist an opportunity to display comparable skills. So, the desire of artists and patrons to keep up with artistic fashion may partially explain a new phenomenon which creeps into fifteenth-century depictions of the Massacre of the Innocents. The Massacre becomes a battle, in which the women are subject to as much violence as their babies, and occasionally fight back.

In works such as Domenico Ghirlandaio's *Massacre of the Innocents*, painted as part of the decoration of the Tournabuoni chapel in Santa Maria Novella in Florence (completed 1490), the fashionable intention is evident (Figure 1.8). Ghirlandaio provides an antique-style setting for the massacre, complete with ancient reliefs which invite the connoisseurial viewer to compare the Renaissance painter's skill with that of his ancient Roman forebears. Ghirlandaio even includes 'quotations' from these ancient sculptures such as the rearing horses, or the prostrate warrior in the foreground. The latter is particularly incongruous in the context of the narrative, unless one assumes that he has been felled by an especially ferocious mother.

We can partly explain the mothers' shift from passive grief to active defence in terms of humanist ideas about the propriety of emotional expression or the desirability of imitating ancient art, but to rely on such explanations attaches too much importance to Renaissance high culture, and neglects these images' relationship to more popular forms. Other tendencies may also contribute to the change in interpretation of the Massacre, and these tendencies are most explicit in fifteenth-century popular drama.

At the beginning of this paper it was suggested that medieval dramas of the Massacre of the Innocents inclined towards tragedy or comedy, and that a comic element had been present even in the solemn church dramas known from the eleventh century. In liturgical dramas on the Feast of Holy Innocents and in the days before Christmas sacred elements predominated, but nevertheless Herod had consistently been portrayed as a farcical figure. During the celebrations of Epiphany this spirit of mockery and misrule was allowed freer expression.[11] At Padua, for example, not half a mile from

Figure 1.8 Domenico Ghirlandaio, *The Massacre of the Innocents,* fresco. Santa Maria Novella, Florence, c.1485-90 (Soprintendenza per i beni artistici e storici, Firenze)

Giotto's evocation of maternal love and grief in the Arena Chapel, a very different sort of representation went on in the cathedral on the eve of Epiphany. A cleric representing Herod, wearing an untidy liturgical tunic, entered the church from the sacristy and hurled a wooden spear at the choir. He then proceeded to read the lesson 'furiously' whilst his henchmen reenacted the Massacre of the Innocents in a novel manner, attacking the bishop, canons and choristers with an inflated pig's bladder.[12]

In other Italian cities in the fourteenth and fifteenth centuries, notably Milan and Florence, spectacular outdoor pageants celebrating the Feast of the Magi seem to have been the norm at Epiphany. In these, the ridiculous figure of Herod featured prominently, ranting at the Magi and his courtiers, sometimes killing himself in a burlesque fit of pique. In 1390 in Florence, a chronicler recorded a 'feast of the Magi' performed on the streets of Florence. The magnificent displays of the Magi's mounted retinues, 'very honourably dressed with horses and with many attendants,' together with the costumes of Herod and his courtiers, were the primary object of the chronicler's attentions. His account ends with the casual observation that the 'celebration' ended at five o'clock in the afternoon, when Herod 'caused to be killed many children represented in the arms of their mothers and nurses'.[13]

It appears that during the course of the fifteenth century, dramatic representation of the Massacre of the Innocents ceased to be a visualization of God's plan for human salvation, and became instead a source of popular entertainment, part of the general fun-and-games of a public pageant. In many places, the representation of the Massacre was not even attached to the liturgical calendar. In England, for example, it seems to have been associated with midsummer festivities and to have assumed a uniquely knockabout character.[14] In one version from Chester, performed in English in the open air, the combat between mothers and soldiers is clearly played for laughs. The soldiers, named Sir Grymball Launcher and Sir Waradrake, swagger onto the playing area brandishing their swords and taunting the audience. The mothers are foul-mouthed harridans who respond in kind, attacking the soldiers with boots and pot-ladles and engaging in sexual banter with them. One mother claims that her child is the soldier's bastard, another graphically explains that her child should not be slaughtered as it is a girl, and invites the soldier to investigate for himself: 'Nay, freak, thou shalt fail; my child thou shalt not assayle; he hath two holes under the tayle; kiss and thou might assay'. The children are murdered with a flourish nonetheless.

Whilst the Chester play is within a specifically English tradition, and the sexual antagonism accompanying the violence is unusually explicit, it nevertheless expresses a misogyny which was pervasive throughout medieval Europe, and which took new forms in the fifteenth century. It was suggested earlier that the liturgy of the Feast of Holy Innocents had allotted women three roles: to mother, to grieve and to defile. The first two of these roles were amply represented in the images of nursing mothers and demented mourners, excluded from knowledge of God's plan and unable to rise above the limits of their supposed feminine natures. The third of these roles, that of woman as defiler, may not be made explicit in representations of the Massacre, but it may be sensed behind the bawdy violence seen at Chester.

Returning to the Italian Renaissance painting of the *Massacre of the Innocents* by Ghirlandaio, one can discern similar misogynistic currents beneath its humanist sophistication. In Ghirlandaio's fresco men and women are shown in violent physical contact, contrary to all contemporary norms of sexual decency (Figure 1.8). To appreciate its impact, we may usefully contrast the scene with another by the painter in the same chapel. In the *Visitation* a group of respectable ladies (one of whom is identifiable as Giovanna degli Albizzi, the patron's daughter-in-law) stands on the right of the picture, witnessing the encounter between the Virgin Mary and Saint Elizabeth (Figure 1.9). Their upright and composed demeanour exemplifies the restrictive standards of behaviour expected of upper-

Figure 1.9 Domenico Ghirlandaio, *The Visitation*, fresco. Santa Maria Novella, Florence, c.1485-90 (Soprintendenza per i beni artistici e storici, Firenze)

class women at the time. By contrast, in the *Massacre*, the mothers of the Innocents are without dignity or modesty; their breasts and shoulders are uncovered as they grapple with the soldiers, and as their sex is revealed, so their femininity is lost. Virago-like, one mother attacks a soldier and pulls him back by the hair. Another mother has been decapitated; a third steps over her body. The violence here is violence against women, inflicted not only by the soldiers but by the artist himself, and for the viewer's delectation. The bloody confection of severed members and penetrated flesh here offers an aestheticized retribution against the castrating 'other'.

Women, of course, are not the only feared 'other' represented in the Massacre of the Innocents, for xenophobia also found expression in the scene. Exotic costumes and swarthy or malformed facial features are common in depictions of the murdering soldiers, signifying their generic otherness. A German altarpiece from the church of St Lawrence in Nuremberg features Hebrew lettering on the clothes of one soldier, signifying more specifically that he is Jewish.[15] The soldiers in Matteo di Giovanni's *Massacre of the Innocents* (1482), comprise a grimacing array of racially exotic caricatures in pseudo-oriental headgear, urged on by Herod (Figure 1.10). The turban sported by the latter makes it likely that this image refers to contemporary fears of Muslim expansion, made especially pressing by the Turkish fleet's destruction of Otranto only

Figure 1.10 Matteo di Giovanni, *The Massacre of the Innocents*, altarpiece. S. Agostino, Siena, 1482 (Soprintendenza per i beni artistici e storici, Siena)

two years earlier. A German broadsheet of the sixteenth century even reused a woodcut of the Massacre of the Innocents to illustrate an 'eye-witness' account of the Turkish invasions. Such propagandistic practices may have been common, and deserve separate study.

What have the dramas and popular pageants, the carved pulpits and the painted chapel walls considered in this paper to do with the massacre in history? They are not evidence of how massacres actually looked, for they are not based on the real thing but on fantasies – God's plan for Man's salvation, and men's desire for women's subordination. Yet this does not negate their value to historians, for the visual culture of the period intersects with all other areas of cultural activity, including war. Medieval art and drama may not tell us how massacres looked, but in their fantasized association of sex, violence, race and religion, they may tell us something about why massacres happened.

Notes

1. The texts of these are most fully published in K. Young, ed., *The Drama of the Medieval Church*, 2 vols. (Oxford, 1933), vol. 2, 102-24.
2. Young, *Drama*, vol. 2, 117-22.
3. Young, *Drama*, vol. 2, 109-17.
4. Such literature is usefully surveyed in C. Casagrande, 'The Protected Woman', and S. Vecchio 'The Good Wife', in C. Klapisch-Zuber, ed., *A History of Women in the West*, vol. 2, *Silences of the Middle Ages* (Cambridge, Mass., 1992), 70-104 and 105-35.
5. M.R. Miles 'The Virgin's One Bare Breast: Nudity, Gender and Religious Meaning in Tuscan Early Renaissance Culture', in S. R. Suleiman, ed., *The Female Body in Western Culture: Contemporary Perspectives* (Cambridge, Mass., 1986), 193-208. Reprinted in N. Broude and M. Garrard, eds, *The Expanding Discourse: Feminism and Art History* (New York, 1992), 27-38.
6. It is difficult to establish the latter point; all that can be said for certain is that Rachel plays a major part in the documented church dramas of the eleventh and twelfth centuries, and is inconspicuous or absent in the documented vernacular dramas of the fifteenth century. The paucity of (published) texts from the intervening period does not allow firm conclusions about the relationship between these dramatic genres over time.
7. I. Ragusa and R. B. Green, eds, *Meditations on the Life of Christ: An illustrated Manuscript of the Fourteenth Century*, trans. I. Ragusa (Princeton, 1977), 38-39.
8. Evidence for these practices is discussed in L. Jacobus, 'Gesture in the Art, Drama and Social Life of Late-Medieval Italy' (Ph.D. diss., Birkbeck College, University of London, 1994), 49-51.
9. D. Freedberg, *The Power of Images: Studies in the History and Theory of Response* (Chicago and London, 1989), 192-201.
10. Sharon T. Strocchia, *Death and Ritual in Renaissance Florence* (Baltimore and London, 1992), 11-12.
11. See K. Young, *Drama*, vol. 1, 104-10, and G. Wickham, *The Medieval Theatre* (London, 1974), 51-55.

12. Young, *Drama*, vol. 2, 99-100.
13. Rab Hatfield,'The Compagnia de' Magi', *Journal of the Warburg and Courtauld Institutes*, 33 (1970): 107-61, esp. 108.
14. R. Axton, *European Drama of the Early Middle Ages* (London, 1974), 180-82, from which the following summary of the Chester play derives.
15. Discussed and illustrated in Ruth Mellinkoff, *Outcasts: Signs of Otherness in Northern European Art of the Late Middle-Ages* (2 vols. Berkeley, 1993), vol. 1, 105, and vol. 2, plate IV.17.

CHAPTER 2

THE 'MASSACRE' OF JEWISH CHRISTIANS IN CÓRDOBA, 1473-1474

John Edwards

A casual action, considered to be a deliberate insult to the Old Christians, provoked the disturbance. [The Brotherhood of Charity] was marching in a long procession, when a young convert girl had the idea of throwing some water out of the window on to the canopy that was covering the image of the most Holy Virgin. At once, the blacksmith shouted out frantically that what had been thrown was urine and that it had been done as an insult to holy religion. These words gave rise to much whispering among the people, but such mutterings reached their climax when the blacksmith, in stentorian terms, harangued them thus: 'I offer you my condolences, honoured citizens, for the manifest insult that these abhorred heretics have dared to offer to holy religion, without any fear at all of the punishment of their crimes. We are going to avenge it on these reprobate enemies of the faith and of charity.[1]

In these words, one of the most significant chroniclers of fifteenth-century Castilian history, Alfonso de Palencia, describes the outbreak of one of the most violent riots which took place in that period in the southern Spanish city of Córdoba, in March 1473. According to Palencia's account, the vengeance announced by the blacksmith, one Alonso Rodríguez, took the form of an attack on numerous houses, owned by *conversos*, or Christians of Jewish origin, in the neighbourhood. A Cordoban knight, Pedro de Torreblanca, said to be popular in the town, who attempted to block the path of the enraged participants in the procession, was wounded and trampled on, after which it became clear that a major riot would develop. Torreblanca's supporters engaged the *conversos*' attackers in combat, and the struggle extended into the surrounding streets. The blacksmith and his supporters took refuge in St Francis' church, while the chief magistrate (*alcalde mayor*) of the city, Don Alonso de Aguilar, took decisive action. Offering negotiations, he inveigled Rodríguez out of the sanctuary of the church and stabbed him with a lance, a commoner presumably being regarded as unworthy of dispatch by means of a sword. The blacksmith was taken home, near to death, by his supporters, while the *conversos* prepared to defend the streets in which they were mainly concentrated, also hiding away their precious possessions. A crowd gathered round the house of Rodríguez, who had by this time died, and were told that, Christ-like, he had been resurrected, and was once again demanding vengeance against the *conversos*.

This macabre reenactment of the Christian story led to the looting of *converso* houses, which Alonso de Aguilar tried to stop by arriving outside the blacksmith's house with a squadron of his personal retainers, on horseback. This show of force did not, however, have the desired effect of ending the violence. Instead, another councillor (*veinticuatro*) member of the Cordoban lesser nobility, Pedro de Aguayo, said by Palencia to be 'a factious man and a friend of the *converso* tanners', rallied them and their supporters to resist the 'Old Christian' attackers, thus exacerbating the situation. At this point, Alonso de Aguilar was driven out of the eastern part of the city, by a hail of weapons and missiles, and fled westwards to his official headquarters in the castle (Alcázar).

Given the prospect of looting the houses of wealthy *conversos*, labourers in from the countryside, and villagers from nearby, joined the ranks of Córdoba's own inhabitants. Don Alonso responded by offering protection to the likely victims and their property in the old castle (Castillo Viejo), which adjoined his own fortress. While the richest were able to follow this advice, the less well-off saw their best chance in defending themselves at the street corners, using for protection whatever remnants still remained of the walls which divided the western and eastern halves of the city. Worse was to follow.

By Palencia's account, it was at this stage that Don Alonso and his brother Gonzalo Fernández de Córdoba, later to be known as the 'Great Captain' for his military exploits in Italy, decided that it was expedient to abandon the *conversos* to their fate. Thus it was on 16 March 1473, no fewer than sixteen days after the disturbances started, that they felt the full effect of the hatred of the majority of their fellow citizens. In Palencia's studied and mannered words, 'By this time, no-one among the Old Christians was on the side of the *conversos*: on the contrary, they rushed to set fire to their houses, to steal their jewellery, and generally to loot. They violated maidens and cruelly despoiled matrons, or else made them suffer a horrible death.' The chronicler goes on to claim that a beautiful young girl was cut open from top to bottom, so that her embroidered undergarment could be removed more rapidly, and retails the rumour that one man violated the corpses of young women who had been killed in the riot. According to Palencia, the sack of 16 March followed a two-day stand-off, during which the rioters were already armed but did not act. Apart from the violence against individuals, and the looting of property, numerous houses were set alight and, as a result of the riot, some *converso* families fled the city. In the chronicler's view, while those who left in this way suffered further assault in the countryside as they travelled, the further looting and theft which took place in towns subject to the rule of Córdoba – Montoro, Adamuz, Bujalance, La Rambla and Santaella – was due to the active encouragement of Don Alonso and his brother the 'Great Captain'. Whatever the truth of this, it seems that many of Córdoba's *conversos* fled towards Seville, where further riots occurred in the following year. For many, the final refuge was Gibraltar, where *converso* refugees from various parts of Andalusia put themselves under the protection of the duke of Medina Sidonia, while others fled to Italy or Flanders.[2]

Alonso de Palencia's account, which does not differ substantially from that given by his contemporary, Diego de Valera, who was also based in Andalusia, may be supplemented from other sources.[3] But before looking more carefully into the nature of the 1473 riot, its immediate causes and its short- and long-term consequences, it is necessary to examine the history of the target-group, the Jewish Christians, or *conversos*. In the early summer of 1391, Córdoba still possessed one of the largest Jewish communities in Spain, but, by the middle of June of that year, there had been a major outbreak of violence in the city, which was to alter its demographic constitution for ever. Within a few weeks, attacks were suffered by urban Jewish communities from Seville in the south west, where the outbreak started on 6 June, to Catalonia in the north east. Various explanations – religious, political, social and economic – have been offered for this unique phenomenon in Spanish history.[4] As far as Córdoba is concerned, a good short description of what occurred in 1391 is to be found in a letter sent by Henry III of Castile to Burgos city council, on 16 June of that year:

> Understand that it has become known how, in the last few days, in the most noble cities of Seville and Córdoba, through inducements and persuasion exercised by the archdeacon of Ecija [Ferrán Martínez], some of the lesser people of the said cities, behaving like troublemakers

and men of little understanding, without thought for our interests ... or fear of God or my justice, ... attacked the Jews living in the communities [*aljamas*] of the said towns, killed some of them, robbed others, and forced others to become Christians. As a result, the Jews who used to live in these communities have been driven out, about which I am very angry, because this does me great disservice.[5]

While this contemporary, if hardly objective, source dismisses the notion that a thousand or more Jews died in Córdoba in the first half of June 1391, it indicates the main consequence of the attack, which was the end of the city's Jewish quarter as such, with the departure of those who remained faithful to the Jewish religion, and the conversion of many of those who remained to Christianity. By 1399, the *Judería* had been made into a new parish, which was dedicated to St Bartholomew by 1410, while the converts largely moved eastwards into the central political, economic and social areas of the city – indeed to the very streets where the 1473 riot was to take place.[6] Thus by the time of the outbreak on 16 March, *conversos* were living in the parishes on either side of the Calle de la Feria (Fair Street), St Mary, St Saviour and All Saints to the west, and St Nicholas 'in the Ajarquía', St Peter and St Andrew to the east [see map]. It was on this area that the 1473 riot was centred.

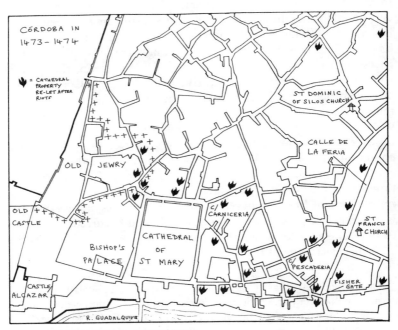

Figure 2.1 Córdoba in 1473-1474

Evidence from the periods preceding and following the riot gives a clear indication that many of these *conversos* and their descendants had achieved considerable success in fifteenth-century Córdoba. When the agents of the Cathedral attempted to re-let their properties after the riot, they operated in the main trading streets in this central quarter, such as the Calle de las Carnicerías (Butchers' Street), the Calle de la Pescadería (Fisher Street), and the Calle de la Feria itself. The twenty-seven tenants affected included (ironically, or perhaps significantly) two blacksmiths, as well as a carpenter, a second-hand clothes dealer, a bootmaker, a silk merchant, a surgeon, a tavern keeper, a cloth merchant, a surgeon, and various other workers in leather trades.[7] But before the nature and consequences of the 1473 riot are examined in greater detail, it needs to be asked what economic circumstances these converted Jews were operating in, during the years immediately preceding the outbreak of violence against them.

The Calle de la Feria, and the area surrounding it, had been economically active since the thirteenth century, when the city returned to Christian rule. The street itself, named after the two annual fairs which were held in it under a 1284 charter of Sancho IV, was also a centre for permanent traders, as were the neighbouring parishes of St Mary and St Nicholas. On the street itself, and in its vicinity, a wide range of goods were available, from basic foodstuffs such as fish to textiles, pottery and jewellery. Trades associated with the horse and with warfare, including the sale of the animals themselves, and the activities of blacksmiths, saddlers, stirrup-makers and armourers, were prominent in these streets. Given the level of national, and even international, interest in the war-making potential of Córdoba's trades and industries, later to come to prominence in Ferdinand and Isabella's Granada campaigns, it is not surprising that the riverside parishes also had a strong association with hospitality, including both hostelries and prostitution.[8] However, all this activity was inevitably subject to the overall trends of the Castilian economy, which was itself strongly influenced by the natural characteristics of the Iberian peninsula.

Generally speaking, Spain is a mountainous and arid country, in which human cultivation is difficult. As far as the 'kingdom' of Córdoba is concerned, there were, and are, three distinct zones of terrain and cultivation. The area to the north of the Sierra, the mountain range which overlooks Córdoba to the south, and forms the southern edge of Spain's central Meseta, was generally poor in soil, and largely devoted to forest products and stock-breeding, though the Mediterranean staples of grain, wine and olive oil were also to be found. The area to the south of Córdoba, known now as then as the Campiña, was, in contrast, a centre for the cultivation of those very crops, and in particular grain. In between lay the valley of the Guadalquivir, with the city on its right bank. Here were concentrated some of the most fertile lands, and highest crops, in the entire region, a relic of the sophistication of the Muslim period, before the Christian reconquest.[9] A certain documentary distortion, caused as much by the records which have survived as by the lack of those which have not, has affected, until quite recently, the economic history of Castile in the mid to late fifteenth century. Because the political upheavals in the kingdom, during the reigns of John II and Henry IV, greatly reduced the power and prestige of the Crown, it used to be assumed that the economy also went into a decline. The truth seems to be, however, that the king's loss of revenue meant no more than the transfer of money and resources from his coffers to those of the nobles, and of others who were economically active.[10] The climate of the kingdom, including the Córdoba region, paid scant regard, however, to the ambitions of any king, magnate or farmer. Between 1447 and 1473, there is evidence of seriously bad harvests in part or the whole of Andalusia in no fewer than eighteen of the twenty-seven years involved.[11] In addition, the Castilian coinage had been heavily debased, particularly during the reign of Henry IV, with inevitable effect on the living standards of the poorer members of the community.[12] Thus it is not hard to find causes of economic and social discontent in the city and countryside of Córdoba in the early months of 1473, and yet politics played at least as important a part in the build-up to violence against the city's *conversos*, in the 'massacre' itself and in its ending.

The reigns of John II and Henry IV of Castile were notorious for complex faction-fighting among the upper nobility, the main aim of which was for individual aristocratic dynasties to secure as much as possible of the patronage and other economic resources which were theoretically invested in the Crown. A notable feature of this period was the strengthening control exercised over the royal towns by upper noble families. In the case of Córdoba, the battle for power over city and countryside was largely fought out between the two senior branches of the Fernández de Córdoba family, led by Don Alonso de Aguilar and the count of Cabra respectively. By 1470, the Aguilar faction had emerged victorious, and was in effective control of the city, with its leader Don Alonso installed in the Alcázar as chief magistrate (*alcalde mayor*). Both the count of Cabra and Córdoba's bishop, his relative and ally Don Pedro de Córdoba y Solier, lived outside the city in the first years of the 1470s, and Henry IV's attempt, in May 1472, to reverse this situation was unsuccessful. Don Alonso's wings were not to be clipped until 1477-8, when Henry's sister Isabella removed him from public office.[13] Before considering the role of the *conversos* in these developments, it is perhaps worth noting that the factions supporting these Cordoban magnates, which were generally known as *bandos*, were wider in scope and more amorphous than conventional feudal retinues. They included not only blood relatives of the faction leaders, but also those with any kind of military, financial link to them, or even geographical proximity, in terms of residence in particular streets of the city.[14] In such circumstances it was as difficult for a *converso* as for any other Cordoban citizen to avoid some kind of involvement with the *bandos*. Whether or not that involvement caused *conversos* to be unpopular, and even helped to precipitate the violence of 1473, is a matter to be considered when the available sources for the riot and its consequences have been examined more fully.

Since the Mosque-Cathedral (*Mezquita-Catedral*) owned a large amount of property in the parishes worst affected by the rioting, it is fortunate that enough documentation survives in the Cathedral archive to provide quite a striking picture of the consequences, not in terms of violence against people, on which chroniclers such as Palencia and Valera focus, but in the damage done to property. The matter was discussed at the chapter meeting on 1 April 1473, a fortnight after the riot.

> On this aforementioned day, the lords dean and chapter gave power to Antón Martínez, minor canon [*racionero*], and to Fernand Ruiz their steward, to let all the properties of the [Cathedral] church which they find to have been vacated by those who had been their tenants, because of the robbery of the converts [here *confesos*, the fifteenth-century term] which was committed in this city, and the destruction of their possessions and houses. [They are to let them] for the period from now to St John [the Baptist's day, 24 June], securing good guarantors, and if they do not find people to take [these properties], they should seal them up with stones and mud [*piedra lodo*], or in whatever way seems best to them. [The chapter] orders that whatever they spend on [these houses] should be agreed by its accountants under the steward's account.[15]

The seriousness of the depredations of March 1473 is made all too clear in this dry and practical account, most obviously in the fact that so many tenants had clearly departed for good after the riot. The researches of Nieto Cumplido and Escobar Camacho indicate that, in the twenty or so cases in which relettings by the Cathedral chapter are recorded, the houses concerned had been rented by economically active people in some of the busiest commercial streets. These included both the Calle de la Feria, where the incident of the water-spilling occurred at the Rastro cross, during the procession from the

Franciscan church, and its destination the Fisher Gate [*Puerta de la Pescadería*].[16] The Cathedral's agents did not find it easy, however, to restore their masters' property portfolio in the riot-stricken area, as a capitular minute of 5 November 1473 clearly shows:

> We, the dean and chapter of the [Cathedral] church of Córdoba, state that, in as much as in the past year of 1472, which was completed on St John [the Baptist's] day in the present year of 1473, there occurred in this aforesaid city great fires and robberies and scandals, because of which many of the farmers of [our] rents and tenants of our properties, and their guarantors, absented themselves from this aforesaid city, and others have come into such poverty that they cannot, at present, pay the rents and interests that are owed to us, because of which you, Ferrand Ruiz, our steward, have not been able to gather or collect certain quantities of *maravedís* [the Castilian money of account] that are owed to us from the aforesaid year of '72 by the aforesaid, our rent-farmers and tenants. Neither have you been able to accomplish against them all the things that you were obliged as our steward to do. For this reason, since things are as they have been described above, and as it is our wish to treat you kindly, and in order that there may be a final drawing up of your stewardship accounts for the Community [of the Cathedral] and the dole [the Cathedral charitable fund] for the aforesaid year of '72, and so that the order may be given for the lords of the church [Cathedral] to be paid the *maravedís* which may be found from the aforesaid account books to be owing to them, we are in concord and agreement with you, our aforementioned steward, in this matter.[17]

In a cold and mercenary fashion, these Cathedral documents reveal the horror of the species of 'ethnic cleansing' which invaded Córdoba in 1473, as a ghastly replica of the attack on the city's Jews in 1391. But if the canons were right, and, living in the relevant area, they were in a good position to know, even if they had not been property owners, the riot was a cause of 'major fires and thefts and scandals'. The question is, were these acts the responsibility just of craftsmen, and of other victims of the poor economic conditions of the early 1470s, or were grander people involved? The chronicler Alonso de Palencia more than hints that they were. Unfortunately, and perhaps significantly, this cannot be confirmed from official municipal records, such as the minutes of council meetings, which begin to survive in a systematic fashion only from 1493, but some useful fragments of evidence may be found in the still existent registers of the city's notaries.[18]

On 10 August 1478, five years after the riot, Luis de Córdoba, a full member [*veinticuatro del número*] of Córdoba city council, made his will before two notaries. A resident [*vecino*] of the parish of St Dominic, to the east of the Calle de la Feria, Luis asked to be buried in his own chapel in the Dominican church of St Paul. The will was witnessed by three members of the office-holding nobility of Córdoba, Alfonso de Angulo, Juan de Angulo and Diego Muñiz de Godoy. After the usual pious benefactions, Luis instructed his executors, the parish councillor [*jurado*] Gonzalo Cabrera and the theologian Diego Fernández, who was on the staff of the Cathedral, to settle various of his debts from his estate. One of these is of particular interest in the context of the troubles of 1473. After instructing Cabrera and Fernández to spend 8,000 *maravedís* on 'those things which they understand to be for the benefit and utility of the community of this aforesaid city of Córdoba', councillor Luis acknowledged a further debt:

> And in as much as I am responsible that, when the robbery of the *conversos* happened in this city, on account of 5,000 *maravedís* [I took] from my neighbours, the *conversos* who used to live near my house, I order that my executors distribute and pay from my goods the aforesaid 5,000 *maravedís* to those of my *converso* neighbours whom they find living nearest, because I am under obligation. And because I took, when the aforesaid robbery happened, two pieces of local cloth [*paño de la tierra*], one piece blue, I order [my executors] to find out whom they belonged to, and give them back to them.[19]

Cabrera cites two further examples of later references to the 'robbery' of 1473. In 1499, Bartolomé Ruiz de la Mesa ordered a payment to be made from his estate to 'a son of Rodrigo Alfonso Çabán [of] 1,500 *maravedís*, which he owes him for certain things which came into his power when the robbery of the *conversos* took place'. Just two years after the 'riot', Luis Muñiz de Godoy, a councillor [*veinticuatro*], was still in dispute with one Juan de Córdoba over a silver cup, which was claimed by the *veinticuatro*, but which Juan refused to return to him, on the grounds that it was the latter's property and had been stolen during the 'robbery' of the *conversos*.[20]

Thus there is evidence of burnt-out houses, of the looting of property, on occasions even admitted by leading citizens in the writings of the notaries to whom they had access. The walled-up houses of the Cathedral parish and its neighbours bore testimony to the loss, more through departure than death, of numerous productive families – a loss felt keenly by landlords and their stewards. Who, though, were the members of the confraternity of Charity [*La Caridad*] whose violent reaction to a supposed provocation from a child brought such devastation to some of Córdoba's busiest streets? The chroniclers Palencia and Valera are united in describing the Caridad as an 'Old Christian' confraternity, in other words one which consisted of Catholics who were not, or proclaimed themselves not to be, of Jewish origin. Palencia says that the overt purpose of the organization was to raise money for the ransoming of Christian captives from Muslim hands, but both writers more than imply that it in fact existed to rouse religious fervour not so much against the traditional Islamic foe but rather against its members' own *converso* neighbours. In fact, Valera roundly describes the so-called confraternity as a 'conspiracy in the city under the colour of devotion'.[21] As far as the social composition of the Caridad is concerned, although the only member whose specific occupation is known is the blacksmith Alonso Rodríguez, the ringleader of the violence, contemporary evidence suggests that it was primarily a lower-class organization. Palencia, for example, describes the rioters as 'the plebs of the Old Christians', though one of the company, Juan de Buenosvinos, later became an Inquisition prosecutor.[22] However, the involvement of the upper classes in the disturbances is not only indicated by notarial evidence but also more than hinted at by the chroniclers.

The best indication of the issues underlying the robbery and destruction of 1473 is to be found in a measure taken by Don Alonso de Aguilar after order had been restored. In Palencia's words, 'it was declared through the voice of the town crier that all *conversos* were ineligible for public office'. While it is generally asserted, both by the chroniclers of the period and by modern scholars, that the representation of *conversos* among the city's officials was a major source of grievance among the 'Old Christian' population, specific evidence for this contention is hard to find, because of a shortage of reliable records.[23] It is certainly demonstrable that conversion to Christianity, in the decades after 1391, not only allowed Córdoba's Jews to move out of their former quarter into the central commercial streets of the city, but also enabled them to enter fully into its economic and professional life. It is not so easy, however, to identify individuals who profited from the consequences of their baptism. Not only did the neophytes, when taking their baptismal names, supposedly obliterate their religious identity as Jews, but they also took on a new social identity. For both reasons, the extent of *converso* office-holding in the city cannot be reliably estimated. Cabrera states that 'identity of names, professional dedication and similarly their social connections are quite a good indication to deciding the matter, but not always a sufficiently safe one'.[24] An example of the use of this method is the suggestion that Gonzalo González, a public notary [*escribano público*] was a *converso* on the basis that he made personal notes on the riots of 1473 and 1474 in his registers.[25] In reality, the only hope of finding greater security in identifying *converso* families, and their true role in Cordoban life, will be lengthy archival research, both locally and nationally.[26] In the meantime, it is only possible to work on the basis of the recorded perception that *conversos* were disproportionately prominent in the economic and social life of the city. Their offence would not have been identifiable in such terms, however, had it not been for religious categories.

It seems undeniable that 'Old Christian' hostility towards Jewish Christians, most of them, by 1473, the descendants of converts rather than those who personally changed religion, became mixed with both economic discontent and opposition to the 'one-party rule' of Don Alonso de Aguilar, after the expulsion of the Cabra faction from Córdoba. As with politics, the background to the assault on the *conversos* was national, in that the first prohibition of public office-holding by Jewish Christians was introduced by a rebel regime in Toledo in 1449. Although that particular measure was repealed soon afterwards, when John II's government regained control of the city, its influence clearly reached Córdoba. When the precentor of the Cathedral, Ferrand Ruiz de Aguayo, made his will in 1466, and founded a chantry there, he explicitly excluded 'New' Christians from ministering at its altar, 'notwithstanding that in this generation of *conversos* there are many virtuous and good persons, and of good conscience and life'.[27] The suspicion and threat against the converts were already more than implicit before the political confusion of the early 1470s gave their opponents a chance to wreak revenge, as they saw it. The ambiguity of the situation, in which even fellow converts admitted to having sympathized with the rioters and looters, is exemplified by some verses addressed by Antón de Montoro, a Cordoban and *converso* himself, to Alonso de Aguilar. The main theme of the poem is a rebuke to Don Alonso for his failure to protect the city's 'New' Christians at the vital time, but, in his honesty, Montoro could not avoid adding his own confession of guilt:

> I, in my misfortune,
> was the first to put on
> the livery of the blacksmith [Alonso Rodríguez].[28]

These lines indicate all too clearly the real threat of the Caridad and the Cruz del Rastro. A limited degree of coexistence, which had existed in the city for the first half of the fifteenth century, was coming to an end, and more institutional means of dealing with such conflicts were about to be introduced, in the form of an Inquisition, which was to put the terror of the 1473 rioters into a new and more effective dimension. At the request of the new sovereign of Castile,

Isabella, and of her consort Ferdinand, Pope Sixtus IV established a new Inquisition for her kingdom on 1 November 1478. Four years later, one of its tribunals began operations in Córdoba. On the scale of violence of the Spanish Inquisition, it seems unlikely that the 1473 riot qualified as a massacre, but there was a postscript. According to the account of the supposedly *converso* notary Gonzalo González, on the night following the death of Henry IV, 'On Sunday, at night-fall on the 11th of this month of December of [14]74, the second robbery of the *conversos* was carried out in this city, and on the following Tuesday, they hanged six men in the afternoon, and flogged three, and banished another three.'[29] Don Alonso de Aguilar and his supporters, including, as they no doubt did, the *conversos* who either had not fled after the riot of the previous year or had subsequently returned, could not have known that, on the following day, Isabella was to claim the throne of Castile in Segovia. Nonetheless, it is possible to surmise that even that highly independent magnate had decided that governmental office should be exercised, four years before he was suspended from his magistracy, for dereliction of duty, by the new queen. Even if the 1473 disturbances had resulted in more damage to property than to persons, their psychological impact was to last well into the sixteenth century.

Thus, even if it was not a 'true' massacre in terms of numbers killed, the 'riot', or 'robbery', of 1473, together with its sequel in the following year, was a prelude to the institutional violence of the Cordoban Inquisition which, after 1480, was to claim dozens of lives. The difference was that the violent repression of Christians of Jewish origin, motivated as it was by social and economic greed and jealousy, and political faction, moved its location and changed its nature, in terms of the agencies primarily responsible. No longer was such action to depend upon street-fighting, initiated, whether officially or not, in that busy commercial thoroughfare, the Calle de la Feria. After the establishment of the Inquisition on the opposite, western, side of the Mosque-Cathedral, in the royal castle, where the *corregidor*, who was the symbol of Ferdinand and Isabella's rule, also had his headquarters, such action was to be firmly in the hands of the authorities, and carried out in 'legal' form. Thus the succession of *autos de fe*, rather than the riot of 1473, was perhaps the 'true' Cordoban 'massacre'.

Notes

1   Alfonso de Palencia, *Crónica de Enrique IV*, ed. and trans. A Paz y Melia, *Bib-*
     ...ca de Autores Españoles, vol. 257, 86.

2. Palencia, *Crónica de Enrique IV*, 86-87, 130A.

3. Mosén Diego de Valera, *Memorial de diversas hazañas*, ed. Juan de Mata Carriazo (Madrid, 1941), 240-41.

4. For example, Philippe Wolff, 'The 1391 pogrom in Spain: social crisis or not?', *Past and Present*, 50 (1971): 4-18; John Edwards, *The Jews in Christian Europe, 1400-1700* (second edn, London, 1991), 28-29.

5. Fritz (Yitzhak) Baer, *Die Juden im christlichen Spanien*, vol. 1 part 2 (Berlin, 1936; reprinted Farnborough, 1970), 232-33, translated in Edwards, *The Jews in Western Europe, 1400-1600* (Manchester, 1994), 47-48. In 1395, the young king visited Córdoba, and instructed one of his courtiers, the *aposentador real*, to compile a report, but no further results appear to have followed [Baer, *Die Juden*, vol. 1, 245].

6. Manuel Nieto Cumplido and C. Luca de Terna y Alvear, 'El Alcázar Viejo: una repoblación cordobesa del siglo XIV', *Axerquia* (1980): 244-46; José Manuel Escobar Camacho, *Córdoba en la Baja Edad Media. Evolución urbana de la ciudad* (Córdoba, 1989), 77; Edwards, 'The *Judeoconversos* in the urban life of Córdoba, 1450-1520', in *Villes et sociétés urbaines au Moyen Age. Hommage à M. le Professeur Jacques Heers* (Paris, 1994), 288-89. On the similar situation in Seville, see, in the same volume, Angus MacKay, '*Conversos*, urban culture and religion in fifteenth-century Castile', 282-83.

7. Nieto Cumplido, 'La revuelta contra los conversos de Córdoba en 1473', in *Homenaje a Antón de Montoro en el V centenario de su muerte* (Montoro, 1977), 43-44, 47 and 49.

8. Escobar Camacho, *Córdoba en la Baja Edad Media*, 134-48.

9. Edwards, *Christian Córdoba. The city and its region in the late Middle Ages* (Cambridge, 1982), 2-6.

10. See the forthcoming work of John Edwards, *The Spain of the Catholic Monarchs, 1474-1516*, in Blackwell's History of Spain (Oxford).

11. Angus MacKay, 'Popular movements and pogroms in fifteenth-century Castile', *Past and Present*, 55 (1972): 33-67; 56-58, reprinted in *Society, economy and religion in late medieval Castile* (London, 1987).

12. MacKay, 'Popular movements', 34 and 53-54, and *Money, prices and politics in fifteenth-century Castile* (London, 1981), esp. 42-104.

13. Edwards, *Christian Córdoba*, 148-50; Emilio Cabrera Muñoz, 'Violencia urbana y crisis política en Andalucía en el siglo XV', in *Violencia y conflictividad en la sociedad de la España Bajomedieval* (Zaragoza, 1995), 5-25, esp. 16-18.

14. Edwards, *Christian Córdoba*, 152.

15. Nieto Cumplido, 'La revuelta contra los conversos', 47.

16. Nieto Cumplido, 'La revuelta contra los conversos', 43-44. For details of the relevant streets in the period, see Escobar Camacho, *Córdoba en la Baja Edad Media*, 134-48.

17. Nieto Cumplido, 'La revuelta contra los conversos', 49.

18. Council minutes [*Actas Capitulares*] survive for 1473 (a fragment not relevant to the riot of that year), 1479, 1493 and continuously from 1495, in the Archivo Municipal. One set of registers for the period, Office 14, is available in the Archivo Histórico Provincial, in the section of *Protocolos Notariales* [hereafter AHP, PN].

19. AHP PN Of. 14-12-14- fol.16.

20. AHP PN Of. 14-05 (05) fol. 9v, no date, and 14-06 cuad. 7 fol. 25r, 28.1.1475 [Cabrera, 'Violencia urbana', 23n].

21. Palencia, *Crónica de Enrique IV*, 86-87; Valera, *Memorial de diversas hazañas*, 240-43.

22. Cabrera, 'Violencia urbana', 22n.
23. For a good example of the genre, see F. Márquez Villanueva, 'Conversos y cargos concejiles en el siglo XV', *Revista de Archivos, Bibliotecas y Museos*, 63 (1957): 503-40, especially 519-20.
24. Cabrera, 'Violencia urbana', 21.
25. Cabrera, 'Violencia urbana', 20n, citing a paper by Margarita Cabrera Sánchez, 'El problema converso en Córdoba. El incidente de la Cruz del Rastro', given at the Congreso Internacional, 'La Península Ibérica en la Era de los Descubrimientos, 1391-1492', Seville, 1994.
26. For a possible method of research see Edwards, 'Los conversos de Córdoba en el siglo XV: un proyecto de la historia social', in *Andalucía entre Oriente y Occidente. Actas del V Coloquio Internacional de Historia Medieval de Andalucía* (Córdoba, 1988), 581-84.
27. Nieto Cumplido, 'La revuelta', 35-36.
28. Antón de Montoro, *Cancionero*, eds Marcella Ciceri and Julio Rodríguez Puértolas (Salamanca, 1990), 322.
29. AHP, PN, Of. 14- 11 (08), cuad. 12 fol. 55.

Chapter 3

Hidden Transcripts

Secret Histories and Personal Testimonies of Religious Violence in the French Wars of Religion

Mark Greengrass

'Massacre' first gained its modern meaning as a word in sixteenth-century France. Up to the 1540s, it had been the word used for the butcher's chopping block; and the butcher's knife was the 'massacreur'. In 1545, however, the judges of the sovereign court of Provence undertook a campaign of religious cleansing, stripping heretics out of the region of Mérindol, Cabrières and the surrounding districts, which had long been refuges for Waldensian communities. It was one of numerous provincial campaigns to extirpate the growing Protestant heresy from the body of traditional France in the 1540s and 1550s. In a famous pamphlet, however, it was referred to as 'un massacre', and the term stuck.[1] Writing later, Calvin's successor Beza described 'the savage massacre that the judges at Aix perpetrated upon the Waldensian brethren ... not upon one or two individuals but upon the whole population, without distinction of age or sex, burning down their villages as well'.[2] It became the peculiarly (though not uniquely) Protestant term for the popular sectarian hatreds which would be the bloody litany of the French civil wars of the second half of the century, culminating, of course, in the most spectacular moment, the ecktype massacre, that of St Bartholomew, in August 1572.[3] It was from France that the term entered the English political vocabulary, not least through the appearance of translated French Protestant pamphlets and Sylvester's metrical version of Salluste du Bartas' *Divine Weekes and Workes*.[4] 'The bloodie massacre at Paris' was the familiar way of referring to the St Bartholomew's Day massacre by the end of the century at the time of the publication of Christopher Marlowe's play.[5]

It is not difficult to delineate some of the chronology and even the common features of this period of sectarian hatred, common features which are doubtless not unique to sixteenth-century France. Firstly, there were clearly defined cycles of sectarian violence, running out of phase with the more formal militarized conflicts of the civil wars themselves. So the periods of greatest sectarian tension on the streets of Paris, and provincial cities like Rouen, Lyon, Troyes and Dijon, tended to occur just prior to, and on the eve of, the more formal periods of warfare: in 1561-2, 1567-8, 1572 and then, finally, in 1588-9.[6] Secondly, the sectarian tensions were inevitably most bloody in those communities where the two religions, Catholic and Protestant, were mixed. The scale and intensity of the massacres tended to decrease markedly after 1577 because, in so many French cities, particularly of northern France, the Protestant minority had been forced out of town or become an insignificant force. It was still one which could be taunted, or treated as a scapegoat for the ills of the community at large; but it was no longer capable of putting up much of a fight. Thirdly, there were familiar patterns to the diffusion of sectarian violence both across a city and from one city to another. There were copycat incidents, the most famous of which involved the massacre of St Bartholomew itself which, as the nineteenth-century French historian Michelet pointed out was 'une saison de la Saint-Barthélemy', encompassing a score of provincial cities in the two months following the events in Paris.[7]

There was also a degree of stereotyping of responses amongst the massacring mobs as well as from amongst the sometimes complicit municipal authorities. So certain streets were well known as the battle-zones for the enactment of religious violence, each one a 'Shankill Rd' (to draw on the contemporary resonances of sectarian tension in Northern Ireland) for the local inhabitants: the rue Moyenne in Troyes, or the rue du Taur in Toulouse.[8] Certain quarters of particular cities became the 'Bogsides' of provincial France: the quartier Hugon of Tours (which may have given its name to the 'Huguenots'); the riverside quartier dominated by the cutlers in Toulouse, or the parish of St Eloi in Rouen; the quartier bourg St Michel in Paris, close by the quartier Latin.[9] In many cities, the first sectarian troubles gave rise to lists of proscribed Protestants, suspects who would be regularly rounded up in subsequent periods of tension, their property sequestered, their friends investigated, actions by municipal authorities which were part and parcel of the rituals attached to sectarian incidents in the French civil wars.[10] The edicts of pacification (1563; 1570; 1576; 1577; 1598) provided the Protestant minority with guaranteed places of worship, generally well outside the walls of major cities in northern France. This, however, resulted in the Protestants being particularly exposed as they made their way to and from the services or *prêches* on Sundays, a slow-moving procession and target for popular vengeance. So, in Troyes, Rouen, Paris and elsewhere north of the Loire, the typology of massacres was subtly modified by edicts whose ostensible objective was to prevent their occurrence.

The most notable common feature of the French massacres has been, however, the ritual objects of violence – such as those identified by Natalie Zemon Davis in a notable article, first published in 1973.[11] She indicated how very wide the range of sectarian incident could be, partly because the possibilities of sacral offence could be generously conceived; whether it was taunting a priest, ridiculing a monk, mocking a religious procession, throwing mud against a statue, desecrating a font or destroying an altar. Although she has been criticized for overstating the ritual of purification to be found within the French massacres, there is no doubt that she was right to stress the asymmetry between the ritual massacral space afforded by the traditional religion and the lack of ritual objectives provided by the reformed religion. She cites the Protestant *Histoire Ecclésiastique des églises réformées* ..., published in 1581, as asserting that 'those of the Reformed Religion made war only on images and altars, which do not bleed, while those of the Roman religion spilled blood with every kind of cruelty'.[12] Whilst she accepts that there were numerous distinctions to be drawn, 'nevertheless, when all this is said, the iconoclastic Calvinistic crows still come out as the champions in the destruction of religious property', whilst 'in bloodshed, the Catholics are the champions'.

A more sophisticated explanation for this asymmetry has recently been advanced by the French historian, Denis Crouzet, in his monumental book *Les Guerriers de Dieu*.[13] Crouzet seeks to explain the distinctively different attitudes to religious violence amongst Catholics and Protestants in the wars of religion. To do so, he immersed himself in the printed literature, particularly the pamphlets and broadsheet collections of the *Bibliothèque Nationale*. What he discovered in this literature was a powerful strand of apocalyptic and prophetic forces supporting the traditional Catholic religion at the popular level from the earliest decades of the French reformation. For Crouzet, the notion that the world would shortly come to an end was part of a belief system in which holy power was immanent, engaged mystically and prophetically in a mighty struggle against the forces of darkness. Everything in the world, spatially and temporally, had sacral significance. For traditional Catholics the novelty of heresy 'on the doorstep', within their midst as it were, was yet one more sign, alongside portents in the skies, monstrous births and miracles, of the imminent end of the world. To fight the heretics, to massacre and to destroy them, says Crouzet, was not just a desire to purify the world from the pollution of heresy; it was a more fundamental desire to be the conduit of God's wrath and to become part of God's immanence in the Last Days. The Old Testament provided a lexicon of language, symbols and gestures with which to evoke this immanence. So, innocent children were reported as playing a prominent part in the stomach-turning popular violence of the civil wars because they were seen as Christ-like bearers of God's blessing in the Last Days. Far from reflecting a 'natural' violence to be expected in sixteenth-century societies, the popular bloodshed of the civil wars took place in moments, according to Crouzet, of abnegation of society, when individuals were engaged in a sacral act. Hence the particularly gruesome cruelty meted out towards Protestants, the perverted mutilation of their bodies after their death. This was not sadism as we might understand it. Rather, the heretics were nonhumans, diabolic agents, and their pursuants were God's secret, avenging angels.

Huguenot propaganda, by contrast, sought to undermine the hidden agenda of Catholic violence by suggesting that it arose from profanity. Its perpetrators lusted after Protestant wealth and Protestant offices. Their motives were base and their emotions perverted. Their violence was a sign of a negation of God, rather than his immanence. Yet there was a calvinist violence too, although its psychological roots were different. It was human, rationalistic, cool – calculated and targeted to achieve a total Protestant reformation. Their first attack was upon images because calvinists did not accept the semiotics of Catholic holy power. Images were not the embodiment of God's immanence in this world. They were idols, profaning and desecrating His sovereign majesty. They had to be destroyed and, although in northern France iconoclasm remained at an elementary stage of gesture, in southern France it was more systematic, paralysing the lawcourts which sought to control it. Then came an iconoclasm towards other aspects of holy power. Preachers were interrupted during sermons, clergy were mocked in the streets and Catholic processions were held up to ridicule. Dislike and fear of priestly power was revealed in satirical broadsheets. The Roman church was portrayed as a world of 'fools', 'dogs', 'beasts', 'ravening wolves'. The priests, their animal lusts mocked before the public, were the inevitable victims, and the gruesome rituals of their suffering – disembowelling a speciality – took on the gestures and images appropriate to their circumstances.

Let us, without going at this stage into further detail, accept that, for whatever reasons, there was an asymmetry in the attitudes to religious violence in the French sectarian violence of the wars of religion between Catholics and Protestants. There is, however, another, and more fundamental, element of asymmetry and this is in respect of the evidence which we have of these massacres. On the one hand, there was a good deal of published printed propaganda relating to the events which occurred within French provincial cities and in Paris during this period. The first so-called massacre of the civil war period, that which occurred at Vassy in March 1562, was itself the object of various contemporary printed pamphlets.[14] There were numerous local incidents written up after the event, by one side or the other.[15] Many of these became the basis for compilations of massacre tales and stories, such as those which filled the later editions of Jean Crespin's Protestant martyrology, the already-cited *Histoire ecclésiastique* and other anthologies of such publications.[16] The hand of the energetic Genevan-based Simon Goulart (the Elder) is to be seen amongst many of those prepared amongst the Protestants. But the existence of these anthologies indicates that these pamphlets had a more enduring readership than we might imagine.[17] Such accounts of course each proclaimed themselves to be a 'true history' or a 'true account'; and each sought to dismiss the claims of the other side as to who had started the massacre and what its true intentions and purposes were, whilst advancing its own explanation for events.[18] They claim to reveal the secret intentions of the actors in the events, to spill the beans as to the secret political intentions of the participants, or the parties manipulating the events from a distance. As Simon Goulart said in his preface to the *Mémoires de l'Estat*:

> The memory of the massacres committed in several cities of France in the months of August and September of 1572, engraved in the hearts of an infinite number of men, made many wish that the treachery of the authors of these massacres not remain hidden in the shadows of forgetfulness and that the executioners of these abominable cruelties be punished as they deserved. So when it pleases God to bring us a good peace in which justice may be done, good people hope that innocent blood, spilled with such inhumanity, will win vengeance on the guilty. As for those who already by death have escaped from human punishment, or others who in various ways escape in the future, clearly people must be informed of what they did.[19]

So it is in these pamphlets that we find the well-articulated explanatory frameworks which became the focal points for later historical debate. The Duke of Guise has a secret aim to eliminate protestantism from the kingdom. The Prince of Condé has a plot to subvert the French monarchy and is using the Protestants to further his aims. The queen mother has an agenda all of her own to protect her sons and preserve the authority of the monarchy at no matter what cost to the nation. The seeds for the elaborate 'metahistory' of the massacre of St Bartholomew were already laid in the decade of sectarian tension before 1572 and the highly publicized debate which each successive cycle of incidents aroused.

We shall return to some aspects of the construction of this 'metahistory' later. Despite what Goulart claimed in his preface, however, the fact is that these were generally histories without actors – sometimes even without events described in a detailed form. They are detached and at several removes from the massacres which had actually taken place and the *dramatis personae* who had witnessed them. In these accounts, the question of what actually happened is subordinated to questions of why, and of whom to blame. Those descriptions which we do possess are second or third hand, manipulated and doctored for public consumption in various ways, and influenced by the accumulated stereotypes of how heretics in the Middle Ages had been expected to manifest themselves, or how the suffering martyrs of the early church had behaved in subtle fashions which are not easily taken into account. This is particularly so of the notorious massacre of St Bartholomew. Without exception, the contemporary published accounts which appeared in the few years after 1572 seek to exemplify the killing in varieties of familiar topoi: the patient, stoic Protestant magistrate, the corrupt and base-motivated assassin, etc. They explain the events as the responsibility of a young and weak king, unable to control his council, or the Machiavellian machinations of a wicked Jezebel of a queen mother, Catherine de Medici, who would stop at nothing to reinforce and sustain her authority over her son Charles IX, or the cynical plotting of a grandee, especially the Duke of Guise and his faction, or again the manipulations of a distant foreign power (Spain). The 'evidence' (such as it is) is generally so far removed from what actually happened, that it is, in one respect or another, almost always unsatisfactory. This is reflected in the ongoing debate about the responsibility for the massacre of St Bartholomew which has received additional recent supplies of popular oxygen from the success of the film *La Reine Margot*, with its replication of the conventional nineteenth-century *argot* account of Alexandre Dumas.[20] It is therefore impossible to use such evidence without substantial reserve and qualification as accurate accounts of what actually went on; since 'true histories' or 'summary and true discourses' is what they signally fail to provide.

For this reason, we need to pay more attention to the 'hidden transcripts' of the massacres, the personal testimonies, the secret histories of what went on, and to why there are (relatively) so few of them. They will not enable us to resolve the problems posed by the printed pamphlet evidence, but they will enable us to explain more clearly why they should not be expected to do so. By letting these more personal and individual testimonies speak for themselves in their more unguarded ways, we shall be able to learn more about the asymmetries of evidence which are fundamental to the limits of our understanding of them. The term 'hidden transcripts' is the one used by James C. Scott to describe the gossip, the stories, the gestures, the rituals used by the poor peasants of south-east Asia when talking about their lords and masters.[21] Such 'hidden transcripts' provide a measure of independence from the authority of their lords, and thus a degree of validation for themselves and their condition. The accounts of Huguenot victims who survived the massacres and were prepared to tell the tale of what they had seen and heard was not merely marked by a surprising independence (and hostility) towards established (especially princely) authority. They also reflected the networks of internal support and communication, of economic and psychological sustenance, which sustained the Huguenot remnants, especially after the massacre of St Bartholomew.

The first example of a personal testimony from a survivor is the tale of Jean de Mergey, a companion of François, Count of La Rochefoucauld.[22] Like many others, he survived by means of disguise and deception; by becoming other than he was. At the same time, he drew upon the multiple resources of clients and friends to secure his protection. La Rochefoucauld himself had been killed in the massacre, but his son (M. de Marcillac) had, like many of the survivors, found unexpected refuge in the house of one of the most extreme Catholics, someone who happened to be his kinsman, the sieur de Lansac. Jean de Mergey sent letters to Lansac's house on the rue Saint-Honoré asking to be rescued. For Mergey it was a miracle that his letters got through, for Lansac kept his house tightly barred and guarded during the events of the massacre. The first missive was refused by the porter and the second had to be sent almost as a secret message. They eventually met up, with a Catholic gentleman sent to give Mergey cover. He arrived at Mergey's door and said 'in a rude and threatening voice: "allons"'. Mergey's first thought was that he was about to be assassinated and he drew his sword. Once his fears were overcome, he was escorted to the relative safety of the rue Saint-Honoré. But, in Mergey's account, it is when he finally met up with Marcillac which he remembered most. For both men, the emotional tensions of the previous three days of massacre around them welled up along with their shared sense of an experience which could bear no discussion, and a solidarity which was born out of their anguish: Marcillac 'on seeing me threw his arms round my neck, holding me in this embrace for a long time, without saying a single word, with tears and sighs, and I the same'. This was what most stuck in Mergey's memory, the moment when he awoke from the trauma of the preceding events which he had more or less elided from his consciousness. Of the events themselves, he tells us almost nothing.

For Maximilien de Béthune, writing some thirty years after the events which he had experienced aged eleven-and-a-half, it is perhaps not surprising that the memory had faded.[23] Like Jean de Mergey and Marcillac, he was in Paris in 1572 to celebrate the marriage of Henri de Navarre to Marguerite of Valois, the famous 'noces brulantes' which was the prelude to the St Bartholomew massacre. He remembered being left alone by his governor and his tutor, whom he never saw again. He recalled shouts, the sound of the tocsin, and lots of confusion. He remembered deciding to try to make it from the rue de Reims to the collège de Bourgogne, not far away, where he knew he would be able to meet up with some school friends. He put on his school uniform and tucked a Book of Hours under his arm. He was stopped three times along the way by soldiers who expressed astonishment when he said that he was going to school. Of the scenes of carnage which he witnessed, he would only say that he remembered as though it were yesterday hearing 'the streets incessantly reverberating with these cries: "Kill, kill the Huguenots", and the clamour of those being murdered.' When he finally arrived at the college, he remembered having to bribe the porter to let him in and the fear of the college principal who told him that he had heard the rumour that they wanted to kill all the Protestants 'even infants at the breast, and Catholic women who were known to be pregnant by a Huguenot, on the model of the Sicilian Vespers against the French'. And here he firmly closes the door on further reminiscence – a childhood memory only half-opened up for investigation. But then, it was not altogether prudent for a minister of the first Bourbon king in the years after the civil wars to dwell too much on what had happened in the recent, turbulent past. That king was devoted to erasing the turbulent past, selectively and prudently shaping it to his own purposes. Here is one of the most remarkable features of the French civil wars; that individuals carried with them their memories, and knew that others with whom they had daily dealings, did so too. Leading massacrers, perhaps, saluted politely those who had seen members of their family suffer or their property sequestered; and yet, about such memories, all parties judged it best to remain silent, seeking (for all sorts of reasons public and private) to internalize them. Jacques-Auguste de Thou, for example, writing over thirty years after the events of 1572, elaborates the history of one of the massacrers, a member of the Paris militia, ensign Thomas Croizier (or Crozier). De Thou explains that he had often heard Croizier, a 'murderer deserving the scaffold', hold his hand up, 'raise his arm with inhuman vanity', and boast 'that he had killed more than four hundred men with this arm in the carnage' of Paris.[24] Even in this apparently personal reminiscence, however, things are not exactly as they might appear. Barbara Diefendorf, who has carefully examined the testimony and compared it with the other accounts of Croizier's exploits given by Goulart and by Crespin, notes that de Thou had every reason to want to paint Croizier in as black a light as possible.[25] He made him responsible for the death of the *parlementaire* judge Jacques Rouillard, and portrays him as personally cutting off the magistrate's head after toying with him as to whether he was going to die or not. The other accounts, however, claim that de Thou's own father, Christophe, was the instigator of Rouillard's death on the grounds that he (Rouillard) was an independent-minded judge who was pursuing a case of fraud against a fellow-judge who happened to be de Thou's close friend. De Thou, therefore, had every reason to want to find a scapegoat in his history for this assassination and Croizier provided a convenient name and face. The testimony is valuable, however, as a reminder of the way in which the continuing memories of the massacres interwove themselves into a metahistory of what had happened, even in the minds of individuals who had been present at the time.

Some Protestants interpreted their survival as an example of God's mysterious and remarkable secret providence. This was how Jacques de Caumont, another Gascon noble cadet like Marcillac, interpreted what had happened to him in Paris in August 1572.[26] He had expected to be part of the Protestant army and his first reaction to the bloody events unfolding before him had been to want to join what Protestant contingent would be formed to protect themselves. But his efforts were forestalled by a brother who was recovering from illness and whom he felt he could not leave. So he remained in his lodgings. He saw the Catholic troops batter down the door and pillage their property. He saw his father offer his own life providing that his sons were spared. He remembered a king's ransom being negotiated for his life (2,000 *écus*) before being led downstairs and ordered to tear his handkerchief into strips to make the sign of the cross which would be then pinned to his hat as a protection for him as he negotiated his way through the Paris mob.

They managed to reach the Louvre, which was where Caumont remembered the moment of his greatest fear: 'they fully believed that they were to be dispatched; because they saw many of their religion killed and thrown into the Seine, which in many places was already red with blood, they saw many dead bodies, including that of the sieur de Piles'. From there they were led by their Catholic captain to a safe house. Held captive by some Swiss soldiers, they waited until the ransom could be raised from amongst their kinsmen. They did not attempt to escape, or to evade their captors. The word of honour of a gentleman had been given and, in any case, Caumont's father declared that he was too old to do other than to be 'resolved to await God's providence, who will dispose of us according to His will'. Such passivity is common amongst Huguenot victims; it is as though they were complicit actors in the drama which was unfolding around them. For Diefendorf, there was much in the Huguenots' particular understanding of God's protection, their reading of the Bible (especially the Psalms) and their experience of the earlier civil wars, to explain this passivity. But, again, we must remember that so many of our examples of it come from the indirect and 'fashioned' accounts of the experience of massacre, designed to present to us a particular picture of Protestant endurance. However, in the case of the Caumonts, this was not the end of the story because, on the Tuesday morning, they were told that they were wanted for questioning by the king's brother, Henri de Valois, Duke of Anjou. They had their capes, hats and bonnets stripped from them and set out, accompanied by a lackey, to return to the Louvre, with the streets around it surrounded by soldiers. Suddenly and without warning, the soldiers cried '"Kill! Kill!"' 'First of all the eldest of the children was stabbed several times, crying as he fell:"Oh, my God! I am dead."' His father turned to try and help his eldest son, but was himself set upon and stabbed, falling on top of him. Jacques:

> covered in blood, but miraculously not wounded, cried too, as if inspired by heaven: "I am dead!", and at the same time fell between his father and his brother, and whilst on the ground, received yet more fierce blows, though not even his skin was pierced. God protected him so visibly that although the murderers robbed and stripped them, they never realised that one of them was not even injured.

There he remained until the end of the afternoon, his face on the ground, in his shirt-sleeves, lying beside his dead father and brother, until a groundsman from a tennis court tried to take his shirt off him and turned him over. 'Seeing him so young, he cried out: "Alas! This one's only a poor child. What a terrible shame, what could he have done wrong?"'. Encouraged by this expression of sympathy, Jacques de Caumont blinked and shook his head to indicate that he was not dead and the man pushed him back down on the ground, hissing that he wasn't to make a move 'because they're still here'. He returned somewhat later, put a cape around his shoulders and lifted him to his feet. He pretended to kick him and make him walk ahead of him. Some of the bystanders asked him what he was doing. 'Oh! This is only my little nephew who is drunk', he said. 'I'm taking him back to give him a good hiding'. He was led by the linesman back to his house, was given a back room and a straw mattress, and forced to part with the three jewels which he possessed. He was then given a disguise and only then, on Wednesday 27 August, did he finally make his escape.

Writing in 1595 for the benefit of her son, Philippe, the story of Charlotte Arbaleste's time in Paris in 1572 was told within the same Calvinist pieties; but, through them, an extraordinary tale emerges.[27] She wanted her son to learn, mark and inwardly digest her own life-story, just as she had done that of her father and her husband, both of whom were dead by the time of the massacre of St Bartholomew. Indeed, she was in Paris to settle the remnants of their affairs at the time that the massacre took place. In bed when her maid brought her first word of what was going on outside – things can scarcely have begun – she went to the window of her lodging to look out onto the rue Saint-Antoine and saw the town-guard and a crowd assembling, everyone with the (Catholic) white crosses in their hats. She recalled the confused succession of news as it became daylight, especially that of the death of her brother, one of the Admiral Coligny's adherents. Her main thoughts were for her three-and-a-half-year old daughter whom she despatched with a maid to the comparative safety of a relative, M. de Perreuze, living not far away in the rue Vieille-du-Temple. She followed later, leaving her house not long before a contingent arrived to look for her, and ransack it. They did not need long to work out where she might have gone and she resorted to hiding in a loft, from where, wondering whether they included those of her own child, she could make out the 'strange cries of men, women and children who were being massacred in the streets'. For a week, she led a shadowy, hidden existence, sheltering where she could, spending one night in the house of the captain of the watch and ward, a leading figure in the massacres. On Monday 2 September, she made her escape from Paris, dressed as a common wench, on a boat destined for Sens. Even then, her disguise evidently could not cover her accent, background and evident fear. When asked for a passport (which she did not have) 'they began to say to me that I was a Huguenot and that I would have to be killed'. It required the testimony of one of her friends in high places and the quick-wittedness of a good woman who stood up for her, before she could proceed on a journey with more frightening incidents until she finally reached the safety of Sedan.

These accounts of survivors are fascinating (and there are others which might also be cited – Charlotte d'Arbaleste's future husband, Philippe du Plessis Mornay, for example, or Renée Burlamachi), but not in the way that we might expect. They tell us remarkably little about the massacre of St Bartholomew itself. Their protagonists were too young, too frightened, too surprised or too hidden to have any general perspective on what was happening around them. They provide us with fragments of history, fractions of reality which we (any more than they) cannot piece into a whole. Individuals could neither explain to themselves or to others, the curious mixture of events in which they had been involved. They could not provide any sense of the larger picture; how many had been killed in Paris during the three days of St Bartholomew; how it had all started, and why. Denis Crouzet cites a contemporary verse which struggles with this perplexing ignorance:[28]

> Numbering the dead
> Is an impossibility.
> Endless, ceaseless the bodies
> During the terrible fury.
> Men as well as women
> Bundled into the river
> To carry the news
> Boatless to Rouen.

They could not even explain adequately to themselves the paradoxes of the affronts which they experienced to all known sociabilities, deferences, ways of behaviour. Nor could they account for the curious, unknown, inexplicable acts of kindness, common humanity and decency which also happened to them, and which had helped to save them. Above all, they had no means of explaining to others, in language which could possibly convey it, the full emotional intensity of what they had experienced. 'Incredible' and 'extraordinary' rival 'inhumane' 'barbarous', 'barbarism', 'butchery' and 'massacre'; but they barely served the turn. The reality could be measured only in impression and poetic reality. The scale of things, for example, was to be conveyed by the colour of the river Seine, turned to red by the number of bodies dumped in the river. To re-present the reality was to testify to a horrible dream, where reality seemed no longer what it had been, or what it should be:[29]

By the Gods, what is before my eyes? Is it not some dream
Which makes me slumber and imagine something untrue?
Have I really seen this trouble, or rather is it true
That all those here mentioned have felt the dread
But equitable hand of the great God, the Father
Of all that is here below ...?

For the survivors, in any case, the emphasis was as much upon the
sense of relief and release once they had escaped to comparative
safety as upon witnessing to what they had experienced in Paris.

The Protestant survivors from the St Bartholomew massacre in
Paris were, in any case, not in any state to tell their story immediately afterwards. It is no coincidence that all four of the testimonies
which we have alluded to come from accounts at least twenty-five
years after the events they are describing. An equivalent lapse of
time has been noted for many victims of the Holocaust in our own
century. Some were doubtless heavily traumatized. Poor little
Gillette Le Mercier, for example, was forced (according to Crespin)
to witness the execution of her parents before being 'baptized' in
their blood during the massacre in Paris. Her tormenters issued the
horrible threat that, if she ever became a Huguenot, 'the same
would happen to her'. In a petition, filed before the courts on 28
February 1573, she is described as a 'poor little girl unable to
speak'.[30] There must have been many who were incapable, if not of
speaking, at least in the short term, of contemplating what they had
witnessed, and who elided it from their immediate consciousness.
There were prudential as well as deeper reasons, in any case, for
keeping quiet. The Protestants had relied on their private networks
of support and sustenance during the early civil wars. It was only
amongst friends of the faith that they had really trusted themselves
to speak. And, at least in northern France, many of those networks
were cut away by the massacres of 1572. Even this private world
(our testimonies all come from the relative security of exile in Sedan,
in Geneva, or in the Midi) found it difficult to confront the uncomfortable reality – which was that the Protestants, on the whole, had
not fought back and resisted massacre; and, more serious still, that
many of their coreligionists had decided to convert back to catholicism in the wake of St Bartholomew. For those that abjured, their
survival of the massacre represents nothing if not their humiliation.
Hugues Sureau du Rosier, writing from the position of one who had
abjured only to reconvert once more thereafter, put it like this: it
was 'evidence of the indignation of God, as if he had declared by
this means that he detested and condemned the profession and exercise of our religion ..., as if he wished entirely to ruin this church

and favour instead the Roman'.[31] The amnesia of silence prevented their recalling this particular wrath of God.

Amongst Catholics, too, there is an equivalent absence of direct testimony, albeit for somewhat different reasons. The butchers themselves, for evident reasons, kept quiet. What would induce them, beyond the folly of bravura, to lay themselves open to possible revenge attack, if not legal recrimination? One of the most striking features of the troubles on French streets in the civil wars is how few names one can put to the faces of the Catholic crowd in comparison with the vulnerable, exposed specificity of the Protestants involved. As Barbara Diefendorf points out for Paris, we know the details of only a handful of individuals for the events of 1572. The same asymmetry is, incidentally, to be noted in Crespin's martyrology for the riots or other incidents which occurred during the trial and executions of heretics before 1560 and in the early 1560s.

For the notables, there were some who faced the wall, locked, bolted and guarded the doors, and waited for the fury to subside. Jacques-Auguste de Thou, for example, reported that he spent most of the days during and after the massacre shut up in the family home, afraid to go out because the sight of blood made him physically sick.[32] In those cases where there was some warning of the sectarian tensions to come, some notables, both Catholics and Protestants, found it convenient to head for their country estates and await better times.[33]

Local notables had also little to be proud of during these disturbances. Their position was, generally speaking, an unenviable one. They were frequently compromised by the elected officers of the watch upon whom they had to rely for keeping the peace. At the moments of greatest tension – in the spring of 1562, for example, or again in the immediate aftermath of the St Bartholomew massacre – they were also unsure of the steer from above.[34] Toulouse was certainly not unique in finding that its local élite was divided and fighting amongst itself – divisions which made their mark upon the city's insurrection and resulting massacre in May 1562.[35] It is not surprising that city magistrates as well as sovereign court judges willingly collaborated with the clauses of royal edicts of pacification to erase all mention of sectarian troubles from their registers. Some, like the Parlement of Paris, chose to strike through the relevant judgments (leaving them legible without too much difficulty). Others, such as (for example) the consuls of Lyon, instructed their town secretary to tear the passage out relating to the treatment of the city's Protestants in 1572, but to cover themselves with a note as to what the offending passage had contained.[36] So, although the destruction of the legal record is far from complete, it is certainly so patchy that, in only a few instances can the secondary accounts be confirmed (and even then only in the most general terms) by first-hand reports, carrying some degree of legal veracity.[37] For ordinary Catholics, their sense of 'chaos and confusion' (the terms used by Etienne Pasquier – usually a curious and well-informed contemporary) was perhaps a reflection of their knowledge that, in times of panic, rumour and misinformation were as significant as anything else; a shrewd awareness that they were witnessing moments when group fears and group activities were out of the control of any one individual or set of individuals. Their fear was transparent, and well founded. One anonymous account from Paris in 1567, told of his receiving orders to keep a good watch at night, to have arms at the ready, to stay indoors, keep a lantern alight until daylight, and keep buckets of water at the ready. 'That night', he continued, 'they found in the street the skin of a man who had been flayed alive, which terrified pious souls. If someone said a word in favour of the authors of the rebellion, it was permitted to kill him, which was the fate of many'.[38] These were not the circumstances to enquire too closely about the activity, beliefs and behaviour of one's neighbour.

It was only to be expected that, in the relative absence of coherent 'explanations' of what had happened from those who had either suffered, perpetrated, or been nominally responsible for keeping order during these massacres, the myth-making metahistory to which we have already referred should have taken over. The myth-makers were able to provide (inevitably partial, one-sided and speculative) explanations where none were otherwise available. Explanations – or exculpations – were certainly needed, especially by those in authority; and, equally so, for incomprehending foreigners, for whom the events in France were as bafflingly barbaric as the affairs of Bosnia to the majority of Western Europe this past two years. Reacting to the news of the St Bartholomew massacre, the Earl of Leicester wrote of 'that cruelltye that I think no Christian synce the heathen tyme hath hard of the lyke', whilst Lord Burghley declared, 'these French tragedies ... cannot be expressed with tongue to declare the cruelties'.[39] Propagandists and pamphleteers therefore created a history where there was none. But, in doing so, they inevitably drew on their imaginations and on a complex and inherited stock of absorbed stereotypes. To illustrate the point, let us cite the example of the famous 'affaire Saint-Jacques', when a secret conventicle of Protestants meeting in Paris was sprung, a riot ensued and many Protestants were arrested. It was described in the diary of a Provins priest, Claude Haton.[40] He recounted the granting of sexual favours ('fraternal and voluptuous charity') which went on at the conventicle before the candles were extinguished, along with incest,

infanticide, and cannibalism. His description owes almost nothing in
detail to the events in Paris; but, as Luc Racaut has strikingly
demonstrated, it owes a good deal to the accounts of the early Christian
Church to be found in Tertullian along with an explicit
borrowing from a passage from Guibert of Nogent's autobiography
which refers to the heretics at Soissons at the beginning of the twelfth
century.[41] Similarly, Georges Bosquet, the magistrate from Toulouse,
whose account of the insurrection and subsequent massacres in that
city in May 1562 constitutes one of its major sources, chronicles the
diabolic and monstrous elements of heresy.[42] The latter was a dangerous
and wicked monster, 'hideous and detestable ... nourished
and suckled, engendered even, by the ambition and avarice of its
miscreant perpetrators who, without any vestige of religion, secretly
plotted the entire overthrow of the human race'. When he comes to
describe the early Protestant meetings in Toulouse, his views are
entirely dominated by this set of stereotypes, and this was with an
explicitly didactic purpose. It was in a publication in 1561 by his fellow
judge in Toulouse, Jean Gay, that Bosquet had found
conveniently assembled all the materials from Toulouse's Albigensian
past which confirmed the prejudices underlying his views.[43]
Protestant accounts of massacres were similarly influenced by stereotypes
from the past and also carried a didactic message. The account
of the sufferings of the 'martyrs' of Lyon in 1572 drew implicitly on
those of its early Christian martyrs – indeed in a later edition it was
bound alongside a homily against idolatry and an account of the
persecution under the Roman Empire.[44]

The published pamphlets and accounts of the massacres compete
with one another, contradicting each other's claims and counter-
claims. The process is highly complex and often impossible to
unravel. How wary we should be, therefore, of taking the published
accounts of French massacre at their face value! Georges Bosquet's
history of the Toulouse events of 1562, for example, is a kind of
hidden agenda for a Protestant riposte in the *Histoire Ecclésiastique*
almost two decades later. The two accounts are mirror images of
one another, the one a tit-for-tat response to the other. Should we
take these published sources as evidence for distinctive underlying
group consciousnesses towards religious violence? This is the
essence of Denis Crouzet's magisterial work. An (unpublished)
Protestant recital of the impact of St Bartholomew at Troyes suggests
we should be wary of constructing too neat a typonomy, either
of Catholic 'immanence', their destructive violence embodying
God's will, or Protestant 'human' violence, their iconoclastic energies
reflecting the need for mankind to reform the world in
accordance with God's will.[45] The account begins with the Protes-

tant recalling that he had a distinct sense that these tragic events in the city had been predicted, portended by heavenly numerology, astrology and geology. The peace of Saint-Germain had been signed in September 1570. The ninth month of the year, according to some poets, was an auspicious month, it being the period of a conception leading to the birth of an infant. But, looking back on things ('my remembrance of the past'), this author had strong doubts. A child 'having been nourished and clothed for about two years became a great monster and cruel murderer of men'. He noted that Mars dominated over all the other planets throughout 1572, a bad omen for the Protestants. Then came the strange tremors and earth movements in the city of Troyes, which led to joists falling to the ground, a house collapsing onto the street, and a further structural collapse in a building which led to a woman being trapped and killed. To these ill-omens he attached the devaluation of foreign coin, high prices, a poor harvest, and 'several illnesses ... most of which [were] very strange and principally [affecting] the young'. This individual (it may have been Pierre Pithou) sought to explain the subsequent rounding-up of Protestants in the city and their murder in the city's prison in the wake of the news from Paris, not merely in terms of greedy and unscrupulous individuals driven by the devil, but as immanent within the world, predicted by strange and unnatural events. In the extraordinary fears and suspicions aroused by sectarian tension and fed by rumour, people could see what they wanted to see (hawthorn trees, for example, blooming suddenly in late summer after St Bartholomew in Paris, touching which apparently worked curative miracles) and even the sceptical could be disposed to believe what they wanted to believe.

Notes

1. *Histoire mémorable de la persécution et saccagement du peuple de Merindol et Cabrières et autres circonvoisins appelez Vaudois* (1556).
2. G. Baum, E. Cunitz and E. Reuss, eds, *Corpus Reformatorum (opera Calvini)* (59 vols, Braunschweig, 1863-80), vol. 49, col. 136.
3. Towards the end of the sixteenth century in France the term 'massacre' would be appropriated by the Catholic League to describe (in particular) the assassination of the Duke and Cardinal of Guise at Blois in December 1588; this is particularly evident in the numerous League pamphlet publications of that period; e.g., *Portraict et description du massacre proditoirement commis ... en la personne de Henry de Lorraine ...* (Paris, 1588?); *Discours en forme d'Oraison funèbre sur le massacre et parricide de Monseigneur Le Duc et cardinal de Guyse* (Paris, 1589?); *Remonstrance faicte au Roy par Madame de Nemours [Anne d'Este], sur le massacre de ses enfans* (Paris, 1588; 1589); *La nullité de la pretendue innocence et justification des massacres de Henry de Valois ...* (Paris?, 1589).

4. 'Massacre' occurs six times in the English translation of Du Bartas; animals 'massacre' one another, people are 'massacred' and the 'Machiavellian Brains' of politique princes acting without God's blessing also engineer 'publique, (lawfull) Massacre'.

5. See, for example, the phrase occurring in William Warner's verse epic, *Albions England* (1592 edition); Christopher Marlowe's *The Massacre at Paris* (written *c*.1592; published in the incomplete surviving edition, 1593/4), incorporates both the 'massacres' of 1572 and the 'massacres' of 1588 with the play culminating in the death of the Machiavellian duke of Guise and the lines: '*Vive la messe!* Perish Huguenots!/ Thus Caesar did go forth and thus he died'.

6. This pattern was noted in Denis Richet, 'Aspects socio-culturels des conflits religieux à Paris dans la seconde moitié du XVIe siècle', *Annales E.S.C.*, 32 (1977): 764-89, esp. 770-71.

7. Janine d'Estèbe, *Tocsin pour un massacre* (Toulouse, 1974), chap. 9, 143-55, citing Michelet, 143.

8. Penny Roberts, *A City in Conflict: Troyes during the French Wars of Religion* (Manchester, 1996); Mark Greengrass, 'The Anatomy of a Religious Riot in Toulouse in May 1562', *Journal of Ecclesiastical History*, 34 (1983): 367-91.

9. Philip Benedict, *Rouen during the Wars of Religion* (Cambridge, 1981), chaps. 3 and 4; Barbara Diefendorf, *Beneath the Cross: Catholics and Huguenots in Sixteenth-Century Paris* (New York and Oxford, 1991).

10. J. M. Davies, 'Persecution and Protestantism: Toulouse, 1562-1575', *Historical Journal*, 22 (1979), 31-51.

11. N. Z. Davis, 'The rites of violence', *Past and Present*, 59 (1973); reprinted in her *Society and Culture in Early Modern France* (Stanford, 1975), chap. 6.

12. Ibid., 173.

13. Denis Crouzet, *Les Guerriers de Dieu: la violence au temps des troubles de religion (vers 1525–vers 1610)* (2 vols. Paris, 1990).

14. E.g. *Destruction du saccagement exerce cruellement par le Duc de Guise et sa cohorte, en la ville de Vassy*, in L. Cimber and F. Danjou, eds, *Archives curieuses*, 1st series (14 vols. Paris, 1834-40), vol. 4, 103-56.

15. Many of these titles are recorded in the splendid bibliography to Crouzet, *Guerriers de Dieu*, vol. 2, 633-93. This is a listing constructed, however, from the Bibliothèque Nationale and should not be regarded as entirely exhaustive. Provincial publications are not always represented there. So, for example, the interesting *Discours du massacre de ceux de la religion reformée fait à Lyon par les Catholiques Romains* ([Lyon], 1572), probably written by Jean Ricaud, is not recorded in it – a title which may serve as one example of the richness of the pamphlet record for these incidents.

16. Jean Crespin, *Histoire des Martyrs*, eds D. Benoit and M. Lelièvre (3 vols. Toulouse, 1899); Simon Goulart, *Mémoires de l'Estat de France sous Charles Neufiesme contenant les choses les plus notables, faictes et publiés tant par les catholiques que par ceux de la Religion ...* (3 vols. Meidelbourg [Geneva], 1576); cf his later collections for the later period of the Catholic League: *Mémoires de la Ligue, contenant les événemens les plus remarquables depuis 1576 ...* (6 vols. Amsterdam, 1758).

17. On Simon Goulart, see L. C. Jones, *Simon Goulart, 1543-1628* (Geneva and Paris, 1917); and R. M. Kingdon, *Myths about the St Bartholomew's Day Massacres, 1572-1576* (Cambridge Mass. and London, 1988), esp. 2-6.

18. E.g., amongst numerous titles which might have been cited: Nicolas Regnault, *Discours veritable des guerres et troubles advenus au pays de Provence ...* (1564); *Histoire véritable de la mutinerie, tumulte et sedition faite par les prestres de sainct-Médard ...*, in Cimber and Danjou, eds, *Archives curieuses*, 1st series,

vol. 4, 49-62; *Advertissement particulier et veritable, de tout ce qui s'est passé en la ville de Tholose depuis le massacre et assassinat* ... (Toulouse, 1589); *Discours veritable de l'entreprise sur Troyes a demy prises par les heretiques* ... (1590).

19. Goulart, *Mémoires de l'Estat*, vol. 1, fols. I-IV; translated and cited in Kingdon, *Myths*, 4-5.

20. For the debate, see Jean-Louis Bourgeon, 'Les légendes ont la vie dure: à propos de la Saint-Barthélemy et de quelques livres récents', *Revue d'histoire moderne et contemporaine*, 34 (1987), 102-16, and the same author's, *L'assassinat de Coligny* (Geneva, 1992); Marc Venard, 'Arrêtez le massacre', *Revue d'histoire moderne et contemporaine*, 39 (1992), 645-61. Denis Crouzet, *La Nuit de la Saint-Barthélemy: un rêve perdu de la renaissance* (Paris, 1994). The latter is a remarkable reappraisal, including a review of the evidence as to whom (if anyone) was incriminated in the events leading up to the massacre. It has substantially influenced the argument of this chapter in the section which follows.

21. James C. Scott, *Domination and the Arts of Resistance: Hidden Transcripts* (New Haven and London, 1990).

22. *Mémoires de Jean de Mergey, gentilhomme champenois in Collection complète des mémoires relatifs à l'Histoire de France* (ed. M. Petitot), vol. 34 (Paris, 1823), esp. 70-76.

23. David Buisseret and Bernard Barbiche, eds, *Oeconomies royales*, vol. 1 (1572-1594) (Paris, 1970), esp. 12-15.

24. Jacques-Auguste de Thou, *Histoire de Monsieur de Thou des choses arrivées en son temps* (3 vols. Paris, 1659), vol. 3, 369.

25. Diefendorf, *Beneath the Cross*, 169.

26. Le Marquis de La Grange, ed., *Mémoires authentiques de Jacques Nompar de Caumont duc de la Force* ... (4 vols. Paris, 1843), vol. 1, 46-50.

27. *Mémoires de Madame de Mornay. Edition revue* ... (Paris, 1865), vol. 1, esp. 51-71.

28. Crouzet, *La nuit de la Saint-Barthélemy*, 33.

29. Ibid., 35; cited from *La Mort prodigieuse de Gaspart de Coligny, qui fut Admiral de France* ... (Paris, [1572]).

30. Jean Crespin, *Histoire des martyrs*, vol. 3, 678-80; Diefendorf, *Beneath the Cross*, 220.

31. [Hugues Sureau du Rosier], Confession et recognoissance ... (Basel, 1574), 7-8, cited in Diefendorf, *Beneath the Cross*, 142.

32. De Thou, *Mémoires* ... (*Nouvelle collection des mémoires*, J-F. Michaud and J-F. Poujoulat, eds) (Paris, 1838), vol. 11, 276.

33. To take a Protestant example, Nicolas Pithou from Troyes was absent from the city at the moments of greatest danger for the Protestant church there. His account of its turbulent history in those periods must have been constructed from the testimony of others: see M. Greengrass, 'Nicolas Pithou: experience, conscience and history in the French civil wars', in Anthony Fletcher and Peter Roberts, eds, *Religion, Culture and Society in Early Modern Britain* (Cambridge, 1994), 18.

34. For the confusions surrounding royal orders after St Bartholomew, see Philip Benedict, 'The Saint Bartholomew's Massacres in the Provinces', *Historical Journal*, 21 (1978), 211-34.

35. Greengrass, 'The anatomy of a religious riot', 367-91.

36. Charles Péricaud, *Notes et documents pour servir à l'histoire de Lyon* ... (Lyon, 1842), 71.

37. For one example of confirmation, see Diefendorf, *Beneath the Cross*, 101, where she was able to find some elements of corroboration for Crespin's story of the death of the Paris passementier, Philippe Le Doux and his wife at St Bartholomew.

According to Crespin, his wife was so close to giving birth that the midwife was already in attendance. She pleaded with her assailants to be allowed to have the baby and even attempted to escape. She climbed to the attic but was caught, stabbed, and thrown into the street below. The half-born child, its head poking out of the mother's abdomen, was left to die in the gutter. In this case, we have part of the judgement (sentence) in a subsequent lawsuit involving the distribution of the property taken from their house. The legal documentation tells us the name of the assailant (which Crespin had either not known or neglected to mention). But the depositions only tell us 'that they were killed'. They present a clinical and minimalist account of what had happened in comparison with Crespin's stomach-turning recital.

38. B. Diefendorf, *Beneath the Cross*, 80.

39. Edmund Lodge, ed., *Illustrations of British History* (4 vols. London, 1791), vol. 2, 74-76.

40. Claude Haton, *Mémoires contenant le récit des événements accomplis de 1553 à 1582* (2 vols. Paris, 1857), vol. 1, 50-53.

41. Luc Racaut, 'Incest, infanticide and cannibalism: the use of medieval typology to describe French protestants in sixteenth-century catholic polemic' (unpublished paper). I am grateful to the author for his permission to cite this paper here.

42. G. Bosquet, *Histoire sur les troubles advenus en la ville de Tolose, l'an 1562* (Toulouse, 1595). This account had originally been published in Latin in the immediate aftermath of the affairs it describes; but it was banned and copies of it confiscated by orders of the *conseil privé* on the grounds that it contravened the clause of the edict of pacification of 1563 obliterating the memory of sectarian incidents during the previous civil wars.

43. Jean Gay, *Histoire des scismes et heresies des Albigeois conforme à celle de present ...* (Paris, 1561).

44. The *Discours du massacre de ceux de la religion reformee fait à Lyon* [originally published in 1572], was republished in 1574 with, *Une ... remonstrance aux Lyonnais lesquels ... continuent à faire hommage aux idoles and an Epistre des anciens fideles de Lyon et de Vienne, contenant le récit de la persecution qui fut dressé contre eux sour l'Empereur Antoninus Verus.*

45. Bibliothèque Nationale, Paris, MS Dupuy 333, fols. 65v-75.

CHAPTER 4

MASSACRE AND CODES OF CONDUCT IN THE ENGLISH CIVIL WAR

Will Coster

On Christmas Day, 1643, the inhabitants of the Cheshire village of Bartholomy became aware of approaching soldiers.[1] The troops were royalists under one Major Connaught. Around twenty neighbours, probably all men, retreated to the greater security of the tower of St Bartoline's church. The pursuing royalists entered the body of the church and set fire to rushes, pews and forms. Surrounded with smoke and threatened by flame, the occupants called out for quarter and, when their surrender had been accepted, they left the tower. Once outside, they were stripped of possessions and clothes, then stabbed, or had their throats slit. Twelve, including the minister John Fowler, died from their wounds.

This incident gives a very different impression from that which was once the prevailing view of the English Civil War, as a civilized conflict, fought according to chivalrous codes of gentlemanly conduct: in the striking phrase of the parliamentary general William Waller a 'war without an enemy'.[2] As recently as ten years ago Blair Worden concluded that the English experience of civil war was 'uncommonly civil'.[3] This image has often been contrasted sharply with that of the Thirty Years' War in Europe, which has been seen as a bloody and vicious contest.[4] John Morrill and John Walter have noted that the English war was not 'stained by the bloody violence that marked religious conflict on the continent'.[5] Ironically, as views of the real level of violence in the European wars have become generally more optimistic, recent historiography has emphasized the impact of the civil wars: which affected all three Stuart kingdoms, dragged on for almost twenty years and, at times, saw one in five of the male adult population in arms.[6] An important part of this new image of the war are the numerous atrocities carried out on soldiers, and civilians, by forces from both sides. This paper will investigate the reasons behind those acts of this period, like the events at Bartholomy, which may be classified as massacres.

This necessitates some definition of what a massacre is.[7] The first criterion is one of scale. Although not all would agree, the assumption of this paper is that massacres are distinctly different from murders of individuals; although it is not possible to set inalterable rules about when multiple murders become massacres. Equally important is that massacres are not carried out by individuals, but by groups. Numerous fatalities inflicted by one person (although very unlikely given the state of seventeenth-century weaponry) are multiple, or mass murders, not massacres. To define a killing as a massacre also implies the use of superior, even overwhelming, force: a more equal struggle would simply be a battle. The force is also usually concentrated, as the use of the term massacre implies not only numerous deaths, but that they be in relative proximity. Finally, as all the above suggest, the term is most often employed when the act is outside the normal moral bounds of the society witnessing it. Thus legal, or even some quasi-legal, mass executions, like those of leveller leaders at Burford in 1647, have been excluded from this study. In any war, but perhaps especially in a civil war, death is usually inflicted on a large scale, but this killing is often acceptable to the society or societies involved, because it is placed within prescribed moral bounds. In peace, these bounds are defined by state and civil law, in war new criteria are applied. Under these rules killing is usually more likely, but rarely unrestrained. In the context of the seventeenth century these codes of conduct are usually referred to as the 'laws of war'.[8] Barbara Donagan has recently demonstrated how widely accepted and disseminated these laws were, through military handbooks, soldiers' catechisms, and articles of war, which were required to be read by officers to their troops.[9] However, in the sudden transition from civil peace to armed conflict of the summer of 1642, these laws may not have been clearly understood or applied. What is more important, their significance may have been lost on the majority of the population, who did not take up arms.

It has become fashionable of late to refer to the distinct conflicts of the middle decades of the seventeenth century, which involved the three Stuart kingdoms of England, Ireland and Scotland, as the 'British Civil Wars'. However, this paper is largely concerned with the events of the first civil war in England and Wales, which began in the summer of 1642 and ended in the spring of 1646. Nevertheless, it remains important to note that this 'First Civil War' was both preceded and succeeded by other conflicts and all three kingdoms were involved, in some respect, in military encounters with each of their counterparts between 1638 and 1651.

The wars in Scotland and Ireland have generally been depicted as more brutal and bloody than the conflicts in England. In the most recent major study of the experience of war in seventeenth-century Britain, Charles Carlton upholds the generally accepted view that the level of violence in peacetime England and Wales was low in comparison with the other two Stuart kingdoms. He notes that, 'the fighting in England, at least, was remarkably free from atrocities, largely because of the lack of ethnic or ideological differences'.[10] In contrast, the massacres of Irishmen and women at Drogheda and Wexford are usually considered the most serious blots on Cromwell's moral record.[11] Similarly, the destruction of the remnant of the Marquis of Montrose's army and its camp followers, after surrender at Philiphaugh, is a byword for excessive covenanter zeal.[12] However, contrary to the previously dominant image of a civilized and limited war in England, it is possible to find a number of instances that fit the above definition of massacre in the war in England and Wales; more than in the immediate, preceding, contemporaneous, or subsequent conflicts in Scotland or Ireland.

There is no need to look for a complex reason why atrocities of this sort appear to have been more prevalent in the kingdom of England than elsewhere. The strategic nature of the war in England, and its longer duration, both suggest that massacres would be more likely. The First Civil War was, by most standards, a confused struggle, without clear strategic battle lines. Battles were numerous, with over fifty set-piece conflicts in the field and innumerable lesser actions, such as raids and clashes between scouting parties. These conflicts were rarely decisive, and this, added to the localism that dominated the early part of the war, made sieges and assaults the most effective means of securing territory. The total numbers of this form of conflict are difficult to ascertain, but there were almost certainly in excess of two hundred formal sieges, assaults and opposed raids in England alone.[13] In a siege, but particularly an assault, massacres were far more likely. As can be seen in the table, fifteen out of eighteen massacres took place after (or during) an attack on some form of garrison. However, the prevalence of certain types of military conflict does not in itself explain why massacres occurred.

The chronology of massacre in the war is also interesting: six of the identified massacres were in 1643, seven in 1644 and five in 1645, but none in the part-years of conflict of 1642 and 1646. This appears to suggest that level of military activity, which was greatest

Figure 6.1 Massacres in the First English Civil War

Place	Date	Perpetrators	Victims
Abbotsbury, Dorset	–/10/1644	Parliamentarians (Ashley Cooper)	20+? Soldiers
Bartholomy, Cheshire	25/12/1643	Royalists (Connaught)	12 Civilians
Basing House, Hampshire	14/10/1645	Parliamentarians (Cromwell)	100+ Soldiers and Civilians
Birmingham, Staffordshire	3/4/1643	Royalists (Rupert)	? Soldiers and Civilians
Bolton, Lancashire	28/5/1644	Royalists (Rupert)	78+ Soldiers and Civilians
Bradford, Yorkshire	1/7/1643	Royalists (Newcastle)	10 Soldiers and Civilians
Burton-on-Trent, Staffordshire	9/7/1643	Royalists (Henrietta Maria)	30 Soldiers and 20 Civilians?
Canon Frome, Herefordshire	22/6/1645	Scots Covenanters (Leven)	? Soldiers
Cheriton, Hampshire	29/3/1644	Parliamentarians (Waller)	120 Prisoners
Holt Castle, Denbighshire	–/2/1644	Parliamentarians	13 Soldiers
Hopton Castle, Herefordshire	13/3/1644	Royalists (Woodhouse)	31 Soldiers
Howley Hall, Yorkshire	22/6/1643	Royalists (Newcastle)	? Soldiers
Leicester	29/5/1645	Royalists (Rupert)	? Soldiers and Civilians
Naseby, Northamptonshire	14/6/1645	Parliamentarians (Fairfax)	100+? Women
Newcastle-upon-Tyne, Northumberland	19/10/1644	Scots Covenanters (Leven)	? Soldiers and Civilians
Preston, Lancashire	20/3/1643	Royalists (Derby)	? Soldiers and Civilians
Shrewsbury, Shropshire	22/2/1645	Parliamentarians (Mytton)	50 Irish Soldiers
White Sykes Close, Marston Moor, Yorkshire	2/7/1644	Parliamentarians (various leaders)	? Soldiers

in the middle years of the war, was more significant in the creation of massacres than any growing animosity between the protagonists. Between August 1642 and the winter of 1642/3, warfare was at its most mobile, as both King and Parliament expected to decide the issue in a single clash between concentrated armies.[14] However, the much-anticipated encounter, at Edgehill in Warwickshire on 23 October, proved anything but decisive. When the royalist advance on London stalled at Turnham Green, the two sides went into winter quarters and the scene was set for another three-and-a-half years of conflict. The next two years saw the peak of military activity, with the adversaries balanced until the battle of Marston Moor, on 2 July 1644. This, the largest battle fought on British soil, involved a combined parliamentary force under the Scottish commander Alexander Leslie, the Earl of Leven, Lord Fernando Fairfax, and the Earl of Manchester. They decisively defeated the royalists under the King's nephew, Prince Rupert, and the royalist commander in the north, the Marquis of Newcastle. From this point, the north ceased to be an effective theatre of war and the royalists were on the defensive. A clash between the reorganized parliamentary New Model Army and the King's only remaining significant field army, at Naseby in Northamptonshire on 14 June 1645, doomed the royalist cause and almost all that remained were mopping-up operations.

Geographically, the distribution of massacres approximates to the major areas of conflict in the war. Although there were no borders and lines of defence in the conventional military sense, there were zones controlled by the two sides. The only region largely to escape conflict was that south and east of London and East Anglia, which remained in parliamentary hands throughout the war. Parliament also dominated throughout the war in the East Midlands, south-west Yorkshire and the Pembroke peninsula. Until 1644 the royalists were the major force in the north, the west and Wales. Many of these 'royalist' areas were disputed twice, once when initially gained by the King in 1642-3, and again in the later stages of the war when overall defeat meant their fall to the victorious New Model Army. As a result of these factors the war was fought out across a border zone that ran from the south coast to the Humber. Both sides made frequent sallies into this zone, like those carried out by the royalists that resulted in defeats at Cheriton in 1644 and Naseby in 1645. Thus, as can be seen from the accompanying map, rather than conveying any grand significance, the geography of massacres reflects closely the confused nature of the war, and that it affected most regions of the country.

The responsibility for the eighteen massacres identified was distributed evenly between the royalist forces and the parliamentarians

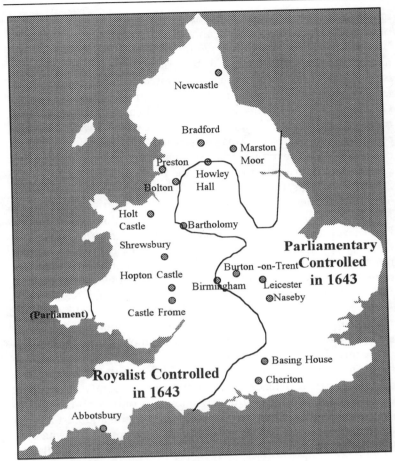

Figure 4.2 Massacres in England and Wales 1642-1646

combined with their Scots allies (who crossed the border in January 1644). However, six of the nine massacres carried out by royalists occurred in 1643, two in 1644 and only one in 1645. In contrast, massacres perpetrated by the Scots and parliamentary forces, were evenly distributed between 1644 and 1645. As the fortunes of the parliamentarians generally waxed throughout the war, this again indicates that it was victory that tended to lead to massacre. However, it is also possible to suggest that parliamentary soldiers were becoming less tolerant of the defeated, perhaps in a response to real or alleged royalist atrocities.

In the relatively recent body of academic interest in this topic, historians have tended to search for psychological, or sociological, explanations of behaviour among those carrying out massacres.[15]

Such explanations tend to work better for Ireland and Scotland than for England. Here racial and religious enmity was a constant. Furthermore, the soldiers perpetrating the crimes, like the New Model Army in Ireland, were often more professional, and therefore arguably more inured to the brutalities of war, than the 'civilians in uniform' who found themselves fighting in 1642 or 1643. Clearly such factors are a part in any comprehensive explanation of the problem, but they are not sufficient in themselves. It is important to note that the actions of those perpetrating atrocities have a specific historical context and a local dynamic. An examination of the historical context is crucial to understanding massacres in the civil wars. Apart from these conflicts, such acts were almost unheard-of events in early modern England. The argument of this paper is that it was the context of war that made such atrocities possible and, at the same time, notable.

Atrocities were a key propaganda tool in the pamphlet war that shadowed the physical one. Part of the explanation, on the one hand, for brutal acts of war and, on the other, for their definition as barbaric atrocities (a contradiction that plays a part in the perception that they were massacres), was their employment as propaganda. A demonstration of partiality in the reporting of massacres can be seen in one parliamentarian broadsheet of 1646 which referred to the Bartholomy incident. It exclaimed, 'how could wee forget that bloody massacre of Byron in Cheshire, that in coole blood murthered no less than 1500, that fled to a Church for shelter, by fiering the same, and all these innocent poore soules burnt therein'.[16] The incident has often been attributed to Lord John Byron, the royalist commander in Cheshire at the time. This is because of an 'intercepted' letter from him to the Marquis of Newcastle, which was subsequently printed by his parliamentary opponents. In it, he is supposed to have boasted of having put the villagers to the sword, 'which I find the best way to proceed with these kind of people, for mercy to them is cruelty'.[17] Since there is no collaborative evidence that Byron was even at the massacre, and despite his reputation as the 'Bloody Braggadocio', it seems somewhat unlikely that he wrote such a letter. But what cannot be ignored is that the events like those at Bartholomy (especially when the figures were inflated by a factor of over one thousand) presented the protagonists with clear propaganda victories.

The use of atrocities as propaganda creates a number of problems for their study. Firstly, it indicates just how unreliable newspaper accounts of such events could be. Secondly, it is possible to suggest that massacres were created out of the moral discrepancy between the codes of soldiers and of the people in general. The former were subject to the demands of necessity and the laws of war, and the latter still concerned with preserving values and laws more easily applicable in peace.

The laws of war current in the period were in many ways highly draconian. Attacks on neutral civilians were not acceptable under these laws, neither were prisoners, once captured, available for execution (unless they were specifically found guilty of particular crimes).[18] However, most importantly for the study of massacres, a besieging force was entitled to slaughter an entire garrison on entry, if quarter had been refused when offered. Besieging troops who stormed a town were also within their rights to sack and plunder. In such a case the position of civilians within a town was anomalous. With no universal uniforms until 1645, and often no uniforms at all, men in particular, might be considered in a similar light as defending troops, easily becoming victims of soldiers hot in pursuit of their property.

The potential severity of these rules in a successful assault may explain a number of massacres during the war. Events at Leicester in May 1645, which were used against the King at his trial, horrific though they were, were also within the rules of military conduct. The town was taken by storm after a breach had been made in its defences by artillery. The parish registers of the town suggest that at least seven hundred people died in the short period of combat, and the longer period of sack that followed.[19] Given the overwhelming force possessed by the attacking royalist army, this seems likely to have included large numbers of defending parliamentary soldiers and civilians. Stories of orders for mass slaughter, used against the King, should be treated with scepticism, but the most generous parliamentary account speaks of the deaths of 'some women and children amongst the multitude of the rabble of common soldiers', and one royalist recalled plundering turning to slaughter with 'no quarter given in the heat'.[20]

Although the King was present at Leicester, the command of the operation was undertaken by his nephew, Prince Rupert. Rupert had an unenviable reputation during the war as a merciless and inhuman slaughterer.[21] The accusation was not hard to make, as he was in command of the perpetrators of two very similar massacres, at Birmingham (in 1643) and Bolton (in the following year). As at Leicester, in each case the massacre was part of the sack of a town, which resulted from storming through a breach in the defences.

Estimates for the dead at Bolton have ranged from two hundred up to two thousand. Even the lower figure would make this the worst massacre of the war for loss of life. However, the parish register of the town gives the names of only seventy-eight individuals, noting, 'All these of Boltonn slayne on the 28 of May, 1644', which seems to imply the list is comprehensive.[22] Perhaps more significantly, all three individuals mentioned as murdered in the anonymous parliamentarian eyewitness account published three months later, were also named in the register.[23] However, the parish register may exclude defending troops not from the town, who are known to have been present, and those buried elsewhere. The parliamentary account mentions the number of 1,200 or 1,500 murdered. Such a figure is given credence by the fact that royalist accounts speak of 1,600 or even two thousand killed. But these versions may have taken their lead from parliamentary propaganda. It is only the seventy-eight named individuals, including two women, but at least some soldiers, that can be said with any certainty, to have been killed.

Rupert's unenviable record in this regard may result from a number of factors, not least his position as an important general, and therefore the likelihood that he would command in more sieges. Perhaps, more significantly, he was an impatient, even impetuous commander. Therefore it is not surprising to find him attempting to take towns by the risky technique of storming, rather than the time-consuming one of a full siege. However, the most important factor may have been that Rupert considered himself to be a professional soldier and the obvious fact that he was a German prince. He was probably more aware of continental practice regarding the laws of war than many of his colleagues and perhaps less willing to mitigate their effects. Rupert's career appears to present a number of instances where massacres were carried out within a set of military moral bounds. Many Englishmen (particularly when they were likely to receive a sensational and partial account of events) would not have accepted these bounds.

Other massacres can be placed within the bounds of the laws of war. The assaults on Newcastle, in October 1644, and Canon Frome Castle in Herefordshire the following year, by the Scots under the Earl of Leven, were almost certainly accompanied by sack and the death of defenders and inhabitants, although the Scots strenuously denied it.[24] Leven was also an experienced soldier: as former commander of the Swedish army he was well used to conditions and codes prevalent in the Thirty Years' War. Again, he did not originate from the society in whose war he participated. Neither, of course, did Queen Henrietta Maria, nominal commander at the taking of Burton-on-Trent in July 1643. The royalist paper *Mercurius Aulicus* claimed that 'her majesties goodnesse and clemency was so exemplary, and like her royall selfe, that she forbad any violence to be offered to the town'.[25] Hostile accounts stated that thirty soldiers had their throats cut and twenty civilians were drowned.[26] What is clear is that the town was taken by assault and plundered.

If these are instances of the brutal laws of war being applied by foreigners, there are also instances of their implementation under the leadership of native-born Englishmen. This was the case when the Earl (later Marquis) of Newcastle, ordered the storming of Howley Hall in Yorkshire in 1643.[27] However, by personal intervention Newcastle did manage to save the life of the parliamentarian governor, suggesting he did not welcome his soldiers' excesses. A more obvious example of the application of the laws of war can be seen in the career of Oliver Cromwell. The events at Drogheda and Wexford have already been noted and are dealt with in detail in the essay by Robin Clifton in this volume. Cromwell also commanded at the final assault on Basing House in Hampshire, on 14 October 1645. The dead included a quarter of the 400-strong garrison, a number of refugee noblemen, and six Catholic priests. A woman also had her head smashed in when she attempted to defend her father from attack.[28]

But surely Charles Carlton is right to suggest that although the laws of war allowed such brutality, this does not in itself explain why they were enforced.[29] Of the hundreds of actions against garrisons in the First Civil War, only a small proportion resulted in the sack of the town, house, or castle concerned. Many of these actions ended in success for the defenders, and others, where the garrisons were defeated, were ended by terms. The governors of towns, houses and castles had an unenviable task once a siege began. If they surrendered too soon, they faced the very real possibility of execution by their own side. If they miscalculated and were successfully stormed, the sack of the town was likely. Once through the defences, attacking troops expected plunder as a reward for their face-to-face encounter with death. Such behaviour has also been seen as a natural reaction to the sudden relief brought by victory.[30] Having waded through smoke, bullet, cannon ball and over the bodies of their comrades, often in a realistic expectation of imminent death, to breach the defences of a town, soldiers often experience an acute elation and sense of release. This state is akin to drunkenness and is frequently the precursor to acts of extreme irrationality and violence, like the royalist cavalry after they forced the breach of Bolton in 1644 crying, 'kill dead! kill dead!'.[31] Just as important is the reaction of the defeated defenders here described as, 'the poore amazed people', who also tend to move into a state akin to drunkenness, but becoming passive in attitude.[32] This not only invites attack, but facilitates it.

Warfare in built-up areas is also notoriously vicious. Such surroundings radically alter the circumstances of battle. Enemies confront each other suddenly and at much closer quarters in buildings, than they do in the field. Flight, the most common resolution of conflicts on a battlefield, is frequently unavailable in such areas and physical combat is much more likely. Use has also been made by military historians of the concept of 'critical reaction', originally developed by the zoologist Hediger.[33] This suggests that reaction to a threat is determined by distance. Beyond a certain distance animals tend to retreat when threatened, but within it they attack. John Keegan applied this concept to the French attack on Hougoumont farmhouse during the battle of Waterloo. He argued that breaches of the perimeter by a storming party triggered just such a critical reaction among the defending British Foot Guards. This resulted in the massacre of every intruder except the drummer boy, but a similar reaction may be triggered by successful invaders when coming face-to-face with their defeated enemy.

It is also important to note the psychological function of defences that exist besides the physical one. While walls, ramps and ditches provide cover from enemy weapons and slow assaults, they are just as important in supplying a definition of territory for both defender and attacker. The attacker has a clear, but often imposing objective. The defender has a line to hold and a sense of ownership. In this way assaults are territorial battles and so have been seen as arousing particular anxiety and aggression that perhaps made bloody resolutions more likely. But, although these general points must be kept in mind, each massacre varied greatly in its particulars.

What can be seen is that massacre was more likely where casualties among the attackers had been high. This appears to have been the case both at Leicester and Hopton Castle, in Herefordshire, which fell to the royalists in March 1644. Thirty-one defenders were stripped, tied back-to-back, then had their throats slit and were thrown in a ditch.[34] It is also evident that commanders in these situations often did not attempt to restrain their men. We have the account of the parliamentarian Sir Anthony Ashley Cooper, who commanded at the taking of the Abbot's House, Abbotsbury in Dorset, in October 1644. Unable to fight their way in, his troops wrenched open a window and forced-in burning faggots of furze through the gap. The flames began to rage out of control, then, he wrote, 'they cried for quarter, but having beat diverse men before it, and considering how many garrisons of the same nature we had to deal with, I gave the command that there should be none given'.[35] The slow death of the defenders was, however, cut short as their powder store exploded, killing soldiers from both sides. Other commanders have rarely left us such frank descriptions of their motives, but they can occasionally be glimpsed. For Rupert at Bolton, it was perhaps the hanging of a captured Irish soldier over the walls by the defenders, that resulted in an unwillingness to restore order.[36] It may also have been the town's religious reputation as 'the Geneva of the North'. For Cromwell at Basing House, it may have been that the owner, the Marquis of Winchester, was a known Catholic and the garrison was considered a haven for his coreligionists. As they stormed the defences at dawn the New Model Army's battle cry was 'down with the papists'.[37]

Events at Bolton and Basing suggest race and creed were major reasons why military violence occasionally spilt over into massacre. Their effects can be seen exacerbating a situation which a general, willingly, or unwillingly, had allowed to develop. The impact of religious and racial tensions, can also be seen in a number of massacres that were apparently in contradiction of the laws of war. The destruction of the Marquis of Newcastle's Whitecoats at White Sykes Close, towards the end of the battle of Marston Moor, may have been because their parliamentary opponents assumed they were Catholics. We know that a member of one of these regiments, who had been taken a few weeks before, had red and blue crosses of silk on his undyed uniform. One captor took these for 'an ensigne ... of some Po[p]ish Regiment'.[38] After the parliamentary victory of Cheriton, Hampshire in 1644, 120 prisoners, many of them Irish, were executed.[39] At Naseby, the horse of the New Model Army slashed the faces of poor women found in the royalist baggage train, and according to some accounts, killed a hundred of these camp followers. Apparently the troopers believed these to be prostitutes and/or Irishwomen. In reality, most were probably Welsh, as a number may have been the wives of royalist infantry.[40]

Fear of foreigners and Catholics combined in the hatred of the Irish, which can be seen as a major element among those atrocities committed by parliamentarians. However, it is important to note that this was not simply xenophobia, or religious fanaticism, suddenly being expressed, but instead the outcome of a long history of perceived atrocities and threats on both sides. In the case of Catholics, the parliamentarians may have had the sixteenth-century massacres of St Bartholomew's Day in France and the Spanish Fury in the Netherlands in mind. In England such events were widely reported and printed in accounts like that of the poet George Gascoigne on the horrific sack of Antwerp by the Spanish in 1576.[41] In addition, more recent events like the sack of the Protestant city of Magdeburg in 1631, built on this fearsome picture of Catholic inhumanity.[42] These events may have done more than simply create tensions that found expression in massacre. Such circumstances placed the Catholics, but the Irish in particular, outside the laws of war. Thus they were exempted from the normal protection of these codes. The use by Charles I of both Irish troops and of the returning English army under the Earl of Ormonde (which had been sent to put down the rebellion, but which the parliamentarian press managed to label as Irish), gave Parliament another propaganda victory. These troops were in an exposed position if captured by the enemy. In the eyes of many they had acted outside the acceptable codes of conduct and were thus excluded from them. From October 1644 in England, and December 1645 in Scotland, this exemption was formally recognized by acts of Parliament, which stated that any Irishman captured in arms was to be put to death.[43] Irishmen were legally dehumanized and demonized, a group outside the laws of war and therefore uniquely vulnerable to the danger of massacre.

The Irish and Catholics were not, however, the only groups excluded from these codes. It appears that any enemy believed to have broken the laws were placed outside their protection. One example of this occurred at the battle of Adwalton Moor in July 1643, when the defeated parliamentary troops fled from threats of 'Bradford Quarter'. This was a reference to the indiscriminate killing of a royalist officer in front of that town, six months before.[44] At Hopton Castle a number of the attackers were Irish, and therefore less likely to have respected codes of conduct from which, after all, they were themselves excluded.[45] Finally, the massacre of prisoners after Cheriton was justified by accusations that houses were to be set alight by retreating royalists.[46] In cases like these, it is possible to see why the laws of war did not prevent massacres from occurring. But codes of conduct remained important even when breached. Those writing on the side of the perpetrators of these massacres were often careful to justify such atrocities by indicating how the rules did not apply. What can also be seen is that each event had its own dynamic. Detailed sources, where they exist, suggest a gradual breakdown of codes of conduct. Rarely was there a sudden violent and isolated expression, of social, religious, or racial tensions.

However, one instance where these factors do not appear to have played a part was at Bartholomy on Christmas Day 1643. The most reliable source is parliamentarian in bias and states specifically that quarter had been given to the villagers who took refuge in the church tower, and that the massacre was 'contr'y to the Lawes of Armes'.[47] The massacre was all the more horrific because it occurred on a holy day and violated ideas of sanctuary; because the victims were not soldiers, and because they were stripped before being attacked (perhaps to prevent their clothes from being ruined). The incident is puzzling because by retreating to the tower the villagers must have left their property (and perhaps their womenfolk) less well defended. Whatever they were carrying hardly seems worth the effort of smoking them out. Finally, once captured, and when the situation was relatively orderly, they were then cut down, apparently in cold blood. But the sources may not reveal all the circumstances behind the massacre of which we can gain only hints and indications. An unsubstantiated local tradition, gathered from the great-grandson of a survivor, suggests that the incident was sparked off by the shooting of a royalist, from the tower, by the son of the local clergyman.[48] We also know that one of the perpetrators was a local Cheshire man. After the Restoration he cited the incident as evidence he should be granted a pension. This seems to indicate that events were not regarded locally with the shame such an atrocity might be expected to attract. The only justification we have for the incident is that the victims were 'malignant persons', which might suggest that their attackers did not realize they were civilians. Finally, we have the name of the leader of the royalists, Major Connaught, and the position, only a few miles from Nantwich where the garrison included a number of Irishmen. Even here, it is possible that what appears to be a cold-blooded and irrational killing, was part of a wider history of racial mistrust, and escalating hostility. What is more important, the use of the incident as a tool of national propaganda indicates how important the existing codes of conduct were in shaping actions and allegiances in the war.

There also remains the problematic issue of whether these breakdowns of the codes of conduct were a common, or a rare occurrence. Such a calculation is a difficult one. It has to be noted that most sieges, and even a large number of assaults, ended relatively peacefully, or even amicably. Perhaps, more revealingly, massacres after battles were very rare. This contrasts sharply with circumstances north of the border. Here each of the Marquis of Montrose's string of victories was followed by a long and bloody pursuit, accounting for the deaths of up to half the enemy's numbers. The usual figure in England was between 10 and 20 percent. In England, when a battle was lost, surrender was by far the most common result for soldiers who could not escape. Last stands, like those at White Sykes Close, were extremely rare, suggesting quarter was usually offered, and even expected. Perhaps because English and Welsh private soldiers could change sides, while officers might be exchanged, massacres were unnecessary and even likely to detract from a victorious army's strength.

The relatively low homicide rate of early modern England, and the rarity of massacres in the rest of the period, was perhaps due to the racial unity and relative peace of the kingdom. These were benefits not available to those in large sectors of the continent. Nevertheless, there were vulnerable groups within a society that was imbued with a heady mix of xenophobia and anti-popery. In 1642, when the physical and moral upheaval of the civil war destroyed stability and created an explosive racial cocktail, the spectre of massacre raised its ugly head. Such events were minor compared with even the most conservative estimates of the atrocities of the Dutch Revolt and the Thirty Years' War. They can, however, be seen as an unavoidable consequence of any protracted warfare in early modern Europe. The urban nature of much of the combat of the Civil War made massacre increasingly likely as the conflict became a war of attrition. Thus, the First Civil War suggests that the English were not so different from their Celtic or European contemporaries: that they were subject to similar prejudices and codes of conduct. When suffering circumstances similar to those of their neighbours, seventeenth-century Englishmen reacted with a similar mixture of brutality and horror.

Notes

1. J. Hall, ed., *Memorials of the Civil War in Cheshire and the Adjacent Counties by Thomas Malbon of Nantwich, Gent., and Providence Improved by Edward Burghall, Vicar of Acton, near Nantwich*, The Record Society for the Publication of Original Documents Relating to Lancashire and Cheshire [hereafter RSPODRLC], 19 (London and Redhill, 1889): 158-59.
2. Cited in R. Ollard, *This War Without an Enemy: A History of the English Civil Wars* (London, 1976), 85.
3. B. Worden, 'Providence and politics in Cromwellian England', *Past and Present*, 109 (1985): 141.
4. For the debate on Germany, see H. Kamen, 'The economic and social consequences of the Thirty Years' War', *Past and Present*, 39 (1968); T. K. Raab, 'The effects of the Thirty Years' War on the German economy', *Journal of Modern History*, 36 (1962); S. H. Steinberg, *The 'Thirty Years' War' and the Conflict for European Hegemony, 1600-1660* (London, 1966), 91-122 and J. Theibault, 'The rhetoric of death and destruction in the Thirty Years' War', *Journal of Social History*, (1993), 245-90. However, for a rather more pessimistic comparison see I. Roy, 'England Turned Germany? The Aftermath of Civil War in its European Context', *Transactions of the Royal Historical Society*, 5th ser., 28 (1978).
5. J. S. Morrill and J. D. Walter, 'Order and disorder in the English Revolution', in A. Fletcher and J. Stevenson, eds, *Order and Disorder in Early Modern England* (Cambridge, 1985), 141.
6. C. Carlton, *Going to the Wars: The Experience of the British Civil Wars, 1638-1651* (London, 1992), and B. Donagan, 'Codes of Conduct in the English Civil War', *Past and Present*, 118 (1988): 65-95. M. Bennett, 'Contributions and assessment: financial exactions in the English Civil War, 1642-46', *War and Society*, 4 (1986), and S. Porter 'The fire raid in the English Civil War', *War and Society*, 2 (1984).
7. For an alternative definition see, E. Carlton, *Massacres: an Historical Perspective* (Aldershot, 1994), 1, and B. Bailey, *Massacres and Account of the Crimes Against Humanity* (London, 1994), 1.

8. G. Parker, 'Early Modern Europe', in M. Howard, G. J. Andreopoulos and M. R. Shulman, eds, *The Laws of War: Constraints on Warfare in the Western World* (Yale, 1994), 48; J. Childs, *Armies and Warfare in Europe, 1648-1789* (Manchester, 1982), 22-24; and for a more problematic contribution to the debate, see T. Merton, *Henry's Wars and Shakespeare's Laws, Perspectives of the Law of War in the Later Middle Ages* (Oxford, 1993), esp. 89 and 95-101.

9. Donagan, 'Codes of Conduct', 73-87.

10. Carlton, *Going to the Wars*, 260.

11. See the assessment in A. Frasier, *Cromwell Our Chief of Men* (London, 1973), 357.

12. C. V. Wedgewood, *Montrose* (London, 1952), 115.

13. Carlton, *Going to the Wars*, 154-55, identifies 198 out of 645 actions in England as 'sieges', however this is clearly an underestimate as preliminary research indicates that there were at least this number of opposed attacks on towns alone.

14. For a recent and balanced account of operational aspects of the war see M. Bennett, *The English Civil War* (London, 1995).

15. Carlton, *Massacres, an Historical Perspective*, 2.

16. Anon, *England's Wolfe with Eagles Claws, The Cruel Impieties of Bloud-thirsty Royalists, and Blasphamous Anti-Parliamentarians, under the Command of that Inhumane Prince Rupert, Digby, and the Rest. Wherein the Barbarous Crueltie of our Civil Uncivil Warres is Briefly Discovered* (London, 1646).

17. J. Vicars, *Magnalia Dei Anglicana, Gods Arke Overtopping the Worlds Waves, or the Third Part of the Parliamentary Chronicle* (London, 1646).

18. G. Parker, 'Early Modern Europe', 48.

19. J. Wilshere and S. Green, *The Siege of Leicester: 1645*, (Leicester, (1970) 1972), 11.

20. Anon, *A Perfect Relation of the Taking of Leicester with the Severall Marches of the Kings Army Since the Taking Thereof* (London, 1645), and R. Symonds, *Diary*, Camden Society (London, 1859), 18.

21. The most recent biography provides a useful guide to Rupert's military career, but virtually ignores this important aspect of Rupert's image, see F. Kitson, *Prince Rupert, Portrait of a Soldier* (London, 1994), 176.

22. A. Sparke, ed., *The Registers of the Parish Church of Bolton*, Lancashire Parish Register Society (Privately Printed, Bolton, 1913), 465.

23. G. Ormerod, ed., *Tracts Relating to Military Proceedings in Lancashire during the Great Civil War*, Chetham Society (1844).

24. R. Howell, *Newcastle-upon-Tyne and the Puritan Revolution: a Study of the Civil War in North England* (Oxford, 1967), 166-67. P. Gaunt, *The Cromwellian Gazetteer: An Illustrated Guide to Britain in the Civil War and Commonwealth* (Stroud, 1987), 79.

25. *Mercurius Aulicus*, 18 July 1643.

26. I. G. Phillip, ed., *The Journal of Sir Samuel Luke*, Oxford Record Society (Oxford, 1947), 117. See also the balanced assessment in R. Sherwood, *The Civil War in the Midlands, 1642-1651* (Stroud, 1992), 45-46.

27. P. R. Newman, ed., *Companion to the English Civil Wars* (New York, Oxford, Sidney, 1990), 74-75.

28. P. Young, *Oliver Cromwell and his Times* (London, 1962), 74.

29. Carlton, *Going to the Wars*, 258.

30. P. Watson, *War the Mind, The Military Uses and Abuses of Psychology* (London, 1978), 242-50.

31. Ormerod, *Tracts*, 192. Not, as stated in Carlton, *Going to the Wars*, 175, the siege of Preston.

32. H. Arendt, *On Violence* (London, 1969), L. Branson and G. W. Gothals, eds, *War Studies from Psychology, Sociology, Anthropology* (New York, 1964).

33. J. Keegan, *The Face of Battle: A Study of Agincourt, Waterloo and the Somme* (London, 1976), 147-48.

34. Historical Manuscripts Commission, *Calendar of the Manuscripts of the Marquis of Bath, Preserved at Longleat Wiltshire*, vol. 1, 29-30.

35. Cited in Carlton, *Going to the Wars*, 172-73.

36. Ormerod, *Tracts*, 190.

37. W. Emberton, *Love, Loyalty, the Close and Perilous Siege of Basing House, 1643-1645* (Privately Printed, Bedfont, 1972), 89-90.

38. Cited in P. Haythornthwaite, *The English Civil War, 1642-1651: An Illustrated Military History* (Poole, 1983), 86. See also P. Young, *Marston Moor 1644: The Campaign and the Battle* (Warwick, 1970), 136-37.

39. J. Adair, *Roundhead General: A Military Biography of Sir William Waller* (London, 1969), 148.

40. M. Ashley, *The Battle of Naseby and the Fall of Charles I* (New York, 1992), 90.

41. G. Gascoigne, *The Spoyle of Antwerpe* (London, 1576).

42. Donagan, 'Codes of Conduct', 68-70.

43. On the treatment of the Irish see the important survey in R. N. Dore, ed., *The Letter Books of Sir William Brereton*, SPODRLC, (2 vols. 1990), vol. 2, 594-602.

44. Newman, *Companion*, 15.

45. Charles Carlton indicates that the royalists believed that poison bullets were being used against them, but gives no source. The account of the parliamentarian Captain Priamus Davies does mention that they believed the royalists were using such bullets at Brampton. Historical Manuscripts Commission, *Bath*, vol. 1, 23 and 36-39. See Carlton, *Going to the Wars*, 259.

46. Adair, *Roundhead General*, 148.

47. Hall, ed., *Memorials of the Civil War*, 159.

48. E. Hinchliffe, *Bartholomy: In Letters From a Former Rector to his Eldest Son* (London, 1958), 95.

CHAPTER 5

'An Indiscriminate Blackness'?

Massacre, Counter-Massacre, and Ethnic Cleansing in Ireland, 1640-1660[1]

Robin Clifton

I

Between 1640 and 1660 all three of Charles I's kingdoms were ravaged by civil war, and atrocity and massacre marked the wars in all three. But, as the 'English', 'Scottish' and 'Irish' essays in this collection show, there were marked differences between the three kingdoms concerning the nature, extent, and causes of these episodes of unregulated killing. Though historians now increasingly agree that England's civil war was more desperate and bloody than has been commonly supposed, the number of massacres committed was low, perhaps surprisingly so. In Scotland too massacre was limited by circumstance, time and place. Among the three kingdoms it was only in Ireland, it seems, that civil war unleashed humanity's full capacity for wholesale and pitiless slaughter.

There are good reasons for regarding the civil war in Ireland as more atrocity- and massacre-ridden than those of the other two kingdoms. The core of the conflict was a struggle for land and power between Protestant settlers and the native Catholic Irish, and the religious division was intensified by differences in language, social structure and cultural values. Protestant Englishmen in the seventeenth century felt a contempt for Irish people, culture and religion so deep and comprehensive that it could fairly be called 'racial'. Many examples could be given of this attitude to the Irish and their religion; two of the more notorious will suffice here. In 1644 the English Parliament ordered that any Irishman captured under arms in England was not to be treated as a prisoner of war: he was to be summarily executed. And secondly, in 1649, no less a person than Oliver Cromwell bluntly told an Irish garrison that this same English Parliament would 'never permit the public practise of catholicism' in Ireland.[2] Death for any armed Irishman captured in England; no toleration for his faith in his home country. Such intolerance and hatred should lead, one would suppose, to a particularly 'dirty' war in Ireland.

As indeed it appears to have done. To the present day two massacres and a third 'celebrated atrocity' are remembered from mid-seventeenth-century Ireland. The first massacre was the one which began Ireland's civil war, in October 1641; it accompanied a rebellion by the Catholic Irish against the Protestant settlers, which developed into a hysterically reported mass killing of the latter. Then, after a long and bitter civil war, prolonged and made more savage by multiple foreign interventions, the Irish fighting was ended by Oliver Cromwell's whirlwind campaign of 1649-50, during which his troops massacred the garrisons of two towns they besieged, Drogheda and Wexford – a second set of massacres, still remembered with bitterness today. And finally, following the Cromwellian reconquest, Protestant settler hegemony was cemented by an 'ethnic cleansing' atrocity, the forcible mass deportation of the defeated Irish to the far west of Ireland, the infamous choice of 'Hell or Connaught' of the 1650s.

Further evidence for a massacre-ridden civil war in Ireland appears to come from population figures. Though military and civilian deaths from civil war were not light in England or in Scotland, in neither country did war inflict a clear drop in population level. It was otherwise in Ireland. Up to 1641 the population had risen steadily: one million in 1500, 1.4 in 1600, 2.1 in 1641; but then there occurred a sharp fall so that numbers stood at 1.7 million by 1672. After this, renewed growth took the population to 2.2 million in 1687, and 2.8 in 1712. By far the greater part of this massive decline – some four hundred thousand people or 19 percent of the 1641 population – took place in the 1640s and 1650s, and was the direct or indirect result of over a decade of warfare. By comparison, England's civil wars cost approximately 180,000 lives, or 4.5 percent of a population of over four million.[3] Ireland's civil war death toll is comparable to the devastation suffered during the Second World War by countries such as the Soviet Union, Poland, or Yugoslavia, and suggests that the war-time massacres, which so contributed to these horrific modern figures, also occurred in mid-seventeenth-century Ireland.

Three propositions then seem to emerge about the Irish civil war. First, that there existed ample causes for massacres to accompany any fighting between the settlers and the native Irish: divisions over culture, religion and language; English hatred and contempt for the 'backward' Irish; competition for land, office, work. Secondly, several large-scale and well-known massacres did take place in the 1640s, and many more may be presumed to have occurred, given the desperate nature of the fighting, and the evidence of the population figures. Thirdly, as a consequence of these two points, that this was indeed a time of 'indiscriminate blackness' for Ireland. However, this essay will argue that while these propositions are true in part, each needs substantial qualification; and that the qualifications discussed below not only modify our view of Irish history during a truly crucial period, but also extend our understanding of the process of massacre in significant ways. Four key events will be considered: the rebellion and massacres of 1641, the civil war which ensued, the Cromwellian massacres at Drogheda and Wexford, and the forced population clearances of the 1650s.

II

If the subject was not so grim, and its results not so dire, the events of 1641 in Ireland could be termed 'massacre by mismanagement'. On 22 October 1641, without any warning or obvious immediate cause, large numbers of the Irish Catholic population rose in revolt against the English settlers, who held an increasing proportion of the land and political power.[4] The initial rebellion took place mostly in the north-eastern province of Ulster, but though a simultaneous attempt to seize Dublin failed, within days the rising spread to other areas. The rebels normally attempted to capture strongpoints such as castles and fortified houses, though many ordinary farmhouses were also taken. Settlers who resisted were sometimes killed, but in its first days the rebellion was relatively bloodless. This followed the strict instructions of its leaders, who within days had issued a proclamation asserting their loyalty to the King, declaring indeed that they had his warrant for their action, and calling for a calm and non-violent takeover of power by the Irish under their sovereign lord, King Charles I.

Events, however, very quickly slid out of the control of the Irish leaders, or of anybody else. Many settlers were expelled from their farms and houses to die on the roads of cold, exhaustion or mal-treatment; or after a while they were simply killed in cold blood by their captors. But others began successfully to resist the rebels, and in turn killed them mercilessly when opportunity offered. By early 1642 a spiralling war of rebellion, resistance, and revenge had engulfed Ireland. Perhaps as many as two thousand settlers were directly killed in the first three months of the rebellion, and another four thousand died from exposure, and other causes, after being expelled from their homes. These figures were greatly exaggerated by English pamphlet writers, for whom the rebellion became a constant news item: week by week Protestant death tolls in the tens of thousands were reported, totals of one to two hundred thousand were announced, and by 1646 the quasi-official account produced for Parliament by Sir William Temple set the number of Protestant 'casualties' at three hundred thousand. This when the total Anglo-Scottish settler population in the whole of Ireland numbered no more than 125,000.[5]

What had happened? Recent work on the rebellion has led to several important conclusions. It is clear that neither the Irish leaders nor their followers had any general intention or plan to massacre the settlers. It is equally clear that the rebellion was prompted by no recent intolerable oppression of the Irish by the Anglo-Scots settlers. It was planned and initiated by some of the leading aristocratic figures of Irish society who had very limited aims, but who then lost control when the mass of the Irish population joined in to follow their own agenda which, it became evident, was more sweeping than that of their leaders.[6] Even so, the mass of the participants also did not plan or intend any massacre. But thousands of deaths did follow from the rebels' actions, and these must be examined in more detail.

The core aim of the aristocratic plot which detonated the rebellion was limited and specific: to secure recognition of the so-called 'Graces', a set of measures guaranteeing that Irish land-holding tenures would not be overturned by the imported forms of English law, so giving more security to Irish landholders. The Irish believed that in 1628 they had been given a promise that the Graces would be implemented, in exchange for generous taxes voted to the Crown by the Irish Parliament. However, the promise and the Graces were ignored by successive Lords Lieutenant, particularly Strafford, who treated both the Irish and the settlers with impartial contempt and severity. Irish leaders nursed their grievance until the King's crisis with the Scots in 1637 appeared to give them their opportunity. For three years, tortuous negotiations took place with Strafford and with the King over the possible raising of an Irish army to beat down the Scots, in return essentially for action over the Graces.

But though Strafford was prepared to raise a small (and mostly Protestant) Irish army of four thousand men, both he and the King shrank from the dangers of using large Irish Catholic forces against the Scots, and the talks lapsed. They were revived again, however, at the end of 1640 when the King faced a new crisis, this time with his English Parliament. Accepting that Charles would still refuse to use an Irish Catholic army against his mainland critics, the Irish lords planned this time to follow the example of the King's Scottish and parliamentary opponents. They would mount a coup – bloodless, non-violent, and ostensibly in support of the King – against his enemies, which would force Charles to negotiate with them; just as first the Scots, and then the English Parliament had forced the King into negotiations and concessions with them. In one coordinated blow they would seize strongholds in Ulster, Dublin and elsewhere, thus cancelling the political strength of the settlers, and forcing the King to treat with them if he wanted to maintain his authority over Ireland. In this way the Graces would be secured, and Charles might also be forced to allow public celebration of the mass in Ireland, and the repeal of Poynings' Law, thus ending the Westminster Parliament's control over business in the Dublin Parliament.[7]

Several points were crucial if the scheme was to succeed. There must be no violence: negotiations could only follow from a bloodless coup (as in Scotland and in England). The King's ultimate sovereignty over Ireland must be respected: there could be no hint of real independence. There could be no general demand for the reversal of land confiscations made up to 1640: the settlers were here to stay, and the Graces were strictly a guarantee for the future, not a reversal of the past. There would be no attack upon Scottish settlers: the English Parliament was the target, and so only English strongholds would be seized. (Leaving the Scots alone would also divide the Protestant opposition, and demonstrate the measured and controlled nature of the action). Demands concerning the Catholic Church would have to be kept muted. Tactically, the seizure of strong points must be sudden, coordinated, and quickly successful. And above all, the lords must remain in control of events from first to last.

The rebellion failed in virtually every one of these conditions. To carry out their limited and non-violent 'loyal' coup, the Irish lords needed the 'muscle' of their servants, retainers and dependants, to seize the Protestant strongpoints. But these dependants, the middling and lower sorts of the native Irish, had their own grievances against the settler community. The newcomers had taken from them land, employment, prosperity, and (consequently and at least as important) social standing. They had done this over many years, and more by the 'normal' processes of economic competition, purchase and debt than by crude political land confiscation: the settlers were simply more attuned to the growing market, and more determined to get ahead in a new land, than their local Irish competitors. This did not, however, make the Irish any less determined to get back their lands when opportunity offered.

Besides land, religion was the other problematic area. Though effectively tolerated in Ireland (but no more than that), the church, its clergy, and many of the laity, wanted the full restoration of catholicism to its former authority, power and role in Ireland; and they wanted it no less urgently than other Irishmen wanted their lands back. The opportunities implicit for Irish catholicism in the 1637-41 crisis were quite evident, and the clergy and their supporters played a critical part in 1641. Catholic clergy were very active in rousing religious opposition to the settlers before the rebellion, particularly the Franciscans. This order was increasing rapidly in numbers (trebling to six hundred nationwide by 1640); as mendicant friars they kept the closest contacts with the mass of the population; and they were also the most powerfully pro-Spanish element in the clergy, and the most imbued with the crusading, uncompromising spirit of the Counter-Reformation. Their provincial assembly at Multyfarnham in early October 1641, only days before the rising, actually debated whether the Protestant heretics in Ireland should be removed 'by violence', or whether they should be more peacefully 'banished'. In either case they should be removed from Ireland, a significant formulation of, and justification for, 'cleansing' attitudes which developed during the rising. Some Irish clergy also seemed genuinely to fear that the English Parliament's intermittent preoccupation with Catholic priests and plots in 1641 presaged a wholesale attack on them, and the wildest tales of atrocities against Catholics in England accompanied the rebellion in Ireland – such as the story that the Queen's confessor had died in her arms, following torture by Parliament.[8] For such people a pre-emptive strike seemed the only hope.

When the coup temporarily paralysed settler power, clergy and people had the opportunity they had awaited for years. Local Irish ransacked the farms and houses of their Protestant landlords, employers and neighbours, destroying the indentures and mortgages registering their land sales and debts to the newcomers. They seized money, valuables, clothing, and household goods; they seized buildings, crops and cattle; and above all they seized land, and drove the settlers and their families on to the roads and away from their neighbourhood. At this early stage of the rebellion, the sources are quite clear, there was very little killing: the near-universal activity was simply theft and expulsion. Indeed the first instructions of the Parliamentary Commission to gather evidence from settlers against the rebels referred to 'robbery' practised against them, but not to killing. (The instructions were later revised.) Again, for the first few weeks of the rebellion most material collected in the depositions taken by the commissioners refers to theft and expulsion and not to homicide.[9]

Where violence did initially take place the reasons were often local, personal and 'exceptional'. Occasionally the settlers resisted strongly, and killings followed. Some farmers, merchants or employers – notorious locally for their harshness – had personal scores against them to be settled. Several of the Protestant clergy were particularly unpopular, and were killed; sometimes as unpopular symbols of their detested faith, sometimes because of their severe exaction of tithe to support their alien church. Such actions however were, at first, untypical. But within weeks this changed, and 'ethnic cleansing' to obtain possession of land and goods, turned into mass killing. Why?

Sometimes settlers were killed when the first, local, group of Irish who seized their homes were joined, a few days later, by other elements coming from farther afield. The settlers were strangers to the latecomers, and killing was easier. More frequently, deaths occurred when the settlers had been expelled and put on the road. As they laboured toward safety they were exposed, powerless, to the hatred and revenge of Irish villagers whom they passed and to whom they were, again, strangers. Stoned and beaten, their few possessions and even their remaining clothes forcibly stripped from them, injured and exhausted they struggled on, suffered and died. Others fell victim to bandits, 'wood-kerne', Irish who had often taken to banditry for lack of any other occupation, and who blamed the settlers for their desperate plight, and duly took revenge upon them. Sometimes the refugees met one of the many troops of disbanded soldiers roaming the countryside, desperate men also, who would kill to rob. Where the expelled settlers had been provided with a local escort to see them well away from the district, they could be killed either because their escort eventually became tired of their slow progress and made an end of their burden, or because the settlers were handed over to a new escort, who had no reason to cosset these helpless strangers, and who would also make an end of them.

But the biggest killer of those on the roads was 'natural causes': hunger and thirst, cold and exhaustion. For those expelled from their homes often the only sure shelter they knew of, and tried to make for, was Dublin, for many a hundred miles or more away. And in late October-November the Irish winter was beginning. For every one settler deliberately killed, probably two or three more died from exposure. In the late nineteenth century, W.E.H. Lecky tried to calculate the number of settlers who died, using the extremely difficult

'Depositions' of surviving settlers as his source. He suggested that some four thousand were killed, and eight thousand died from 'ill-usage'. These figures however relate to a two-year period after the beginning of the rebellion, i.e., to late 1643, when the civil war was well under way. For deaths during the first two or three months of rebellion, before civil war really started and introduced a new factor into the equation, we should probably halve each of Lecky's estimates, giving approximately two thousand killed, and four thousand dying from exposure, etc. Recent writers echo this order of magnitude, with estimates of settler deaths from all causes ranging from five to eight thousand.[10]

The first of our massacres was therefore the uncontrolled consequence of a political coup which went badly wrong. It was not the spontaneous and justified reaction of native Irish to gross settler ill-usage of modern nationalist legend; nor was it the massive, cold-blooded and deliberately planned massacre long denounced in Protestant legend. But its effects, at the time and later, were nevertheless devastating. It made civil war in England close to inevitable – by demonstrating the reality (it seemed) of violent Catholic conspiracy, by making English Protestants fear a parallel plot in England, and by appearing to implicate both the King and the Queen in the massacre of thousands of their subjects. It most powerfully reinforced Anglo-Scottish prejudices that the Irish were an infamous and barbarous race, with whom no compromise was possible. It served as a public justification for English domination of Ireland for over two centuries.[11] And, most immediately and fatally, it awoke an appetite for revenge which would infect the whole subsequent Irish civil war.

III

Mass killing therefore began the civil war in Ireland, just as the massacres of the Cromwellian reconquest ended it. Between these two episodes, during the decade of the war itself, much less is known, for the detailed history of the Irish civil war is only now beginning to be written – though it is probable that intermittent massacre of civilians and prisoners continued. Two critically important points can however be made about the war period. The first concerns its impact upon the civilian population. This was catastrophic. Ireland's massive population loss in the 1640s and 1650s was entirely the consequence of a decade of brutal war; not through death in battle or massacre, but principally by starvation and disease caused by and spread by the armies.

No less than four separate armies fought for control of Ireland, totalling between forty to sixty thousand men: not far short of the numbers raised in England, but supported by a civilian population less than half that of England, and by an agriculture considerably less productive. Taxes fed those forces, and impoverished the people: just one of the armies, that of the earl of Ormond, raised £607,000 in one year, this alone being seven times the annual peacetime revenue of the Irish government. Requisitioning, free quarter, and simple looting took even more than the taxes: a modest force of five thousand men campaigning in 1647 consumed ninety tons of cornmeal and cheese each month, every month. Besides stripping the economy of its productive surplus the armies also deliberately destroyed resources which they could not control. Forays into 'hostile territory' burned mills, destroyed crops, killed livestock, smashed wagons and farm equipment: 'resource denial' or scorched earth, seventeenth-century style.[12]

The result was that by the second half of the 1640s starvation had begun. In 1648 the Earl of Inchiquin reported that 'divers of my men have dyed of hunger, after they lived for a while on catts and doggs, as many [others] have done'. In the same year another eye-witness reported that famine had taken hold, 'killing thousands of the poorer sort'. With famine came dysentery and typhus, and then in 1649 the bubonic plague. That summer thirteen hundred per week were dying in Dublin alone, and twenty thousand died in Galway. In short, the war caused what a recent essay has soberly termed 'the total collapse of the Irish economy'.[13] This collapse, coupled with the plague and disease, in turn killed off over a third of a million people. Such figures put the massacres of 1641-2 and 1649-50 into a sobering context: each sectarian tradition remembers the massacres they suffered – the Protestants 1641-2, the Catholics 1649-50 – but both miss the factor that really made the 1640s such a dreadful decade for Ireland: bitter, protracted and destructive warfare.

A second point about the war, no less obvious, also needs to be made. This is its strongly confessional nature. Protestants saw nothing remarkable in their church's and clergy's commitment to the defeat of the Irish rebels. But a similar commitment by the Catholic Church and clergy to the rebellion and the war confirmed their most paranoid fears of Rome's insatiable desire to crush protestantism. The Catholic clergy's role in causing the initial rebellion, referred to in section II above, only slowly became known to Protestants at the time. What quickly became evident, however, was the clergy's public role during the first disturbances, and the fiercely Catholic nature of the rebels' words and deeds. Priests were seen among the crowds who attacked settlers' homes (though they were often trying to save

Protestant lives). But these acts were lost in the wave of Catholic iconoclasm which accompanied the rising: bibles were cut up, defaced, burnt; churches were thoroughly scrubbed out before ceremonial rededication to catholicism; Protestant graveyards were opened up, and the corpses dumped in pits outside holy ground. Fragments of conversation reported from among the rebels showed the ugly process of turning one's (religious) enemy from a human into an animal or a thing: 'it was no more pity to kill English than to kill dogs'; all English 'were God's enemies'; none but 'were christened at Mass were Christians'; dead English were bound for hell but all 'Irish souls were to go to God'.[14] Such attitudes ease killing the unarmed and the helpless: dehumanization precedes many a massacre. During the French religious wars, victims on both sides were dehumanized before being killed, and graveyards were opened up for the dead to be desecrated. In this century Nazi propaganda regularly portrayed Jews as rats living in filth: a notorious sequence in the film *Der Ewige Jude* (1940) identified Jews with rats pouring out of cellars and sewers.[15]

Once Ireland's civil war was under way the Catholic Church and clergy played an increasingly important and public role. This was probably inevitable given the church's historic role in Irish society and politics, and the absence of any other nation-wide organization to coordinate and lead resistance, but it powerfully fed Protestant conspiracy theories. The process became visibly 'official' when a provincial synod, meeting under the Archbishop of Armagh at Kells in March 1642, called for an assembly of clergy and laity to be set up to direct the war effort. The response was a meeting of clerical and lay representatives at Kilkenny in May of that year, which agreed to set up a permanent assembly. This met a few months later. The May meeting also issued an Oath of Association for the rebels, calling on 'all Catholics of Ireland' to support the war. Subsequent declarations from Kilkenny laid emphasis upon the war's religious aims, including recognition of catholicism as the official religion of Ireland, public acceptance of its hierarchy and disciplinary courts, etc., and the restoration of all monastic and other church lands seized at the Reformation. Rome's involvement grew from sending a papal agent to Kilkenny in 1643 to full control two years later, when Cardinal Giovanni Rinuccini arrived with the Vatican's full backing, a large war chest, and an inflexible commitment to nothing less than total victory – commitment pressed to the point of repudiating Kilkenny's past agreements, and the excommunication of any Irish Catholic who spoke for anything less than complete victory.[16]

If priestly influence was one prong of the Catholic fork, armed intervention from foreign, Catholic, powers was the other. Once again opinion in England saw nothing remarkable in the despatch of Scottish and English Protestant forces to subdue the rebellion, but panicked at the thought of outside intervention on the Catholic side. Limited English aid had in fact begun to turn the war against the rebels when in 1643, Owen Roe O'Neill led a thousand other Irish mercenaries in Spanish service back to Ireland, and reversed Protestant gains. Rebel diplomacy worked tirelessly to gain the release of more Irish soldiers serving in French, Spanish and German armies; and parliamentary representatives at these courts worked no less hard to block such appeals. Papal intervention, at first with advice, but then with men, money and orders, apparently completed Protestant fears of an international Catholic conspiracy to drive them out of Ireland.

And once driven from Ireland, then what? In the obvious interests of their own long-term security, as well as for revenge and plunder, the Irish Catholic armies, it seemed, would have to invade England: catholicism in Ireland could never be safe until its powerful, heretical, neighbour was neutralized. And there would never be a better opportunity than when England was divided and distracted by its own civil war. Hence Parliament's order of 1644 to hang all Irish prisoners taken in England: this was not simply a typical piece of English brutality against the Irish, but a savage reaction to a very real fear that Catholic intervention would first win Ireland and then spill over to conquer England. In the same way, Oliver Cromwell's celebrated blunt warning that Parliament would permit no toleration of catholicism in Ireland did not spring from a blind hatred of catholicism, but from the full knowledge of the deep political part it had played in the Irish civil war, and the not unreasonable conviction that given half a chance it would do so again.

The civil war in Ireland was therefore fought more bitterly than that in England partly because its immediate causes were far more violent and bloody than those obtaining in England; but also because in Ireland the stakes were far higher – foreign invasion and Catholic rule was never a likely consequence of parliamentary defeat in England, but Protestant defeat in Ireland raised these very frightening possibilities.

IV

Thus far we have a massacre (in 1641) which took place, but which was not intended and was certainly exaggerated in its reporting; and scattered war-time massacres which also occurred, but which were of less significance than other aspects of the war. But the massacres committed by Cromwell's troops at Drogheda and Wexford in 1649 are commonly accepted as being deliberate, are at least as well known as those of 1641, and involved a large and non-exaggerated number of victims.

Judgement on these massacres has been unsparing, from both historians, and the general public. A textbook history of Ireland speaks of 'a general massacre at Drogheda' where '3,500 people, both soldiers and townsfolk of both sexes, were put to the sword'; and in the same work 'Cromwell … treated Wexford the same way.' A specialized study of the 1650s land confiscation refers to 'the violence and ruthlessness' of the two sieges, which gained Cromwell 'everlasting hatred in Ireland'. A more popular work notes both Cromwell's 'typical English racial contempt for the Irish', and its consequences – at Drogheda 'some 3,500 men, women and children … killed', and at Wexford (in more detail) 'the soldiers slaughtered nearly 1,500 of the inhabitants, including 250 women, as many children, five Franciscan priests [sic] and two Franciscan friars'. At nonspecialist level, judgements are even more assured and sweeping: a recent article in a reputable English Sunday newspaper asserted that, 'were Cromwell alive today, the U.N. would prosecute him as a war criminal'. Nationalist Irish circles today are certain that Cromwell saw the Irish as 'a racially inferior people'; that his reconquest was 'exceptionally cruel and bloody' even by the standards of the time; and that in achieving it 'the New Model Army massacred the residents of Drogheda, Wexford and some smaller towns'.[17]

Though strongly felt, these views are mistaken, being based upon ignorance of the 'laws of war' at the time, or ignorance of the circumstances of the sieges, or (concerning Cromwell) upon ignorance of what he actually said.

The number and identity of the dead need first to be established. The garrison at Drogheda numbered 2,870 officers and men, and the much smaller force at Wexford had been reinforced just before the siege to approximately two thousand. The troops at Wexford were Irish, but about half those at Drogheda were English Protestant royalists, their commander a well-known English royalist, Sir Arthur Aston, who among other services had held Oxford for the King. Each of these fairly small towns also held three to four thousand civilians.[18]

The total death toll among the defenders is usually set at around three thousand for Drogheda, and about half that number for Wexford. On each occasion the majority of the garrison was killed, perhaps as many as three-quarters of them, and several score, perhaps hundreds, of civilians died as well. Cromwell is usually held directly responsible for the high death toll at Drogheda, because at the height of the battle, as his men were breaking into the town, he gave an order that no prisoners should be taken. At Wexford, though he gave no orders to refuse quarter, it is clear that his troops were again very reluctant to take prisoners. Furthermore, at Drogheda, where several hundred prisoners were taken, one-tenth of them were executed and the remainder transported to Barbados. Finally, a number of civilians were killed at both sieges, perhaps two to three hundred, including several priests. Why did all this happen, and were these sieges 'massacres'?

First, it is clear that the actions of Cromwell and his troops at both sieges were 'lawful', in the sense of being within the contemporary 'laws of war'. Sieges are a very old form of warfare, and give rise to moral difficulties because of the unavoidable presence of innocent noncombatants within the battlefield. Quite precise rules had therefore been developed to govern sieges, giving rights to defenders, civilian population and attackers, while also recognizing the realities of battle. The central point was that if a town surrendered when formally summoned to do so, the lives of all within it were to be spared. They might also receive a further summons, and a further chance to surrender without harm, when the siege guns had been drawn up and were ready to commence firing. But once the formal summons had been refused and heavy fighting started, the garrison and the residents had no automatic right to quarter when the town was stormed. Mercy, then, lay entirely with the attacking commander and his troops, and applied to garrison, prisoners, and civilians alike.[19]

This was not only law, it was recognized practice. As late as the nineteenth century, and to a commander as eminent as the Duke of Wellington, these rules were accepted as normal, reasonable and lawful.[20] This was because the laws relating to sieges were no arbitrary set of rules played in an unreal 'war game', but the product of harsh experience. Surrender could be accepted before any serious fighting began because the attacking troops had not suffered any losses, and were still immediately responsive to orders. But once fighting started, smoke and confusion, anger at losses, fury at the enemy who had inflicted them, and the adrenalin charge of killing, all drove out thoughts of mercy in the attackers, and made control and restraint by commanders for a time impossible. Contemporary opinion also regarded a period of killing and looting at the end of a siege as a 'payment' or recompense to the attackers for the loss and hardship they had suffered during it; and accepted too that the best way of bringing troops under discipline again was to allow them licence to do what they pleased for a fixed period of time after a town was stormed.

By the laws of war, therefore, Cromwell and his men were guilty of no 'war crime', for each town was properly summoned before the attack began. But not every siege in the seventeenth century ended in a bloodbath, and Drogheda and Wexford were the only Irish sieges conducted by Cromwell which did end in mass killing. What was particular about these two, and not about the other towns he besieged?

An important point is that these were the first two battles fought by Cromwell's army after it landed in Ireland. Cromwell's chances of success in Ireland depended upon his fighting a very short campaign. He intended these first encounters to be exemplary – as his surrender summons to Dundalk shows, where he explicitly warned the garrison of the consequences of refusal. In this he succeeded: after Drogheda and Wexford most towns he summoned surrendered quickly and there was no fierce siege, and no mass killing. Cromwell's opponent, the Earl of Ormonde, conceded 'how great the terror is [caused by] those successes', and lamented that his own forces 'are yet so stupefied' that he could not get them to 'act anything like men toward their own preservation'. Cromwell was right in his calculation that extreme (though lawful) severity in the first sieges would (in his often overlooked explanation) 'tend to prevent the effusion of blood for the future': the 'Hiroshima' justification of brutality to shorten a bloody war. And the seventeenth-century laws of war also accepted this aim as a proper reason for refusing quarter in a siege.[21]

A second reason for implacable attack in these opening sieges was that both towns were crucial for the campaign's further progress. Drogheda controlled the road from Dublin north to Ulster, with its core of settler support for Cromwell; while Wexford was the key to the south where the bulk of rebel strength lay and had to be defeated. Furthermore, the enemy recognized this, assembling at Drogheda what Cromwell termed 'the flower of all their army', and powerfully reinforcing the troops at Wexford.[22]

But probably stronger than these tactical considerations, for most of the soldiers at least, was the motive of revenge. The massacres of 1641 were very much in the mind of the army as it marched into Ireland – Cromwell's Drogheda despatch to Parliament referred to that garrison as 'these barbarous wretches, who have imbrued their hands in so much innocent blood'.[23] Only three years before, in 1646, Sir William Temple, a distinguished parliamentary lawyer, had published a semi-official account of the 1641 rebellion, apparently sober and factual, full of grisly detail, and setting total Protestant casualties at the appalling figure of three hundred thousand. With this recently published work in mind, reviving memories of the flood of atrocities of 1641-42, the English army's first encounters with rebel forces were likely to be savagely vengeful; though moderating later as killing sated the appetite for revenge.

At least as important as these general reasons, however, were particular factors operating in each siege, leading to the mass killings. An obvious but often neglected fact is that both sieges were in fact desperately hard-fought battles, a point often blurred by talk of the 'massacre' of (presumably helpless) soldiers and civilians. At Drogheda Cromwell's men only broke into the town on their third attempt, with Cromwell himself in the lead. Even then resistance continued, first from improvised street barricades, then from a high point known as Mill Mount, and then from the tower of St Peter's church. It was this continued resistance, pointless since most of the town had been captured, which exasperated Cromwell – adrenalin-charged from leading the fighting – into ordering that no prisoners be taken. Shots fired by persistent defenders the following day led to renewed fighting, and the death of more prisoners.[24]

Similarly, at Wexford the besiegers were first angered by the rebel commander's misuse of surrender negotiations to smuggle reinforcements into the town; and then, when cannon had made a breach in the wall, he resumed negotiations and attempted to impose his own terms of surrender upon Cromwell. But while these talks were taking place, a senior rebel officer made his own peace and allowed the besiegers into the town's castle. From here they swarmed into the town, but met fierce resistance in the streets – not least from Irish sailors who had long made Wexford a pirate base preying on English shipping. As at Drogheda, the narrow streets and enclosing town wall made flight difficult, and escape impossible, and the fighting became a slaughter. But at Wexford the tragedy was compounded, for part of the town ran down to the harbour, and when a struggling mass of townsfolk, seamen and soldiers were driven down to the water's edge they tried to escape in boats. Heavily overloaded with a panic-stricken crowd, these sank. Several hundred drowned, including at this point many women.[25]

These two episodes suggest several practical reasons why sieges sometimes become massacres. For some time the attacking force must expose themselves to the defenders' fire, without being able to reply effectively themselves, until they break into the town. They are then unlikely to be merciful when the defenders, having now lost their advantage of firing from cover and finding themselves at a severe disadvantage, offer to surrender. Next, surrender is usually simply not a practical option in savage hand-to-hand fighting, and during sieges the closeness and confusion of fighting down narrow, winding streets made offering and accepting the surrender of individuals or small groups extremely difficult. Finally, the key point of battle at this time was to put the opponent to flight: the victor then won control of the battlefield, rendered his opponents incapable of further resistance, and most importantly, left them helpless against pursuit by the cavalry, part of whose purpose was to ride down and kill a fleeing enemy. On an open battlefield flight might bring safety for the defeated, but in a fortified town men in flight could run, but not hide. Pursuit would always catch them – and soldiers were after all trained to kill a fleeing enemy. And, finally, civilians could easily be killed as well, since most armies did not wear distinctive uniforms, and it was not easy to distinguish soldier from civilian in the confusion of a running fight. Moreover, as the pirates at Wexford show, some 'civilians' had every reason to become totally involved in the fighting.

As to Cromwell's personal responsibility for the killings, his critics invariably point to his own acknowledgement of guilt at Drogheda: 'I forbade them to spare any that were in arms in the town'; and to the harsh note of vengeance present in his reports: 'I am persuaded this is a righteous judgement of God upon these barbarous wretches' (at Drogheda), and God's 'righteous justice brought a just judgement upon them' (at Wexford). What is often omitted however is Cromwell's further reflection that, had this not been evidently God's will, and had not there been the hope of quick surrenders in future, 'such actions ... otherwise cannot but work remorse and regret'.[26] It could be noted too that Cromwell's notorious acceptance of responsibility at Drogheda (quoted above) may be beside the point. His order was made in the heat of close action, with fighting going on in all streets of the town. Few of his soldiers, apart from those very close to him, could have heard it and Cromwell's words possibly 'legitimated' something that he knew was happening in any case.

V

Half of the Irish indictment against Cromwell lies in these two notorious sieges; the other half in the equally notorious post-war land settlement which bears his name. This settlement is popularly understood in apocalyptic terms. Irish Catholic bishops at the time charged England with aiming to 'extirpate' the Irish people and their religion and seize all their land, and this language is repeated today: 'a blue print for the destruction of a nation'; 'a policy of expulsion and confiscation which is nowadays dignified with the term "ethnic cleansing"'; 'wholesale clearance to the worst land in Ireland'; and, in a recent nationalist history, 'England was confident that it had at last devised a final solution [sic] to its Irish problem'.[27]

There are two misunderstandings here. One event which did occur, a very large-scale seizure of Irish land, is developed into one which did not take place, a massive population expulsion. And secondly, the English Parliament's initial proposals are mistaken for the completed event. In 1653 Parliament legislated to confiscate Irish land, to pay for suppressing the rebellion. The amount seized varied in twenty-eight counties from 4 percent to 77 percent, with a median of 46 percent. Total Irish landownership fell from around 60 percent of the island in 1640 to little more than 20 percent. This was a political and cultural disaster of the first magnitude for the Irish, because it reduced their landowning class to political and social impotence for two centuries and created an all-powerful ruling caste of Protestant landowners.[28]

But the massive seizure of land was not accompanied by a massive population transfer; there was no full-scale ethnic cleansing. This is the event which did not occur. The great majority of the Irish population stayed where they were, most because they had no land anyway and were needed by the Protestant settlers as labour to work the land; and others because they were stripped of between one-third and two-thirds of the land they held, but were permitted to remain on the rest. It was the greater Irish landowners only who were uprooted to Connaught and their numbers were quite small, between one to two thousand families. They were allotted land in Connaught as compensation, though considerably less than they had formerly held. Parliament had indeed originally considered moving virtually the whole Irish population to the western counties. But it abandoned the plan because the settlers protested that they needed Irish labour, because the expected wave of new English colonists did not materialize, and because driving over a million people hundreds of miles from their homes was simply not within the administrative compass of a small seventeenth-century state. Parliament's final action was a great deal less draconian than its first intention – but the two are often merged into one.

On direct punishment for the rebellion, too, Parliament's first thoughts were much more bloodthirsty than its final actions. The 1653 Act put all Irish participants in the 1641 rising in jeopardy of the law, estimated at some eighty thousand people or over a tenth of all adult males. But the trials of 1653-54 actually resulted in little over a hundred executions, not a large slaughter considering the number 'at risk', and the anger still aroused by the rebellion. Equally, the tens of thousands of Irish once thought to have been rounded up for transportation to slavery in the West Indies has been revised downwards to a few thousand; and the notion that this was an atrocity reserved by the English for their Irish subjects alone has died as it became clear that transportation had become a regular punishment for rebels, convicted criminals and poor vagrants, of English no less than Irish origin. Many more Irish were permitted to leave voluntarily to seek their fortune on the Continent in the 1650s, than were transported.[29]

VI

Several points seem to emerge from this study. The period was indeed one of 'blackness' for Ireland, but the savage events which took place were not wholly 'indiscriminate', in the sense of being completely random, irrational and meaningless. Understandable calculations and causes lay behind the mass killings of 1641 and 1649, and the huge land seizure of the 1650s. Even the appalling religious bigotry of the period shows rational causes, with the Catholic Irish trying to cleanse their land of what they saw as foreign heresy, and the Anglo-Scots settlers reacting violently to the dominant part played in Ireland's civil war by the Catholic Church and clergy, assisted by foreign Catholic powers. Even the hatred and contempt felt by the Anglo-Scots for the Irish – and vice versa – can be seen as not so much an early form of racial prejudice, and more as the understandable though appalling consequence of a desperate struggle over land, power and religion, in a winner-takes-all situation.

A second point is that much of this violence, on both sides, was unplanned and unintended. It was often the unforeseen (and sometimes undesired) consequence of accident, miscalculation and mischance, the unpredictable sum of countless small acts and decisions. Nobody deliberately planned the spiral of killings in 1641, nor consciously set out to exterminate town garrisons in 1649; and the land settlement of the 1650s took an entirely different form from the one originally intended by Parliament. But in the popular memory of these events, for both the Nationalist and Unionist communities, cold-blooded premeditation by the other side explained all. It is the same with the numbers involved: each side grossly exaggerated the number of its victims to prove the insensate ferocity of its opponent – then and now. However, if the necessary explanatory qualifications were imposed upon both intent and number, some of the poison might be taken out of communal relations today in Northern Ireland. In particular, it would help if the real tragedy of mid-seventeenth-century Ireland, for both communities, was seen to be the war itself, and not individual actions during it.

Finally, this study has shown some of the problems concealed in the use of the term 'massacre'. Two key components of a massacre are deliberate intent, and victims who are either helpless or who are not formally involved in the fighting. But 'deliberate intent' is not a simple, single thing: as the cases of 1641 and 1649 show, it is a web of many limited and confused aims and actions, leading often in directions few foresee or desire. And the 'helpless victims' may turn out to be soldiers wishing to surrender who were, a short while before, full of fight; or include as 'nonparticipatory civilians' clergy or other civilians very active in directing the war, sailors who doubled as pirates, or civilians who were involved simply because their town was besieged. Involvement and helplessness are also not simple, single factors.

Obviously the term and concept of massacre cannot be abandoned. But two improvements might be suggested. The criminal law interposes a category of manslaughter between death by accident, and death by murder. We seem to need a similar mid-point category for mass death, to denote a lessened and indirect though still culpable, degree of responsibility. And secondly, we should note that our difficulties with 'massacre' arise, in part, through a wish to distinguish between 'acceptable' situations of mass killing (such as formal warfare), and other 'non-acceptable' areas. Perhaps the answer is that we should recognize more clearly the fundamental criminality of all forms of mass killing, whether 'legitimated' by the State or not, and consign to oblivion the concept of a 'just' war.

Notes

1. 'Indiscriminate blackness' was coined by W. D. Love, 'Civil War in Ireland', *Emory University Quarterly*, 22 (1966), 57.
2. S. R. Gardiner, *History of the Great Civil War* (London, 1889), vol. 2, 33-4, 24 October 1644; T. Carlyle, ed., *Oliver Cromwell's Letters and Speeches* (London, 1857), vol. 2, 48, Letter CIII, 12 September 1649.
3. T. W. Moody et al., eds, *A New History of Ireland* (Oxford, 1976), vol. 3, 389; C. Carlton, 'The Impact of the Fighting', in J. Morrill, ed., *The Impact of the English Civil War* (London, 1991), 20.
4. There is a large amount of literature on the 1641 rising: this account derives from N. Canny, 'What really happened in 1641?', in J. H. Ohlmeyer, ed., *Ireland from Independence to Occupation, 1641-1660* (Cambridge, 1965); R. Gillespie, 'The End of an Era', in C. Brady and R. Gillespie, eds, *Natives and Newcomers: Ireland 1534-1641* (Suffolk, 1986); Love, 'Civil War in Ireland', 57-72; M. Percival-Maxwell, 'The Ulster Rising of 1641, and the Depositions', *Irish Historical Studies*, 21 (1977-78): 144-167; Percival-Maxwell, *The Outbreak of the Irish Rebellion of 1641* (Dublin, 1994); A. Clark, 'The Genesis of the Ulster Rising of 1641', in P. Roebuck, ed., *Plantation to Partition*, 29-45.
5. Love, 'Civil War in Ireland', 58-60, 66; K. J. Lindley, 'The Impact of the 1641 Rebellion upon England and Wales, 1641-45', *Irish Historical Studies*, 18 (1972): 143-76 passim.
6. Canny, 'What really happened', 29-32; Clark, 'Genesis of the Ulster Rising', 30-38; Gillespie, 'End of an Era', 203-4.
7. Percival-Maxwell, 'The Ulster Rising', 147-51, 162-64; Gillespie, 'End of an Era', 212; Canny, 'What really happened', 31-37.
8. Gillespie, 'End of an Era', 197-98, 208; Moody et al., *New History of Ireland*, vol. 3, 296-99; Canny, 'What really happened', 29, n.12.
9. Love, 'Civil War in Ireland', 60-63. For the 'Depositions' see A. Clark, 'The 1641 Depositions', in P. Fox, ed., *The Treasures of the Library of Trinity College Dublin* (Dublin, 1986), 111-23; and for a selection from the Depositions see

    M. Hickson, ed., *Ireland in the Seventeenth Century, or the Massacres of 1641* (London, 1884), 2 vols.

10. W. E. H. Lecky, *A History of Ireland in the Eighteenth Century* (London, 1892), vol. 1, 46-47, 60, 74-79.

11. Canny, 'What really happened', 37-40; Love, 'Civil War in Ireland', 62; T. C. Barnard, 'The Uses of 23 October and Irish Protestant Celebrations', *English Historical Review*, 106 (1991): 889-920, and, 'Crises of Identity among Irish Protestants 1641-1685', *Past and Present*, 127 (1990): 39-83.

12. S. Wheeler, 'Four Armies in Ireland', in J. Ohlmeyer, ed., *Ireland from Independence to Occupation*, 43-65; L. M. Cullen, 'Economic Trends 1660-1691', in Moody et al., *New History of Ireland*, vol. 3, 387-407.

13. R. Gillespie, 'The Irish Economy at War 1641-52', in Ohlmeyer, ed., *Ireland from Independence*, 169, 176-78.

14. J. Ohlmeyer, 'Ireland Independent', in Ohlmeyer, ed., *Ireland from Independence*, 89-104; Canny, 'What really happened', 40.

15. On dehumanization see N. Z. Davis, *Society and Culture in Early Modern France* (Stanford and London, 1975), 152-87; on exhuming corpses, see P. Roberts, *A City in Conflict: Troyes during the French Wars of Religion* (Manchester, 1996), 89-90. I am indebted to my colleague Dr. Penny Roberts for these references.

16. B. Fitzpatrick, *Seventeenth-Century Ireland* (Dublin, 1988), 172-73; P. Corish, 'The Rising of 1641 and the Catholic Confederacy, 1641-45', in Moody et al., *New History of Ireland*, vol. 3, 296-97.

17. E. Curtis, *A History of Ireland* (London, 1936), 250; K. S. Bottigheimer, *English Money and Irish Land* (Oxford, 1971), 116; P. B. Ellis, *Hell or Connaught* (London, 1975), 3-4, 21; *Observer*, 3 September 1995 (I owe this reference to the kindness of my colleague Professor B. S. Capp); K. Kelley, *The Longest War* (London, 1982), vol. 15, 4-5.

18. S. R. Gardiner, *History of the Commonwealth and Protectorate* (London, 1894), vol. 1, 124 and 143. Gardiner's account of the two sieges is still the fullest and most reliable. Some popular histories are also sceptical of the charge of massacre: see for example J. C. Beckett, *The Making of Modern Ireland, 1603-1923* (London, 1966), 102.

19. M. Howard et al., eds, *The Laws of War* (Yale, 1994), chap. 4 and esp. 48-51.

20. Howard et al., *Laws of War*, 48; Gardiner, *Commonwealth and Protectorate*, vol. 1, 132 and n. 2.

21. T. Carlyle, ed., *Cromwell's Letters and Papers*, vol. 2, 48; Howard et al., *Laws of War*, 49, 51.

22. W. C. Abbot, *Writings and Speeches of Oliver Cromwell* (Cambridge, 1939), vol. 2, 127; Gardiner, *Commonwealth and Protectorate*, vol. 1, 144.

23. Abbot, *Writings and Speeches*, vol. 2, 127.

24. Gardiner, *Commonwealth and Protectorate*, vol. 1, 131-34.

25. Gardiner, *Commonwealth and Protectorate*, vol. 1, 145-47.

26. Abbot, *Writings and Speeches*, vol. 2, 127, 142.

27. P. Corish, 'The Cromwellian Conquest', in Moody et al., *New History of Ireland*, vol. 3, 344; *Observer*, 3 September 1995; *BBC Radio 4*, 7.30 a.m., 20 April 1996, 'Farming Today' programme from County Kerry, Eire; Kelley, *Longest War*, 5.

28. K. S. Bottigheimer, *English Money and Irish Land* (Oxford, 1971), chap. 5, and 3, 215.

29. P. J. Corish, 'The Cromwellian Regime', in Moody et al., *New History of Ireland*, vol. 3, 355-65, 369.

CHAPTER 6

SLAUGHTER UNDER TRUST

CLAN MASSACRES AND BRITISH STATE FORMATION

Allan I. Macinnes

I

The process of state formation in early modern Europe has become a dominant, if at times insular, theme of the 'new British history'.[1] Integral to this process was frontier pacification along the Anglo-Scottish Border and throughout Irish and Scottish Gaeldom, in order to promote, change, confederate and, ultimately, incorporate the United Kingdom. In anticipation of regal union, and as a first step in clamping down on frontier feuding among clans and families, James VI of Scotland (later I of England) made a significant statutory change to the laws of treason in 1587. Henceforth, perpetrators of premeditated massacres of rivals were indictable for slaughter under trust.[2] During the seventeenth century, the proponents of British Union successively viewed premeditated massacres within Scottish Gaeldom as uncivilized embarrassments, as diversionary acts of retribution and as exemplary punishments.

The charge of slaughter under trust became indelibly associated with the political fortunes of the House of Argyll who, as chiefs of ClanCampbell, Scottish magnates and British statesmen were among the foremost exponents of Anglo-Scottish union. This acquisitive House had benefited territorially from the treasonable ramifications of slaughter occasioned by the civilizing policies pursued by James VI and I in the wake of the regal union of 1603. However, the House, in the personage of Archibald Campbell, Marquis of Argyll – who actively promoted the covenanting revolution against Charles I and confederation between the Scottish Estates and the English Parliament – was eventually indicted for slaughter under trust as a consequence of covenanting reprisals against royalist clans during the 1640s. Most notoriously in terms of folk memory, the House of Argyll was implicated in the massacre of Glencoe, when the Whig regime of William of Orange exacted exemplary reprisals against Jacobitism in the 1690s, reprisals effected to demonstrate that social disorder and political unrest within Scotland was not an insurmountable obstacle to the imposition of incorporating union at the behest of the British court.

II

By no means confined to Scottish Gaeldom, feuding was endemic in town and country during the sixteenth century. However, while the incidence of feuding was probably no higher in Gaeldom than elsewhere in Scotland, frontier societies in the Highlands, as on the Borders, certainly had more extensive and intensive feuds involving clans and families in a range of atrocities varying from freelance banditry to premeditated slaughter. Within Gaeldom, feuding was essentially the product of the mismatch between feudal landholding and territorial settlement: that is, while the élite of most clans had charters conveying estates from the Crown or other landlords, these charters did not always relate to the territories actually settled by their clansmen. Thus, the *oighreachd*, the heritage of the clan élite as landlords, was not always coterminus with their heritage, their *duthchas*, as trustees over the territories settled by their clans.[3]

At the same time, the forfeiture of the Lordship of the Isles by the Scottish crown at the end of the fifteenth century not only shattered the fragile unity of the powerful ClanDonald, but left a political vacuum in which feuding clans accorded priority to military might over social order and political stability. Disorder and instability were further compounded by the prospects for mercenary employment opened up by Tudor endeavours to assert English hegemony over Ireland. The chiefs and leading clan gentry of the Scottish Gaels developed a lucrative trade in the seasonal provision of fighting men both to aid and contain the military ambitions of the Irish Gaels. The seasonal mercenaries from the Highlands and Islands, who were supported by bounties and food levies, became known as the redshanks or *buannachan* in the course of the sixteenth century. When not engaged in Ireland, the *buannachan* formed a military caste who expected to be supported by the clan peasantry. At the same time,

they formed a ready reservoir of manpower to perpetuate feuds instigated by the territorial ambitions of rival clan élites.

In the course of such feuding, massacre featured as an occasional,
if notorious ingredient. Distinctions must be drawn, however,
between opportunistic and premeditated acts of vengeance in the
furtherance of feud. Opportunistic massacres were hot blooded and
tended to happen in a confined space, such as a cave, church or even
a tower-house where the means of escape could be readily blocked
off. Premeditated massacres were cold blooded and tended to take
place after an offer of, or request for, hospitality had been proffered
or after articles of capitulation had been agreed for besieged parties.[4]

Feuding had reached such particular intensity during the minority of James VI, that he marked his majority in 1587 by the passage
of two acts which had a particular bearing on both Highlands and
Borders. The first was the general band which bound over chiefs
and other heads of families for the conduct of their clansmen and
followers. In the process, the clans were recognized as *de facto* agencies of central government with chiefs and leading gentry liable to
punitive fines if they countenanced disorder. The second act,
designed to promote greater discipline within landed society, was to
define premeditated murder or slaughter as not just a capital, but a
treasonable offence. Thus, clan chiefs or any other members of
landed society authorizing the massacre of rivals by whom they had
accorded hospitality or articles of capitulation, were liable to be
charged with slaughter under trust. If convicted, their property as
well as their lives were forfeited.[5]

The first clan chief to face indictment under this amended legislation was the inveterate feudatory, Lachlan Maclean of Duart.
During 1588, he so objected to the prospect of John MacDonald of
Ardnamurchan becoming his step-father, that he murdered eighteen
followers of MacDonald after their wedding party had retired for
the night. Only the pleas of his mother spared the step-father who
was subsequently tortured and incarcerated. Maclean of Duart also
commissioned one hundred Spanish troops, who were shipwrecked
on the break-up of the Armada, to assist his clansmen despoil the
territories of various branches of the ClanDonald and lay siege to
Mingarry Castle, the seat of MacDonald of Ardnamurchan. Lachlan Maclean, though outlawed and denounced rebel, was not held
to account for this campaign, which reputedly neither spared men,
women or children, and was deemed treasonable as 'the like barbarous and shamefull crueltie hes [seldom] beine hard of amangis
Christeanis in any kingdome or age'.[6]

The legislation of 1587, indeed, had more a descriptive than a
disciplinary impact on Scottish Gaeldom where occasional acts of

extreme violence continued, though some have been greatly exaggerated.[7] The primary intent of the Crown and the Scottish Privy Council was to license rather than monopolize violence by issuing commissions of fire and sword which empowered clan chiefs and other members of landed society to mobilize their followers to inflict summary justice. The award of commissions, which contained dispensations for massacres, slaughter and other atrocities carried out in hot blood by those licensed to execute fire and sword, tended to favour the rights of *oighreachd* over those of *duthchas*. Although routinely awarded against parties who transgressed rights of property or threatened a localized breakdown of public order, the commissions too often legitimized feuding rather than terminated violent conduct. Nonetheless, the commissions did give advance notice to parties liable to summary justice; they usually operated with a winter close-season and were subject to periodic review – usually on an annual basis as the seventeenth century progressed.[8]

No major cold-blooded incident involving the massacre of clansmen in the guise of slaughter under trust can be verified between the 1590s and the 1640s. This situation can in no small measure be attributed to the Union of the Crowns which opened up more effective ways of containing feuding and military engagements after 1603. The accession of James VI of Scotland as James I of England not only facilitated coordinated action in Edinburgh, London and Dublin to subdue frontier societies, but placed the resources of the English navy at the service of the Scottish Privy Council to terminate the mercenary trade of the *buannachan*. Feuding among the clans was further checked by the Crown's military and legislative offensive on the western seaboard of Scottish Gaeldom, an offensive that complemented the plantation of Ulster in driving a permanent wedge between the Gaels of Ireland and Scotland. The Crown's offensive was particularly marked by the expropriation of four notoriously troublesome clans: by the reaffirmation of the general band to promote the annual accountability of the clan elite at Edinburgh, and by the redundancy of the *buannachan* as priority was accorded to productive estate management over fighting men.

The MacDonalds of Kintyre, Islay and Jura were the most prominent clan whose élite were expropriated, a task facilitated by the internal divisions between the chief, Angus MacDonald of Dunyveg, and his eldest son, Sir James MacDonald of Knockramsay. For his attempt to immolate his parents at their house of Askomull in Kintyre twelve years earlier, Sir James was indicted for wilful fire-raising in 1609. These treasonable charges, which were preferred two years after the authorization of expropriation, gave judicial gloss to the forfeiture of his clan élite. Although over two hundred armed followers were alleged to have participated, this attempted arson was reputedly not premeditated but carried out in hot blood. Sir James, who was detained in prison rather than executed, escaped in 1615 to conduct a desperate and unsuccessful resistance to the annexation of his clan's territories by the ClanCampbell.[9] From 1607, when the House of Argyll first secured title to Kintyre, the Campbell élite were not only the principal beneficiaries of the Crown's selective policy of expropriation, but also to the fore in using the terms 'North British' for Scotland and 'British' for colonists settling in Ulster.[10]

III

The suppression of the ClanDonald Rebellion of 1615 led to the reinvigoration of legislative measures to hold chiefs and leading gentry annually accountable for the conduct of their clansmen and, in the process, carry through the redundancy of the *buannachan*. However, the productive redeployment of their energies in agriculture rather than warfare or banditry took over two decades to accomplish. Indeed, redeployment was only made effective when the unprecedented demands for manpower during the civil wars of the 1640s was compounded by the need for labour to promote recovery from the extensive devastations perpetrated throughout Scottish Gaeldom. As the main Scottish theatre of warfare, political polarity between covenanters and royalists was intensified by reprisals in which clans revived feuding in the guise of military campaigning for and against the House of Stuart.

Two infamous incidents stand out: clan massacres which led to charges of slaughter under trust being eventually preferred against Archibald Campbell, Marquis of Argyll, in 1661. These charges were but part of a massive arraignment against Argyll at the Restoration to hold him treasonably to account for his conduct as the leading covenanter of the 1640s and as collaborator with the Cromwellian occupation of the 1650s. The two principally victimized clans, the Lamonts of Cowal and the MacDougalls of Lorne, had originally served in the covenanting forces in association with the Campbells, but had changed sides in 1645 to participate in the renewed devastation of Campbell territories in Argyll and the Perthshire Highlands. These devastations, masterminded over successive winters by Alasdair MacColla, commander of the royalist clans and their allies from the Confederation of Irish Catholics, had inflicted damages in excess of £1.3 million Scots (almost £110,000 sterling) on the Campbells and their associates. A fringe member of the clan élite of the expropriated MacDonalds of Kintyre, Islay and Jura, MacColla had split with the supreme royalist commander, James Graham, Marquis of Montrose, to maintain a bridgehead with Ireland on the western seaboard. Their joint campaign of guerrilla warfare during 1644-5, had combined the intensity of Irish warfare to the continental devastations experienced during the Thirty Years' War. In taking revenge, the Covenanting Movement was particularly vindictive towards the Irish Confederates who were drawn mainly from the estates of Randal MacDonnell, Marquis of Antrim. As head of the Irish branch of the expropriated ClanDonald, he viewed the royalist cause as a means of reclaiming Kintyre, Islay and Jura from the ClanCampbell.[11]

In June 1646, a contingent of covenanting irregulars, mainly Campbells, under the command of James Campbell of Ardkinglass, who had served in Ireland against the Catholic Confederates, laid siege to the Lamont strongholds in Cowal. Although their chief, Sir James Lamont of Inveryne was spared under the terms agreed for the capitulation of his clan, thirty-six of their gentry and possibly another one hundred clansmen, women and children were massacred in the confusion that followed the surrender of the castles of Toward and Ascog. Lamont prisoners taken to the town of Dunoon were summarily hanged over the next seven days following exhortations from a local presbyterian minister, Colin MacLachlan from Lochgoilhead. In the following June, three hundred clansmen, mainly MacDougalls, were massacred several days after surrendering Dunaverty castle, which they had garrisoned for MacColla, to covenanting forces commanded by Lieutenant-General David Leslie. This slaughter on the Kintyre peninsula, committed eleven months after Charles I had commanded the royalist forces on the western seaboard of Scottish Gaeldom to disband, was instigated by two presbyterian zealots – John Nevoy, a chaplain and Thomas Henderson, a clerk – who were accompanying the army. The Marquis of Argyll, who held the rank of colonel, was in attendance as a more than interested onlooker. As hereditary justiciar of Argyll and the Isles, the marquis was empowered to try all civil and criminal charges except treason. He subsequently instigated legal proceedings in his own court to strip the surviving clan élite of both the Lamonts and MacDougalls of title to their estates on the grounds of excessive debts owed to his house and other Campbell creditors. Arrears of public dues to the Covenanting Movement compounded their delinquency.[12]

The massacre of the Lamonts was the culmination of acts of retaliation perpetrated on both sides of the North Channel by Campbells. In the course of the massacres in June 1646, damages in excess of £600,000 Scots (£50,000 sterling) were reputedly inflicted on Toward, Ascog and other Lamont estates in Cowal. Some of those hanged at Dunoon only died after being suffocated by the earth heaped upon them when cast into graves. Sir James Lamont of Inveryne, though spared, was held in various Campbell strongholds before being brought to Stirling castle in 1651 to answer for his participation with MacColla in his devastations of Argyllshire. The Lamont chief was only spared from trial by the abortive march on England by the covenanting and royalist forces who united in the patriotic accommodation with Charles II. Although the Lamont chief was released after Oliver Cromwell's forces seized Stirling, Argyll raised further actions for debt under the Cromwellian regime to recover costs in excess of £2,900 Scots (almost £245 sterling) for the entertainment and lodging of Sir James as a prisoner.[13]

Reprisals after the massacre at Dunaverty were no less vicious and not restricted to the MacDougalls whose estates in Lorne and the island of Kerrera in particular were laid waste as the covenanting army swept north from the Kintyre peninsula. Their chief, Dougall MacDougall of Dunnolly, was imprisoned for eighteen months in the Campbell stronghold of Inchconnel and obliged to surrender estates to the House of Argyll. While Dunaverty had been besieged, the neighbouring royalist stronghold of Lochhead had been allowed to surrender and its garrison, mainly MacAllisters, who had also switched from being covenanting allies of the Campbells to royalist followers of MacColla, were initially allowed to disperse. Once the majority of the garrison at Dunaverty had been massacred, the survivors together with clansmen in Lochhead were pressed into the French army. However, sixteen of the leading MacAllister gentry were recalled from parole and hanged, their estates being forfeited to the House of Argyll.[14]

Undoubtedly, the vindictive but successful combination of political reprisals and territorial acquisitiveness were the hallmarks of Argyll's deliberate confusion of public and private advantage, first as a leading covenanter and then as a Cromwellian collaborator. Such a prejudicial combination, however, left the marquis fatally open to indictment for slaughter under trust fourteen years after the massacres in Cowal and Kintyre were committed. Nonetheless, Argyll was able to muster a selectively robust defence for his conduct during both massacres, a defence enhanced by his absence from the slaughter in Cowal and by his presence in the subordinate capacity as colonel in the covenanting army in Kintyre. Indeed, at the time of the massacre of the Lamonts he was in England as a covenanting negotiator making his celebrated speech to the Grand Committee of both Houses in favour of sustaining constitutional confederation between the Parliamentarians and the Scottish Estates.[15] Thus, he could attest at his trial that he had given no special direction for the reprisals against the Lamonts. As no document could be produced proving the contrary, he contended he was not liable for the crimes committed either under statute or common law. At the same time, he challenged the existence of articles of capitulation for the garrison at Lochhead. He claimed that the offer of surrender to the garrison at Dunaverty was unconditional and their fate left to the discretion or mercy of the covenanting army's council of war, a situation subsequently supported by another colonel, Sir James Turner. A veteran of the Thirty Years' War, he affirmed that Lieutenant-General Leslie's decision to authorize the massacre, though against the prevailing European practice, was neither a breach of law or custom.[16] In effect, Argyll argued that his indictment for slaughter under trust was not relevant in Cowal because the covenanting irregulars were under the trust of another, namely Campbell of Ardkinglass, and not relevant in Kintyre because no assurance had been given to the surrendered garrisons that their lives would be spared.

However, articles of capitulation, if not extant for the garrison at Ascog, certainly survived for the garrison at Toward, having been subscribed on 3 June 1646 by Sir James Lamont of Inveryne on behalf of his clansmen, and by James Campbell of Ardkinglass and six other leading gentry of the ClanCampbell for the covenanting irregulars. While the articles of capitulation were manifestly breached by massacre, they also contained the explicit admission of the Lamonts' current association with Alasdair MacColla's royalist forces and their past military involvement against the Campbells. Accordingly, Argyll was able to use a supplementary defence for reprisals against the Lamonts in Cowal as against the MacDougalls and the MacAllisters in Kintyre. The three clans were acknowledged adherents of MacColla and the royalist forces on the western seaboard whom he had been empowered to prosecute with fire and sword under a commission of lieutenancy authorized by the covenanting Parliament of 1644. This commission – which was still current throughout the summer of 1647 – was upheld by the Treaty of Breda in 1650, which formalized the patriotic accommodation between covenanters and royalists to uphold Charles II as King of Scots and work for his restoration elsewhere in the British Isles. Although this defence glossed over the statutory distinction between reprisals carried out in hot and cold blood, Argyll was able to argue persuasively that the conduct of himself and his clansmen, no less than that of the covenanting army under David Leslie, was covered by the Act of Oblivion which accompanied the ratification of the Treaty of Breda by the Scottish Parliament prior to the coronation of Charles II as King of Great Britain at the outset of 1651. While all charges against Argyll for his conduct during the 1640s were consequently dropped, he was convicted for his treasonable collaboration with the Cromwellian regime during the 1650s and subsequently executed on 27 May 1661.[17]

IV

By 1665, however, the eldest son of the marquis, also Archibald Campbell, had been fully restored to the family estates and heritable jurisdiction. As ninth Earl of Argyll, he reasserted the territorial acquisitiveness of his clan, most notably at the expense of the Macleans of Duart who were eventually expropriated from Mull, Tiree and Morvern by 1681. While Argyll had the full backing of John Maitland, Duke of Lauderdale, the most powerful Scottish politician in the two decades following the Restoration, the armed resistance of the Macleans to expropriation was supported by the former royalist clans on the western seaboard. Having defied an order obtained by Argyll in his own heritable jurisdiction to effect their eviction for outstanding private debts and arrears of public dues amounting to almost £232,000 Scots (£19,333 sterling), the Macleans were deemed to be in rebellion against the Crown. Their legal position was further compromised when the Macleans and their former royalist allies mounted predatory raids on the Argyll estates that culminated in the wanton sacking of the Garvellach Isles in October 1675. Although the number of lives lost cannot be determined accurately, their hot-blooded action was reported to have exhibited such cruelty, barbarity and inhumanity as 'can scarcely be credited amongst savages, let alone in any part of the Christian world, where law and justice are supposed to prevail'. Not only did the Macleans become subject to a commission of fire and sword, but the ninth earl was authorized to mobilize the militia of the shires of Bute, Dumbarton and Inverness, as well as Argyll, to enforce expropriation.[18]

In keeping with central government's escalation of its military presence in the Highlands during Lauderdale's dominance of Scottish politics, commissions of fire and sword were backed up by the presence of regular troops and the raising of Independent Companies of trusted clansmen. Ostensibly, this military escalation was to curtail banditry and predatory raiding. In reality, the military were most frequently deployed as tax collectors. At the same time, by propagating a climate of disorder among the clans, the Highlands were used as a military training ground to further Lauderdale's ambitions to introduce absolutism on the cheap in Scotland. In order to maintain his personal exercise of provincial government north of the Border, Lauderdale was also prepared to promote incorporating union as a political diversion that would emasculate parliamentary opposition to the British court in England as well as Scotland.[19]

Integral to Lauderdale's absolutist endeavours was the deliberate confusion of clans with cateran bands. The latter, who had all but thrown over the social restraints of clanship, were primarily responsible for banditry and predatory raiding in the Highlands. However, there were three clans, in and around the district of Lochaber, who continued to engage in predatory raiding and episodically hire themselves out as enforcers, usually for landlords on the Lowland peripheries of the Highlands, in territorial disputes with neighbours. Of these three clans, the MacGregors were proscribed outlaws having been expropriated at the outset of the seventeenth century, the MacDonalds of Keppoch had had the charters to their estates rescinded for their involvement in the ClanDonald Rebellion of 1615, and the MacDonalds of Glencoe had also lost title to their estates for persistent banditry during the 1630s. All three clans had fought on the royalist side during the 1640s and had figured prominently in MacColla's winter devastations of Campbell estates in 1644 and 1645. All three had also sided with the Macleans against the House of Argyll during the 1670s. They added to their notoriety by their role in suppressing the Argyll Rebellion in 1685. This rebellion had been occasioned by the forfeiture of the ninth earl for refusing to recognize that the Catholic James, Duke of York, could become supreme governor of the Kirk of Scotland when he acceded to the throne as James VII and II. Although Argyll received limited backing from his clan, his rebellion was supported by the militant Protestants from the west of Scotland who formed the bedrock of the Whig regime which came to power at the Revolution in 1688-9. The three bandit clans and their former royalist associates utilized the ninth earl's rebellion as an opportunity for vengeance against his territorial interest in Argyll. Under the nominal command of John Murray, Marquis of Atholl, the Lochaber clans ravaged indiscriminately. At a stroke, Lowland prejudices about Highland lawlessness were reaffirmed by the depredations on what was termed the Atholl Raid. Central government felt justified in intensifying its military presence to contain disorder in the Highlands.[20]

All three clans participated in the last clan battle fought at Mulroy in Lochaber on 4 August 1688. This battle, fought by the MacDonalds of Keppoch and their bandit associates against the endeavours of their landlord, Lachlan Mackintosh of Torcastle, chief of ClanChattan, to evict them from their lands of Glenspean and

Glenroy, breached the official script. As a result, a punitive expeditionary force was despatched by central government in September, 'to destroy man, woman and child' pertaining to the MacDonalds of Keppoch. Their houses and their corn were to be burned. Although the MacDonalds of Keppoch retreated to the hills, the government troops indulged in four days of systematic devastation in Glenspean and Glenroy. The MacDonalds of Keppoch were only spared further reprisals by the advent of the Revolution against James VII and II towards the end of 1688. On the outbreak of hostilities between the Jacobites and the Whigs in 1689, the MacDonalds of Keppoch were in the anomalous position of being deemed rebels by the outgoing government of James VII and II for the events at Mulroy and by William of Orange's incoming Whig regime for their active Jacobitism. However, the clan's adherence to the Jacobite cause was marked less by principled commitment than by predatory opportunism. Instead of participating in the military campaign which was instigated by the Jacobite victory at Killiecrankie on 27 July 1689, the MacDonalds of Keppoch targeted the territories of the Clan-Chattan and their associates for reprisals, inflicting damages in excess of £35,950 Scots (£2,996 sterling).[21]

The MacDonalds of Glencoe and, to a lesser extent, the MacGregors also went on the rampage after Killiecrankie with the MacDonalds of Keppoch. The MacGregors were not only proscribed, however, they were also dispersed throughout the southern and eastern Highlands. The two branches of the MacDonalds were particularly vulnerable as their respective territories were easily identifiable and their manpower was not extensive. A further irritant for the incoming Whig regime was that the Jacobite clans, though unable to break out of the Highlands when their victory at Killiecrankie was reversed at Dunkeld in August 1689, took over two years to enter peace negotiations. The frustrations among William of Orange's British forces were made manifest by the general destruction wreaked in the Highlands by the army commanded by Hugh Mackay of Scourie and the particular ravaging of the island of Eigg in May 1690, when the naval commander from Ulster, Edward Pottinger, condoned murders and rapes perpetrated against a Catholic community associated with the MacDonalds of Clanranald.[22]

V

Although the MacDonalds of Keppoch were first choice for exemplary discipline by a Whig regime determined to eradicate Jacobitism, the MacDonalds of Glencoe became a more opportune target when their ageing chief, Alasdair MacIain failed to take an oath of allegiance to William of Orange by 1 January 1692. His failure was technical in that he had arrived at Inverlochy in Lochaber to give his oath just before the deadline, only to be redirected to Inveraray as the location of the sheriff court for Argyll where he duly made his submission by 5 January. Nonetheless, his technical default served as the pretext for the summary execution of himself and around thirty-seven of his clan. The resultant Massacre of Glencoe on 13 February 1692, was carried out by two companies of the Argyll Regiment under the command of Sir Robert Campbell of Glenlyon, who had asked for and received hospitality in Glencoe since 1 February. This massacre, the most commemorated in Highland history and whose historiography includes contributions by Beethoven, stands out as an atrocity not so much for the numbers massacred as for the legal circumstances. The breach of hospitality amounted to slaughter under trust that exposed not only the government but the Crown to charges of treason.[23]

Public perceptions bolstered by folk tradition and the contemporaneous reaction of Gaelic poets, have tended to view this atrocity as part of the ongoing feud between the Campbells and the MacDonalds.[24] While there was a legacy of feuding engendered primarily by the territorial acquisitiveness of ClanCampbell at the expense of the ClanDonald since the break-up of the Lordship of the Isles, it would be erroneous to depict the MacDonalds of Glencoe as inveterate enemies of the House of Argyll. Certainly, their notoriety as deprecators was resented by the chiefs of ClanCampbell who, as landlords to the unruly Glencoe men, were held accountable for reparations by central government. Nonetheless, the Campbell élite never wholly denied the Glencoe men their clientage. John Campbell, first Earl of Breadalbane, was instrumental in employing the MacDonalds as well as contingents of MacGregors in the Independent Companies from 1680. Breadalbane's employment of these poachers-turned-gamekeepers was part of a wider strategy to transform the Lochaber district from the epicentre of Highland disorder to the strong-arm of the Crown. The establishment of a permanent garrison at Inverlochy was to be complemented by the erection of Lochaber and its environs into a separate royal jurisdiction. As well as revoking the heritable jurisdictions of the House of Argyll and other leading landowners, their feudal titles to the territories of the Lochaber clans were to be bought out by the Crown at a cost of £126,000 Scots (£10,500 sterling). In addition to serving as a judicial centre, the garrison town was to be a regimental base for a thousand Lochaber clansmen recruited as a standing force to march on command 'upon all occasion of any troubel or insurrection'.

However, Breadalbane's suggestion that the Crown should productively tap the support of the clans which had formed the bedrock of the royalist campaigns during the civil wars was discredited by the Atholl Raid of 1685, albeit never entirely abandoned by James VII and II prior to his deposition by Scottish Whigs at the Revolution.[25]

Despite his Jacobite sympathies, Breadalbane remained neutral during the Scottish rising in support of James. With the Jacobite clans remaining armed in open defiance of the post-Revolution regime and with the continuous fear of an Irish invasion to oust the Whigs, Breadalbane was commissioned by William of Orange to negotiate a peaceful conclusion to the war in the Highlands. A treaty finalized at Achallader in Argyllshire on 30 June 1691, offered a pardon and indemnity for all chiefs who took an oath of allegiance to William at the sheriff court in their county of domicile by 1 January 1692. Breadalbane also took the opportunity to revive his strategy to transform Lochaber: £1,200 sterling (£14,400 Scots) was to be given to chiefs and clan gentry to purchase charters enabling them to hold their lands directly from the Crown rather than other chiefs and landlords like the House of Argyll which was again restored to its estates and heritable jurisdiction under Archibald Campbell, the tenth earl, at the Revolution. However, in a move that was to make him both a villain to the Gaelic poets and a ready scapegoat for central government in the wake of the massacre, Breadalbane purportedly agreed to a secret treaty with the Jacobite clans. The public agreement to recognize William was to be null in the event of an invasion from France in support of James VII and II. Moreover, if the forces loyal to the Whig government went abroad, the clans would rise and Breadalbane would join them with a thousand followers. At the same time, the public agreement required the assent of the exiled King James at Saint-Germain.[26]

When the public agreement offering a pardon and indemnity was confirmed officially on 26 August, William of Orange threatened defaulters with 'the utmost extremity of the law'. Two days later, the private articles agreed at Achallader were leaked to the Whig military establishment who duly informed the leading Scottish politicians at court. Breadalbane came under sustained pressure to contrive exemplary punishment for defaulters. By November, Breadalbane was acutely conscious that delayed submissions by the Jacobite clan élite were both undermining his revived strategy to transform Lochaber and leaving him vulnerable to political machinations at court. Delayed submissions were, on the one hand, encouraging unruly elements in Lochaber to resume their association with cateran bands and, on the other, preventing the release of up to four regiments of Scottish troops whom William wished to redeploy against the French in Flanders. His willingness to devise a scheme to disarm and emasculate the clans depended on the fulfilment, not the abrogation, of the public treaty of Achallader. In furtherance of his desire to raise a clan regiment solely licensed to bear arms in the Highlands, he planned to convert his castle of Kilchurn in Glenorchy into a military barracks. Breadalbane, while venting his frustrations over delayed submissions, may have sought to rechannel money due to the MacDonalds of Glencoe to secure feudal titles into reparations for cattle stolen by them during the Jacobite rising. However, there is no convincing evidence that he was prepared to interpret the utmost extremity of law as a massacre, far less to push beyond the extremity and perpetrate slaughter under trust. Indeed, after the deadlines for submissions had passed, but before the technical default of the Glencoe chief was known outside Inveraray, Breadalbane confided to his Edinburgh lawyer on 5 January 1692, that he was a spent force in the shaping of Highland policy at court.[27]

The methods for exemplary punishment of defaulters had already been decided before Breadalbane's arrival at court in late December. The principal architect of the massacre was the Secretary of State for Scotland, Sir John Dalrymple, Master of Stair, who had first backed then compromised Breadalbane over his negotiations with the Jacobite clans. The day before he informed the earl that he expected to hear either about prompt submissions or a scheme to maul the Jacobite clans, he had affirmed to Breadalbane on 2 December 1691 that he thought 'the Clan Donald must be rooted out'. He went on to question whether the £1,200 sterling set aside to buy feudal titles 'had been better employed to settle the Highlands, or to ravage them'. Stair, not Breadalbane, had the premeditated design to go beyond the limits of legality. Stair was also able to exploit the acerbic political rivalry between Breadalbane and the recently restored Earl of Argyll, who used his political interest at Edinburgh to query the legality of MacIain's delayed oath and to ensure that the Glencoe chief was excluded from the indemnity issued by the Scottish Privy Council in the new year. The news of MacIain's technical default was first conveyed to Stair privately at court by Argyll on 11 January. Both rejoiced that the way was now clear for exemplary action against the MacDonalds of Glencoe.[28]

Stair's motivation was essentially political. Having been a member of the outgoing regime who switched sides at the Revolution, rather than go into exile with James VII and II, Stair was a Whig by expediency not by commitment. Stair was not a firm upholder of a Revolutionary Settlement that allied constitutional limitations on the monarchy to a presbyterian establishment in the Kirk of Scotland. He supported proposals at court for an incorporating parliamentary union with England which would remove the necessity of the Crown being accountable to the Scottish Estates. The price of parliamentary accountability at the Revolution had been a resurgence in constitutional opposition to the court running Scotland as an English satellite, much to the frustration of William of Orange who considered such opposition as an intolerable irritant to his designs to check the military ambitions of Louis XIV of France. Simultaneously, Stair was intent on demonstrating to William that he was the hard man of Scottish politics who could deliver a compliant regime north of the border that would vote troops and supplies for William's continental campaigns. The contrived massacre of one or more Jacobite clans would strengthen his position to retain sole responsibility as Secretary of State for Scotland.[29]

Critical to this strategy was a propaganda campaign of religious disinformation. The Jacobite clans targeted for reprisals, particularly the ClanDonald, were branded as 'popish'. While the catholicism of the MacDonalds of Clanranald was a contributory factor in the atrocities perpetrated on the island of Eigg in May 1690, the vast majority of the Jacobite clans, including the MacDonalds of Glencoe, were episcopalian – like the Master of Stair, himself.[30] Albeit Stair had targeted both the MacDonalds of Keppoch and the MacDonalds of Glencoe for exemplary punishment, the Keppoch chief successfully made his peace with the Whig regime at Inverness just prior to the deadline for submissions. But, Alasdair MacIain, chief of the MacDonalds of Glencoe, having presented himself before Colonel John Hill, commander of the garrison of Inverlochy, on 30 December was redirected to the shire court at Inveraray. An eventful journey through the snows delayed his arrival there until 2 January 1692. The technical default of MacIain played into the hands of Stair. On being informed at court on 11 January, he exalted that 'it's a great work of charity to be exact in rooting out that damnable sect, the worst in all the Highlands'. Five days later, he instructed the commander-in-chief of the Whig forces in Scotland, Sir Thomas Livingstone, that for a just example of vengeance, 'I entreat that the thieving Tribe of Glencoe may be rooted out in earnest.[31]

That same day, Livingstone had been informed by William of Orange that if the MacDonalds of Glencoe could be separated from the rest of the Jacobite clans, 'it will be a proper vindication of publick justice to extirpate that Sect of Thieves'. Having simultaneously accepted belated submissions from five other Jacobite chiefs, William was clearly prepared to countenance the isolation and the annihilation of the MacDonalds. However, as William made clear in a letter to Livingstone on 11 January, defaulters were to be proceeded against by fire and sword. Albeit this was couched in terms of the traditional dispensing of summary justice, the military were to be the sole exponents of this commission which was to be directed against houses, livestock, plenishing, goods and clansmen – but not women and children. Moreover, the conditional nature of William's authorization of action against the MacDonalds of Glencoe on 16 January exonerates him both from direct complicity in the massacre and from treasonable charges arising from slaughter under trust. However, William can be accused of crassness when he established a royal commission of inquiry in April 1695, with the claim that he knew nothing of the massacre until eighteen months after the event; a charge compounded by his rescinding of the £1,200 sterling promised to the Jacobite clans at Achallader and, above all, by his pardoning Stair after the discredited Secretary of State was accorded prime responsibility for the massacre by the Scottish Estates in July 1695.[32]

In effect, Stair translated the King's conditional authorization to extirpate into a reality. Moreover, he withheld for nineteen days information about MacIain's technical default at court while he contrived punitive action with Livingstone. Stair was determined that this action was not only to be exemplary but also to be done quietly without either the commotion or limitations traditionally associated with commissions of fire and sword. Two days after MacIain's default was circulated at court, troops of the Argyll Regiment moved into Glencoe on 1 February. In requesting hospitality in anticipation of orders to move against another prominent defaulter, Alasdair MacDonald of Glengarry, the troops were unaware that Stair's instructions for a massacre had been communicated to Colonel Hill at Inverlochy with the admonition that action 'be secret and sudden'. Only the pleadings of Hill, a humane Ulsterman distraught by his orders, stopped Stair transporting the survivors of the massacre. Indeed, Stair was still determined to remove survivors from Glencoe when he was dismissed from office in 1695.[33]

In his meticulous planning of the massacre, Stair had two willing accomplices among the military. Livingstone, the Scottish commander-in-chief, though ranking as a brigadier, was still being paid as a colonel. Stair used his twelve months arrears of pay as an effective bargaining counter. The career ambitions of Lieutenant-Colonel James Hamilton, second-in-command at Inverlochy, were utilized by Stair and Livingstone to force compliance from Hill. Hamilton was brought into play as early as 23 January, when he received instructions from Livingstone that his garrison was to carry out the wishes of the court for punitive action in Glencoe, 'that the thieving nest might be entirely rooted out' without troubling central government with prisoners. Hamilton, in turn, secured the compliance of Major Robert Duncanson of the Argyll Regiment who sent the fatal instruction to Campbell of Glenlyon on 12 February, that the massacre was to commence the following morning at five o'clock. Yet, Hamilton and Duncanson were under instructions to assist Glenlyon from seven o'clock – a critical two-hour gap which strongly suggests that Glenlyon's troops, two-thirds of whom were drawn from Campbell estates, were set up for blame. Glenlyon, moreover, made a highly plausible stooge. A drunken, vengeful bankrupt who, despite his long-standing local association fortified by marriage alliances with the MacDonalds of Glencoe, had lost livestock to them during the Jacobite rising.[34]

Nonetheless, news of the massacre on 13 February 1692 seeped out once Glenlyon mislaid his order papers in a coffee house after his troops withdrew to Edinburgh. His orders were spirited to France where they were published in the Paris *Gazette* on 12 April and subsequently exploited to embarrass the Whig regime by Jacobite polemicists based in London. The resultant controversy in Scotland was not abated by the royal commission of inquiry which served to reinvigorate parliamentary attacks on court influence in general and to denigrate William's ambitions for a political union in particular. While the Scottish Estates were intent on retribution against Stair, no endeavour was made to secure reparations for the MacDonalds of Glencoe despite the poignant petition of the survivors on 26 June 1695, that their clan had been murdered and butchered, 'against the laws of nature and nations, the laws of hospitality, and the publick faith, by a band of men quartered amongst them, and pretending peace, tho' they perpetrated the grossest crueltie under the colour of his Majesties authority'.[35]

Notwithstanding the political opportunism of the Scottish Estates, the most jarring and salutary, yet most neglected and incongruous, feature of the massacre was the disregard for clan affinities. Not only did the Argyll interest countenance Stair's setting up of their kinsman Breadalbane as the public scapegoat for the slaughter under trust, but the minority Catholic faction within the Jacobite clans led by Alasdair MacDonald of Glengarry provided ready, if unwitting, accessories of Stair. Breadalbane's negotiated indemnity at Achallader, confirmed by William of Orange on 26 August 1691, left four months for the Jacobite clan élite to swear allegiance. Why, therefore, did MacIain and the other chiefs persist in a policy of brinkmanship? In part, blame can be attached to the exiled James VII and II who did not authorize their transfer of allegiance until 12 December. In the interim, however, the chiefs were dissuaded from seeking indemnity by false rumours of French assistance for their cause. These rumours were circulated primarily by Glengarry, who was also instrumental in leaking details of Breadalbane's secret treaty to Stair. Glengarry actively discouraged chiefs like MacIain and Sir Ewen Cameron of Lochiel, the leader of the majority episcopalian faction among the Jacobite clans, who were prepared to make their peace with William. Glengarry was the first Jacobite chief to receive news of the authorization from Saint-Germain on 23 December. But, he delayed informing Cameron of Lochiel until 30 hours before the indemnity expired. Lochiel, who just managed to reach Inveraray before the prescribed deadline expired, was designated to inform MacIain. Arguably, the Glencoe chief had insufficient time to seek indemnity at Inveraray before 1 January 1692; hence, his fateful decision to travel the shorter distance to the garrison at Inverlochy.[36]

VI

While the massacre of Glencoe certainly stiffened the resolve of the Jacobite clans to maintain support for the exiled House of Stuart, its historical significance rests primarily on the subsequent willingness of the British political establishment to escalate reprisals. At the same time, the negative political ramifications arising from slaughter under trust as a treasonable offence, meant that the exemplary punishment of clans could no longer be conducted covertly in the manner of Stair. Despite siren voices within the British establishment calling for further exemplary measures along the lines of Glencoe, reprisals after the next major Jacobite rising in 1715-16 were relatively lenient, partly because of the need to establish the House of Hanover as the new ruling dynasty, but primarily because of the widespread Jacobite affiliations of the Scottish nobles and gentry. However, the greatest severity awaited the failure of the last major Jacobite rising in 1745-6, when the front-line role of the clans in a campaign that reached as far as Derby, provoked rampant Scotophobia. In marking out the Jacobite clans for special treatment, the salutary examples of summary justice inflicted directly by the military not only at Glencoe, but also at Toward, Ascog and Dunaverty, paved the way for the genocidal intentions of 'Butcher William', Duke of Cumberland, to eradicate any future Highland threat to the British State.[37]

Notes

1. c.f. S.G. Ellis and S. Barber, eds, *Conquest and Union, Fashioning a British State, 1485-1725* (London, 1995); R.G. Asch, ed., *Three Nations – A Common History? England, Scotland, Ireland and British History, c. 1660-1920* (Bochum, 1993); A. Fletcher and P. Roberts, eds, *Religion, Culture and Society in Early Modern Britain: Essays in Honour of Patrick Collinson* (Cambridge,

1994); P.S. Hodge, ed., *Scotland and the Union* (Edinburgh, 1994); R.A. Mason, ed., *Scots and Britons: Scottish Political Thought and the Union of 1603* (Cambridge, 1994); A. Grant and K.G. Stringer, eds, *Uniting the Kingdom? The Making of British History* (London, 1995); J. Robertson, ed., *A Union for Empire: Political Thought and the Union of 1707* (Cambridge, 1995); B. Bradshaw and J. Morrill, eds, *The British Problem c. 1534-1707: State Formation in the Atlantic Archipelago* (Basingstoke, 1996); S.J. Connolly, ed., *Kingdoms United?* (Dublin, 1998).

2. *Acts of the Parliaments of Scotland (APS)*, 12 vols, T. Thomson and C. Innes, eds, (Edinburgh, 1812-75), vol. 3 (1567-92), 451 c.34, 461-67 c.59.

3. A.I. Macinnes, *Clanship, Commerce and the House of Stuart, 1603-1788* (East Linton, 1996), 30-55.

4. D. Gregory, *The History of the Western Highlands and Isles of Scotland, 1493-1625* (Edinburgh, 1836, reprinted 1975), passim.

5. *Register of the Privy Council of Scotland (RPCS)*, first series, 12 vols, J.H. Burton and D. Masson, eds, (Edinburgh, 1870-98), vol. 2 (1569-78), 9-11; vol. 3 (1578-85), 9, 61, 278-80, 505-6; vol. 4 (1585-92), 55-57, 787-92, 802-3, 812-14. K.M. Brown, *Bloodfeud in Scotland, 1573-1625: Violence, Justice and Politics in Early Modern Society* (Edinburgh, 1986), 32, 46. The episode which purportedly triggered the passage of the act concerning slaughter occurred as part of a long-standing feud between the MacDonalds of Dunvyeg whose territories extended through Kintyre to Islay and Jura, and the Macleans of Duart whose heartlands were in Mull, Morvern and Tiree, but who also claimed influence in Islay and Jura. In the course of 1586, Angus MacDonald of Dunvyeg had captured Lachlan Maclean of Duart and around forty of his clansmen while they were his guests in Kintyre. The endeavours of the Macleans to resist capture led to two of them being burnt. While the Maclean chief was liberated, contemporaneous reports that all the hostages were beheaded – one each day until their numbers were used up – were countered by a remission issued by the Privy Council on 16 April 1587. No charges were to be pressed against MacDonald of Dunvyeg on condition that he delivered up the remaining hostages and that he, like the other chiefs involved in the Irish mercenary trade, subscribe to the general band.

6. *RPCS*, vol. 4, 156-61, 290-91, 341-42. The chief of ClanGillean was neither held to account for this episode, nor for subsequent excesses prior to his death fighting against the MacDonalds of Kintyre, Islay and Jura in a naval engagement at Gruinard off the island of Islay in 1598.

7. Gregory, *The History of the Western Highlands*, 272-73, 280-89, 296; D. Stevenson, *Alasdair MacColla and the Highland Problem in the Seventeenth Century* (Edinburgh, 1980), 1-33; I.F. Grant and H. Cheape, *Periods in Highland History* (London, 1987), 14-21.

8. Macinnes, *Clanship, Commerce and the House of Stuart*, 56-87.

9. Gregory, *The History of the Western Highlands*, 305-12, 326-28, 357, 361-86; *Ancient Criminal Trials in Scotland*, 3 vols, R. Pitcairn, ed. (Bannatyne Club, Edinburgh, 1833), vol. 1, 15, 21; vol. 2, 366; A. Matheson, 'The Trial of Sir James MacDonald of Islay', *Transactions of the Gaelic Society of Glasgow*, V (1958): 207-22.

10. Inveraray Castle Archives (ICA), bundle 63/3; ICA, Argyll transcripts, vol. 8 (1600-10), nos. 114, 256; vol. 9 (1611-20), no. 163; Scottish Record Office (SRO), Breadalbane Collection, GD 112/1/378. Material collected from ICA was funded by Major Research Grants from the British Academy.

11. Macinnes, *Clanship, Commerce and the House of Stuart*, 88-121; *State Trials*, W. Cobbet, ed. (London, 1809), vol. 5, 1369-499.

12. ICA, Argyll Transcripts, vol. 12 (1638-49), nos. 357, 423; vol. 13 (1650-59), nos. 15, 63, 136; H. MacKechnie, *The Lamont Clan* (Edinburgh, 1938), 168-93; D. Stevenson, 'The Massacre at Dunaverty', *Scottish Studies*, 19 (1975): 27-37.

13. *State Trials*, vol. 5, 1379-94. Reprisals, which commenced in 1645, continued for nine years. Three months before the actual massacres of June in which he participated prominently, Duncan Campbell of Ellangreig and a party of armed accomplices murdered forty adults and children while seizing possession of the Lamont lands of Cowston and Stroan. Two of the four leading gentry imprisoned with the Lamont chief were hanged after trial in Argyll's justiciary court at Inveraray. Their estates were forfeited respectively to Argyll and Ardkinglass.

14. Ibid., 1409-11; Stevenson, *Alasdair MacColla and the Highland Problem*, 214-17, 226.

15. *The Lord Marques of Argyle's Speech to a Grand Committee of Both Houses of Parliament* (London, 1646).

16. Sir J. Turner, *Memoirs of His Own Life and Times, 1632-70*, T. Thomson, ed. (Bannatyne Club, Edinburgh, 1829), 45-47. Turner's statement, that the treatment of prisoners at Dunaverty was not outside the bounds of restraint, have particular force in a European context with respect to reprisals against armies perceived to be in opposition to the State – in this case the Covenanting Movement in 1647, albeit the trial of Argyll was brought in the name of the Crown at the Restoration. (G. Parker, 'Constraints on Warfare in the Western World', in *The Laws of War*, M. Howard, G.J. Andreopolous and M.R. Shulman, eds (New Haven and London, 1994), 40-58, 233-40).

17. *State Trials*, vol. 5, 1458-62; ICA, Argyll Transcripts, vol. 12 (1638-49), no. 313. By giving up Toward, Sir James Lamont, his clansmen and their families were to have safe conduct to rejoin MacColla. In return for delivering up weapons taken from the Campbells, either from their ransacked houses or during skirmishes in the field, the Lamont chief and gentry were free to transport all baggage and provisions but not ammunition from Toward. Ardkinglass undertook to provide boats for this purpose, which Lamont guaranteed to return. The Lamonts agreed to move out with their baggage before 8 o'clock the next morning, having delivered the keys and the keeping of Toward to Ardkinglass.

18. ICA, bundles 47/1, 48/2, 49/1, 54/4-5 and /329, 69/2-3, 70/6-7 and /9, 100/51 and /99; Macinnes, *Clanship, Commerce and the House of Stuart*, 130-37; Stevenson, *Alasdair MacColla and the Highland Problem*, 285-87.

19. W. Ferguson, *Scotland's Relations with England: a Survey to 1707* (Edinburgh, 1977), 153-7; *History of the Union of Scotland and England by Sir John Clerk of Penicuik*, D. Douglas, ed. (Edinburgh, 1993), 78-81.

20. ICA, Argyll Transcripts, vol. 11 (1629-37), nos. 727, 757; Historical Manuscripts Commission (HMC), 12th Report, Appendix 8, *MSS of the Dukes of Atholl*, (London, 1891), 12-24; *An Account of the Depredations committed on the ClanCampbell and their followers during the Years 1685 and 1686 by the Troops of the Duke of Gordon, Marquis of Atholl, Lord Strathnaver and others; when the Earl of Argyll Rose in Arms to Oppose the Tyranny of James VII* (Edinburgh, 1816), passim. Regardless of any involvement in the rebellion, Campbell clansmen had their livestock and household furnishings removed, their crops and mills destroyed, and their houses demolished. Depredations, which continued throughout the winter, were perpetrated particularly in areas settled by Lowland migrants invited into Cowal and Kintyre to promote the work of recovery in the wake of the civil wars.

21. Macinnes, *Clanship, Commerce and the House of Stuart*, 42-46. In order to reinforce his commission of fire and sword, Mackintosh of Torcastle had been

given a contingent of government troops to overpower and evict the MacDonalds of Keppoch. However, not only was the battle lost by the ClanChattan, but
the commander of the government forces, Sir Kenneth MacKenzie of Suddie,
was killed at Mulroy.

22. *APS*, vol. 9 (1689-95), 45, 190-1 c. 143, 233 c.2, 365, appendix, 126; SRO,
Leven and Melville MS, GD 26/13/31-2 and /40; P. Hopkins, *Glencoe and the
End of the Highland War* (Edinburgh, 1986), 234-35.

23. L. von Beethoven, *On the Massacre of Glencoe: Das Blutbad von Glencoe* (New
York, 19nd); D.J. MacDonald, *Slaughter under Trust* (London, 1965); J. Preb-
ble, *Glencoe, the Story of the Massacre* (London, 1966); M. Linklater, *Massacre:
The Story of Glencoe* (London and Glasgow, 1982); Hopkins, *Glencoe and the
End of the Highland War*, 286-350.

24. *Orain Iain Luim: Songs of John MacDonald, Bard of Keppoch*, A.M. MacKenzie, ed. (Scottish Gaelic Texts Society, Edinburgh, 1973), 198-201; J.A.
MacLean, 'The Sources, Particularly the Celtic Sources for the History of the
Highlands in the Seventeenth Century, (Ph.D. thesis, University of Aberdeen,
1939), 340-47.

25. *RPCS*, third series, 16 vols, P.H. Brown, H.E. Paton and E.W.M. Balfour-
Melville, eds (Edinburgh, 1908-70), vol. 2 (1665-69), 329-32; National Library
of Scotland (NLS), Campbell Papers, MS 1672, fos. 40-41; SRO, Breadalbane
Collection, GD 112/1/682. In 1667, the clan elite of the MacDonalds of Glencoe
were arraigned before the Scottish Privy Council for leading a predatory raid the
previous autumn into Aberdeenshire, a raid that purportedly inflicted damages
in excess of £18,930 Scots (£1,578 sterling) for loss of livestock, furnishings and
crops on the estates of Dame Magdalene Scrimgeour, Lady Drum. As their landlord under the terms of the general band, Archibald, ninth Earl of Argyll, had
been obliged to part with £7,082 Scots (£590 sterling) to recoup Lady Drum's
losses. Nonetheless, Archibald Campbell of Inverawe had not only brokered a
reconciliation with the House of Argyll by 1669, but acted as the persistent protector of the Glencoe men in the Restoration era.

26. *Highland Papers: Papers Illustrative of the Political Condition of the Highlands
of Scotland, 1689-1696*, J. Gordon, ed. (Maitland Club, Edinburgh, 1845), 33-
166; Glasgow University Library (GUL), Papers on the Massacre of Glencoe,
MS Gen. 533/38; J. Drummond of Balhaldie, *Memoirs of Sir Ewen Cameron of
Lochiel*, J. MacKnight, ed. (Maitland Club, Edinburgh, 1842), 255-314.

27. Dumfries House (DH), Loudoun Papers, A517/12-14; Prebble, *Glencoe, the
story of the Massacre*, 181-82, 226-29

28. *Highland Papers*, 49-55; GUL, Papers on the Massacre of Glencoe, MS Gen.
533/38.

29. P.W.J. Riley, *King William and the Scottish Politicians* (Edinburgh, 1979), 81-
102; A.I. Macinnes, 'The Massacre of Glencoe', *The Historian*, 35 (1992):
16-19.

30. W. Ferguson, 'Religion and the Massacre of Glencoe', *Scottish Historical
Review (SHR)*, XLVI (1967): 82-87, and SHR, XLVII (1968); J. Prebble, 'Religions and the Massacre of Glencoe', *SHR*, XLVI: 185-86; Hopkins, *Glencoe
and the End of the Highland War*, 44.

31. GUL, Papers on the Massacre of Glencoe, MS Gen. 533/38. The administration
of the oath of allegiance had been held up further by the new year festivities. The
bucolic sheriff-depute of Argyll, Sir Colin Campbell of Ardkinglass (the grand-
son of the chief executioner of the Lamonts in 1646), did not appear at
Inveraray until 5 January.

32. Ibid.

33. Ibid.; *Highland Papers*, 91-92, 121.

34. GUL, Papers on the Massacre of Glencoe, MS Gen. 533/38.

35. *Highland Papers*, 119, 150-1; J. Hay, [1st Marquis of] Tweeddale, *The history of the feuds and conflicts among the clans in the northern parts of Scotland from the year 1031 to 1519, now first published from a manuscript of the reign of James VI: With an authentic narrative of the massacre of Glencoe, contained in a report of the Commission given by His Majesty William III 20th June 1693* (Aberdeen, 1842); G. Ridpath, *The massacre of Glencoe: being a true narrative of the barbarous murther of the Glenco-men in the Highlands of Scotland by way of military execution on the 13th of Feb. 1692* (London, 1703).

36. DH, Loudoun Papers, A517/12-14; Drummond of Balhaldie, *Memoirs of Sir Ewen Cameron of Lochiel*, 305-13.

37. *Highland Papers*, 162-66; A.I. Macinnes, 'Scottish Gaeldom in the Aftermath of the '45: The Creation of the Silence', in *Jacobitism and the '45*, M. Lynch, ed. (The Historical Association, London, 1995), 71-83.

CHAPTER 7

THE CIRCASSIANS

A FORGOTTEN GENOCIDE?

Stephen D. Shenfield

Who Are (or Were) the Circassians?

This is the question I am usually asked if I ever mention my interest in the Circassians. Except for specialists in the Caucasus, there are few people in the Western world (although more people in the Middle East) who remember who the Circassians were, where they came from or what happened to them. They are an almost forgotten people. You will find no place called 'Circassia' on any contemporary map. The nearest you will get to it, and then only should you happen to know that the Russian word for 'Circassian' (borrowed from the Turkish) is *cherkess*, will be the Karachai-Cherkess Autonomous Province in southern Russia. This area in fact lies somewhat to the north of the historical Circassia: it is where some of the Circassians were resettled following the tsarist conquest of their homeland. Moreover, the name of the territory is now somewhat misleading, inasmuch as the Circassians, who theoretically share it with the Turkic Karachai people, actually account for a mere 10 percent of its roughly half-million population.[1]

Perhaps, however, you like poring over old maps, as I do. If so, take a look at a map of Russia dating from the early-nineteenth century, and you will find Circassia clearly marked – a country in the north-western Caucasus and along the north-eastern shore of the Black Sea, stretching southwards from the banks of the River Kuban, which at that time marked the southern boundary of the Russian empire. And you can read about Circassia in the old books of nineteenth-century western travellers such as the French consul Gamba (1826), the English adventurer James Bell (1841), the French couple de Hell (1847), the American George Leighton Ditson (1850), and the Dutch consul de Marigny (1887). And if you go back in time a few more decades and inspect a map drawn in the middle of the eighteenth century, then you will see the name 'Circassia' boldly straddling both banks of the River Kuban, from the lowlands east of the Sea of Azov, between the Kuban and the Don, all the way to the borders of Ossetia and Chechnya up in the main Caucasus mountain range and along the Black Sea coast from the isthmus of the Sea of Azov to Abkhazia.[2] Circassia at that time, prior to tsarist imperial conquest, occupied an area of 55,663 square kilometres – rather greater than the area of Denmark – and possessed an indigenous population in excess of two million.[3]

The origins of the Circassians can be traced back as far as the Bosphoran Kingdom of the eighth century BC, and possibly to the Cimmerian Empire that existed along the shores of the Azov Sea before 1500 BC. They enjoyed close cultural and trading ties with the ancient Greeks, especially with the Athenians, and even participated in the Olympic Games. Their gods also closely corresponded to the Greek gods: Shi-bla, God of Thunder, was their Zeus, Tlepsh, God of Iron and Fire, their Hephaestos.[4] For most of their history they were an agricultural people. They had a feudal and patriarchal social structure consisting of princes, nobles, freemen and serfs. Most accounts describe them as having consisted of 'tribes', the exact number and designation of which seem to have varied over time. These tribes were too closely related to be considered separate ethnic or even sub-ethnic groups. Circassians' identity was defined by a series of overlapping kinship groups, stretching outwards from the individual's closest kin to the Circassian nation (or proto-nation if one prefers) as a whole.[5]

Circassia was Christianized under Byzantine influence in the fifth and sixth centuries. While Daghestan in the north-eastern Caucasus was Islamized as early as the eighth century, Circassia long stayed outside the sphere of Arab and Muslim influence.[6] From the sixteenth century it entered into alliance with Georgia: Georgians and Circassians regarded themselves as constituting a single Christian island in the Muslim sea and jointly appealed to Russia for protection. Tsar Ivan the Terrible had a Circassian wife. Muslim influence among the Circassians dates no earlier than the seventeenth century, and only in the eighteenth century, under the threat of impending Russian invasion, did they accept Islam, with a view to facilitating a defensive alliance with Ottoman Turkey and the Crimean Tatar Khanate.

The Circassians fought against Russian conquest for over a century, from 1763 to 1864 – longer than any other people of the

Caucasus, even the Chechens. Their final defeat in the 1860s led to massacre and forced deportation, mainly across the Black Sea to Turkey, in the course of which a large proportion of them perished. Many Circassians were also utilized by the Ottomans in the Balkans to suppress the rebellious Serbs, but almost all of these were later relocated to the interior of Anatolia.

Since that time, the great majority – about 90 percent – of people of Circassian descent have lived in exile, mostly in Turkey, Jordan and elsewhere in the Middle East. Only isolated remnants, currently about three to four hundred thousand people altogether, remain in Russia and other parts of the post-Soviet region. During the last decades of the tsarist regime, the emptied and devastated Circassian lands were resettled by Russian, Ukrainian, Armenian and other colonists. Later many Georgians also settled in Abkhazia, feeding resentments that culminated in the recent Abkhaz-Georgian war – a conflict which can only be understood against the background of the Circassian trauma of the last century.

Massacre and Deportation

In 1860, having failed to subdue the Circassians in ninety-seven years of warfare, the Russian government decided to enforce their mass migration to other regions of the empire or to Turkey. General Yevdokimov was entrusted with the execution of this policy, and advanced into the still unconquered parts of Circassia with newly formed mobile columns of riflemen and Cossack cavalry. In the northern areas that he first penetrated, the Circassians submitted to his will: that same year, four thousand families set sail for Turkey from the estuary of the Kuban without offering any resistance.[7] However, the tribes living further to the south-east did prepare to resist. At the place where now stands the popular Black Sea resort of Sochi, the Abadzekhs, Shapseghs and Ubykhs formed an assembly and appealed— in vain – to the Ottomans and Britain for help.

In September 1861, the Emperor himself, Tsar Alexander II, visited Yekaterinodar, the Russian town closest to the scene of the action, and there received a delegation of Circassian chiefs. The chiefs expressed readiness to recognize Russian suzerainty provided that Russian troops and Cossacks were removed from Circassian lands beyond the Rivers Kuban and Laba. Their proposal was rejected. The Abadzekhs, however, agreed to move to new lands offered them further north (many of the titular people of the Adygei Autonomous Province are their descendants) while the chiefs of the other tribes refused to uproot their people.

Subsequent military operations against them began in the spring of 1862.[8] The Russian soldiers systematically burned the Circassian villages – all the villages of the Shapsegh without exception were burned down – while the crops growing in the fields were trampled under the hooves of the Cossacks' horses.[9] Those inhabitants who then declared their submission to the Tsar were marched off, under the control of Russian superintendants, for resettlement on the plain to the north while those who refused to submit were sent down to the seashore to await deportation to Turkey. Many others – men, women and children – fled from their burning villages only to perish of hunger and exposure in the forest and mountains.

Having conquered the Shapsegh and Abadzakh, recounts the Circassian historian Shauket, the column of General Babich followed the seashore southwards, destroying villages as it went:

> They were on the border of the land of the Ubykh. From the side of the Goitkh pass another column came to meet them. Little Ubykhia became the last citadel of Circassian freedom. The Ubykh made a last attempt to prolong the agony, but the Russians compressed the ring ever tighter. From the south, troops were landed in the very heart of the Ubykh land, while from the north three columns advanced through the mountains and along the seashore. The last resistance was broken.[10]

Trakho, another Circassian historian, continues the story:

> There remained only the small coastal tribes: the Pskhu, the Akhtsipsou, the Aibgo and the Jigit. In the course of May 1864 these tribes were annihilated almost to the last man, woman and child. Seeing this, Circassians gathered from all corners of the country in a frenzy of despair threw themselves into the valley of the Aibgo. For four days (7-11 May) the Russians were repulsed with great losses. Heavy artillery was then brought up and began to belch fire and smoke into the little valley. Not one of the defenders survived. The capture of this little valley, lost in the mountains, was the last act in the long tragedy of the Circassian people. On 21 May the Great Prince Mikhail Nikolaevich gathered his troops in a clearing for a thanksgiving service.[11]

Of this same final battle-pogrom Shauket writes :

> The last battle took place in the area of the Black Sea near Maikop, in the Khodz valley [i.e., the valley of the Aibgo] near the town of Akhchip. That rough mountainous area was the last stronghold at which women and children assembled for protection from the Russian advance. The women threw their jewellery into the river, took up

arms and joined the men in order to fight the battle of death for the sake of their homeland and honour, lest they should fall captives in Russian hands. The two parties met in a horrible battle which turned out to be a massacre unprecedented in history. The objective of that battle [for the Circassians] was not to achieve success or victory, but to die honourably and to leave a life which had no honourable hope left. In that battle men and women were slaughtered mercilessly and blood flowed in rivers, so that it was said that "the bodies of the dead swam in a sea of blood". Nevertheless, the Russians were not content with what they had done, but sought to satisfy their instincts by making the surviving children targets for their cannon shells.[12]

The subsequent deportations to Turkey began on 28 May. They took place under horrendous conditions. The Russian historian Berzhe bore witness to the state of the Circassians even as they awaited deportation on the Black Sea shore:

> I shall never forget the overwhelming impression made on me by the mountaineers in Novorossiisk [New-Russian] Bay, where about seventeen thousand of them were gathered on the shore. The late, inclement and cold time of year, the almost complete absence of means of subsistence and the epidemic of typhus and smallpox raging among them made their situation desperate. And indeed, whose heart would not be touched on seeing, for example, the already stiff corpse of a young Circassian woman lying in rags on the damp ground under the open sky with two infants, one struggling in his death-throes while the other sought to assuage his hunger at his dead mother's breast? And I saw not a few such scenes.[13]

Those who had survived this ordeal thus far were now herded by the Russian soldiers en masse on to barges and small Turkish and Greek ships, loaded with several times as many passengers as they could carry. Many of these sank and their passengers drowned in the open sea. For those who survived the voyage, conditions on arrival in Turkey were no less horrific. Arrangements that had been made by the Turkish government for receiving and resettling the migrants were grossly inadequate. Moshnin, the Russian consul in Trapezund on the Turkish coast, reported as follows:

> About six thousand Circassians were landed in Batum, [and] up to four thousand were sent to Churuk-su on the border [with Turkey]. They came with their emaciated and dying livestock. Average mortality seven people per day. About 240,000 deportees have arrived in Trapezund and its environs, of whom 19,000 have died ... Average mortality two hundred people per day. Most of them are sent to Sam-

sun; 63,290 remain. In Kerasund there are about fifteen thousand people. In Samsun and its environs over 110,000 people. Mortality about two hundred people per day. Typhus is raging.[14]

How many Circassians, then, perished from death in battle, by massacre, drowning, hunger, exposure and disease? Prior to the Russian conquest, the Circassians (including the Abkhaz) numbered about two million. By 1864, the north-western Caucasus had been emptied of its indigenous population almost in entirety. About 120-150,000 Circassians were resettled in places elsewhere in the Empire set aside by the Russian government. (By the time of the 1897 census, there were 217,000 Circassians in Russia). According to Brooks, about 500,000 were deported to Turkey;[15] in addition, thirty thousand families – perhaps 200,000 people – had emigrated voluntarily in 1858, prior to the deportations. That still leaves well over one-half of the original population unaccounted for, to which must be added those who died at sea or on arrival. The number who died in the Circassian catastrophe of the 1860s could hardly, therefore, have been fewer than one million, and may well have been closer to one-and-a-half million.[16]

Was It Genocide?

Did the Russian conquest and deportation of the Circassians constitute the deliberate genocide of a people, or was it 'only' a case of ethnic cleansing carried out with brutal disregard to human suffering? My approach to this difficult question firstly involves examining the background of previous and concurrent Russian treatment of newly conquered peoples. Had the Russian empire already perpetrated, or was it perpetrating, genocide in other places, outside the Caucasus? Secondly, I consider the attitude of the nineteenth-century Russian political and military élite towards the Circassians. Had the possibility of genocide been contemplated as a solution to the problem posed by the Circassians' resistance to conquest? Or, to use the phrase made famous by Norman Cohn, was there 'a warrant for genocide'?[17] And thirdly, why was the decision taken in favour of deportation? What was the thinking of the Tsar and his advisers that underlay this decision? Does it appear likely that their real purpose was genocide?

On this score it should suffice to consider two other important examples of Russia's relations with newly conquered peoples: the conquest of the native peoples of Siberia in the seventeenth century, and the incorporation of the Kazakh nomads in the nineteenth century.[18] This latter process reached completion at about the same time as the conquest of Circassia (1864).

The indigenous peoples of Siberia lacked the numbers, political unity or military strength with which to block the steady Russian advance eastwards to the Pacific, but on occasion they did resist their economic exploitation. Thus, Russian brutality in collection of the pelt tax (*yasak*) sparked a rebellion among the Yakuts and the Tungusic-speaking tribes along the River Lena in 1642. The Russians responded with a reign of terror: native settlements were torched and hundreds of people were tortured and killed. The Yakut population alone is estimated to have fallen as a result by 70 percent between 1642 and 1682. However, it was the intention of the government in Moscow to exploit, not exterminate, the indigenes, and in order to resuscitate declining fur deliveries steps were taken towards the end of the century to protect them: for instance, no executions were to be carried out without Moscow's consent. Moscow again intervened after the most cruel episode of all, the 1697-9 invasion of the Kamchatka peninsula by the commander Vladimir Atlasov. His force of one hundred men killed twelve thousand Chukchi, and eight thousand Koryaks and Kamchadals respectively. Yet following an epidemic of suicides, local authorities were ordered to restrain natives from taking their own lives.[19] Thus, though a large proportion of indigenous Siberians did perish as a consequence of the Russian conquest of their lands, this was the result of economic exploitation, the brutal suppression of uprisings and the murderous zeal of individual military commanders rather than of any deliberate state policy of genocide.

A similar conclusion may be drawn regarding the treatment of the Kazakh nomads. Russian outposts were established along the northern edges of the Kazakh steppe as early as the sixteenth century, but the interior was incorporated only in the nineteenth century, between the 1820s and the 1860s. Like the Siberian indigenes, the Kazakhs bowed to the inevitable and did not offer widespread resistance to the Russian advance. There were, however, some local uprisings (as in 1836-7), provoked by the confiscation of traditional grazing grounds. As the nineteenth century wore on, the Kazakhs were greatly impoverished as they and their herds were squeezed into ever smaller areas of the steppe to make room for new Russian settlers, leading to population losses, though not on a truly genocidal scale.[20] The idea of getting rid of an entire people, whether by means of forcible deportation or by genocide, therefore, does not appear to have arisen in previous Russian practice. The decision to deport the Circassians represented something new.

We find an interesting reflection of contemporary Russian perceptions of the Circassians in the books of western travellers
sympathetic to Russian ambitions in the Caucasus. The Circassians
are typically portrayed as primitive warlike barbarians and savage
bandits. 'The peoples of Circassia and Abkhazia,' a French diplomat writes, 'have lived by piracy and brigandage from time
immemorial ... Anger, vengeance and greed are their dominant passions.' A French tourist couple entertain their readers with the story
of how a Polish lady was kidnapped by Circassians while on her
way to take the waters at the spa of Kislovodsk, and recount how
they managed to escape from pursuing Circassian horsemen as they
rode through frontier territory from Stavropol to Yekaterinodar.[21]

Do these hostile stereotypes constitute a warrant for genocide?
Reading some authors, it is hard to avoid answering yes. Thus
George Ditson, who claims to be the first American to visit Circassia and who dedicates his book to the Russian governor of the
Caucasus, Prince Vorontsov, draws a direct parallel between the
subjugation of the Circassians and that of the American Indians
being accomplished at the same period. It turns out that this
thought was suggested to him by the Russian Prince Kochubei,
whom he approvingly cites as saying: 'These Circassians are just like
your American Indians – as untamable and uncivilized ... and,
owing to their natural energy of character, extermination only
would keep them quiet' – though he does admittedly offer the alternative of 'employing their wild and warlike tastes against others.'[22]

Historians of tsarist Russia conventionally stressed the desire to
put an end to Circassian raids on existing Russian settlements and
to clear new fertile lands for the settlement of landless peasants
migrating from Central Russia in the wake of the abolition of serf-
dom as the motive behind the decision to deport the Circassians. As
one influential account puts it:

> In Chechnya and Daghestan [the central and eastern parts of the
> northern Caucasus] the Russians were satisfied with the natives' sub-
> mission, but on the Black Sea coast they intended to gain possession
> of the wide and fertile Circassian lands to provide for a part of the
> great wave of Russian peasant migration resulting from emancipation
> of the serfs in 1861. Every year Cossacks and peasant migrants from
> central Russia were penetrating farther and farther up the affluents of
> the [Rivers] Kuban, Laba, Belaya and Urup. These new villages and
> *stanitsy* [Cossack settlements] were frequently raided by the Circas-
> sians who resented the Russian settlement of their tribal lands.[23]

As the same authors point out, the resettlement of the Circassian
lands was a partial failure. 'The Kuban region was thickly settled,

but along the Black Sea coast the Russian, German, Greek and Bulgarian colonists proved unable to support the humid climate and the forest environment, and today the wilderness has conquered the Circassian orchards and gardens.'[24]

More recently, Brooks has put forward an alternative view, more soundly based on detailed research into the writings of prominent Russian officials and generals of the time.[25] He argues that their main motive was simply to secure reliable politico-military control by Russia of a strategically important area of the Caucasus. This goal seemed suddenly much more urgent in the 1850s after the Crimean War, which had underlined the danger of foreign intervention in the Black Sea region and the necessity of pre-empting it. However, close to a century of unsuccessful fighting had convinced frustrated Russian policy-makers that the Circassians could not be subdued, but only deported or exterminated. Thus the military campaign was not a response to the extraneous needs of settlement. On the contrary, it was only *after* victory was achieved that the generals pressed (in vain) for accelerated settlement to consolidate the conquest. Similarly, though the order of the Tsar was to deport the Circassians, not exterminate them, we have seen from the remark of Prince Kochubei, quoted above, that Russian officials and generals were not averse to the idea of exterminating a large proportion of the Circassians. General Fadeyev also attested to this when he wrote that the Russians decided 'to exterminate half the Circassian people in order to compel the other half to lay down their arms.'[26]

So was it genocide? The deportation of the Circassians can certainly be regarded as an example of 'ethnic cleansing', in which massacres and the burning of villages served to force the Circassians into emigration. 'This great exodus', concludes Henze, 'was the first of the violent mass transfers of population which this part of the world has suffered in modern times.' He goes on, however, to suggest that it set a precedent for the Armenian genocide, implying that what happened was at least comparable to genocide.[27] There was no obsession to wipe out every single Circassian, but there was a determination to get rid of them without delay, in the full knowledge that a large proportion of them were bound to perish in the process. As Count Yevdokimov recounts: 'I wrote to Count Sumarokov, why does he remind us in every report of the frozen bodies covering the roads? Do the Great Prince and I really not know this? But can anyone really turn back the calamity?'[28] Such cynically feigned inadvertence reminds one of the tsar who 'commuted' a death penalty imposed on a soldier to a hundred lashes of the knout, knowing that he could hardly survive such an ordeal.

The End of the Circassians?

The catastrophe that befell the Circassians in the 1860s put their survival as a people at risk both inside the Russian empire (and later the Soviet Union and its successor states) and in exile. The impact of the deportations on the different Circassian sub-groups varied widely. Worst affected were the western and central tribes, several of which disappeared completely from the Caucasus, most notably the Ubykh, while others left behind only small remnants.[29] A native population compactly residing throughout Circassia was thereby reduced to fragments, 'islands' that in the course of time were separated by an intervening 'sea' of Slav and other settlers. By 1917, the descendants of the Circassians remaining in Russia were scattered over many non-contiguous areas, in most of which they formed a minority. No single town had a Circassian majority.[30]

The effect of this process was to weaken pan-Circassian identity and raise the salience of narrower identities. Thus the removal of the Ubykh, who had constituted the geographical and linguistic bridge between the Abkhaz and the northern Circassians, facilitated the development of a more distinct Abkhaz identity. Similarly, the isolation from other Circassian communities of those Shapsegh villages that remained in the Tuapse area heightened the sense of a separate Shapsegh identity. In the new geodemographic conditions created by conquest, deportation and the influx of settlers, tribes naturally tended to evolve into separate ethnic groups. The sense of being Circassian was not altogether lost, but what had previously been perceived as a single people came to be seen as a family of closely related but distinct ethnic groups.

The effects of the Soviet period on the ethnic identity of the Circassians, as on that of other indigenous peoples, were complex and shifting. In the 1920s and early 1930s, the policy of 'indigenization' (*korenizatsiya*) helped preserve Circassian language and culture from Russifying pressures. Four ethnic territories were created specifically for different groups of Circassians within the Russian Federation.[31] In addition, the Abkhaz enjoyed considerable autonomy within the Republic of Georgia, and for some years (1921-31) even had a union republic of their own, loosely associated with Georgia. On the other hand, certain aspects of the indigenization policy did serve further to weaken and fragment Circassian identity. In 1927 what had previously been a single Circassian literary language was split into two separate literary languages: Kabard-Cherkess and Adygei.[32] Also Circassian groups were, both in the 1920s and later, arbitrarily put together with the Karachai and Balkar, who speak a Turkic language, to form mixed ethnic territories.[33] The later Soviet period witnessed a return to the policy of Russification – or, in the case of the Abkhaz, whose cultural rights were suppressed under Stalin – Georgianization.[34] From the 1960s onwards, the Circassian language was only taught as a subject in the schools of the ethnic territories but was no longer employed as a vehicle of instruction.

With the collapse of the USSR, the lifting of controls over movement and communication facilitated a modest revival of shared Circassian identity. In some families, an 'unauthorized ethnic history' stressing the common Circassian roots of Kabardian, Adygei, Cherkess, Abaza and Abkhaz had been transmitted secretly from generation to generation, and this history could now be openly propagated.[35] Links with the descendants of the Circassian exiles have been established, though efforts to attract the latter back 'home' have so far yielded scant results.

However, among the great majority of Circassians living in exile, the Circassian identity was better able to hold its own against narrower identities. The challenge it faced was of a different kind – that of gradual assimilation into the host societies of Turkey and the Middle East. Over time the exiled 'Circassians' tended to become 'Turks (or Jordanians, etc.) of Circassian descent'. Nevertheless, even in Turkey the younger generation still speak Circassian – albeit only poorly, as a second language – and profess a sentimental pride in the Circassian heritage.[36] In Jordan, Palestine-Israel, Saudi Arabia and other countries that formed part of the Ottoman empire, compact communities of Circassians still exist. In Jordan Circassians exercise important functions as military officers and businessmen. Two Circassian villages remain in the Balkans, one in Kosovo and one in Transylvania.

So the Circassians have survived as a people. I expect that they will continue to survive in the foreseeable future – especially taking account of the social climate in the post-Soviet region and in a world now more conducive than ever to the preservation and revival of ethnic identity. Even Circassian sub-groups that were thought to be on – or over – the verge of extinction may survive. For example, Ubykh is often described as a dead language, and the death of the last living speaker of Ubykh has been reported more than once. However, a prominent Canadian specialist on the Circassians, Professor John Colaruso,[37] informs me that among the descendants of the Ubykh living in Turkey there is now a small group of young people who are learning the Ubykh language from their grandparents and are intent on keeping the Ubykh identity alive. The Circassians, their stubborn and heroic resistance to conquest and to the horrors perpetrated against them by their conquerors will not be forgotten after all. And yet how close they came to slipping into oblivion. If the fate of the Armenians in Turkey and of the Jews of Europe is still widely remembered today, is that not largely thanks to the status and influence enjoyed by many of the Armenian and Jewish communities fortunate enough to survive elsewhere? The contrary case of the Circassians brings home to us how easily the genocide of a people can, under less favourable circumstances, still fade out of our historical consciousness.

Notes

1. The figure is derived from the results of the Soviet population census of 1989, which recorded the total population of the Karachai-Cherkess Autonomous Province as 415,000 (see Goskomstat SSSR, *Natsional'nyi sostav naseleniya SSSR po dannym vsesoyuznoi perepisi naseleniya 1989 g.* (Moscow, 1991), 42. If one counts the closely related Abazins as Circassians, the proportion of the latter in the population rises to 16 percent. The rest of the population comprises Karachai, Russians, Nogai and other ethnic groups. The Circassians call themselves in their own language 'Adyghe'.

2. The Abkhaz, like the Abaza and the almost extinct Ubykh, are sometimes counted as Circassians and sometimes not. But they are certainly all closely related to the Circassians, and I include them as such.

3. These figures are taken from the book of the Circassian historian, R. Trakho, *Cherkesy (Circassians-Northern Caucasians)* (Munich, 1956), 113. At various times earlier in its history Circassia also extended further northwards, to the lands lying beyond the Sea of Azov.

4. Trakho is of the opinion that the Circassians adopted the Greek myths. Another Circassian historian claims that, on the contrary, it was the Greeks who took their myths from the Circassians! See Shauket Mufti (Habjoka), *Heroes and Emperors* (Beirut, 1944).

5. There is a theoretical controversy, to which I do not intend to contribute here, concerning whether 'nations' can be said to have existed before the modern period. Be that as it may, it is undeniable that there have existed since ancient times certain groups with a strong sense of common descent, culture and identity, though not necessarily ever united in a single political entity. These we may call 'proto-nations.' One such is the Circassians.

6. The Circassians' adoption of both Christianity and Islam was opportunistic and superficial. One ethnographer describes the religious beliefs of the Abkhaz, for instance, as an eclectic mixture of pagan, Christian and Muslim elements. See Sula Benet, *Abkhasians: The Long-Living People of the Caucasus* (New York, 1974).

7. In fact, large-scale emigration to Turkey had started in 1858, when thirty thousand families had departed. However, news of the bad conditions awaiting the refugees there almost stopped the migration by the end of that year.

8. The following account draws on W.E.D. Allen and Paul Muratoff, *Caucasian Battlefields: History of the Wars on the Turco-Caucasian Border, 1828-1921* (Cambridge, 1953), 107-8; Willis Brooks, 'Russia's conquest and pacification of the Caucasus: relocation becomes a pogrom on the post-Crimean period', *Nationalities Papers*, 23, 4 (1995): 675-86; Trakho, *Cherkesy*, 32-56; Shauket, *Heroes and Emperors*.

9. The burning of villages was by no means a new practice. In the country of the Abadzakh alone, over a thousand settlements had burned between 1857 and 1859. Shauket, *Heroes and Emperors*, 237.

10. Shauket also tells us that the Ubykh had been weakened by a series of natural disasters in 1859: tremendous swarms of locusts had damaged the fields, a live-stock epidemic had destroyed most of their cattle and horses, and a large proportion of their people had died from a disease similar to cholera. See Shauket, *Heroes and Emperors*, 245.

11. Trakho, *Cherkesy*, 50-51.

12. Shauket, *Heroes and Emperors*, 250.

13. Trakho, *Cherkesy*, 52-53.

14. Ibid. Moshnin's figures imply mortality rates following arrival in Turkey in the region of 2.5 to 5 percent per month.

15. See Brooks, 'Russia's conquest', 681.

16. This is a very rough estimate pending more detailed research. Another method of estimating the number of survivors would be to extrapolate backwards from later data for the population in Turkey descended from the deportees. In spite of its undoubtedly high birth rate, it was not until the middle of the twentieth century that this population again reached two million.

17. Norman Cohn, *Warrant for Genocide: The Myth of the Jewish World Conspiracy and the Protocols of the Elders of Zion* (New York, 1967).

18. 'Kazakh' is a transliteration of the Russian word for this people. The government of Kazakhstan initiated a switch to 'Kazak,' which is a transliteration from the Kazakh language. Here I follow the more familiar usage.

19. See John J. Stephan, *The Russian Far East: A History* (Stanford, 1994), esp. 23-24. Also useful is Yuri Slezkine, *Arctic Mirrors: Russia and the Small Peoples of the North* (Ithaca and London, 1994).

20. See Martha Brill Olcott, *The Kazakhs* (Stanford, 1987), esp. chap. 4; and Shirin Akiner, *The Formation of Kazakh Identity: From Tribe to Nation-State* (London, 1995).

21. See Le Chevalier Gamba [Consul of the King(of France) at Tiflis], *Voyage dans la Russie Méridionale et particulièrement dans les provinces situées au-delà du Caucase, fait depuis 1820 jusqu'en 1824* (Paris, 1826), vol. 1, 78; Xavier Hommaire De Hell, *Travels in the Steppes of the Caspian Sea: The Crimea, The Caucasus &c.* (London, 1847), 286, 301-3.

22. George Leighton Ditson Esq., *Circassia; or A Tour to the Caucasus* (New York and London, 1850), x-xi; and Paul B. Henze, 'Circassian Resistance to Russia', in Marie Benningsen Broxup, ed., *The North Caucasus Barrier: The Russian Advance towards the Muslim World* (London, 1992), 80. Gamba, *Voyage*, 91-92, on the other hand, thought that the Circassians could be 'civilized' by a few years of orderly government and hard work. For other West-European writers, hostile to the expansion of the Russian Empire, the Circassians were indeed 'a wild people, known through so many centuries for their barbarism' – but *noble* rather than contemptible savages, friendly and hospitable to foreign visitors who have named a reputable *konak* (protector). See The Chevalier Taitbout de Marigny [Consul of His Majesty the King of the Netherlands at Odessa], *Three Voyages in the Black sea to the Coast of Circassia: including descriptions of the ports, and the importance of their trade: with sketches of the manners, customs, religion &c. of the Circassians* (London, 1887), 17; and the Englishman James Stanislaus Bell, *Journal of a Residence in Circassia During the Years 1837, 1838, 1839* (Paris, 1841), who found the Circassians to be of a pure and hardy character reminiscent of the ancient Greeks.

23. Allen and Muratoff, *Caucasian Battlefields*, 107-8. One specific concern attributed to the Russian government was the need to secure safe access to and use of the new Black Sea port of Novorossiisk, at risk from its Circassian hinterland.
24. Ibid., 108.
25. Brooks, 'Russia's conquest'.
26. Quoted in Trakho, *Cherkesy*, 51, from General Fadeyev's *Pis'ma s Kavkaza* (Letters from the Caucasus) of 1865.
27. See Henze, 'Circassian Resistance', 111.
28. Trakho, *Cherkesy*, 51.
29. Ronald Wixman, *Language Aspects of Ethnic Patterns and Processes in the North Caucasus* (University of Chicago, Dept. of History, Research Paper No. 191, 1980), 78-79.
30. For an account of the position of the Circassians in the Soviet period, see Rieks Smeets, 'Circassia,' *Central Asian Survey*, 14, 1 (1995): 107-125.
31. These were: (1) the Adygei-Cherkess Autonomous Province, created in 1922, in 1936 renamed the Adygei Autonomous Province; (2) the Cherkess Autonomous Province, 1926; (3) the Kabardian Autonomous Province, 1921; and (4) the Shapsugh National County, 1922.
32. See Wixman, *Language Aspects*, 145.
33. That is, the Karachai-Cherkess Autonomous Province (in 1922-26 and again from 1957) and the Kabardino-Balkar Autonomous Province or Republic (from 1922 until the deportation of the Balkars in 1944, and then again from 1957).
34. The ethnic territories for Adygei, Cherkess and Kabard were formally retained. However, the Shapsegh lost their ethnic territory after the war, and repeated appeals for its restoration have been rejected at the insistence of the provincial authorities.
35. See Paula Garb, 'Ethnicity and Alliance Building in the Caucasus' (paper presented at 'The International Spread and Management of Ethnic Conflict' Conference, University of California, Davis, March 1995). The 1990-onwards cultural festivals organized by the Confederation of Mountain Peoples of the Caucasus and the participation of Circassian volunteers from the Northern Caucasus on the Abkhaz side in the Georgian-Abkhaz conflict have been additional factors in the revival of Circassian identity.
36. Divergent assessments on the degree of Circassian assimilation in Turkey can be found in Henze ('Circassian Resistance', 63), who argues for the continuation of a meaningful Circassian identity among them, and Smeets ('Circassia', 109, 125), who is sceptical.
37. Of McMaster University, Hamilton, Ontario.

CHAPTER 8

'UNUSUALLY CUNNING, VICIOUS AND TREACHEROUS'

THE EXTERMINATION OF THE WOLF IN UNITED STATES HISTORY[1]

Peter Coates

'Violence is as American as cherry pie' (H. Rap Brown)[2]

Many recent historians of the American frontier endorse the sentiments captured in this famous catchphrase of the militant wing of the 1960s 'black power' movement. Though Hollywood has traditionally packaged frontier violence in terms of 'High Noon'-style confrontations between individual gunslingers, it often took the distinctive form of the massacre. These were frequently the final expression of conflict stemming from considerations – frequently intertwined – of class, ethnicity, religion and race. The most infamous feature of the Ludlow Massacre of 1914, an assault by the Colorado state-militia (mostly Anglo-American) on the tent city erected by striking coal miners (mainly Greek, Italian and Serb immigrants) was the incineration of two women and eleven children who sought shelter in a dugout. Mormons were both subject to persecution and its instigators. Driven from the Midwest in the 1830s by various massacres, they dished out violence too. At Mountain Meadows, Utah in 1857, frontier Mormons (in alliance with Paiute Indians) slew around a hundred 'gentiles' – men, women and children – from a California-bound wagon train.

The most notorious massacres, however, involved non-whites. Anti-Oriental riots in the latter part of the nineteenth century could result in numerous deaths; a nativist mob killed fifty-one Chinese coal miners in Wyoming in 1885. But indigenous peoples were the main victims.[3] William Hubbard might have regarded Indians as sole perpetrators, even eschewing the term 'history' for his *Narrative of the Troubles with the Indians in New England* (1677) because his subject matter was composed more of 'Massacres, barbarous inhumane Outrages, than Acts of Hostility, or valiant Atchievements [*sic*]' normally associated with war,[4] yet massacre of Indians by whites was more common.

Words formerly employed to describe European occupation of North America, such as 'colonization' and 'settlement', are now overshadowed by the less benign and euphemistic language of invasion, conquest, subjugation and massacre. Triumphalist accounts of the winning of the West dotted with Anglo-Saxon heroes have given way to sometimes strident critiques of the losing of the West in which Indians loom large among the casualties of white brutality. A non-fictional bestseller detailed the atrocities U.S. troops inflicted in the name of progress, civilization and manifest destiny. An eyewitness at the Sand Creek Massacre (Colorado, 1864) related that, 'I heard of numerous instances in which men had cut out the private parts of females and stretched them over the saddle-bows and wore them over their hats while riding in the ranks', while others dangled female genitalia from the tips of their bayonets.[5] Indeed, the collective trauma of the Native American experience at Euro-American hands prompted Indian rights activist Russell Means to announce that, 'Columbus makes Hitler look like a juvenile delinquent',[6] and scholars to introduce the concepts of 'genocide' and 'Holocaust' unambiguously into the discourse over European relations with American Indians.[7]

Though the terrain of North America is patently heavily saturated with blood, Indians were actually not the ultimate victims. The blood and guts of other indigenous beings were spilled in even greater quantities. The most lurid (if under-appreciated) massacres in the continent's history involve the massive destruction and, in some instances, wholesale eradication, of wild species, tragic losses that one 'new' Western-cum-environmental historian also treats in terms of Holocaust and genocide, specifically labelling capitalist democracy's attitude to wildlife 'biocidal'.[8] Seeing massacre in this way is not as outlandish as it might first appear. The *Concise Oxford English Dictionary* refers to 'general slaughter, carnage, (of persons, occas. of animals)'. In fact, livestock butchery has long been central to understandings of massacre. In Old French, *machacre* was slaughterhouse, and few who visited the Essex port of Brightlingsea in 1995 and saw the posters in windows protesting against live exports of animals (the posters depicting sheep weeping tears of blood into the North Sea) will have failed to make the connection. Moreover, while we may be more accustomed to thinking about massacre in exclusively human terms, there are instances when the metaphor of animal-world slaughter (including that of American animals) has been applied to human predicaments, as when the Anglo-American media at the end of the Gulf War of 1991 referred to the 'turkey shoot' of the Iraqi army fleeing Kuwait.

Certainly, the *Oxford English Dictionary* entry extends its coverage of massacre beyond 'the unnecessary, indiscriminate killing of human beings', to include 'also occas. the wholesale killing of wild animals'. The example provided is the massacre of deer and hogs in early colonial Virginia. But this was hardly an isolated case. The reduction of an estimated sixty to seventy-five million buffalo that roamed North America in 1492 to about five hundred in 1900 was accomplished, after the Civil War, by hide-hunting outfits systematically butchering herds with round the clock, industrial efficiency in what became effectively an abbatoir *al fresco*. An arresting photograph in Bill Couturie's recent film, *Earth and the American Dream*, shows relics of the Great Plains killing fields: a huge pyramid of buffalo skulls topped by a man with the demeanour of a conquering mountaineer, the camera moving slowly from base to summit up a slope that seems to go on forever. Similarly, a restrained estimate puts the passenger pigeon population throughout its American range on the eve of white settlement at between three and five billion. Yet the bird was extinct in 1914, when the last specimen, Martha, died in Cincinnati Zoo. John James Audubon, the prominent nineteenth-century artist and naturalist, recounts a massacre in a Kentucky wood in 1813. Pigeons were knocked down with poles, shot, stunned with pots of sulphur and corn soaked in alcohol, chopped out of their roosts and netted – a deafening slaughter lasting all night. In the morning, 'the authors of all this devastation began to move among the dead, the dying, and the mangled, picking up the Pigeons and piling them in heaps. When each man had as many as he could possibly dispose of, the hogs were let loose to feed on the remainder.'[9]

The buffalo and passenger pigeon, like the beaver and sea otter, fell 'victim to commodification' and were converted from their status in aboriginal eyes from 'other-than-human persons' into 'animals of enterprise'.[10] The devastating assault on such creatures is often cited to evoke the profligacy, rapacity, myth of superabundance, thoughtlessness and crude commercialism that were the leitmotifs of natural resource exploitation in frontier regions, not to mention the crass disregard for other species' right to existence.

They were readily killed, an easy source of money and, in the case of the buffalo, in the way of crops and cattle. Some whites certainly thought them stupid and ungainly but buffalo (and pigeons and furbearers) were not detested or mutilated, as Indians sometimes were. For comparable pathological hatred, we must turn to lesser-known, yet no less ruthless, campaigns against wild predators. Hatred towards them – and wolves in particular – is peerless in Euro-American relations with other creatures.

Though the massacre is a flexible, ever-shifting concept, integral to most definitions and instances is the idea of gratuitous and usually unprovoked attack on non-combatants. Despite being maligned as the supreme perpetrators of wanton and calculated slaughter in the animal kingdom, predators actually fit this bill neatly. The history of predator extermination in the United States is not that of a rational response commensurate to the scale of the threat or tangible record of transgression, but an indiscriminate, open-ended war. Hatred is not necessarily vented through violence, let alone that specialized form known as massacre. But in this instance, massacre was the end product and logical conclusion. The organized, systematic killing of predators was sanctioned by the wider community and its objective was not simply control but complete eradication – thus, surely making it the quintessential type of massacre.

The campaign was directed against the species as a whole ('species specific' in contemporary predator control parlance) rather than individuals with a proven record of killing livestock. Any predator was under automatic suspicion. It is revealing that 'control' was not adopted as an official term until the 1930s. Previous terminology spoke more candidly of elimination, extermination and destruction. Addressing delegates of a sport hunting association dedicated to building up supplies of game animals in 1920, a wildlife manager declared with missionary fervour that 'it is going to take patience and money to catch the last wolf or lion in New Mexico. But the last one must be caught before the job can be called fully successful.'[11]

Two million is a prominent early twentieth-century nature writer's 'conservative' estimate of wolf numbers in North America on the eve of European contact.[12] In 1800, there were hardly any left in New England.[13] By the early 1900s, a scorched-earth policy had reduced total North-American numbers to two hundred thousand, most of these relegated to Canada and Alaska. By 1945, the very few that remained in the U.S. outside of Alaska, were largely immigrants from Mexico and Canada. Already by the 1930s, predator extermination campaigns were focusing on coyotes, which were occupying the niches vacated by their larger wolf cousins.

Today, only about two thousand wolves cling on in the continental U.S., beleaguered in the wildlands of central Idaho and northern Michigan, Minnesota, Wisconsin and Montana. Wolf eradication in North America has been more successful than many efforts to eliminate groups of undesirable people, stimulating a contemporary nature writer, Barry Lopez, to dub what were effectively counterparts to ethnic cleansing, 'an American Pogrom'.[14]

II

This study of wolf extermination thus explores the nature and dimensions of vilification, investigating the role in the construction of its *bête noire* identity played by association with hated groups of people and through the projection of pejorative human qualities. This, in fact, requires a wider perspective, for there is nothing peculiarly American or modern about attitudes and behaviour towards wolves. Nor has the wolf been alone in its traducement: most animals 'red of tooth and claw' have suffered defamation of character, if not quite to the same degree. Our discussion particularly focuses on the various organized anti-wolf crusades as distinct from their uncoordinated killing primarily for pelts or trophies. The region west of the Mississippi between the 1860s and the 1920s has been chosen for special attention because this regional phase represented the zenith of wolf killing in the United States, both official and informal, in quantitative terms. The body count was the largest, and the resources invested in the programme the greatest.

Some preliminary remarks are warranted, however, because wolves have been persecuted throughout history. The practical impossibility of coexistence between animal predators and people, especially livestock raisers, may seem sufficient explanation. But the wolf has been a casualty of civilization in a much larger sense: Americans who shot, trapped and poisoned the obnoxious wolf and obliterated its haunts carried with them a heavy baggage of history and culture. Indeed, the wolf's malevolent reputation – one handed down from Aesop's fables – still permeates popular culture. Disney's *Beauty and the Beast* portrays wolves as merciless aggressors drooling with bloodlust. 'Wolf' crops up frequently in everyday expression: slang usages convey notions of voracious and insatiable appetite, of preying on the defenceless and of stealing property (not least the appropriation of another man's woman). Unflattering examples can be located at most times in Western culture and in most places: the British described German U-boats in World War Two as wolf packs, a term some West Germans were to apply to Baader-Meinhof terrorist cells in the 1970s.[15] By contrast, it is difficult to locate positive images aside from that contained in the fable of Romulus and Remus, the wolf children who founded Rome, and its derivative in Kipling's story of Mowgli.

Western civilization's overwhelmingly negative appraisal of wolves is evident not only in ancient Greek allegories but also in early Christianity. The Bible casts the devil as the wolf from hell and enemies of the faith are wolves. Wolves were beyond the moral pale. They had no souls, beauty or utility (nobody ate wolf except in an emergency). Elaborate wolf drives in medieval France (*battues*), launched when a wolf was accused of attacking someone, led to hundreds of their deaths.[16] Natural histories of the wolf from the Renaissance onwards were on a par with the crassest racism, focusing on their murderous savagery, cannibalism, cunning, deceit, cowardliness, perversity, depravity, exponential reproduction, and stench. Most menacing were the supernatural powers of evil attributed to them, epitomized by the werewolf and the belief that people were metamorphosed into wolves through demonic intervention (known as lycanthropy).[17] Customary Christian identification with the wolf's victims, the idea of the good shepherd protecting the innocent and vulnerable, and the smearing of unbelievers as wolves were traits particularly evident in colonial New England. Spiritual leader John Winthrop characterized himself as 'a poor shepherd ... among the small flock of sheep I daily fold in this distant part of the wilderness ... to secure them from the wild rapacious quadrupeds of the forest.'[18] Just as the killing of Indians was thought to be divinely sanctioned, the struggle against the wolf assumed all the elements of a sacred mission against a creature with a propensity for massacre most foul.

The Euro-American tendency to blur the distinction between Indians and wild animals worked to the predator's disadvantage. Indians inhabited a grey zone between man and beast, people, who, if not literal beasts, possessed beastly qualities. Impelled by untempered lust and other base instincts, they became scapegoats for, and the personification of the evils the Puritans saw lurking under every human skin. An account of a notorious 'Indian hunt' in New England in 1675, that led to the killing of the chief the English called King Philip, told how, with reference to the beseiging of a swamp, 'it is ill fighting with a wild Beast in his own Den'. Descriptions of the killing of Indians were wrapped in all the conventions applied to the exorcistic slaying of mythical beasts. And one seventeenth-century chronicle pointed out that the so-called 'Indian wars' were actually more akin to the extermination of vermin than to standard Christian notions of warfare.[19]

Moreover, settlers deemed predators and Indians alike to have no claim on the untamed land, which, as hunters, they ranged instead of inhabited. The wolf was designated an outlaw and you defended your property against it as you would against Indians, claim jumpers, cattle rustlers and trespassers in general.[20] If they returned to their old stomping grounds after eviction, Indians and wolves simply confirmed their status as renegades. In these manipulative ways, wolves, wilderness and Indians became a fused object of hatred, an unholy trinity that jeopardized the economic, social and spiritual health of the colonies.

Similarly, Francis Jennings points to the distinction European colonists made between savage war and civilized war, the latter being rational, measured, purposeful and progressive while the former, practised by Indians and wild beasts, constituted 'unchecked and perpetual violence' and 'unredeemed retrogression', aimless apart from satisfaction of the mindless force of appetite.[21] These concepts were adopted simultaneously by wolfers, who waged civilized war against these other practitioners of savage warfare. The way of fighting and killing was important in bolstering the connection. Indians skulked through the woods and ambushed their victims like 'a pack of wolves.' As Euro-Americans dissolved into paroxysms of self-righteous indignation over Indian scalping (when not engaging in it themselves), so they also considered the wolf's methods to be of unparalleled brutality.

Senator John R. Kendrick of Wyoming, a rancher himself (like many western American politicians), believed there was 'nothing so vicious in its cruelty as the method employed by the gray wolf in destroying his prey. His prey is literally eaten alive, its bowels torn out while it is still on its feet in many cases.'[22] Theodore Roosevelt, the future president, who lost cattle to wolves on his Dakota Territory ranch in the 1880s, railed against 'the archetype of ravin, the beast of waste and desolation', not least because of distaste for its alleged practices of hamstringing cattle (and horses) from behind, bob-tailing them, disembowelling them through biting the flank, and devouring nothing but the unborn calves of pregnant cows.[23]

Ironically (in view of their own exploits), buffalo hunters (who had ample opportunity to observe since wolves were camp followers, feeding on the carrion) contributed to the mood of hysterical hatred, one of them hailing the wolf as 'the very incarnation of destruction with his powerful jaws of shark teeth ... and the cunning of man'.[24] Such rhetoric assisted the rise of the wolf killer to the status of supreme protector of the animal kingdom's meek and mild. And there came a juncture on every frontier when the Indian 'menace' had been snuffed out and settlers began to perceive the wolf as the greatest threat – and not only to their domestic stock and pastoral economy but to the general welfare of civilization itself. The height of the stakes involved – and the impossibility of compromise – were bluntly articulated in a vituperative letter by an Iowa sheepman, from a report in 1892, on the condition of the local sheep industry: 'The wolf, not merely figuratively, is at the door of many an Iowa farmer ... Much of the best sheep lands of the State ... cannot be pastured with sheep ... Sheep can't live there now on account of the wolves ... Really it is a stain, a foul stigma, on the civilization and enterprise of the people of Iowa that these wolves remain and are frequently seen crossing the best cultivated farms, and even near the best towns in our State.'[25]

Segregation in ghetto-like confinement or the erection of a cordon sanitaire were, therefore, never considered options. Raise the bounty to an attractive level, the sheepman argued, and 'the boys will then arm themselves with the best rifles of long range ... and speedily exterminate the lupine race'.[26] Yet it was the trap rather than the rifle that served as the most potent and eloquent symbol of this holy war. According to its leading nineteenth-century designer, writing in the era's standard text on woodcraft, the trap, 'going before the axe and the plow, forms the prow with which iron-clad civilization is pushing back barbaric solitude', replacing former 'occupants of the soil', with 'the wheatfield, the library and the piano'.[27]

The first and most enduring weapon in the war against the wolf in North America, however, was a classic one that probably originated in ancient Greece: the bounty payment. In medieval England, bounties took the form of land grants, and regular participation of the peasantry in wolf hunts was often a feudal duty. Some New England colonies required Indians to submit an annual wolf tribute and extended bounties to all species suspected of endangering livestock and game or of preying on crops, which were designated 'vermin' ('varmints' in American English).[28] In this way, the wolf also became 'an animal of enterprise' in the sense that a price was pinned to its head and wolfing became a lucrative source of income for a clutch of enterprising colonists and Indians.

But bounties (derided by their critics as 'rural welfare') were problematic: the potential for fraud – ersatz ears were a favourite ploy – was enormous. So habitat clearance, which also had European precedents, was seen as a longer-term solution as well as a direct means of flushing them out of their lairs. The draining of wetlands ('an annoyance and prejudice to the town ... both by miring of cattle and sheltering of wolves and vermin') assumed the dimensions of a profound civic duty in colonial New England, and as late as 1928 woods were burned for this end in Arkansas.[29]

With the installation of the 'cattle kingdom' in the American West after 1865, making the region a safe area for livestock was the priority of wildlife management, especially in the face of an upsurge in cow and sheep predation which reflected dwindling supplies of the wolf's traditional prey of antelope and buffalo. One cattleman portrayed the wolf as 'a specialist in carnage ... [that] brought professional skill to the slaughter of cattle', and by the 1870s, local and state authorities offered bounties as well as stockmen's associations.[30] This phase of the perennial crusade was accompanied by advances in the technology of extermination. The rifle, trap and snare were supplemented by the broadcast of strychnine (not least because wolves were good at avoiding traps). The deadly qualities of the 'vomiting bean' were already known in seventeenth-century New England, where it was mixed with meat to despatch troublesome birds. But supplies had to come from abroad and more liberal distribution awaited the start of domestic manufacture in the 1830s. Strychnine arrived in the American West during the California gold rush of 1849, and jars of the substance in crystalline sulphate form swiftly became a familiar feature on the shelves of trading posts.

Wolf pelt hunters catering to the considerable demand for overcoats from the Russian army were strychnine's first major customers and use peaked between 1860 and 1885. This period, during which the interests of stockmen and the fur trade coincided, was the heyday of the private wolfer, many of whom were former beaver trappers and soldiers mustered out of the frontier army. Wolfing also provided out of season work for cowboys and a bonanza for a motley crew of frontier types. Stockmen provided poison and a bounty, leaving the wolfer to locate his prey by following the buffalo herds. He then shot a buffalo and laced the carcass with strychnine, after which he was free to sell the pelt. One poisoned buffalo carcass ('bait station') could yield thirteen wolves, fifteen coyotes and forty skunks in a night (and numerous other non-target species).[31] Two ex-government wolfers explain that the 1870s were marked by 'a sort of unwritten law of the range that no cowman would knowingly pass-by a carcass of any kind without inserting in it a goodly dose of strychnine sulphate, in the hope of eventually killing one more wolf'.[32] In Montana alone, 80,730 wolves were brought in for bounty payments totalling $342,764 between 1883 and 1918, while in a single week in Arizona in 1913, one cowboy-cum-wolfer earned $9,000 by killing eighteen wolves.[33] By 1900, they had been eliminated from much of the West, for the offensive was carried even into areas where livestock raising had not yet penetrated.

Many would agree that the killing of unarmed women and children is a crucial ingredient that sets the human massacre apart from other acts of violence, random or planned. The justification for killing children – even babies – offered by Colonel Chivington of the Colorado Cavalry shortly before the Sand Creek Massacre was that 'nits make lice'.[34] Similarly, the killing of wolf pups in breeding dens was urged by the U.S. secretary of agriculture in 1907.[35] This reflected a conviction that wolves were fast-breeders. Such was the paranoia of one of the most renowned wolf hunters, Ben Corbin, that he claimed that if unchecked, their numbers in North Dakota would outstrip the State's livestock. According to his feverish arithmetic, the State housed over a million wolves, and with each one eating two pounds of beef a day, this cost an astronomical $44 million a year.[36] No method was considered illegitimate. Kerosene was poured into dens which were then set alight. Whether the object was dog, bitch or pup, wolf-hunting was a popular recreation west of the Mississippi in the late nineteenth century. The carcass would be hung from a pole and paraded along main street on a Saturday night. As Lopez emphasizes: 'A lot of people didn't just kill wolves; they tortured them. They set wolves on fire and tore their jaws out and cut their Achilles tendons and turned dogs loose on them.'[37]

But why did emotions run so high over wolves and other predators? Victims of hatred in the human world are often scapegoats – those blamed for taking jobs, threatening morality and spreading crime. In like-style, stockmen blamed cattle losses – which might be attributed to drought, severe weather, rustling, disease, drowning and other natural causes – exclusively on a wolf that might simply have been scavenging. It is not hard to see why. Ranching was (and still is) a precarious enterprise, at the mercy of forces beyond the rancher's control. The wolf, by contrast, was a tangible target: as Lopez explains, 'You couldn't control storms or beef prices or prevent hoof and mouth disease, but you could kill wolves.'[38]

Conservationists shared the stockman's view that the only good wolf was a dead wolf. The sympathies of William T. Hornaday, the leading turn-of-the-century wildlife protectionist, did not extend to predators: 'Of all the wild creatures of North America, none are more despicable than wolves. There is no depth of meanness, treachery or cruelty to which they do not cheerfully descend.'[39] He wanted all predators wiped out, except one pair of each species, whose proper place would be in his zoo (he was director of the New York Zoological Park). Conservationists and humanitarians (many of the latter were vegetarians) – and even the most radical advocates of animal rights (invariably vegetarians) – were only interested in so-called good or harmless animals as they strove for a more perfect natural world with no place for rapacity. This reflected a strong belief that animals had moral sense and ought to live by human values: those who did not abide by civilized human standards forfeited consideration. For the sake of desirable birds (in other words, game species appealing to sports hunters, and many conservationists at this time fell into this category of outdoorsman), the Audubon Society destroyed owls and hawks on its bird refuges (which granted sanctuary from predatory creatures, if not from the human variety), describing them as disturbers of the peace.[40]

Accordingly, it would be a mistake to approach predator elimination exclusively in terms of the coercion of public and politicians by special interest groups like stockmen and hunters. As Donald Worster stresses, this desire to clean up and re-order the natural world was not only central to the mentality of conservation but also to the general orientation of reform during the Progressive era.[41] The hallmark of this period (1890s-1910s) was a comprehensive campaign to improve American life by eliminating the useless and those elements injurious to the useful, variously expressed through legislation governing working hours and adulteration of foodstuffs, slum clearance, teaching immigrants about hygiene, the purification of politics with measures to counteract the authority of the city machines and bosses – and wolf elimination. So while the basic justification for eradicating the predator may have been economic – it made life harder for ranchers and competed with sportsmen – these groups went much further in their bid to whip up a frenzy of hatred, especially when lobbying for funds. It was elevated to a moral issue and predators were criminalized and 'dehumanized' through the agency of anthropomorphism. Every undesirable and negative human quality was heaped onto wolves and coyotes. The utopian feeling (already detectable in seventeenth-century New England) that the purging of predators from the body politic would lead to a paradise of game and a cornucopia of beef, wool and mutton, reached its apogee during this period. At fundamental issue here were threats to national prosperity and security. Corbin identified his quarry as 'the enemy of the state ... for what greater enemy can the state have than one that is able to wage war on the state's chief industry day and night?'[42]

During the 1920s even *Scientific American* lambasted the coyote as 'piratical' for its crimes against property, tarring it as the 'original bolshevik.'[43] (Between 1915 and 1927, two million coyotes were slaughtered). By 1945, with Nazis and Japanese the archetypal enemies, Wisconsin sportsmen could rebuke a plea for the toleration of predators (in view of their beneficial role in checking populations of wild grazers) with the public statement that: 'The wolf is the Nazi of the forest. He takes the deer and some small fry. The fox is the sly Jap who takes the choice morsels of game and the song birds.'[44] It was, thus, only appropriate that those defined as state enemies should eventually be hounded by the apparatus of the State itself. Bounty payments had long been endorsed by authorities at the State and local levels but in the early twentieth century the federal government itself weighed in with its might, and in a more direct capacity. The predecessor of the Bureau of Biological Survey (BBS), the Office of Economic Ornithology and Mammalogy, began testing poisons in 1885 and soon after its establishment in 1896, the BBS was furnishing ranchers with advice on predator elimination. For instance, that spring was the best time to locate wolf dens and that destroying the young was a cheap and easy method of elimination.

Wolves that had eluded the wolfers tended to retreat to undeveloped federal lands and stockmen complained that national forests and national parks were increasingly serving as safe havens and breeding grounds. Extermination in the national forests (also serving the interest of deer hunters) began in 1907, during which BBS agents notched up 1,800 wolves and 23,000 coyotes across thirty-nine national forests, with an estimated saving in stock worth $2 million.[45] Those who have come to associate U.S. national parks with dedication to wildlife preservation may be surprised to learn that the federal predator extermination business also infiltrated this most protected category of public lands. Poisoned carcasses had been used to kill predators in the first national park, Yellowstone (established 1872), since 1877, with a pack of hounds brought in to hunt mountain lions (also known as cougar and puma) in 1893. The enabling legislation of the U.S. National Park Service (1916) formalized such arrangements by allowing for killing of animals and plants judged 'detrimental' to park purposes compared with the deer, elk, and antelope which were seen as a prime tourist attraction and a way to sell the fledgling parks to the public.[46]

Over the next decade, park officials, in cooperation with the BBS, and further supported by state and county authorities, sportsmen's clubs and magazines, conservationists, stockmen, civic organizations and their various political representatives, pursued predators throughout the grand nature parks of the American West. They did so with the zeal of a Wyatt Earp wiping out a nest of bandits. In 1920 the park service's director happily noted the increase in deer and other prey species. With the eradication of the last gray wolf from Yellowstone by the late 1920s, the entire park system of the continental United States had been cleansed of the species. Attention now shifted to the coyote, on which the recently retired park service chief Horace Albright, recommended, in 1937, that his successor declare 'open war'.[47]

These federal campaigns had their counterparts beyond the national forests and national parks. For regardless of the efficacy of existing measures, other public (as well as private) lands were regarded as sources of reinfestation. In 1914, Congress finally responded to a tenacious western stockmen's initiative for 'control' at public expense on private lands and public lands beyond the parks and forests by appropriating $125,000 to establish a crack government unit. Similarly, predator control among the activities of the BBS was so prominent that, following his perusal of the agency's archival materials, the writer Charles Bowden remarked that the 'records are a bit like a history of the Jews as Hitler might have written it'.[48]

The contempt that the federal agent felt for the freelance wolfer introduces a fascinating sideline: relations between professional and amateur agents of massacre. Casual wolfers might have been protecting the interests of civilization but were not themselves held in high regard. The college-trained government corps looked down on their activities as haphazard, unregulated, unscrupulous, and, not least, attractive to the dissolute and depraved. The authorities responsible for official massacre prided themselves on their unemotional approach, frowning on acts of brutality by private parties such as the scalping of coyotes and wiring shut their mouths. (The most powerful argument that officials advance nowadays in defence of their agency is that abolition of federal predator control will simply lead ranchers to take the law into their own hands, meaning 'a pure, goddamned disaster for wildlife'.)[49] Bounty hunters certainly had a vested interest in perpetuating supplies of the noxious animal, and often engaged in 'wolf farming' by killing the pups but sparing the mother.

Moreover, professional exterminators sometimes held their victims in high regard. Stanley Young, who worked for the BBS's Predatory Animal and Rodent Control Service (PARC) between 1919 and 1937, and was the agency's head from 1937 to 1939, was ambivalent. Though he believed that the wolf is '100 percent criminal, killing for sheer blood lust', and, 'All wolves are killers', he developed a grudging admiration: 'in spite of all that is bad about the wolf, I personally consider this animal our greatest American quadruped and have often wished that it would change its ways just a little so that the hand of man would not be raised so constantly'. And he was prepared to grant the species an asylum, if only in places 'where these large killers can exist in no direct conflict with man'.[50]

In any event, BBS agents had a tougher job than their private predecessors as there were fewer wolves around. Nonetheless, they did perform an effective mopping-up operation: New Mexico's wolf population was pared down from three hundred to thirty between 1917 and 1920.[51] Government agents' entry into the fray may not have inaugurated a numerically significant new phase of wolf massacre, but the best known of these agents, Bill Caywood, did ultimately nail some of the most famous diehard or 'outlaw' wolves of the West, many of them battle-scarred trap survivors, such as three-legged Old Lefty of Burns Hole, Colorado. These incorrigibles were invariaby personalized in the manner of human bandits and public interest in their nefarious deeds was enormous. The Custer Wolf of South Dakota was credited with destroying $25,000 worth of cattle during a seven-year spree, while the most notorious, Three Toes of South Dakota, apparently gave 150 men the slip for thirteen years. The 'outlaw' wolf was invariably wanted dead and the capture of such a beast was the occasion for parades, speeches, banquets and other acts of thanksgiving, with the successful hunters receiving gifts such as engraved gold watches.

As far as predators in general were concerned, the annual 'body count' peaked in the decade following the First World War, when BBS agents were poisoning 35,000 coyotes per annum.[52] By 1931, three-quarters of the bureau's budget was earmarked for predator 'control', while a decade later, almost $3 million was expended annually for this purpose.[53] Within a few years the most lethal chemical of all was adopted; sodium fluoroacetate, better known as compound 1080 (which destroys the nervous system and causes cardiac arrest). The crusade against predators of all stripes continued apace: between 1961 and 1970, the ADC's 'gopher chokers' (as critics called them) scattered seven million tallow pellets laced with strychnine over the western plains; as late as 1989, the unit enjoyed an annual budget of $29.4 million.[54]

However, though such policies initially had widespread public support this was never universal and eroded over time. Turn-of-the-century alternatives to the hegemonic image of the wolf could be found in Jack London's bestseller, *The Call of the Wild* (1903), and the tales of Ernest Thompson Seton (the most popular author of wildlife stories in North America), which celebrated the wolf's exceptional strength and intelligence. Yet one suspects that an urban sophisticate could enjoy these writers while tacitly approving of predator elimination.

The earliest genuine efforts to rehabilitate the wolf must be sought elsewhere. Just as the prevailing image was heavily anthropomorphic, so was the counter-offensive. The tactic – one article by Seton was entitled 'The Natural History of the Ten Commandments' (1907) – focused attention on the wolf's moral qualities and virtues. The two most laudable traits were monogamy – in which respect Seton compared wolves favourably with dogs ('domesticity is notoriously bad for the morals of animals') – and male chivalry – Seton defining the latter as 'consideration by a male for a female, on account of her sex, when the sexual passion is dormant'). Moreover, male wolves were 'good fathers' as well as 'good husbands', doing their share of the child-raising. Family values were uppermost as the wolf's champions trumpeted the benefits to offspring of being raised within this stable family unit (Seton called it a 'life-long union'). Unencumbered by the disadvantages of single parenthood, cubs enjoyed the 'advantage of two wise protectors'. (This also worked to the wolfer's advantage; both parents were often to be found in the dens.) Another commentator went so far as to compare the wolf's clean living and freedom from sexually transmitted diseases with the promiscuous lifestyle and disease-ridden status of rabbits. The elaborate studies of wolf sociology undertaken by another lupine champion drew attention to other genteel and civilized traits.[55] In contrast to the popular image of gluttony, William J. Long believed the wolf's dining sessions were 'as peacable as a breakfast table' (1909).[56]

On a more practical level as well as on rather different grounds, predator eradication in Yellowstone National Park had been opposed since 1924 by a citizens' watchdog group, the National Parks Association. This was largely due to the resulting surplus of prey species, particularly elk, that devastated trees and led to mass starvation during harsh winters.[57] Other dissenters during the inter-war years, notably Joseph Grinnell, director of the Museum of Vertebrate Zoology at the University of California, Berkeley, and the American Society of Mammalogists, underscored other unforeseen consequences: the proliferation of grass-eating rodents such as rabbits and pocket gophers, which now also needed to be wiped out to serve stockmen's interests. Moreover, by the early 1930s, only a trickle of dead wolves were coming in from the parks while the amount spent on eradication on public lands as a whole was vastly in excess of the value of stock lost to predators. The influence of the Bureau of Biological Survey's critics (who, in the 1920s, dubbed the outfit the 'Bureau of Destruction and Extermination') was reflected in the 1934 moratorium on predator extermination in parks, a policy officially terminated at the end of the decade following a report showing that coyotes did not menace other park creatures.[58]

Nevertheless, federal biologists striving to secure a new deal for predators in the parks, during the 1930s, remained alert to the superimposition of human norms of morality and behaviour upon them: 'There is sometimes a tendency in men in the field to hold any predator in the same disreputable position as any human criminal. It seems well to comment that no moral status should be attached to any animal. It is just as natural (just as much a part of nature) for coyotes to prey upon other animal life as it is for trees to grow from the soil, and nobody questions the morality of the latter.'[59] Increasingly, in this period, these ecological arguments, offered by biologists, stressed the value of predators to healthily functioning ecosystems in the face of commonplace anthropomorphic stereotyping. The almost Pauline conversion of Aldo Leopold, the guru of modern American environmentalism, from gung-ho wolf killer to wolf appreciator, has become emblematic of the birth of modern ecological consciousness in the United States. In a 1944 essay, which has since attained the status of gospel among U.S. environmentalists, the trigger-happy young forest ranger relates how he was shocked into a reappraisal of the conventional wisdom of predator hatred one day in New Mexico back in the 1910s. As he watched the 'fierce green fire dying' in a female wolf's eyes ('In those days we had never heard of passing up a chance to kill a wolf'), he learnt how to think ecologically, or, to use his resonant phrase, 'like a mountain':

> Since then I have lived to see state after state extirpate its wolves. I have watched the face of many a newly wolfless mountain, and seen the south-facing slopes wrinkle with a maze of new deer trails. I have seen every edible bush and seedling browsed, first to anaemic desuetude, and then to death ... In the end the starved bones of the hoped-for deer herd, dead of its own too-much, bleach with the bones of the dead sage.[60]

However, many scientists with access to political authority still believed that protection was exclusively for 'good animals' and extermination on other public lands continued unabated until the 1960s, when government advisory committee reports promoted intensified questioning of the value of control on economic and ecological grounds. The wolf's status as an upright and valuable member of the ecological community was popularized at this time by Farley Mowat's *Never Cry Wolf* (1963), a fictional account of a biologist's wolf studies in the Canadian far north, and, more recently, the Disney film of that name. Poisoning effectively ended in 1972, with the banning of compound 1080, strychnine and cyanide on public lands and passage of the Endangered Species Act (1973), under which the wolf is classified as 'threatened'. Other predators have yet to win a reprieve. A covert photograph of the heads of thirteen Arizona mountain lions decapitated in 1990 by Animal Damage Control (which had succeeded PARC in 1974) provoked a howl of public protest, but two years later the unit (which has since changed its name to the even more euphemistic and consumer-friendly sounding 'Animal Services') killed 2.2 million wild animals. Many were crop-eating birds and 'nuisance' animals such as garbage bears and foxes that raided hen coops, but the biggest non-avian offender was the coyote, with a body count of 97,966.[61] Friends of the predator argue that the best way to resolve actual (as opposed to perceived) conflict with stock are non-lethal methods of deterrence: time-honoured, low-tech solutions such as guard dogs, and high-tech gadgets such as strobe and siren scare devices. Despite their effectiveness, livestock interests currently show little interest in such practices, which they intepret as appeasement rather than *détente*.

The unreconstructed hatred of the hunter intolerant of competition flourishes as nowhere else in the wolf's last American stronghold – Alaska. In his study of Alaska in the 1970s, journalist John McPhee recalls the bravado of the late Joe Vogler, gold-miner and fierce advocate of Alaskan independence, who 'picked up and tossed idly in his hand a piece of dry wolf feces [*sic*] with so many moose hairs in it that it looked like a big caterpillar. "Greedy gut-ripping son of a bitch," he said. "Stinking dirty cowardly predator. I'd kill the last pregnant wolf on earth right in front of the President at high noon."' And though there is no prospect of a reprise of past massacres, official or unofficial, Alaskan hunters have recently called for a reduction of wolf numbers to levels likely to benefit their prized game species.[62]

Yet the most sensitive current flashpoints are to be found in the areas, notably around Yellowstone National Park, where wolves were reintroduced in 1995 in accordance with the Endangered Species Act.[63] Since it sheds the protection conferred by endangered status if it kills stock, the wolf still serves ranchers as a scapegoat for any loss. Autopsies on a wolf shot by an Idaho rancher in 1994, and its alleged victim, indicated that the calf 'probably died of causes related to birthing and was dead at the time the wolf scavenged the carcass', and that the calf had been moved from its birth site to its location next to the wolf 'by persons unknown'. Federal investigators were forced to withdraw after a taste of the intimidation and threat of violence with which right-wing extremists are currently greeting representatives of the federal 'Gestapo' across the mountain West.[64]

Despite the new tenderness in some quarters, old attitudes die hard. Given the persisting bias against predators not only among ranchers and hunters but throughout popular culture, this is likely to remain an intriguing subject for the historian of the more violent aspects of the dialogue between humans and other carnivores.

Notes

1. H. E. Anthony, *Animals of America* (Garden City, NY, 1937), 65.
2. Harvard Sitkoff, *The Struggle for Black Equality, 1954-1992* (New York, 1993), 203.
3. For an overview, see Richard Maxwell Brown, 'Violence', in Clyde A. Milner et al., *The Oxford History of the American West* (New York, 1993), 393-425.

4. Richard Slotkin, *Regeneration through Violence: The Mythology of the American Frontier, 1600-1890* (Middletown, CT., 1973), 88.

5. Dee Brown, *Bury My Heart at Wounded Knee: An Indian History of the American West* (New York, 1971), 89.

6. *Guardian*, 19 August 1991.

7. David Stannard, *American Holocaust: Columbus and the Conquest of the New World* (New York, 1992); Kirkpatrick Sale, *The Conquest of Paradise: Christopher Columbus and the Columbian Legacy* (New York, 1990); Lyman H. Legters, 'The American Genocide', *Policy Studies Journal*, 16, 4 (1988): 768-77.

8. Donald Worster, 'Other People, Other Lives', in *An Unsettled Country* (Albuquerque, 1994), 70-71, 73, 78. A book on deforestation, entitled 'The Great Chainsaw Massacre' is yet to appear. Historians accustomed to historical study that confines itself to relationships between people, and those whose ethical system firmly subordinates wild creatures, will undoubtedly feel uneasy about an approach that, in their view, places the killing of wildlife more or less on a par with that of humans. They will be even less happy with definitions of genocide that have been stretched to include wildlife. In particular, historians of the Jewish Holocaust in Nazi Germany and survivors of Nazi extermination camps may find these analogies glib at best, outrageous at worst. Needless to say, environmental historians applying terms such as genocide and Holocaust to relations between humans and wild animals intend no offence. We certainly have no desire to belittle human sufferings or to trivialize the concept of massacre.

9. Scott Russell Sanders, ed., *Audubon Reader: The Best Writings of John James Audubon* (Bloomington, 1986), 121.

10. Richard White, 'Animals and Enterprise,' in Milner, *Oxford History*, 243, 237-38.

11. Aldo Leopold, quoted in Susan L. Flader, *Thinking like a Mountain: Aldo Leopold and the Evolution of an Ecological Attitude toward Deer, Wolves and Forests* (Columbia, 1974), 3.

12. Ernest Thompson Seton, *Lives of Game Animals* (Garden City, NY, 1925), vol. 1, 261.

13. The Eastern timber wolf (*Canis lupus lycaon*) was the major subspecies east of the Mississippi. The gray wolf (*Canis lupus*) dominated west of the Mississippi.

14. Barry Holstun Lopez, *Of Wolves and Men* (New York, 1978), 167. Use of 'pogrom' is increasingly common among environmentalists. See Donald G. Schueler, 'Contract Killers', *Sierra* (November/December 1993): 70. For a discussion of hostility to predators that also covers bears, mountain lions, vultures and bald eagles, see Lisa Mighetto, *Wild Animals and American Environmental Ethics* (Tucson, 1991), 75-93. For a detailed case study see Richard P. Thiel, *The Timber Wolf in Wisconsin: The Death and Life of a Majestic Predator* (Madison, 1993).

15. These observations apply to other predators too. British television advertisments for 'cracking' auto-crime deploy snarling hyenas stalking their 'prey' in a multi-storey car park.

16. Lopez, *Of Wolves and Men*, 147, 149. The most eminent of wolf experts contends that, in North America, 'no scientifically acceptable evidence is available to support the claim that healthy wild wolves are dangerous to man'. L. David Mech, *The Wolf: The Ecology and Behavior of an Endangered Species* (Garden City, NY, 1970), 291.

17. Conrad Gesner, *Historiae Animalium* (5 vols. Tiguri, 1551-1587); Edward Topsell, *The Historie of Foure-Footed Beastes* (London, 1607); Georges Louis Le Clerc (Count de Buffon), *Histoire Naturelle* (44 vols. Paris,1749-1804). For an imaginative and polemical probing of wolf symbolism and Western culture's historic fear and loathing of the wolf (lycanphobia), see James C. Burbank,

Vanishing Lobo: The Mexican Wolf and the Southwest (Boulder, 1990), 54-86. Also useful (and more authoritative) is Peter Steinhart, *The Company of Wolves* (New York, 1995), xi-xvii, 30-48, 51-52, 338-45.

18. Valerie M. Fogleman, 'American Attitudes towards Wolves: A History of Misperception', *Environmental Review*, 13, 1 (1989): 66.

19. Slotkin, *Regeneration*, 167, 154, 170, 88. For analogies between wolves and Native Americans from the American West in the second half of the nineteenth century, see Bruce Hampton, 'Shark of the Plains: Early Western Encounters with Wolves', *Montana, The Magazine of Western History*, 46, 1 (1996): 11.

20. In the terminology of seventeenth-century English law, a wolf-head was an outlaw, and the popular expression 'to cry wolf-head' meant to sound the call for hunting down an outlaw.

21. Francis Jennings, *The Invasion of America: Indians, Colonialism and the Cant of Conquest* (New York, 1976), 146.

22. This particular instance of a widely held view is from the 1890s. See U.S. Senate, Committee on Agriculture and Forestry hearings, *Control of Predatory Animals*, 71st Congress, 2nd and 3rd Sessions, 8 May 1930 and 28/29 January 1931 (Washington, 1931), 6.

23. Theodore Roosevelt, *The Wilderness Hunter* (1893; reprint, New York, 1927), 305, 310-11; *Hunting Trips of a Ranchman: Sketches of Sport on the Northern Cattle Plains* (1885 reprint, New York, 1900 [1885]: 42, 45; U.S. Department of Agriculture, *Yearbook* (Washington, 1920), 297. On the basis of recent studies, Mech, *The Wolf*, 204-5, doubts that hamstringing (severing the Achilles tendon), was a widespread method of killing.

24. Lopez, *Of Wolves and Men*, 175.

25. Stanley P. Young, *The Wolves of North America, Part 1. Their History, Life Habits, Economic Status, and Control* (1944, reprint New York, 1964), 360.

26. Ibid.

27. Sewell Newhouse, *The Trapper's Guide* (1865, reprint, Community, NY, 1887), 212.

28. William Cronon, *Changes in the Land: Indians, Colonists and the Ecology of New England* (New York, 1983), 132-34, 154; James B. Trefethen, *An American Crusade for Wildlife* (New York ,1975), 163-67.

29. Cronon, *Changes*, 133.

30. Lopez, *Of Wolves and Men*, 159.

31. Young, *Wolves of North America*, 327, 331.

32. Ibid., 335.

33. Edward Curnow, 'The History of the Eradication of the Wolf in Montana' (Master's diss., University of Montana, Missoula, Montana, 1969), quoted in Lopez, *Of Wolves and Men*, 183. See also Rick McIntyre, *A Society of Wolves: National Parks and the Battle over the Wolf* (Stillwater, MN, 1993), 67; David E. Brown, *The Wolf in the Southwest* (Tucson, 1983), 45. For a thorough account of the campaign in another western state, see Peter M. Zmyj, '"A Fight to the Finish": The Extermination of the Gray Wolf in Wyoming, 1890-1930', *Montana, The Magazine of Western History*, 46, 1 (1996): 14-25, though Zmyj does not reflect on the broader issues posed by wolf hatred.

34. Brown, *Bury my Heart*, 89.

35. Young, *Wolves of North America*, 382.

36. Benjamin Corbin, *Corbin's Advice; or, the Wolf Hunter's Guide; Tells How to Catch 'Em and All About the Science of Wolf Hunting* (Bismark, 1900), quoted in Lopez, *Of Wolves and Men*, 184-85; Steinhart, *Company of Wolves* , 37.

37. Lopez, *Of Wolves and Men*, 159, 139. Montana even resorted to germ warfare; between 1905 and 1916, a law instructed the state veterinarian to capture

wolves, infect them with sarcoptic mange and then release them (McIntyre, *Society of Wolves*, 67).

38. Lopez, *Of Wolves and Men*, 180.
39. William T. Hornaday, *The American Natural History* (New York, 1904), 22, where he also repeats the time-honoured charge of cannibalism. Wolves and coyotes are also dealt with in his classic text on wildlife conservation, *Our Vanishing Wild Life* (New York, 1913), in the chapter entitled 'Unseen Foes of Wild Life'. Jay D. Hair, a recent president of the National Wildlife Federation, contended in 1993 that while other predators like the cougar were also ruthlessly suppressed, 'none evoked the mysterious frightfulness nor were so thoroughly scourged as the wolf'. (McIntyre, *Society of Wolves*, 7).
40. Thomas R. Dunlap, *Saving America's Wildlife: Ecology and the American Mind, 1850-1990* (Princeton, 1988), 15, 85.
41. Donald Worster, *Nature's Economy: A History of Ecological Ideas* (Cambridge, 1985), 261-73.
42. *Corbin's Advice*, quoted in Lopez, *Of Wolves and Men*, 185.
43. *Scientific American*, 122 (6 March 1920): 246.
44. Flader, *Thinking like a Mountain*, 211-12. Returning soldiers who embarked on zealous wolf assaults in Minnesota also called them Nazis (Lopez, *Of Wolves and Men*, 150).
45. Young, *Wolves of North America*, 381-83; Cameron Jenks, *The Bureau of Biological Survey: Its History, Activities and Organization* (Baltimore, 1929), 46.
46. Alfred Runte, *National Parks: The American Experience* (Lincoln, Neb., 1979), 111; McIntyre, *Society of Wolves*, 51-65.
47. Alston Chase, *Playing God in Yellowstone: The Destruction of America's First National Park* (Boston, 1986), 23, 21, 52, 120-21, 127.
48. Young, *Wolves of North America*, 382-83; McIntyre, *Society of Wolves*, 75.
49. *Sierra* (November/December 1993): 75.
50. Worster, *Nature's Economy*, 277-78; Young, *Wolves of North America*, 8. See also Worster, 'Other People, Other Lives', 80.
51. Flader, *Thinking like a Mountain*, 60.
52. Dunlap, *Saving America's Wildlife*, 49. For details of government campaigns of the periods 1890-1925 and 1906-1928 respectively, see Brown, *Wolf in the Southwest*, 41-71, and Jenks, *Bureau of Biological Survey*, 42-52.
53. Worster, *Nature's Economy*, 264.
54. Jeremy Rifkin, *Beyond Beef: The Rise and Fall of the Cattle Culture* (New York, 1992), 209.
55. Ernest Thompson Seton, 'The Natural History of the Ten Commandments', *The Century*, 75 (Nov. 1907): 24-33; also his *Life-Histories of Northern Animals*, vol. 2, *Flesh-Eaters* (London, 1910), 756-57; *Lives of Game Animals*, vol. 1, 276, 330; and Woods Hutchinson, 'Animal Marriage', *Contemporary Review* (October, 1904): 493. Though modern studies have confirmed the quality of wolves' parental care, they have found it hard to corroborate that they mate for life. Nonetheless, research does reveal a preference for long-term relationships (Mech, *The Wolf*, 142-46, 114).
56. Quoted in Mighetto, *Wild Animals*, 89. Long was one of the best known of the so-called 'nature fakers' – those writers who insisted that extraordinarily human-like animal activities could be scientifically verified.
57. John Ise, *Our National Park Policy: A Critical History* (Baltimore, 1961), 319-20, 585.
58. Dunlap, *Saving America's Wildlife*, 95, 128.
59. U.S. Department of the Interior, National Park Service (George M. Wright, et al.), *Fauna of the National Parks of the United States: A Preliminary Survey of*

Faunal Relations in the National Parks (Washington, DC, 1933), 48. For the emergence of more sympathetic attitudes toward predators within the Park Service, see Thomas R. Dunlap, 'Wildlife, Science, and the National Parks, 1920-1940', *Pacific Historical Review*, 59, 2 (1990): 187-202.

60. Aldo Leopold, *A Sand County Almanac* (New York, 1949), 130-32. For the reassessment of the predator's value, focusing on developments in ecological science, see Thomas R. Dunlap, '"The Coyote Itself": Ecologists and the Value of Predators, 1900-1972', in Kendall E. Bailes, ed., *Environmental History: Critical Issues in Comparative Perspective* (Lanham, MD, 1985), 594-618.

61. *Sierra* (November/December 1993): 70-76, 97. The grand total of 2.2 million included 114 wolves.

62. John McPhee, *Coming into the Country* (New York, 1977), 303-4. For the massive national controversy in 1992 over Alaska's proposed aerial 'control' project, see McIntyre, *Society of Wolves*, 104-5, and Steinhart, *Company of Wolves*, 267-95.

63. Hank Fischer, *Wolf Wars: The Remarkable Inside Story of the Restoration of Wolves to Yellowstone* (Missoula, MT, 1995); Steinhart, *Company of Wolves*, 212-66.

64. Odean Cusack, 'Reprieve for Minnesota's Wolves', *Sierra* (March/April 1984): 41-42; Ted Williams, 'Defense of the Realm', *Sierra* (January/February 1996): 34-39, 121-22. In the 1980s, farmers in northeastern Minnesota killed about 250 wolves a year.

CHAPTER 9

THE CANUDOS MASSACRE, A HUNDRED YEARS ON

Robert M. Levine

In October 1897, thousands of men, women and children residing in an isolated Roman Catholic religious community in the backlands of the State of Bahia died defending their homes against a furious attack by the Brazilian army. Captives had their throats slit, often with family members forced to watch. The so-called Canudos War was no isolated massacre; its events were reported daily over a period of months by newspaper correspondents and, from a safe distance, by the Brazilian Minister of War. When Canudos finally capitulated, after months of resistance, the community's 5,200 homes were burned to the ground. The few surviving women were evacuated to the coast, where they were made servants (and in some cases, prostitutes); some of the surviving children were 'adopted' by some of the onlookers or otherwise taken as trophies of war. This chapter examines the background to Canudos and explores the reasons for the distorted way that it came to be seen as a threat so dangerous that only its destruction could ensure the survival of the Brazilian Republic.

The early 1890s were a powerfully disturbing period for Brazilians worried about their nation's uncertain transition from monarchy to Republic after the little-resisted military coup of 15 November 1889. Republican government had come to Brazil nearly seven decades later than to most of its neighbours. Legislation separating church and state had established secular primacy. The army assumed the mantle of defender of national unity and ruled dictatorially between 1889 and 1894. Much of Brazil was mired in economic stagnation and chronic impoverishment, especially in the vast Amazon basin and in the destitute northeast, the historical centre of Brazil's population and economic activity. Streams of migrants headed south, seeking regular employment and sustenance; but few gained either. Landowners, convinced that the newly freed slaves would not work efficiently for wages, attempted through government-subsidized colonization schemes to recruit agricultural workers from Northern Europe, although in the end most of those who came were from Italy, Spain and Portugal. Rural Brazilians in general were considered to be unwilling to work hard and incapable of being productive.

Sensing the climate of change, the London *Statesman* euphorically called the Emperor's exile, in late 1889, the most important event in the world. In Brazil, however, the slow pace of industrialization forestalled the momentous transformations that were affecting city life in Western Europe and in the United States. Nonetheless, new technology and new ideas challenging the orthodoxies of the nineteenth century were filtering in from abroad to Brazilian coastal cities at a quickened pace. Even agriculture, at the heart of the oligarchy's traditional hold on power, was undergoing rapid change. Within the space of a decade and a half (from the early 1880s to the mid-1890s), centralized refineries supplanted the centuries-old system of mills driven by water or animal power. The eastern coast's sugar plantation economy became permanently transformed, especially in Pernambuco, Alagoas, Rio de Janeiro, and Bahia. Railway networks and port improvements, built with foreign capital, sharply lowered the cost of bringing export staples to markets. The accelerating changes were disruptive, however, and did not proceed smoothly. Coffee culture in the southwest, which had absorbed much of the migratory stream, began to experience overproduction. Northeastern plantations hired fewer workers as rates paid for sugar and cacao stagnated or fell. Prices of staple foods such as corn, beans, and rice almost tripled. Warehouses erected at railway hubs supplanted the market system in rural towns and altered trading patterns. More people, many from outside the traditional aristocracy, were able to make fortunes from these innovations, disrupting the status quo and destabilizing daily life. Foreign investment poured in. Oligarchic hegemony became undermined by cycles of boom and bust, fuelled by speculation and deflationary pressures.[1]

The Republic ushered in an era of extreme federalism. Each of the former provinces, now states, could tax its exports, raise its own armed forces, and to the limits of its fiscal resources, pursue its own railway, road, port facilities, and urban construction programmes. As a consequence, the dynamic units of the federation, without exception in the south (Rio Grande do Sul, Minas Gerais, and especially São Paulo with its expanding coffee frontier), jumped ahead in material growth and political power while the rest of the country languished. The state which lost the most in national influence as a measure of its shrivelled economic base was Bahia. Its large population brought few political benefits because representative government meant little. The federal government soon came to be dominated by the commanding southern states, and the northeast's economic base stagnated. The Bahian political élite became extremely splintered by partisan infighting throughout the 1890s, while the southeastern élite became strong, and united state republican parties began reaping the benefits of the new federal system. In this framework, the national government did little more than arbitrate, sometimes lending its support to an oligarchic faction, at other times negotiating directly with local bosses, the interior *coronéis*, who in Bahia and the backlands of the northeast were so powerful that throughout the region on both sides of the São Francisco River, 'nations of coronéis' were said to flourish.[2]

As elsewhere in the hemisphere, the crude forms of government which had prevailed for decades gave way to pragmatic and nuanced prescriptions for national progress. These tended to combine nineteenth-century economic liberalism with measures designed to stifle popular expression and to block effective social mobilization. Brazilian élites agreed to accept a rural solution but only so long as it kept power in the hands of the traditional landed oligarchy and its clients.[3] A consequence was an assault against autonomous folk societies; Canudos was one of these victims of Europeanized 'progress' imposed by the nation's coastal élites.

Canudos (or Belo Monte) was a religious settlement founded by a pious lay Catholic mystic, Antônio Vicente Mendes Maciel, known to his followers as Antônio Conselheiro (the Counsellor). Belo Monte took form on the grounds of an abandoned cattle ranch owned by the Jeremoabo clan in the parched backlands interior of the State of Bahia. Lying in the 'backlands' known as the *sertão*, the region was afflicted by a severe climate and generally inhospitable terrain that intimidated visitors. The backlands conjured up images of backwardness and inhospitability of place and people, although on the whole its dry climate was neither intolerable nor oppressive. Backlands residents – *sertanejos* – were not peasants like the sedentary rural peoples of the Andean highlands or Middle America, where the term 'peasant' is used mostly to describe poor rural families with little freedom or independence, living and working on land once communally shared but now either divided into minifundia (units too small to yield profit) or larger properties owned by others.[4] Most rural backlanders lived as renters or sharecroppers under miserable conditions, but they retained a limited freedom of movement and a grudging spirit of self-reliance. Before 1893, few outsiders passed through the Bahian *sertão* except en route to the São Francisco River 130 kilometres to the north.

Conselheiro's 'New Jerusalem' grew precipitously and contained more than five thousand mud-and-wattle huts scattered in close proximity below a ring of hills and low mountains. Its population of twenty-five thousand (at its height in 1895 probably closer to thirty-five thousand), made it the largest urban site in Bahia after Salvador, the capital, seven hundred kilometres to the southeast. Canudos drained labour across several states, especially from the Rio Real in southern Sergipe to Inhambupe in Bahia. Between 1893 and 1897, it became the expression of a popular movement atavistic to outsiders but vigorous and pragmatically adapted to the region's limitations. Conselheiro was a product of this unique backlands religious environment. Since colonial days, the São Francisco Valley was known for the powerful influence of flagellant penitential brotherhoods. The backlands population, largely self-instructed in its catholicism, tended to blend everyday stoicism and resignation with messianic hopes. It sanctioned an apocalyptic view of life, indulgences, and the cult of personal saints. The *beatos* (lay persons living as if they were members of a religious order) and other late nineteenth-century wanderers were laymen in religious garb.[5] They offered quasi-sacramental functions and combined moral and practical advice with fire and brimstone millenarian allegories becoming, in the words of a present-day cleric, 'an institutionalized form of popular religion'.[6] Herein lay the heart of the clash between the 'modern' and 'backwards' cultures embodied in the Canudos conflict: the characteristics which coastal observers disapproved of and scorned were the very ones which brought vitality to Conselheiro's followers.

The drain of surplus labour from surrounding regions as well as exaggerated tales of religious fanaticism told by visitors to Conselheiro's self-proclaimed 'holy city' led local élites to demand intervention. When Conselheiro stubbornly held firm, the decision was made first to disarm the 'rebels' and ultimately to destroy their city.[7] After three military expeditions failed, a fourth expedition of more than eight thousand men, commanded by three generals and the minister of war, shelled Canudos into submission in October 1897. Only a handful of survivors – all women and children – survived. Canudos went down in Brazilian history as a glorious victory for the forces of civilization against the dark forces of primitivism and insurrection.

The attitudes and erroneous suppositions held by educated coastal Brazilians about the nature of life in the rural hinterland made even greater the shock news about the army's inability to subdue Conselheiro's *jagunços*. Although their stereotypes of the rural poor conjured up images of resistance to authority and latent violence, at the same time they subscribed to the long-standing myth that, even in the northeast, the period after 1850 represented a kind of golden non-violent age.[8] In reality, the region was swept by both urban and rural conflict between 1850 and 1900, including food riots in Salvador and slave revolts in the interior; no fewer than fifty-nine violent conflicts were enumerated by the provincial Ministry of Justice up to 1889 and undoubtedly many others went unreported. Major outlaw gangs roamed the backlands. The immediate region, in fact, produced more violent gangs (*quadrilhas*) than any other part of Bahia. Nor did the government's victory over Canudos mean any cessation of politically linked violence. The 1899 municipal elections pitted anti-incumbent interests against Governor Luiz Vianna's allies, just as before, with the usual attendant beatings, attacks on commercial establishments, and murder.[9]

Because they aimed their actions against the dominant classes of the region, bandits in some ways brought balance to the dominance that powerful landowners and others in the backlands exerted, but *sertão* brigands did not help the poor – in spite of the Robin Hood myth wishfully appropriated by some commentators. The bandits stole everything they could: cattle, jewellery, agricultural implements, guns, food, even holy images from churches.[10] Some *quadrilhas* not only rustled cattle and committed armed robberies, but also attacked tax revenue agencies. The police, in turn, frequently lashed out in frustration, making arbitrary arrests and in general casting suspicions on *sertanejos*. Insurrections, when they occurred, inevitably led to suppression, although when mobs looted warehouses or food stores they initially made away with what they wanted without being caught. Once the police arrived, though, mass imprisonments followed and sometimes judges fined entire populations to pay for damages.

Conditioned by centuries of obligation, the Brazilian rural poor were intimidated and dominated by the landowners and their politician clients.[11] Perhaps in response to their helplessness against secular power, many of the revolts took on a millenarian character, sometimes rooted in mystical visions or notions of divine revenge. However, these left no more of a mark on the mass of the rural population than folktales which eventually became half-legend, half-myth. Historically, insurrectionary leaders fared poorly: like Conselheiro, three of the major rebels in earlier centuries – Zumbí in the seventeenth and Tiradentes in the eighteenth (and Lampião in the twentieth) – had their heads severed and displayed on pikes by forces representing the law.[12]

In the mid-nineteenth century certainly less than 5 percent and probably less than 1 percent of the rural population owned land. The persistence of slavery and the smooth transition from colony to monarchy influenced nineteenth-century Brazilian life. The author Machado de Assis, one of the few mulattos accepted as a member of the élite, with unconscious irony complained in 1876 that '[we] are what came over in Columbus's Caravel'.[13] Safely conservative, Brazil avoided the worst forms of Spanish American *caudillismo* and the terribly destructive forces of racial civil war; yet power remained distributed within a narrow spectrum of interlocking élites.

As far as the largest portion of the population was concerned, the substitution of Republic for monarchy had little impact. In contrast, the last quarter of the nineteenth century in Catholic France experienced the implementation of compulsory education in 1883, which in turn led to the ascendancy of village school teachers and a new prominent role for public education. This was accompanied by a decline in the importance of the village priest and his sometimes old-fashioned and narrow teaching methods. In Brazil, no such change appeared, even on the horizon. Only seven hundred primary schools functioned in the entire nation, prompting the Secretary of Public Instruction to complain that another 1,300 were urgently needed but could not be built for lack of funds and qualified teachers.[14]

In 1894, there was in the region in which Conselheiro preached hardly a single town or hamlet with a school with more than fifty children enrolled. Many had fewer than twenty-five. The élite's resistance to finding new sources of tax revenue doomed any hope for real change. In 1896, the largest single source of state income came from the sale of tax stamps, as befitting a society mired in bureaucracy, duties on property transfer, from professional and business license fees, and – fourth on the list – export duties. There were no real estate or land taxes, virtually no levies of any kind in rural areas, and no assessments on income or inheritance. All improvements had to be funded through bond issues and annual foreign loans, which in the first decade of the Republic were floated to yield sums in excess of all combined sources of income.[15]

Much of the way Canudos was seen in the intervening decades derived from the unprecedented success of *Os Sertões*, a passionate account of the campaigns against Canudos published in 1902 by Euclydes da Cunha, who had covered them as a war correspondent. Like Emile Zola, who descended the mines at Anzin in 1884, to see for himself the terrible conditions of coal miners' lives before writing his novel *Germinal*, da Cunha internalized his subject to the point where he remained tormented for the rest of his life.[16] But, whereas in France, Hugo and other socially conscious critics achieved some measure of political influence, da Cunha's leverage was neutralized by relegating him to lionization, by his own unhappy end, and by the failure of Brazilian society to concretely tackle any of the terrible circumstances he exposed. Nevertheless, due to him, the legacy of the backlands tragedy persisted even after the public's fascination with it had subsided.

Da Cunha's view of the backlanders drew on the idea of progress which had gained wide acceptance in Europe and in North America during the second part of the nineteenth century.[17] Sensitive to the suffering he saw during the final military assaults on Canudos and to the brutality exhibited on both sides of the conflict, his account reflected his dualist view of Brazilian society as irrevocably divided between the archaic primitivism of the backlands and the progressive culture of the coastal cities. The way da Cunha saw Canudos frightened coastal Brazilians who knew, deep down, that the material progress of the capital cities and the façade of civic modernity, symbolized by the new Republican form of government, represented more show than substance. Ambivalence tormented him; he deeply respected the perseverance of the rural peasants but he accepted the prevailing belief that they were racially inferior. He was influenced by Comptean positivism's appeal to science and its loathing of superstition and backwardness. This led him to believe that the Republic was threatened by Conselheiro's stubborn resistance to the new order, of which one aspect was nostalgia for the Empire. Dismayed by both military factionalism and monarchist plots after the Republic's birth, internecine jockeying among the states, and a severe economic depression in the early 1890s, da Cunha, and others of like mind, came to see Canudos as a challenge to the new civilian government in the federal capital and a threat even to the nation itself.

His epic narrative was painstakingly written and rewritten in the five years following the destruction of Canudos. On the one hand, it was a political statement of anger and revolt. On the other, it was a personal declaration, written at a crisis point in the author's troubled career, a means, perhaps, for the failed military officer who had left under the cloud of a nervous breakdown to purge the trauma he had witnessed from his mind. In his writing and research, he was aided by others, including the engineer and regional historian, Teodoro Sampaio, and academicians, Francisco Escobar and Lúcio de Mendonça. Strangely, da Cunha initially had trouble finding a publisher for his long and angry narrative written, as Joaquim Nabuco put it, 'with a stiletto'.[18] Yet within a year of publication of

Os Sertões, da Cunha, the soul-searching critic of the Republic's Vendée, was voted into both the Instituto Histórico e Geográfico Brasileiro (the Brazilian Historical and Geographical Institute) – a stronghold of traditionalism founded by Emperor Dom Pedro II – and to the august, self-important Brazilian Academy of Letters. After some brief carping, critics rushed to lionize the military engineer and amateur historian, who acknowledged that he had been waiting with a 'schoolboy's' fear for approval.[19]

As for Antônio Conselheiro; in twenty years of wandering through the northeastern backlands up to mid-1893 and until the destruction of Canudos itself, he had exercised the role of a dedicated lay missionary counselling against civic and religious disobedience. Conselheiro had intense feelings about social justice and personally opposed slavery. His followers were not aberrant primitives mesmerized by religious superstition, as chroniclers insisted, but a heterogenous community whose members included emancipated slaves (*crioulos*), rural sharecroppers of Indian-Caucasian descent (*mamelucos*), men and women from small towns and settlements, and a few linked by family ties to leading élite networks on the coast.

Most rural backlanders lived at subsistence level. They survived in the ravaged landscape by raising garden crops on land which had access to water owned by others. Some performed farm labour or worked as herders responsible for raising domestic animals and cattle owned by local landlords. Religion touched nearly every aspect of their lives. Some men and women imposed penitential restrictions on themselves; many fasted through much of the day. For Conselheiro and his closest followers, Belo Monte represented an earthly 'vale of tears', a transitory passage awaiting the final judgement and the coming of the end of the world. Conselheiro's rhetoric contained apocalyptic references which disturbed outsiders seeking evidence of more orthodox religious practices in the community.

Among *Canudenses* were a thousand or so backlands men who had been *vaqueiros* (cowhands); some may have been army or police deserters as well, and some had been fugitive slaves or bondsmen before emancipation. Da Cunha and others gave them the pejorative collective name *jagunços*, meaning both 'a race of mestizos … virile and adventurous', and 'incoherent, uneven, and turbulent in character'.[20] The term burrowed into the national psyche and for years came to be used for backlanders of any vocation although even within Canudos only a small portion of its population – Conselheiro's bodyguards, and some of his fighters – were true *jagunços*. During the military conflict, the name became the generic term for Conselheiro's fighters: tenacious rural ruffians quick to violence. It also conjured up images of sympathy; the children in Conselheiro's settlement were dubbed *jaguncinhos* (little *jagunços*), as if they had been raised by wolves or satan-worshippers.

From these ranks Conselheiro drew fighters who were invariably skilled with rifles, knives, and had an uncannily intimate knowledge of the topography. They resembled the gauchos (*gaúchos*) of Brazil's far south, but the backlanders herded their cattle in great, open spaces, and were more at the mercy of the rocky and sun-baked terrain, epizootic cattle infections, alternating flood and drought, and the need to constantly defend themselves against marauding cattle thieves. The backlands *jagunços,* to da Cunha, were 'less theatrically heroic, stronger, and more dangerous' than their *gaúcho* counterparts.[21] These differences were probably exaggerated. Both groups of cowboys brought a savage resilience to battle, showed little regard for their own lives, and were considered by army commanders to be without equal as cavalrymen as well as footsoldiers. An important difference which da Cunha did not take into account was the fact that the *gaúchos* lived in a more abundant environment and could thrive by hunting wild cattle, though this was changing in Rio Grande do Sul, by the late 1890s, with the introduction of barbed wire which facilitated cattle herding. It is significant that da Cunha characterized the entire *sertanejo* population as pastoralists, although most of the population lived from sedentary agriculture or petty commerce.

Thus, the men and women who made up Conselheiro's legions were diverse, drawing equally from the rural and urban portions of the region and representing a broad spectrum of ethnic and economic origins. They came from the Recôncavo, the towns of Alagoinhas and Esplanada in the hill-plateau *tabuleiro* region near the coast, and distant *sertão* hamlets several hundred kilometres away in western Pernambuco and Paraíba. Rural folk from neighbouring towns comprised the majority; in the main they were *caboclos,*[22] but the residents of Canudos represented a much broader socio-ethnic spectrum than conventionally believed. Their towns were not indolent; they were not, as residents of the coast believed, all as miserable as beggars.

Canudos quickly became an irritant but it hardly posed a real danger to the foundation of the Republic. Until the settlement was attacked by soldiers and earmarked for destruction, it coexisted peacefully with its neighbours. Up to twenty-five thousand men and women flocked there, but hundreds of thousands more in the region did not and showed no inclination to do so. Canudos also became a victim of circumstance; its birth and explosive growth fatally coincided with the opportunity to mount a propaganda campaign depicting it as a monarchist plot. In the aftermath of the ensuing carnage, the shaky civilian government was able, through a carefully orchestrated and jingoistic patriotism, to facilitate and consolidate what became known as the 'politics of the governors' – a brokered arrangement through which the strongest states in the federation gained unprecedented power – and in which alliances between state machines and *coronéis* secured for the agrocommercial oligarchy an unopposed control over rural Brazil.

It was the scale of the Canudos challenge within the context of a rising incidence of post-1889 rural intransigence and urban discord which, thus, so unnerved the affluent and politically-conscious sector of urban society. Yet the Republic, except for some local élites in the southern states, remained unpopular among landowners in much of the countryside. Nationwide disorganization characterized all levels of government from the *municípios* to the federal capital, and the two-party system of the Empire – which for all its failings had at least run smoothly – lay in shambles. State-based parties now dominated, but in most cases they remained divided along traditional lines based on local, clan-based rivalries. Added to this was the presence of the 'eleventh-hour Republicans', old political hands who, at the last minute, had seen the light and become nominal Republican converts as a strategy of political survival.

What, then, was unique about Canudos? It differed from all of the other episodes in large as well as small ways. Conselheiro preached salvation of the individual soul, not for his entire community. His vision was messianic and millenarian although from the standpoint of its theology and prescriptions for social behaviour it was not a threatening one. He never sought to impose it on others. Violence was brought to bear against Canudos; it was not exported from Canudos to the surrounding region, even though residents of at least one nearby city, Juazeiro, on the Pernambuco shore of the São Francisco River, were stampeded into panic by unsubstantiated rumours that the *conselheiristas* would besiege and loot the city in retribution for the nonreceipt of promised timber.

The conflict at Canudos, moreover, occurred at a distinctive juncture in Brazilian history, concurrent with the imposition of a new (and feared) political system which aggravated long-standing conditions of deprivation.[23] Those cut off from the source of social change – in this case, from the world of the coastal élites and hence of the modernizing government of the Republic – found that change could come as much in the form of ultramontanist clerics, seeking to reform backlands Catholic practice, as in the less discrete impact of the railway on the rural environment.

At stake here was a broadening, end-of-century gulf between the gentrified religion (or, its repudiation in the influential masonic lodges and parlours of the secular humanists) of the emerging national élite culture on the one hand, and that of a backlands on the other, aspects of which bear remarkable similarity to the remote mental universe of the eighteenth-century French village, described by Robert Darnton. The religion of the latter 'presented man as a slave of passion', filling his head 'with visions of threatening, occult forces … miracles, and hagiography'; though Darnton, picking up on a hypothesis of Robert Mandrou, has noted that the popular literature of the Old Regime also served as an ideological substitute for class consciousness among the masses.[24] In the Brazilian case, the pervasiveness of rural folk religious belief, so different from orthodox catholicism in its coastal (and ultramontanist) form, not only provided the common basis of attraction to holy men like Conselheiro but deflected attention 'from the real world of toil and exploitation'.[25]

To Conselheiro's followers, then, the State represented 'structural, cataclysmic upheaval' in its efforts to extend its power to the remote rural interior.[26] They, thus, willingly accepted prescriptions for life which provided comforting structure and direction. *Canudenses* were assigned work, and lived according to a set routine which must have brought a sense of security to those who had been traumatized by deprivation and by the vicissitudes of drought, disputes between clans, and economic uncertainty. Many other ordinary citizens of the backlands questioned the secularized Republican order. Some viewed the new requirement for civil registration and census questions about racial origins as a threat to restore the slavery abolished by the monarchy a year before it fell. Conselheiro had pulled down and burned notices of new municipal taxes in 1893. Even the election of a president rather than the lifetime investiture of a fatherly monarch raised fears; many backlanders preferred to seek refuge in Canudos, a communal settlement led by a protective patriarch.

What outsiders wanted to see as a rebellion was, thus, a collective statement by an integrated and unified community demanding the right to move to a place they considered a haven from an unfriendly world. Belo Monte had to be crushed because it upset the stability of the status quo in the *sertão*. It affected two major elements of rural oligarchical power: the pliant labour system and the 'herd vote' – the Old Republic's practice through which rural bosses captured all the votes under their control and delivered them in exchange for local power. Outmigration from all parts of the backlands to Canudos posed an immediate, real threat to this system. Had not the punitive expedition sent to meet Conselheiro at Masseté been overcome, there would have been less apparent justification for retaliation, but another pretext would have come sooner or later, given the political realities of the day.

Educated, coastal Brazilians were easily terrified by notions of Conselheiro and his followers as renegades and savages because of the image of rural folk – even before the introduction of scientific racism – as unsophisticated and prone to disaster. It is noteworthy that Conselheiro was not remembered as an abolitionist, even by contemporaries and later historians seeking lessons of social injustice in the Canudos drama. Conselheiro declaimed regularly against the evils of slavery but those who feared him distrusted his motives, remembering that he also advocated restoring the monarchy and, if only by implication, the paternalistic (and non-modern) social order it represented. A visionary and a prophet, his message deeply disturbed commonplace assumptions about social and institutional relationships. The hold exerted on his followers was evidently related to their insecurity and desperation for new lives. His protesting voice allowed enemies to label him an insurrectionist, and to justify his destruction on grounds of law and order.

Even so, the settlement at Canudos was always peaceful and nonviolent. The *Canudenses* did not proselytize. In this sense, they were heirs to the hapless participants of the Rodeador movement eight decades earlier. Of them, anthropologist and psychiatrist René Ribeiro notes that testimony from participants arrested by police revealed the 'essential gentleness' of their conception of their holy crusade by which they sought to establish, at Jerusalem, the Kingdom of God on earth.[27] A politically motivated uprising in the same region, in 1817, hardly affected these religious folk and their dreamlike concept. Prayer and waiting for King Sebastian took precedence over militancy. So, too, in Canudos. The holy city was a centre of refuge, theocratically organized though pragmatically connected to the surrounding environment – an achievement that bespeaks considerable flexibility on the part of Conselheiro and his aides.

Yet neither Conselheiro's personal mannerisms nor the way he comported himself as a mendicant preacher were particularly unusual for the backlands. His career followed the standard pattern of apostolic missionaries. His coarse blue robe knotted at the waist by a cord was the standard garb not only for *beatos* in northeastern Brazil but of several religious orders throughout Latin America, including the Capuchins, the principal clerical order in the northeast in the late nineteenth century. Missionaries in cassocks were more frequent visitors to backlands' villages than urban priests dressed more conventionally, and thus the sight of Conselheiro was nothing extraordinary. Only in founding Canudos and attracting so many followers to it did he overstep the mark by disrupting the region's economic life.

But Conselheiro never claimed to be the Messiah. His supernatural charisma was always attributed to him by others. He did, of course, exercise a powerful spell over his flock, and his acerbic (and anti-social) personality frightened many. What has never been questioned is his unshakeable personal faith and determination to shield his followers from the sins and temptations of modern life. To those who encountered him he projected a 'sense of foreboding ... pervasive and unappeasable'.[28] Conselheiro broke the hold of the traditional system of social control, and offered new lives for the faithful, especially in the heady period before the settlement was attacked by its enemies.

Never revolutionary, the Canudos community shared only a few similarities with other historic millenarian experiments. As individuals, Conselheiro's faithful embraced millennial expectations by voluntarily leaving their homes and coming to Canudos because their region was in crisis. Although Conselheiro failed to maintain and capitalize on his early alliances with some landowners and backlands *coronéis* in the region, his was no idealistic utopia. Millenarians of his stripe did not repudiate hierarchy and the unequal distribution of wealth *per se*; rather, most condemned selfish, immoral acts of new (and threatening) kinds of patrons. Deprivation and Conselheiro's spellbinding explanations about the evilness of encroaching modern life brought them together, but they were not 'fanatics' until circumstances united them in common defence against armed outside attack. After the carnage started, those who did not flee may well have capitulated to the mood of fiery prophecy and determination described by da Cunha. They also knew of their likely fate if captured outside the settlement – fears borne out at least in the first weeks after Canudos's destruction.

Canudos residents thus behaved rationally. They consciously and courageously abandoned their former lives to enter Conselheiro's holy city. They displayed the same characteristics ascribed by Roderick J. Barman to the Quebra-Quilo rioters: an 'independent, aggressive group possessing a well-established way of life which they were capable of defending with concerted, effective action and without much regard for the wishes of those usually considered to be the dominant elements in rural society'.[29] It is, thus, insufficient to dismiss Canudos and like movements as responses to *anomie*, or breakdowns of the traditional extended family owing to the rise of urbanization, the decline of paternalism, and other factors.[30] Nor was Belo Monte simply a kind of 'dumb theatre', as outsiders tended to regard it – a pathetic, year-round version of the carnivalesque practice whereby the poor become rich and enact waking dreams of social inversion.[31] Those that elected to live in Conselheiro's austere commune were probably motivated by the dislocations caused by the accelerating pace of change bringing instability to the backlands, and to the always-present hardship in individual lives.

Before Canudos was besieged, its residents were too busy building the settlement and following Conselheiro's austere precepts of
daily behaviour to be crazed by end-of-the-world fantasies. Many
residents did not participate in the religious routines of the community. The truly faithful were conceivably predisposed to follow
Conselheiro as a prophet because of the predilection of rural folk
catholicism for saints and the possibility of personal saintly inter-
cession in their lives. Conselheiro also served as a kind of regional
coronel, exerting the same level of power over his flock as traditional backlands *coronéis*.[32] His paternal theology protected his
subjects from the leviathan in the guise of the new Republican government which they believed to be evil for mystical reasons (the
coming millennium; the 'kidnapping' of the fatherly Emperor), and
on concrete grounds (the threat to legitimacy and inheritance posed
by obligatory civil registry of births, marriages, and deaths).

Observers who see in popular religious movements signs of anti-
social or pathological behaviour often fail to realize that what may
seem pathological or crisis-provoked to them may be considered as
perfectly reasonable and normal within the world view of their
practitioners. While the outcome of individual millenarian movements in Brazilian history may be disappointing or tragic they are
part of a long-established tradition of millenarian hope and expectation, which was a systemic element in backlands culture. This,
too, may explain the usual passivity and gentleness of the faithful –
until outsiders reacted against, or moved to neutralize or destroy
them. In a country where institutionalized religion has been popularly perceived to be allied with the interests of the State, and where,
until relatively recently, the Catholic hierarchy has left the majority
of the population to its own devices, it is little wonder that a dis-
satisfied believer, committed to millenarian precepts, could rise to
capture the imagination of others who shared his dreams of imminent salvation and emerge as a thaumaturge or charismatic leader.

It is, however, important to repeat, and remarkable to note, that
despite the tenacious resistance of Conselheiro's community – far
beyond what could have been expected – its behaviour up until the
initial engagement with government troops was both quiescent and
passive. George Rudé and others have found in preindustrial populations in Europe, as well as in Africa and Asia during the nineteenth
century, a 'hatred' of the rich and powerful that seems to have been
totally lacking at Canudos.[33] Riots did occur in Brazil's northeast
over changes in regulations governing the weekly markets but they
were brief and discontinuous. Day-to-day behaviour did not indicate
any lasting hatred or class conflict. Rather, the rural poor accepted
their condition, even if Canudos showed that their deep, almost

mystic fatalism did not prevent them from defending themselves when provoked. Only in the most diffused sense can it be said with accuracy that Canudos was influenced by social conflict.

Studies of rural populations have evolved through several stages of interpretation. The first generation of peasant studies debated whether their subjects were revolutionary or conservative, and whether it was the development of capitalism or the demands of the State which pushed rural inhabitants into revolt.[34] In the next 'generation' historians emphasized the diversity of the peasant experience through detailed case studies of individual localities. The third 'generation' synthesized the findings of the first two. It is now generally acknowledged that the causes of rural anger are usually seen in reductions of autonomy, security, or mobility. These tensions are compounded by deep grievances and perceived opportunity to sabotage the existing system or to flee from it.

In the case of Canudos, it seems that the grievances of the faithful produced not aggressiveness but deeper psychological regression. Deep-rooted local customs, including those bearing on race and on the poor's self-image, undermined the rural population's autonomy and its capacity for collective action, without the kind of charismatic leadership provided by Conselheiro.[35] Instead, spiritual revolt at Canudos yielded messianic hope and the determination to take leave of the secular world by finding refuge in a disciplined, protected community. The willingness of rural men and women to accept authority and to shrink from confrontation itself predisposed many of them – perhaps the most depressed members of the population – to heed Conselheiro's message, to have the courage to follow him, and to accept the strictures of Belo Monte's austerity.

There is ambiguous evidence about whether rural mores restrained the rural poor from casting off their docility. To be sure, northeastern *caboclos* lived 'far away' from the State in the sense that their behaviour was incomprehensible to coastal observers and even to the landowning élite; but they also lived all too 'close' in terms of their awareness of the unwritten nuances of regional, factional, and clan rivalries, not to mention the incursion of local and state officials under the Republic.[36] The remarkable tenacity of those faithful who did not flee Belo Monte but who resisted to the end may possibly be explained by theories about the 'density' of popular culture. Social psychologists have suggested that belonging to or joining a group demands greater sacrifice from members, who in turn may give greater prestige to association with it.[37] This seems to fit with what we know about behaviour within Canudos under Conselheiro's leadership. That same determination which outsiders considered primitive might alternatively be viewed as an assertiveness in which group cohesiveness under Belo Monte's utopian framework was reinforced by Conselheiro's imprecations that the faithful, not the outside world, would be redeemed.

However, Conselheiro's decision to remove his followers to the relative safety of a defended holy sanctuary was not insurrectionary, although it did threaten the *status quo*. This sense of threat was exacerbated by the ways in which he dealt with local landowners and with civil and ecclesiastical authorities. Conselheiro, stubborn and quick-tempered, was as quick to label his enemies heretical agents of the anti-Christ as his detractors were ready to see in him a crazed fanaticism. Perhaps he genuinely believed that the millennium would bring divine intervention. Nevertheless, neither Conselheiro nor his community were deliberately subversive or provocative. The characterization of Canudos, by da Cunha and his contemporaries, as a backlands 'rebellion', was accurate only insofar as one considers the physical act of abandonment by the backlanders of their former residences as rebellious. At the outset of the community's founding, Conselheiro knew all too well that overt rebellion would result in immediate military retaliation.

Assuming that he was not promised protection from landowners and others sympathetic with him in the region, Conselheiro's own outlook must have changed dramatically during 1895 and 1896. Either he became more arrogant, convinced of his city's invincibility, or he believed that the millennarian scenario was irreversible and that armed conflict would speed the Day of Judgement. Had Conselheiro been concerned with the day-to-day secular world, not, as he was, entirely consumed by a spiritual emphasis, he might have encouraged his followers to emphasize everyday forms of resistance – foot dragging, deception, dissimulation, feigned ignorance, false compliance, sabotage, sit-downs, malicious gossip, and so on – avoiding direct symbolic confrontations with authority or with élite norms. Rural folk culture's tolerance for malefactors may signal vicarious admiration for their noncompliance. Then there is the matter of women's roles in Belo Monte. There, at least to a limited extent, women exchanged their traditional social roles for new ones within the community. While they were physically segregated because of Conselheiro's personal misogyny, including in church, they were more independent than they would have been outside of the settlement. They were assigned tasks as hard as those given to men, and their daughters were permitted to attend primary school alongside their sons.

Overall, Conselheiro's invitation for backlanders to join him in a utopian settlement seems a half-way point between passivity and promoting open defiance. Here, the dour, psychologically depressed condition of rural backlanders – not only in the nineteenth century but well into the twentieth – probably acted against more outward manifestations of aggressiveness. The normative, raw material accompanying daily experience itself provided an education in interpreting who held power, how that power might be used against oneself, and what conduct would and would not be tolerated. Elsewhere in the many parts of the world where a wide gap separates the powerful from the dispossessed, passive compliance is the strategy overwhelmingly adopted in the face of punitive retribution.[38] In the high São Francisco *sertão*, only in rare and isolated individual acts perpetrated by aggrieved squatters against representatives of individual landowners, was there, in the words of James C. Scott, a rejection of 'the denigrating characterizations the rich deploy against them'.[39]

Only very recently has Brazilian scholarship started to distance itself from da Cunha's manichaean vision and to consider Canudos's inhabitants as victims. If one reason was the magisterial quality of da Cunha's work, another was the fixation by literary scholars on da Cunha as a writer. Brazilian historians, as well, have been loath to look for causes, being seemingly content to consider the consequences – usually from the perspective of the victors.[40]

What is remarkable about the Canudos region today is that so little has changed. Sharecroppers still live in mud huts of exactly the same size and primitiveness as one hundred years ago. The Bahia *sertão* remains on the margin of Brazilian life. Many residents live outside the market economy, eking out their existence by scratching the dry ground and by hiring themselves out for less than the legal minimum wage as day labourers. Textbooks still characterize Conselheiro's followers as barbarous rebels, although a new feature-length movie filmed in 1996 by Sérgio Rezende depicted Conselheiro – played by the popular actor José Wilker – less one-dimensionally than in the past, and emphasized themes of social injustice and misery.[41]

Notes

1. Some suggest that the roots of the Brazilians' pre-World War One identity crisis and the crumbling of the previously entrenched moral foundation of Western society may be traced to accelerating events during the last decades of the nineteenth century. See, for example, Eric J. Hobsbawm, *The Age of Empire, 1875-1914* (New York, 1987), 10-11.
2. Boris Fausto, 'Brazil: Social and Political Structure, 1889-1930', Leslie Bethell, ed., *The Cambridge History of Latin America*, vol. 5, c. 1870-1930 (Cambridge, 1986), 791.

3. See Charles A. Hale, 'Political and Social Ideas in Latin America, 1870-1930', in Bethell, ed., *Cambridge History*, vol. 4, 368-69, 382.

4. See, for example, Colin Henfrey, 'Peasant Brazil: Agrarian History, Struggle and Change in the Paraguaçu Valley, Bahia', *Bulletin of Latin American Research*, 8, 1 (1989): 1-24.

5. Ralph della Cava, 'Brazilian Messianism and National Institutions: A Reappraisal of Canudos and Juaseiro', *Hispanic American Historical Review*, 48, 3 (1968): 405. *Beatos* and *beatas* were not simply pious lay persons: their status had to be conferred by a priest.

6. Luiz Gomes Palacin, S.J., in *Historia da Diocese de Paulo Afonso* (Goiania, 1988), n.p.

7. For a full account, see this author's *Vale of Tears* (Berkeley, 1990).

8. Brazilian authors favourable to the monarchy contributed to this interpretation, arguing that the 'democratic' monarchy under Pedro II had entered after 1850 a 'golden age'. See Manoel de Oliveira Lima, *América Latina e América Inglesa: a evolução brasileira comparada com a hispano-americana e com a anglo-americana* (Rio de Janeiro, 1914), and the North American missionaries D.P. Kidder and J.C. Fletcher, *Brazil and the Brazilians, Portrayed in Historical and Descriptive Sketches* (Philadelphia, 1857).

9. The unusually high level of violence during the campaign was noted in the study by Francisco Marques de Góes Calmon, commissioned for the commemorative edition of the one-hundredth anniversary of the founding of the *Diário Oficial da Bahia, Vida Econômico-Financeira da Bahia. Elementos para a História de 1808 a 1899* (Reprinted, Salvador, 1982), 120-21.

10. Linda Lewin, 'The Oligarchical Limitations of Social Banditry in Brazil: The Case of the 'Good' Thief Antônio Silvino', *Past and Present*, 82 (1979): 116-36; Hamilton de Mattos Monteiro, 'Violência no Nordeste Rural' (PhD Diss., University of São Paulo, 1978), 70-73.

11. José Honório Rodrigues, *The Brazilians: Their Character and Aspirations* (Austin, 1980), 12; Janaína Amado, *Conflicto Social no Brasil: a Revolta dos 'Mucker'* (São Paulo, 1978).

12. Clóvis Moura, *Rebeliões da senzala: quilombos insurreições guerrilhas* (Rio de Janeiro, 1972), 190.

13. Rodrigues, *Brazilians*, 24.

14. Information based on data from the Arquivo Estudual da Bahia.

15. 'Relatório do Inspector do Thesouro ... ao Dr. Governador do Estado em 12 de maio de 1896', *Correio de Notícias* (Salvador, 1896), 4-20.

16. Tom Wolfe, 'Stalking the Billion-Footed Beast', *Harper's Magazine*, 279, no. 1674, (November 1989): 55.

17. In Brazil this view was expressed as early as 1871 by Sergipe-born Sílvio Romero (1851-1914), who studied themes as diverse as animal magnetism, evolution, literature, and the songs and poems of rural northeasterners and whose characteristic personal mood throughout the period was one of depression. Romero's writing clearly anticipated Da Cunha's fears that Brazil's cultural, social, and racial gap between its coastal and hinterland population imperilled the nation's future. Decades later, the emergence of northeastern regionalist literature continued this preoccupation. Unlike the *paulistas*, who emphasized the more exotic Indian heritage, José Lins do Rêgo and his contemporary writers dwelled on what they considered to be the anthropological liabilities of *caboclo* and *mulato* race mixture. See Flora Süssekind, *Tal Brasil, qual romance? Uma ideologia estética e sua história: o naturalismo* (Rio de Janeiro, 1984); Dain Borges, 'Progress and Degeneration in Brazilian Social Thought of the 1930's', paper presented at LASA Congress, Miami, 5 December 1989.

18. Nicolau Sevcenko, *Literatura como Missão* (Rio de Janeiro, 1983), for the best of many works interpreting da Cunha's literary style and significance. Also Gilberto Freye, *Perfil de Euclides e outros perfis* (Rio de Janeiro, 1944) and F. Venâncio Filho, *Euclydes da Cunha e seus amigos* (São Paulo, 1938), for his letters to fellow writers and academics.

19. Letters, Euclydes da Cunha to José Veríssimo, Lorena, 3 December 1902 and to Francisco Escobar, 27 November 1903, reprinted in Filho, *Euclydes*, 79-80, 113.

20. Euclydes da Cunha, *Rebellion in the Backlands* (Chicago, 1944), 72 ff; for the original Portuguese edition, see *Os Sertões* (São Paulo, 1985), 87 ff.

21. Da Cunha, *Rebellion*, 94-95; *Os Sertões*, 101.

22. The term *caboclo* has varied meanings in Brazil, in the most general sense as the Brazilian approximation of the Spanish-American *mestizo*, i.e., a lower-class peasant. However, whether the *caboclo* is essentially a northern type or a phenomenon of the south is a matter of some dispute: James B. Watson, 'Way Station of Modernization: the Brazilian Caboclo', in James B. Watson et al., eds, *Brazil: Papers Presented in the Institute for Brazilian Studies, Vanderbilt University* (Nashville, 1953), 9.

23. See Yonina Talmon, 'Millenarism', in David Sills, ed., *International Encyclopedia of the Social Sciences* (New York, 1979) vol. 10, 349-60, esp. 354.

24. Robert Darnton, *The Kiss of Lamourette: Reflections in Cultural History* (New York, 1990), 239-40, commenting on Mandrou's, *De la culture populaire aux 17e et 18e siècles* (Paris, 1964).

25. Darnton, *Kiss*, 240.

26. Pierre Clastres, *Society Against the State* (New York, 1987), 202.

27. René Ribeiro, 'Brazilian Messianic Movements', in Sylvia L. Thrupp, ed., *Millenial Dreams in Action: Studies in Revolutionary Religious Movements* (New York, 1970), 55-69.

28. Ironically, this description was written about John Calvin but it fits Conselheiro perfectly. See John Gross, review of William J. Bouwsma's, *John Calvin: A Sixteenth Century Portrait* (Oxford, 1987), in *New York Times*, 8 December 1987, 29.

29. Roderick J. Barman, 'The Brazilian Peasantry Reexamined', *Hispanic American Historical Review*, 57, 3 (1977): 404.

30. See, for example, Maria Isaura Pereira de Queiroz, *O campesinato brasileiro*, 42-45; 59-63; and her 'Messiahs in Brazil', *Past and Present*, 31 (1965): 62-86; and Todd Alan Diacon, 'Capitalists and Fanatics: Brazil's Contestado Rebellion, 1912-1916' (Ph.D diss., University of Wisconsin, 1987), 381-84, for an evaluation of the Pereira de Queiroz view.

31. See Roberto Da Matta, *Carnavais, malandros e heróis: Para uma sociologia do dilema brasileiro* (3rd edn, Rio de Janeiro, 1981).

32. Duglas Teixeira Monteiro, 'Um confronto entre Juazeiro, Canudos e Contestado', in Boris Fausto, org., *História Geral da Civilização Brasileira*. Tomo III. *O Brasil Republicano*. Vol. 2. *Sociedade e Instituições (1889-1930)* (São Paulo, 1977), 42-45.

33. G. Rudé, *The Crowd in History: A Study of Popular Disturbances in France and England, 1730-1848* (London, 1981), 61-64; Juan R. I. Cole, 'Of Crowds and Empires: Afro-Asian Riots and European Expansion, 1857-1882', *Comparative Studies in Society and History*, 31, 1 (1989): 131-32.

34. Ian Roxborough, review of John Tutino, *From Insurrection to Revolution in Mexico*, *Social History*, 13, 3: 373-74.

35. See David Hunt, 'The Measure of Popular Culture', *Comparative Studies in Society and History*, 31, 2 (1989): 363.

36. See Eugene Weber, *Peasants into Frenchmen: The Modernization of Rural France, 1870-1914* (Stanford, 1976).

37. See Hunt, 'The Measure', 368, esp. note 3.

38. Antonio Gramsci explicates this process as one of ideological intimidation where ruling class hegemony is assured by 'symbolic' as well as physical production: *Selection from the Prison Notebooks* (London, 1971). Also Friedrich Engels, *The Condition of the Working Class in England* (Moscow, 1973), 162-63, where he proposes that English rural folk were entirely removed from the institutional circuits of symbolic power. Also cited in James C. Scott, *Weapons of the Weak* (New Haven, 1985), 321.

39. Scott, *Weapons*, 304. See also, 315-16.

40. A recent exception is a new book by Marco Antonio Villa, *Canudos: o Povo da Terra* (São Paulo, 1995).

41. See *Jornal do Brasil* (Rio de Janeiro), 9 March 1996, 5.

CHAPTER 10

'A Certain Rigorous Treatment of All Parts of the Nation'

The Annihilation of the Herero in German South West Africa, 1904

Tilman Dedering

In order to define genocide, Helen Fein has proposed a catalogue of questions which not only seek to ascertain the degree of organization of the perpetrators and the authoritative level at which their genocidal strategies are conceptualized, but also the ideologies, myths and articulated beliefs which justify (or question) such strategies.[1] This chapter, in describing how a German colonial war escalated into the near-annihilation of a whole African people, seeks to consider both the contemporary and historiographical debate regarding the policy making, planning and, indeed, rationalizations of the perpetrators.

A myth that is still prevalent in the literature claims that they did not know any better, because they were captives of their own *Zeitgeist* (spirit of the age) and *Weltanschauung* (worldview). Consequently, the ethical standards that influence the scholarly analysis of genocide are irrelevant because they ignore the fact that the German perpetrators could not transgress their own moral universe. Such a view underestimates the cultural diversity of ideas even within a society as authoritarian as Wilhelmine Germany. The first part of our chapter summarizes the events which led to the genocide of the Herero people in German South West Africa (today's Namibia). The second part focuses on the debate, regarding their fate, among politicians, journalists and memoir writers within Imperial Germany.

The German-Herero War, 1904

The Herero rose against colonial rule in 1904, twenty years after
the Germans had officially annexed the territory. There were a variety of reasons for their rebellion. Since the *rinderpest*, which
devastated the whole of southern Africa in 1897, had destroyed
large numbers of their cattle, the Herero had become more vulnerable to the colonial pressure on land and livestock resources.[2] A
sense of disempowerment had begun to pervade Herero society,
intensified by the increased colonial interference with chiefly authority. Moreover, the Herero had been encouraged by European traders
to buy goods on credit. Considerable debts were soon accumulated
and many Herero found themselves at the mercy of unscrupulous
traders, who compensated themselves by taking away their cattle.[3]
All these factors disrupted an African pastoralist society whose culture revolved around the possession of livestock.

The moment when the Herero opened hostilities, in January
1904, had been carefully chosen. The Governor, Theodor Leutwein,
had transferred most of his troops from Hereroland, in the centre of
the colony to the south, in order to quell an uprising by the Bon-
delswart-Nama. The whole of the Imperial *Schutztruppe* consisted
of only eight hundred white volunteers, apart from a small African
auxiliary force. During the initial stage of the rebellion about 150
Europeans were killed as the Herero attacked farmers, traders and
soldiers.[4] Those whites who survived the first outburst of violence
flocked to the military stations in order to seek protection.

The incredulous reaction to these events, by the German administration and settler population of less than five thousand, is striking.
They had been taken completely by surprise, provoking demands for
revenge compounded by lurid tales of a general slaughter of the whites
by black 'barbarians'. In fact, the Herero were targeting mainly German men, a conscious political strategy aimed at discouraging other
European settlers in the colony from siding with the Germans. Orders
from Samuel Maharero, the supreme Herero chief, specifically stated
that missionaries, Britons and Boers were not to be harmed.[5] Though
the order did not prevent several instances of brutal murder, in most
cases the Herero warriors followed Maharero's instructions to the letter and spared women, children, missionaries and non-Germans.

Settler shock was also provoked by the tenacity and fighting
skills of the Herero in engagement with Leutwein's *Schutztruppe*,
following the latter's hasty return from the south, in February.[6]
Sometimes Herero warriors appeared on the battlefield clad in German uniforms, and organized themselves according to the Prussian
model of platoons and squadrons.[7] Moreover, their repeated attacks

caused serious *Schutztruppe* losses.[8] For a brief period, the Germans were thrown into confusion as telegraph wires were cut, railway lines destroyed, farms pillaged, cattle driven off and smaller military stations overrun. Lacking an overall strategy, however, the Herero failed to build on their initial success, half-heartedly besieging bigger settlements, such as Windhoek, and mainly harassing cattle posts and stragglers.[9]

The war increasingly brutalized the participants on both sides. Apart from the killings and mutilations committed by the Herero, the mere fact that 'savages' had the audacity to challenge white claims of superiority sharpened racist attitudes which had always been rife among the settler population. News about the refusal of the colonial troops to take prisoners reached Germany through letters written by soldiers during the first months of the war. This was grist to the mill of the *Reichstag* opposition, August Bebel, the leader of the Social Democratic Party, accusing the government of committing atrocities against helpless Africans. Leutwein was unable to disprove these accusations, which also were confirmed by the Rhenish missionaries in the colony.[10] The British Magistrate of Walfish Bay, John Cleverly, reported in May 1904:

> The general feeling among the Germans at present partakes of an unreasoning and vindictive bitterness which is almost as nearly allied to barbarism as the unbridled passions of the Hereros themselves. I have heard, myself, Germans who were in action describing boastfully how their troopers bayonetted Herero women. The position is most serious and the vindictiveness displayed on both sides is almost without parallel.[11]

At the beginning of the war, the only reinforcement that reached the shores of the colony was a small detachment of marines from the gunboat *Habicht*, which had been anchoring, at its outbreak, in Table Bay, at the Cape. Five hundred more marine volunteers arrived in February.[12] Further reinforcements were poured into the country during the following months. By March, 1,567 men, a thousand horses, six machine-guns and ten pieces of light artillery had arrived, though this was not yet enough to enable the inexperienced German troops to launch a decisive strike against an enemy who had several thousand warriors in the field and were, initially, freely roaming the country.[13] Moreover, typhoid soon began to devastate the ranks of the *Schutztruppe*.[14] The British military attaché in Berlin recorded that the unsuccessful colonial campaign had caused a stunned reaction in the German capital and admitted that it was 'difficult to avoid feeling a certain amount of *Schadenfreude* (malicious pleasure) on learning of the misfortune of these "superior" people'.[15]

When the newly appointed military commander, General Lothar von Trotha, arrived in the colony, in June 1904, to replace the luckless Leutwein, the bulk of the Herero forces with their women, children and livestock had already begun to concentrate at the Waterberg, in its northeast. The environmental conditions prevailing in the area certainly contributed to their decision to gather on this plateau in large numbers, not least because it offered plenty of water and grazing at a time when there was little rain.[16] As cattle were central to pastoralist Herero culture (and with livestock raiding a main objective of their traditional warfare) it is not surprising that in some skirmishes Herero warriors were prepared to fight desperate rearguard actions to prevent their cattle from falling into German hands, while on other occasions they rapidly slipped several thousand kine, plus women and children through the German lines.[17] If the withdrawal to the Waterberg has been described as 'a shrewd tactical move' because it forced the Germans to overextend their supply lines, the presence of several tens of thousands of Herero with their livestock, over a four-month period, however, exerted tremendous pressure on its natural resources, resulting in famine and disease among both humans and animals.[18] Worse, the concentration of the mass of the Herero people gave the Germans the opportunity they had been looking for: to encircle and annihilate them.

Kaiser Wilhelm, however, had quickly lost interest in a colonial war that had failed to bestow glamour on the *Schutztruppe*, his attention being instead absorbed on the emerging conflict between Russia and Japan.[19] Von Trotha had, therefore, not received precise instructions from him, apart from the order to 'crush the rebellion by all means available'.[20] Leutwein's strategy to break the resistance of the Herero and then to negotiate peace with them had clearly failed, spelling, in turn, the demise of his divide-and-rule policy, the so-called 'System Leutwein', which had irritated settlers and colonial ideologues alike for whom the consolidation of colonial rule had not proceeded sufficiently rapidly.

The arrival of von Trotha on the scene, was also ominous for other reasons. Appointed for his role in the extirpation of the Boxer rebellion in China and the Wahehe rising in German East Africa, the new commander was, significantly, only answerable to Alfred von Schlieffen, the Chief of the General Staff in Berlin. This meant that neither the Colonial Office, nor the governor in South West Africa had any authority over him, or hence the possibility to moderate his proposals for dealing with the Herero.[21] Even before his departure from Germany he had declared a state of emergency for the whole colony thereby giving absolute power to the military authorities.[22] Ensconced therein, von Trotha categorically rejected any negotiations with the Herero, ostensibly on the grounds that they had not only killed settlers and soldiers but also mutilated their dead bodies. Von Trotha described his strategy in his diaries:

> My initial plan for the operation, which I always adhered to, was to encircle the masses of Herero at the Waterberg, and to annihilate these masses with a simultaneous blow, then to establish various stations to hunt down and disarm the splinter groups who escaped, later to lay hands on the captains by putting prize money on their heads and finally to sentence them to death.[23]

While von Trotha's use of the term 'annihilation' (*Vernichtung*), therefore, may not have initially implied the physical extermination of the entire Herero people, his line of reasoning clearly blurred the distinction between their military defeat and their wholesale destruction. Moreover, von Trotha, as 'man on the spot', clearly intended to use his power in order to give to the war a far more radical bent than that of his predecessor, whom he depised as too 'soft' not least because of his attempts to negotiate a peace. 'Conquered the colonies have to be, nothing of that can be withdrawn. The natives have to give way, see America. Either by the bullet or via (the) mission through brandy.'[24]

His views on colonial policy thus highlighted the split not only between himself and the more subtle political and economic considerations that characterized Leutwein's thinking, but also within the ranks of the *Schutztruppe*, between the so-called 'old Africans' and new arrivals from Germany. While the former, who were better acquainted with the African mode of warfare, emphasized the priority of capturing Herero livestock instead of 'annihilating' the enemy, the latter often expressed their discontent regarding what they deemed as an unheroic 'fighting for oxen'.[25]

Meanwhile, von Trotha's annihilation battle plan was put into effect at the beginning of August 1904 as he lined up some four thousand German soldiers, in the Waterberg area. They faced approximately six thousand Herero fighters – many of whom did not have firearms but fought only with their *kerries* (war clubs)[26] – and an unspecified number, certainly several tens of thousands of Herero non-combatants. By contrast, the German troops were equipped with all the paraphernalia of modern European warfare: thirty-six pieces of artillery, fourteen machine-guns, as well as communication detachments using heliograph, telegraph and wireless.[27]

Despite the technological superiority of the colonial troops, however, the battle at the Waterberg did not develop according to plan. Even before it had begun some officers had warned von Trotha that placing the weakest German contingent in the south-east, near the

Omaheke desert, could result in a flight of the Herero into the so-called sandveld.[28] This was precisely what happened on 11 and 12 August. After fierce resistance, a main mass of Herero slipped through the lines of the concentric attack and escaped through the south-eastern gap. Retrospectively, it is not exactly clear why von Trotha tried to encircle them given that he neither had enough men, nor, due to lack of roads and transport, sufficient mobility with which to accomplish it.[29] Later, when it became necessary to justify the apparent strategical failure of the battle, members of von Trotha's staff explicitly denied, in patent contradiction to the announcements made by their former commander-in-chief, that they had wanted a 'second Sedan' at the Waterberg.[30]

However, after the battle-worn Germans had temporarily abandoned their pursuit of the fleeing Herero, von Trotha adopted an overtly genocidal strategy. All along, von Trotha seems to have considered only two real options: either the crushing of the Herero by mainly military means or, if that failed, their physical destruction by pushing them into the desert. All escape routes to the west, south and north-east were now blocked, the Germans' cordon extending for approximately 250 kilometres, and including, so they claimed, control of almost all the water-holes in the area. In fact, they were not able to seal off the Omaheke completely, some Herero bands succeeding in returning to the central areas through the German lines. But with their sorties into the desert during the dry season and the stepping up of these operations, in February 1905, when the rainy season began, the German plan succeeded in preventing most Herero from returning from it.[31]

Yet despite murmurs of discontent both from Rhenish missionaries and high-ranking officers about chasing half-dead Africans into the desert,[32] not to say an offer to surrender from the now completely broken Herero, von Trotha refused to even countenance peace.[33] The official publication of the German General Staff makes it clear that not only did he believe 'the acceptance of a more or less voluntary surrender to be the biggest political mistake, because a reconstruction of the old tribal organization would lead to renewed bloodshed sooner or later', but that he conceived his strategy in terms of a 'race war' aimed not at the surrender of the Herero but at the destruction of the social core of their existence.[34]

However, the extermination of the Herero did not mean the end of African resistance to German colonial rule. On the contrary, the battle at the Waterbeg precipitated a new round of warfare in the south of the colony. The Nama, who until this point had kept quiet where they did not actively support the Germans in their campaigns, had been increasingly alienated by the all-out hysteria among whites, including open discussions as to how the last vestiges of African independence were to be abolished after the war. When, after the battle, the Nama leader, Hendrik Witbooi, who had been coopted into an alliance by Leutwein in 1894, declared war against the Germans, they realized that they faced the prospect of a protracted guerrilla conflict against a formidable enemy.[35] But before von Trotha could concentrate on this new task, he had to mete out the final blow against the Herero. He drew up a proclamation, which was read to the *Schutztruppe* after a religious service on the western border of the Kalahari desert, on 2 October 1904. The next day it was translated to some Herero captives who were chased back to their people after the exemplary execution of some prisoners. It was also sent, the following day, to the Chief of the General Staff.[36] The proclamation read:

> I, the Great General of the German soldiers, address this letter to the Herero nation. The Herero are no longer German subjects. They have murdered and stolen and cut off the ears, noses, and other body parts from wounded soldiers. Now they don't have the courage to continue the fight. I say to the people: anyone who hands over one of the captains as a captive to a military station, will receive one thousand marks. The one who hands over Samuel will receive five thousand marks. The Herero people will have to leave the country. If the people refuse, I will force them with cannons to do so. Within the German boundaries, every Herero, with or without firearms, with or without cattle, will be shot. I won't accommodate women and children anymore. I shall drive them back to their people or I shall give the order to shoot at them. This is my message to the Herero nation.[37]

In a supplementary order, von Trotha stated that his soldiers were to shoot over the heads of women and children in order to drive them away – which still left them no option but to return to the desert and perish there. Moreover, the General explicitly stated that he did not expect his troops to take male prisoners.[38] The fact that von Trotha did not make the slightest attempt to conceal his genocidal intentions indicates that he believed he was acting in accordance with generally accepted rules of military conduct. He explained to von Schlieffen that he did not agree at all with the 'old Africans' among his officers, who wanted to preserve the Herero as a labour force for the colonial economy. Instead he insisted that 'the nation must be annihilated as such' and that he accepted responsibility for these actions, which, more euphemistically, he described as 'a certain rigorous treatment of all parts of the nation'.[39] In a letter to Leutwein, he continued to defend his strategy thus: 'Throughout my period of duty here, the eastern border of the colony will remain sealed off and terrorism will be employed against any Herero showing up. That nation must vanish from the face of the earth. Having failed to destroy them with guns, I will have to achieve my end in that way.'[40]

Meanwhile, in Berlin, von Schlieffen, who had initially supported von Trotha's policy, on 23 November, offered the following comments on it to Chancellor Bülow with a view to rescinding the proclamation. 'Trotha's plan that the whole nation should be either destroyed or driven out of the country can be supported ... The erupted race war can only end with the annihilation (*Vernichtung*) or complete enslavement of one side ... General von Trotha's intentions can be sustained. However, he does not have the power to translate them into reality.'[41] Bülow, who also had been petitioned by the Rhenish Mission, then asked Wilhelm II to order von Trotha to accept the surrender of the Herero.[42] He reminded the Kaiser that his farewell address to the German expeditionary corps leaving for China, in 1900, had 'already caused much trouble', because Wilhelm's sabre-rattling and bloodcurdling remarks had earned the Germans the unflattering nickname of 'Huns'.[43] Apart from political considerations, the Chancellor also worried about the moral implications of von Trotha's action, not to say the impending shortage of African labour in the German colony.[44] According to Bülow, the Kaiser reluctantly consented after several hours (though according to Drechsler, only after several days).[45]

In ensuing debates in the *Reichstag*, Bülow put on a brave face in order to defend von Trotha against the fierce attacks by the Social Democratic Party, who accused him not only of exterminating an African people, but also of being responsible for the brutalization of German soldiers who had been encouraged to abandon any 'civilized' military code of ethics.[46] While Bülow in reply claimed that 'seldom or never has a colonial war been conducted in such a patient and humane manner',[47] von Trotha himself initially flew into a rage 'that bordered on open insubordination' against his new orders, only very hesitantly following through his now required remit to accept prisoners, who were to be rounded up with the help of the Rhenish missionaries.[48] In a letter to Bülow, von Trotha pointed out that his 'harsh views' on the treatment of the Herero had, previously, neither been countermanded by the Kaiser nor the Chief of the General Staff. Acidly he added – in capital letters, for effect – 'QUI TACET, CONSENTIRE VIDETUR' (he who keeps silent, seems to consent). Only extremely grudgingly, given that he reiterated his objections to the peace efforts of the Rhenish Mission, did he promise 'to work according to Your Excellency's wishes from now on'.[49] As a result, by April 1905, about six thousand Herero were in 'concentration camps' (the name deriving from the British camps for Boer civilians during the South African War), the number rising to about fifteen thousand, in May 1906. Several thousands of these, however, died due to the disastrous conditions prevailing in the camps. They were eventually closed in August 1906.[50]

It is difficult to assess accurate numbers of survivors. Population figures before the war are necessarily based on European estimates, mainly missionary sources. Consequently, high casualty figures have repeatedly been questioned – often with the specific aim to belittle the impact that the war had on the Herero.[51] On the basis of an official census in 1911, Drechsler has suggested that out of an original population of eighty thousand Herero, about fifteen thousand may have survived the war, an estimate which includes those Herero who survived the German concentration camps.[52]

Several years later von Trotha attempted to exculpate himself in a newspaper article, arguing that his proclamation had only been intended to convince the Herero 'that their rule was over' and that he would have accepted their surrender if they only would have asked for peace.[53] He did not miss the opportunity, however, to make another jibe at his pet-hate, the Rhenish Mission, whom, he claimed, had incited the Herero with images 'of the bloodcurdling Jewish history of the Old Testament'.[54]

The Debate about the War

The German public was well informed about the the fate of the Herero whose mass flight into the sandveld was, graphically if not morbidly, described by contemporary authors and observers. Not least in the published documentation of the General Staff which seems to have taken some delight in the knowledge that 'the majority of the people ... must have perished on their flight through the Omaheke'.[55]

> No efforts, no hardships were spared in order to deprive the enemy of his last reserves of resistance; like a half-dead animal he was hunted from water-hole to water-hole until he became a lethargic victim of the nature of his own country. The waterless Omaheke was to complete the work of the German arms: the annihilation of the Herero people.[56]

German press support for von Trotha's policy was, often, a good deal less enthusiastic. While, thus, the *Deutsche Kolonialzeitung* explicitly defended his refusal to negotiate with the Herero in spite of their enormous casualties, the *Berliner Zeitung* pointed out that the General had, nevertheless, failed in his attempt to defeat them.[57] Others inveighed against the government because of the enormous costs of the combined Herero-Nama war, which eventually amounted to almost 600 million marks.[58] Some colonial propagandists considered the criticisms to be so outspoken that they talked about a large-scale 'anti-Trotha campaign'.[59]

German press and parliamentary criticism of von Trotha's 'more drastic measures' were also published in newspapers in Great Britain and Cape Colony, from as early as October 1904.[60] The Cape press particularly seized on the denunciations made in *Reichstag* debates by the Social Democrats against the military leadership's inhumane warfare.[61] Its gleeful repetition of these reports was, however, tempered by anxiety that the war in the German colony might spill over into the Cape and encourage the African population to rise against white domination. This was particularly so after the Nama had declared war on the Germans, exciting much more direct Cape Colony interest in Namibian events and against a background of growing African political consciousness and the rise of the so-called Ethiopian movement in South Africa.[62]

In the many accounts of the war in contemporary newspapers, magazines and memoirs in Germany, however, discussion of the ethics of von Trotha's campaign was often omitted in favour, for instance, of a concern at the damage done to the colonial economy due to the number of cattle that had perished in the desert.[63] By contrast, the annihilation of a whole people was described in a matter-of-fact way, undoubtedly informed by social-Darwinian ideas that deemed the destruction of 'savage' Africans as the inevitable result of colonial warfare with 'civilized' Europeans. The official documentation of the German General Staff, which does not contain von Trotha's proclamation, but does give a detailed account of his attempt to destroy the Herero 'as a nation', was thus, not only enthusiastically reviewed in the *Militär-Literatur-Zeitung*, but recommended by it as the most appropriate Christmas present a German boy could receive from his father.[64] The *Deutsche Kolonialzeitung* similarly delighted in announcing, in December 1904, that 'the sandveld has delivered the final judgement ... to the pathetic remnants of the once so powerful Herero'.[65]

Many authors, thus, believed that the Kaiser's first war had not only stabilized German rule in Namibia, but had resuscitated the martial spirit of a nation weakened by a period of protracted peace.[66] Veterans of the conflict, claimed a writer who indulged in racist depictions of the Herero as subhumans, 'will point to the high seas, where the storms howl towards foreign countries, where the German Reich has to participate in the cultural struggle if it does not want to sever its own life line'.[67] Less extravagantly, some military experts emphasized that the war had given 'officers and men the opportunity to prove to the world and the fatherland that they are equal to the fighters of Belle-Alliance and Sedan; it permits the testing of new military technology that did not exist in 1870-1 in the face of the enemy under the most difficult conditions'.[68]

Some contributions to this debate were characterized by a racist terminology that makes the comparison with national socialist statements tempting. There was a great deal of ranting and raving against 'hazy humanitarian ideals' in booklets and memoirs. One pamphleteer even suggested making a 'clean slate in South West Africa', though he stopped short of making 'precise suggestions as to the final solution (*definitive Regelung*) of the native question'.[69] Several eye-witness accounts also depicted the Herero as faceless 'others', on the lowest rung of the social-Darwinian ladder. Less than human, their complete extinction could be contemplated with equanimity. 'What makes the Herero so revolting', argued a Captain Maximilian Bayer, who had served on von Trotha's staff, 'is the fact that their way of thinking is completely different from ours. Their logic is not like our logic ... How can we communicate with people whose vocabulary does not even contain words such as 'gratefulness', 'obedience', 'patriotism', 'affection', 'loyalty'?'[70]

Bayer repeated his charge on a public lecture tour across many German cities, implying, thereby, that this rendered the Herero useless for 'the further development of the colony'.[71] Another officer explained that the Herero had to be pushed into the Omaheke because German firearms had been 'too humane,' by which he actually meant inefficient, while a former member of the *Habicht* marine corps described 'niggers on the rampage' who raped and mutilated German women and impaled their children on broomsticks.[72] His view that there could be no more talk 'about mercy towards such bestiality; our password was and remained: "No mercy!"', was not mere rhetoric. The repeated shooting of Herero prisoners is thinly veiled in his account.[73] Their dead, however, could supposedly be of use to science. A book by an anonymous author contains a picture of three German soldiers filling a crate with human skulls. The caption explained:

> A crate with Herero skulls was recently packed by the troops in German South West Africa and sent to the Pathological Institute in Berlin, where they are going to be used for scientific measurements. The skulls, whose flesh had been removed by Herero women with pieces of broken glass before they were put in the mail, belong to Herero who were hanged or killed in action.[74]

Significantly such overtly racist statements were often accompanied by bitter complaints not only about the 'unpatriotic' opponents of 'world policy', but also about the noticeable lack of enthusiasm for the war that prevailed in Germany, despite the propagandistic efforts of the German Colonial Society.[75]

Thus, the shrill calls for a 'final solution' for the Herero were opposed by a substantial section of the German public. There were also critics, who did not question the right of a 'superior' people to colonize Africans, but argued for an 'enlightened' form of colonialism. A former judge from the colony, for example, suggested that the proletarianization of indigenous Namibians implied 'respecting their human rights and paying them fair wages'.[76] Another writer recommended the African-American educationist, Booker T. Washington, because he had proven 'that human nature in all of its forms remains the same, irrespective of the colour of skin ... thus, one has to revise racial prejudice before one can solve the native question in South West Africa'.[77] Another published account of the Herero war emphasized that the author had only survived because of the assistance he had received from some loyal Herero and even tried to put chief Maharero's actions into perspective.[78] Under the circumstances, such comments constituted a remarkable critique of the biological determinism propagated by conservatives.

Conclusion

Since Horst Drechsler and Helmut Bley published their studies of German colonialism in Namibia in the 1960s, scholars have continued to ask whether or not the mass killing of the Herero amounted to genocide. The actual numbers of victims has been questioned and the accusations raised against the German colonizers in the official British documentation, the so-called Blue Book of 1918, has been depicted as malicious anti-German propaganda.[79] Similarly, von Trotha's murderous announcements have been belittled as harmless rhetoric. Some scholars have rejected the use of the term 'genocide'[80] with regard to the Herero, because of its connotations with the Holocaust, while others have adopted it for this very reason, emphasizing the Herero war as a milestone on an authoritarian and inhumane 'special path' in German history that extended from Bismarck to Hitler.[81]

What are the specific features of the German-Herero war? Clearly, its mass murder, for which major responsibility lies with von Trotha, the 'man on the spot'. Briefly, he had the power to conceive and pursue a radical, genocidal policy. Yet the annihilation of the Herero was clearly not the product of a homogeneous cultural environment: the idea that Africans could simply be exterminated was debated in public and eventually rejected by Germany's decision-makers. Ethical considerations thus played some part in influencing the decision to stop von Trotha's killing machine, though many contemporaries were also appalled by his fanatical determination to wipe out the Herero in the face of political and economic rationality.

The war was also characterized by the use of advanced military technology, a modern industrialized nation using South West Africa as a testing ground for machine-guns, modern communication technology as well as concentration camps and the newly developed vaccination against typhoid fever.[82] In a confidential report to the British General Staff, Major T. Wade, the British military attaché with the *Schutztruppe* in Namibia, stated: 'There can be no doubt, I think, that the war has been of an almost unmixed benefit to the German colony. Two warlike races have been exterminated, wells have been sunk, new water-holes discovered, the country mapped and covered with telegraph lines, and an enormous amount of capital has been laid out.'[83]

Some authors, therefore, have suggested that the Germans experimented with a 'totalitarian' type of social engineering that anticipated aspects of national socialism.[84] It is beyond the scope of this account to discuss this view, though recent research suggests that the control exerted by the Germans over Africans in the aftermath of the war was less efficient than previously has been assumed.[85]

Were, then, the mass killings in South West Africa a crude prequel to Nazi industrial extermination?[86] If one searches for similarities, instead of a neat line of historical continuity, the German-Herero war more closely resembles the actions of German soldiery on its eastern front during the Second World War, rather than the specificity of Nazi death camps. In South West Africa as in the Soviet Union, the Germans 'too often behaved as if the alleged barbarism of their opponents ... justified barbaric behaviour'.[87] Eric Hobsbawm has pointed out that during the twentieth century, 'more human beings had been killed or allowed to die by human decision than ever before in history', perhaps up to 187 million people.[88] Though we cannot discard questions about the destructive aspects of German history or of its continuity, to focus on it alone could impede our analysis of the origins of genocide as a regular feature of our 'age of extremes'.

Notes

1. Helen Fein, *Genocide. A Sociological Perspective* (3rd edn, London, Newbury Park, New Delhi, 1993), 25-27.
2. The classic studies are: Horst Drechsler, *'Let Us Die Fighting'. The Struggle of the Herero and Nama against German Imperialism (1884-1915)* (London,

1980); (German edn, Berlin, 1966); Helmut Bley, *South West Africa under German rule, 1898-1914* (London, 1971); (German edn, Hamburg, 1968).

3. Drechsler, *Let Us Die Fighting*, 117-19.

4. On the history of the war: Jon Bridgman, *The Revolt of the Hereros* (Berkeley, 1981); Jan-Bart Gewald, *Towards Redemption: A Socio-Political History of the Hereo of Namibia between 1890 and 1923* (Leiden, 1996); Gesine Krüger, 'Kriegsbewältigung und Geschichtsbewußtsein. Zur Realität, Deutung und Verarbeitung des deutschen Kolonialkrieges 1904-1907' (PhD Diss., University of Hanover, 1995); Walter Nuhn, *Sturm über Südwest. Der Hereroaufstand von 1904 – Ein düsteres Kapitel der deutschen kolonialen Vergangenheit Namibias* (Koblenz, 1989); Gerhard Pool, *Die Herero-opstand, 1904-1907* (Cape Town, 1989); Arnold Valentin Wallenkampf, 'The Herero Rebellion in South West Africa, 1904-1906. A Study in German Colonialism' (PhD Diss., University of California, Los Angeles, 1969). Gewald suggests that the war was precipitated by white paranoia rather than by organized African resistance to colonial rule. However, the question of whether or not the war erupted merely because of a 'series of misunderstandings' should remain open in the light of inconclusive evidence. See Gewald, *Towards Redemption*, 178,191-6.

5. Drechsler, *Let Us Die Fighting*, 143.

6. Ibid., 97.

7. Andreas Selmeci and Dag Henrichsen, *Thomas Pynchon und die Geschichte der Herero* (Bielefeld, 1995), 59-60.

8. Drechsler, *Let Us Die Fighting*, 149.

9. Drechsler, *Let Us Die Fighting*, 144; Nuhn, *Sturm über Südwest*, 75-76.

10. Drechsler, *Let Us Die Fighting*, 151. Vereinigte Evangelische Mission (United Protestant Mission) (hereafter VEM), Records of the Rhenish Mission Society, vol. 2, 603, Herero-Aufstand, A. Kuhlmann, Karibib, 18 May 1904, 104-109.

11. Public Record Office (PRO), London, FO, 64/1645, 'Native Rising in German South West Africa', John Cleverly, Magistrate Walfish Bay, to Secretary of Native Affairs, Cape Town, 18 May 1904.

12. Nuhn, *Sturm über Südwest*, 96-100.

13. John J. Grotpeter, ed., *Historical Dictionary of Namibia*, African Historical Dictionaries, no. 57 (New Jersey and London, 1994), 198. When the Nama entered the war after the defeat of the Herero in October 1904, the Germans were forced to increase the number of troops in South West Africa dramatically. This peaked at about fifteen thousand soldiers (but with only a minority fighting troops), Drechsler, *Let Us Die Fighting*, 186.

14. Drechsler, *Let Us Die Fighting*, 149. 689 members of the *Schutztruppe* died of diseases during the war, 676 were killed in action, and seventy-six were recorded as missing: Großer Generalstab, *Die Kämpfe der deutschen Truppen in Südwestafrika* (Berlin, 1907), vol. 2, 335.

15. PRO, FO, 64/1645, Military Attaché Gleichen, British Embassy, Berlin, 8. April 1904.

16. Arnold von Engelbrechten, *Der Krieg in Südwestafrika* (Berlin, 1906), 58.

17. See the study by the Rhenish missionary Jakob Irle, *Die Herero. Ein Beitrag zur Landes-, Volks- und Missionskunde*, (Gütersloh, 1906). Nuhn, *Sturm über Südwest*, 123, 195.

18. Drechsler, *Let Us Die Fighting*, 152. Belwe, Max, *Gegen die Herero, 1904-1905* (Berlin, 1906), 105; Generalstab, *Die Kämpfe*, vol. 1 (1906), 160, 217.

19. Wilhelm II was reported as saying: 'I urgently require that South [West] Africa won't be mentioned in my presence until the first sign of victory', *Berliner Zeitung*, 323, 13 July 1904.

20. G. Spraul, 'Der "Völkermord" an den Herero. Untersuchungen zu einer neuen Kontinuitätsthese', *Geschichte in Wissenschaft und Unterricht*, 39, 12 (1988): 718-19.
21. Nuhn, *Sturm über Südwest*, 203. Several government departments were involved in the organization of the war: the Prussian Ministry of War, the Supreme Command of the *Schutztruppen*, the Imperial Naval Office and the General Staff of the Prussian Army.
22. Ibid., 205.
23. Quoted in Gerhard Pool, *Samuel Maharero* (Windhoek, 1991), 251.
24. Pool, *Maharero*, 248. See also Drechsler, *Let Us Die Fighting*, 148.
25. Nuhn, *Sturm über Südwest*, 221.
26. See for instance Belwe, *Gegen die Herero*, 27-28, 100.
27. Drechsler, *Let Us Die Fighting*, 155; Nuhn, *Sturm über Südwest*, 221.
28. Drechsler, *Let Us Die Fighting*, 155.; Nuhn, *Sturm über Südwest*, 229.
29. Drechsler *Let Us Die Fighting*, 154-55, has therefore suggested that von Trotha had always planned the complete destruction of the Herero; see also Nuhn, *Sturm über Südwest*, 229.
30. Maximilian Bayer, *Der Krieg in Südwestafrika und seine Bedeutung für die Entwickelung der Kolonie. Vortrag gehalten in 35 deutschen Städten* (Leipzig, 1906), 23, 25. Bayer claimed that the Germans did not expect that they could prevent the Herero from breaking through their lines but was unable to explain why then von Trotha had adopted a concentric attack in the first place. In his 4 August 1904 instructions he had announced his intention to attack the 'enemy' simultaneously 'in order to annihilate him', Nuhn, *Sturm über Südwest*, 227.
31. Generalstab, *Die Kämpfe*, vol. 1, 196, 213-14, 216-17. Pool, *Samuel Herero*, 269.
32. See especially Ludwig von Estorff, *Wanderungen und Kämpfe in Südwestafrika, Ostafrika und Südafrika, 1904-1910* (private pubn, Wiesbaden and Fontainebleau, 1968), 116-17.
33. On 13 September 1904, von Trotha noted: 'Veld Hereros, women and children, come in big numbers to ask for water. Have given orders to chase them back by force, because an accumulation of a big number of prisoners would constitute a danger to the provisioning and health of the troops.' Pool, *Maharero*, 270.
34. Generalstab, *Die Kämpfe*, vol. 1, 212.
35. Tilman Dedering, 'Hendrik Witbooi, the prophet', *Kleio*, 25, (1993): 54-78.
36. Pool, *Maharero*, 271-72; Spraul, 'Völkermord', 723-24.
37. Bundesarchiv Potsdam (Federal Archives Potsdam) (BAP), Reichskolonialamt (Imperial Colonial Office) (RKA), vol. 2089: 7. Von Trotha's proclamation was only published in Germany a year later in *Die Deutschen Kolonien*, no. 8, August 1905, 245-7.
38. Drechsler, *Let Us Die Fighting*, 157; Nuhn, *Sturm über Südwest*, 283.
39. BAP, RKA, vol. 2089, von Trotha, 4 October 1904, 5.
40. Ibid., von Trotha to Leutwein, 27 October 1904. For a description of the altercation between Leutwein and von Trotha see Drechsler, *Let Us Die Fighting*, 161-62; Nuhn, *Sturm über Südwest*, 285.
41. Quoted in Spraul, 'Völkermord', 727-8.
42. Nuhn, *Sturm über Südwest*, 302.
43. 'The Kaiser became excited and we did not part in a friendly mood', Bernhard Fürst von Bülow, *Denkwürdigkeiten* (Berlin, 1934), vol. 2, 21.
44. Drechsler, *Let Us Die Fighting*, 163-4.
45. Bülow, *Denkwürdigkeiten*, 21; Drechsler, *Let Us Die Fighting*, 164. See also Spraul, 'Völkermord', 719, 734.

46. For instance *Stenographische Berichte über die Verhandlungen des Reichstages*, vol. 11, 2 December 1905, 91-2, 110. The German press had levelled their criticisms against the General even before the events at the Waterberg became known in Germany. The *Berliner Zeitung* published a leader on 7 January 1905, entitled, 'Trotha, the annihilator' ('*Trotha, der Vernichter*'), and criticized his announcement to the settlers' council in Windhoek that 'the annihilation of the rebellious tribes is the objective of all military operations'.

47. *Stenographische Berichte*, vol. 11, 9 December 1905, 193. In his memoirs, however, Bülow painted a different picture of von Trotha: 'In order to deal more quickly with the Herero, he suggested driving them with their women and children into a waterless desert, where they would have had to face a certain and painful death.' Bülow, *Denkwürdigkeiten*, 21.

48. Spraul, 'Völkermord', 720. Von Trotha indignantly told the *Windhuker Nachrichten* in August 1905 that he had been ordered by Chancellor Bülow to pursue a new policy of clemency, Spraul, 'Völkermord', 734, n. 64.

49. BAP, RKA, vol. 2089, von Trotha to Bülow, 6 January 1905.

50. Drechsler, *Let Us Die Fighting*, 207-8.

51. Brigitte Lau, 'Uncertain Certainties: The German-Herero War of 1904', *Mibagus*, 2 (1989): 4-5, 8; Karla Poewe, *The Namibian Herero. A History of their Psychosocial Distintegration and Survival* (Lewiston, N.Y., 1985); Jürgen Sudholt, *Die deutsche Eingeborenenpolitik in Südwestafrika. Von den Anfängen bis 1904* (Hildesheim, 1975). See also Dedering, 'The German-Herero War of 1904: Revisionism of Genocide or Imaginary Historiography?' *Journal of Southern African Studies* 19, 1 (1993): 80-88; Joachim Zeller, 'Ohne Land und Vieh, aber mit dem "Merk des Kaisers"', *Geschichte-Erziehung-Politik*, 6, 12 (1995): 738-49.

52. Drechsler, *Let Us Die Fighting*, 213-14. 80 percent of the Herero population, therefore, would have perished between 1904 and 1907, when the war officially ended. Moreover, 50 percent of the Nama population may have died.

53. Pool, *Maharero*, 274.

54. VEM, vol. 2, 602, Herero-Aufstand, Rhenish Mission Inspector Spiecker to Friedrich Lange, 24 February 1909, 0001-2.

55. Generalstab, *Die Kämpfe*, vol. 1, 216.

56. Ibid., vol. 1, 211. See also, 203, 209, 217-8.

57. *Deutsche Kolonialzeitung*, vol. 44, 3 November 1904, 434. 'The Herero escaped! We just don't have any luck with South West Africa', complained a newspaper which continually criticized von Trotha for his apparent lack of success, *Berliner Zeitung*, no. 344, 25 July 1904.

58. Horst Gründer, *Geschichte der deutschen Kolonien* (3rd edn, Paderborn and Munich, 1995), 122.

59. *Die Deutschen Kolonien*, vol. 9/10, September-October 1904, 220; vol. 9, September 1905, 269.

60. *The Owl*, 18 November 1904; *Cape Times*, 3 February 1905.

61. The *Cape Times* approvingly cited the Berliner *Vossische Zeitung* when the latter declared that 'General von Trotha's methods of conducting the campaign have brought discredit upon Germany in the eyes of civilization', *Cape Times*, 21 August 1905.

62. '...the threat of extermination in General von Trotha's proclamation is not likely to render the position on the border easier', *Cape Times*, 19 May 1905. These fears focused on the border crossings of African fighters replenishing their supplies south of the Orange River before returning to resume their struggle in the German colony.

63. 'But the cattle? Where are the cattle?', asked one journalist who wondered whether it would be possible to push the Herero into the desert, because 'the country is too

big', *Deutsche Kolonialzeitung*, vol. 36, 8 September 1904, 356. See also G. Maercker, *Unsere Kriegführung in Deutsch-Südwestafrika* (Berlin, 1908), 11. Also Nuhn, *Sturm über Südwest*, 109, on Governor Leutwein's initial concern that the Herero would drive their spoils of war – and one of the most important assets of the colonial economy – across the border into British territory.

64. *Militär-Literatur-Zeitung*, vol. 8, August 1906, 294, and vol. 10, October 1906, 371.

65. *Deutsche Kolonialzeitung*, vol. 50, 15 December 1904, 495.

66. For instance H. Auer von Herrenkirchen, *Meine Erlebnisse während des Feldzuges gegen die Hereros und Witbois* (Berlin, 1907), 110, a view also reiterated by former Chancellor Bülow thirty years later, *Denkwürdigkeiten*, vol. 2, 20.

67. E. Freimut, *Gedanken am Wege. Reiseplaudereien aus Deutsch-Südwestafrika* (Berlin, 1909), 199. See also Bayer, *Der Krieg*, 65.

68. Boethke,' Die Verkehrstruppen in Südwestafrika', *Beihefte zum Militär-Wochenblatt* (1906): 39.

69. C. Otto, *Südwest-Afrika. Wohin steuern wir? Ein nationaler Notschrei und anderes* (Berlin, 1906), 104.

70. Bayer, *Der Krieg*, 8.

71. Ibid., 7. Regarding the Nama, he was even more outspoken: 'In times of peace we do not have to bother whether or not a few thousands of Hottentots wander around in a vast territory such as South West Africa. We don't have to exterminate them because they are absolutely useless for the cultural development. Nature itself will achieve that task ... The day will come when the Hottentots will disappear, but not to the detriment of mankind, because they are only born robbers and thieves, nothing else.' (Bayer, *Der Krieg*, 10-11).

72. Maercker, *Unsere Kriegführung*, 47. M. Unterbeck, ed., *In Südwestafrika gegen die Hereros. Nach den Kriegstagebüchern des Obermatrosen G. Auer* (Berlin, 1911), 60-1. German soldiers and officers often commented on the reputedly extraordinary resilience of Africans to physical pain which, however, was seen as another proof of their inferior place in the social and racial ranking order. See M. Belwe, *Gegen die Herero*, 11; H. von Ortenberg, *Aus dem Tagbuch eines Arztes. Feldzugskizzen aus Südwestafrika* (Berlin, 1907), 22.

73. Unterbeck, ed., *In Südwestafrika gegen die Hereros*, 46, 61-62, 106, 166.

74. Anon., *Meine Kriegs-Erlebnisse in Deutsch-Süd-West-Afrika. Von einem Offizier der Schutztruppe* (Minden, 1907), 114.

75. 'Unfortunately our war in South West Africa is not "popular" in the usual sense', *Militär-Literatur-Zeitung*, no. 12, December 1906, 426. The *Deutsche Kolonialzeitung*, mouthpiece of the German Colonial Society, repeatedly complained about the 'indifference' regarding the Herero war that prevailed in Germany, because 'the public is fed with only a few short telegrams' from the theatre of war (See no. 43, 27 October 1904, 423).

76. Victor Fuchs, *Ein Siedelungsvorschlag für Deutsch-Südwestafrika* (Berlin, 1907), 86-7.

77. A. Kuhn, *Zum Eingeborenenproblem in Deutsch-Südwestafrika. Ein Ruf an Deutschlands Frauen* (Berlin, 1905), 27. See also, however, 28, where the author defends the maintenance of corporal punishment in the colony.

78. G. Spittler, *Ansiedler-Erlebnisse aus den Anfängen des Hereroaufstandes* (Berlin, 1913), 64.

79. BAP, RKA, vols. 4704-705, Englisches Blaubuch (Bericht über die Eingeborenen Südwestafrikas und deren Behandlung durch die Deutschen. Hergestellt im Verwaltungsbureau Windhuk, Südwest-Afrika, January 1918).

80. Genocide argues Fein (*Genocide*, 24), 'is sustained purposeful action by a perpetrator to physically destroy a collectivity directly or indirectly, through

interdiction of the biological and social reproduction of group members, sustained regardless of the surrender or lack of threat offered by the victim.' See also George J. Andreopoulos, ed., *Genocide: conceptual and historical dimensions* (Philadelphia, 1994); Frank Chalk and Kurt Jonassohn, *The history and sociology of genocide. Analyses and case studies* (New Haven and London, 1990).

81. See Ludwig Helbig, 'Der koloniale Frühfaschismus', in N. Mbumba, H. Patemann and U. Katjivena, eds, *Ein Land, eine Zukunft. Namibia auf dem Weg in die Unabhängigkeit*, (Wuppertal, 1988), 102-18. A recent account in Italian establishes a line of continuity from the Knights Templars to the 'final solution of the Herero', Franceso Lamendola, *Il genocido dimenticato. La 'soluzione finale' del problema Herero nel Sud-Ouest Africano 1904-1905* (Pordenone, 1988). In his travelogue Sven Lindqvist has recently claimed an overall European tradition of genocide which is reputedly rooted in colonialism. Sven Lindqvist, *Exterminate all the Brutes* (London, 1996), 149-51, 155-60. It is problematic, however, to assert such clear-cut 'traditions' without examining other important influences on twentieth-century European concepts of genocide such as the brutalizing experience of the First World War. When Lindqvist equates the atrocious treatment the Native Americans, Herero, Bushmen and Ndbele received from Europeans with the Holocaust, he blurs important historical differences, Lindqvist, *Exterminate all the Brutes*, 160. Significantly, the Bushmen (San) in South Africa were also the victims of ruthless persecution and killings at the hands of other Africans.

82. During the later course of the war, the Germans installed a technically superior telegraph network to that used in British South Africa. Museum für Post und Kommunikation, Berlin, vol. AM 10/93, Imperial Post Office Windhoek, 18 May 1908.

83. Quoted in Michael Fröhlich, *Von Konfrontation zur Koexistenz: Die deutschenglischen Kolonialbeziehungen in Afrika zwischen 1884 und 1914* (Bochum, 1990), 256.

84. Bley, *Kolonialherrschaft*, 314.

85. Philipp Prein, 'Guns and top-hats: African resistance in German South West Africa, 1907-1915', *Journal of Southern African Studies*, 20, 1 (1994): 99-121. The records of the German colonial administration contain many references to the lack of control over the African population after the war. For instance BAP, Zentralbüro Windhoek (Records of the Central Office, Windhoek), Kaiserliches Gouvernement von Deutsch-Südwestafrika (Imperial Government of German South West Africa) (microfilm), Geheimakten (Secret Files), vol. 7 d., District Commandant, Gobabis, to Government, Windhoek, 12 October 1910, 1-4; vol. 7: l, Native Commissioner Ebeling, Warmbad, to Government Windhoek, 24 February 1914, 43-4.

86. As claimed by Henning Melber, '"Es sind doch auch Menschen!"'. Die Kolonisierten aus der Sicht deutscher Reichstagsabgeordneter', in Mbumba et al., *Ein Land*, 119-131; and again in 'Kontinuitäten totaler Herrschaft: Volkermord und Apartheid in "Deutsch-Südwestafrika". Zur kolonialen Herrschaftspraxis im Deutschen Kaiserreich', in *Jahrbuch für Antisemitismusforschung*, ed., Wolfgang Benz (Frankfurt and New York, 1992), vol. 1, 91-116.

87. John Keegan, *A History of Warfare* (London, 1993), 373. See also Omer Bartov, *Hitler's Army: Soldiers, Nazis, and War in the Third Reich* (Oxford, 1992); Stephen G. Fritz, *Frontsoldaten: The German Soldier in World War II* (Lexington, 1995).

88. Eric Hobsbawm, *Age of Extremes. The Short Twentieth Century 1914-1991* (London, 1994), 12.

CHAPTER 11

'KILL ALL, BURN ALL, LOOT ALL':

THE NANKING MASSACRE OF DECEMBER 1937 AND JAPANESE POLICY IN CHINA

Callum MacDonald

Introduction

The Nanking massacre in December 1937 was the biggest single atrocity of the China Incident, which began five months earlier, and of the entire Pacific War into which Sino-Japanese hostilities merged after Pearl Harbor. It was also one of the best documented for it took place in the conquered capital of Republican Kuomintang (KMT), China under the horrified eyes of the foreign community. When the city fell to the Central China Expeditionary Army under General Matsui Iwane on 12 December 1937, Japanese troops embarked on an orgy of murder, rape, arson and looting which lasted for over six weeks. As the *Associated Press* correspondent, Haldore Hanson, remarked, until then atrocities had been largely ignored: 'Smaller Japanese units had run amuck in hundreds of Chinese towns and villages. Most of these stories were liberally discounted; the Japanese were still given the benefit of the doubt. The crimes committed by twenty thousand soldiers under the direct supervision of officers were so heinous that no one could refrain from publishing the facts.'[1] Estimates of the total number of victims varied. After the war, the Chief Prosecutor of Nanking District presented a figure of 278,586 murders to the International Military Tribunal at Tokyo. Witness testimony suggested a minimum of 42,000 killings and anything between eight thousand and twenty thousand rapes.[2] This imprecision was inevitable for the Japanese kept no record and the Chinese Red Swastika Society, which was responsible for collecting many of the bodies, 'did not dare to keep an accurate account'.[3] At the time the Japanese Army itself issued a report stating that twenty-three Chinese officers, fifty-four NCOs, and 1,498 enlisted men had been executed for looting or for disguising themselves in civilian clothes.[4] The defendant at Tokyo, General Matsui, however, denied that any massacre had ever occurred. There had been a few incidents, but those responsible were severely punished. Chinese claims were 'absolutely untrue'.[5] His account was backed up by a number of staff officers. The testimony of Mamoru Iinuma was typical. There had been some cases of rape and plunder, 'but as for the alleged tens of thousands of slaughtered bodies, never did I see them, even in a dream'.[6] The prosecution, however, was in no doubt, arguing that Nanking differed only in scale from what had happened throughout China. It 'was no isolated instance. It was typical of numerous incidents of this character' designed to 'crush forever all will to resist on the part of the Chinese people ... This was the Japanese pattern of warfare.'[7]

Matsui was condemned to death and hanged at Sugama Prison in Tokyo on 21 December 1948. Despite the verdict and the overwhelming evidence of what had occurred in Nanking, ex-officer groups and revisionist Japanese historians have continued to deny that any crime was ever committed.[8] As for successive Japanese governments, their desire to draw a veil over the wartime period and their failure to apologize for what happened in China, a failure that amounted to denial, cast a long shadow over postwar relations between Tokyo and Peking. Not until the new Emperor, Akihito, visited China in October 1992, was there a symbolic acknowledgement of the past when he confessed to 'a deep sense of grief' about the 'unfortunate period when our country brought profound suffering to the Chinese people'.[9] Although it is futile to deny the reality of Nanking and of many other Japanese war crimes, it is important to examine the background against which they occurred. As Eastman has argued, shocking and repulsive as the conduct of the Japanese Army often was, 'within the total context of the Japanese occupation, atrocities were the exception rather than the rule. In areas where the Japanese had consolidated their control, life and labour went on more or less normally ... The Japanese were, it is true, often harsh and arrogant toward the conquered Chinese.' Usually, however, these qualities 'resulted only in frictions and unpleasantness, rarely (relatively speaking) in atrocities'.[10] In this respect the Japanese occupation of China differed from the Nazi occupation of Poland. What factors, then, specifically lay behind the Nanking massacre and the many other atrocities which made the record of the Japanese armed forces between 1937 and 1945 such a shameful one?

Race and Empire

During the Second World War, the answer seemed simple. The Japanese committed hideous crimes because they were Japanese and did not accept the norms of behaviour observed by the civilized world. This view, which reflected racist thinking, inverted the myth of Japanese uniqueness fostered by the Japanese themselves, and ascribed negative qualities to the supposed exceptionalism of the 'Yamato race'. Nothing better could be expected from 'the monkey men of Asia'.[11] Even after the war, explanations based on Japanese exceptionalism remained popular in the West. One view of Japanese conduct stressed the absence of internalized moral codes in Japan and the prevalence of a 'situational ethic'. The behaviour of individual Japanese was shaped by the behaviour of the group. Drafted into the army and placed in a context in which atrocities were encouraged or condoned, Japanese soldiers simply followed the line of least resistance.[12] There is some evidence for this in a postwar novel by Tasaka Hanama, *The Long Imperial Way*, which he based on his experiences as a soldier in China. According to Tasaka, while military discipline was fierce, there was little official concern with issues like gambling, looting or visiting brothels: 'The lofty pretensions of the Imperial Army sprang primarily from a belief in the Emperor's divinity and in the divinity of the race also, and they were concerned very little with ideals of moral conduct or with codes of ethics.'[13] The behaviour of soldiers from other countries who were involved in atrocities, however, for example Germans in Russia, or Americans in the Philippines, Korea and Vietnam, suggests caution about any explanation centring on the supposed absence of an absolute moral code amongst the Japanese. The experience of the twentieth century is that where race is a powerful factor wars tend towards barbarism and atrocity whatever the nationality of the troops involved.

Certainly, during the period of the Meiji restoration the Japanese officer corps promoted among the troops a belief in the divine origins and unique qualities of the 'Yamato race' as a tool of social integration. Indeed, it was an article of faith that this ideology had brought victory over a larger rival in the Russo-Japanese war. If, however, the mystical union of the Japanese race under a divine Emperor constituted the special 'moral' ingredient which made the Army invincible, this carried with it the danger that it would lead to a rejection of technology. As a result the army was in the curious position of requiring an industrial sector to produce armaments, while rejecting the social consequences of modernization as a threat to the very values that made Japan unique.[14]

This contradiction became obvious in the 1920s, a period of relative liberalism and military retrenchment, when the army feared for its traditional place in national life. The collapse of Imperial Germany and even more the Russian revolution, which Japanese soldiers had witnessed at first hand during the abortive Siberian expedition, convinced young officers of the need to construct a total warfare state. In this system all resources, human and material, would be mobilized behind the national war effort. In their social-Darwinist world view, spiritual mobilization was as vital as physical rearmament. Indeed for Japan, a small power faced by larger rivals, 'moral' factors would make the difference between defeat and victory. The army therefore rejected liberalism, materialism and capitalism, the 'way of the West', elevating instead the cult of the Emperor and the divinity of the Japanese race. Only by a return to the past could social disintegration be averted. Army doctrine emphasized 'spiritual training' (*seishin kyoku*), the unique moral qualities that made the Japanese a superior people. It called for aggression, attack and heroic self-sacrifice.[15] The military handbook, *Basic Principles of the Imperial Army*, as revised during this period, eliminated words like 'surrender' and 'retreat'. The cult of the bayonet was stressed as part of the warrior image. The army was the Emperor's army, trained in 'the way of the heavenly sword'. There was a self-concious appeal to an extreme version of the samurai past, particularly the Kyushu tradition which proclaimed: 'When touched by a horse, cut down a horse; when touched by a man cut down a man.'[16] This made the Japanese army, unlike the navy, an anti-scientific and in some ways obscurantist organization that denied the importance of material factors. Spirit (*seishin*) 'became the army's substitute for weapons'.[17] This ideology became national doctrine after 1931 when the army once again held the levers of power. Although claiming legitimacy by an appeal to samurai origins, it was 'a perversion' which encouraged war crimes: 'It generated a range of mental attitudes that bordered on psychopathy: a view of death as sublime and beautiful, the falling cherry blossom; surrender as the ultimate dishonour, a belief whose corollary was total contempt for the captive; reverence for the sword ... which gave beheading as a punishment a special mystical significance.'[18]

As John Dower argues, therefore, while Westerners turned to pseudo-science to bolster their theories of racial superiority, the Japanese 'turned to mythohistory where they found the origins of their superiority in the divine descent of their sovereign and the racial and cultural homogeneity of the sovereign's loyal subjects'. Japan was a divine land and the Japanese a chosen people: 'The race had no identity apart from the throne and the mythic and religious (Shinto) traditions that had grown up around it. No outsider could hope to penetrate this community. This was blood nationalism of an exceptionally potent sort.'[19]

Such thinking fuelled an arrogant and racist attitude towards other Asians. The self-defined Japanese mission was to free Asia from communism and Western domination but this did not mean that all Asians were equal. Chinese, Koreans and others were at best dependent members of a family headed by the Japanese. And just as it would be unnatural to treat women and children as equals, so also must Asians be treated as dependants and controlled for their own good. The Japanese were thus wholly unable to understand those who resisted their unique mission. As early as 1934, Harry Emerson Wildes, a former professor of sociology at Keio University, noted that the Emperor cult had convinced most Japanese they were 'different from and far superior to the residents of any other land. The kami blood was not to be insulted by the belief that outsiders were equals ... Tokyo's resentment at being baffled by a people she despises shows itself in Japan's public attitude towards China.'[20] The Chinese were typically described as insincere in their relationship with Japan. This attitude often produced statements that appeared bizarre to outsiders. General Matsui, a convinced pan-Asianist who boasted of his acquaintance with Sun Yat-sen, argued that the war in China was no different from an older brother thrashing a younger one to bring him to his senses. It was waged 'not out of hatred but out of love'.[21] General Tojo Hideki adopted a similar argument: 'There was real fighting to be sure, but it was considered to be a family quarrel in which the younger brother, China, was being made to reconsider its various illegal acts typified by such anti-Japanese phrases as *konichi* (oppose the Japs) and *hainichi* (expel the Japs). The basic purpose was always the fostering of good neighbourliness and friendship and for that reason the thing was never called a war nor was there a declaration of war.'[22]

The troops in China reflected these beliefs. In an officially approved account, *War And Soldier*, published in 1940, Hino Ashei-hei, an educated enlisted man assigned to an army propaganda company, expressed sympathy for the sufferings of Chinese peasants and compared them to children. At the same time, however, he expressed his contempt for the Chinese as a people: 'It always surprised us Japanese to see how the inhabitants of the towns which we occupied greeted us with smiles and tried to be so friendly ... Japanese would sooner die than be friendly with an enemy ... how could we help despising them as a nation, when they would sell their smiles and flattery to an enemy for the price of their own skins ... To us soldiers they were pitiful, spineless people.'[23] Hino also confessed to discomfort at the fact that Chinese and Japanese looked so alike when they were in fact so different. It gave him 'a certain queer feeling' to find the face of the enemy at once alien yet familiar: 'They look like us, indeed, too much; it is almost embarrassing.'[24] But while they were inferior, the Chinese combined cowardice with cunning. The despised enemy was also a figure of fear. As Hino remarked, 'we had to regard every one of them with suspicion, in order to be effectively on our guard'.[25] If not kept in their place they might take a terrible revenge. Similarly, Tasaka's novel contains a revealing debate amongst Japanese troops ordered to burn a village for sheltering guerrillas. They justified their action by arguing that 'if we had not burnt it they would have thought us weak'. If Japan lost the China war, the enemy would come to Japan and 'do more terrible things than we are doing. Our homes would be wrecked ... The women of Japan would all be raped ... that is why we have come this far ... to suffer our hardships and to fight.'[26] The Chinese were thus docile but bloodthirsty. They combined the contradictory qualities of child and devil. It was an approach which fitted what Dower calls an abiding Japanese sense of 'being always the threatened, the victim, the aggrieved – and never the threat, the victimizer, the giver of grief'.[27] Soldiers who shed tears for the suffering of a favourite horse and were painfully shy in the presence of Japanese women, were capable of killing and raping Chinese, apparently without compunction.

   This kind of thinking occurred in an organization, the Japanese army, which was both brutal and rigidly hierarchical. Soldiers were taught that they had no other duty but to obey. The Imperial Rescript, read to the troops every day, emphasized that an order from a superior should be treated as an order from the Emperor himself. Discipline was enforced by beatings, often for no apparent reason. New recruits were routinely beaten by first-year soldiers to teach them the habit of blind obedience and their humble position in the military hierarchy. They in turn would hand out beatings to conscripts when they became senior privates. This practice was called 'injecting willpower'.[28] It was a form of socialization that crushed the individual and educated the mass in routine brutality. As Tasaki recalled, there were 'no individuals in the Imperial Army – only absolute servants of the Emperor – and no rights except the right to die gloriously for the Emperor. Punishers and punished, superiors and subordinates, the soldiers of the Japanese Imperial

Army suffered together under a system which tried to make destructive machines of them ...'[29]

During the China War this deliberate encouragement of brutality was reinforced by supplying the troops with live prisoners for bayonet practice. New officers were expected to decapitate victims with a single blow from their samurai swords, reintroduced in 1935 to encourage notions of Japanese exceptionalism and a unique warrior past. These bloody demonstrations took place in front of the group, ensuring that nobody would risk the shame of losing their manhood by appearing a coward. Uno Shintaro, a former intelligence officer in North China, recalled that such displays were part of the education of new drafts from Japan: 'Most officers did this. If they didn't their authority was weakened The men would say, "He's nothing but appearances". Nobody wanted to be called "spineless".'[30] Azumi Shiro, a former private and one of the few veterans to speak out about Nanking, implied that his company had not been involved in the atrocities because their commander was 'a coward ... too squeamish for executions'.[31] Bayoneting and beheading were a routine part of anti-guerrilla operations. They were also used against Chinese passers-by who showed disrespect for the divine Emperor by failing to bow to his representative, the Japanese soldier. According to the American correspondent, Carroll Alcott, peasants in the occupied zones had to go down on their knees and kowtow to Japanese sentries or be 'stuck by a bayonet'.[32] Edgar Snow had no doubt that this was the inevitable product of the bastardized Bushido code celebrated by the Japanese Army: 'Less than a hundred years ago any samurai ... could test his sword whenever the urge moved him, by cutting off the head of the first commoner unlucky enough to meet him. He could be embarrassed only if he failed to remove the offending object with one blow. It is not hard to see where the Japanese soldier finds traditional sanction for the same practice in China today.'[33]

Racism and calculated brutality were necessary preconditions for atrocities but they did not make the Japanese unique or exceptional. Other imperial systems rested on similar foundations, often with similar results. One contemporary comparison was the mass murder of at least six thousand Abyssinians in Addis Ababa by the Italian occupying force in March 1937, following a bomb attack on General Graziani.[34] Nor were they the entire explanation of Japanese conduct at Nanking and elsewhere. After all, atrocities were the exception and were visited on only a small proportion of the Chinese population. Something more was required to create a massacre on the scale of Nanking. As Christopher Browning argues in *Ordinary Men*, 'war and especially race war, leads to brutalization, which leads to atrocity'. But atrocities fall into different categories. One type is described by Browning as 'battlefield frenzy'. Although atrocities of this kind 'were too often tolerated, condoned or tacitly ... encouraged by elements of the command structure, they did not reflect official government policy ... such ... atrocities represented a breakdown in discipline and the chain of command. They were not "standard operating procedure".' Another type of atrocity such as taking and shooting hostages or the activities of the Nazi *Einsatzgruppen* in Russia were the result of 'cold calculation'.[35] Such atrocities represented official policy and were sometimes but not always associated with deliberate genocide. It is with this distinction in mind that the events at Nanking should be examined.

The Campaign

War blunts normal human sensibilities. The soldier quickly comes to focus on the survival of himself and his unit. There is no time for remorse or second thoughts about the morality of killing. Hino Ashihei, viewing a pile of bloodsoaked Chinese corpses in a trench near Hsuchow, later noted that he 'did not feel any pity whatsoever ... Surely, it would have been only right that I should feel some kind of remorse at seeing the bodies of the enemy dead?'[36] Even by the standards of the China war, the campaign in the Yangtse valley, which began in August 1937, was particularly harsh and bloody. Faced with a Japanese threat in North China after the Marco Polo Bridge Incident on 7 July, the Chinese leader, Chiang Kai-shek moved his best troops, two Central Army divisions trained and equipped by the Germans, into Shanghai. His objective was to threaten the Japanese position there and perhaps also to provoke Western mediation by fighting in a city that contained the largest concentration of foreign capital in China. In the first week the Chinese almost drove the small Japanese Naval Landing Party, which was defending the Japanese concession, into the sea. The navy had to call on the army for help and a Shanghai Expeditionary Force was hastily created under General Matsui Iwane. Shortage of shipping and the precarious position in Shanghai meant that these troops had to be fed into the fighting piecemeal and they took heavy casualties in bitter street fighting. It was an unpleasant shock for people conditioned to believe that the Chinese were a worthless nation who could not fight. Only after landings at Hangchow Bay, by the 10th Army under General Yanagawa Heisuki, on 5 November 1937, did Chinese resistance collapse.[37] As the Japanese advanced up the Yangtse Valley towards Nanking, the Central China Expeditionary

Army was formed from the Shanghai Expeditionary Force and 10th Army. Matsui was given command of this new body which was in effect a headquarters organization. By his own account its function was limited to coordinating the operations of the two field commands. 10th Army remained under General Yanagawa while Matsui's old position with the Shanghai Expeditionary Force was filled on 1 December by Prince Asaka, a member of the imperial family by marriage to a daughter of the Emperor Meiji.[38]

As Eastman notes, the troops advancing on Nanking 'had been engaged in the most sustained fighting of the entire China war. Blood had flowed in horrendous quantities: there had been approximately forty thousand Japanese and considerably more than 250,000 Chinese casualties in the Shanghai fighting alone ...'[39] Some Japanese units had lost 80 percent of their number. In addition, they had outrun their supply lines and were existing on grass soup, tinned plums and biscuits. A Japanese doctor later told Hanson of one case in which soldiers from his unit captured two Chinese rice barges and then started fighting amongst themselves over the contents. A cholera epidemic had also taken its toll. The Japanese medical service was unable to deal with this and infected soldiers simply fell out along the line of march to either recover or to die. While three hundred had died of the disease by the middle of October, Hino records that many others were also suffering from bowel and bladder infections which made them pass blood.[40] At the Tokyo Trial, Matsui rehearsed some of these facts, implying that his soldiers and not the Chinese had been the real victims of the Yangtse campaign.[41] As a result, the Japanese troops were hardly in a charitable mood towards the Chinese. Harassment by snipers in the streets of Shanghai had encouraged them to think of anyone who was not Japanese as the enemy. According to Hidaka Shinrokuro, a Japanese diplomat who testified at the Tokyo Trial, their attitude to the civilian population was one of 'hostility ... and suspicious watchfulness'.[42]

It was in this mood that the Japanese Army reached Nanking. Against the advice of his German military advisers, Chiang had ordered a last stand in the city rather than surrender his capital without a fight. He had placed his troops in a trap, for Nanking was situated within a bend of the Yangtse and there was no way for the forces there to escape once the Japanese had sealed the land approaches. The garrison of around fifty thousand consisted of the remnants of two élite Central Army divisions, decimated in Shanghai, along with provincial units from Canton, Kwangsi and Hunan. Despite the collapse of the Yangtse front, morale was described as good. The Chinese sandbagged the city gates and burned villages within a fifteen-mile radius of the walls to deny the enemy shelter and create a field of fire. The British and U.S. embassy staffs were evacuated to gunboats on the river along with those foreign nationals who were prepared to go, but a few remained behind for humanitarian reasons. An international safety zone was organized by a committee under the German businessman, John Rabe of Seimens, to provide a haven for refugees. It was modelled on a similar zone established earlier in Shanghai by the French priest, Father Jacquinot.[43] The Chinese cooperated with the committee by removing troops and anti-aircraft guns from the demarcated area. Informed of the existence of the zone, the Japanese refused to recognize it, on the grounds that Nanking was a defended fortress. They promised, however, not to attack the zone deliberately if it was not used for military purposes.[44] On 9 December 1937, Matsui issued an ultimatum to the Chinese garrison, calling on it to surrender by noon the next day. Without a capitulation 'the horrors of war' would be let loose on Nanking. But according to Matsui: 'Though harsh and relentless to those who resist, the troops of Japan are kind and generous to non-combatants and Chinese troops who have no enmity to Japan. The Japanese Army earnestly desire to protect oriental culture.'[45]

Already the day before Matsui had issued his ultimatum, on 8 December, the Chinese commander, General Tang Sheng-chih, had abandoned the city, slipping away by boat. According to Chinese official accounts he had ordered the garrison to break out but there is no evidence of this.[46] When the assault began with an air and artillery bombardment on 10 December, the Chinese troops, finding themselves leaderless, panicked. On the evening of 11 December, with the Japanese closing in, they swarmed towards the river in an attempt to escape. At the Hsiakwan Gate, trucks and cars 'jammed, were overturned, caught fire ... a terrible holocaust and the dead lay feet deep. The gate blocked, terror mad soldiers scaled the wall and let themselves down on the other side with ropes, punees and belts tied together ... Many fell and were killed. But at the river was perhaps the most appalling scene of all.' Panic-stricken men fought for places on the few available boats: 'The overcrowded junks capsized ... thousands drowned. Other thousands tried to make rafts of the lumber on the river front, only to suffer the same fate.'[47] Many, finding no boats, turned back to the city and sought refuge in the international zone, throwing away their weapons and equipment. The Ministry of Communications which contained large stores of ammunition caught fire and exploded throwing a ghastly flickering light on the surrounding chaos: 'The horror of the scene was accentuated by the wounded who were crawling around imploring aid.'[48] But the long agony of Nanking was only just beginning.

As Chinese authority collapsed many looked to the Japanese to retrieve the situation. According to the *New York Times* correspondent, F. Tillman Durdin, 'When the first column of Japanese troops marched from the South Gate up Chungshan Road ... small knots of Chinese civilians broke into scattered cheers, so great was their relief that the siege was over and so high were their hopes that the Japanese would restore peace and order.'[49] The international committee also looked forward to the day when 'people would be able to return to their homes and get back into normal life again'.[50] Matsui, who was sick with tuberculosis in Soochow, later testified that he shared this objective and had issued strict orders for the occupation of the city.[51] According to his staff, this directive was hand delivered to General Yanagawa and Prince Asaka as the army approached Nanking. Matsui called for the maintenance of strict discipline amongst the troops who were to gain the respect of the Chinese by their behaviour. Only specially selected units were to enter the city. The occupation of the enemy capital was to dazzle the world with the glory of Japan.[52] In the same testimony, however, he maintained that it was up to the field and divisional commanders to enforce this order. He had no direct control over troops and was therefore not responsible for discipline.[53] This ambiguity about the chain of command was never resolved at the Tokyo Trial and was to obscure, perhaps deliberately, the real responsibility for what followed.

Within hours the Japanese had begun a search for soldiers in civilian clothes which rapidly escalated into a campaign of indiscriminate massacre. The victims were shot, bayoneted or doused in petrol and set on fire. The troops seemed to treat this activity as a sport. John Magee witnessed the murder of an old Chinese man in a long traditional gown by two Japanese privates: 'The soldiers walked in front of him and couldn't have stood more than five yards in front of him, and both of them shot him in the face – killed him. They were both laughing and talking as though nothing had happened; never stopped talking or smoking their cigarettes ... they killed him with no more feeling than taking a shot at a wild duck, and then walked on.'[54] Durdin recorded the shooting of two hundred men against the wall of the bund: 'Then a number of Japanese trod nonchalantly around the crumpled bodies, pumping bullets into any that were still kicking. The army men performing the gruesome job had invited navy men from the warships anchored off the bund to view the scene. A large group of military spectators apparently greatly enjoyed the spectacle.'[55] Thousands of women were raped and butchered. Neither the very old nor the very young were spared. Shops and houses were looted and set on fire. Foreign property and even embassy buildings were destroyed.[56]

Members of the international committee did what they could for the Chinese, often at great personal risk, but their protests were ignored. Rabe tried to protect the refugees by wearing a swastika armband which he thrust in the faces of Japanese troops, surely the only time the Nazi symbol was used as a humanitarian symbol. But despite the developing relationship between Berlin and Tokyo, symbolized by the Anti-Comintern Pact of 1936, he was treated with no more consideration than any other foreigner. Things did not improve even when military police appeared on the scene. According to John Magee, chairman of the Red Cross in Nanking, 'these very gendarmes began to do some of the things the other soldiers were doing'.[57] General Alexander von Falkenhausen, the chief military adviser to the Chinese government, reporting on the massacre to Berlin, condemned Japanese conduct as 'indescribable for regular troops'.[58]

Why did this bloodbath continue for six weeks, apparently unchecked? Japanese diplomats in Nanking, appalled by the conduct of the Army, tried to intervene, but to no effect. According to Bates, they were 'honestly trying to do what they could in a very bad situation, but they themselves were terrified of the military', and could do nothing except forward the complaints of the international committee to Tokyo.[59] In the Japanese capital the Foreign Minister, Hirota Koki, 'alarmed and worried' by the reports, asked Ishii Haro of the East Asian Bureau to raise the matter with the army at the regular Liaison Conference meeting. Hirota himself spoke to the War Minister, General Sugiyama Gen, but there is no evidence that immediate action was taken and the issue could not be discussed in cabinet since it was not considered the proper place for questions relating to the army in the field.[60] In January 1938, Lieutenant-General Honma Mashaharu was despatched to investigate conditions in China, but although Matsui, Asaka and eighty other officers were subsequently recalled, it remains unclear whether this had anything to do with Nanking. Matsui argued that the postings were part of a major troop reorganization at the end of the Yangtse campaign which required the deactivation of some headquarters units. The ten divisions of the Central China Army were being reduced to five 'and these officers were superfluous'.[61] Certain conclusions can be drawn from this paralysis both in Tokyo and at a local command level. As a letter in the *South China Morning Post* remarked, there were only two possible explanations: 'Either those in authority do not want to control their troops or they can't.'[62] The anonymous writer thus suggested alternatives which have remained central to the debate about the Rape of Nanking ever since.

Battlefield Frenzy

It could be argued that the Nanking massacre fitted the first of Browning's types, and resulted from a breakdown of discipline and the chain of command. The troops, maddened by the strains of the campaign, simply broke loose, with the tacit collusion of at least some of their divisional officers who 'were in a far from normal state of mind'.[63] According to a Japanese journalist, Imai Masatake of the Tokyo *Asahi*, the excuse for mass murder was an order to clear the city of stragglers before the ceremonial entry of General Matsui.[64] Sasaki Toichi, who commanded the 30th Brigade of the 16th Division, commented that his men had been out for revenge since the battle of Shanghai: 'Prisoners surrendered in droves, several thousand in all. Our enraged troops ignored superior orders and slaughtered one bunch after another. We had suffered heavy casualties in the bitter ten-day fighting. Many of our men had lost good friends. The unit hated the Chinese and there was a feeling of wanting to kill every one of the bastards.'[65]

A parallel to this explanation of the Rape of Nanking might be the sack of Magdeburg in 1620, when Imperial troops under General Tilly murdered some 25,000 of its inhabitants, despite the General's wish to spare the city. Some foreign observers at Nanking argued that no similar atrocity had occurred since the Thirty Years War. Insofar as he admitted anything at the Tokyo Trial, this is what Matsui also implied as an explanation, noting that while the discipline of the troops under fire was 'excellent', their 'conduct and behaviour was not ... I think there were some lawless elements in the army'. He admitted that there might have been 'some excited young officers and men' who had 'committed unpleasant outrages'. When he reached Nanking on 17 December and was informed by the *Kempeitai* (Military Police) about a few cases of indiscipline he had felt 'shame and sorrow'. He had reiterated his orders regarding good conduct and three or four incidents were severely dealt with by court martial.[66] Similarly, his Deputy Chief of Staff, Muto Akira, the only witness to admit that anything extraordinary had occurred, categorically denied that the troops had been acting under orders: 'I regret that you ask such a question. There is no army in the world or no government in the world that will instruct their people to shoot or kill children or the civilian population'. What happened at Nanking in 1937 and at Manila in 1944 was the product of poor indoctrination: 'The troops that committed the atrocities in Nanking and Manila were men mobilized in a hurry and they were not trained properly in military conduct.'[67] Their actions reflected badly on the honour and prestige of the Imperial Japanese Army.

Matsui, however, insisted that his soldiers were 'experienced troops, officered by experienced men', leading American witnesses to the conclusion that the atrocities had been either ordered or condoned by the higher command.[68] According to John Magee: 'If there had been any real effort to stop this conduct, it could have been stopped, but it was looked upon entirely too lightly ... If they had shot twenty-five men then the thing would have stopped.'[69] On one occasion the chairman of the international committee, John Rabe, had returned to his compound with a Japanese officer to find a soldier in the act of rape: 'All the Japanese officer did was to slap the Japanese soldier's face ... Herr Rabe was utterly disgusted.'[70] Searle Bates also noted that, while some of the looting was by soldiers for their own use, there was also evidence of organized looting under the control of officers. He had seen a convoy of lorries almost a mile long, loaded with antique Chinese furniture and other precious items.[71] This pointed towards something more than a military riot, suggesting method and purpose.

Matsui certainly knew more than he was prepared to admit, though there is evidence to support his claim that he tried to prevent the atrocities. At the time a Japanese journalist informed a British friend that when Matsui arrived from Soochow on 17 December and witnessed the situation in the city, he called the commanders to a conference 'on the steps of the Sun Yat-sen Monument at the Purple Mountain. For half an hour he harangued them. He told them that what had happened in Nanking would be a permanent stain on the honour of the Japanese army and that they should all feel everlasting shame. Nevertheless this process of murder and pillage continued right up the Yangtze Valley.'[72] When Matsui was repeatedly questioned after the war about why his orders had been disobeyed, his replies remained consistent. He could only act through his subordinate commanders for he had no direct control over troops. If atrocities had occurred, it was their responsibility.

This, however, put under the spotlight the role of Prince Asaka, whose 16th Division of his Shanghai Expeditionary Force was responsible for policing the captured city. Matsui was asked to comment on rumours that Asaka had in fact ordered the massacre but had been shielded from blame as a member by marriage of the imperial family. His reply was categorical: 'I do not think so. Prince Asaka had joined the army only about ten days before its entry into Nanking and in view of the short time he was connected with this army, I do not think that he can be held responsible. I would say that the Division commanders are the responsible ones.'[73] This devolved guilt downwards onto Lieutenant-General Nakajima Kesago of the 16th Division, a former *Kempeitai* officer and a known political extremist. According to some accounts, Nakajima had been wounded during the final assault on Nanking and was in 'a rather excitable state'.[74] It was certainly convenient to blame someone who was not a member of the imperial family. Nevertheless, there were those, both then and since, who believed that Asaka had played a key role. According to the American journalist, Hallett Abend: 'Prince Asaka was the man who permitted the shocking rape of Nanking, but since he is related to the imperial family his name was never mentioned in connection with that ghastly ... reign of savagery',[75] while Edward Behr implies that Matsui sacrificed himself to save Asaka: 'It is one of the grim ironies of history that the International Military Tribunal handed out the death sentence to the one Japanese general who was appalled by the Nanking atrocities and did his best to prevent them.'[76]

A War of Punishment

But any explanation that seeks an answer in the actions of a single commander, like Asaka or Nakajima, or even of the entire Central China Army, fails to address certain questions. The atrocities at Nanking, like most Japanese atrocities, took place within a specific context. They were neither normal nor universal. This suggests that Nanking was an act of policy, different in scale rather than in kind from what happened elsewhere and under certain precise conditions. In other words, its 'irrational' atrocities were directed towards a specific 'rational' goal.

Deliberate atrocity had a long history in the Japanese army. During their first colonial campaign in 1895, Japanese troops slaughtered thousands of civilians to suppress guerrillas and secure the island of Taiwan. According to the Belgian diplomat, Baron D'Anthan, their conduct was 'arbitrary, arrogant and cruel'.[77] After the proclamation of the protectorate over Korea in 1905, great brutality was used to put down the 'Righteous Armies' which rose against Japanese rule.[78] In 1919, following mass demonstrations for Korean independence, Japanese troops were again unleashed on the population in a campaign of terror. In the village of Hwach'ang-myon, Wiwon County, North P'yong-an Province, the inhabitants were burned alive on suspicion of having supplied food to guerrillas. Similar atrocities were committed in Kyonggi Province.[79] In 1920, the Japanese sent a punitive expedition across the border to attack Korean settlements around Chientao in eastern Manchuria, methodically shooting young men and burning villages. Some three thousand were murdered in a three week campaign.[80] When the Japanese Kwangtung Army seized

Manchuria and created the puppet state of 'Manchukuo' in 1932, it resorted to the same tactics. Western sympathizers described the new state as a 'benevolent despotism' which was civilizing an area traditionally associated with only two crops, 'soya beans and bandits'.[81] Others were less impressed. The British Consul in Mukden, P.D. Butler, reported, in June 1936, that 'Manchukuo' was 'under the control of a military despotism whose methods can only be described as savage. The Kwangtung Army rely upon terrorism as an instrument of policy, convinced apparently that Chinese antagonism can be cowed by the unrestricted use of machine guns and torture.'[82]

Butler was referring to the so-called 'bandit suppression campaigns', launched by the Kwantung Army to stabilize the political situation in the new state. The Japanese experienced major problems in 'Manchukuo' with banditry, both traditional and political. Manchurian peasants had always turned to banditry as a seasonal economic activity, but after 1932 there was also an outbreak of political banditry, often directed by the Chinese Communist Party. Amongst these bands was the North-East United Anti-Japanese Army which contained within its ranks a young Korean named Kim Il-Sung who rose to supreme power in the North Korean State after 1945.[83] The Japanese fight against Manchurian bandits was an expensive one. In 1937 alone it cost them 175 million yuan, or over half of the Manchukuoan defence budget.[84] The French military attaché in Tokyo calculated in June 1937 that at least 1,148 soldiers had been killed since 1932. A source on the Japanese General Staff put the casualty list at four a day.[85] The Japanese were anxious to crush the partisans. Armed revolt challenged their claims to have brought peace and justice to the province and endangered lines of communication in what was intended as their main concentration area in any future war with Russia. In this situation they applied the lessons already learned in Korea, aiming to cow the population and destroy the infrastructure which supported guerrillas. John Paton Davies, the U.S. Vice-Consul in Mukden, recalled that the Kwangtung Army organized Manchurian villages on the basis of collective responsibility. If a village was suspected of collusion with bandits, a punitive column would arrive and 'at the whim of the pacifiers, arbitrarily shoot from one to all the men of the village'.[86] According to Davies, similar methods were later used in China. Anti-partisan operations followed 'the same saturnalian procedure on the Yangtze as on the Sungari [in Manchuria]: a certain part of the male population (depending on the "guilt" of the village) is shot outright, the women raped and some killed, the houses are burned ...'[87] This became known as the 'Three Alls Policy' – 'Burn All, Kill All, Loot All', and was an established tool of Japanese occupation policy.[88]

Japan, like other imperial powers, had thus a well-established concept of the punitive expedition, designed to break resistance and create a situation in which the civilizing mission of the dominant race could be carried forward. The entire Yangtse valley campaign fitted into this concept of a war of punishment. It was not only in Nanking that murder, rape and looting occurred on an unprecedented scale. One foreign witness estimated that at least 300,000 Chinese were killed during the Japanese advance:

> A considerable proportion of these people were slaughtered in cold blood. The observer spoke of old men and boys having been forced by the Japanese soldiers to carry burdens far beyond their strength and, when they fell down from sheer exhaustion, having been bayoneted and flung into a ditch by the roadside. Nor were the dead spared ill-treatment. At many points along the road ... Chinese graves were opened up and the coffins burned. It was the considered opinion of this observer that in its advance the Japanese Army has adopted a policy of deliberate terrorism.[89]

Matsui later claimed ignorance of events at Nanking on the grounds that he was detained by illness at his headquarters in Soochow.[90] But exactly the same things were happening there as in Nanking. American missionaries informed the U.S. embassy about terrible scenes of murder, rape and robbery. Every bank and private residence had been looted: 'That this looting was not something done for the sole benefit of the individual soldiers who were doing the work but for the benefit of the Japanese Army and with the knowledge and consent of the officers is proved by the fact that we saw some of the loot being loaded on Army trucks.'[91] In a letter to the *China Weekly Review*, entitled 'Soochow Nightmare', another foreign witness estimated that there had been at least 9,500 cases of rape by the 'lust-mad Japanese army'.[92]

This predilection to rape was mentioned time and again by foreign witnesses and was regarded as a unique Japanese contribution to the horrors of war. Hanson of the *Associated Press* was particularly disgusted by 'the desire of many Japanese soldiers to have themselves photographed in the act of raping Chinese women in daylight', and the captured diaries in which they recorded 'their sadistic prowess'.[93] The practice partly reflected the low status of women in Japanese society and the even greater contempt of Japanese men for women of an 'inferior' race. The Japanese army had its own field brothels or 'comfort stations', often staffed by Korean women forcibly recruited by the colonial authorities, a practice which still casts a deep shadow over Japanese relations with both Korean states.[94] Rape was often used by Japanese officers as a reward for the men after a harsh battle and as an interim measure until the field brothels caught up with the front. But the horrific practice was about more than this. Rape reflected power relationships. As the American writer Emily Hahn remarked, the Japanese used rape as 'the quickest, surest way to humiliate a community. I think that they rape almost as a religious duty, a sacrifice to the god of victory, a symbol of triumphant power.'[95] Rape was a means of punishing a society. It had thus much the same function for the Japanese as the mass rapes committed by the Russians in Germany in 1945. It underlined the powerlessness of the community and the superiority of the conqueror.

The Japanese claimed that their war of punishment was aimed against the Chiang Kai-shek clique. In this connection it is important to understand that Shanghai and the Yangtse valley were fundamental to the KMT's political and economic power. The KMT derived 85 percent of its revenue from the trade and manufacturing sector of the economy centred on Shanghai. It was this which allowed Chiang to maintain a modern army and to exert authority over recalcitrant warlords. The area was also the core of KMT political strength.[96] The destruction of its entire social and economic fabric thus struck directly at the Chinese ability to carry on the war and showed the penalties of resistance. It achieved the same end on a larger scale as burning a 'bandit' village in Manchuria and shooting its population. According to a foreign observer, the area between Shanghai and Nanking, once one of the most densely populated areas on earth, had become 'a desert, with rice crops ungathered and left rotting in the fields as far as I could see. The traveller passes a continuous vista of blackened ruins and burnt-out farms guarded over by gruesomely fattened dogs.'[97] Some of this destruction was undoubtedly the result of scorched earth tactics by the retreating Chinese, but the main perpetrator was the Japanese army. In early 1938, a study by the international committee at Nanking of the rural communities in the immediate area of the city, put 'losses in buildings, labour animals, major farm implements, stored grain and destroyed crops ... [at] ... approximately $41,000,000. Two-fifths of all farm buildings ... were destroyed by fire, 123,000 buffaloes, oxen and donkeys were butchered and stolen, and 661,000 farm implements were destroyed. Thousands of hoes and rakes and water-wheels were broken up and burned, their metal parts collected for scrap and shipped to Japan.'[98] A similar policy was pursued in the Chinese areas of Shanghai, destroyed during the fighting. The factories left standing were stripped of their machinery which was sent to Japan. The ruins of the remainder were scoured for scrap which was used by Japanese war industry.[99] In this way the Japanese hoped not only to secure their Chinese flank for a future war with the Soviet Union by smashing the power base of the KMT, but also to force China to contribute towards preparedness for that war.

The Chinese were thus right in arguing that the evil committed by the Japanese in Nanking 'was done for a purpose'.[100] There is little doubt that Nanking was singled out for special treatment because it was the capital of the New China which the KMT was attempting to create, a China which had been insufficiently subservient to the demands of the Japanese military. In a campaign shaped by atrocity, its agony was prolonged and acute. Durdin of the *New York Times* shared the impression of many observers that the Japanese wanted 'the horrors to remain as long as possible to impress on the Chinese the terrible results of resisting Japan'.[101] According to Hanson, Japan was waging a new form of 'totalitarian warfare' designed to cripple 'not merely the opposing troops but the enemy nation *in toto* – its industries, commerce, finance, education and religion'. This policy made murder, rape and arson inevitable.[102]

Such educated guesses were supported fifty years later when ten former Japanese soldiers testified that they had been acting under orders in a campaign calculated to terrify the Chinese into surrender.[103] Matsui's disclaimers at the Tokyo Trial lose much of their weight in the light of what his troops were doing throughout the area, including around his own headquarters at Soochow. It should also be remembered that he was the one who had promised to subject Nanking to 'the horrors of war' if the garrison did not surrender, a pledge taken literally by Japanese troops. Against this background the Rape of Nanking should be seen as an act of policy, at least by the dominant group in the Japanese army which had the real power, if not by certain sections of the Japanese government. There is no evidence that the War Minister, Sugiyama, or any other responsible officer did anything about the situation. What they did instead was to prevent information about the punishment policy seeping back into Japan where the population was encouraged to think in terms of the China Expedition as a 'Holy War'. In February 1939 the Military Service Bureau of the War Ministry issued a secret booklet entitled, *Situation of the Army Unit and the Army Man Returning from the Area of the Disturbances*. This outlawed comments like: 'The thing I like best during the battle is the plundering; The prisoners of the Chinese Army are sometimes lined up and killed to test the efficiency of the machine gun. Our company commander unofficially gave instructions for raping as follows – in order that we won't have problems either pay them money or kill them in some obscure place after you have finished.'[104] As Butow remarks, this document revealed a high command issuing orders 'not against the commission of such atrocities, but against revelations concerning them within the home islands'.[105]

Conclusion

The Nanking massacre fits Browning's second type of atrocity better than his first. It cannot be explained away simply in terms of 'battlefield frenzy' or a breakdown of discipline within the local command. In the wider context of the Yangtse campaign and of earlier examples of Japanese atrocities in Taiwan, Korea and Manchuria, it is revealed as part of a considered policy, already long established, of punishing 'inferior' races. In this respect racism and imperialism were intimately associated with atrocity which was a fundamental element of the punishment expedition wherever it appeared. What was dismissed by the West during the war as typical Japanese conduct reflected a more universal tendency inherent in the idea of an imperial 'civilizing mission'. China had already suffered 'punishment' more than once at the hands of the dominant powers within the state system, acting either alone or in concert. The most notorious occasion was the International Expedition to relieve the legations in Peking during the Boxer Uprising of 1900. On their way to the capital, the troops left a trail of devastation in their wake and indulged in 'an orgy of looting and rapine' in the captured city. Thousands of women threw themselves down wells to escape the rampage. When the main German contingent arrived at the end of October, its commander, General von Waldersee, obeyed to the letter the Kaiser's exhortation that his men should act 'like Huns' in revenge for the murder of a German diplomat, launching a series of punitive expeditions in the area around Peking which gave no quarter.[106] One of his officers defended the practice in a letter to the *Cologne Gazette*, comparing it to that adopted towards *franc-tireurs* (partisans) during the Franco-Prussian War. According to the writer, 'all armed resistance and all treachery should be put down with great severity', by shooting suspects and burning to the ground villages which harboured suspected sympathizers. Such harsh treatment was 'a feature of every war and alone renders possible a speedy restoration of tranquillity'.[107] It was a sentiment with which any Japanese officer in the later China War could have agreed.

Notes

1. Haldore Hansen, *Humane Endeavour: The Story of The China War* (New York, 1939), 139-40.
2. *International Military Tribunal, Tokyo* (hereafter *IMT*), 16118-25. Lloyd E. Eastman, 'Facets of an Ambivalent Relationship: Smuggling, Puppets and Atrocities During the War, 1937-1945', in Akirya Iriye, ed., *The Chinese and the Japanese: Essays in Political and Cultural Interactions* (Princeton, 1976), 275-302.

3. *IMT*, 2574.

4. *New York Times*, 25 January 1938.

5. *IMT*, 3455-8.

6. Ibid., 3265.

7. Ibid., 3887-8.

8. Ian Buruma, *Wages of Guilt: Memories of War in Germany and Japan* (London 1994), 112-22. See also Sadao Asada, *Japan and the World, 1853-1952: A Bibilographlc Guide to Japanese Scholarship in Foreign Relations* (New York, 1989), 310-11.

9. *The Times*, 24 October 1992.

10. Eastman in Iriye, *Chinese and Japanese*, 296-97.

11. John Dower, *Japan in War and Peace: Selected Essays* (New York, 1994), 257-85.

12. Eastman in Iriye, *Chinese and Japanese*, 300-1. For a full discussion of this view see Ruth Benedict, *The Chrysanthemum and the Rose Patterns of Japanese Culture* (London, 1967).

13. Hanama Tasaki, *The Long lmperial Way* (London, 1949), 39.

14. Leonard A Humphries, *The Way of the Heavenly Sword: The Japanese Army in the 1920s* (Stanford, 1995), 12-14.

15. Humphries, *The Way*, 79-108.

16. Ibid., 41.

17. Ibid., 100.

18. Meirion and Susie Harries, *Soldiers of the Sun: The Rise and Fall of the Imperial Japanese Army 1868-1945* (London, 1991), 410.

19. Dower, *Japan*, 273.

20. Harry Emerson Wildes, *Japan in Crisis* (New York, 1934), 10.

21. *IMT*, 33815.

22. Robert J. C. Butow, *Tojo and the Coming of War* (Princeton, 1961), 102.

23. Hino Asheihei, *War and Soldier* (London,1940), 219.

24. Ibid., 267.

25. Ibid., 356-57.

26. Tasaki, *The Long Imperial Way*, 102-3.

27. Dower, *Japan*, 276.

28. Tasaki, *The Long Imperial Way*, 72-73.

29. Ibid., 39.

30. Haruko Taya Cook and Theodore F. Cook, *Japan at War: An Oral History* (New York, 1992), 156.

31. Buruma, *Wages of Guilt*, 132.

32. Carroll Alcott, *My War with Japan* (New York, 1943), 276.

33. Edgar Snow, *Scorched Earth* (London, 1941), 70-71.

34. *The Times*, 3 March 1937. According to this report the reprisals were carried out 'with a savagery almost beyond description...every able-bodied Italian in the place appears to have been encouraged to slaughter natives'.

35. Christopher Browning, *Ordinary Men: Reserve Police Battalion 101 and the Final Solution in Poland* (New York, 1992), 160-61.

36. Hino, *War*, 434.

37. Lloyd E. Eastman, 'Nationalist China during the Sino-Japanese War 1937-1945', in John K. Fairbank and Albert Feuerwerker, *The Cambridge History of China*, vol. 13, *Republican China 1912-1949*, Part 2, 550-52; Public Record Office, London (hereafter PRO) WO106/5576, Military Attaché Report, 12 December 1937, XC8599.

38. *IMT*, 32582, 33815-22.

39. Eastman in Iriye, *Chinese and Japanese*, 293.

40. PRO F0371/20960, 'Weekly Intelligence Summary', 9 December 1937, XC8550; F.S.G. Piggott, *Broken Thread* (London, 1950), 295; *The Times*, 14 October 1937; Hanson, *Humane Endeavour*, 143-44; Hino, *War*, 325.

41. *IMT*, 33835-36.

42. Ibid., 21445-61.

43. *The Times*, 9 December 1937; *New York Times*, 9 January 1938.

44. *The Times*, 9 December 1937.

45. Ibid., 10 December 1937.

46. *History of the Sino-Japanese War* (Translated Office of Military History, U.S. Military Advisory Group, China, Tapei, 1967), vol. 1, 71.

47. H. J. Timperley, *What War Means – The Japanese Terror in China: A Documentary Record* (London, 1938), 26-27.

48. *The Times*, 18 December 1937.

49. *New York Times*, 18 December 1937.

50. Timperley, *What War Means*, 68.

51. *IMT*, 33820-22.

52. Ibid., 21934-38.

53. Ibid., 32582, 33875.

54. Ibid., 3901.

55. *New York Times*, 18 December 1937.

56. Timperley, *What War Means*, 35-71.

57. *IMT*, 3928.

58. Ibid., 4599.

59. Ibid., 2638.

60. Ibid., 29974-98.

61. Ibid., 3455-58. Matsui explicitly denied the truth of a report by Hallett Abend in the *New York Times*, 23 February 1938, that Matsui, Asaka, Kanagawa and other officers had been recalled because of lax discipline in the China Area Army. A civilian witness, Ishii Itaro, of the Foreign Office, however, maintained Honma had been sent 'to enforce stricter discipline in the Japanese Army'. *IMT*, 29974-98. In support of Matsui's claim it should be noted that several divisions were transferred at this time to Manchuria and Japan as a precaution against Soviet attack. See Michael A. Barnhart, *Japan Prepares for Total War* (Ithaca and London, 1987),107-8.

62. Shuhsi Hsu, *A New Digest Of Japanese War Conduct* (Shanghai, 1941), 64.

63. Saburo Shiroyama, *The War Criminal: The Life and Death of Hirota Koki* (Tokyo, 1977), 195-96.

64. Saburo Ienaga, *The Pacific War* (New York, 1978), 186-7.

65. Ibid.

66. *IM7*, 3455-8.

67. Ibid., 16129-39.

68. Ibid., 16818-25.

69. Ibid., 3941.

70. Ibid., 3908.

71. Ibid., 2637.

72. Hsu, *New Digest*, 50.

73. *IMT*, 3460-63.

74. Shiroyama, *War Criminal*, 195.

75. Hallett Abend, *My Life In China* (New York, 1943), 274.

76. Edward Behr, *Hirohito: Behind the Myth* (London, 1990), 198.

77. Harries, *Soldiers*, 57.

78. F.A McKenzie, *Korea's Fight For Freedom* (London, 1922), 147-8.

79. Sohn Pow-key, Kim Chol-choon and Hong Yi-sup, *The History of Korea* (Seoul, 1970), 264-5.
80. Wildes, *Japan*, 245.
81. James A. B. Scherer, *Japan's Advance* (Tokyo, 1934), 275-301; see also George Bronson Rea, *The Case for Manchukuo* (London, 1935), and South Manchuria Railway Company, *Answering Questions on Manchuria* (Tokyo, 1937).
82. Butler to Foreign Office, 29 June 1936, *Documents on British Foreign Policy 1919-1939*, Series 2. vols. 893-4.
83. Bruce Cumings, *The Origins of the Korean War*, vol. 1, *Liberation and the Emergence of Separate Regimes 1945-1947* (Princeton, 1981), 34-8; Dae-Sook Suh, *Kim Il Sung: The North Korean Leader* (New York, 1988), 3-54.
84. T. A. Bisson, *Japan In China* (New York, 1938), 399-400.
85. Lieutenant-Colonel Sabattier to Daladier, 30 June 1937, *Documents Diplomatiques Français 1932-1939*, 2nd series, vol. 6, 251-5.
86. John Paton Davies, *Tiger by the Tail* (London, 1974), 180-1.
87. Ibid., 203.
88. Lincoln Li, *The Japanese Army in North China 1937-1941* (London, 1975), 187-216; Cumings, *Origins*, vol 2, *The Roaring of the Cataract 1947-1950* (Princeton, 1990), 286.
89. Timperley, *What War Means*, 85.
90. *IMT*, 32582.
91. Gauss (Shanghai) to Hull, *Foreign Relations of the United States 1938*, vol. 1, 569-70.
92. Timperley, *What War Means*, 87-93.
93. Hanson, *Humane Endeavour*, 144.
94. Buruma, *Wages of Guilt*, 194-5.
95. Emily Hahn, *China to Me* (New York, 1944), 288.
96. Youli Sun, *China and the Origins of the Pacific War* (New York, 1993), 91-2.
97. Timperley, *What War Means*, 85-86.
98. Snow, *Scorched Earth*, 63.
99. Ibid., 84-85.
100. *History of the Sino-Japanese War*, vol. 1, 64.
101. *New York Times*, 18 December 1937.
102. Hanson, *Humane Endeavour*, 146.
103. Behr, *Hirohito*, 198-201.
104. *IMT*, 30125-30.
105. Butow, *Tojo*, 101.
106. Nathaniel Peffer, *The Far East: A Modern History* (London, 1958), 170-1; Christopher Hibbert, *The Dragon Wakes: China and the West 1793-1911* (Newton Abbot, 1971), 351-9; Peter Fleming, *The Siege at Peking* (London, 1959), 244-59.
107. *The Times*, 11 January 1901.

CHAPTER 12

THE INDONESIAN MASSACRES, 1965-1966

IMAGE AND REALITY

John Gittings

Introduction

The large-scale killings which occurred in Indonesia in 1965-66 extended over many months and took place in many locations. Some were conducted directly by the armed forces, others were instigated by the authorities and quite a few were the expression of previous conflict or tension within communities. Because of the secrecy surrounding these events, then and since, it is impossible even to guess at how many separate incidents occurred, how many were killed and how many participated in the killings. They constituted not one massacre but a whole set, loosely connected and with significant regional variations but nevertheless all triggered by events which had occurred and decisions which were taken at the national level of rule. This makes the whole affair an extraordinarily complex phenomenon which it would be hard to analyse even with more adequate information. Yet in spite of many variations in type and character, all of these killings bore the features of a 'massacre' in the usual sense of the word: they involved the mass slaughter of sizeable numbers of individuals who were usually unarmed and defenceless; they happened swiftly and unpredictably; the methods of killing were extremely savage and the victims were treated, dead or alive, with huge contempt.

Several types of question have to be asked about this period. First, was this blood-letting on such a colossal scale sanctioned or even encouraged by outside forces such as the U.S. and Britain? This question has occupied a large part – perhaps the greater part – of academic and journalistic attention in recent years. The answers to it, suggestive but not yet conclusive, tell us more about the nature of Cold War politics elsewhere than about what actually happened in Indonesia. Second, did this protracted sequence of savagery constitute a single all-embracing massacre in the sense of a deliberate and sustained exercise to physically eliminate a large identifiable section of the population? This was contested by the regime which emerged from these events and which, led by President Suharto, remained in power for over three decades. (Suharto was finally overthrown in May 1998 after the mounting internal tensions of Indonesian society were exposed by the Asian financial crisis, leading to mass popular demonstrations and unrest). During all this time the regime avoided analysis of what had happened without seeking to offer its own alternative explanation. Yet, if it occurred as critics claim, then this was a massacre, or massacres, whose 'spontaneous' character was an instrument of sustained policy with a particular end in mind. While all massacres are appalling, this gives a particularly vicious complexion to this case. It helps to explain why, more than thirty years after the events, so little is still known about it, and why it remains an unusually sensitive subject.

A third question, which may begin to be addressed now that the Suharto regime has fallen, has to do with the scale of the massacres. With estimates of those slaughtered ranging from one hundred thousand to more than a million, the possibility of exaggeration and double counting has to be reckoned with. If the process of revolutionary change begun in May 1998 continues, the official files may eventually be opened up, although there will be vested interests among the armed forces opposed to an objective enquiry. Such an enquiry could lead to the higher estimates being scaled down: some aspects of this 'massacre' appear no more immune to myth-making than similar occurrences elsewhere. Yet all contemporary accounts, including those of Western intelligence services, agree that a very substantial number of people was murdered – at least several hundreds of thousands. Statistically this does not begin to match Stalin's purges, the Nazi exterminations, the Khmer Rouge terror, or even the more recent genocides of Rwanda and Burundi. Yet occurring as it did over a short space of time, it may be regarded as comparable in its ferocity and intensity. Serious study of the Indonesian massacres of 1965-66, as and when this becomes possible, will throw light on an important and so far neglected example of a phenomenon which may be abhorrent to humanity, but nevertheless continues to occur – and which still needs to be much better understood.

Coverage of the Massacres

No one who writes about modern Indonesia can avoid mentioning the massacres, though they often get little more than a passing mention. Relatively little research has been conducted on them (with some notable exceptions) and even less is reflected in the secondary literature.[1] They remain to a large extent a series of events located outside any meaningful context, historical framework or explanation. Indeed, the very fact that so little is known or understood about them has become their most noted characteristic thereby serving, perhaps, as a substitute for more extended analysis.

In common journalistic shorthand, the massacres are portrayed as an episode when the 'mob' (not the ruling authorities) moved to 'crack down on the Communists' after the abortive Gestapu coup of 30 September 1965: 'An orgy of violence broke out across the nation, targeting suspected Communists and sympathizers and also ethnic Chinese. An estimated three hundred thousand people died. Soon the Communists were crushed, and the next year Sukarno, a broken man, handed the presidency to Suharto.'[2] The victims, in this view, were targeted by the act of violence itself rather than as a result of conscious action, or even as the consequence of elemental human emotion, though almost assuming the force of a natural disaster such as a flood or typhoon. Thus, they have been described as a 'blood-letting' in which 'more than half a million people were killed'.[3] This use of the passive rather than active mood has led Robert Cribb to observe that, 'the Indonesian killings have been treated as if they fall into an anomalous category of "accidental" mass death'.[4]

This is all the more surprising because, at the time and soon afterwards, there was no secret about the savagery and extent of this 'blood-letting' or about the identity of those who led and participated in it. Contemporary news reports in the Western media spoke of mass slaughter, of nights of terror, of political killings and great purges, and cited totals ranging from three hundred thousand to one million. A remarkably full account was published in the best-selling book by John Hughes, *The End of Sukarno*, with the subtitle 'a coup that misfired: a purge that ran wild.' Hughes, writing for the *Christian Science Monitor*, described the army as 'bent on ruthlessly dismantling the entire Communist Party organization at home', noting how 'few holds were barred' in whipping up anti-Communist sentiment not least amongst Muslim student leaders who were set in motion with the single-word instruction 'Sikat' meaning 'sweep (them away)'.[5]

As for the sequence of events itself, there is little disagreement among scholars and journalists:

1. During the night of 30 September, an abortive coup was launched by a loose coalition of army officers who claimed to be anticipating an imminent move by the Generals' Council against President Sukarno. The coup organizers comprised two main groups. Gabriel Kolko has described the first as 'younger central Javanese who condemned the corruption, Westernization and personal laxity of the leaders of the army living in Jakarta; the second were air force officers, including the commander, who had long-standing complaints against the army over allocation of the military budget and whose careers were dependent on Sukarno remaining in power'.[6] The strong legal Communist Party (PKI) was not involved organizationally, as is shown by the lack of supporting action. But its leader, Aidit, is believed to have provided covert political support through a parallel organization, the Biro Khusus or Special Bureau which reported directly to him.[7]

2. The failure of the 30 September coup left General Suharto, who had fortunately (or mysteriously) not been a target of the conspirators, in a position to exercise decisive leadership. Within a week, an elaborate funeral had been held for the generals murdered in the coup, and lurid tales (which appear to have been unfounded) were published alleging that Communist women had first mutilated the bodies and even, according to some versions, committed sexual orgies with them.[8] The army had found its martyrs and, with the encouragement of the U.S. embassy, 'a cause for a purge of the entire PKI'.[9] On the same day as the funeral, the CIA reported to Washington, that the army had taken the decision to 'implement plans to crush the PKI'.[10] Two days later, the failed coup plotters were labelled, the Gestapu – an acronym for 30 September Movement in Indonesian Bahasa – as if to provide a 'master slogan' for what was to follow and who was to be targeted.[11] PKI premises and support organizations in Jakarta were sacked and their leaders seized. Aidit himself evaded arrest for nearly two months but was executed shortly after capture without being tried.

3. The clean-up in Jakarta moved to central Java, the only area outside the capital where the original coup had been supported. There was also a strong Communist organization in these rural areas. Elite RPKAD commandos under General Sarwo Edhy headed for Semarang: their arrival sparked some futile strikes, which were quickly broken by Edhy's troops. Muslims now began to attack local PKI cadres, some of whom briefly retaliated. A wave of 'murder, torture, arson and revenge' swept across the plain of Klaten and up to the slopes of Mount Merapi with skirmishing around the Communist-held town of Solo.[12] Edhy's commandos drove into the countryside and shot all protestors including women and unarmed

villagers. Then, according to Edhy's own account, the commandos embarked on a full-scale clean-up. Aware that the area was too big and crowded for the troops to tackle effectively, he explains, 'we decided to encourage the anti-Communist civilians to help with the job. In Solo we gathered together the youth, the nationalist groups, the religious (Muslim) organizations. We gave them two or three days' training, then sent them out to kill the Communists.' Thus began, says John Hughes, Indonesia's 'post-coup blood bath'.[13]

4. As the signs of a new direction under the army in Jakarta, and reports of army-inspired action against the PKI and leftists multiplied, the violence spread to other parts of Indonesia. In some cases such as Pasuruan (East Java) and Aceh (Sumatra) the action was spontaneous.[14] Elsewhere local communities acted upon an informal licence to kill from the army. This was true across much of East Java where groups of anti-Communist youth, mostly belonging to the Ansor youth organization of the Muslim Teachers' party, were supported and armed by the army, but often acted autonomously. In Bali the killings began later, after the army initiated reprisals over the murder of a soldier in a clash with Communist youth. A mass movement then developed to the extent that Edhy is reported to have said: 'In Java we had to egg the people on to kill Communists. In Bali we have to restrain them, make sure they don't go too far.'[15] The Bali massacre was conducted 'with an intensity that was second only to what had happened in Aceh'.[16]

5. The biggest wave of killings had expired by the end of 1965 but took time to reach outlying areas. The island of Lombok suffered in early 1966 and West Kalimantan as late as October-November 1967.[17] In the district of Banywangi, on the eastern tip of Java, mass killings occurred from late November to late December 1965, on the anniversary of Gestapu, from 1 to 5 October 1966, and again, from May to December 1968.[18] There are some areas of Sumatra, Kalimantan, Sulawesi and Maluku, where little is known even today of the extent of the killings. Most of West Java was untouched, according to Cribb, because the local Siliwangi Division, having spent many years battling with a fundamentalist Muslim movement, would not allow local Muslim groups to take action.[19]

Anatomy of the Massacres

How did the massacres actually occur? In most contemporary historical cases which are known to us, a great deal of detail is accumulated. Survivors tell their stories; some of those who participated end up on trial; physical remains are disinterred by investigative commissions; and researchers gather together all the available information to provide an authoritative secondary source. None of these materials exist for the Indonesian massacres, except for a very small number of eye-witness accounts, gathered and circulated in secret and which throw light only on a few isolated incidents. No-one has ever been tried for participation in a mass killing: the only trials have been of those accused of complicity in the original Gestapu coup and the murders at the Halim airbase.

Only one investigative commission was ever set up. This was the fact-finding commission under Major-General Sumarno, appointed by President Sukarno, in December 1965, while the massacres were still in progress. According to one anonymous member (interviewed by the author in 1990), it found that the army had set the agenda wherever it went. Loyal citizens were brought forward to present petitions for banning the PKI, and the numbers of dead were grossly under-reported.

For instance, in Denpasar, capital of Bali, a senior commission member eventually smuggled himself out through the kitchen of the hotel where they were quartered, with the help of the *maître d'hôtel*. Late at night he met a policeman who was still loyal to Sukarno, who advised him that the real total of killings by that stage was not three thousand as the commission had been told, but thirty thousand. Similarly, in East Java, a military police chief confessed that the official toll of five thousand should be multiplied 'at least eight times'. On returning to Jakarta, the commission delivered its verdict to the world that seventy-eight thousand had died. Sukarno was secretly advised that the real figure must be four to six times higher. A similar tale about under-reporting was told by a commissioner to the journalist John Hughes, within a year of the events. He calculated that 'about ten times as many people were killed as we actually reported'.[20] The report of the commission was never published, nor did it go into the question of responsibility. An army survey by Kopkamtib (Suharto's Command for the Restoration of Security and Public Order), conducted in 1966, appears to have concluded that around one million people died. It too was never published.[21] Thirty years later, there had still been no proper enquiry or any other form of investigation. This protracted investigative hiatus can be compared to treatment of the Katyn massacre, where reliable evidence proving beyond doubt Soviet responsibility was only unearthed nearly fifty years later, following the collapse of the Soviet Union.

It is probable that persistent enquiry by the media, even long after the event, would still uncover eye-witnesses or participants prepared to reveal what they had seen – or done. The Indonesian media self-evidently has not been in a position to pursue such an enquiry. The mainstream Western media has taken no retrospective interest in the subject, even in years when it could be presented in the light of a significant anniversary (e.g. thirty years afterwards in 1995-6). On the twenty-fifth anniversary, a brief enquiry by this writer was – as far as he is aware – the only attempt of its kind in the British press.[22] A conference held in the run-up to this anniversary produced what remains the most substantial academic monograph on the subject though no more obviously accessible study has been published in book-form.[23] By contrast, other Asian massacres, such as My Lai and Tiananmen Square, have been the subject of numerous successful popular journalistic accounts.

Most of the research so far undertaken has focused on the events in Bali – notorious in folklore surrounding the massacre as scene of the most extreme and savage episodes of violence. In the only book on the subject, Geoffrey Robinson suggests that support in Bali for the abortive Gestapu coup came primarily from within the army. The subsequent aggressive campaign to punish the PKI can be understood as an attempt to deflect attention away from this awkward fact. Local military authorities claimed to uncover evidence that the PKI in Bali were planning to stage their own coup. There was an echo of the accusations made against 'Communist women' at the Halim airbase murder scene. Local members of the Bali chapter of the PKI-affiliated women's organization were said to have been instructed to sell themselves to soldiers and then murder and castrate them. The mass killing began in mid-November, after several weeks of official military action in which PKI-related people were arrested or intimidated, while possessions were stolen, houses burnt and women raped. In the first stage of the massacre, vigilante groups took to the streets and countryside, often with logistical support from the army in the form of trucks, weapons and intelligence.[24]

A glimpse into the next stage was gained by this writer who, on a brief two-day visit to Bali, in 1990, was able to contact one eyewitness who, though he did not admit his participation, gave a reluctant but revealing account. The informant identified a nearby well into which he claimed a hundred bodies had been thrown after the victims were lined up and killed with knives, apparently without resisting. He described a belief, unrecorded elsewhere, that those who were killed must not 'take the picture' of their slaughters to the other world. Consequently their eyes were daubed with whitewash. He claimed too that those committing the deed drank the blood of their victims, 'so that the spirits of the dead would not follow them for seven generations'.[25]

We also possess a remarkable document written for publication in the December 1967 issue of a Bandung student newspaper which reached galley-proof stage but was never published. The writer states that he 'in no way defends the Gestapu/PKI', but takes the view that their 'uncivilized and cruel methods of behaviour' should not have been used against them in retaliation. This is the main source for the assertion that pro-coup army officers encouraged the massacres in order to cover their own traces, and it claims that the main victims were not PKI members but those who were 'deceived by them'.[26] Whether or not the argument is sincere, or used to increase the chance of publication – if so, unsuccessfully – it points to the strong element of score-settling mentioned in many other accounts. There seems little doubt that previous disputes over land played a large part, particularly in Bali where tenancy campaigns had been pursued aggressively by Communist-backed peasant organizations. Kenneth Young also describes attempts to seize land in Kediri (East Java) where, during PKI-inspired land campaigns, in 1963-64, Muslim landlords were attacked by hundreds of peasants armed with sharpened bamboo spears and other crude weapons. It is hardly surprising that two years later the massacres were particularly intense in Kediri.[27]

The Bandung student newspaper's account also discusses another much-noticed phenomenon, suggested also in the eye-witness account quoted above – the passivity of those who went to their deaths:

> There was no resistance in Bali, no resistance of any importance. Those who admitted they were PKI or who were accused of being PKI gave themselves up voluntarily to the authorities. When the killings were being carried out, it often happened that people who had been arrested wanted to be killed because they knew that their days were numbered any way. They preferred to be killed because they were afraid of torture or other methods of mass murder which are totally unacceptable to normal human beings who say they believe in God.[28]

John Hughes gives a similar explanation for what he describes as, 'those eerie stories of party members in Bali donning white burial robes and marching calmly with their captors to execution'.[29] Other explanations have been given in terms of assumed social characteristics: resignation in the face of death, acting out of the appropriate part in a *wayang* shadow-puppet play, Javanese mysticism, etc. But as Young notes with reference to Kediri, 'the victims were mostly trapped in hopeless situations'. Many sought arrest hoping for relative safety but were frequently 'traded off' to vigilante groups for slaughter. The phenomenon of passivity in relation to Java or Bali has also been noted with regard to Jews in the Holocaust.[30]

Evidence of Killings

As with other massacres, the evidence for their commission can be divided into two categories: first, incidents which have been directly witnessed, and second, incidents recounted at second-hand or as hearsay. Not surprisingly, the detail in the first category of incidents is more specific and the numbers involved are more precise and usually smaller. The second category is more likely to recount stories of large numbers being massacred in a single incident, or of many thousands being murdered over a short period of time.

For evidence, particularly of the first kind from Indonesia, we rely on materials collected covertly and made available through the excellent British organization, 'Tapol' (the organization has taken its name from the common abbreviation for political prisoners – who are also probably the source for much of this material). Though the cases which are revealed cannot be regarded as a cross-section, they do reveal an interesting consistency. Most of them describe incidents where a mob of varying size pursues a small number of targeted individuals, who are then butchered often with extreme cruelty. They do not describe mass pogroms or military-type operations. The atmosphere is rather that of an excited witch-hunt or hunting-party. It is probable that such affairs are often led by a few activists with the majority tailing along out of curiosity, although perhaps becoming infected by the atmosphere of violence. (I make this suggestion on the basis of my own study of 'mob' violence during the Chinese Cultural Revolution, also in rural areas, which in several parts of one province involved cases of cannibalism.)[31] Some features of the Tapol reports are worth noting:

(a) In many cases the neighbouring villagers are not involved, having themselves fled or remaining silent out of fear.
(b) There may be a suggestion of vengeance on the part of one or more ringleaders for some previous assumed injury committed by the victim.
(c) There may be some social sanction against the murderer(s), or occasionally intervention by the police or army.

Here are some typical reports, slightly paraphrased from the original source:

1. (from Kediri) It was 3 p.m. and the village was quiet. Suddenly, many people (from the Ansor Muslim youth organization) were heard yelling, 'Allah Huakbar'. A crowd of people arrived at Pranggang village. These people then entered the home of Pak Legi (a peasant) and took him away. Pak Mulyo (another peasant) was

also there. Their hands were tied together with plastic cords. They were taken to a forest on the other side of the river Banjarjo. There they were butchered and their bodies were left on the bank of the river, behind Pak Kalim's orchard. At the time, the village was deserted. All the men had fled and were in hiding. After things quietened down and the gang had left, the villagers who knew the two dead men buried them behind Kalim's house.

2. (Kediri) Sumo Kemin (aged sixty, a peasant) was having a siesta in the early afternoon when, at about 2 p.m., a large crowd of people suddenly appeared at his home. Sumo Kemin's wife was astonished to see this happen: she soon realized that these people were part of an Ansor terrorist gang. In the village of Banjarjo where this incident happened, the villagers were all quiet at the time. Then at 3 o'clock that afternoon, in October 1965, without any questions being asked, Sumo Kemin was butchered, his stomach was cut open, his intestines disembowelled and he was left there, just like that. When she saw what had happened, his wife became hysterical: the neighbours arrived to take care of the body and bury him there on the spot.

3. (Kediri) Tuni, twenty-seven, a Pemuda Rakyat (PKI trade union) member, was taken away by an Ansor gang on 15 October 1965. The district of Kediri became known as a centre of mass murder in that year. The victims were PKI members or people thought to be in the PKI; in some cases, people were just settling old scores. This Pemuda Rakyat member, Tuni, who lived in Pranggang, was visited by a gang organized by the village head who took him to the village hall. Without any questions being asked, he was mercilessly tortured. Maksum, the village head, was in charge of this murder. After having been tortured, he was butchered like a lamb and his headless body was thrown onto a heap of bodies, twenty metres north of the Pranggang health centre. These days, Maksum, the village head, is nowhere to be seen.

4. (From Petemon, Surabaya) One morning in October 1965, a number of PKI members and sympathizers were assembled in the neighbourhood hall, by a group of about one hundred people armed with sickles and machetes, who had been dropped from outside. Then the assembled group of people were killed off quickly. It so happens that a policeman saw what was happening and quickly phoned his commanding officer; the officer said that he had no troops and told him to phone the Mobile Brigade (BriMob). Company D was on picket duty: two teams were sent from it under company commander, Pak Budi. After reaching the place where the killings were going on, the police immediately fired warning shots but the mob took no notice. The BriMob men then began to use their auto-

matic weapons and some of the murderers were shot dead; some of the survivors (from the mob) were captured while others fled.

Even less is known about killings of those taken prisoner and committed to gaol, in some cases many months or even years after the original period of massacre. The same sources have provided some further episodic memories. Murders on Buru island – the island in the Moluccas used from 1969 to 1978 as a large prison camp – were frequent. One case is reported from Ciku and dated 3 October 1973. The soldiers on guard duty were from South Sulawesi and known for their 'extreme bestiality'. Six tapols were said to have been executed, on grounds which are unknown, by soldiers who were ordered to place the barrels of their AK rifles close against the victims' bodies.

Another category of killings arises from the murder of prisoners who had not been sentenced but were being held in detention. The reason for them being taken out and disposed of is usually unclear, though sometimes it occurred when they were being transferred – perhaps into the jurisdiction of a harsher command, or as a pretext for their disposal. An incident on 7 July 1968, in Wonogiri, Central Java, is said to have resulted in the death of 111 tapols, carried out on the orders of the Surakarta Military Commander. 'They were shot one by one, then bayoneted and thrown into a grave.' One named victim was said to have been thrown in while still alive although shot several times. The only survivor was a rich Chinese businessman who bought his freedom on condition that he gave a house to the commander. In another incident, in Wonosari, near Jogjakarta, about forty tapols were summoned and told they were about to be released. They were then taken by an army unit to a place close to a *luweng* or deep well. 'Still alive, they were unloaded from the back of the truck like garbage and tipped into the *luweng*.'[32]

The source for the Wonogiri massacre is said to be a captain in the group which carried out the killings and gave the information after retirement. The source for the Wonosari incident is 'a comrade who was detained in the same camp as the victims and who almost suffered the same fate'. Clearly, such statements cannot be taken as necessarily accurate in detail or even outline. Their credibility depends largely on the way in which they fit in to a wider pattern of reporting. It would require close interrogation to establish how much depends on hearsay or second-hand knowledge. Even long after the event, forensic investigation of reported land-site graves would provide supporting evidence. The use of wells could also be investigated. Rivers and the sea feature in many accounts. There are suggestions that the perpetrators were not only trying to dispose of the evidence but to 'wash away' the crimes which they had committed.[33]

Foreign Involvement

However obscure or poorly reported the Indonesian massacres may have been, those foreign powers with a special interest in the matter (the U.S. and Britain in particular) were more aware than they claimed to be. A note written by a diplomat at the British embassy to his ambassador, unearthed thirty years later when some – but not all – of the archives were opened, is revealing:

> You – like me – may have been somewhat surprised to see estimates by the American embassy that well over a hundred thousand people have been killed in the troubles since 1 October. I am, however, readier to accept such figures after [receiving] some horrifying details of the purges that have been taking place ... The local army commander ... has a list of PKI members in five categories. He has been given orders to kill those in the first three categories. So far, some two thousand people have been killed in the environs ... A woman of seventy-eight ... was taken away one night by a village execution squad ... Half a dozen heads were neatly arranged on the parapet of a small bridge.[34]

The results of the Suharto-led counter-coup were hailed by the White House as 'the great bonus of 1965', leading to 'decisive changes that have permanently altered Indonesia's political face ... [deletion by US censor]. In any event, the PKI is dead in any recognizable form, and Sukarno is apparently doomed ...'[35] A year later a senior State Department official, Deputy Under-Secretary of State, Alexis Johnson, summed up U.S. satisfaction in what has become the classic quotation: 'The reversal of the Communist tide in the great country of Indonesia [is] an event that will probably rank along with the Vietnamese war as perhaps the most historic turning-point in Asia of this decade.'[36] His judgement on Indonesia – though not on Vietnam – was correct: the turning-point ushered in a pro-Western regime which has remained in place to this day.

It is also uncontested that both the U.S. and Britain acted promptly to express their sympathy and support for General Suharto's operation. In another famous quotation, the deputy chief of mission in Jakarta, Francis Galbraith, reported back to Washington that he had made it clear to a high-ranking Indonesian army office, 'that the embassy and the U.S. G[overnment] were generally sympathetic with and admiring of what the army was doing'. Research into declassified U.S. documents reveals, according to one careful study, 'no instance of any American official objecting to or in any way criticizing the 1965-66 killings'.[37] Britain also communicated its sympathy to the 'good generals', as they were described by its ambassador, Sir Andrew Gilchrist. Specifically, it was decided to let the generals know that

Britain (engaged at the time in Borneo against Indonesian armed 'confrontation' over the establishment of Malaysia) would not take advantage of the confusion in Jakarta. It was agreed that the Indonesian army should not be distracted from 'what we consider to be a necessary task'. Gilchrist thereupon sent a 'secret communication' to the generals through 'an American contact'.[38]

The question still waiting to be fully researched and documented is how far the U.S., and to a lesser extent Britain, went beyond approbation and encouragement to provide active, though covert support. The evidence is necessarily fragmentary because so much of the documentation remains out of reach. One researcher concluded, in 1990, that it was premature for any analyst to render final judgement on the CIA's role in the Suharto coup, or in other clandestine activities before or afterwards. 'Few documents relevant to CIA activities have yet been declassified and censors have been skilful in 'sanitizing' ostensibly declassified NSC [National Security Council] staff memoranda.'[39]

However in spite of these difficulties there is sufficient evidence to show that practical assistance, as well as 'moral' encouragement, was provided after the coup and counter-coup. Shortly after the initial events of 30 September, a U.S. official at the embassy, Robert Martens, was 'asked for help' by an aide to the pro-Western minister of trade, Adam Malik. He obliged with a list of several thousand names of Communists which he had carefully compiled. Interviewed in 1990, Mr Martens said that 'I probably have a lot of blood on my hands, but that's not all bad.' After this was reported Mr Martens protested that if he had made this comment, 'it could only have been as a wry remark'. Following these revelations, U.S. sources claimed that Mr Martens had worked entirely alone, without authorization from any senior officials. But Francis Galbraith has described Martens as 'a unique asset' who did 'an amazing job'. Indonesian generals do not deny that information was exchanged with the U.S., but claim with nationalistic pride that they did not need any U.S. data to 'obliterate the Communists': General Suharto was quite capable of doing the job well enough by himself![40]

It has also been well established that in November 1965 the generals asked for weapons and communications gear to arm the Muslim and nationalist gangs who were hampered by primitive equipment. The U.S. quickly promised such covert aid, labelled as 'medicines'. It was described by their ambassador in Jakarta as 'exemplif[ying the] kind of covert low visibility commo[dity] assistance we might be [in the] best position to provide that would have maximum immediate utility [for Indonesian] armed forces'. The ambassador explained that there were constraints upon opening a 'forward-looking dialogue' with the generals, principally because they were 'up to their neck in [the] struggle with [the] PKI'. However this 'hydra-headed adversary' was being attacked 'relentlessly ... and even ruthlessly'. The generals' next task, he concluded with optimism, would be to 'clean out the Augean stable' (i.e., dispose of President Sukarno) and then establish a 'more moderate, truly independent foreign policy course'.[41] The connection between U.S. covert means and strategic ends could not have been more clearly demonstrated. Because of the Borneo connection, the British were also involved in giving their approval to the U.S. supply of radio equipment and the ambiguously referred to 'medicines', to a value of nearly one million dollars. The U.S. had promised to consult Britain before doing anything to support the generals, and it is probable that London was well aware of the real significance of this aid.[42]

One more question remains buried even more deeply in the secret documentation and the disinterest which has surrounded the subject – except among a few determined scholars – over the past three decades. Was there any specific encouragement in advance to the generals to take action, or perhaps even some indirect incitement to the original authors of the failed coup? A termination of the Sukarno regime was in the clear interests of both the U.S. and Britain. A CIA memorandum of June 1962 claims that Prime Minister Harold Macmillan and President Kennedy had agreed in April 'to liquidate President Sukarno, depending on the situation and available opportunities'. It is not clear whether this refers to physical or political liquidation.[43] It was also well understood that, as U.S. Ambassador Jones put it in a pre-coup briefing, 'an unsuccessful coup attempt by the PKI might be the most effective development to start a reversal of political trends in Indonesia'.[44] It is hard to believe that the notion at least of provoking such a coup was not entertained by Western intelligence. Several operatives have hinted after the event that it was a brilliant stratagem, but this type of retrospective boasting should be handled with caution.

The last word – and many preceding sentences, pages and perhaps whole chapters – still have to be written on these external aspects of the Indonesian tragedy. Many more chapters and books remain unwritten on the actual events. These remain buried in what must be one of the biggest black holes of modern history. We must hope that with the long overdue fall of the regime which profited from it, the search for serious answers will at last begin.

Notes

1. Robert Cribb, ed., *The Indonesian Killings of 1965-1966: Studies from Java and Bali* (Melbourne, 1990). This is the only book-length study and is of enormous use both for its analysis (see especially the editor's introductory chapter) and as a source-book.
2. *Los Angeles Times*, 10 August 1996.
3. John McBeth, 'Red Menace', in *Far Eastern Economic Review*, 2 November 1996.
4. Cribb, ed., *The Indonesian Killings*, 16.
5. John Hughes, *The End of Sukarno* (London, 1968), 151-6.
6. Gabriel Kolko, *Confronting the Third World: US foreign policy 1945-1980* (New York, 1988), 178.
7. John Gittings, 'The Black Hole of Bali', *The Guardian*, 8-9 September 1990.
8. This myth is celebrated in the sculptured memorial at the site of the killing at Crocodile's Hole near Halim airbase outside Jakarta. In the central scene, the officers are bound and tipped head first down the well shaft – where their bodies were found – while the women clad in flimsy upper garments frolic in the foreground.
9. H. McDonald, *Suharto's Indonesia* (London, 1980), 50.
10. Kolko, *Confronting the Third World*, 180.
11. Carmel Budiardjo and S. L. Liem, 'The Reckoning with the PKI', unpublished MS, n.d., 60.
12. Budiardjo and Liem, 'The Reckoning', 62; Hughes, *End of Sukarno*, 147.
13. Hughes, *End of Sukarno*, 151.
14. Kenneth R. Young, 'Local and national influences in the violence of 1965', in Cribb, ed., *The Indonesian Killings*, 85.
15. Hughes, *End of Sukarno*, 181.
16. Harold Crouch, *The Army and Politics in Indonesia* (Ithaca, NY, 1978), 152.
17. Cribb, ed., *The Indonesian Killings*, 25.
18. *Tapol*, Bulletin no.15, April 1976, 3.
19. Cribb, ed., *The Indonesian Killings*, 25-6.
20. Hughes, *End of Sukarno*, 183.
21. Cribb, ed., *The Indonesian Killings*, 8.
22. Gittings, 'Black Hole of Bali'.
23. Cribb, ed., *The Indonesian Killings*.
24. Geoffrey Robinson, *The Dark Side of Paradise: Political Revolution in Bali* (Ithaca, NY, 1995), chap. 8, 'After the Coup'.
25. Gittings, 'Black Hole of Bali'.
26. Young, 'Local and National Influences', 82-5.
27. Ibid.
28. Robert Cribb, Soe Hok Gie et al., 'The mass killings in Bali', in Cribb, ed., *The Indonesian Killings*, 252-3.
29. Hughes, *End of Sukarno*, 191.
30. Young, 'Local and National Influences', 85.
31. John Gittings, *Real China: From Cannibalism to Karaoke* (London, 1996), chap. 8.
32. These accounts are translated in, 'Data on atrocities of the Suharto regime', translated by Carmel Budiardjo/Tapol, typescript, n.d. On Buru, see also, 'The Story of the Buru Forced Labour Camp', *Tapol*, no. 128, April 1995.
33. Gittings, 'Black Hole of Bali'.
34. Mark Curtis, 'Democratic Genocide', *The Ecologist*, 26, 5 (1996): 202-4.

35. Frederick Bunnell, 'American "Low Posture" Policy toward Indonesia in the Months Leading up to the 1965 "Coup"', *Indonesia* (Cornell Modern Indonesia Project), no. 50 (1990), 58.
36. Kolko, *Confronting the Third World*, 183.
37. Audrey R. Kahin and George McT. Kahin, *Subversion as Foreign Policy: The Secret Eisenhower and Dulles Debacle in Indonesia* (New York, 1995), 230.
38. Curtis, 'Democratic Genocide', 202-4.
39. Bunnell, 'American "Low Posture" Policy', 30.
40. Kathy Kadane, 'U.S. Officials' Lists Aided Indonesian Bloodbath in '60s', *Washington Post*, 21 May 1990; Robert Martens, letter, *Washington Post*, 2 June 1990; Gittings, 'Black Hole of Bali'.
41. U.S. ambassador, Jakarta, telegram of 6 November 1965, copy in Lyndon B. Johnson Library.
42. Curtis, 'Democratic Genocide', 202-4.
43. Mark Curtis, *The Ambiguities of Power: British Foreign Policy since 1945* (London, 1995), 217.
44. A. and G. Kahin, *Subversion as Foreign Policy*, 225.

CHAPTER 13

THE LEGACY OF MASSACRE

THE 'JASENOVAC MYTH' AND THE BREAKDOWN OF COMMUNIST YUGOSLAVIA

Robin Okey

The blood-lettings in Yugoslavia in the Second World War are among the most notorious of the twentieth century, their memory having been rekindled by the horrors of the 1990s. Together the two episodes open up a potentially vast field for Yugoslav genocide studies, to which this chapter makes only a strictly limited contribution. Its theme is not primarily the killings of 1941-45 themselves, but their legacy, the shadow they cast over ethnic, specifically Serb-Croat, relations in Communist Yugoslavia. The legacy of massacre in that society took various forms, nearly always paralleled elsewhere, but to a greater or lesser extent given a distinctive twist by Yugoslav history. Two particular problems will be broached below. First, what attempts were made to establish the number of victims in intercommunal killing and what difficulties did they encounter? Here the Croat *ustashi* camp of Jasenovac, which was to become a symbol for Serbs of their self-perceived national martyrdom, deserves particular attention.[1] Second, how and why did the question of victim numbers and especially Jasenovac numbers become central to the career of the energetic Croatian historian, Franjo Tudjman, and thereby feed into the growing feud which poisoned relations between Serb and Croat intellectuals well before 1991, in a society ostensibly committed to Communist ideals of 'brotherhood and unity'? More speculatively, a final section will ask if it is possible to locate the roots of the predilection for violence in the west Balkans in a definable historical context. The orientation of the chapter towards Serb-Croat relations, and events in the war-time Croatian State, explains the limited reference to other groups involved in massacre and genocide in war-time Yugoslavia: the Jews of Croatia and Serbia, Gypsies, Albanians and Muslim Slavs.

The immediate background to the Yugoslav civil war of 1941-45 was the collapse of the State created in 1918.[2] Though initially largely supported by Croat bourgeois politicians on the basis of the common language, Yugoslavia deprived these politicians of the limited autonomy they had enjoyed under Hungary. Nor was the new State ever popular with the newly enfranchised Croatian masses, whose Croatian Peasant Party was suspected of separatism by the Serb-dominated regime. The CPP leader Vlatko Maček entered the government in 1939 on the basis of a Serb-Croat compromise (the *Sporazum*) but mutual reservations continued. Maček was critical of the *coup d'état* which overthrew the Serb signatory of the *Sporazum* in late March 1941 and provoked Hitler into attack. Withdrawing to Zagreb, as Yugoslav resistance collapsed, he called on his people not to resist the Nazi-imposed new order while declining a leadership role in it himself.

The so-called Independent State of Croatia (NDH), created under German aegis, was entrusted to Ante Pavelić's far right nationalist *ustashi* movement. This, having been granted Bosnia-Herzegovina by the Germans in accordance with its ideological claims, found upwards of two million Serbs and a million Muslims on its hands out of a total population of six million. The *ustashi* instincts in response to this challenge were reflected in an early statement by one of Pavelić's closest collaborators: 'there is no method that we would hesitate to use in order to make [this country] truly Croatian and cleanse it of Serbs'.[3] Mass arrests of Serbs were ordered, the first massacre of Serbs occurred on 29 April and in August the concentration camps which had sprung into existence were put under Unit II of the *ustashi* security force, the UNS, in the charge of a long-standing Pavelić crony, Vjekoslav (Max) Luburić. Immediately, Luburić set out about building a major camp complex in Jasenovac in western Slavonia, which became one of some seventy-four concentration and collection camps to exist in Yugoslavia in the Second World War. Camp personnel members believed, as they testified later, that Luburić had had instructions for the extermination of the Serbs from Pavelić himself. Faced with German complaints about Luburić's methods, Pavelić appears to have commented that he was worth more to him than a hundred university professors.[4]

Officially Jasenovac, which was made up of several units, was known as a 'collection and work camp'. Brutal conditions obtained.

'Transports' brought two kinds of prisoner: those without a 'decision' (*odluka*) were immediately taken to their deaths without any formal registration. Those with an *odluka*, nominally for from six months' to three years' detention, were either also killed at once if physically weak, or put to work. The frequency and average size of transports is, however, unclear. Another source of killing was the practice of culling the inmates when their number exceeded three thousand. Luburić himself is reported to have always carried out at least one killing on his visits to Jasenovac and it is clear he set up his nonchalant sadism as a model. Death was by shooting, bludgeoning with a mallet or slitting the throat, and bodies were burned in a specially prepared oven or, from 1944, thrown into the river Sava. Jasenovac, heavily defended, was (somewhat controversially) never seriously attacked and attempts to escape from it led to heavy loss of life, as late as March 1945.[5]

Naturally, there was sharp resistance to the horrors of which Jasenovac was part – 1,013 execution sites are claimed for Bosnia alone.[6] Serbs took to the woods and mountains, joining the chetnik movement for a monarchist, Serb-dominated Yugoslavia, or the Communist-led partisans. The latter predominated among the Serb minority in Croatia, the former in Herzegovina and east Bosnia. In eastern Bosnia, scene of recent ethnic cleansing, Serbs fell murderously upon Muslims, whom the *ustashi* authorities had declared 'flowers of the Croatian people'. For their part, partisan reprisals reached a climax at the end of the war, when tens of thousands of *ustashi*, chetniks as well as Slovene and Croat non-Communists were handed over to them by the British at Bleiburg, mainly to be killed. In short, the war saw a bewildering pattern of mutual massacre: between *ustashi* and chetniks, chetniks and partisans, Serbs and Muslims, partisans and *ustashi*, not to speak of the genocide of Serbian and Croatian Jews, Serb victims at Magyar hands and the Serb-Albanian imbroglio. The ironic result of these horrors was to help the Communists to power on the slogan of 'brotherhood and unity', but in a longer term they provided a rich quarry of evidence from which opponents, or rival interpreters of that brotherhood could mine.

The Numbers' Game. How Many Victims?

The dimensions of internecine slaughter were a matter of comment and controversy from the start; by Serb escapees to the rump Serbian puppet government in Belgrade, confidants of the Yugoslav government in exile in London, German occupation personnel, Catholic priests and partisans. Figures varied from 200,000 to

700,000, when overall totals were ventured, to talk of 'tens of thousands' in more general comment. Guesswork as such figures appear to have been, they were to be plentifully plundered by postwar polemicists. The real beginnings of organized inquiry came with the State Commission to Investigate the Crimes of the Occupiers and their Assistants, launched by the partisans on the basis of a decision of their quasi-governmental organ AVNOJ in autumn 1943. Yet the difficulties facing the Commission were immense. Leaving aside the invidiousness of such investigations in a wartime society split several ways, the staffs of the National Liberation Army that were entrusted with them were plainly not equipped for the task. When the war was won, progress continued to be frustrated by the paucity of the *ustashi* records. A meeting of 1946, recognizing the weaknesses of work done to that point, ordered the creation of district and local commissions in addition to the existing bodies in each republic. But only three quarters of the district and one sixth of the local commissions came into being before the entire project was wound up in 1948, with a final statement that the absolute number of victims had not been ascertained.

Commission materials were decentralized and remain uncatalogued and unavailable for research, though a number of reports appeared at the time.[7] Thus, the report of the Commission for Croatia of 15 November 1945 estimated that five to six hundred thousand persons perished in Jasenovac and listed sixty-two eye-witnesses of the camp, who spoke of groups of victims varying from twenty-five to seven to eight thousand in size. There were also references to 'daily' burials of two to three hundred from December 1941 and to a lull in 1943 and the first half of 1944. Otherwise, no indication was given as to how the overall figure might have been arrived at.[8] However, this figure was included in Yugoslavia's submission to the Nuremberg War Crimes Tribunal and another of 1,706,000 appeared in Yugoslavia's report to the international reparations conference in Paris in December 1945. It is suspiciously close to the 1,700,000 quoted by the Federal Statistical Office when asked, at short notice, to provide a figure for presentation to the Paris Peace Conference in 1947. As the statistician concerned recalled in 1986, this was meant to represent the demographic loss to Yugoslavia as a result of the war, including thereby not just actual casualties (only partisans were included here), but also the short-fall in births caused by wartime conditions. The Tito regime, however, presented it as the official figure of physical victims, a status it kept thereafter.[9] This was the first of several inconsistencies in Communist Yugoslavia's treatment of the problem.

The matter was next taken up in 1950 by SUBNOR, the League to Commemorate the Fighters of the National Liberation War. The results of its enquiry do not seem to have been collated generally and were never published – 'for reasons beyond our comprehension', in a recent Serb view. They were unavailable in the Croatian office of SUBNOR in 1988 but are kept locally and, therefore, have been used subsequently for local studies.[10] Some estimates of 'demographic losses' were, however, published by statisticians in Yugoslavia and elsewhere in the 1950s, which varied from 1,690,000 to 2,850,000 according to the technique adopted to assess the short-fall in wartime natality.[11] In addition, biographies of wartime camp and prison inmates were compiled by SUBNOR in this period. Some of these were published, including a volume on Jasenovac.

Not until 1964 was another major survey undertaken, on government behest, to provide a basis for reparations negotiations with West Germany. Again, the outcome was declared to be for internal use, though the Croatian figures were revealed to Franjo Tudjman, with consequences described below. Croats argue that non-publication was because the census did not bear out official claims; Serbs cavill that no enquiry was held on the methodological errors which produced what they, sometimes understandably, see as delusory results.[12]

The government initiative of 1964 was sparked by an external factor, the possibility of compensation, and had no successor. But from the early 1960s there was increased grass-roots pressure from veteran groups in adjoining parts of Bosnia. Tito met a deputation in 1961, agreed to a memorial at Jasenovac, but warned against 'lamentation'. A memorial garden and museum eventually appeared in1966-68. A Bosnian group dig at three of 120 grave sites, apparently only lasting a day, extrapolated on the basis of skulls per square metre a total of 550,840 victims. Lengthier and more scholarly excavations in 1964 and 1965, in which Slovene archaeologists but no Croats were prominent, produced a few hundred skulls and criticized the idea of a uniform skull count per metre. Further research proposals were made in 1969 (in which the author stressed the bad effect on public opinion of 'malevolent' writings which downgraded the number of Jasenovac victims), and again in 1977 by the War Victims' Association which proposed a publishing programme on the anti-fascist struggle in the wartime camps, especially at Jasenovac. Work began in 1982 and the first fruits, a multivolume documentary collection on Jasenovac, appeared in 1986.[13] Local studies proliferated. In a 1989 statistical analysis, twenty-one of the forty-nine Croatian local studies consulted dated from 1985 or after, while only seven predated 1975. More strikingly, all but three of the seventeen Bosnian sources were published in the 1980s.[14]

The 1989 analysis, by a seventy-seven year old Croat and long-term UN official, Vladimir Žerjavić, was one of the two first full-length studies of Yugoslav war losses to make a belated appearance. The other was published in 1985 by a sixty-three-year old Bosnian Serb emigré lawyer, Bogoljub Kočović, who had retrained as an economist and statistician. Kočović's introduction stated that after forty years the time for an objective study had come. He estimated nearly two million 'demographic losses' and 1,014,000 'real losses,' with Montenegrins suffering most at 10.4 percent of their population, Serbs following at 6.9 percent, just ahead of Muslims at 6.8 percent and Croats at 5.4 percent. Obviously, the percentages for Bosnian and Croatian Serbs were much higher (16.7 percent and 17.4 percent respectively), but overall their losses in the two provinces, totalling 334,000, were less than half the figure traditionally accepted by Serbs for Jasenovac alone, which Kočović also ridiculed.[15] In view of this objectivity, two of Kočović's interpolations interestingly show how the war crimes issue had already become associated with political scenarios of national strife: after the events in NDH, he wrote, Serbs would have not only a right but a duty to seek modification of the Croatian frontier should Yugoslavia break up; and Bosnian Muslims should remember that only a Serb-Muslim alliance – not a Muslim-Croat one – could prevent the partition of Bosnia at their expense.[16]

Žerjavić's study used similar demographic techniques but sought to provide a cross-check by utilizing the increasingly abundant local studies. It carried a foreword by the Chief Rabbi of Zagreb, a member of the editorial board. 'It is time for us to become a normal country', he urged. 'We must leave the victims, dead almost half a century, to history, demography, victimology and other disciplines.'[17] The overall figure Žerjavić arrived at – 1,027,000 real losses – tallied very closely with those of Kočović. Republican and ethnic breakdowns diverged slightly, but chiefly in their suggestion that the Serb Kočović had underestimated the number of fellow Serb victims and overestimated those of Croats.[18] It was ironic that this first dispassionate study to combine demographic and local historical sources should have appeared at a time when Serbs and Croats were less likely than ever to accept it. How, then, is one to account for the curious situation in which comprehensive treatment of the massacres came so long after the event yet combined with a rise of intransigent prejudice leading to overt politicization of the war crimes issue? Before this latter issue is examined, two general points may be made on the basis of what has been said so far.

Firstly, far from being unique, many aspects of the Yugoslav pattern of response to wartime massacres were replicated elsewhere; in Holocaust studies, which really took off only from the 1970s, and also in the case of German response to its losses in the post-war expulsions from eastern Europe. In this latter case, initial enquiries in the early years after the war, combined with the non-publication of official records, created a received wisdom on the number of victims which only belated academic study challenged as being at least twice as high as the actual losses incurred.[19] Moreover, practical considerations – the need for the post-war generation to get on with building the new Israel, Yugoslavia or Bundesrepublik – as well as psychological ones – a desire to blot out past horrors, the invidious Nazi heritage, or in the Jewish case, the pain of supposed passivity in the face of the Holocaust – hampered serious scholarly examination.

In Communist Yugoslavia, political constraints were especially strong. Its emphasis on multinational 'brotherhood' could be strained by too much picking over old sores in a state where murderers and victims might live side by side. Hence the official party line on the crimes of the 'occupiers', *ustashi* and chetniks being merely designated as their 'assistants'.[20] Indeed, Tito, himself a Croat, was posthumously accused, even by Communists, of allowing his Croatian Communist associates to deceive him into playing down the significance of Jasenovac, which he never visited.[21] In keeping with his distinctive blend of flexible authoritarianism, once the State had endorsed the figures of one million, seven hundred thousand war victims overall, and five to six hundred thousand (sometimes seven hundred thousand) for Jasenovac, historians might omit these figures if they chose but not change or debate them. The gate to interpretation was closed. However, from the 1970s these restrictions became doubly irksome, partly because, as elsewhere, the ageing generation which had survived felt increasingly compelled to transmit its experience to a rising generation that knew little of it, partly because Yugoslavs were less willing to accept Communist tutelage.

These socio-psychological-political factors no doubt played the major role in the failure to come up with a full, objective study of Yugoslav war losses for forty years. But neither, secondly, should the sheer technical difficulties in the way be overlooked. Direct calculation of war victim numbers was inhibited by the lack of Germanic thoroughness in the perpetrators' documentation, and the incomplete, scattered and uncatalogued nature of the data collected in the war's aftermath. Hence the preference in later enquiries for the indirect method based on the notion of 'demographic loss', whereby the actual population recorded in the 1948 census was compared with what it should have been if war had not intervened. Taking away other reasons for a short-fall (such as emigration), one was supposedly left with a residue of violent death. Plainly, this approach bristles with difficulties. On the one hand, calculation of the pre-war birth rate trend and the impact of the post-1918 baby boom on wartime natality, had to be offset with an appropriate deduction for wartime trauma. On the other, statisticians had to grapple with international and internal migration flows, interethnic assimilation rates, international and regional border changes, and changes in census categories, and all this in relation to each of Yugoslavia's many ethnic groups, region by region. Muslims, for example, were treated differently in all censuses from 1931 to 1971, while the 1931 census did not give any internal nationality breakdown among 'Yugoslavs' at all.

Thus, while both Kočović and Žerjavić tackled all these issues with thoroughness and relative transparency, the very complexity of their multifaceted analysis made it easy for critics to dismiss their results as 'manipulation', or alternatively (given the sheer number of different categories of figures), for their numbers which related to one category to be misapplied to another.[22] The transposition of a statistician's demographic loss into a 'real loss' figure in 1947 has already been mentioned. But real loss of population could include loss by emigration, thus to be distinguished from actual wartime deaths, while loss in armed struggle is also distinguishable from unarmed non-combatant victims. Misapplied, figures for these war victims, might be utilized to mean partisans only (as was intended with the one million, seven hundred thousand figure of 1947), or it might include their Yugoslav enemies or, again, it might be applied by those Serbs who tend to identify the totality of war victims with themselves, ignoring the presence of Jews, Gypsies and Croat anti-fascists. Moreover, because Jasenovac has become the symbol of anti-fascist suffering, some Serbs have further confused numbers of camp victims with victims in Jasenovac alone; in fact, as Žerjavić has shown, more people were done to death in situ than in the camps.[23]

Fixation on particular figures, without a grasp of the different categories involved, has had the effect of making academic estimates seem much more out of line with popular perceptions than they need be, thereby creating unbridgeable psychological barriers in the process. In particular, Kočović and Žerjavić's figure of fifty thousand Jasenovac victims not only seems unconscionably low to Serbs who have come to identify Jasenovac with their whole wartime purgatory, but also to fly in the face of their received, 'totemic' wisdom – which only a 'fascist' could challenge – that seven hundred thousand people died there. In fact, Kočović's figure of 334,000 Serbs dead in Croatia and Bosnia and Žerjavić's half a million for those murdered inside and outside the camps, are not much different from what German observers were stating at the time, in passages which war crimes 'maximizers' willingly quote. We are, thus, dealing here with a displacement of concepts which initially may have been due to the sheer complexity of victim categories but which, in the heat of ethnic contestation, has become a wilful irrationality.

The Politicization of War Crimes becomes Overt: Franjo Tudjman and the 'Jasenovac Myth'

What is intriguing about this Yugoslav experience is the way this ethnic contestation arose in an authoritarian state committed to preventing it. This could hardly have happened, certainly earlier on, if the divisions had not had a place at the heart of the Communist establishment itself. The career of Franjo Tudjman, long a member of that establishment, is striking illustration of the process.

Tudjman was born, in 1922, in the same Zagorje region of Croatia as Tito, into a pro-Maček family which switched sides to the partisans, his brother and father being victims of civil war.[24] At thirty-five he became the youngest general in the Yugoslav National Army (JNA) while working in the Military History Institute in Zagreb, specializing in the Second World War. His first major work was a lengthy study of partisan warfare through the ages, *War against War*, whose subtext involved the defence of this kind of warfare against what he thought were centralizing perspectives stressing the regular army aspect of the Yugoslav partisan struggle. Tudjman's thesis became incorporated into the Communist Party programme in 1958, and influenced the reorganization of the JNA in 1959. But gradually the national dimension became unmistakable. Tudjman's rewrite of the topic for the Yugoslav military encyclopedia prepared in Belgrade, and judged unsuitable by the Zagreb Institute, aroused long drawn-out debate – 'you and your Croatia!', as an adjudicating general chided him – before being sent to Tito who passed it with a laconic, 'no comments'.

A bigger row broke out in 1963, when a survey of Yugoslav communism prepared without Croatian input seemed so distorted to Tudjman, now out of the army and founding head of a Croatian institute for the history of the working class movement, that the Croatian Party Central Committee was drawn in. When the meeting came, the Croatian Communist chief, Vladimir Bakarić, delivered a statement condemning the institute for 'bourgeois nationalism'. However, for the first time in twenty years, the Central Committee did not back him in the subsequent discussion. The Second World War was too hot a theme for control even at the highest level. Only this can explain how books – by Tudjman and his former Military Institute director Velimir Terzić – were published which, within a framework of formal Communist orthodoxy, presented provocatively different interpretations of these crucial events. True, the two books were at one in ritually condemning pre-war Great Serbian hegemonism, Maček, chetniks and *ustashi* and upholding the Communists' federal programme. But while Terzić went on to present an essentially sound pre-war Yugoslav state undermined by Croatian separatism, in which Maček's CPP was linked to both *ustashi* and Axis powers,[25] Tudjman, by contrast, depicted an untenable interwar regime of 'lawlessness, terror and violence', and saw the Belgrade *coup d'état* of 27 March 1941 – object of patriotic pride to Serbs – as directed as much against the government's 1939 compromise with the Croats as its pro-German course.[26]

Events now flowed thick and fast. The Academy of Sciences in Zagreb was forced to drop Tudjman's nomination for membership at the last minute because of a phone-call from Belgrade. Tudjman also had to give up plans for an international conference on Marxism and the national question. It was in this period and, in Tudjman's words, by a wholly logical progression that he became embroiled in the issue of war victims and Jasenovac.[27] He succeeded in getting hold of the figure for total concentration camp victims in Croatia from the confidential 1964 census on war losses. At 51,000, these confirmed his long-standing belief that the conventional figures were grossly exaggerated. The matter was particularly germane because of Serbian pressure for the twenty-fifth anniversary celebration of the start of the national liberation movement to be held in Jasenovac. Tudjman opposed the celebration as divisive. 'On Jasenovac you are right', a high official of the Croatian Central Committee told him, 'but for political reasons we can't support you.'[28] In the event, there was no celebration at Jasenovac, and in 1966 the Minister of the Interior, Aleksandar Ranković, identified with the Serb faction in the party, was purged. It seems likely that the persecution of signatories of a petition for the rights of the Croatian language the following year was a *quid pro quo* in the Titoist regime's constant search for the appearance of ethnic evenhandedness. Tudjman lost his post and was expelled from the party, even though he had not signed the petition. In 1972, after the suppression of the Croatian 'mass popular movement' for greater autonomy, which Croatian Communist leaders had backed, Tudjman received a ten months' prison sentence. He believes that then, and in the mid-1960s, Tito protected him from harsher treatment.[29]

Why did Tudjman become so concerned about the exaggeration of what he dubbed the 'Jasenovac myth'? It exemplified what he took from Belgrade historiography to be the subtext of the Serbs' view of the Croats, namely that they were a fascistoid and genocidal people who had brought Yugoslavia down in April 1941, and even whose Communists could not be trusted. He believed it to be a convenient device in the Communist authorities' strategy for keeping Croats on the leash and a main plank of Serb nationalism's bid for power after Tito's death. There was some truth in both surmises. Communist Yugoslavia operated on the principle of ethnic balance. It condemned equally unitarism and separatism (code for Serb and Croat nationalism respectively), reprobated equally *ustashi* and chetniks. But Serbs increasingly felt that the pendulum was swinging too much against them, particularly following the 1974 constitution which consolidated confederal elements in the Yugoslav polity, while virtually depriving Serbia of any control over its Albanian-majority province of Kosovo. 'The equality of [all constituent parts of Yugoslavia] cannot be realized under conditions of inequality for the Serbs', wrote a Serb leader, in 1977.[30] In the Serb view the other nationalities were ganging up to make unitarism the greatest crime, harping on Great Serbianism between the wars as a pretext for splitting up Serbs in the present. And all this when the Serbs saw themselves as more sinned against than sinning, the martyr people of the Second World War, and of Jasenovac.

It was Tudjman's controversial writings about Jasenovac in the foreign press, and in a military encyclopaedia which put its victims merely in the tens of thousands, which basically led, not only to its withdrawal from sale, but to Tudjman's three-year prison sentence in 1981. As the Yugoslav economy crumbled after Tito's death in 1980, the debate as to solutions – further decentralization or recentralization – focused an increasingly disenchanted public ever more on national themes. The intellectual context was one of collapsing Marxist ideals. Tudjman himself records that he had already come to think in the sixties that class approaches obfuscated rather than clarified the national question, even though these had been central to his original embrace of Tito's Marxist federalism.[31] By the 1980s, cynicism had become widespread and 'self-managing socialism' and the nationality arrangements bound up with it were similarly discredited. Repelled by 'the kind of declarative-repetitive discussions on nationalism which have exhausted themselves before our eyes', as one observer put it in 1982, Yugoslavs were increasingly fascinated with subjective issues of national consciousness and its associated symbols, values and past.[32]

In Serb-Croat polemic in the 1980s the Second World War thus provided a magnetic point of attraction, with the killings and Jasenovac at their heart. The flood gates really opened with Veselin Djuretić's pro-chetnik *The Allies and the Yugoslav War Drama*, published in 1985. The style was deliberately opaque, the implications nonetheless plain. Communist Yugoslavia, Djuretić argued,

had pursued an artifical policy of national parity in its treatment of
the war. The prioritizing of social themes had made it appear as if
the partisans had been opposed by equally 'reactionary' Serb and
Croat nationalists in the guise of chetniks and *ustashi*. But this was
to make central what at the time had been marginal and to overlook
the true motives underlying conduct: genocide on the *ustashi*'s part,
self-preservation for the chetniks. Attempts to equate different positions inevitably led to relativism, which invited further manipulation
and led to the destruction of the community it was intended to preserve. It was better honestly to illuminate past contradictions in the
hope of initiating what Djuretić memorably called 'constructive
social negations'.[33] His book electrified Serb public opinion while
drawing the ire of the authorities.

This was also the fate of an article in 1986 on the historical roots
of *ustashi* genocide by a leading Serb historian. Vasilj Krestić traced
the genocidal idea back to the doctrine of 'Croatian state right' as
developed under the Dual Monarchy, whereby all inhabitants of
Croatia were deemed to belong to one (Croat) 'political nation', the
existence of Serbs as a separate national-political entity within
Croatia being denied. Krestić wavered unconvincingly between formal statements that only a small minority of Croats were
atavistically genocidal and an implication that the roots of genocide
went wider.[34] This sort of ambiguity made the old partisan, and Tito
biographer, Vladimir Dedijer's lengthy 1987 attack on the *ustashi*
links of the catholic church in NDH all the more significant, as it
inevitably also spread the blame more generally.[35]

Meanwhile, a three-volume documentary work on Jasenovac by
Antun Miletić appeared, and the *ustashi* State's interior minister
Andrija Artuković was finally extradited from the United States.[36]
Yet the handling of his trial in Zagreb by the Croatian authorities
only further inflamed Serb resentments. Charges that the prosecution
had been deliberately feeble were furiously compounded by a post-
ponement in carrying out the death sentence giving Artuković time
to die naturally.[37] Miletić's documentation – and that published on
Artuković – proved to be a rag-bag of scrappy material, including
name lists retrieved for individual transports, but providing no basis
for calculation of overall victim numbers. On this latter score, earlier
estimates were simply repeated. Expectation that the Miletić work
would produce the smoking gun were therefore not borne out.
Soberer heads commented bleakly that a final synthesis would have
to be based on examination of interlinked situations.[38] Dedijer, an
emotional man caught between strong partisan prejudices and the
self-image of Communist objectivity, in his last work gave arguments
against Serb nationalist exaggerations strong enough to undermine

the six to seven hundred thousand 'middle' position, but did not draw these conclusions himself.[39] It seems most of the urgent calls of these last years for research sprang more from the wish to keep the issue on the boil and expose previous foot-dragging than to accept the inference of any findings. Passions ruled.

So long as the Communist regime lasted, even the dispute about wartime massacres was prevented from becoming a purely intra-ethnic affair. Miletić, the Jasenovac chronicler, was a Croat Communist and in 1989 the Croat Communist leader, Stipe Šuvar, was still saying that hundreds of thousands of Serbs, Jews, and Romany had perished there. Moreover, it was a Croat, the head of the Jasenovac Memorial Grounds Council, Dr. Ante Milković, who put the partisan position most starkly, arguing that the figure of seven hundred thousand victims was 'an integral part of the national liberation struggle and Yugoslav peoples' resistance.'[40] Of course, the highly charged atmosphere of late 1980s Yugoslavia was the product of more than Serb-Croat historical polemic, the major thrust of resurgent Serb nationalism at this time being directed against the Albanian majority in Kosovo, a theme taken up intellectually in the notorious Memorandum of the Serbian Academy of 1986, and politically by Slobodan Milošević.[41]

All this said, the Albanian issue was essentially a catalyst operating to propel the two major Yugoslav nations into ever greater mutual distrust. The nationalist-orientated Croatian Democratic Union (HDZ), with Franjo Tudjman as its leader, having won the April 1990 elections in Croatia, immediately carried out symbolic acts which showed how large the wartime issue loomed in its thinking, including the renaming of the Square of Victims of Fascism the Square of Croatian Heroes, and of a school commemorating wartime child victims after an *ustashi* activist. Such acts intensified the will of the Croatian Serb minority to defy Tudjman's regime and leant wing to Milošević's Greater Serbian strategy, besides, of course, helping Serb propagandists to lift the 'Jasenovac myth' to new heights. Meanwhile, Tudjman not only successively scaled down his own Jasenovac estimates to just twenty thousand victims, but also, against all the evidence, continued to affirm that among them Croat anti-fascists were as well represented as Serbs.[42]

The chief of the official Serb propagandists was Milan Bulajić, who in 1988 had written a book on the Artuković affair. Bulajić was a Montenegrin who had been a child when his father's generation, as he saw it, failed to recognize the *ustashi*'s genocidal intent, on the eve of 1941. Bulajić presented himself as one who had been galvanized by the pro-Artuković slogans of the 1980s to ensure that the same mistake should not recur.[43] It is not an implausible personal scenario. Notoriously, many hard-line Serb leaders like the JNA chief-of-staff in the later conflict, General Blagoje Adžić, had had their families decimated by *ustashi* violence in the Second World War. Bulajić was a polemicist, Adžić a man of the gun, but their core motivation was shared by a figure like Tudjman's former colleague in the Institute of Military History, Jefto Šašić, whose Marxist rationality Tudjman had greatly respected. This was the conviction that the terrible past should not be forgotten but held as a lesson before today's generation, for its victims were 'the basis of our country's freedom'.[44] By contrast, Tudjman's campaign against the 'Jasenovac myth' had been based on the equally passionate belief that Yugoslav society could not and should not be based on memories which he found negative and nationally demeaning. Thus, just as the Yugoslav case offers a particularly complicated example of the problems involved in calculating the scale of massacre and violent death, so it shows in an acute form the dilemma facing a post-trauma society. In what circumstances and to what extent will the commemoration of such terrible events strengthen, or weaken, the society that issues from them?

The Roots of Genocide in Yugoslavia: Some Speculations

The recurrence of massacre and genocide in the Yugoslavia of the 1990s has increased speculation about the possible triggers involved in this embattled part of the world. Early in the crisis journalists wrote much about the malign heritage of communism; later attention tended to switch to the alleged ancient hatreds of the Balkan peoples. Such widely touted perspectives need to be examined. But can the roots of genocide be located in a more specific context than in either of these generalized theses? This final section offers a necessarily tentative answer.

Plainly there were many ways in which the authoritarian Communist system contributed to the malaise it feared. The limits on free discussion of sensitive issues led to suspicions and resentments festering beneath the surface. Yet while Serbs, in particular, were to claim that Jasenovac had become a taboo subject, about which the terrible truth could not be told, the reality was rather that discussion was not open to unsupported individuals but only to those who had institutional backing. The political structures of communism constrained individuals to band together to seek protection for whatever project they had at heart. In a multi-ethnic federation this became almost an open invitation for group mobilization to take place along ethnic lines, which, on a subject as emotive as that of wartime suffering and guilt, the Communist party proved increasingly unable to prevent. Tudjman's whole party career bears testimony to this. Moreover, the federalist structures of the State meant that the trial of Artuković, which was intended to appease the Serbs, was conducted in Zagreb by the very Croatian authorities Serbs were ceasing to trust. The old Stalinist habit, whereby there was a true line flanked by heresies to right and left, also enabled regime supporters to condemn with apparent even-handedness 'fascistoid apologists' who put the Jasenovac victims at only fifty thousand, and 'Serbian extremists' who put them at a million or more. But this exercise increasingly exasperated all sides. Indeed, it came to exemplify the gap between Marxist orthodoxy and private belief, arousing disgust at what was felt to be the artificiality of the whole system. Gut nationalism hereby received its relegitimization as somehow more truly authentic. The political culture of communism played a big role in the final débacle of the dream of brotherhood and unity.

Yet in judging how great that role was it should be borne in mind that the same exaggerations and failures of empathy had already occurred in massacre theme polemics during the Second World War itself. A seemingly arbitrary figure of one hundred and eighty thousand Serb victims, given in the Serbian Orthodox Church's August 1941 memorandum on the initial slaughter – a Croat commentary noted that the estimates given for specified incidents suggested some twenty-nine thousand victims – was raised to over three hundred thousand in transmission to the exiled Yugoslav government in October, on the grounds that more time had passed. Subsequently, it was circulated, in America, as three hundred and sixty thousand.[45] Attempts were made to involve all Croats, including those in the exiled Yugoslav government, in the ignominy of fascist misdeeds. On the other hand, Croat representatives in that same government haughtily rejected the idea of any expression of Croatian remorse for what was being done in Croatia's name and continued to rehearse their constitutional grievances.[46] In other words, it would seem that communism operated to freeze confrontational styles pre-dating it, which were born of an irreconcilable Serb-Croat antagonism.

This, indeed, would seem to be Tudjman's own interpretation in his rambling work, *Wastelands of Historical Reality*. Much of this book is taken up with accounts of and philosophers' reflections upon violence; from Cain and the Israelites in Canaan, to pogroms and the Holocaust. The upshot for Tudjman is a view of history (vouched for, as he sees it, already in the great religions) as a constant cycle of conquest begetting further wars and in which the urge to vengeance by the oppressed yields both creative and destructive impulses indissolubly linked in the human condition, despite all injunctions to the

contrary. Only an acceptance of man's inability to change his circumstances through utopian ideologies (which merely make things
worse) offers a faint hope of future escape from the cycle.

The universal and age-old hatred for the Jews, which Tudjman
obsessively alleges, presumably relates to his version of Hegelian-
ism, in which the historical struggle of opposites in terms of (nation)
states makes the Jew the eternal and unassimilable outsider.[47]
Clearly one of the book's subtexts is the relativization of *ustashi*
wartime massacres, Tudjman referring to similar German concerns
in the *Historikerstreit*, and stressing inconsistencies in figures given
for Auschwitz victims.[48] But he only really concretizes his case when
he takes issue with Vasilj Krestić's argument locating Croatian genocidal tendencies in the late nineteenth-century doctrine of the
Croatian political nation. Remarkably, Tudjman does not deny the
charge but dubs it only 'half correct' in view of Serbian genocidal
designs *vis-à-vis* Croatia. On this score Tudjman cites a notorious
Belgrade newspaper article of 1902 which called for a struggle 'to
the end' between the two peoples.[49]

Tudjman's emphasis on the decades before the First World War is
well-chosen. The ideological seeds of later catastrophe were sown in
this period as modern Serb and Croat national entities struggled to
consolidate themselves in the face of heavy Austro-Hungarian pressure and their own rivalries over Bosnia and incipient Yugoslavism.
Serbs, many living in their own independent state and priding themselves on their rough-hewn peasant democracy, looked with
contempt at a Croat polity at odds with its Serb minority while in
thrall, as they saw it, to its Magyar masters and their gentrified values. Croats could save themselves only if they threw in their lot with
Serbdom, just as they had already borrowed the Serbian language,
leaving only an alien Church as a distinctive marker.[50] Modern Serb
conspiracy theories about the role of Croatian and world catholicism have their origins in this common turn of the century analysis.
As to the doctrine of the Croatian political nation, that was –
according to Krestić – a relic of noble feudalism which discrimi-
nated against Croatian Serbs and should have been relinquished in
the age of democracy. It should be noted that the near unanimity
with which Serb intellectuals supported nationalism by the later
1980s is much better explained (in its historic dimension) in terms
of these relatively concrete and recent national perceptions than by
anything as vague as atavistic hatreds.

As for Tudjman, his absolutization of the principle of the 'Croatian political nation' leads him to utterly reject any limitation on its
historic or state rights to a particular social period. As history proves
that no nation ever voluntarily forgoes its exclusive right to its land,

so the underlying principle of his nation is 'the demand that all inhabitants feel themselves to be citizens of the Croatian State, without regard to religious or ethnic differences, namely that sovereignty over Croatian lands belongs to the Croatian nation ...'[51] In the two halves of this definition there is, at least to West European minds, a sleight of hand conflating a liberal concept of individual citizenship with an exclusive notion of collective national sovereignty. Plainly, it makes Serbs an anomaly in any Croatian polity and gives some plausibility to Krestić's charge. But how has this conflation occurred?

A well-known theory of one form of East European nationalism sees it in terms of a distortion of Western European liberal values as they were transported further east. Western ideas of the nation as an association of free and individual citizens were spatchcocked onto the only institutions in parts of Eastern Europe which, before 1848, bore any national aspect or enjoyed any kind of associational freedom: the group rights of the 'noble nation'.[52] The classic case is Hungary (in which Croatia enjoyed a certain autonomy), where medieval noble constitutionalism, fossilized by socio-economic backwardness, was called in to aid attempts at national revival and modernization. There is much to be said for the view that the roots of exclusivist Croatian nationalism lie in the 'state right' props of a weak and fragmented nineteenth-century society, pitched into *ustashi* violence by the further frustrations of Serbian hegemony in inter-war Yugoslavia.

More recent Serb extremism, too, can be related to the theme of weakness and flawed modernization. For most of this century Serbs saw themselves as a vigorous, successful nation, abreast of the modern world through their democratic traditions and the prestige of Tito's Yugoslavia. Much of the democracy was populism and the vigour Balkan machismo. The Serbs lacked the resources to hegemonize either the first or the second Yugoslavia, and the State's decline after Tito's death increasingly opened their eyes to the mismatch between their self-image and reality. In their mounting paranoia, along with the Albanian threat to their supremacy in Kosovo, and later the alleged rise of Islamic fundamentalism in Bosnia, the 'Jasenovac myth' played an important role.

The link made here between Yugoslav extremism and violence and the problems of the modernization of a backward society can be given some empirical support. The heartland of massacre, both in the Second World War, and the 1990s, has been Bosnia-Herzegovina and the Croatian Krajina. These are traditionally less developed areas; two hundred and fifty-five thousand children in a total Bosnian-Herzegovinian population of two and a half million in 1947 had never attended school.[53] The region forms part of the Dinaric mountain belt, whose inhabitants were described by the famous early twentieth-century ethnologist and geographer, Jovan Cvijić, as characterized by fierce individual and national pride, impulsive violence and a thirst for 'holy vengeance' for historic wrongs.[54] Notoriously, *ustashi* leaders came from this region, just as have the hard-line camarilla of Herzegovinians pressing Tudjman from the right in Zagreb today. The commanders in Jasenovac interrogated after the war showed a common pattern of humble background combined with some years of secondary or seminary education, a combination which would seem to put them in the troublesome category of the *halbgebildete* or 'intellectual proletariat' that Habsburg rulers of Bosnia had sought unsuccessfully to avoid before 1914.[55]

Something of the clash of values which such elements experience in awkwardly developing societies can be seen, at a much higher level, in intellectuals like Tudjman and Krestić. Both combine elaborate pretensions to scientific scholarship with sublime lack of empathy for other views. Tudjman in particular has been deeply affected by the claims of communism to a rational world view and its aspiration to sweep away what he calls the 'historical madness' of rival nationalisms feeding off each other's propaganda. A part of him was plainly sincere in claiming a positive role for the unmasking of exaggeration: the Yugoslav national problem could only be exacerbated by the 'Jasenovac myth'.[56] But another, and it seems a stronger part, is convinced of the power of the past and of the irrational, is in hock to anti-Semitism, cannot see the difference between the Croatian traditions he upholds and the Western values he avers, and ultimately yields to the bleak perspective of unadulterated cultures locked in ineluctable and even genocidal conflict which he so avidly documents.

Much in Tudjman's make-up, as in that of other ex-Yugoslavs, is to be explained by disillusionment with a failed rationalist ideology imposed on unpromising terrain. The argument of this final section is that the Communist episode was only the latest in a series of problematic bids for modernization. The mismatch between Serbs' and Croats' aspirations for Western-style national sovereignty over the last century, and the given circumstances in which they have found themselves, is as close as this contribution can go to the roots of massacre in former Yugoslavia.

Notes

1. See on this, Lj. Boban, 'Jasenovac and the Manipulation of History', *East European Politics and Societies*, 4, 3 (1990): 580-92.

2. For background: A. Djilas, *The Contested Country: Yugoslav Unity and Communist Revolution, 1919-53* (Harvard, 1991); L. Hory and M. Broszat, *Der*

kroatishe Ustascha-Staat, 1941-1945 (2nd edn, Stuttgart, 1965); B. Krizman, Ustaše i treći Reich (2 vols. Zagreb, 1983).

3. Djilas, Contested Country, 120.
4. Krizman, Ustaše, vol 1, 22. For the Ustashi camps, A. Miletić, 'The Ustashi Independent State of Croatia – A Land of Concentration Camps', in M. Bulajić et al, eds, Ustashi Genocide in the Independent State of Croatia (NDH) from 1941-1945 (Belgrade, 1992), 27-30.
5. Based on the interrogations of Jasenovac personnel printed in A. Miletić, ed., Koncentracioni logor Jasenovac 1941-1945 (3 vols. Zagreb, 1986), vol. 2, 1010-89.
6. M. Bulajić, Tudjman's 'Jasenovac Myth'. Ustasha Crimes of Genocide (Belgrade, 1992), 34.
7. J. Šašić, 'Pregled istraživanja genocida u Jasenovcu', Naše teme (1986):1290; V. Žerjavić, Gubici stanovništva u drugom svjetskom ratu (Zagreb, 1989), 104.
8. Commission report on Jasenovac reprinted in Miletić, Jasenovac, vol. 2, 1090-1120.
9. F. Tudjman, Bezpuća povijesne zbiljnosti (Zagreb, 1990), 91, 329.
10. Šašić, 'Pregled', 1291; Žerjavić, Gubici, 96. For the Serb view, Bulajić, Tudjman's 'Jasenovac Myth', 31.
11. For a convincing summary of the issues, see I. Lah, 'Istinski demografski gubici Jugoslavije u drugom svjetskom ratu', Statistička revija, 2 (1952): 214-23.
12. Tudjman, Bezpuća, 332; Šašić, 'Pregled', 1294.
13. V. Dedijer and A. Miletić, Protiv zaborava tabua (Jasenovac 1941-1991) (Sarajevo, 1991), 96-169, 377-84; Šašić, 'Pregled', 1295. For the documentary collection, see Miletić, Jasenovac.
14. Calculated from Žerjavić, Gubici, 185-87.
15. B. Kočović, Žrtve u drugom svetskom ratu u Jugoslaviji (London, 1985), 65.
16. Kočović, Žrtve, 132-33.
17. Žerjavić, Gubici, xvi.
18. Ibid., 82-3.
19. R. Overmann, 'Personalverluste der deutschen Bevölkerung durch Flucht und Vertreibung', Dzieje najnowsze, 26 (1994): 51-63.
20. Thus ustashi crimes were said to have been 'executed according to the preconceived plan of the Italian government with the aim of decimating the Yugoslav peoples', Report on Italian Crimes against Yugoslavia and its Peoples (Belgrade, 1946), 168. Communists like Šašić and Miletić maintained the line of the prior responsibility of the occupiers to the end.
21. Dedijer and Miletić, Protiv zaborava tabua, 383.
22. Šašić, 'Pregled', 1294; Dedijer and Miletić, Protiv zaborava tabua, 67.
23. Žerjavić, Gubici, 102, 116.
24. This and the following paragraph are based on Tudjman, Bezpuća, 21-75.
25. V. Terzić, Jugoslavija u aprilskom ratu (Titograd, 1963), 29-66, 668-74.
26. F. Tudjman, Okupacija i revolucija (Zagreb,1963), 106.
27. Tudjman, Bezpuća, 53-4.
28. Ibid., 56.
29. Ibid., Bezpuća, 57-8, 62. Interestingly, Tudjman (p. 57), calls Tito a 'historical personality ... with the instinct of a great politician and statesman'.
30. I. Banac, 'The Fearful Asymmetry of War: The Causes and Consequences of Yugoslavia's Demise', Daedalus (Spring 1992), 149.
31. Tudjman, Bezpuća, 49.
32. P. Matejević, Jugoslavenstvo danas (Zagreb, 1982), 13.
33. V. Djuretić, Saveznici i jugoslovenska ratna drama (5th edn, Belgrade, 1992), foreword to first edn, and 14.

34. V. Krestić, 'O genocidi nad Srbima u NDH. U periodu do prvog svetskog rata', *Književne novine*, 32, 15 September 1986.
35. V. Dedijer, *Vatikan i Jasenovac* (Belgrade, 1987).
36. See Miletić, *Jasenovac*.
37. M. Bulajić, *Ustaški zločini genocida i sudjenje Andriji Artukoviću 1986 godine* (Belgrade, 1988), 11-26.
38. Miletić, *Jasenovac*, foreword by J. Šašić, vol. 1, 13.
39. Dedijer and Miletić, *Protiv zaborava tabua*, 62-63. In *Vatikan i Jasenovac*, 657-68, Dedijer had cited several of the huge skull count extrapolations from the early sixties, which seem to have become the main Serb counter to the demographic researches of Kočović and Žerjavić.
40. Bulajić, *Tudjman's 'Jasenovac Myth'*, 50, for Šuvar and Milković.
41. For helpful introductions to Yugoslav developments at this time, see particularly M. Crnobrnja, *The Yugoslav Drama* (2nd edn, London and New York, 1996); L. J. Cohen, *Broken Bonds: The Disintegration of Yugoslavia* (Boulder and Oxford, 1993).
42. M. Bulajić, ed., *Suština o neistinama o zločinima genocida 1991-93 godine* (Belgrade, 1994), 30.
43. Bulajić, *Ustaški zločini genocida*, 26-28.
44. Šašić's foreword to Miletić, *Jasenovac*, vol. 1, 13.
45. B. Krizman, ed. *Jugoslavenske vlade u izbjeglištvu 1941-1943. Dokumenti* (Zagreb, 1981), 209 (more than 300,000), 263 (figure of 28,979); Tudjman, *Bezpuća*, 81.
46. Croatian memorandum, December 1941 in Krizman, *Jugoslavenske vlade*, 257-68.
47. Tudjman, *Bezpuća*, 128-305. On Hegel, 226-28; on Jews as outsiders, 271-94, particularly 271-4.
48. Ibid., 294, 156-7.
49. Ibid., 363.
50. For a study of Serb-Croat polemics at this time, based on the leading Croatian Serb paper: M. Artuković, *Ideologija srpsko-hrvatskih sporova (Srbobran, 1884-1902)* (Zagreb, 1991).
51. Tudjman, *Bezpuća*, 361-62.
52. See P. Sugar, 'External and Domestic Roots of East European Nationalism', in I. Lederer and P. Sugar, eds, *Nationalism in Eastern Europe* (Washington, 1969), 3-54.
53. R. Trouton, *Peasant Renaissance in Yugoslavia 1900-1950* (London, 1952), 265.
54. J. Cvijić, *Balkansko poluostrvo* (2 vols. Belgrade, 1922-31), vol. 2, 18-28.
55. See Miletić, *Jasenovac*, vol. 2, 1010-89.
56. Tudjman, *Bezpuća*, 116 (historical madness), 92-3 and passim (Jasenovac myth).

NOTES ON CONTRIBUTORS

Robin Clifton is Senior Lecturer in the Department of History at the University of Warwick. He has published on anti-catholicism in seventeenth-century England, and written a monograph on the Duke of Monmouth's rebellion of 1685. He is currently working on the nineteenth-century revolution in warfare.

Peter Coates is Senior Lecturer in the Department of Historical Studies at the University of Bristol. He is author of *The Trans-Atlantic Pipeline Controversy* (1991); *In Nature's Defence* (1993); (with William Beinart) *Environment and History* (1995); and *Nature: Western Attitudes since Ancient Times* (1998).

Will Coster is Lecturer in History and Director of the Institute for the Study of War and Society at De Montfort University, Bedford. His published works include *Kinship and Inheritance in Early Modern England* as well as the forthcoming *Spiritual Kinship in Early Modern England*.

Tilman Dedering is Lecturer in the Department of History at the University of South Africa in Pretoria. He teaches South African and modern German history and has published on Namibian pre-colonial and colonial history.

John Edwards, formerly Reader in Spanish History at the University of Birmingham, is Senior Research Fellow in Spanish in the University of Oxford. His publications include, *Christian Córdoba. The City and its Region in the Late Middle Ages* (1982); *The Jews in Christian Europe, 1400-1700* (second edn, 1991); and *The Spain of the Catholic Monarchs, 1474-1516* (forthcoming).

John Gittings is Foreign Leader-Writer at *The Guardian*, where he comments on all aspects of current international affairs. He has written or edited books on the Cold War (with Jonathan Steele and Noam Chomsky), Chile, post-war Korea, and the Gulf War. His special field is, however, China, his latest book on the subject being *Real China: From Cannibalism to Karaoke* (1996).

Mark Greengrass is Professor of Modern History at the University of Sheffield. He has published on the French Reformation and Henry IV as well as the European intellectual history of the seventeenth century. His latest book is *The European Reformation, c. 1500-1618* (1998).

Laura Jacobus is Lecturer in the Department of History of Art at Birkbeck College, University of London. She has published on the Arena Chapel in Padua, and on body-language in Italian medieval art. Her research interests are principally focused on late-medieval art.

Mark Levene is Lecturer in the Department of History at the University of Warwick, specializing in modern Jewish history. He is the author of *War, Jews and the New Europe* (1992), and his main area of research is on genocide in the modern world.

Robert M. Levine is Professor of History and director of Latin American Studies at the University of Miami, Coral Gables. In addition to nearly two dozen books on Latin American history, as well as editorship of the Luzo-Brazilian Review, he has also produced four television documentaries.

Callum MacDonald was Professor of History in the joint school of Comparative American Studies at the University of Warwick. He was the author of six books of diplomatic and military history, ranging in geographical scope across the United States, Latin America, Asia and Europe as well as a collaborative prize-winning *Timewatch* documentary on the killing of Heydrich. Professor MacDonald was engaged on a study of Sino-Japanese conflicts of the 1930s at the time of his death in 1997.

Allan I. Macinnes holds the Burnett-Fletcher Chair of History at the University of Aberdeen. In addition to *Charles I and the Covenanting Movement* (1991), and *Clanship, Commerce and the House of Stuart* (1996), he has written extensively on covenants, clans and clearances in Scotland.

Robin Okey is Senior Lecturer in the Department of History at the University of Warwick. He is the author of *Eastern Europe 1740-1945* (2nd edn, 1986) and has also published extensively on Habsburg-South Slav relations in the Dualist period, the Communist experience in Eastern Europe and, more generally, on linguistic and national minorities issues.

Penny Roberts is Lecturer in the Department of History at the University of Warwick. She is the author of *A City in Conflict: Troyes during the French Wars of Religion* (1996), and (with William G. Naphy) editor of a volume of essays on *Fear in Early Modern Society* (1997). She has also published a number of articles on the social and religious history of early modern France.

Stephen D. Shenfield is Assistant Professor at the Watson Institute for International Studies, Brown University (USA). He specializes in the international politics of the post-Soviet region and is also interested in genocide and its prevention.

INDEX